From stage actor and international television star, to block-buster, best-selling author, Judy Nunn's career has been meteoric.

Her first forays into adult fiction resulted in what she describes as her 'entertainment set'. *The Glitter Game, Centre Stage* and *Araluen*, three novels set in the worlds of television, theatre and film respectively, each became instant bestsellers.

Next came her 'city set'. *Kal,* a fiercely passionate novel about men and mining set in Kalgoorlie; *Beneath the Southern Cross*, a mammoth achievement chronicling the story of Sydney since first European settlement; and *Territory*, a tale of love, family and retribution set in Darwin.

Territory took Australia by storm, making Judy one of the nation's top-selling fiction writers, and her following novel, *Pacific,* set principally in Vanuatu, met with equal success. Her next work, *Heritage,* based in the 1950s and set in the Snowies, embraced post-war immigration and the birth of multicultural-ism. The resounding critical and commercial success of *Heritage* has consolidated Judy's position as one of this country's leading fiction writers.

Judy Nunn's fame as a novelist is spreading rapidly. Her books are published throughout Europe in English, German, French, Dutch and Czech.

Judy lives with her husband, actor-author Bruce Venables, on the Central Coast of New South Wales.

JUDY NUNN

FLOODTIDE

RANDOM HOUSE AUSTRALIA

Random House Australia Pty Ltd
Level 3, 100 Pacific Highway, North Sydney, NSW 2060
www.randomhouse.com.au

Sydney   New York   Toronto
London   Auckland   Johannesburg

First published by Random House Australia 2007

National Library of Australia
Cataloguing-in-Publication Entry

Nunn, Judy.
Floodtide.

ISBN 978 1 74166 685 4 (pbk.).

1. Western Australia – History – 20th century – Fiction. I.

A823.3

Cover photo by Jeff Drewitz/Wildlight
Cover design by Darian Causby/www.highway51.com
Map by Caroline Bowie
Typeset in 12/14.5 pt Sabon by Midland Typesetters, Australia
Printed and bound by Griffin Press, South Australia

10 9 8 7 6 5 4 3 2 1

In loving memory of my father, Bob Nunn,
(1908–1978)

ACKNOWLEDGEMENTS

My thanks, as always, and my love forever to my husband, Bruce Venables. My thanks also to the pals and workmates: my publisher Jeanne Ryckmans, Peta Levett, Brandon VanOver and all at Random House Australia; my agent, James Laurie; Colin Julin; and those close friends who have been encouraging and supportive every step of the way, Susan Mackie and Sue Greaves.

Thanks also to my other old friends from Perth who have helped with 'blasts from the past', Sue John and Johanna Fewings, and to those mates who are such experts in their fields and can always be called upon, Warren Brown, Bill Leak and Michael Roberts. For assistance in the research of this book, my sincerest thanks to Bridget O'Brien from Claremont Library for steering me towards her father's books, and to the late Dennis Haselhurst for the extracts relating to the 'Snake Pit', which appeared in *Diversity's Challenge*.

I am indebted to many I met during my research trip to the Pilbara. My thanks to those at Woodside Energy (Public Affairs), in particular Rob Millhouse, Mandy Lorrimer, Luke Blackbourn and Kathryn Robinson; and all the best to the beaut gang at the Karratha Library & Community Centre.

Among my research sources, I would like to recognise the following:

Batavia, Philippe Godard, Abrolhos Publishing, 1993.

Islands of Angry Ghosts, Hugh Edwards, Hodder & Stoughton, 1966.

Diversity's Challenge – A History of the City of Stirling, William S. Cooper and Gilbert McDonald, 1999.

Claremont Yacht Club – 100 Years of History – 1905–2005, Edited Rob Nunn, Claremont Yacht Club Incorporated, 2005.

Burke's Shambles, Anthony McAdam and Patrick O'Brien, Burke Press, 1987.

The Executive State, Patrick O'Brien and Martin Webb, Constitutional Press, 1991.

Author's Note

When I decided to write *Floodtide*, I knew that I couldn't do so without the help of a highly qualified environmentalist, and there was only one person who came to mind – my brother, Robert. In fact, when I approached him I said, 'I'll only do this book if you come on board, Rob.' A case of blackmail? Yes. And it worked.

Here's a potted history of my big brother, Rob:

Rob Nunn is a third-generation West Australian and has spent most of his life on, in and around the Swan River, mostly in the Claremont and Bicton areas. An honours graduate in zoology and geology, he has worked as a marine biologist, a base metals geologist and, finally, as an environmentalist for both the Western Australian government and the international oil industry. He has a long and intimate association with the West Pilbara Region of the state and has worked overseas in the UK, the Netherlands and the Middle East.

Rob has a brilliant mind. Throughout the writing of this book, his contribution in the form of research has been invaluable, and his continuous support deeply appreciated. The journey has proved an enjoyable one for us both, and I'm hoping his involvement with *Floodtide* will inspire him to finish that novel I know he's started.

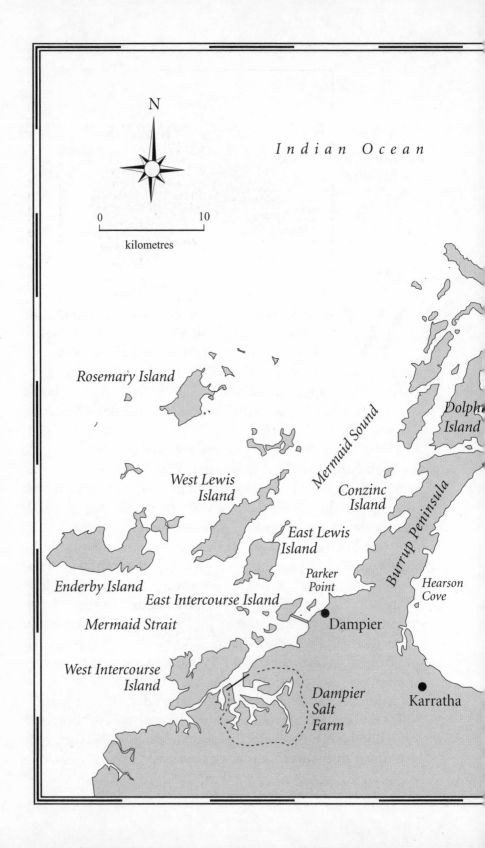

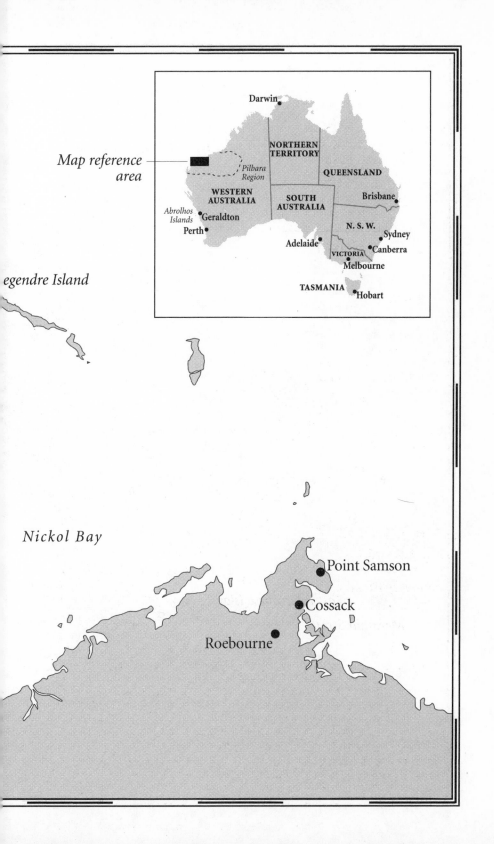

Map reference area

Darwin

NORTHERN TERRITORY

Pilbara Region

WESTERN AUSTRALIA

QUEENSLAND

Abrolhos Islands

Geraldton

SOUTH AUSTRALIA

Brisbane

Perth

N. S. W.

Sydney

Adelaide

Canberra

VICTORIA

Melbourne

TASMANIA

Hobart

egendre Island

Nickol Bay

Point Samson

Cossack

Roebourne

'There is a tide in the affairs of men which, taken at the flood, leads on to fortune'

Julius Caesar, William Shakespeare

PROLOGUE

1965

'Beats me why you wanna go swimmin' with sharks.' The bottles of Swan Lager clinked as Tubby Lard took the cardboard box the kid handed him. 'Only a dickhead'd go swimmin' with sharks.'

'Yeah,' his brother Fats agreed from where he stood up the bow, ready to cast off. 'You wouldn't get me down there for quids.'

'Well, of course you wouldn't, you stupid bastard,' Tubby said, gunning the engine and yelling above the diesel's throb. 'You can't bloody swim!'

Mike McAllister grinned as he stepped nimbly aboard the *Maria Nina*. It was good to see the Lard brothers again.

Tubby eyed the kid's backpack. 'Haven't you got any scuba gear?' he asked.

'At twenty feet I won't need it.'

Mike settled himself on the massive wooden, lead-lined icebox that doubled as a seat and trained his eyes on the distant low-lying rocky islands as the vessel pulled away from the jetty. It was a hot, steamy morning, barely a breath of breeze, the ocean like glass. A perfect day for it, he thought, excited by the prospect of what lay ahead.

Contrary to her name, the *Maria Nina* was no sea sprite. She was an old tub, thirty-eight feet long, stinking of bait and desperately in need of a coat of paint. But that was only her exterior. The brothers cared little for appearances; she was solid and reliable and her engine was meticulously maintained. The *Maria Nina* was a grand old dame of the sea.

Tubby and Fats Lard were cray fishermen who worked the Abrolhos Islands off Geraldton on the coast of Western Australia. During their respective early school years both brothers had been called Lardhead, but not for long, because both were good with their fists. Fred, the elder, had readily accepted Tubby as a substitute. Skinny as a rake, he was amused by the contradiction. Bob, also on the lean side and five years his brother's junior, was an avid jazz fan. He considered his nickname a tribute to Fats Waller.

'Hey Einstein,' Tubby called from the wheelhouse, 'get off your bum and put the grog on ice.'

'Oh.' Mike jumped to his feet. 'Sorry.' He loaded the beer into the ice chest. Beside him, Fats started baiting up the dozen or more hooks on each of the set-lines.

'Want a hand?' Mike asked when the beer was stowed. Fats nodded. Fats Lard was a man of few words; it was Tubby who did most of the talking.

Mike and the brothers had met at the pub in Geraldton just three days previously. It had been early evening, a squally wind blowing in from the sea and alleviating to some degree the oppressive heat of a typical dry and dusty December day.

'You're off the *Pelsaert*, aren't you,' Tubby said. He and Fats were lounging at the bar of the Victoria Hotel when the kid fronted up to buy a round for his mates.

'Yeah, that's right. Three schooners, thanks,' Mike said to the barman.

Tubby eyed the kid up and down. Handsome young bastard – black-haired, startlingly blue-eyed – he should be in the pictures, Tubby thought. Fit too, but just a kid. 'Bit young for a boffin, aren't you?' He glanced at the table where the kid's mates were seating themselves. They were early twenties, he guessed. What were they doing aboard the *Pelsaert*?

'We're students, up from Perth,' Mike said. 'UWA.'

'Ah, right.'

The student part made sense, Tubby thought, but hardly the vessel. He'd seen the MV *Pelsaert* tooling about the Wallabi Islands and upon enquiring had been told it was the State Fisheries' new research vessel on some sort of scientific expedition.

'They give you young blokes a brand new boat just because you go to uni?' He exchanged a look with Fats, who was equally incredulous.

'Hardly.' Mike laughed. He didn't find Tubby's direct manner offensive, he sensed the man was genuinely interested. 'We're here to do the hard yakka,' he joked, 'the stuff the boffins aren't fit enough for.'

'There you go, mate.' The barman placed the beers in front of him.

Tubby waited until the kid had paid for the drinks, then homed in again. 'What hard yakka?' Tubby had an enquiring mind and his questions were invariably relentless.

'We catch tammars.'

It was true. For the past five nights, from eight o'clock until two in the morning, the three students had raced relentlessly around East and West Wallabi Islands, lights strapped to their foreheads, wielding giant butterfly-like nets, the object of the exercise being the capture of the small nocturnal marsupials which would undergo study the following day. Keen athletes, the boys had been selected for their physical fitness.

'Whaddya wanna do that for?' It was the first time Fats had spoken. He was no less interested than his brother, but he always relied on Tubby to lead the way.

Mike, torn between delivering the beers and not wishing to appear rude to the locals, cast a look in the direction of his mates. Muzza was lounging back with a smoke, but Ian, upon catching his eye, gave an irritated wave and a scowl that said 'Hurry it up'.

'The boys are getting impatient,' he said, gathering up the beers. Then he added, 'Why don't you join us?'

'Rightio.' Tubby didn't need any further invitation. He rose from his stool, grabbed his glass, and Fats followed. The brothers liked meeting new people.

They gathered at the table, Mike plonking down the beers, Ian pointedly making a grab for his. As Tubby and Fats garnered extra chairs, the boys shuffled around to make room for them and when they'd settled, Mike made the introductions.

'Murray Hatfield, Ian Pemberton and I'm Mike McAllister,' he said.

'Tubby and Fats Lard.' Tubby leaned across the table, offering Mike a gnarled hand. Ian snorted into his beer.

They shook all round, then Tubby raised his glass. 'Welcome to Gero, boys.'

The others joined in the salutation, taking a swig along with him. Ian Pemberton sipped reluctantly. He was a classically handsome young man, despite slightly protruding ears, but his aquiline features so often conveyed disdain that the effect was invariably ruined. Ian was a snob.

'How long ya been here?' Tubby led the conversation, seemingly oblivious to Ian's contempt.

'A week,' Mike told him.

'How long ya stayin'?'

'Another week.' It was Muzza who replied. Like Mike, he was aware that Ian considered the brothers an intrusion – Pembo could be a real pain at times, he thought. Muzza was keen to follow Mike's lead. He always did. Just turned twenty, Muzza was two years younger than the others and Mike was a bit of hero. He gave one of his lop-sided, baby-faced grins. 'We leave next Saturday.'

'Good-lookin' boat, the *Pelsaert*,' Tubby said, Fats nodding agreement. 'I've seen her holed up in Turtle Bay on East Wallabi – you boys livin' on board, are ya?'

'That's right.' Mike flashed a warning glance at Ian, who was scowling at his beer, before changing the subject and asking the brothers about themselves.

They were cray fishermen, Tubby told him, 'Born and bred right here in Gero.' Although Tubby did the talking, Fats joined in with nods to the table at large. Fats did a lot of nodding.

'The Lards have been cray men for three generations,' Tubby said proudly, 'comin' up for four soon.' Tubby was thirty-nine and his son barely ten years old, but the boy's future was carved in stone. 'We scored the boat off Dad when he bought his new humdinger five years back, didn't we, Fats?' A nod. 'The old man's sixty-three, still in the business, still goin' strong.'

Tubby drained his glass and stood. 'I'll get another round, hey.' It wasn't a question and he was already gathering up the empty glasses.

Ian put his hand over his glass, which still had an inch of beer in it.

Muzza jumped to his feet before Pembo could refuse Tubby's offer. 'I'll give you a hand,' he said.

As the two of them left for the bar, conversation at the table ground to a halt. Ian drained his glass in sulky silence. Fats turned expectantly to Mike. His eyes, set deep in the crinkles of a face weathered well beyond its thirty-four years, appeared eager for another question or some sort of comment, but Mike was at a loss as to what to say. Tubby's potted history of the Lard family had been so succinct that no further question or comment came readily to mind.

But Fats wasn't seeking question or comment, he was seeking an answer. He'd been prepared to wait patiently for Tubby to bring up the subject, as Tubby no doubt would, although, in Fats' opinion, Tubby sometimes took a long time to get to the point. But as Tubby wasn't here now, and there was a hole in the conversation, Fats decided to ask for himself.

'Whaddya wanna catch tammars for?'

Mike was relieved that Fats had started the ball rolling; he was unaccustomed to feeling socially awkward. 'For study,' he said. 'It's a research trip.'

Fats nodded, he'd gathered that.

'We're earning extra money during the summer vacation,' Mike went on, 'assisting in the research for a PhD student on a Fulbright Scholarship –'

'What about the tammars?' Fats asked. He didn't really want to know about the scholarship part.

'Well, they're remarkable animals,' Mike explained. 'They thrive here on East and West Wallabi and we want to find out how. You see, there's virtually no fresh-water source on the islands, particularly on West Wallabi. There's no fresh water at all there, except for rain, of course . . .'

Fats kept nodding as the kid talked, taking it all in slowly, sifting the information. He hadn't known that tammars were so interesting.

Ian Pemberton looked at the cray fisherman, nodding like a metronome, and his irritation grew to boiling point. How dare the yobbos crash their party. How dare Mike ask them to the table. And look at him now! Good old Mike McAllister, everybody's favourite, giving his all to a retard who didn't understand a word he was saying. Ian wanted to deck him. What about the nurses they'd met last night? There was a party on at their flat, starting about now. What the hell were the three of them doing sitting here entertaining a couple of local cretins?

'From an environmental point of view it makes them a very valuable source of study,' Mike said.

'So what is it you do with the tammars?' Fats was fascinated.

'*Protemnodon eugenii* to be precise,' Ian cut in, the disdain in his voice matching the sneer on his face.

Fats turned to look blankly at him, just as Tubby and Muzza arrived with the beers. Ian waited until the glasses had been placed on the table before once again addressing Fats, in exactly the same tone.

'We study the water metabolism of genus *Protemnoden*, species *eugenii*, otherwise known as the tammar.'

There was a deathly silence. Tubby stared at the kid with the bat ears and the pointy face and the built-in bad smell under his nose. He'd sensed his antagonism the moment they'd come to the table, but what had Fats done to rile him? Fats might not be the sharpest tool in the shed, but he was a good bloke, he wouldn't hurt a fly. Well, not unless the fly hurt him, and even then he had to be pushed. Tubby was about to challenge the snotty-nosed little prick, but someone else got in first.

'Stop being a smartarse, Pembo,' Mike said good-naturedly. 'Sit down, Tubby, there was no offence intended. Was there, Ian?' The question was pointed.

'Course not.' Checked by Mike's warning tone and the threat of danger, Ian attempted a smile, which wasn't successful.

Tubby sat. Very slowly, his eyes darting about the group, like a cat ready to pounce.

Fats, too, looked around the table, aware of the sudden tension. He'd gathered that some sort of insult had been intended, and while he wondered what he'd done to warrant it, he wasn't particularly offended. But he could tell that Tubby was ready to do battle, and he was prepared to join in. Tubby only ever picked a fight when there was good cause for it.

'I'm here on a dual study period myself,' Mike said to the brothers, as if nothing had happened. 'Doing some advance research for my PhD next year, and the topic's right up your alley.'

'Oh yeah?' Tubby said, distrustful. One word in the wrong direction and these little uni pricks wouldn't know what'd hit them. But he couldn't help himself, he was impressed by Mike. It was obvious the other two took their lead from him. Muzza wasn't a bad kid, but he seemed younger than the others and, Tubby suspected, a bit of a 'yes' boy. As for the bat-eared snotty-nosed bastard . . .

'And how exactly would your *advance research* be right up our alley?' he asked, his tone a dangerously supercilious imitation of Ian's.

Mike turned to Fats. 'What do you reckon I'm studying, Fats?'

'Eh?' Fats was caught out; people usually addressed their questions to Tubby.

'The topic I'm studying – what do you reckon it is? What's right up your alley?'

'Crayfish?' Fats asked hopefully.

'Spot on.' Mike once again addressed the older brother. 'As well as the study of tammars, the *Pelsaert* and her crew are doing a pre-season cray census. The object of the exercise will lead to a better estimate of the catchable cray population later in the season, and maybe even the following year as well. Does that interest you?'

'My oath it does,' Tubby said. Any insult was forgotten, the kid had won him.

Twenty minutes later, as they were polishing off the next round of beers – Muzza's shout – Mike was still talking, Tubby was still asking questions, and Fats was still hanging on every word. The brothers knew only too well that the whole of the Abrolhos was a hatchery and nursery area this time of year. All down the west coast the cray season ran from mid-November until the end of June, with the exception of the Abrolhos where it didn't start until mid-March. They'd been wondering what the *Pelsaert* was doing laying pots, and now Mike was explaining the mark-and-recapture techniques employed in the research.

'Tail-punching,' he said. 'It leaves an identifiable mark when they're recaught.'

'Well, bein' a Fisheries vessel, we didn't exactly think you were doin' something illegal,' Tubby said. Fats nodded, although they'd both had their doubts. 'Whatever experiments they're up to, I bet they're keepin' a good few crays on the side,' Tubby had said as he'd watched them blatantly setting their pots, and Fats had agreed.

Mike didn't go into detail about the recent break-through. The discovery of *puerulus* in numbers – the elusive settling phase before the juvenile hard-shelled crayfish emerged – had caused much excitement in academic circles. But it wasn't necessary to explain the finer points; both brothers understood the impact of the research. An advance and accurate prediction in the numbers of mature crayfish would revolutionise their industry.

'Time to go.' Ian replaced his empty glass on the table with a little more force than was necessary. Aware that he'd overstepped the mark earlier, it was the only way he could signal his boredom and irritation. He stood. 'The girls are waiting.' He forced another smile, his second of the evening, and again it didn't work. 'Nice to meet you, Tubby, Fats.'

Muzza looked to Mike for his cue. He was a bit bored himself. The cray fishermen had lost their appeal now that the girls were beckoning.

'Sorry, Muz.' Mike smiled apologetically. 'I got a bit carried away. You go and have a good time.'

Muzza shook hands with the brothers as he rose from his chair, but Ian kept his distance, his eyes on Mike.

'You're not coming?' he asked.

'I never said I was.'

'Jeez, mate,' Tubby said to Mike, nudging Fats as a signal they should make a move. 'If you've got women lined up don't let us stand in your way.'

'You're not.' Mike's tone was definite, but his reply was directed to Ian. 'I told you from the start I didn't want to be in it.'

Fats rose from the table, a decision seemed to have been made. 'Goodo then,' he said. 'My round.'

'No, it isn't.' Mike continued to look at Ian. He was wondering how on earth he'd remained friends with Pembo for the past several years. But he knew the answer. He was sorry for the bloke. 'It's Ian's round. Isn't it, Ian?'

Tubby watched, intrigued by the second or so of power play between the two young men, but it was no competition.

'Sure,' Ian said, 'my shout', and he went off to the bar where he ordered three beers. He and Muzza certainly weren't hanging around with the Lard brothers when there were women to be had. Mike had turned into such a square, he thought. God, Mike McAllister had been the biggest womaniser of them all – the bloke could score in a convent, women always gravitated to him. But he'd changed since he'd met Johanna. What a bastard, Ian thought as he paid for the beers. Without Mike he probably wouldn't score tonight. Mike had always been his lucky draw card, and now he was left with young Muzza who, in his opinion, was a definite loser.

He returned to place the three beers on the table. 'You ready, Muzza?' he asked, and Muzza once again stood.

Mike leaned back in his chair, raising his glass to them

both. 'Thanks, Pembo,' he said pleasantly. 'You guys have a great night.'

Ian made his farewells tightly but politely.

'See you, Muzza,' Mike called as they left. 'Don't do anything I wouldn't do.'

'Leaves me plenty of licence,' Muzza called back over his shoulder.

'You sure you don't want to go with your mates?' Tubby's question was incredulous. Why didn't Mike want to chase after women? Crikey, they'd be queuing up for a young stud like him.

'Yep, quite sure. I'm not interested.'

As he said it, Mike realised that he genuinely wasn't. He certainly would have been six months ago – six months ago he would have been leading the troops – but since he'd met Jo, he'd lost the urge to bed other women. Not because he felt the need to remain faithful – he'd made no commitment and neither had she – but for some reason the thrill of the chase no longer seemed important. Funny about that, he thought.

'I've got a girlfriend in Perth,' he said to avoid any further questioning.

'Ah,' Tubby replied, sharing a nod with Fats. The kid was in love – that explained it. He took a long draught of his beer and settled back in his chair. 'So, where were we up to, Einstein?' He could listen to the kid all night.

'The *Batavia*.' Mike decided it was his turn to ask the questions.

'Eh?' The non sequitur took both brothers by surprise.

'Do you know about the wreck of the *Batavia*?'

'Do I what!' Tubby's grin was triumphant. 'She was a Dutch East India trading vessel that foundered on the Abrolhos in 1629.' He looked like a schoolboy who'd topped his class; he was glad of the opportunity to show off his knowledge to the kid. 'There was a bunch of muti-neers on board and they were going to pirate her, but she hit the reef instead. And after the shipwreck they murdered just about all the survivors.'

'Women and children as well,' Fats interjected, the gleam of morbid fascination in his eyes. 'Them islands is covered in bones.'

It was more historical fact than Mike had anticipated from the brothers. 'Do you know where the wreck is?' he asked.

'Too right.' It was Fats again, suddenly and uncharacteristically articulate. 'Tubby and me was on hand when it was discovered a couple of years back. We know the exact spot, don't we, Tub?'

'Yep, we helped the expedition team when they were diving on it. They needed our local knowledge of the area,' Tubby said with a touch of pride.

'I've heard it's in shallow water, is that right?'

'Around twenty feet or so.'

'Could you take me to it?'

The look Tubby exchanged with Fats was dubious. 'Well, we *could*,' he said tentatively.

Mike presumed the brothers were concerned about money. 'I'll pay . . .' he added hastily.

'Nah, nah, it's not that.' Tubby waved a hand airily. 'It's just that you need the right day. If the weather's crook, you can't make an approach, it's bloody impossible.'

'So if the weather's right, will you take me out there?'

Fats was nodding vigorously. Fats had taken to Mike. But then so had his brother.

'Yeah, if the weather's right,' Tubby agreed.

Mike tried to negotiate a price, but the brothers would have none of it. 'Well, at least let me pay for the fuel,' he insisted.

Tubby shrugged. 'If you like, but we'll be takin' the boat out anyway. We gotta make a living.'

Prior to the commencement of the cray season, the brothers fished with set-lines for dhufish and baldchin grouper, both prize table fish for the West Australian market.

'Okay, it's a deal. And I'll bring along a case of beer.'
'You're on, Einstein.'

Three days later, the squally winds had died down and the weather was perfect.

Tubby followed the deep channel that led from the safe anchorage behind the reefs out into the open ocean. He and Fats would lay their set-lines before taking Mike to the wreck site. The *Maria Nina* churned smoothly through the gentle swell, the sea and the sky so peacefully clear they seemed to merge as one. Mike sat on the icebox helping Fats bait up the lines. An hour or so later, when they'd set them, floats bobbing on the ocean's surface, Tubby turned the vessel about.

'You can only approach the wreck from the open sea,' he said as Mike joined him in the wheelhouse. 'Treacherous bastard of a place – no way you can come into it from the land. That's Beacon Island,' he pointed at the low, rocky island up ahead. '*Batavia*'s Graveyard, it's known as. The wreck's just a mile south of it.'

Mike gazed at the island, barren and desolate like the rest of the Abrolhos. *Batavia*'s Graveyard, he thought, and couldn't help feeling a thrill of anticipation. This was the highlight of his trip. It was strange, he hadn't expected it to be – there'd been far too much else to preoccupy him. He'd been intrigued by the lunatic notion of nightly tammar chasing, and excited by the prospect of next year's PhD study when he'd be working as a field assistant with Dr Bruce Phillips of the CSIRO, the man who'd made the breakthrough *puerulus* discovery. Not once had the *Batavia* entered his mind, and why should it? He'd known little about its actual history when he'd left Perth – only that the site of an old Dutch wreck had created headlines when it had been discovered on the Abrolhos in 1963. But he'd been enthralled by the tales he'd heard aboard the *Pelsaert* on the night of his arrival, the crew members infecting him with their own fascination with the *Batavia*'s brutal past. The very vessel that was accommodating them, he'd been told by the crew, was named after the actual commander of the *Batavia*, Francisco Pelsaert. And then they'd embarked upon the grisly story of mutiny, murder and acts of such atrocity that surely the leader of the mutineers must have been the devil himself.

Ever since that night, young Mike McAllister had viewed the islands of the Abrolhos through different eyes, perhaps through the eyes of a seaman. He was seeing them now with a sense of history.

Ecologically, their make-up was simple – in studying the ecology of the crayfish, Mike had also studied their habitat – the islands were formed of coral shale and sand built up by the conflicting currents on the shallow plateaus. Plants sprouted from seeds in bird droppings to form sparse vegetation, binding the sand with roots and resulting in a series of low-lying islands that somehow defied the elements. It was that very defiance which he found remarkable. For hundreds of years, these desolate and insignificant-looking outcrops, little more than a combination of reef and sandbank, had withstood the full force of nature. They, and the treacherous submerged reefs surrounding them, had become indestructible demons feared by seamen over the centuries. Infamous graveyards to many a ship and its sailors. In fact, as the crew of the *Pelsaert* had told him, the very name Abrolhos meant in old Dutch, 'keep your eyes open'.

No longer did the islands appear insignificant to Mike. The islands of the Abrolhos were to be respected. They were a timeless and impressively powerful force in the landscape: pristine, primitive and untameable.

'We're coming in nor'-east on the original course of the *Batavia*. That's the reef up ahead, a bit to port.'

As Tubby's voice broke into his thoughts, Mike looked to where the man was pointing. The only giveaway sign of the reef was a ripple of white frills playing teasingly across the ocean's surface.

'We picked a good day for it,' Tubby said, cutting back the speed until they were idling. 'You can get ripped to pieces out here – in crook weather the place is like a bloody cauldron. Let her go,' he called to Fats who was standing by ready to drop anchor. They were barely a hundred yards from the reef.

When the *Maria Nina* was securely at anchor, Tubby cut the engine. 'We'll hang back fine in this breeze,' he said. 'Grab us a beer, will ya, Einstein?'

Mike lifted out an icy cold bottle. Fats was already handing around three grimy plastic beakers. 'Not for me thanks, Fats,' he said, stripping down to his Speedos.

The brothers swigged on their beers while they baited up – two hooks on each handline. They had no intention of sitting idly by while the kid explored the wreck.

'She should be about dead ahead of us,' Tubby said as Mike donned his flippers. 'Take your time, we'll be jake, there's good fishin' here.' He couldn't resist adding, 'And where there's good fishin', there's sharks.'

'You wouldn't get me down there,' Fats said, slinging his line over the side and watching it spiral from its reel down into the depths. The fact that their baits might well be an added attraction to sharks was of little concern to either Tubby or Fats. If the kid was mad enough to go swimming in shark-infested waters then that was his problem.

'No worries.' Mike grinned at the brothers' dire warnings. They didn't alarm him, he'd dived many a time with sharks.

He slid over the side and trod water while he rinsed his facemask and snorkel. When he was ready to take off, he gave the brothers the thumbs up.

'Good luck, Einstein,' Tubby called, chucking his own line into the water and holding his beaker out to Fats for a refill. He watched the kid's easy style as he swam towards the reef, sliding through the water as if he was born to it. Just like Murray Rose, he thought. The kid was pretty to watch.

As Mike swam, a slow energy-conserving freestyle, his powerful flippers barely moving, he relished the sensation of the water and his sense of oneness with it. He always did. It wasn't something he analysed, but neither was it something he took for granted. He was always aware that in the water he felt as if he were in his element, as if he and the sea shared something special.

Through the surface swirl he could see the reef below, and he made a shallow dive, just about seven or eight feet, to get a clearer view.

Then that exhilarating moment when sound ceased to exist and everything stopped, even time itself. It was what he loved most about free diving. There was no echo of laboured breathing through scuba equipment, there was just him and the world under the sea. A world where colour and action abounded and drama unfolded all in breathtaking silence.

Beneath the dappled silver canopy of sun and sea, the visibility was perfect and the colours vivid. The blues and greens of the corals, the fiery reds of the sponges, the delicately wavering mauves of the anemones, all were as riotously colourful as a spring garden in full blossom. He pressurised and swam a little deeper, following the reef's terrain, through castle-like turrets where gaudily painted fish disappeared like magic, past ledges from which crayfish watched, their protruding feelers the only giveaway of their presence, down canyons where silver schools of skipjack and kingfish maintained their restless patrol.

He'd be around twenty feet now, he guessed, but no sign of the wreck. Time to go up. He stopped swimming and allowed himself to slowly drift upwards, just a gentle flick of the flippers now and then, depressurising as he went, watching the dappled silver above grow closer and closer.

When he broke surface, he heaved in a lungful of air and looked back at the *Maria Nina*. She was a good two hundred yards or so away. He must have drifted with the current. He circled back with slow, easy strokes, regaining his breath, studying the reef beneath him, conserving his energy. Perhaps, even from the surface, he'd be able to see the wreck. Given the calm conditions and the fact that she was lying at only twenty feet, surely it was possible. But try as he might, he could see no sign. Perhaps the brothers had got it wrong, he thought. He dived again, allowing himself more distance this time, he'd go with the flow of the current.

He was down about fifteen feet, once again lost in a world of silence and colour, and his attention was so focused on a vivid blue cluster of staghorn coral that he failed to notice the sinister grey shape that had appeared out of nowhere. It was the disturbed reaction of a school of silver bream that caught his attention, and he turned to see the shark gliding towards him effortlessly with no apparent movement of its body, like a robot on automatic pilot, majestic and omnipotent.

He anchored himself against the reef and watched, prepared to lunge forward in attack should the creature show any interest in him – attack was always the best form of defence. The shark was around ten feet in length. Barrel-shaped, yellow-eyed, with long gill slits and a high tail fin, it was a whaler, a dangerous species. But it paid him no attention as it passed by barely four feet away; he could have reached out and touched it.

He watched as the shark cruised a little deeper, gliding through a shallow valley in the rocks below. Perhaps it was unaware of his presence, or perhaps it was merely uninterested. He continued to admire its shadowy form as it cleared the valley and disappeared into the misty beyond.

Then the glint of something caught his eye, drawing his attention to a shape resting amongst the valley's coral growth. It was a long, cylindrical shape at odds with its surrounds, far too regular to be fashioned by nature. And, as the sun's light played teasingly through the ocean's surface above, it glinted again.

His lungs told him he needed to resurface. He had no time to examine the shape, but he knew what it was. A cannon. He'd found the site. The wreck itself must be nearby.

When he broke surface, heaving in air, he looked towards the *Maria Nina*. In his excitement he wanted to shout to the brothers, 'It's here! I've found it!', but they were paying him no attention. Tubby was heaving a dhufish over the side and Fats, having also struck lucky, was hauling in his line.

He trod water for a minute or so, keeping himself stationary against the current, careful not to drift over the spot while he prepared himself. And when he was fully recovered, he dived again.

The moment he was beneath the surface, he spotted the telltale glint and saw the cannon nestled in its rocky valley below. But as he swam downwards, he realised that the valley wasn't a valley at all. It was the encrusted wreck of the *Batavia*.

There she was, a flattened-out skeleton moulded into her grave. The rocks had hollowed out a tomb over the years, protecting her in part from the destructive forces of tide and surf, and the stern and ribs of the vessel were in an extraordinary state of preservation. He was lost in awe, it was beyond his wildest expectations. He wasn't sure what his expectations had been, but certainly not this.

Briefly, he examined the cannon. It was covered in sea growth, and he assumed it to be bronze but couldn't be certain. It was the refraction of sunlight through relatively shallow water that had lent it the deceptively metallic glint. The giant anchor nestled nearby also seemed to glint from behind its thick encrustation of barnacles. It appeared to signal a life that belonged to its past glory.

But it was the skeletal remains of the *Batavia* that he found truly overwhelming. For centuries, the Abrolhos had kept her hidden, storing her here, preserving her like a trophy, as if in her amazingly recognisable condition she was proof of their own indestructibility.

He swam over what had been the belly of the ship, aware that he must resurface, that he must maintain enough breath in order to breathe out continuously on the way up and release the air pressure in his lungs. But he wanted to remain a part of it all for just one moment longer, to savour the image. It would never be the same on a second dive.

He locked himself between two of the mighty beams that formed the skeleton of the hull and stayed motionless, feeling himself a part of the vessel. Part of a vessel that was four hundred and thirty-six years old! The thought was staggering. And even more so as he recalled the tales the crew aboard the *Pelsaert* had told him. Names flashed through his brain. Pelsaert, the commander; Jacobsz, the skipper; Cornelisz, the wealthy merchant, the leader of the mutineers who'd tortured and murdered at random. And hundreds of nameless others, soldiers, sailors, passengers – over three hundred had been on board when she'd foundered. He pictured them as he looked about the wrecked hulk that was the *Batavia*. He felt their panic and heard their screams.

He must go up, he told himself, this was foolish. His lungs were now bursting, and he was asking for problems shooting to the surface from twenty feet without depressurising. But what the hell, it wouldn't kill him, he'd wait just a moment longer.

He could see them now, their faces tormented, their screams ringing in his ears. Which voice, which face, he wondered, belonged to Jeronimus Cornelisz? Which one amongst them was the torturer, murderer, killer of children?

He stared at the faces that now came at him from every gloomy corner of the wreck. Men, women, children, terrified and tortured every one of them. He searched amongst them for the face of evil.

It was strange, his lungs were no longer at bursting point. In fact, he felt peculiarly at ease, as if he could stay for as long as he wished. As if he could breathe underwater.

It was then that the last vestige of common sense told him he was hallucinating. He was on the verge of drowning. He kicked away from the wreck and made for the surface, the voices behind him screaming for him to come back, screaming for him to save them. But the silvery glint of the sun was now screaming at him to save himself.

Closer and closer he came to the light. The sun was his life, but it was teasing him. It was so close and yet he was unable to reach it, his lungs once again bursting, panic setting in, a fist of iron clamping around his heart telling him he wasn't going to make it.

Tubby was keeping a watch out for the kid. He hadn't seen him for a while and he was wondering whether he should start to worry. Then he saw him break surface and breathed a sigh of relief. Silly of him to worry, the kid could swim like a fish. But his relief was short-lived. Something was wrong. The kid was clutching at his chest, gasping, his face contorted.

'Einstein!' Tubby yelled. And, sharks or no sharks, he hurled himself into the sea.

BOOK ONE

CHAPTER ONE

Young Michael McAllister could swim before he could walk. At least that was his mother's claim. 'He just crawled into the river one day and started swimming,' Maggie would say. 'He was barely a year old.'

Three years later, Mike's baby sister, Julie, followed his lead. Literally. Baby Jools crawled across the sand into the river and dogpaddled out to her brother.

It wasn't really that extraordinary. Their father, Jim, was a boating man and a prodigious swimmer himself. His children, like many youngsters brought up by the banks of the river, were born to the water, and throughout the years of their childhood the river would continue to serve as a never-ending playground.

For hours, Mike and Jools and their mates would chuck bombies off the end of the jetty, or hurl tennis balls with all their might out into the river and try to reach them before Baxter, the McAllisters' two-year-old black Labrador, beat them to it. It was some time before they met with success – Baxter was an obsessive ball-chaser and a powerful swimmer. There were also the repeated attempts to break the record of eight aboard the inflated tractor-tyre inner tube, an exercise that met with no success at all. But as the children grew older, Baxter would concede defeat, the tractor tube would be replaced by dinghies and sailing boats, and the competition would begin in earnest.

The McAllister home, a rambling old colonial house, fronted on to Victoria Avenue and sloped down the hill to Freshwater Bay, with Claremont jetty to its right and, further along the beach, the old Claremont swimming baths to its left.

Built in the latter part of the nineteenth century, during the early development of the area, the house had seen better days, but it had a ramshackle elegance. Deceptive in design, it appeared from the street to be a single-storey bungalow with surrounding verandahs, but steps at the rear led from the balcony, which overlooked the river, to a below-stairs area that had once been the 'batman's quarters'. The original owner had been a military man. The 'batman's quarters' now housed mainly storage space along with a large playroom, Jim's extensive workshop and a laundry.

The house's sprawling back garden was abundant with fruit trees and grape vines, and a large vegetable plot yielded corn, tomatoes, beans or peas according to the season. Beyond the garden was a flat grassy area with an open boatshed where the dinghy and tackle was stored, and beyond the boatshed was the Swan River where, fifty yards from shore, Jim's modest twenty-four-foot yacht, *Alana*, named after his mother, rested peacefully on her mooring.

It was a comfortable home that offered a comfortable lifestyle. Perth was a sleepy town in the fifties, and there were many such homes along the banks of the river, providing an idyllic childhood for those like Mike and Jools.

On hot summer nights Mike and his best mate, Spud Farrell, who was in the same class at school, would trawl for prawns. They wore old sandshoes to protect themselves from cobbler stings, and Spud's brother Billy, two years younger, carried a hurricane lamp. Wooden poles over their shoulders, Mike and Spud would drag the twenty-foot funnel of netting behind them, while Billy led the way, the lamplight attracting the prawns to the net and warning the boys of snags up ahead. Relentlessly, they trawled between the jetty and the baths; it was hard work but rewarding. Each time they returned to the beach Jools would be jumping up and down excitedly, Baxter by her side letting out the odd bark, both of them eager for the thrilling moment when the contents would be spilled from the net's pocket onto the sand and the prawns would jump and glitter, pink-eyed, in the light of the lamp.

Jools was always allocated 'guard duty'. She wasn't strong enough to haul the net and too young to be trusted with the lamp, but Mike had assured her of the importance of her role. 'Someone could come along and nick our catch,' he told her, and so, during their absence, she paraded the beach like a diminutive pig-tailed sergeant major. Upon the boys' return, she and Baxter had a tendency to get over-excited and Mike had to constantly warn her, as they sifted through the weed and gobbleguts and other small fish, to keep Baxter away and to be wary of cobblers. The stings of even the smallest cobblers occasionally caught in the net were shockingly painful.

The boys would boil up the prawns in the laundry's old copper, and after they'd feasted there was always an ample supply for both the McAllister and Farrell households. Mike invariably gave Spud the lion's share though – there were five Farrell kids so it seemed only fair.

The old copper came in for a great deal of use. The blue manna crabs that Mike and Jools caught at dusk in their witch's-hat drop nets off the end of Claremont jetty ended up in the copper. So did the mussels they dived for during the baking hot afternoons of midsummer, when others were indoors beside fans praying for the arrival of the Fremantle Doctor – the welcome afternoon breeze that came in from the sea.

The mussels, which grew in abundant clusters on the pylons of the jetty, were Jim McAllister's personal favourite. When the children returned with their catch, he'd pour himself a glass of beer and join them, hauling a bucketload of steaming mussels from the copper and emptying them out in a heap onto the old wrought-iron table that lived in the back garden and served the specific and ingenious purpose of mussel strainer.

Jim always made his own contribution to the exercise, mixing the vinegar and mussel juice in the pickling jars, and concocting a hot dipping sauce which the kids avoided like the plague. They'd sit around the table, each with a pickling jar, and Mike and Jim would do their best to ignore Jools who always insisted on chanting 'One for me, one for the pot', and was quick to catch her father out if he ate two in a row without contributing to his pickling jar. Not that it mattered. By the time they'd pickled and eaten their way through the first lot they were bloated, and the second bucketload from the copper was purely for pickling.

The old copper had proved very efficient over the years. Maggie had gladly donated it in order to preserve her kitchen from the stench of seafood and the assault of grey gunge boiling out of huge pots over her stove. By then she'd acquired her brand new washing machine with its labour-saving hand-operated wringer, so she didn't need the old copper.

Jim McAllister was not a wealthy man. He was an agriculturalist employed by the government, and the comfortable middle-class existence he provided for his wife and children was the direct result of hard work. He'd put a deposit on the old house shortly before his marriage with a small inheritance he'd received from his grandparents, and after that it had been his own labours and Maggie's clever budgeting that had paid it off.

A stalwart member of Claremont Yacht Club and a keen

yachtsman, Jim was also a talented carpenter, and boat-building had become his leisure-time passion. *Alana*, his pride and joy, was the result of a year's relentless weekend labour, and he raced her regularly in the CYC meets. But, unlike many a boating man, Jim shared his yacht with his family. *Alana* had provided successful Christmas holidays at Rottnest Island for the past several years, despite the cramped living accommodation aboard, and her mooring at Rotto's Thomson Bay had become the McAllisters' annual retreat.

Jim was currently applying his boat-building skills to the restoration of a dilapidated second-hand Vee Jay he'd acquired for his son. Mike would soon be twelve, and twelve was a good age for a boy to have a racing yacht.

Jim and Maggie McAllister were caring parents, but they weren't physically demonstrative. It wasn't the nature of either to cuddle and cosset their children, and Jim could at times be a strict disciplinarian. He was rarely unfair and rarely lost his temper, but when true disobedi-ence demanded retribution he believed in corporal pun-ishment. That was when the slim bamboo stick, which remained threateningly on top of the wardrobe, came into play. It was pliable and whip-like, and several smart blows to the bended backside, even through clothes, delivered a hefty sting. But Jim wasn't without a sense of humour. The day the kids nicked the stick and replaced it with the rolled-up and firmly taped newspaper that was reserved for Baxter when he was going through one of his chewing or digging phases, and which made a heck of a racket but didn't hurt, Jim allowed himself to see the funny side.

Maggie McAllister, far less conventional than her husband, had a very clearly defined sense of humour. She was not a water baby herself, and remained seated on a deckchair under a large-brimmed hat reading a book while her husband and children cavorted in the river or the sea.

Nor was she a boating person, and steadfastly refused to adopt the jargon. 'Port' and 'starboard' remained 'left' and 'right', 'aft' and 'forward' were the 'blunt end' and the 'pointy end', and the galley, the cabin and the head were the kitchen, bedroom and toilet respectively. It became a running family gag, and Maggie enjoyed being the butt of the joke during the annual holidays at Rotto, which was the only time she ever set foot on *Alana*.

An attractive woman, she'd been a dedicated teacher, but had given up her career to raise a family, as most of her contemporaries had done. But unlike her contemporaries, she'd returned to work when her children were both of school age. 'Relief teaching – just three days a week,' she'd assured her husband. Jim, a conservative man, had found his wife's decision confronting at first, but he hadn't stood in her way. Maggie was a clever and imaginative woman who needed mental stimulation, and he decided to ignore the odd critically raised eyebrow and admire her for her independent spirit.

Maggie instilled her own form of discipline in her children by appealing to their basic common sense.

'Wendy Halliday's mum chops it up fine.' Nine-year-old Jools was propped against the kitchen's Laminex-topped island bench, chin on fists, critically watching her mother tear up the lettuce.

'Oh dear, I suppose that makes me a bad mum.'

'Well, no . . .' That hadn't been exactly what Jools had meant.

'It's a pity they don't teach you how to be a mum. I wonder if I could start taking lessons?'

'I just meant that –'

'Mind you, there are probably quite a lot of different ways to make a salad when you consider it. What do *you* think, Jools?'

Jools pondered the question, which had been offered in all seriousness, and, as she viewed the array of salads and herbs on the kitchen bench, she also pondered the options it raised.

'Yep,' she said. 'I bet there'd be lots and lots of different ways.'

The quickly developing independent streak in Jools came directly from her mother.

Jim McAllister's effect upon his children, apart from his disciplinary measures, was by example. He was an accomplished man. Heralded during his university days as a sportsman, he'd retained his fitness, and at forty could defeat men half his age on a tennis court. Furthermore, he was academically respected. One of the government's leading agriculturalists, he was currently working on the Ord River Scheme, the audacious and innovative irrigation system intended to cultivate the arid north of the state. Jim was an all-rounder, good at anything he tackled, and it rubbed off on his children. They wanted to be able to swim like Dad, and to handle a boat like Dad, and to gather mussels from down deep just like Dad did. They'd been emulating him from their earliest years.

Now that Mike had turned twelve, and was about to embark the following year upon his secondary school education, he wanted more than ever to emulate his father. He wanted to do important work, work that really meant something, work like his dad did.

'I'm going to be a scientist.'

'You mean space rockets and all that sort of stuff?' Spud Farrell was impressed.

It was lunchtime and, having kicked the footie around, the boys were sitting on one of the benches in the school's gravel playground, empty lunchboxes beside them, swigging back the remnants of their milk. The miniature bottles were doled out at midday and were always lukewarm, particularly on a hot summer's day like today. But the kids drank them uncomplainingly nonetheless.

Claremont Primary School was a couple of blocks from the McAllister house, in Bay View Terrace, which led up the hill to the suburb's village centre. Its location was even more convenient for Spud, who lived just around the corner in Pennell Road.

The boys had been discussing their forthcoming exams. The students of sixth standard A were to sit for the Perth Modern School state-wide scholarship and entrance examinations, which were held every year. Perth Modern School, or 'Mod' as it was known, took the top sixty boys and top sixty girls across the state into their seventh standard. It was the beginning of secondary school and serious stuff, and the boys' conversation had progressed to ambition. Spud's was simple – he wanted to be rich.

'No, not rockets,' Mike corrected him. 'I'm going to be a scientist, like my dad.'

'But your dad works for the Department of Agriculture.'

Spud's tone was dismissive and Mike couldn't help but register it.

'Yeah, but he's still a scientist,' he protested.

There was a pause. Spud's scepticism was so obvious that Mike took offence.

'He is so! You should do your homework, Spud,' he said as scathingly as possible. 'Agriculture's a science, you know.'

'All right, all right, keep your hair on.' Spud backed away, hands in the air in mock surrender, a look of wounded surprise on his face. 'Strewth, I didn't even *say* anything, there's no need to jump down my throat.'

His reaction was so successfully that of the wrongfully accused that Mike felt guilty, just as Spud intended he should.

'Sorry,' he muttered, aware that he'd over-reacted, but still smarting at Spud's inferred slur upon his dad.

'Cripes, Mikey, I wouldn't say anything against your old man.' Spud chose a different tack. 'Your dad's a top bloke.' Manipulative as he was, Spud was genuinely keen to make amends. Mikey McAllister was his best mate – heck, they were so close that he was the only one allowed to call him Mikey, and that really meant something.

'I only wish my old man was more like him,' he said, and this time it wasn't altogether an act. Not that he'd swap his old man for Mr McAllister – well, not when the old man was halfway sober, anyway – but cripes, look at what Mikey had! That great big house, holidays at Rotto on his dad's yacht, and his old man had just given him a Vee Jay for his twelfth birthday! Whether Mr McAllister qualified as a real scientist or not – and Spud was doubtful of the fact – the bloke was one heck of a dad. 'My old man could take a leaf out of your dad's book,' he added, 'and that's the truth.'

Spud had been two years old when his family had emigrated from Ireland and he was a dinky-di Aussie – all the Farrells were, they'd embraced citizenship and were proudly Australian – but Spud had adopted quite a few of his father's phrases, and on occasion sounded very like Sean Farrell himself.

Mike was tempted to call Spud's bluff and tell him to stop bunging on. He admired his friend's talent as a con man – it had got them out of trouble on many an occasion – but he didn't like it when Spud practised his talents on him, which he suspected might be the case right now. But then he couldn't be sure. It was often the way with Spud – it was hard to tell sometimes when he was conning and when he wasn't, even for Mike, and they were best mates, which, he supposed, showed just how clever Spud was. But for all Spud's cleverness, Mike sometimes felt sorry for him. Spud did it hard. An early morning paper run before school, babysitting his little sister every Saturday while his mum and his older brother and sister worked, and a dad who was drunk most of the time. Spud's wasn't an easy life.

Mike decided against confrontation and changed the subject instead, reverting to their original discussion about the entrance exams.

'So do you reckon we'll get in?' he asked, ignoring Spud and picking up the footie that sat on the bench beside him, bouncing it idly between his knees on the pavement.

Spud, aware that he couldn't get around Mikey as well as he could others, was grateful that he'd been let off the hook. He really hadn't meant to insult Mikey's dad. Heck, Mikey idolised his old man.

'Sure we will,' he replied with his cheekily irresistible grin. Snub-nosed, freckle-faced and ginger-haired, Spud could be very beguiling. 'If anyone can get us through, you can bet your last quid Mr Logan can.'

Mr Logan was a sure-fire topic for conversation. The one-eyed ex-POW, survivor of Changi, the infamous Japanese prison camp in Singapore, was a hero to every boy in his class.

Colin Logan made a habit of sharing his wartime experiences with his students. He'd tell his stories to each new classroom of pupils who came under his tuition. Never in a gruesome way, and nor was he boastful – his stories were often funny, invariably informative and always downright compelling. He had his pupils eating out of his hand, and he knew it. Colin Logan was a born teacher.

Spud's and Mike's altercation was forgotten as they talked about the forthcoming exams. Mr Logan had them all fired up.

'There's not one among you,' he'd assured his students of sixth standard A, and he'd taken a slight dramatic pause, 'not one who isn't capable of making the grade and getting into Perth Mod. It's simply a matter of application and hard work.'

'I reckon he's right, Mikey,' Spud said, with a self-assurance he didn't really feel. 'Mr Logan wouldn't try and con us.'

Spud's doubts were not of Mr Logan, but rather of himself. He wouldn't be able to cheat his way through these exams as he had so often in the past, and even at his tender age he realised this was a defining moment in his life. He needed to get into Mod, it was his only chance. And he needed a full scholarship what was more, other-wise he'd be doing the paper run full-time, or working as a brickie's labourer like his big brother Eamon. And he sure as hell didn't want to finish up at the Swan Brewery like his dad, washing out the beer kegs and replacing the old seals with new ones. That was the end of the line in Spud's opinion. Not that his old man thought so. Sean Farrell thought his job was the best thing since sliced bread. Well, he would, wouldn't he? The brewery turned on free beer for its ten-minute morning and arvo smokos, and for another ten minutes at lunch break too. No wonder his old man was in seventh heaven.

''Tis a God-given job, Eileen,' his dad'd say to his mum when he came home via the pub, pissed as an owl and happy as a pig in shite. 'What other employer would so appreciate its workers?' And then he'd regale the whole family with tales about his buddies at work and the jokes he'd heard that day, omitting the filthiest ones for the sake of the kids. Spud had to admit that although his dad was a drunk, he was always a happy one. People liked Sean Farrell, they found him funny. Spud did too. His dad was always good for a laugh, but it didn't stop him being a loser.

'He's a good man, your da,' his mother would say when she sensed her son's disapproval. 'He's grand with you kids and he's never laid a hand on me in anger. You've no cause for criticism, Patrick.' She always called him Patrick when she was ticking him off and Spud hated it. 'You could do a lot worse than your da, you know.'

Eileen herself knew only too well. Both her sisters back in the old country did it a lot worse than she did. One had a husband who beat her when he was on the grog, and the other had no husband at all – Seamus had run off and left Mary with four kids just a year back. Eileen sent her a bit of money every now and then, from the wages she earned cleaning the houses of the rich who lived around the bay in Peppermint Grove.

The Farrells had emigrated from Ireland shortly after the war. The Australian government's call for migrants and its ten-pound Bring Out a Briton campaign had been an offer too good to refuse for many who were feeling the hardship of post-war Britain. Sean and Eileen, together with their three children, of whom Spud was the youngest, had been housed at the migrant hostel in Bicton on Point Walter Reserve, the other side of the bay from Claremont. But when Sean had scored his job at the brewery, they'd moved across the river to the little rented cottage in Pennell Road. From there it was just a short walk up the hill to the Stirling Highway and the regular buses which, en route to the city, passed the imposing brick edifice of the Swan Brewery where it sat on the banks of the river in Crawley.

Eileen had been happy with the move. She loved the cottage with its verandah and tiny front garden. She'd never had a garden before, or a verandah for that matter – they didn't exist in the back streets of Dublin. But after Billy's birth two years later, with their finances stretched to the limit, she'd told Sean they were to practise the rhythm method in order to avoid another pregnancy. 'If God considers it a sin, then so be it,' she'd said defiantly, more for her own benefit than her husband's. Sean was a lackadaisical, if not altogether lapsed, Catholic who only went to church to keep his wife happy. Their birth-control strategy had worked for a good seven years, until 1953 when a mishap had occurred, resulting in baby Caitlin. But by that time, Eamon, the oldest of the boys, was fourteen and had left school to work for a mate of Sean's who had a milk delivery truck, so there was an added income to the household. And it wouldn't be long before twelve-year-old Maeve opted out of school. Maeve had her mind set on working in a shop.

Neither Sean Farrell nor his wife had received a secondary education themselves, and although they didn't urge their children to leave school and seek employment, they saw no problem if that was what the kids wanted. But Spud did. Spud saw a huge problem. His brother Eamon was sixteen now, a bricklayer's apprentice with no ambition beyond being good at his job. 'Brickies are always in demand,' he'd boast to Spud. 'You can earn a big quid if you're good.' And fifteen-year-old Maeve now served behind the counter at the Claremont newsagency. Her sole aim in life was to be a shop assistant in Boans Department Store in the city where she'd get to wear a snazzy uniform. Spud had set his sights far higher than his siblings. He was going to be rich and successful. At what, he wasn't sure. But the way to success was through education. And the way to education was a scholarship to Perth Mod.

For the first time in his short life, Spud had truly applied himself. He'd received special encouragement from Colin Logan, who believed it his duty to inspire the under-privileged to seek an education, and who secretly had a soft spot for the canny little Irish-Australian.

'You're a smart boy, Spud,' he'd said. 'You could land a full scholarship if you tried.' A scholarship was the kid's only option, Colin knew it. There was no way his parents could afford school fees. 'But you'll have to study hard. No bludging. No trying to take the easy way out.' The one eye had flashed a distinct warning – Colin had never caught the kid openly cheating, but he'd had his doubts.

'Yes, sir.' And Spud had studied as hard as he knew how.

'I dunno about the others, Mikey,' he now said with his customary bravado, 'but you and me, we'll get in, no two ways about it. Like my old man says, *carpe diem*.' His dad had picked up the expression in some pub somewhere. 'It's Latin,' Sean Farrell had boasted to his son, 'means "seize the day",' and Spud had adopted the expression ever since.

Spud was really firing himself up more than Mikey. What did it matter if Mikey didn't get in? Mikey didn't need Mod, his parents could afford to send him to private school. Heck, they already had him booked into his dad's old school, Scotch College. The only reason Mikey was sitting for the entrance exams was because his mum had gone to Mod, and his dad reckoned that she'd had a better scholastic education than he had. 'Dad reckons Mod offers the best education in the state,' Mikey had said. Jeez, Mikey had it easy.

Spud was envious, but not bitter. It was a simple fact of life: there were the 'haves' and the 'have nots', and he was one of the latter. But he didn't mind firing Mikey up. Mikey was his mate and, besides, they were always best when they worked as a team.

'We're winners we are, you and me,' he said.

Spud proved right about a number of things that summer. He was right about Mr Logan getting them through. Ten students from Colin Logan's class found their way to Perth Modern School the following year. The previous record for Claremont Primary entrants had been five.

The grateful students of sixth standard A, knowing their hero to be an inveterate smoker, pooled their resources and bought him a Ronson cigarette lighter, which Maggie McAllister took to the jewellers and had personally engraved.

'I told you we were winners, Mikey,' Spud said. He'd been right about that too. He and Mike McAllister had been amongst the ten selected. But it had been Spud who had won the full scholarship. And he hadn't cheated once!

'Look out, Mod, here we come,' he crowed. Spud Farrell was on his way.

Chapter Two

At nearly fifteen, Mike and Spud were obsessed with sex, or rather with the thought of it: neither had actually performed the act yet. But it was only a matter of time. They talked at great length about losing their virginity, and Spud had definite views on the subject. Their female contemporaries at Perth Mod were out of the question in his opinion. 'Too young,' he said with a worldly wisdom. And the final-year female students, the objects of both boys' lust, were simply out of their league.

'A woman outside of school – older, and with experience – that's what we need,' he declared. 'You shouldn't pick a virgin first time round anyway. Best to set your sights on one who knows the ropes.' It was a direct quote from his old man.

The fact was, Spud was getting desperate. He'd tried to score with any number of girls at Mod but he'd rarely got beyond the kissing stage, and that was only with the younger ones who were interested in their own form of experimentation and saw him as a fellow innocent. They'd been shocked when his hands had groped at their budding breasts. And when, in a reckless attempt, he'd tried to chat up one of the older students, she'd told him to get lost.

Spud hadn't changed much since he was twelve, not in the physical sense anyway. His mind had certainly matured, he was well advanced for his age mentally, but in appearance he was younger than his contemporaries. He was below average height, his body hadn't yet filled out, and he remained the snub-nosed, freckle-faced boy he'd always been. It annoyed the hell out of him when girls called him Smiley after that simpering kid in that puke-making picture.

He envied Mikey. Mikey had been shaving for a whole year now, and Spud didn't even have bum-fluff on his chin. Mikey was already as tall as the final-year blokes and he had a body to match. He could easily pass for seventeen – eighteen even. Christ, Mikey had it made. The girls thought he looked like Tony Curtis, not bloody Smiley. If Mikey hadn't been his best friend, Spud could easily have grown to hate him.

But Mikey *was* his best friend, wasn't he? And they'd always been a team. If he stuck with Mikey, Spud thought, he was bound to get lucky. Mikey attracted the girls like flies to shite, as his old man would say. At the bowling alley or the Claremont footy club, away from Mod and out of school uniform, Mikey had no trouble conning girls about his age. Hell, he'd nearly made it all the way with that bird Jeannette after the Saturday night jazz session at the Dalkeith Hall. And she had to be at least seventeen.

'Yep,' Spud said, 'I reckon we should aim for older women. What do you say?'

'I reckon you're right.'

Mike knew exactly what Spud was after, but he wasn't prepared to pave the way for his mate and risk crippling his own chances. This was one time when he and Spud weren't a team, he'd decided. It was each man for himself, and Mike had his own plans, which involved Hilary, the new teller at the Claremont post office. Hilary was nineteen, blonde and sexy as all get out. He'd been flirting

with her for a whole month now, and she'd agreed to go
to the pictures with him this Saturday night. But he wasn't
about to tell Spud that. Spud'd probably front up at the
pictures and blow his cover. Not deliberately, of course,
but he'd blow it simply by being there.

'You're a bit young for me, aren't you?' Hilary eyed the kid
up and down. God, but he was handsome. He'd come in
to the post office a number of times since she'd been
working there – buying a few penny stamps, flirting with
her outrageously – and now he was asking her to the
pictures. 'How old are you? Seventeen?'

'Eighteen.' Mike decided to go for broke. 'I'm off to uni
next year.'

'Really?'

It had worked, he could tell she was impressed.

'So what do you say? Want to come to the pictures?'

'Why not?' Hilary's casual shrug successfully masked a
faint shimmer of excitement. She normally preferred men
in their twenties, they had more style, but heck, if a bloke
was this good-looking what did it matter if he was a bit
younger? And a uni student too!

'How about the Windsor?' Mike kept his eyes intently
trained upon hers, for fear they might stray towards the
dramatic cones of her breasts, which were pointing,
machine-gun-like, at him through her tight knitted top.
'*Bus Stop*'s on at the Windsor.'

He'd decided to opt for the cinema in Dalkeith. In Claremont, everyone knew everyone, and if he chose the local
just down the road he was asking for trouble. Besides,
Marilyn Monroe was in *Bus Stop* – although he doubted
whether he'd be watching Marilyn if Hilary was sitting
beside him. She might not be up to Marilyn's standard, but
hell, Hilary was the real thing! The breasts and blonde hair
and big red lips were flesh and blood, not a fantasy up on
the screen.

But she shook her head. 'I've seen *Bus Stop*,' she said. 'Why don't we go to the open-air pictures? I love the deckchairs, and *Trapeze* is on. They say it's terrific.'

'Sure,' he agreed with a nonchalant grin. Damn, he thought. The open-air pictures meant Claremont.

Spud was suspicious when Mikey said he wasn't coming bowling with the gang that Saturday night. Fairlane, the brand new ten-pin bowling alley in Adelaide Terrace, was a great place to meet girls.

'I'm studying,' Mike said. 'Exams next week, remember?'

'Studying!' Nobody studied on a Saturday night. 'You're *studying*?'

It was a pretty lame excuse and Mike knew it, but he hadn't been able to come up with anything else. He and Spud always spent Saturday nights together.

'Yep,' he said firmly, and Spud walked off in a huff, convinced that Mikey had something lined up and wasn't letting him in on the action. Mikey was a bloody awful liar.

Mike and Hilary met outside the Claremont open-air picture theatre.

'You wait here, and I'll get the tickets,' he said as they stepped into the foyer. He could see old Tom Russell in his customary position behind the counter.

'G'day, Mike,' Tom said jovially, looking up at him – crikey, but the boy had grown this past year or so. 'Spud not with you?' He was surprised. Young Mike McAllister and his mate Spud Farrell were normally joined at the hip.

'Not tonight, Mr Russell,' Mike muttered. 'Two tickets, thanks,' and he put his money on the counter.

'One child, one adult, is it?' Tom asked, peering over Mike's shoulder at Hilary, who had taken her lippie from her clutch bag and was doing a quick touch-up.

'Yeah.' Mike focused on the spidery hands as they care-

fully tore off two tickets from two different-coloured rolls
– one for the grown-ups and one for the children.

'Got yourself a new girlfriend, have you?' A bit of a
wink, harmless, just a joke.

Mike gave him a sickly grin and bought a box of Jaffas.
He wished to hell they'd gone to the Windsor.

As they walked to the open-air auditorium with its well-
trodden grass and its sea of canvas deckchairs, he surreptitiously slipped the tickets to the usherette, careful to hide
them from Hilary so that she wouldn't notice the different
colours. Then he took her boldly by the hand and led her
up the back.

Hilary didn't mind. She knew what the seats up the back
signified, and she stowed her clutch bag under her deckchair and settled herself comfortably.

It was still half-light, and while they watched the ads
and then the trailers, they sat in silence, sucking away the
sugar coating of their Jaffas, but Mike wasn't tasting
the chocolate inside. Only six months previously, if it had
been an indoor picture theatre and he'd been with Spud,
he'd have been rolling the lollies down the aisle like all the
kids did. But Jaffas were the last thing on his mind tonight.

As dusk faded and the Movietone News started, he
quietly slipped the box of lollies under his chair. He
reached out and took Hilary's hand, and his heart
pounded wildly as he felt her fingers entwine with his.

Mike had taken girls to the pictures before and he'd
discovered that indoor theatres were better than outdoor.
You could drape your arm around the back of the seat and
your hand could casually creep over the girl's shoulder,
and if she didn't react, you could let it rest there, sometimes teasingly close to her breast. You couldn't do the
same thing with deckchairs. But tonight was different.
Hilary was not a fourteen-year-old school girl, she was the
real McCoy, and the deckchairs were working to Mike's
advantage. His hand, linked with hers, was resting on her

knee, and she was bare-legged beneath the flimsy cotton skirt. The proximity of her naked skin was unbelievably tantalising.

Tom and Jerry came and went, and the support feature started – a black and white British comedy with Alec Guinness and the regular Ealing line-up – and Hilary made no objection when, ostensibly seeking a more comfortable position in his deckchair, Mike's hand moved a little higher up her thigh, her own hand moving with it. He frantically considered what his next move should be, but all of a sudden she started guffawing and rocking about in her chair. Hilary adored Terry-Thomas. And then she disengaged hands to light up a cigarette, so Mike decided to save his move for the main feature.

During interval he went off to buy them a couple of Smacks while Hilary made a quick trip to the ladies. He would normally have bought the threepenny tubs rather than the expensive chocolate-coated ice-creams, but as he forked over two sixpences he didn't give a damn that tonight was costing him a whole week's pocket money. He'd do anything to impress her.

Back in their seats and half an hour later, with the Smacks demolished and the film well under way, he once again reached out and took her hand. Again, his mind could encompass little other than the thought of the naked skin beneath her skirt, but for the first time since they'd entered the cinema, he found himself taking in what was happening on the screen. Gina Lollobrigida had to be the sexiest woman on the planet, he thought. And what an excellent choice *Trapeze* had been – it was one of the hottest pictures he'd ever seen, a real turn-on. He stole a glance at Hilary. Was it having the same effect on her? It appeared to be. She was gazing at the screen mesmerised, her mouth slightly open, lips glistening invitingly, and through her thin skirt he could feel the warmth of her thigh. He wondered whether he dared relinquish his hold on her hand and make direct contact with her skin as he desperately wanted to.

He sat motionless. Up on screen, Tony Curtis was about to kiss Gina Lollobrigida. Jeez, he thought, they looked as if they were on heat, the two of them. Then, beneath his hand, he felt Hilary's thigh move as she wriggled slightly in her deckchair. He glanced at her again. She remained, as before, mesmerised, her focus solely on Tony and Gina who were now hungrily feeding off each other. Then she gave another slight wriggle.

He swivelled his body in the deckchair and leaned forward to kiss her neck. It seemed safer to start there – if she pulled away from him then he'd immediately back off. But she didn't pull away. She turned to him instead, and the open mouth and glistening lips he'd been admiring were suddenly devouring him, just like Gina and Tony up on the screen.

Mike was on fire. They both were. He could feel the whole of her mouth, her tongue and her teeth, and she made no protest as he freed his left hand from hers and found his way beneath her skirt. Far from it. She was clutching at him, running her fingers over his chest and his shoulders, just the way Gina had been doing to Tony. Mike's right hand sought frantically from one rigid pointy breast to the other, desperate for the feel of flesh beneath the formidable brassiere, but to no avail. He started to lift the knitted top from the waistband of her skirt.

Then, as quickly as she'd initiated the action, Hilary called a halt. She pulled away from him, adjusting her skirt and top, and sat back in her deckchair, her breathing a little laboured but her eyes once more steadily focused upon the screen.

Mike, forced to follow her lead, also sat back, fiercely willing his erection to disappear, and both remained eyes front, no bodily contact, throughout the rest of the film, conscious of other couples in clinches in nearby deckchairs.

'It was terrific, wasn't it?' Hilary said, as the credits started to roll and the shadowy shapes of people moved towards exits, beating a hasty retreat before the lights came up and the general exodus started.

'Yep.' Mike had forgotten the picture. He'd even forgotten Gina Lollobrigida. All he could think of was the pashing session and whether she'd let him go further. Was tonight the night it was going to happen? How was he to go about it? Where could he take her?

'All of my girlfriends who've seen it told me it was terrific.'

Her girlfriend Maureen had told her that *Trapeze* was sexy and that she had the hots for Tony Curtis. Well, Hilary thought, Maureen hadn't been wrong. God, she'd been turned on. She'd surprised herself, she shouldn't have allowed it to go that far. A bit of a cuddle was all right, but groping like that . . . and on a first date. Crikey, she'd been so hot and ready she could have done it right there and then.

'Shall we go?' she said, picking up her clutch bag and making a move in her chair, about to join the shadowy figures.

'No hurry.' Mike wanted to race out of the cinema right now. He'd thought of the boatshed – the perfect place if he could get her there. He'd ask her to go for a walk by the river, and then he'd take her to the boatshed at the back of the house. But he'd seen the Brown brothers, Len and Brucie, rising from their chairs two rows down. Len was in his class at school. He couldn't afford to bump into one of his mates on the way out. 'Let's wait until the rush dies down,' he suggested.

'Oh. Right then.' Hilary settled back and contemplated lighting up another cigarette.

He sensed she was a little restless, so he took her hand again, half-expecting she might withdraw it, but she didn't. Then the lights came up and he smiled winningly, praying that she'd forgive him for having groped her, and praying that she'd let him do it again.

My God, she thought. The heavy-lashed, earnestly boyish eyes – she'd just seen them up on the screen. 'You look like him,' she said.

'Who?'

'Hasn't anybody ever told you?'

'What?'

'You look like Tony Curtis.'

'Really?' Jeannette had told him exactly the same thing the night he'd nearly scored with her. He didn't think he looked at all like Tony Curtis. Tony Curtis was a bit girlie, he thought – he'd much rather look like Burt Lancaster. But if it turned girls on – as it had Jeannette, until she'd discovered he was only fourteen – then he was more than prepared to go along with it.

'Tony Curtis, eh?' He looked impressed. 'Gosh.' And he smiled again.

God, he was sexy, Hilary thought.

'Come on,' he said several minutes later. The theatre had rapidly emptied and, having scanned the faces of the few remaining, he could see no-one he knew.

But as soon as they stepped into the foyer, he ran into trouble.

'Young Mike McAllister!' It was Mrs Hewson, chatting to old Tom Russell. 'My goodness, haven't you grown.' Molly Hewson eyed him up and down. She'd seen the boy only about nine months ago and he'd been a big lad for his age then, but my goodness, she thought, he must be nearly six foot now. 'I'd hardly have recognised you –'

'G'day, Mrs Hewson. Good to see you after all these years.' Mike grabbed Hilary by the hand and bolted, leaving Molly Hewson in a state of bewilderment.

'What was that all about?' Hilary asked.

'Silly old bat. She hasn't seen me for five years. You want to walk down to the river?'

'Sure,' she shrugged, and they strolled hand in hand through the balmy night down Bay View Terrace towards the jetty.

'Shall we go out to the end?' she asked when they got there.

'Nah, let's walk along the beach.'

He headed off to the left, and Hilary followed obligingly, taking off her sandals and relishing the feel of the sand between her naked toes.

'Do you want a ciggie?' she asked, delving in her clutch bag.

'Yeah, thanks.'

He didn't, but he took a cigarette from the packet she proffered him, and produced a lighter from his top pocket. It had been Spud's suggestion that he always have a lighter at the ready whether he smoked or not. 'Girls like it, mate,' he'd said. Spud was already a seasoned smoker. Mike didn't much care for cigarettes, although he'd practised diligently in order not to look like a novice.

Heads together, hands shielding the flame from the light breeze off the water, they lit up, then sat side by side on the sand looking out at the river, dark and dappled in the moonlight.

'It's beautiful,' Hilary said.

'Yep.'

They were silent for a moment, and Hilary, listening to the gentle lap of the waves licking the shore, thought how romantic it was and wondered when he'd kiss her again. She wouldn't let it get out of hand like she had in the pictures though. She rarely did it on a first date, it was a rule of hers.

Mike wasn't listening to the lap of the waves or feeling the romance of the moment. He was aware that they were only twenty yards from his home and the boatshed. He stubbed his half-smoked cigarette out in the sand and waited impatiently for her to finish hers.

'That's my dad's boat,' he said, making conversation so that she wouldn't sense his restiveness. He pointed at *Alana*, silhouetted and bobbing on her mooring barely fifty yards away.

'Is it?' She turned to him, eyes wide. 'Really?'

'Yeah, really. He built her himself. She's called *Alana*, after my grandmother.'

'Gosh.' Hilary looked back at the yacht. She hadn't known that people built boats. Not that she'd given it much thought, but she'd presumed they came out of factories, like cars. 'That's fantastic.' She took a final drag and dug her cigarette butt into the sand. 'Really fantastic.'

'I can show you where he built it.'

The words sounded juvenile and clumsy, and he cursed himself. He'd rushed things, she must surely guess what he was thinking. But her look was blank.

'I live just there.' He pointed along the beach.

'You live right by the river?' That was even more impressive than the home-made boat.

'Yeah, come on and I'll show you.'

She picked up her purse and sandals and he helped her to her feet.

There was no rear gate to the McAllister property, just a gap in the bamboo where the sand led directly to the grass, and the grass led directly to the boatshed. The narrow strip of bamboo that grew along much of the foreshore protected the privacy of a number of riverside homes, and like many other property owners Jim McAllister had deemed it unnecessary to construct any further form of barricade.

'This is where Dad built *Alana*,' Mike said, leading her into the open boatshed. 'And he restored a Vee Jay for me too. There she is.'

In the half-gloom of the boatshed it was impossible to see the Vee Jay, which was buried beneath its tarpaulin anyway, but Mike was so bent on seduction that he wasn't thinking clearly.

'Wow,' Hilary said dutifully, presuming he was showing off and prepared to make the right response. But through the far end of the open boatshed she could see the shapes of trees and vines, which interested her far more. 'Can I look at the garden?' she asked, not waiting for an answer.

'Oh. Yeah. Right.'

Mike followed her as she walked in the direction of the house. Once past the grape vines she could be seen from the balcony, and his dad often sat out on the balcony in the late evening, having his nightcap and looking at the river. But she stopped at the grape vines. Old, with thick gnarled trunks and dripping with great clusters of as yet unripened fruit, the vines formed a perfect arbour, beyond which Hilary could see a rambling garden of fruit trees and grassy slopes.

'Oh,' she whispered. In the light of the moon, it was quite breathtaking.

She appeared entranced and it seemed the right moment to kiss her. Besides, he was emboldened by the need to stop her before she stepped out into full view of the house. His kiss was tentative at first, in case she feared that he'd grope her as he had in the cinema, and as he so urgently wanted to right now.

Hilary dropped her sandals and clutch bag. It was perfect. The grape vines and the moonlight and the fact that he looked like Tony Curtis. She responded with fervour.

They sank to the grass, Mike trying not to rush things, but, with an instant and raging erection, finding it difficult. He ran his hands over her breasts, but when he investigated beneath the knitted top, the brassiere appeared so impregnable that he quickly gave up, lifting her skirt instead, caressing her bare thigh, making his way upwards. He was glad there was no suspender belt anchoring the panties in place as had been the case with Jeannette. Jeannette hadn't let him get any further than this. 'Not now,' she'd said, as they'd pashed behind the Dalkeith Hall. 'Not now, not here,' – the suggestion being that another time and another place she'd let him go all the way. But she hadn't. The next time she'd seen him she'd cut him dead. She'd turned on her heel and walked away without a word. Someone had obviously blabbed.

Mike's senses were assailed by the taste and the touch and the very smell of Hilary. It was about to happen! God, he prayed, as his fingers slid beneath the crotch of her panties, don't let her stop me now. Please God, don't let her stop me now!

Hilary was aroused. Like there was no tomorrow, she realised as she felt his fingers slide beneath her panties. She was hot and wet and ready, and with her mouth still glued to his, she pulled up the knitted top, reached her hands behind her and unfastened her brassiere. As her breasts sprang free, Mike threw all caution to the wind, his right hand groping from one to the other while his left, which had been at her crotch, disappeared to struggle frantically with his trousers.

Hilary was aware that he seemed to be having some trouble, so she dived her own hand down to help him, slipping off her panties at the same time. They were fumbling now, both of them, flustered and urgent.

'Have you got a rubber?' she whispered.

'Eh?' Mike halted. He hadn't thought of a condom.

'Doesn't matter.' She grabbed her clutch bag and fossicked about. She didn't make a habit of doing it on a first date, but she always carried a rubber because you just never knew.

Hilary had been sexually active for the past three years, but she didn't consider herself promiscuous. Rather she was a modern woman. She had no intention of being married at twenty-one like her mum – a shotgun wedding, she was sure, although her mum had never said so – and then deserted at twenty-six with three kids to bring up on her own. Hilary was going to be a woman of the world, with lovers, and when she was thirty she was going to marry a rich bloke and settle into a life of luxury. Hilary had plans.

She found the condom and ripped the packet open with her teeth.

Mike couldn't see what she was doing, but suddenly her hands were on him and she was feeding the condom down the shaft of his rigid penis with great expertise. Then, before he knew it, she was guiding him into her as she lay back on the grass.

Any vestige of control deserted him as he felt himself engulfed. He moaned at the indescribable pleasure of it. A long, heart-felt, incredulous moan of euphoria. His penis felt like a lost soul that had finally found its way home. Then he started pumping for all he was worth.

Hilary was about to tell him to slow down. 'It's not a race,' she was going to say. But it was too late – he'd ejaculated.

'Oh,' she said as he lay panting over her. She had a nasty feeling that perhaps he'd been a virgin.

Mike rolled away from her onto his back and looked up at the stars, which seemed alarmingly bright as they glittered at him through the grape vines.

'Haven't you done it before?' she asked bluntly, doing up her brassiere and searching about for her panties. It was more an accusation than a question.

'Yeah.' Mike leaned up on one elbow, struggling to regain his breath. 'Tons of times.' He knew he'd rushed things and come far too fast, and that he should feel terrible for not having given her more pleasure, but he couldn't help it, he felt elated. He'd finally done it! And sex was every bit as wonderful as his wildest imaginings.

'I'm sorry, Hilary, I got too excited.' What would Spud say at a time like this, he wondered. 'I'm really, really sorry,' he said in all earnestness. 'But it's because you're so sexy, you see? You're such a turn-on – that's why I got carried away. It'll be better next time.'

The boost to her ego was some mollification, but Hilary wasn't sure if there'd be a next time. 'Yes, well, I have to go now.'

He walked her back along the beach and up the hill of Bay View Terrace to Stirling Highway where he waited half an hour with her for the late-night bus service. He kissed her again while they waited, but her response wasn't the same. She was guarded, and now that his euphoria had faded a little, Mike felt genuinely apologetic.

'It really will be better next time,' he whispered. 'I promise.'

Hilary reserved her judgement. 'We'll see,' she said primly, but agreed to go swimming with him at Cottesloe on Wednesday. She'd bring her bathers and meet him after work, she said.

It was half past one in the morning when Mike snuck quietly into his bedroom. His curfew was midnight on Saturdays, but his parents didn't wait up for him and it was unlikely they'd hear his return. His bedroom was a section of the side verandah that his dad had converted into a sleepout when Mike had first started at Mod. 'The boy's nearly a teenager,' Jim had said, 'he needs his own room for study and privacy.' Before that, Mike had shared a bedroom with Jools.

He lay on his back staring up at the ceiling. So that was what it felt like to be inside a woman! He wanted to relive the moment and relish the feeling, but there was no time, sleep was claiming him. His last waking thought was his promise to Hilary. Next time would be better, he'd make sure of it.

But there was no next time. At least, not with Hilary.

'Don't you come near me,' she hissed as he greeted her outside the post office on Wednesday. It was the same scathing look Jeannette had given him, and he knew in an instant. But how had she found out so soon? She didn't even live in Claremont!

Mike's expression of Tony Curtis-like boyish bewilderment infuriated Hilary, and she wasn't about to give him the satisfaction of knowing how she'd found out. It had actually been her friend, Maureen. On Sunday she'd boasted to Maureen that she'd been to the pictures the previous night with a bloke who looked just like Tony Curtis.

'*Trapeze*, what's more,' she'd said. 'And the lights came up and there I was looking at him! Tony Curtis, I swear it, and just as sexy!'

Hilary had drawn a personal veil over the fact that Mike hadn't been sexy at all when it had come to the crunch. She'd decided he was too good a prospect not to be given a second chance. But she wasn't going to tell Maureen she'd gone all the way on a first date. Not yet, anyway. Not until she was wearing Mike on her arm. Then, who knew, perhaps she'd boast about the fact that she'd set her sights on him and scored on the very first night.

'What's his name?' Maureen asked.

'Mike McAllister. He lives by the river and he's got his own boat, and I'm going swimming with him on Wednesday.'

Maureen worked in the haberdashery department of Boans in the city, and at her shift's morning tea break on Monday she'd told the girls that a friend of hers was going out with a Tony Curtis look-alike who lived by the river and had his own boat.

'Wow, what's his name?' someone asked.

'Mike McAllister.'

That was when Maeve Farrell, who worked the same shift but was in cosmetics, had dropped the bombshell. 'He's my little brother's best mate,' she'd said. 'He's fourteen.' And Maureen had rung Hilary that night. Perth was a very small place.

'If you tell anybody what happened, I'll say that you're a liar,' Hilary muttered. She didn't look angry now, she looked embarrassed and insecure. 'I could lose my job, you know.'

'I won't tell anyone.'

'And don't come to the post office any more,' she said. Then she walked off, head held high, maintaining her dignity but inwardly terrified that Mike would show off to his mates.

Mike did show off. Just to Spud. He couldn't resist.

'I've done it,' he said.

Spud didn't have to ask 'Done what?' There was something different about Mikey. He could see it in his face.

'You've had it off.' It wasn't a question.

'Yep.'

'Who with?'

But Mike refused to say.

'It's bullshit. You're lying. How am I s'posed to believe you've had a root if you won't say who with?' Spud tried every trick under the sun, but still Mike wasn't forthcoming, so he gave up the interrogation. 'What was it like?' he said instead.

'Fan-bloody-tastic!'

Spud was eaten alive with envy. It wasn't fair, Mikey got all the breaks. But if Mikey could score, then so could he, he told himself, and he set out to conquer with a renewed vigour. It only landed him in trouble. He was reported to the headmaster for touching up a final-year student and threatened with expulsion if it happened again.

The following year, Spud embarked upon a money-making scheme. His plan was simple. If he couldn't seduce a girl, he'd buy one. But he'd need at least double the going rate, he figured. For a prostitute to take on an underage client, he'd need to make it worth her while.

Hub caps started disappearing from luxury vehicles

parked in the wealthy areas of Peppermint Grove and Mosman. Mercedes-Benz fetched the best price, Spud found. He had a good contact in a wrecker's yard through Ernie, his dad's friend who ran the milk delivery service. No questions asked.

For months he squirrelled away his money. He'd set his sights on ten quid. A good earn for a hooker was a fiver, he'd discovered – he'd asked outright at the Sun Majestic Massage Parlour in Roe Street, West Perth. Of all the brothels in Roe Street, the Sun Majestic held the greatest attraction for Spud. It had a mystique about it the others didn't, and the sign out the front promised 'a touch of the Orient'. Madam Ruby who ran it was a top-looking sort, what's more – raven-haired, almond-eyed and exotic.

'Whaddya mean, what would it cost?' From behind the desk in the soft, rose-lit reception area, Ruby Chan looked the kid up and down, her amusement evident. 'Whaddya want to know that for, sonny?'

The strong Aussie accent surprised Spud, but he found the smile encouraging, and gee, she was a looker. Her breasts in the low-cut décolletage were creamy and perfect.

'I'm doing a project for school.' He flashed his cheekiest grin and Ruby threw back her head and laughed. The kid was cute.

Ruby Chan was really Ruby Smith and second-generation Australian. Her grandfather had worked as a coolie on the goldfields out of Darwin, and her mum had married a man called Smith and come to Perth to open a laundry shop. But Ruby was enterprising, she'd moved up in the world. The Sun Majestic Massage Parlour was an extremely popular brothel, and the efficiency with which it functioned was due to Ruby's expert management.

'Well, you tell your teacher my girls cost five quid,' she said, 'just in case he wants to pay us a visit sometime.'

'Five quid.' Spud contemplated the sum. It was a lot of

money and the prospect of doubling it was daunting. There might be other places with cheaper rates, he thought, but then he'd set his sights on the Sun Majestic, hadn't he?

'Rightio,' he said, 'I'll tell him.'

'And you come back yourself when you're older.' Ruby laughed again.

'Rightio. I will.'

It was three months later, and Spud had amassed the impressive sum of five pounds, but doubling it was proving difficult. He had to work further afield these days – people in nearby areas were keeping a close watch on their cars since the outbreak of hub-cap thefts – and Mercedes-Benzes seemed in short supply. Then he had a stroke of luck. More than a stroke of luck, he decided. The wallet was manna from heaven.

Five of them found it one wintry Friday night on their way to the bowling alley. Spud, Mike, the Brown brothers and Ivan the Pole were walking along Adelaide Terrace towards the Fairlane bowling centre and, as they passed the modest brick building that housed the Australian Broadcasting Commission, there it was, just lying in the gutter. Brucie Brown spotted it first, black leather glistening in the light of a streetlamp. He picked it up.

'Cripes,' he said, peering inside at the fiver and the one-pound note. 'Six quid.'

'Don't open it here, you bloody moron.' His older brother Len snatched it from him and hid it under his duffle coat as a gang passed them by and walked through the front doors of the nearby bowling centre.

'I reckon we should hand it in,' Mike said.

'Hand it in where?' Len asked.

'The ABC.' Mike gestured behind him. 'It's right outside the front door. It probably belongs to someone who works there.'

'And what'll they say when we hand it in and there's no money in it?' Len's sneer said 'you moron', and the others appeared in agreement.

'I don't think we should keep the money.'

Spud intervened before the other three could howl Mike down. 'Let's find out who owns it first,' he said, and they walked down to the corner of Victoria Street away from the Friday-night busyness of the bowling alley.

Under a streetlamp, outside a sleepy block of flats, Spud took the wallet from Len and explored its contents. The driver's licence read 'Anthony Wilson'.

'Jeez,' he said, recognising the name and handing the licence to Mike, who passed it around. They all recognised the name. Anthony Wilson was the recently elected MP for Nedlands and he received far more publicity than his counterparts from other local electorates. Exactly how or why, no-one seemed to know. His views were not radical, yet he was always available for a quote, saying the right thing at the right time in true pollie fashion, and he and his wife appeared regularly in the social pages. Spud's dad, Sean, had very definite opinions about Anthony Wilson.

'The man's a self-promoter, it's all bleedin' hype. He'd sell his constituents right down the river if it served his purpose! He's a used-car salesman and he always will be.'

Sean didn't really have his facts right. Anthony Wilson had not joined the family business of Wilson & Sons Prestige Cars, but had pursued a career in politics from a very early age, achieving a degree in economics and joining the Young Liberal Party. None of which impressed Sean Farrell.

'Young Wilson's a crook, just like his father and his brothers, you mark my words,' Sean said.

'Well, we know whose wallet it is and we've got the address,' Mike said as Spud handed him one of Anthony Wilson's business cards. 'Waratah Avenue, Dalkeith. Easy, we can return it to him personally.'

The Brown brothers and Ivan the Pole looked at Mike as if he'd come from another planet. But Spud didn't. Spud was too busy sifting through the other business cards he'd pulled from the wallet. Important people, he realised – a corporate executive, several government officials, and the deputy commissioner of police. He turned over the deputy commissioner's card and saw a phone number written in biro on the back. F3397. A home phone number. I bet Mr Wilson wouldn't want that to go missing, Spud thought.

'So after we nick the money we return the bloke's wallet, do we?' Len asked Mike, again with derision. 'That's really bright.'

'No.' Mike shook his head. 'Like I said, we don't keep the money.'

'Oh yes we do.' Len ripped the wallet from Spud who was left holding the business cards. 'If you don't want your share,' he said to Mike, lifting out the six pounds, 'then you just say so.' Bloody Mike McAllister, it was all right for him, with his rich parents and his regular pocket money week in week out!

'I *am* saying so! I don't want to keep the money!'

Mike and Len were eyeballing each other, it was becoming an issue.

'Hang on, hang on,' Spud said. 'We'll take a vote.' He knew damn well which way it'd go. 'Who says we keep the money, who says we don't?'

The Brown brothers and Ivan the Pole voted for the money.

'That's it then. You blokes keep the money and Mikey and I'll ditch the wallet.'

Len looked at Mike who just shrugged. He'd been outvoted and he didn't want any part of it.

Spud held out his hand for the wallet, but Len didn't immediately return it – he was too surprised. Spud's family was even poorer than his.

'Six quid splits easier between three,' Spud said reasonably. 'You lot stick with the money. I'm with Mikey on this – I'll give it a miss.'

Len shrugged and handed over the wallet. 'Suit yourself.' Spud Farrell had turned into a real wimp, he thought, copying Mike just to stay in his good books. Well, Len didn't give a shit about Mike McAllister and his family and their posh house by the river. Fuck the lot of them. Kowtowing wasn't the way to get on in life.

Spud replaced the business cards and tucked the wallet into the top pocket of his windcheater. 'I'll leave it where we found it,' he said.

They walked back to the Fairlane centre, and while the others went inside Spud checked that the coast was clear before walking on to the ABC. But he didn't leave the wallet.

It was after eleven o'clock when he rang the front doorbell of the smart-looking two-storey house in Waratah Avenue. He'd left the bowling alley at ten. Mike had bowed out of a final game in order to chat up a knockout brunette who had to be at least twenty, so Spud had called it quits too, bidding the boys good night and giving Mikey an encouraging wink that said 'You're on to a good thing there.'

He'd caught the bus home and it had been a twenty-minute walk to the house in Waratah Avenue. He was glad to see the lights on inside and the car parked in the driveway; he'd thought being a Friday night, the Wilsons might be out. The car was a Mercedes-Benz, he noted. An old one, second-hand, courtesy of Wilson & Sons Prestige Cars, but the hub cabs'd fetch an excellent price.

The door opened. Ah, Spud thought, the man himself. Things were going like clockwork.

'Mr Wilson?' he asked.

'Yes. And what can I do for you, young man?'

The expression was benign, but there was the slightest

reprimand in the voice, as if he was really saying 'Do you know how late it is?'

'It's more a case of what I can do for you, sir.' Spud's intention was to sound respectful, but it didn't seem to work.

'Oh, is that so?' Anthony Wilson smiled. 'And what would that be?'

There was a touch of condescension now. The bloke was a smarmy bastard, Spud decided.

'I thought you might want this back.' He produced the wallet from his windcheater pocket and held it out, pleased by the response.

'Where did you get that?' Anthony Wilson's complacency vanished and he took the wallet, staring at it in disbelief as if it couldn't be his. He didn't even know it had gone missing. Was the kid a pickpocket? If so, why was he returning the wallet? Did the cheeky little prick expect a reward?

'We found it sir, me and my mates.'

'You *found* it?'

'Yes, sir, lying in the gutter.' The man's incredulity was now focused upon him. 'Didn't you know you'd lost it, sir?'

'Exactly *where* did you find it?'

'In Adelaide Terrace sir, outside the ABC. Like I said, it was lying in the gutter.'

The live interview he'd done following the six o'clock news – Anthony remembered now. He'd collided with Megan Hetherington at the ABC's front door as he'd belted out after the interview, already running late for the cocktail party at Government House. She'd followed him to his car, nagging him about a fundraising dinner for the Cancer Research Foundation, and he'd fobbed her off with a card, telling her to ring his secretary. He'd shoved the wallet in his greatcoat pocket instead of returning it to his jacket as he normally would – or at least he thought he had. In his haste, he must have dropped it. How extraordinary.

'Come in,' he said to the boy, suddenly aware that he was cold standing in his shirtsleeves at the open front door. 'Come in, come in.'

Spud stepped inside and Anthony closed the door. A woman's voice called from upstairs.

'Who is it, darling?' Again, the petulant edge of 'Don't they know how late it is?' Melanie was getting ready for bed.

'A young man who found my wallet,' her husband called back.

'Good heavens, I didn't know you'd lost it.'

'Nor did I.'

Anthony shepherded Spud into the warmth of the lounge room.

'I'm afraid the money's gone missing, sir,' Spud said, gesturing at the wallet. 'My mates took it. I'm sorry about that.'

'Your mates took it?'

'Yeah, but I can't dob them in, you know how it is.'

'You didn't keep any of the money for yourself?'

'No, sir, I didn't,' Spud said in all honesty, his face a picture of innocence. 'I didn't think it was right.'

'What's your name, son?'

'Patrick Farrell, sir – they call me Spud.'

'Well, Spud. It's nice to make the acquaintance of such an honest young man.' Anthony took his wife's purse from her handbag which was sitting on the coffee table. He wasn't really sure whether the boy was honest or whether he was being conned, but he was deeply thankful for the return of his wallet and he owed the boy a favour. Anthony believed in the recognition and exchange of favours. The practice had stood him in good stead over the years.

'Thank you for your time and your trouble,' he said as

he handed Spud a five-pound note.

'Wow!' Spud said, in full Smiley mode. 'Thank *you*, sir.'

Early the following evening, Spud presented himself at the Sun Majestic Massage Parlour. They hadn't actually opened for business yet, but he'd been waiting across the road for Ruby to arrive. He saw her pull up in her bright red Toyota and after she'd gone inside he waited for another minute or so. Then, bold as brass, he walked into the reception area and rang the bell on the counter. Ruby appeared.

'I'm back,' he said. 'And I'm older.'

She wanted to laugh, but she didn't. She could tell the kid was serious. 'But not old enough, sonny.'

'I'll be sixteen next birthday.'

Something about the way he said it told Ruby that he wasn't lying. She'd have picked him for thirteen at first glance, the impish face was deceptively young, but there was a maturity in his manner that certainly didn't belong to a thirteen year old.

'Come back after your birthday, sweetie,' she said kindly, 'and bring your birth certificate with you.'

'I'm not lying.'

'I didn't say you were. But they'd shut me down if I took you on. You're not worth the risk.'

'Double the going rate.' Spud pulled out the neatly folded wad of money – a fiver and five one-pound notes. 'There you go,' he said, 'ten quid,' and he placed it on the counter.

Ruby looked from the boy to the wad of notes, then back to the boy. Ten pounds was a lot of money, he'd probably stolen it.

'I've been saving up,' Spud said. 'I've been saving up for months now.'

She studied him. Whether the kid had stolen the money or whether he'd saved it was really immaterial. He was desperate for sex – a virgin, she presumed – and prepared to pay double her top rate. She found both his money and his earnestness appealing.

'What are you like with a lawnmower?' she asked, picking up a biro and scribbling on the notepad that sat on the counter.

Spud made no reply – she didn't seem to require an answer.

Ruby tore the page off the notepad and gave it to him. He glanced at it – an address in Subiaco.

'Come around tomorrow afternoon about two,' she said. 'My grass needs trimming.' And she tucked the ten pounds into her décolletage.

Ruby's house in Subiaco was of the old-fashioned variety – weatherboard, with a front verandah and a dunny out the back. But it was pretty, freshly painted and as neat as a pin. Except for the grass, which had grown a little straggly.

'What's your name?' she asked as she led him down the side path to the backyard.

'Spud. Spud Farrell.'

She was dressed in a pair of cords and a jumper, her black hair in a ponytail and wearing no make-up. In the harsh glare of day she looked older than she had in the rose-lit reception room of the Sun Majestic, Spud thought. He'd taken her to be about twenty-five then, but she'd probably be in her thirties. Hell, not that he was being critical, she was an absolute stunner. He'd thought about nothing but Ruby all day.

'There you go.' She pointed at the old rotary-blade lawnmower leaning against the side of the dunny. 'Give me a yell when you've finished.' And she went into the house, the back flywire door slapping shut behind her.

What? Spud stood there bemused. He'd paid her ten quid for the privilege of mowing her lawn? He hadn't thought she was serious. Hell, he'd get all sweaty. He'd showered in readiness just before he'd come out, and he was wearing his best shirt under his windcheater.

The day was nippy, but he stripped down to his singlet and for the next twenty minutes ploughed back and forth pushing the old mower until the lawn was finished and he was dripping with sweat.

He picked up his shirt and windcheater and crossed to the back door, about to give her a call, but she was there waiting for him with a glass of water. She ushered him in. She was wearing a silk wrap-around, tied at her breasts, and her hair was down now, black satin falling on ivory-skinned shoulders.

'Thanks.' He gulped down the water and handed the glass back. 'Um . . .' He wished she'd say something, he wasn't sure what he was supposed to do. 'Would you mind if I had a bit of a wash?' He gestured at his sweaty singlet.

'I have a much better idea,' she said, taking him by the hand.

She led him into the bathroom where the big old enamel tub was full and brimming with soap bubbles. 'Take your clothes off,' she said, and he did. Then she untied the knot of her wrap-around. It dropped to the floor and she stood there, naked and glorious. Spud had never seen anything like it.

'I'll wash you myself,' Ruby said. For ten pounds the boy deserved the full service.

Spud had never had a bubble bath before. At first he tried to grope Ruby's breasts and touch the mat of black hair between her thighs – apart from the men's magazines that were passed around at school, he'd never seen a woman's pubic hair before. Well, he'd caught a glimpse of his sister Maeve's gingery bush one night when he'd been perving through the window of the bedroom she shared with Caitlin. Maeve had screamed the house down and he'd been well and truly ticked off by his mum, but if the truth were known he hadn't really found Maeve's gingery offering all that fascinating. Probably because she was his sister, which was just as well. But Ruby's bush was a real turn-on, he thought, making another grab for it.

'Later,' she said, smacking his hand away as she had each time he'd tried to grope her. 'Time for that later.' So Spud relaxed, as Ruby had planned he should.

Ruby's determination to give Spud his money's worth was a matter of honour and personal pride. She'd been good at her job for eighteen years and now, at thirty-five, she managed the brothel as madam and kept her few regular clients, servicing their friends if they wished her to, but she'd given up the nightly trade. Her feelings about virgins, however, remained the same.

Working girls always welcomed virgins. In and out, a speedy job, no complications. You didn't have to work virgins up like you did the old guys. It was all too easy – bring them on quick and get ready for the next trick. Ruby didn't see it that way, she never had. A young man's first time should be an experience, she thought, something to remember.

Spud had hit it lucky, and this Saturday afternoon would stay locked in his memory for as long as he lived.

She dried him down and took him into the bedroom where she allowed him to explore her body. 'Gently, slowly,' she kept saying, 'you'll last longer that way.' And Spud curbed the urge to thrust himself into her; he wanted to learn everything Ruby had to teach him.

She caressed him with her hands and her tongue, careful not to bring him to the brink, pausing now and then, telling him to breathe deeply. Finally, she allowed him to enter her. And when he did, she told him not to move. They stayed like that for a full minute, Spud lost in heaven, and then she undulated her muscles and he moved in perfect unison – only for twenty seconds or so; by that time he'd lasted as long as he could.

She left him when it was finished, and as Spud lay on his back in the little bedroom in the little weatherboard house in Subiaco he thought of Mikey McAllister. Mikey had said it was fan-bloody-tastic, he remembered. Well, Mikey McAllister didn't know the half of it, Spud'd bet his last bob on that!

Ruby offered him a cup of tea before he went. She was in her cords and jumper again and as they sat in the kitchen she looked out at the backyard.

'You did a good job of the lawn.'

'If I come back and mow it again,' he said, 'will you give me a discount?'

Ruby roared with laughter. 'No way,' she said.

'The mystique of the Orient, Mikey – there's nothin' like it!'

Spud couldn't wait to boast of his conquest, but just as Mike had done, he refused to name names, except to say that she was Chinese. Mike was fascinated, but made no further queries, respecting Spud's protection of the girl's identity. In actuality, Spud was protecting himself. If he told Mikey he'd been with a hooker, he thought, Mikey'd wonder where he got the money – prostitutes weren't cheap. But he gave his mate a full account of what had gone on and basked in Mikey's open-mouthed envy. Shit, it felt good, he thought. Mikey McAllister, envious of *him*! It was a first.

For the following month Spud went on a spree. He branched out from hub caps to car radios, and the house in Waratah Avenue was his first port of call. All four hub caps and the radio from Anthony Wilson's Mercedes went missing.

Four weeks to the day, he was back at Ruby's.

'I've come to mow your lawn,' he said very loudly for the benefit of the neighbours, and when she led him down the side path to the backyard, he handed her five quid.

'I reckon I shouldn't cop double rates if I do your lawn, eh?' he asked hopefully.

Ruby nodded and accepted the five quid. It was only fair, she thought. Besides, the kid was gutsy and she liked him for it.

Over the ensuing monthly visits they came to an understanding. Spud mowed the lawn and paid the going rate whenever he could – he had a business on the side now, running a book on all the school's sports events and keeping a 10 per cent cut for his troubles. But when he was a quid or so short, Ruby lined up odd jobs for him to do about the house – he was a proficient handyman – and they called it quits.

As the months stretched into a year and Spud turned sixteen, there was even the odd occasion when she gave him a freebie. Ruby had grown really fond of the kid by then.

During their final year at Mod, sex continued to dominate the lives of Mike McAllister and Spud Farrell, with rugby coming a close second and study a poor third. At seventeen, Mike had finally stopped growing and Spud had finally started. He would never be a tall man, but he'd certainly filled out. He was chunky and muscular and girls now found him attractive – in a cute kind of way.

As the leaving exams loomed, Mike realised that he'd have to pay a bit more attention to his studies. He'd need a good matriculation result to get into the sciences at UWA, and if he bombed out his father would be deeply disappointed. In his day, Jim McAllister had been one of Perth Uni's finest students, academically and athletically, and Mike was aware that he expected no less of his son. Besides, Mike wanted to go to uni – his desire to emulate his father had not waned over the years. So he took his mind off girls, as much as was humanly possible, and applied himself to his work.

Spud didn't. Uni held no attraction for him, and he studied only those courses which he found interesting and felt would be useful. Particularly maths – Spud liked playing with numbers.

Mike's matriculation placed him amongst the top ten students that year. Spud, after cruising through his exams with no expectations, was surprised to discover that he'd passed all seven subjects, with distinctions in maths A and B and physics. He'd received only a conceded pass in English, however, which was essential to matriculation, so he wasn't eligible for university. Who the hell cared, Spud thought.

That summer, the river seemed to play a more important part than ever in their lives. They swam and fished and prawned and crabbed with carefree abandon. Even girls seemed to take a back seat for a while. Perhaps they sensed this was the end of their boyhood.

'Look!' Mike pointed at the bird feeding frenzy out in the bay. 'Grab the outboard and tackle.'

The sun was setting, painting the sky with orange, and he and Spud had just hauled the Vee Jay into the boatshed following an afternoon sail.

While Spud grabbed the outboard and fishing tackle, Mike dragged the little dinghy down to the beach. They both knew what the birds signalled. The tailor were running.

Ten minutes later they were out in the bay, surrounded by gulls swooping and diving, the water all around them swirling and writhing with the tailor that were feeding in their own frenzy on the same school of whitebait.

With a spinner each trailing behind the dinghy, Mike and Spud were pulling in tailor hand over fist. They blooded each fish as soon as they got it aboard, and the moment their line was out they were hauling in another. Half an hour later, when the bucket was full, they decided to call it a day. They'd be cleaning and filleting fish all night otherwise. But they were exhilarated. Hauling in tailor like that was always a buzz.

It was dusk when they dragged the dinghy into the boat-house. They took the bucket of fish up to the laundry where Mike turned on the outside light and grabbed the cutting boards and knives that were stored there. Then he spread newspaper over the wrought-iron table and they sat side by side and started cleaning the fish.

'You could have taken me with you!' a voice behind them said accusingly. It was Jools, hands on hips.

Mike turned to her. 'There wasn't time,' he said.

'Yes, there was. I was watching from the balcony. The birds are still feeding. And it's *my* boat!'

She had a point. The dinghy belonged to Jools. It wasn't really a dinghy at all, it was a Pelican, or Junior Trainer, a little sailing boat with a detachable mast. Jim had built it for her the previous year as a thirteenth birthday present. But it had also replaced the old dinghy and now served as a tender for *Alana*, so came in for general use. Still, Mike thought, with a touch of guilt, he should have asked her permission.

'Sorry, Jools,' he said. 'You want to lend a hand?' He gestured at the mess of scales and guts.

She nodded, mollified by the apology and keen to accept the invitation. For some inexplicable reason, Jools loved cleaning fish.

'Grab us a cold beer then.'

Although Mike was underage, it was understood that a cold beer went with cleaning fish, which was fine by Jim and Maggie McAllister. As for Spud, well, he'd been known to get legless with his dad on a lost Sunday after-noon.

'Rightio.'

Jools belted eagerly up the back stairs. Just turned fourteen, she was a late developer. Still very much a tomboy, she couldn't understand some of her girlfriends who talked about nothing but boys or the fact they'd just got their first bra. She'd much rather be cleaning fish.

Spud started filleting the several fish they'd already scaled and gutted. He enjoyed filleting. With the super-sharp, scalpel-like knife reserved for the purpose, he felt for the backbone of the fish with all the delicacy of a surgeon.

Mike watched him for a moment; he was doing an excellent job. It had been Mike who'd taught Spud how to fillet fish, just as his own dad had taught him. 'Filleting fish is an art,' Jim McAllister had said, holding up a back-bone with the remaining flesh so transparent you could see right through it. Mike had worked hard at perfecting the art, and had passed his expertise on to Spud. They'd shared so much, he thought, watching Spud's deep con-centration.

'What're you going to do, Spud?' he asked.

'Eh?' Spud looked up. The question had come out of nowhere.

Mike was a little surprised himself. He hadn't really intended to talk about their futures, but he couldn't envisage going to uni without Spud.

'If you sat for your leaving English next year and got a good pass you'd get your matric.'

'What do you mean? Go to uni?'

Mike nodded encouragingly. Hell, Spud was one of the cleverest blokes he knew. Spud could do anything he set his mind to; he'd be mad if he didn't give uni a go.

'Nah,' Spud said. 'Don't want to, don't need to and couldn't afford to anyway. It's all right for you, mate, your folks have got money.'

Though he'd often thought it, it was the first time Spud had said the words out loud, and he said them without rancour. But Mike felt the need to correct him.

'No, they haven't,' he said. 'We're not rich.'

'Oh, aren't you.' Spud laughed. 'Well, it's one helluva life.'

This time there *was* a touch of rancour, but Mike failed to notice.

'Yep,' he grinned. 'We're paupers who live like kings, Dad says.'

It was one of Jim McAllister's favourite sayings – he believed in drilling home to his children the fact that they should never take their privileges for granted.

'Paupers who live like kings!' Spud let out a guffaw. Jesus, Mikey was naïve, he thought. But he loved him for it. 'I'll swap you, mate,' he said, just as Jools arrived with the beers.

Over the wrought-iron table and the bloodied newspaper and fish guts, they toasted each other.

'Mates forever,' they said.

CHAPTER THREE

'You're Mike McAllister, aren't you? I'm Ian Pemberton.' Ian proffered his hand as he joined Mike in the queue at the canteen. He'd made a point of seeking him out. It was time they got to know each other, he thought, they had a lot in common. To Ian, they were plainly the brightest in their first-year science course, and Mike came with an excellent pedigree, given his father's university sporting record.

'G'day, Ian.' Mike shook his hand. He'd seen Ian at the lectures – they were doing the same subjects: geology, zoology, maths and chemistry – but it was less than a fortnight into the term and they'd not as yet actually introduced themselves. 'How're you enjoying it all?' he asked. 'Bit different from school, isn't it?'

Ian was surprised at the ingenuousness of the remark. He – and all the other freshmen, as far as he could tell – was doing his very best to embrace the student ethos and appear blasé. Apart from sifting out which college a fellow student had graduated from, one didn't refer to 'school' in such a manner. At least, Ian certainly didn't. But far from seeming gauche, Mike's lack of inhibition lent him a confidence the others seemed to lack.

'Yes, I suppose it is,' Ian agreed.

They shuffled up in the queue, reaching the counter where conversation halted as they made their selections.

'Why don't we grab that table by the window?' Ian said when they stood with trays in hand.

Mike had been about to join his mates from Mod, who were sitting up the far end of the canteen, but he could see there was only space at the table for one more, and as Ian seemed to have latched on to him, he decided it'd be rude to give the bloke the flick.

'Right you are,' he said, and they crossed to the table Ian had indicated.

'Your dad's Jim McAllister, isn't he?' Ian asked once they were settled.

'Yeah, that's right,' Mike said, before taking a mouthful of his ham and salad roll.

'Awarded more full Blues than any other student in the sporting history of UWA.' Ian made the announcement sound as impressive as it was.

Mike was surprised. 'How'd you know that?'

'With a record like his, who wouldn't?'

'Just about every other first-year student around, particularly when they've been here less than a fortnight.'

Ian decided to cough up to the truth, rather than sound as sycophantic as he obviously had. 'My mother told me actually. She went to uni with your dad.'

His mother hadn't told him about Jim McAllister's sports record at all; Ian had checked it out for himself just the previous day. But Cynthia Pemberton had certainly boasted about having been to uni with Mike's dad.

'That'll be Jim McAllister's son,' she'd said when she'd asked Ian for the names of his fellow students – at least, those who'd made an impression upon him and whose names he'd remembered. 'Jim was a wonderful sportsman,' she'd said, hinting at a familiarity which hadn't existed. 'He held all sorts of records,' she added vaguely.

Cynthia hadn't really known Jim McAllister, he'd been two years ahead of her, but like every other female student on campus at the time, she'd fancied him. She liked to dine out on her university years whenever she could though – it gave her a background of her own and an academic edge over most of her friends. The fact that she'd completed only eighteen months of an arts course before marrying Gordon Pemberton was something she didn't mention, instead hinting that she'd given up a promising academic career – in exactly what area was always hazy – to devote herself to her husband.

'Really?' Mike asked. 'What's your mum's name?'

'Cynthia. It would have been Randall then. Cynthia Randall.' Ian was glad to have garnered Mike's interest.

'I'll remember her to Dad.'

'Yes, she'd like that, I'm sure.' Ian picked up his chicken sandwich. 'So you graduated from Scotch College like your dad, did you?' he asked before biting into it.

Mike found Ian's knowledge of his dad a bit suspect – the bloke seemed to be trying too hard to make an impression. Christ, he thought, I hope he's not queer.

'No, Perth Mod,' he said rather abruptly.

'Oh.' Ian was surprised. A government scholarship school, he hadn't expected that. He associated Mod with a rather motley crew. Perhaps he'd made the wrong choice, after all. He'd decided to select his friends with care.

'What about you?' Mike asked.

'Guildford Grammar.'

'Ah.' Mike wondered whether that explained Ian Pemberton's arrogance. He'd heard the Guildford Grammar blokes were up themselves.

It wasn't the most auspicious of beginnings.

'I met a bloke whose mum went to uni with you,' Mike said to his dad over dinner that night.

'Oh, and who would that be?' Jim asked.

'Her name was Cynthia Randall.'

His father looked blank.

'One of your conquests?' Maggie asked with a smile. She hadn't known her husband during his uni days, but she was aware that he'd been quite a lad. 'Don't gobble, Jools,' she said admonishingly. Eager to leave the table, Jools was scoffing down her casserole at a rate of knots.

'Cynthia Randall.' Jim gave it a second or two of thought, then shrugged. 'Never heard of her,' he said.

'She's Pemberton now. Her son's called Ian.'

'Pemberton.' Jim knew the name. 'Gordon Pemberton owns *Trusan*.' *Trusan* was a custom-built, forty-foot luxury yacht that sailed out of Royal Freshwater Bay Yacht Club. Designed as much for pleasure as she was for racing, she was much admired in boating circles.

'Does he?' Mike asked, surprised. 'I thought Vic Nelson did.'

'No, Vic just skippers her.' Jim grinned. 'He probably likes people to think he owns her, and who can blame him? But Pemberton employs him full-time, he doesn't race himself. He's an orthodontist – lives in Peppermint Grove. Would he be your mate's dad?'

'Probably,' Mike said.

'Can I leave the table now, Mum?' Jools asked.

'No ice-cream and fruit salad?'

'Nup. I'll be late for rehearsal.'

Fifteen-year-old Jools was heavily involved in an amateur production of *The Crucible* at Patch Theatre. She'd decided she was going to be an actress.

'See ya,' she said to no-one in particular. Slinging her bag over one shoulder, she disappeared from the dining room, ponytail bouncing, and they heard Baxter yelp as she tripped over him in the hall.

'Home by ten.'

Maggie's call went unheeded and the front door slammed shut.

'Gordon Pemberton, eh?' Jim was interested to hear that his son had met up with the Pemberton boy. 'She's a beautiful vessel, *Trusan.*'

Mike didn't check out whether Ian Pemberton was Gordon's son. He wasn't sure he particularly liked Ian Pemberton, and he didn't want to appear to be seeking his friendship. But as it turned out, Ian stopped seeking his. Having decided that it was safest to adhere to the 'old school tie' principle, Ian stuck to the company of his ex-Guildford Grammar friends, avoiding Mike and his mates from Perth Mod.

As the months passed, however, and first term became second, the freshmen of 1962 relaxed into university life. Familiar cliques, embraced for safety's sake, dissolved and new ones formed, and Mike and Ian did achieve a friendship of sorts – mainly forged on the rugby field where both excelled. Mike, strong and fast, played centre, and Ian, a superb kick, played fullback, where he avoided tackles whenever possible.

By that time, Mike had embraced university with a passion. He loved everything about UWA – the landscaped gardens and lily ponds of its campus, the elegance of its sandstone arches and walkways, the graceful simplicity of its central bell tower. He loved the lifestyle university offered too – the intellectual stimulation, the camaraderie and the sport. But above all, he loved the girls. And the girls loved him.

Ian Pemberton was resentful of Mike McAllister's popularity. What did Mike have that he didn't, he wondered. His sporting prowess was equal to Mike's, his academic skills superior, and, like Mike, he was good-looking. Yet, for some unfathomable reason, he wasn't the hit with the girls that Mike was, much as he tried to compete.

Second term came and went, and in the popularity stakes things remained the same. Ian had hit a stalemate.

Finally, in the late spring with their first-year exams barely a month away, he gave up trying to compete with Mike McAllister. There seemed little point. Swallowing his resentment, he decided once again to cultivate Mike's friendship. It appeared he had no alternative.

'Want to come on the twilight this Friday?'

They were sitting on the sidelines of the rugby field doing some warm-up stretches before the training session when Ian casually dropped the invitation.

'What? Aboard the *Sea Witch*?' Mike asked.

They'd discussed their respective backgrounds on a number of occasions and discovered they had other common interests besides rugby. Ian, although a latecomer to the sport, was a keen yachtsman and regularly crewed on *Sea Witch,* an eighteen-footer belonging to a friend of his dad's at Royal Freshwater Bay Yacht Club.

'No. *Trusan.* Dad's taking out a couple of his cronies and their wives, and I'm crewing for him. He said I can bring a mate along.'

'Sure. Great,' Mike agreed. He'd planned to take Natalie Hollingsworth to the jazz session at Claremont footy club, but theirs was a casual, easy relationship – she wouldn't mind if he changed it to Saturday, he was sure.

Ian grinned. He'd known it would be the clincher. No-one knocked back a sail on *Trusan.* 'Freshie at five thirty,' he said. 'Berth 21.' And they jumped to their feet as the coach's whistle sounded.

The cosy little yacht club in Claremont, of which Mike was a member along with his father, was a poor cousin indeed to the spectacular Royal Freshwater Bay Yacht Club. The grand colonial clubhouse of 'Freshie' sat in splendour on its green hill at Peppermint Grove where it could be admired from every vantage point about the bay. And nestled in its marina was a king's ransom in craft – some devoted to the noble sport of yacht racing, some offering quality leisure time acquired through hard-earned labour, and some the trappings and playthings of the wealthy.

Trusan mingled with the other yachts, dwarfing most, as vessels of all size and description jostled for pride of place, sails luffing in the stiff sea breeze. All were awaiting the boom from the small cannon that would signal the commencement of the twilight race. At the helm, Vic Nelson manoeuvred the huge yacht with consummate ease amongst the hordes of boats, which somehow, miraculously, managed to avoid each other, and when the cannon sounded he was in perfect position.

Twenty minutes later they were well in the lead with the rest of the field far behind them. Gordon Pemberton gave his skipper the customary signal. Vic Nelson in turn signalled Ian to lower the jib and they changed course, leaving the race to set off on their leisurely sail upriver.

Mike was disappointed they weren't completing the race, but Ian had warned him.

'It's only a social sail,' he'd said apologetically. 'We'll take off with the starters – Dad likes to prove a point, but Mum hates racing. The boat's really more about entertaining for her.' He gave a rueful shrug. 'Bloody shame. *Trusan* races like a dream.'

As they neared Point Resolution, Gordon took over the helm.

Gordon Pemberton was an older version of his son. A handsome man in his late forties, hair greying at the temples, his classic looks were marred by slightly prominent ears and he bore himself with an ease of confidence bordering on arrogant. It was like looking at Ian thirty years from now, Mike thought.

'Well, thank goodness that part's over,' Cynthia said gaily to her husband's two colleagues and their wives. She particularly addressed poor little Glenda, who'd never been on a yacht before and was looking positively green.

'I hate it when it *leans* like that.' She and the other four had been comfortably seated in the broad open cockpit and hadn't been required to move once since they'd set sail. She turned to Gordon, who was manning the wheel at the stern, Vic now having taken over the mainsheet from Ian. 'Darling,' she called good-naturedly, 'it's *still* leaning a bit, can't you *stop* it?'

'We'll have the wind behind us soon, dear,' Gordon responded mildly. Cynthia made the same complaint every time they sailed, and every time he made the same response, even if they weren't about to have the wind behind them.

Gordon would have liked to devote more time to racing, but he was a busy man and there simply weren't enough hours in the day. So he enjoyed an occasional social sail and basked in the racing honours accorded *Trusan* under the expert helmsmanship of Vic Nelson. Vic, who always assembled a first-class crew, had skippered the yacht to victory in many a major long-distance ocean race. Gordon was immensely proud of *Trusan* and her triumphs. *Trusan* was a symbol of his success.

'Ian, pet, drinks, please.' Cynthia trotted down the several broad steps into the main cabin.

'I'll give you a hand,' Mike said as Ian obediently followed his mother. The wives were now chatting, and the men, colleagues of Gordon's from Sydney, had started talking shop. They were in Perth for a conference – one was a periodontist and the other an endodontist – and Mike didn't feel he had much to contribute by way of conversation.

Trusan's main cabin bore the semblance of a comfortable living room. Spacious and open plan, the galley on the aft starboard side was complete with refrigerator, full-size stove, bench and sink. Aft portside was a cosy nook with armchair and captain's log table, and stretched along both sides were built-in sofas that pulled out to form additional bunks when the central dining table was removed. A door led to a narrow passageway and the head, and then to the forward cabin, which housed a large double bed and ample wardrobe and drawer space.

Mike, looking about the main cabin, thought of *Alana*'s icebox and primus stove, and the sleeping bags he and Jools rolled out in the cockpit at night. This sort of opulence didn't seem to belong on a yacht, he thought. But then *Trusan* was unlike any other yacht he'd seen. Her interior was that of a luxury motor cruiser and yet, under sail, she cut through the water like the sleekest of racing craft.

Cynthia was busily lifting platters of food out of the refrigerator – she had them made up by a gourmet caterer – and she handed Mike a bottle of champagne.

'Be a darling,' she said with a dazzling smile. 'And Ian, pet, the smoked salmon first.' She indicated one of the platters and Ian disappeared with it into the cockpit where the men and their wives were admiring the first rays of what promised to be a magnificent sunset.

Mike wondered what his reaction would be if his mother called him 'pet' as Cynthia did Ian, although Ian didn't appear to notice. It was obvious she doted on her only child, but Mike wasn't sure what to make of Cynthia Pemberton. She was beautiful in a manufactured way – white designer-label shorts and shirt displaying a neat, trim body, wind-tousled hair blonde-streaked to perfection. She was charming and vivacious and seemed far too young to be Ian's mother. But was she really as vacuous as she appeared?

'You're Jim McAllister's boy, how lovely to meet you,' she'd said the moment he'd stepped aboard *Trusan*. 'I went to university with your father.' It was said very loudly, for the benefit of the others who were already seated in the cockpit having a glass of champagne before the boat left the pen.

'Yes . . .'

Mike had fortunately been required to make no further comment as Cynthia had introduced him to her husband's colleagues and their wives.

'And this is Vic Nelson,' she said, leaving Vic until last.

'G'day, Mike,' Vic said as they shook. 'How's your old man?'

'He's great. Sends his regards.' Mike had been pleased by Vic's recognition. 'Give Vic Nelson my best,' Jim had said when his son had told him he was doing the twilight sail on *Trusan*.

Fifteen minutes later, Vic had started the engine. As *Trusan* glided out of her pen, Ian and Mike standing by to raise the sails when they were clear of the yacht club, Cynthia had collected the champagne flutes. 'There's plenty more where that came from,' she'd promised, 'but we have to get the *nasty* part over first.' She'd given a girlish laugh of apology to the men and their wives and disappeared below to rinse and dry the glasses, and Mike had wondered what the 'nasty part' was. He knew now. The nasty part was sailing.

'Thank you, dear,' Cynthia said as the champagne cork popped. 'The glasses are in that cupboard.' Then a directive to Ian, who had reappeared, 'Don't forget the napkins, pet.' Cynthia, expert hostess that she was, was in full party mode.

'Dad and Vic'd prefer a beer,' Ian said when he and Mike had returned to the cabin, having served champagne to the guests in the cockpit.

'Yes, of course.' They always did, although for the life her Cynthia couldn't understand why they'd prefer beer to vintage Taittinger. She handed Ian the platter of patés and cheeses, opened a bottle of Swan Lager and poured two glasses. 'Be a dear and give one of those to Vic,' she asked Mike. Cynthia always made a point of serving Vic last. He was, after all, the hired help.

'Sure.' Mike picked up the glass.

'Thank you, pet.' She gave him another dazzling smile, but this time there was something personal in it, something coquettish even. 'You've been *such* a help.' She patted his cheek, and the gesture was so intimate that Mike was shocked. My God, she's coming on to me, he thought.

'I'm *so* glad you're Ian's friend,' she said. Then she swanned out to the cockpit with Gordon's beer. 'Well, you won't see a sunset like *that* in Sydney,' Mike heard her announce to her guests as he followed in her wake.

They all admired the now amber-pink sky, and as Cynthia handed around platters and chatted to the group, Ian went below and poured a couple of beers for himself and Mike. 'You'd go a beer rather than champagne, wouldn't you?' he'd muttered and Mike had nodded.

Cynthia was laying on the charm for all it was worth and, as Mike watched her, he realised that she hadn't been coming on to him at all. Well, no more than she was now coming on to the other men, and in open view of their wives, not to mention her own husband. She was flirting unashamedly with them – guiding the conversation with an impish wink of encouragement here and there, or a touch on the arm to emphasise her agreement with some point one of them had made. Now she was even taking one by the hand – blatantly turning to his wife as she did so.

'He's a remarkable man, your husband, Glenda,' Cynthia said, and Glenda basked in the praise.

Mike couldn't help but admire her skill. She was manipulating both the men and the women with absolute ease. In flattering the men, she was flattering their wives, and she made sure not to exclude her husband. 'Oh, Gordon's of the same mind. He's said that so *often*! Haven't you, dear?' And Gordon would nod benignly.

Gordon Pemberton was happy to leave the socialising to his wife, and thankful that no effort was required on his part. The twilight sail was a return of the hospitality he'd received from his colleagues in Sydney, and both men bored him. He'd rather be chatting to Vic about *Trusan*'s forthcoming return race from Perth to Albany.

Ian returned with the beers and he and Mike sat, freely observing the social exchange. They were expected to make no contribution. Cynthia was ignoring them both completely, just as she was ignoring Vic Nelson. But then she'd ignored Vic from the outset. She always did – there was nothing to be gained from giving her attention to the skipper. Just as there was nothing to be gained now in giving her attention to her son, much as she adored him, or to his friend, much as she approved of him.

'Do you mind if we sit up the bow for a while?' Ian asked his father, who was still at the helm. 'We'll come back when we go about.'

They were in Perth waters with the breeze behind them. It was a gentle sail now, but when the yacht went about, the return trip would be rougher.

Gordon nodded his permission, and Ian and Mike took their beers up the bow where they sat on the deck, the babble of conversation from the cockpit a blur, replaced by the rhythmic sound of the water against *Trusan*'s prow.

'I thought you might want a rest,' Ian grinned. 'Mum can be a bit much when she's working the room.'

Mike wasn't sure what he was supposed to say by way of reply. He couldn't tell whether Ian was being sardonic or not. 'She's certainly something, your mum,' he remarked with what he hoped sounded like admiration.

'Oh yes, she's very good at her job. Dad always says she's his greatest asset.' No dig was intended; Ian's response was made in all seriousness. 'She gave up uni for Dad – he's her career, she says, and they make a good team.' There was genuine respect in his voice as he spoke of his mother. 'Mum's bloody smart actually. She knows as much about the share market as Dad does – more, probably. In fact, I don't know why he doesn't give up his practice altogether. He doesn't need it.'

It seemed to Mike a rather callous dismissal of Gordon Pemberton's achievements. He'd heard that Ian's father was considered one of the top orthodontists in the country.

'He probably likes working,' he suggested mildly.

Ian nodded. 'Yes, he says he does, but I think it's more the social prestige he enjoys. Dad likes being the best in his field. He only went into orthodontics to make money. He told me I should do the same thing and cash in on his reputation. Dad reckons there's big money in mouths.'

It wasn't exactly the way Gordon had put it, but the gist had been much the same. 'A career in dentistry can be very rewarding, Ian,' he'd advised, 'particularly if you specialise. You should give it some thought.'

Ian laughed. 'I couldn't quite come at the prospect of spending a lifetime in people's mouths myself, so I opted for a science course. I don't know exactly where it'll lead me yet, but I don't think Dad'll be too disappointed, so long as I make money.'

Mike found the way Ian spoke of his parents brutally direct and faintly shocking, but there was no malice in what he said. In fact, there was something refreshing about his honesty, Mike decided. It surprised him that Ian had no particular aspirations though. He was the most gifted student in their course, a natural academic.

'But there must be something you want to achieve?'

'Oh, tons of things.' Ian laughed again, deliberately misunderstanding. 'A boat like this for starters.'

'Fair enough.' Mike grinned in return and took a swig from his beer. Ian's unashamedly frank reply had left him with nothing to say.

'How about you?' Ian asked. 'Following in your old man's footsteps?'

'Sort of, yes. I want to work with the environment like Dad, but preferably in marine biology if I can – marine science and conservation really fascinates me.' Mike couldn't disguise his enthusiasm. 'Probably because of my childhood and all this,' he added, looking about at the waterways he'd sailed and fished his entire existence. 'I love the river and the life in it and everything it stands for. I mean, what a way to grow up.'

Aware that his response may have appeared over-earnest in Ian's eyes, Mike shrugged. 'I'm just a river rat at heart,' he said with a smile. 'An academic Huckleberry Finn.'

'You're an idealist, that's what you are.' Ian had expected as much. 'You want to do something meaningful, don't you?'

Mike studied Ian warily, expecting to see derision, but there was none. 'Probably, yes,' he admitted. 'Well, if I pass, anyway. I'm not as brainy as you.'

'True, but you'll get there. Commitment's the thing.' Ian raised his glass in a toast.

They swigged back the remains of their beer and sat in comfortable silence for a while. The sunset had long faded and they watched the lights of Perth blinking against the sky and, overlooking the city, the war memorial, illuminated and hanging like a fairy castle in the air, high on the darkened hill of Kings Park.

'We'd better go back,' Ian said, and they returned to the cockpit. *Trusan* would be going about shortly. They'd be tacking close to the wind, the boat would be leaning, Cynthia would be complaining and Glenda would be turning green.

Forty minutes later, *Trusan* joined the mêlée of boats returning to the yacht club and Vic Nelson took over the helm. He turned the yacht into the wind, the boys lowered the mainsail, and, under power, he guided *Trusan* into the pen.

Another obligatory round of champagne followed while Vic and the boys stowed the gear, Mike glad of the opportunity to avoid the social chat, and half an hour later they were saying their farewells in the yacht club's car park. Cynthia had arranged a stretch limousine, which had been waiting for a good twenty minutes, and she insisted Mike accept a lift home with her husband's colleagues.

'I can call a taxi,' he said. He would certainly have preferred to.

'Nonsense. They're staying at the Parmelia. Claremont's right on the way.' Cynthia wasn't even looking at him, she was too busy brushing cheeks with the men and their wives. 'Just give the address to the driver. It's been *divine*,' she said, taking Glenda's hands in hers. 'I do hope I see you again before you go back to Sydney.' She wouldn't. All hospitality debts had been repaid. Gordon would see the men at the conference, but Cynthia had fulfilled her duties.

As the limousine cruised off, Mike looked out the window. Gordon was already walking towards his Bentley parked nearby, but Cynthia stood, one arm draped over the shoulder of her handsome young son, striking a pose as she waved farewell to her guests.

Mike decided that he didn't particularly like Cynthia Pemberton. She was not vacuous as he'd first thought – far from it. As Ian had said, she was smart. But he'd come to the conclusion that she was the most awful snob. He'd found her treatment of Vic Nelson as they'd left the boat exceptionally rude. She'd ignored him completely. Even as Vic had helped her from the boat onto the jetty, as he had each of the women, Cynthia had kept chatting to the others as if the man were a lackey simply doing his duty. She hadn't even said goodbye to him as she and the group had walked off down the jetty.

Mike had been a little surprised by Gordon's and Ian's treatment of Vic too, although both had been pleasant enough.

'See you, Vic,' Ian had said, and Gordon, last off the boat, had shaken his hand. 'Thanks, Vic. Well done.'

But then father and son had walked off to join the others, leaving Vic to clear away the bottles and refuse on his own.

Mike had watched them go. 'I'll take the garbage ashore, shall I, Vic?' he'd asked.

'No, thanks, Mike, that's my job.' Vic had offered his hand. 'Give my best to your dad,' he'd said as they shook.

The Pembertons seemed to live by a different set of rules, Mike thought. The rules of the rich, he supposed. It explained a lot about Ian. No wonder he was a snob. What option had he had? He'd been born and bred one. Mike suddenly felt a bit sorry for Ian Pemberton – no wonder he put people off with his arrogance. And what a pity his only aspiration was to be rich like his dad. The bloke had the brains to be successful in any field he chose.

'Spud, this is Ian. Ian Pemberton, Spud Farrell.' Mike made the introductions and the boys shook hands.

The three of them had met up outside Claremont Yacht Club early Saturday evening, just two weeks after Mike's sail on *Trusan*. Mike had considered it only fair to reciprocate Ian's invitation with one of his own, although it was quite possible Ian would consider CYC beneath him, and God only knew what he'd make of Spud. But then God only knew what Spud would make of Ian. If there was one thing Spud Farrell couldn't stand, it was a snob. Mike hoped Ian wouldn't start pissing from a height as he had a tendency to. If he did, Spud'd probably deck him.

Despite having gone their separate ways, Spud and Mike had kept in touch over the past year. A day's work at the yacht club now and then to earn free beers on a Saturday evening – as they'd done that very afternoon; and the occasional night of jazz at the footy club – as they intended to do that night. The bond between the two remained strong, and Spud, as if needing to reaffirm it, would often say the words out loud. 'Mates forever, Mikey,' he'd toast as he raised his illicit glass of beer, and Mike would respond with fervour.

Claremont Yacht Club remained a prime venue for Mike

and Spud's illicit drinking. They were still legally under-age, but at CYC the stalwart older members – permanent fixtures in the bar on a Saturday night – would shout them beers in return for a day's sweaty labour sanding back and anti-fouling a boat on the slips, or slaving away at some dogsbody work about the clubhouse, which always seemed in need of repair.

Mike, Spud and Ian found their way through to the bar, which was smoky and crowded, as it always was on a Saturday. A chook raffle was in progress, and several men were gathered around the old poker machine the club had recently garnered – the one-armed bandit was proving CYC's most successful fundraiser to date. Down the end of the bar, old George was tucking into his blue manna crabs, chin dribbling yellow as he noisily sucked out the mustard before ripping the shells apart. It wasn't a pretty sight, but everyone was used to it.

Mike and Spud were greeted all round, and very soon they had beers in their hands, as did Ian – any friend of the boys was welcome, the old blokes agreed. Besides, they could do with an extra worker about the place.

The three of them gathered at a table by the window overlooking the narrow strip of beach and the modest gathering of boats in the marina below.

'Bit different from Freshie, eh?' Spud said to Ian with just the touch of a sneer.

Mike had told Spud about Ian and the Pembertons and the sail aboard *Trusan* that very afternoon as they'd worked on the hull of the old clinker dinghy, and Spud had been impressed.

'*Trusan*, eh? Shit, she's got to be worth a quarter of a million. They must be stinking rich.'

'Yep,' Mike had agreed. 'Rich as Croesus, I'd say.'

It had got Spud thinking. He'd had a number of links with the wealthy of Peppermint Grove over the years. He wondered whether his mother had ever cleaned for the

Pembertons, or whether he'd ever stolen Gordon Pemberton's hub caps. Now, as he looked at Ian in his trendy silk
sports jacket, Spud's old edge of resentment crept back.
Ian Pemberton represented everything he detested and
everything he yearned for. Christ, he thought, he used to
be envious of Mikey and his family, but the McAllisters of
Claremont were paupers compared to the Pembertons
of Peppermint Grove.

'Yeah, it's different from Freshie all right,' Ian agreed,
looking around at the cosy camaraderie of the bar. He
hadn't picked up on Spud's derision. 'I wouldn't be able
to do this at Freshie.' He saluted them with his glass and
took a hefty gulp of beer.

Mike and Spud raised their glasses to follow suit, but
before they could drink, Spud got in with the toast. 'Mates
forever, Mikey.' It was a deliberate exclusion of Ian. Spud
was staking his claim in a friendship to which Ian did
not belong.

Mike recognised the toast as another put-down to Ian,
just as he'd registered the comment about Freshie. Why
was Spud being so antagonistic?

'Yeah. Mates,' he said, burying his head in his beer glass.

Then Ian, who hadn't put a foot wrong so far, waved the
proverbial red flag.

'Mikey?' he queried mockingly. '*Mikey*! You're joking!'

He was about to make some witty comment about how
the A team rugby squad might react to their leading star
centre's nickname, when Spud turned with a vengeance.

'That's right. *Mikey*.' His voice matched Ian's for
mockery, and had a touch of his father's Irish, as it often
did when he was bent on making an impact. 'You can
always tell when people like you, *Ian,* because that's when
they give you a nickname. I'm *Spud*. He's *Mikey*. Who are
you, *Ian*?'

Ian was floored. What had he done?

Mike wondered whether he should just get up and leave

and take Ian with him. He had no idea why Spud was being so belligerent.

'Go and score us another beer, Spud,' he said reasonably, hoping it'd give Spud time to cool down. 'Old George should be good for a round after the work we did on his clinker this arvo.'

Spud went off for the beers, aware that he'd gone too far and that Mikey wasn't happy.

'Well, what's got up *his* nose?' Ian said with a supercilious arch of his eyebrows.

'Wouldn't have a clue,' Mike replied. He changed the subject. 'You want to come on to the footy club later? We're meeting up with Natalie and a couple of her girlfriends.' At least they would be, Mike thought, if Spud cooled down. If not, he'd go without him.

'Sure,' Ian agreed. Hell, of course he wanted to come – he'd had the hots for Natalie Hollingsworth all year. So had every other male student on campus, but of course Mike had got there first. Still, Natalie's girlfriends sounded promising, particularly if they were the dolly birds she hung around with at uni.

When Spud returned to the table it was obvious he'd decided to toe the line. 'There you go, Ian.' He plonked a beer in front of Ian and gave him a guarded but friendly enough smile. It wasn't an apology. Rather it was a promise that he was prepared to behave himself, for Mikey's sake.

'Thanks, Spud.'

'Ian's coming with us to the footy club,' Mike said.

It had been a foregone conclusion. 'Well, you'd be mad not to with girls lined up, eh?' Spud grinned. He couldn't wait himself.

'Our last night out on the tiles,' Mike announced, taking a hefty swig of beer.

Spud commiserated with them – he knew they started their final first-year exams in two weeks. You wouldn't get him studying again for quids, he said. 'School was enough for me.'

Then he turned to Ian. 'Mikey tells me you're the brainiest bloke in the class.' He said it as a compliment and with admiration, but he was waiting for just the tiniest reaction. If Ian up-himself Pemberton dared take the piss out of Mikey's nickname, Spud'd go him.

But Ian knew better than to make any comment. He thought about correcting Spud in his use of the term 'class', but decided against that too.

'Uni's just a means to an end really.' He shrugged with what he hoped was a touch of humility. Ian had figured Spud out – the bloke was working class with a chip on his shoulder. 'Anyone can make a go of it.'

'And which particular end do you have in sight, Ian?'

'Money.'

Spud laughed, not unpleasantly. 'What for, mate? You've already got it.'

'No, I haven't – my dad has.'

'Same thing, isn't it?'

'Nope. Not at all.' Ian was no longer trying to placate Spud. He meant every word he said. 'My dad's a self-made man. He didn't inherit a penny himself, and I'm not relying on inheriting from him. Hell, I'd have to wait too long for a start, and he might spend it or lose it anyway. Dad built his own fortune, and that's exactly what I'll do.'

Mike watched the exchange with amusement. He could tell that Spud suddenly found Ian interesting. And why shouldn't he? They were alike, after all – both money-obsessed.

Spud was thinking exactly the same thing. Ian Pemberton was an arrogant shit, there were no two ways about it, but in a bizarre way they had a lot in common. They both wanted to be rich and they'd both been inspired by their fathers. Ian wanted to be just like his old man, and Spud wanted to be everything his old man wasn't.

'Well, good luck to you, Pembo,' he said. He was taking the piss all right, but in a friendly way.

Ian didn't react. He was sure the nickname was intended to be derogatory, but Spud Farrell was a tough little bloke and it wasn't worth crossing him. Ian abhorred violence – he'd run a mile from a fight.

An hour or so later, they left for the Claremont footy club. Spud's old Austin was undergoing repairs at the garage, as it often was, and Mike didn't own a car, so the two had been prepared to walk. It wasn't far – the club was just across the railway line opposite the Claremont pub. Instead, they arrived in style, pulling up right outside in Ian's brand new, bright red Ford Falcon Pursuit. As they piled out, Spud produced a flask from the inside pocket of his denim jacket.

'My contribution,' he said, and they took a quick swig each before they went inside. It was Bundaberg rum – overproof and with a kick like a mule.

Mike was the only one who scored that night. He and Natalie left early. Ian and Spud gave up trying to flirt with the other two girls: it was obvious from the start that they weren't really interested.

'What do you do?' one of them had asked Spud.

'I'm a bookie,' he'd said with a worldly air. Being a bookie at nineteen was no mean feat – it was bound to impress.

It didn't. In fact, it put the kybosh on things for Spud, and the girls hadn't been interested in Ian from the outset. They knew him from uni and thought he was up himself.

After Mike and Natalie had left, Spud and Ian took their Cokes outside – they weren't going to share their Bundy with the girls if there was nothing in it for them. They walked around the side of the club, away from the lights of the main entrance, and leaned against the wall while Spud spiked their drinks.

'Why'd you say you were a bookie?' Ian asked with a touch of admiration. He rather respected Spud for taking the piss out of the girls like that. They'd asked for it in his opinion.

But Spud hadn't been taking the piss at all. 'Because I am. Well, as good *as*,' he said in response to Ian's disbelieving look. 'I'm a bookmaker's *clerk* – it's only a matter of time.'

'You can't be a bookie's clerk,' Ian countered triumphantly. 'You're too young. Clerks can't be accredited until they're twenty-one.' *So there*, his voice said, like a kid who'd won an argument.

Spud wasn't deterred. 'Sure, I can't go to the race meetings for a couple of years, but I can still do the books, can't I?' He swilled back half his rum and Coke in one fell swoop. 'Ever heard of Big Bet Bob?'

'Yeah. Who hasn't?' Everyone, even those outside betting circles, knew of Robert 'Big Bet Bob' Wetherill. He was one of Perth's top bookmakers and always in the news. A clever self-promoter, Bob made sure of it.

'Well, that's who I work for.'

'You're joking.' Ian sounded less confident now; Spud's assurance was very convincing.

'Nup. I work out of his offices in Dalkeith.'

'Really?'

'Yeah, he took me on six months ago. I'm good with numbers, see.' Spud drained his glass. 'Finish your Coke,' he said. 'We'll drink the last lot neat,' and he took the flask from his pocket.

While Ian manfully skolled his nearly full glass, Spud made his announcement.

'I'm going to become the youngest bookmaker ever registered in Western Australia,' he said, 'and that'll be just the start. Being a bookie's like uni, you see, Pembo. It's just a means to an end.'

As Ian downed the last of his rum and Coke, head whirling, he saw no reason to doubt that Spud Farrell was destined for success.

The rum, on top of the beers they'd imbibed at the yacht club, had lent a glow of bonhomie to the night and, as Ian dropped Spud off outside the cottage in Pennell Road, both a little the worse for wear, it was as if they'd been mates for years.

'See you, Spud,' Ian said.

'See you, Pembo.'

A bizarre, and rocky, friendship was in the making.

CHAPTER FOUR

Maggie McAllister was a little concerned about her son. It didn't worry her that Mike seemed to have turned into a bit of a lair – she agreed with her husband that it was just a phase he was going through. But she had deep reservations about the whopping great one-cylinder 500cc Matchless motorbike he'd insisted on purchasing for his twenty-first birthday. He hadn't wanted presents or a party, just the equivalent in cash, and when they'd obliged him, to Maggie's horror he'd gone out and bought the second-hand bike.

'It's just part of the phase he's going through,' Jim had once again assured her, but this time he hadn't allayed her fears.

'A bloody dangerous part,' she said.

Jim personally thought the bike a safer vehicle than the little 125cc Lambrettas so popular amongst the students these days, but he lectured Mike nonetheless. His lecture was more about Mike's application to his studies than anything else though. The boy was of legal drinking age now, and it was a naturally wild time in a young man's life. Jim understood the temptations on offer, but the student drinking culture could be the downfall of some, he warned.

'You've had excellent passes so far, Mike,' he said reasonably. 'It'd be a shame to let it all go in third year, don't you agree?'

'Don't worry, Dad,' Mike promised. 'I won't let that happen.'

Mike meant it. He had no intention of flunking the final year of his basic three-year science course. He planned to complete a further honours year and then embark on his PhD. But it was true he was finding it difficult to knuckle down and study. He was too busy revelling in everything life had to offer. Not that drinking was any novelty – he and his mates had been drinking illegally for years – but pubs and beer gardens had now become the common meeting ground, and the partying was intense. Mike was sensible enough, however, to leave his bike at home when he went out on a spree with his mates.

Ian Pemberton's twenty-first promised to be a slap-up party, and even those students who disliked him accepted the gilt-edged invitations. Ian's popularity had picked up, however, since he'd been getting around with Mike. He seemed to have lost some of his arrogance it was agreed, and although his fellow students didn't know exactly when or how the nickname had evolved, somewhere along the line Pembo had become one of them – more or less.

The twenty-first was celebrated at the family home with all the pomp and ceremony the Pembertons had at their command. A marquee was erected on the grass tennis court and a twelve-piece band and dance floor set up beside the pool. Cynthia's gourmet caterers provided the continuous buffet laid out on long linen-clothed trestle tables in the marquee, and waiters in dinner jackets paraded about the gardens with trays of beer, champagne and soft drink, and endless bottles to top up empty glasses.

The champagne wasn't vintage Taittinger. It wasn't even champagne if the truth be known, although it said so on the label. It was a local sparkling wine – Cynthia's one economy for the night. She doubted whether the students would value the real thing, she said, but secretly she was sure that they wouldn't know the difference. And, to give her her due, she was probably right.

Two burly men in dinner jackets – members of the three-man security team Cynthia had employed – stood either side of the wrought-iron gates that led directly into the lavishly landscaped back gardens of the Pemberton property. The third equally burly security man was posted around the block by the circular driveway to the front door, with orders to redirect all arrivals to the rear entrance. Cynthia didn't want a mob of unruly students traipsing through her house.

'How do you do. So nice of you to come.'

The band was playing 'Three Coins in the Fountain', which seemed very apt as Cynthia stood, radiant and per-fectly lit, beside the fountain near the gates, greeting each and every guest. The indirect lighting throughout the garden was most effective, emphasising the beauty of the statues and rockeries and imported palms. Beside Cynthia stood her husband, and both were flanked by tray-bearing waiters.

'Welcome, welcome.' Gordon's approach was one of bonhomie, shaking everyone's hand and gesturing to the waiters. 'Help yourself to a drink.'

'Hello, Mike, how lovely to see you.'

Cynthia smiled dazzlingly and shook his hand. The smile froze just a fraction as she turned to greet the ginger-haired young man who had arrived with Mike McAllister. He was dressed in jeans and a denim jacket. She didn't approve. The invitations had said 'cocktail dress' for the women and 'smart casual' for the men. Smart casual did not mean jeans.

'How do you do,' she said. 'So nice of you to come.' She didn't offer her hand.

'Good to meet you, Mrs Pemberton.'

Spud was aware of the disapproval. He could have worn his decent gear – he had a number of classy sports jackets these days. He would have too, if there'd been anything to gain by it – he was quite happy to ingratiate himself when necessary. But Gordon Pemberton? An orthodontist with no interest in gambling? He'd opted for the denim instead. It made a statement.

'And what's *your* name?' Cynthia's smile remained frozen. The boy looked rather common, she thought, he couldn't possibly be one of Ian's fellow students. But he'd arrived with Mike McAllister. She was a little confused.

'Spud,' he said. 'Spud Farrell.'

Inwardly, she cringed. 'Your *real* name, dear. What's your *real* name?'

Cynthia Pemberton was every bit as up herself as Mike had told him, Spud thought, but he had no intention of being rude. He didn't want to spoil Pembo's party.

'Patrick,' he admitted. 'But I prefer Spud.'

The boy was most certainly from the wrong side of the tracks, Cynthia thought. Where on earth had Ian *met* him?

'Well, *Patrick*, I hope you have a lovely evening.'

She turned to the next guest, and Gordon saved the moment. 'Help yourselves to a drink, boys,' he said.

'Thanks, Mr Pemberton.' Mike took a beer from the waiter's tray. Cynthia was certainly behaving true to form, he thought. 'Let's find the birthday boy,' he said to Spud.

Spud grabbed a beer and, as they moved off, he yelled, 'Hey Pembo, where are you?' at the top of his voice.

Behind them, Cynthia once again cringed. The boy was not only common, he was a thug. And *Pembo*. She'd heard one or two of the other students refer to her son as Pembo that evening – it was unutterably ghastly, she'd have to put a stop to it.

'How do you do. So nice of you to come.'

*

Ian was not immediately in sight so the two mingled for a while. Spud left Mike chatting to Murray Hatfield. Murray was still in first year, but he and Mike and Ian had become good mates – an unusual situation between third-year students and freshmen, but Muzza, baby-faced and popular, was the best halfback the A team had ever had.

Spud finally found Ian beside the miniature waterfall of the rockery, which was at the rear of the pool. He was chatting up Natalie Hollingsworth. The nearby band was now playing 'Unchained Melody'.

Ian had been coming on strong to Natalie for the past several months – she and Mike had long ceased their casual affair – but his efforts had been to little avail.

'Hello, Spud.' He grinned as he looked Spud up and down – the jeans wouldn't have been a hit with his mother. He deliberately hadn't invited Spud home in the past, knowing what his mother's reaction would be; the ensuing interrogation simply wouldn't be worth it. But this was *his* twenty-first, he'd decided, on *his* terms, and he'd wanted Spud here. 'Glad you could make it,' he said. Then he gave Spud the nod to disappear, signalling he was making inroads with Natalie. But Spud wasn't to be deterred.

'G'day, Natalie,' he said. 'Need a word with you, Pembo.'

'Don't go away.' Ian flashed Natalie a grin. She smiled politely in return – she still considered Ian Pemberton insufferably arrogant.

'You said your folks wouldn't be here,' Spud hissed when he'd taken Ian aside. Bugger it, there was no way he could spring his surprise if that stitched-up mother of Pembo's was around.

'They'll be leaving soon,' Ian assured him. 'They're going to the ballet. Mum just wanted to do the meet-and-greet thing, that's all.'

'Bit of a dampener.' A real dampener, Spud thought – the red-carpet royal welcome was a bloody disaster. Everyone was standing around like stale bottles of piss, trying to be on their best behaviour and freezing in the fucking cold. 'So when are they coming back then?'

'One o'clock, they said. They're having supper with friends.'

One o'clock was the promise Ian had exacted from his mother. Cynthia had tried to negotiate for midnight but he wouldn't be in it. He'd also refused his parents' offer of a formal dinner, which he'd known would have been predominantly for their friends, not his, with speeches and the classic twenty-first 'key' and all the other bullshit such an event entailed. The party was to be for his mates, he'd said, or he didn't want a party at all. Gordon had been surprisingly understanding, and Cynthia had been forced to give in with ill grace. 'Well, we'll just have to have it in the back garden,' she'd insisted, despite the fact that it would be late August and probably chilly. She'd arranged for the marquee to be heated, and had decided that the toilet facilities in the cabana by the pool would be more than adequate, but she'd prayed it wouldn't rain. They'd have to come inside if it did.

'One o'clock, eh?' Spud was safe. His surprise was planned for the dot of midnight. 'Right you are.' And he disappeared, leaving Pembo to resume his pursuit of Natalie Hollingsworth. But Natalie had gone.

Damn Spud, Ian thought as he went off in search of her.

Cynthia was miffed that less than half the guests had arrived when, twenty minutes later, she and Gordon left for His Majesty's Theatre. The invitations had stipulated seven o'clock. Ian had tried to warn her.

'No-one arrives at parties until at least nine, Mum,' he'd said.

'Then you must simply tell them to be punctual, pet,' she'd answered. 'I shall consider it the height of rudeness if they're late.'

Her instructions had apparently been ignored, and now Cynthia was forced to leave without having vetted all the guests. It was intolerable. She gave strict orders to the security guards that all gatecrashers were to be turned away. Anyone without an invitation was not to be admitted, she said, and any potential troublemaker was to be instantly evicted. Then she and Gordon drove off in the Bentley to the strains of 'April in Portugal'.

After the departure of the Pembertons senior, the party picked up. The band instantly segued into 'It's All Over Now', the smash hit from a hot new group called The Rolling Stones, and followed it up with a string of every-one's favourites from The Beatles. Within seconds, the girls in their smart, flimsy cocktail dresses had ventured out from the warmth of the marquee into the chill night air to throw themselves about on the dance floor.

Shortly after nine, a bunch of students arrived with the stash of marihuana Ian had paid for in advance. They were the hippie set from uni, the 'Ban the Bomb' mob. He didn't normally mix with them, but they could be relied on for dope, and with the promise of endless free food and booze they'd eagerly accepted the invitation. Ian himself wasn't a regular 'head' but he was determined to give his guests the very best time possible – it was the sole purpose of the night. His twenty-first birthday party was a bid for friend-ship. Ian Pemberton was enjoying his newfound accept-ance. He liked being Pembo – one of the boys.

Joints were passed around, surreptitiously at first, then, as the mixture of grog and grass freed inhibitions, with a careless abandon. Tony and Bobbo, the bouncers by the gates, exchanged knowing looks and grins – they could smell the pot.

Around eleven thirty, Bobbo left his post to have a bit of a prowl about the garden, and returned with his report. The kids were getting bombed out of their brains, he said, but there was no sign of trouble. They were having a ball

– staggering around the dance floor, snogging all over the place, and one couple was all but having it off by the grove of palm trees near the back verandah. The bouncers had no intention of interfering. Let the kids have a good time, they thought – who cared? Their orders were to keep gatecrashers away and evict troublemakers. Besides, they couldn't stand the insufferable Cynthia Pemberton.

'Hey, you blokes want a beer?'

It was a quarter to twelve when Spud fronted up to the bouncers at the gate.

'Can't, mate, we're on duty,' Tony said.

'Thanks all the same,' Bobbo added. The offer had been made in the spirit of friendship – the kid wasn't giving them cheek. He didn't seem as out of it as some of the others either, Bobbo thought. He certainly wasn't stoned – you could always tell.

Spud stayed chatting with them for ten minutes or so. He held his liquor well and he never smoked grass – booze and dope didn't mix, he'd found. But he'd had quite a few beers and was on to the Bundy now. The Pembertons hadn't provided spirits, but Spud always had his flask handy.

'Are you punters?' he asked. 'I've got a couple of good tips for Belmont tomorrow.'

'Oh yeah?' Tony raised an eyebrow.

'Too right. Whack a fiver on Lightning Ridge in the fourth for starters, he's a dead cert.'

'You reckon, do you?' Bobbo, too, appeared sceptical.

'Yep, a fiver on the nose and you'll be laughing.'

'And you'd know, wouldn't you.' The kid was a cocky little bastard, Tony thought.

'It's my job to know, mate. I clerk for Big Bet Bob Wetherill.'

The men dived into their pockets for pen and paper, and five minutes later they had a list of red-hot tips – 'Straight from the horse's mouth,' as Spud said.

Tony and Bobbo were still writing down the last of the tips when the taxi pulled up. Spud gave Cyrenne a wave as she stepped out of the car.

'She's a friend of mine,' he said to the bouncers. 'She left her invitation at home, I've got it right here.' He took the gilt-edged invitation from his pocket and handed it to Bobbo. 'We've got a surprise lined up for my mate, you know what I mean?'

A tall platinum blonde sashayed towards them on six-inch gold stilettos, her belted trenchcoat flapping open to reveal a healthy expanse of silk-stockinged thigh.

'Right.' Bobbo and Tony shared a grin. The kid had hired a stripper – where was the harm in that? But wouldn't it just get right up the nose of that pain-in-the-arse Pemberton bitch.

Bobbo checked the invitation. 'Seems to be perfectly in order,' he said, and Tony shrugged agreement. The stripper would be gone before the Pembertons returned, and even if word got back to the harridan of the house, they couldn't be blamed. They'd collected the invitation, which was perfectly legitimate. How could they have known?

'Great.' Well, that was easy, Spud thought. 'G'day, Cyrenne,' he said. 'Come on in.'

'Hello, Spud.' Cyrenne greeted him, and then, with the sublime confidence of one used to men drooling over her, she winked at the bouncers. 'Hi, boys,' she said as she walked through the gates. Tony's and Bobbo's heads swivelled, eyes ogling the wriggle of her backside.

A minute or so later, they heard the band strike up a raunchy introduction and the kid yell 'Surpriiiise!' Tony said to Bobbo, 'My turn for a bit of a recce, I reckon.'

Ian Pemberton's jaw dropped the moment Cyrenne walked onto the dance floor, the others clearing the way and yelling their approval. He knew who she was. Cyrenne was no stripper. She was one of the top hookers from the

Sun Majestic Massage Parlour. Spud had introduced him
to the brothel over a year ago, and he'd been there several
times since. But Cyrenne had always been booked in
advance – it seemed she was a favourite amongst the high-
flyers who frequented the place.

'Happy birthday, Pembo.'

Spud appeared beside him and started clapping along
with the others as the band launched into 'Hey Big
Spender', and before Ian could comment, Cyrenne's trenchcoat landed on his head. He struggled out from beneath it
and stood gawking.

For a non-professional, Cyrenne's performance was
extraordinarily competent – in fact, it was far more seduc-
tive than the average stripper. But then she'd had a great
deal of experience on more intimate occasions. Beneath
the trenchcoat she was dressed in a bright red satin
miniskirt and matching braless halterneck top. The skirt
was split to waist high on one side, displaying black silk
suspenders and stockings, and the top was low cut,
exposing voluptuous breasts.

Cyrenne herself had requested the band play 'Hey Big
Spender'. It was the highly suggestive number the chorus
of hookers sang in the new Cy Coleman musical, *Sweet
Charity*, and the girls from the Sun Majestic had proudly
adopted it as their own. They knew the lyrics off by heart.

The minute you walked in the joint . . .

She took Ian by the hand and led him to a chair beside
the dance floor, where she dangerously placed a stilettoed
foot on his crotch while she divested herself of her shoe.

I could see you were a man of distinction . . .

When her other shoe had been removed in the same
manner, she threw them both to Spud, who deftly caught
them, then she proceeded to circle the chair, gyrating to
the music and whispering the lyrics huskily to Ian. She was
no singer and didn't pretend to be, but the way she said
the words was a personal come-on.

Good looking, so refined . . . The band was into the second chorus by now.

Positioning herself legs astride in front of him, she thrust her pelvis at him with the obvious invitation that he undo the miniskirt.

Say, wouldn't you like to know what's going on in my mind . . .

A cheer went up when the skirt dropped away to reveal perfect buttocks, enhanced by a G-string and suspender belt, and everyone started chanting a countdown as she teasingly released each suspender, her foot once again in Ian's crotch.

So let me get right to the point . . .

When both silk stockings were removed, she draped them around his neck, then snapped off the suspender belt.

I don't pop my cork for every man I see . . .

It was the third and final chorus and the crowd was going wild. 'Get it off,' they yelled.

She sat on his lap and whirled the suspender belt about her head like a lasso.

Hey big spender . . .

When that, too, had been hurled to Spud, it was time for the top. Cyrenne stood, kicked a leg high over Ian's head and sat straddling him, nose to nose, arms about his neck, G-stringed crotch grinding against his now healthy erection.

Hey big spender . . .

She wriggled her pelvis in time to the music. The number was reaching its crescendo.

Hey big spender . . .

Slowly, she untied the halterneck top.

Spend a little time with me.

Then she stood and, as the top landed at Spud's feet, she thrust her glorious breasts right into Ian's face.

'Hey Big Spender' was over, as was the strip, and Cyrenne, clad in only her G-string, took Ian by the hand, raised him to his feet and bowed to the crowd, who madly applauded.

The band struck up 'Happy Birthday', everyone joined in, and Spud, having collected Cyrenne's gear, returned it to her. She donned the trenchcoat and pocketed the rest of the paraphernalia – the show was clearly over. Everyone went back to their partying, the band embarked on an Elvis bracket, and Cyrenne winked at Spud as, hand in hand, she led Ian towards the verandah and the back door to the house.

Shit, Tony thought, watching from the shadows by the rockery, the kids weren't supposed to go inside the house unless it rained – those were the Pemberton bitch's orders. But what the hell, the kid was her own bloody son. And there'd been no trouble, had there? He and Bobbo had kept guard by the gate – how could they possibly have known that the party boy had snuck inside for a quick root? Tony returned to the gate.

Inside the house, the caterers, who had permission to use the kitchen, were far too busy with the constant replenishment of food platters to take any notice of the young couple quietly sneaking upstairs.

From the garden, Spud watched as one of the upstairs bedroom lights went on, then very quickly went off again. He smiled. He hadn't had to pay a penny for Cyrenne. She'd been a present from Ruby. He'd sent any number of big punters Ruby's way and she'd owed him a favour. Now Pembo did too. Spud liked doing things for his mates, but he also liked racking up favours. You never knew when they'd come in handy.

It'd been a bloody good night, he thought, grabbing a Coke from the tray of a passing waiter. He poured half of it into a pot plant and drained the last of his flask into the glass.

The Pembertons senior arrived home a quarter of an hour earlier than expected, but their premature return posed no threat. Cyrenne had left a good twenty minutes previously. She'd brought the kid on quickly, no mucking about, she had a client booked in for one o'clock.

The band was playing 'As Time Goes By' when Cynthia walked through the house to the back garden – the bouncers had reported that the Bentley was pulling up in the front driveway.

But the music was drowned out by the raucous screech of voices.

'*A smile is just a smile . . .*'

Cynthia was appalled when she stepped onto the verandah and was confronted by the sight of two dozen students in a drunken sing-along, arms linked, swaying unsteadily on the dance floor, some barely able to stand. And amongst the shadows of the garden, she was sure she could see some highly suspicious activity. She stepped back inside and turned on the burglar deterrent switch by the door.

The whole of the garden was suddenly and starkly floodlit. The band stopped playing, those on the dance floor shielded their eyes from the glare, and, amongst the previously darkened nooks and crannies, couples sprang apart startled, in various states of disarray. It was certainly the way to end a party.

The students, drunk and stoned for the most part, lurched out into the night. Cynthia did not stand by the gates farewelling them as she had intended. But she did have a sharp word with the security men.

'What on earth's been going on?' she demanded as she took them aside.

'There's been no trouble, ma'am,' Bobbo reported. 'The kids have been on their best behaviour.'

'But they're all drunk!' she said furiously.

'Can't stop them drinking, ma'am,' Tony said. 'The alcohol was provided.' And by you, his tone clearly indicated.

Ian said much the same thing when everyone had gone

and she accused his friends of being drunken reprobates.

'Well, you've only got yourself to blame,' he said accusingly, swaying on his feet, none too sober himself.

'I beg your pardon?' Cynthia wished Gordon would give her some back-up, but he'd gone to bed, apparently unperturbed.

'All that Taittinger . . .' The remark dripped sarcasm, he'd known it was local bubbly. 'What else can you expect? They're *common*, aren't they? They're not *used* to it. If you feed them vintage Taittinger it's *bound* to go to their heads.'

Cynthia was shocked. Ian was mocking her. Why? His friends weren't common at all. Most came from excellent families – she knew the parents of many of them. Why was her son attacking her?

'You shouldn't have done it, Mum,' he said, starting to slur his words a little. 'You shouldn't have turned the lights on.'

'Good heavens, Ian, I was only doing what any decent mother –'

'You shouldn't have done it, that's all. I'm going to bed.'

He couldn't be bothered taking the confrontation any further, he was too far gone. And besides, he'd had too good a time. She'd killed the night, certainly, but it would have been over the moment she got home anyway. His mum was just being his mum. She couldn't help the way she was.

'Great party though,' he said, resisting the urge to add 'before you fucked it up' – he'd hurt her enough, he could tell. 'Really really, great great party. The best night of my life, in fact.'

Cynthia watched in dismay as her beloved son weaved his way upstairs. What had she done that was so very wrong? He'd never in his life spoken to her in such a manner. She was more than hurt. She was cut to the quick.

*

It *had* been the best night of his life, Ian thought as he switched on the bedside lamp and collapsed into bed fully clothed. He gazed up at the ceiling, still seeing the halo of Cyrenne's silver-blonde hair reflected in the glow from the garden's lights as she straddled him. It hadn't lasted long, he'd been as randy as hell – she'd been bringing him on ever since she'd started playing with him during the strip – but the experience had been amazing nonetheless.

Strangely enough, it hadn't been the sexual act itself which had been the biggest thrill. He'd had hookers before, although perhaps none quite as impressive as Cyrenne. Indeed, he'd lost his virginity to a hooker – just over a year ago, when Spud had taken him to the Sun Majestic. He hadn't told Spud he'd been a virgin at the time. It was obvious that Spud regularly introduced new clients to the Sun Majestic – in fact, Ian suspected that he scored freebies in exchange – and it had all seemed so worldly that he'd been too ashamed to admit that at nearly twenty years of age he'd never slept with a girl. He'd been back to the brothel a number of times since then – he'd become quite a regular. He liked buying a woman. The process was less complicated than trying to chat up the girls at uni. When he paid, there was no need to try and win favours, nor was there the fear of rejection.

But tonight had been something new and exciting. Cyrenne had been *here,* he thought, here in this very room!

He looked about at the past of his childhood. At his sporting trophies from school and university where they sat on their shelves, silver-plating kept buffed and shining by the cleaning lady upon Cynthia's instructions. They were all there, from his first junior track and field medal at Guildford Grammar to the hundred yards hurdles cup he'd won last year at UWA. He looked at his posters of Elvis, which had been sticky-taped to the walls for a number of years now. They hadn't met with his mother's approval, but she'd allowed them anyway. Sticky-tape didn't do too much damage, Cynthia had declared, and she'd decided that he'd get over the teenage need for posters eventually. He had. But he kept refreshing the sticky-tape and the posters remained, either as a gesture of defiance or a declaration of his personal space, he wasn't sure which.

Hell, he thought, and laughed out loud. He'd had one of the top hookers in Perth right here in his room. It was mind-bogglingly exciting. The secrecy, the daring of it! What would his mother say if she knew? That was the thrill – far more than the sex. It was the highlight of his life.

Spring arrived, hot and early, and third year was coming to its conclusion with exams on the horizon. For Mike and Ian it was the culmination of their basic three-year science course, although following second year Ian had decided upon a new direction. He'd tried to persuade Mike to join him.

'Geology, mate, that's where the money is. Nickel. The hunt's already on – it's only a matter of time.'

Ian had done his homework. Nickel, the new wonder additive in the production of improved high-tensile steels, was in heavy demand, and the recent strikes at Sudbury in Canada had had a huge impact upon the global stock market. The search was now on in the mineral-rich state of Western Australia.

'Half the lecturers are already doing side-line work consulting,' he urged. 'There's a shortage of qualified geologists in WA – in the whole of Australia for that matter. We'll be able to write our own ticket. A double major in Geol 30 and 31, that's what we need. You're mad if you don't make the switch.'

Mike shrugged. 'Then I'm mad. I'm sticking with zo-ol.' He had no interest in joining Ian on his get-rich-quick campaign. His commitment to the field of environment and marine biology remained unchanged.

At the moment, however, his commitment seemed to be taking a back seat as the weather, hot and welcoming, beckoned him to the beach. Often on the weekends, instead of studying, he'd lair off down Stirling Highway on his motorbike to throw himself into the surf at North Cottesloe before joining the gang of his like-minded mates for a quick beer at the Ocean Beach Hotel.

Occasionally Jools would nag him into taking her along. She'd ride pillion, refusing to wear the safety helmet, her cropped brown curls riotous in the wind. She loved the bike. Mike found her company no hardship; he was fond of his little sister, and besides, he was between girlfriends at the time. Not that he had any wish to reserve the pillion seat. He preferred to play the field, and did so openly and unashamedly.

Jools loved their days together at North Cott. They'd go body-surfing and eat dagwood dogs – frankfurters on wooden skewers battered and dipped in tomato sauce. Jools always complained loudly about the way the sauce ran out after the second bite. 'Have a pie instead then,' Mike would say every time. But she never did. North Cott wouldn't be the same without a dagwood dog. Then, in the beer garden at the OBH, she'd sit with her lemonade – at eighteen she was still underage – while Mike and his mates would slip her a beer on the sly. Finally, they'd lair back to Claremont on the bike, Mike taking the corners at breakneck speed, just the way she liked it.

Jools adored her big brother, and her time with him was particularly special now – she'd be leaving home next year.

'I'm going east,' she'd announced at the dinner table just the previous month. 'To Sydney. Next year.'

It hadn't been altogether unexpected. Jools's desire to be an actress had come under much discussion over the past year. Maggie, realising that her daughter was not to be swayed in her choice of career, had suggested that perhaps they should consider the National Institute of Dramatic Art.

'If she passes the audition it's a two-year course,' she'd said to Jim. 'Formal training seems the way to go, don't you think?'

But Jim had been surprisingly adamant in his refusal. 'If she wants to set her sights on university she has my full support,' he'd said rather stuffily, 'but what sort of career is it – dressing up and pretending to be someone else?' He was honestly mystified. Acting wasn't a career at all, it was a hobby. 'Let her do her plays and things in her spare time,' he'd said, 'I'm not sending her to NIDA.' He was disappointed in his daughter – Jools was a clever girl, she could have done well at uni. He'd refused to budge on the subject.

Jools had taken up the gauntlet. The tomboy had become the rebel, and far from being deterred by her father's decision, she considered it a challenge. She'd make it on her own, she told him defiantly.

After leaving school, she wisely took her mother's advice and did an evening course in shorthand and typing at Perth Technical College, at the same time auditioning for the ABC and becoming a regular performer in radio dramas and children's programs. Then, upon completing her secretarial course, she took up part-time office work while appearing in several productions at the Perth Playhouse.

Already Jools was proving her point, and Jim had to admit he admired her tenacity.

'She said she'd make it on her own, and I'm sure she will,' he told his wife by way of self-vindication. He knew Maggie hadn't agreed with his decision regarding NIDA.

Jim secretly believed that his daughter would give up her acting nonsense when she met the right man and settled down to have a family. Just as he secretly believed that most women were destined to follow the same path eventually, even those who embarked upon an academic career. Jools's decision to waive a tertiary education was therefore a disappointment only. Had his son made a similar decision, it would have been a catastrophe.

And now Jools had dropped her bombshell. She was heading east next year and, like her father, she refused to discuss the matter any further.

With the exams only two weeks away, Mike realised that his father's warning had proved ominously true. He'd let his studies go downhill, and he'd have to swot like mad if he was to cram a year's study into the fortnight ahead. He stopped seeing the voluptuous Sophia – a second-year medical student with whom he'd been having a brief fling – and applied himself with a vengeance, managing to scrape through by the skin of his teeth. Ian Pemberton gained straight As as usual, with the minimum of effort.

Jim McAllister wisely didn't make any 'I told you so' comments about his son's disappointing exam results. He was aware that Mike had given himself a scare, and that it was a lesson learned. Instead, he gave permission for Mike and his mates to take *Alana* to Rotto for a week.

Rottnest Island had always been the favoured choice for students celebrating the end of a year's hard slog, and 1964 proved no exception. The beer garden at the Quokka Arms overlooking Thomson Bay teemed with young people rejoicing in their freedom and bent on having as wild a time as possible. Amongst them were Mike McAllister and his mates Ian Pemberton and young Murray Hatfield. In bathers and open shirts, the three downed jugs of beer, sang raucous rugby songs and flirted with the girls.

Surprisingly enough, baby-faced Muzza, although hardly in Mike's league, was popular with the girls. Gregarious, earnest, there was an innocence about him that girls trusted. He was the boy next door and they let down their guard, realising only too late that, like all fit young men with raging libidos, Murray Hatfield was really interested in only one thing. But by then it was too late, they genuinely liked him. Everyone did. It was impossible to dislike Muzza.

Ian Pemberton, however, continued to have trouble with girls. Despite his good looks, they didn't warm to him, and he always came off second best when he was in the company of Mike and Muzza. But fortunately for Pembo, this week at Rotto was not about girls. For once, beer and camaraderie took priority over scoring as the three gave themselves up to the sea and the sun and the Quokka Arms.

Every now and then they'd wander down to the beach and throw themselves into the sea to sober up. Then, at the end of a boozy afternoon, they'd row themselves out in the dinghy to *Alana* where they'd share another few beers, have a swim off the boat, and finally collapse.

Occasionally, they took a break from the frenzy of partying, and went fishing. They'd haul in by the dozen the herring and skipjack and garfish attracted to the oil streak and burley they'd put out from the stern of the boat. Or they'd drift beside the deep reefs and fish for snapper and dhufish. And when they returned to the mooring at Thomson Bay, they'd clean and fillet and cook up their catch on the old primus stove.

Sometimes they'd walk around to Armstrong Bay and North Point on the extreme north side of the island, where they'd dive for crayfish. They'd build a campfire on the beach and boil up the crays in the old kerosene tin with the top cut off, and they always took several bottles of beer with them.

Conversation inevitably turned to the future, a prospect which excited all three, although Ian tended to play it blasé. He enjoyed sending his mates up.

'My God, I'm marooned on an island with two idealists,' he said mockingly one hot afternoon as they sprawled on the sand, bellies full of cray and into their fifth beers.

'I'm not an idealist,' Muzza countered fuzzily, the combination of heat and alcohol clearly evident.

'Oh yes, you are. Anyone who undertakes a degree in medicine has to be.'

'I'm interested in the human body – that doesn't make me an idealist.'

'Of course it does; you're the same as Mike. He wants to save the environment, you want to save lives. What's the difference?'

Muzza liked being compared to Mike. Mike was his mate, but also a bit of a hero. He lapsed into contemplative silence, gazing at the sand for a moment or so. He'd never considered himself an idealist, but perhaps, deep down, he was. He certainly wanted to do something meaningful with his life. Perhaps his choice of medicine over architecture, which had also interested him, had been a subconscious decision to serve humanity in some way.

'You know, I think you're right, Pembo.' Muzza looked up, his face aglow with drunken revelation. 'It never occurred to me before, but I think you're right. I think I *am* an idealist . . .'

'Jesus Christ!' Ian guffawed. Muzza was so bloody gullible, so prone to suggestion – a real innocent. He raised his hands to the sky in prayer. 'Where are you, Spud?' he called out theatrically. 'I need you! Save me!'

Mike laughed at the two of them. They were both pissed, but then again so was he.

The others joined in his laughter, the subject was dropped, and they toasted Spud – the fourth musketeer. No-one knew exactly why Spud hadn't joined them. He'd certainly been invited. 'Too busy, Mikey,' he'd said. 'No time for a holiday. Besides, I haven't earned it the way you uni blokes have.

Mike hadn't been sure what to make of the remark. Spud was hinting at some form of elitism, but was he sending them up? Was it just a good-natured dig, or did he feel excluded, as if they were a club to which he didn't belong? It had been impossible to tell. But Spud had remained adamant in his decision.

'Have a good time,' he'd said. 'Bring me home a few crays.'

Spud genuinely wished his mates well – they'd worked hard; they deserved a break. But they'd be back at uni next year, swotting away like mad, repeating the process with no money to show for it. What a waste of time.

Both of Mike's guesses had been right on the money.

One late afternoon, the boys asked a few girls along to Armstrong Bay and it turned into quite a party. They played the transistor radio at full volume, tucked into the freshly boiled crays, drank copious amounts of beer from the esky and, after they'd watched the sunset, they paired off. They went for a walk along the beach, or a wander around the point, and that night, amongst the nearby rocks and foothills, Ian Pemberton had no trouble at all scoring.

Mike and Pembo and Muzza cemented their friendship at Rotto that year with what they agreed was the best week's holiday they'd ever had in their lives.

The following February, Jools took off for Sydney and Mike embarked upon his honours year. The house seemed strangely quiet without the frenetic energy of Jools, and Baxter, now fat, aged and greying, pined.

Jim's assessment that his son had learned a lesson had been correct. Mike's path in life was clearly defined, and he applied himself with a renewed passion to his chosen subjects of marine biology and ecology. He laid off the long drinking sessions with his mates, the motorbike became simply a mode of transport, and he stopped chasing girls. The latter was difficult, because very often they chased him.

'Mike McAllister. Long time, no see.'

Sophia was the first to greet him as he joined Muzza and the gang of eight, mainly girls, who were seated on communal benches either side of the long table in the centre of the beer garden.

'G'day, Sophe. Two days qualifies as a long time, does it?' He gave her a quizzical grin, pretending that he hadn't got the hint and reminding her that he'd bumped into her in the refectory at lunchtime on Thursday.

'You know what I mean.' She reached out and grabbed his hand, both the gesture and the tone of her voice suggestive.

Of course he knew what she meant. Sophia had been his principal distraction towards the end of last year when they'd spent many a hot summer night in the Scarborough Beach surf club's old boatshed. Sophia's brother was a surf club member and she knew where they hid the key – she found the boatshed exciting, she'd said. So had Mike. Their regular trysts had contributed to his near downfall in the exams. Sophia was dangerous.

'Come here, stranger, you're next to me.' She was seated in the middle, and shuffled along as she dragged him down beside her. He stepped over the bench, smiling an apology at the girl next to Sophia who was also forced to shuffle along and make room.

'G'day, Muzza.'

Mike's tone was pointed as he called to Muzza who was at the end of the table on the opposite side, his arm about a girl and in the throes of a serious chat-up.

'Mike. G'day, mate.'

Muzza, noticing Mike's arrival for the first time, gave him an apologetic shrug. It was Saturday arvo and the two had planned to meet for a quiet beer at the Nedlands Park Hotel, affectionately known as Steve's, but Muzza hadn't been able to resist joining his fellow medical students. Particularly as there'd been only two blokes at the table.

Mike grinned – apology accepted and situation understood – but he wouldn't stay long, he decided. With the exception of Muzza, the others had obviously been here for some time and most seemed pretty well loaded. He was riding his bike, he couldn't afford to get legless. Besides, he'd planned to study this afternoon.

Muzza made the introductions starting from his end of the table. There were several present whom Mike recognised from uni but didn't really know – they were all in second year. 'And Johanna Whitely.' Muzza finished with the young woman seated beside Mike at the end of the bench. 'Jo, Mike.'

'Hello, Mike.'

'Hello, Jo.'

He'd seen her around the campus – it was difficult not to, she was very good-looking, in a different sort of way. A willowy girl, with fair hair and classical cheekbones, there was an elegance about her he'd admired. But there was also something a little aesthetic and remote, and he'd decided she was an intellectual, probably pretentious and not his type. But now, as her eyes met and held his, he did a quick rethink. There was nothing of the pseudo-intellectual about Johanna – to the contrary, there appeared no pretension at all. In the hazel-green eyes he saw candour, and what was possibly an acute intelligence. Whatever it was, he found the directness of her gaze just a little confronting.

'I've seen you around,' he said. The opening gambit sounded pathetic, so he quickly added, 'You're in second-year med, right?'

'Yes.' She'd seen him around too. Who hadn't? And she certainly knew of his exploits. All the girls talked about Mike McAllister – from what she could gather, half of them had slept with him. She could see why, he was devastatingly attractive. But she wasn't interested.

'Hey, stranger.' It was Sophia again, tucking her arm into Mike's and literally hauling him in. 'Where've you been?'

She was a little drunk, but she would have been much the same sober. Sophia pursued men unashamedly. She was forthright and sexy and not accustomed to being ignored, yet here they were, well into first term, and he hadn't even rung her. Not that Mike'd ever promised anything other than a good time, she had to admit, but there were no exams on the horizon now – surely he'd like to pick up where they'd left off.

Mike wondered whether he could avoid Sophia by offering to buy the next round. He didn't have a beer himself, and the jug in the centre of the table was nearly empty, but he decided to meet her head on. Given the mood she was in, she'd only continue the pursuit.

'Actually, Sophe,' he said, leaning in close, his tone intimate, 'I'm keeping pretty much to myself these days – concentrating on my studies, you know? I nearly bombed out last year.'

'Well, we could meet for a coffee or something, couldn't we?' Her arm was still tucked into his and she wriggled beside him, sending a very positive signal that it wasn't coffee she had in mind but rather the Scarborough Beach surf club's old boatshed.

'No,' he said, quietly but firmly, as he disengaged his arm, 'we couldn't.' He stood. 'My round,' he announced to the table, and picked up the empty jug.

'Grab us two, will you, Mike,' Muzza said. 'I'll go you halves,' and he slid a note across the table. Muzza was still legally underage and with his baby face he looked it, so Mike always made his bar purchases for him, just to be on the safe side.

'Right you are.'

When Mike returned from the bar, he plonked the jugs on the table and sat beside Johanna. It appeared perfectly natural to sit at the end of the bench rather than climb over into the centre, but Sophia glowered, taking it as a personal insult.

'Oh, I'm sorry,' he said, suddenly noticing that Johanna wasn't drinking beer but something that looked like a gin, or vodka, and tonic. As a rule, the students avoided the top shelf when they were drinking en masse – it was cheaper to stick to beer. 'What can I get you?' he asked. It was his round, after all. 'Gin and tonic?'

'It's lemonade actually. But no, thanks,' she added as he started to rise. 'Let's face it, you can only take so much of the stuff.'

He sat again, glad that the others were talking amongst themselves. Even Sophia, covering the slight she'd felt at her perceived insult, was now focusing her attention on the young man sitting opposite.

'You don't drink then?' She was about the only uni student who didn't, he thought.

'Good heavens above, no,' she said, wide-eyed, 'I'm underage.'

He looked at her in amazement – she was joking, she had to be. Then she smiled. God, she was gorgeous, he thought.

'Doesn't stop Muzza,' he grinned.

'No. Muzza and I are the babies. Most of the others in our course took a year off after school.'

'And you came straight to uni?'

She nodded.

'Me too. Bit of a culture shock, eh?'

She nodded again. She found his easy manner relaxing – he didn't seem to be chatting her up at all. She'd expected that he would, and she didn't like the routine form of chat-up. When she sensed someone was about to come on strong, she always presented a challenging front, which usually disconcerted them.

'So why don't you drink then?' He gave a mock frown. 'It's a mandatory element of student culture, you know.'

'Did I say I didn't drink?'

'Yes.'

'I lied.'

'Oh.'

'I just can't stand beer.'

He laughed. 'My God, you really are out of step, aren't you?'

'I know, but I can't help it, I hate the stuff.'

'So what'll it be?' He stood. 'I insist. It's my round.'

'Port and lemonade.'

He pulled a terrible face and she shrugged apologetically. She didn't actually like alcohol, but it was her way of joining the brigade – port and lemonade tasted very much like a soft drink.

Johanna, aware of the venomous sidelong glances from Sophia, watched him as he went off to the bar. Well, if this is a chat-up, she thought, which it probably is, then he's very good at it. No wonder they're all mad about Mike McAllister.

'I'm off now,' she said half an hour later, when another two jugs had arrived at the table. She'd enjoyed chatting to Mike. Indeed, she was amazed at the ease with which he'd milked information from her. She came from Manjimup, to the south – 'Karri country,' she'd said, 'a timber town.' And she shared a flat with another girl, also a student, in Kingsway just a quick walk west of the university.

'It must be tough,' he'd said, 'living away from your family.'

It wasn't at all but she hadn't been about to tell him that.

'I'm going too,' Mike said, and he stood. 'Can I give you a lift?'

'No, thanks.' It was a fine autumn day and the flat was barely ten minutes away. Besides, Sophia was staring balefully at her. If looks could kill, Jo thought, I'd be dead as a maggot. 'I feel like a bit of a walk,' she said, not wishing to seem rude.

Johanna had overheard the exchange between Mike and Sophia – she hadn't been able to avoid it. Although Mike had kept his voice down, she'd been right beside him. She'd respected him for his honesty, and she probably would have accepted the lift home, but it simply wasn't worth incurring Sophia's wrath. They were doing the same course and in the same year, and Sophia could be an absolute bitch.

'Bye, everyone.' She gave a general wave to the gang as she left the beer garden, and there were responses of 'See you, Jo'.

Curbing the desire to race after her, Mike called a goodbye to Muzza at the far end of the table and flashed Sophia a friendly smile. 'See you, Sophe.'

'Sure, see you around.' Sophia gave a nonchalant shrug, although inside she was seething. She knew he'd set his sights on Jo. So much for study being top priority, she thought. It was a bloody insult – she'd been given the flick.

Mike sauntered out of Steve's, then leapt on his bike and kick-started the engine. He could see Jo barely thirty yards down the street.

'You sure you don't want a lift?'

She halted as he pulled up abreast of her, the bike's engine idling.

'Oh my God!' She laughed. She'd presumed he'd been offering to drive her, but of course she'd seen him arriving at uni on his bike. 'I must say I'm tempted.' She'd never ridden on a motorbike.

'Great.' He revved up the engine. 'Climb aboard,' he yelled above its roar, 'and hang on to me.'

They took off, Johanna initially clinging to the belt of his jeans, then, as they rounded a sharp corner, putting her arms around his waist and hanging on for all she was worth.

'Lean into the corners,' he shouted back to her. 'Don't try and fight it – go with the bike.'

She did, suddenly loving it. But her flat was nearby and all too soon it was over.

'The brick building ahead there on the left,' she yelled

into his ear, and they pulled up out the front of the squat little block of flats.

She climbed from the bike, running a hand through her windblown hair and laughing with breathless exhilaration.

'That was fantastic! Absolutely *fantastic*!'

'Want to go to North Cott for a swim?'

'What? Now?'

'Why not? Grab your bathers, I've got mine in the back.' He always carried a pair of bathers and a towel on the bike.

'It's a bit cold, isn't it?' It wasn't cold at all, but swimming to Jo usually meant cooling off on a very hot day.

'Come on,' he urged, 'don't be a wimp.' She remained hesitant, but he could tell she was attracted by the prospect of another ride on the bike. 'All right then,' he bargained, 'no swim. Just the run to Cottesloe and back, what do you say?'

'No.'

He was disappointed, until, after a moment's thoughtful pause, she added, 'We'll do the swim. I'll get my bathers.'

When she reappeared, he took the safety helmet from the compartment under the pillion seat and handed it to her. 'Passenger wears the helmet,' he said, 'that's the rule.'

He helped buckle the strap under her chin, then straddled the bike, kick-started the engine and she climbed aboard. By the time they arrived at North Cott, Johanna was riding pillion like a seasoned professional.

They donned their bathing costumes in the public changing rooms and walked down to the beach where the westerly was fierce and the surf rough. She was not a particularly strong swimmer, Mike noted, but she was certainly game. Twice she was dumped, and both times she came up spluttering and laughing. He liked her for it.

They didn't stay long at the beach, and when they were back in their clothes and preparing for the trip home he suggested a beer at the OBH.

'Sorry,' he corrected himself. 'A port and lemonade.'

'Only if it's my shout,' she said.

'You're on.'

They stayed for just the one drink, although Mike could have remained in the beer garden all afternoon. His well-intentioned plans to study had gone out the window, as had his resolution to stop chasing girls. He'd well and truly set his sights on Johanna Whitely, she was irresistible. But when he offered a second round, Jo refused to be in it.

'I think it's home time,' she said firmly.

Twenty minutes later, he dropped her off at the Kingsway flat.

'Do you want to go out tonight?' he asked, as she handed him the helmet. 'There's some good jazz on at –'

'Can't, sorry, I have a date.' She didn't.

'How about tomorrow?'

She shook her head. 'Tied up, I'm afraid.' She wasn't.

She seemed very eager to knock him back – perhaps she was in a relationship, he thought, although he hadn't seen her around with anyone in particular.

'Next week? The week after?' He grinned cheekily. 'You can tell me to piss off if you like.'

She laughed. 'Piss off, Mike.'

'Why?' he asked, the grin disappearing. 'Why don't you want to go out with me? Have you got a steady bloke or something?'

'No.'

'Then . . .?' He left the question hanging. He was bewildered – they'd had such a good time together.

'Actually,' she said, 'I'm keeping pretty much to myself these days – concentrating on my studies. You know how it is.'

It was word for word what he'd said to Sophia. 'You heard?'

'I couldn't help it,' she said. 'I was right next to you, remember?'

'Yeah, well, I meant it . . .' She'd left-footed him a little and he was flummoxed. 'I wasn't bunging on . . .'

'Nor am I.'

It was the truth. Johanna was committed to her studies – she didn't want the distraction of an affair. And to go out with the likes of Mike McAllister would be inviting an affair, she knew it. Platonic friendships were of no interest to him; it was conquests he was after, and she'd simply be another notch on his belt.

'So it's a definite no then?'

His boyishly hopeful last bid was very beguiling, and she wasn't falling for it.

'It's a definite no,' she said, 'but thanks for a fantastic afternoon.'

'My pleasure.' He straddled the bike. 'See you around, Jo.'

'See you, Mike.'

As he revved up the engine, he watched her walk to the ground-floor unit on the right. Flat three, he noted.

At the door, she turned and waved. He waved back, then roared off down the street.

The following weekend, Jo returned with her bags of groceries – she always did her shopping on a Saturday morning – to discover the bike parked outside her flat and Mike leaning against the wall.

'Your flatmate told me you were out shopping,' he said. 'She seems very nice, Kathy – she asked me in for a coffee, but I said no.'

'What do you want, Mike?'

'I thought you might like to go for a spin,' he said. Then before she could answer, he held his hands up in protest. 'It's not a date. Just a quick run down to North Cott and back, that's all.'

She gave in. What was the point of saying no? She'd love a ride on the bike.

'I'll just put these inside,' she said, indicating the groceries.

'Grab your bathers while you're there.' When she gave him a look that suggested he might be pushing things a bit far, he added in all innocence, 'It's a great day for it. The sea breeze isn't in yet, it won't be too rough, and you could do with a few lessons in body-surfing.'

They spent three hours at the beach, Jo stretched it to two ports and lemonade at the OBH, and when he dropped her back at the Kingsway flat, he didn't ask her out.

Mike pursued Johanna Whitely in much the same manner throughout the whole of second term. When the weather became too cold for swimming, they'd rug up and lair down to North Cott anyway, where they'd sit in a milk bar drinking hot chocolate and endlessly talking. They never seemed to run out of conversation, frivolous or serious, but they didn't speak intimately. Jo invited no discussion of her past, nor did she enquire after his – the exchange of personal secrets was reserved for lovers in her opinion, and she didn't wish to encourage him. Instead, they agreed and disagreed on movies, books and music, and they discussed university and their studies with passion, often continuing over a coffee at her flat when he dropped her home. It appeared that perhaps Mike McAllister might be capable of a platonic relationship with a woman, after all.

But he wasn't. Mike found his friendship with Jo frustrating. Much as he liked being with her, and much as he was stimulated by her conversation, to him their relationship lacked the key ingredient – sex. But she'd laid down the rules, and he was determined not to cripple his chances by rushing her. She was the greatest challenge he'd ever come up against.

As the months passed, his obsession with the conquest of Johanna proved surprisingly beneficial to his studies. He didn't chase after other women – although he had the occasional one-night stand – most evenings he devoted to study. And he found Jo's fierce intelligence inspiring – so much so that his plans for seduction gradually took a back seat. Frustrating as the situation was, he didn't want to risk losing her friendship.

It was the beginning of third term, and Johanna Whitely was forced to face the fact that she was head over heels in love and had been for some time. She was angry with herself. How could she have let it happen? During the holidays she'd vowed she'd stop seeing Mike. She'd call the whole thing off, she'd told herself. But what was there to call off? How could she tell him she didn't want to go for a ride on the bike, or have a coffee and a chat? What possible reason could she give? She'd steeled herself nonetheless. She'd tell him that as it was third term, she'd decided to devote every single hour of every single weekend to study. It didn't sound plausible, but she'd give it her best shot. She'd be firm, she told herself – firm and resolute.

But the moment she heard the bike pull up outside, she knew she'd say nothing. She'd continue to play the 'friends' game because she wanted to be with him. In fact, she ached to be with him in every sense of the word – she longed for him to make love to her. But that was a no-win situation too. She'd made the rules quite clear from the outset – friendship only – and it was her non-availability that now kept him intrigued. If she slept with him, she'd become just another conquest and he'd move on. It was a bloody awful mess all round, she thought, and she cursed herself for having allowed it to happen.

'Hi, Mike. How were your holidays?' She greeted him casually at the front door.

'Great. Missed you. How was Manjimup?' he asked as they crossed to the bike.

'Great.'

It had been hideous. She'd hated being under the same

roof again with the stepfather she detested, and the stalemate that had developed between her and her mother had been as awkward and uncomfortable as ever.

'Good to be back though,' she said, buckling the chin strap of the helmet.

'There's an open-air jazz festival on at Scarborough, do you want to give it a burl?' he asked as he kick-started the bike.

'Sounds fab,' she yelled back over the engine's roar. Then she climbed on, wrapped her arms around him and they took off.

It was just one month later that the inevitable finally happened, and it took them both by surprise – even Mike. He hadn't planned it at all.

'Guess what?' he said as he killed the engine and leapt off the bike. She'd heard him pulling up and had come outside, bathers and towel in hand. It was spring now. 'Great news!' He spread his arms wide in triumph. 'Guess. Go on. Guess.'

'What?' She grinned, she had no idea what he was on about.

'I'm going to the Abrolhos. Pembo and Muzza and me. We're going to catch tammars.'

'I think you'd better come in,' she said. 'I'll make us a coffee.'

'During the Christmas holidays, they're doing a ten-day study on the water metabolism of tammars,' he said, talking nineteen to the dozen as he followed her to the door. 'And it's a dual-purpose trip – they're also taking a cray census. I'll be able to tie it in with advance research for my PhD. What do you think of that!'

'It's wonderful, that's what I think.' She was happy because he was.

'It's more than wonderful, Jo.' The moment they were inside the door, he picked her up and whirled her about the poky little lounge room. 'It's fan-bloody-tastic!' he yelled.

They careered crazily around the room together, bumping into the furniture and threatening havoc to the place. 'It's the chance of a bloody lifetime, that's what it is.'

She was clinging to him, dizzy, shrieking with laughter and telling him to put her down. Then, suddenly, they stopped whirling and she stopped laughing. Suddenly, they were kissing. Neither knew who had initiated the kiss, nor did they care – both had been waiting for far too long.

When he started to ease her towards the sofa, she could have stopped it right there and then, but she didn't. She led the way to her bedroom instead.

After they'd made love, and she lay naked in his arms, her head on his shoulder, her leg draped over his, she wondered how on earth to play out the scene. Just as she wondered, with a sense of dread, how long it would be before he moved on.

'What the hell's a tammar?' she asked lightly.

BOOK TWO

CHAPTER FIVE

The news that Mike McAllister had suffered a heart attack while diving at the Abrolhos shocked everyone to the core. Not Mike McAllister! He was twenty-two years old! He was the star centre of the uni A grade team! Mike was young, and as strong and fit as a mallee bull!

Mike himself had discovered that if he hadn't been as young and strong and fit as he was, he'd probably be dead. He'd been told as much by the cardiologist at Royal Perth Hospital, who'd informed him that he had a congenital heart weakness.

'It's nothing that won't allow you to lead a normal life,' the doctor had assured him, aware the news had come as a shock, 'but attempting Mount Everest and deep sea diving are not to be recommended with a condition like yours. If you'd been older and less fit and pushed yourself to the absolute limit as you did, it's quite likely you wouldn't have survived. I'd certainly watch it in future.'

Following his attack, Mike had been taken to the Geraldton Regional Hospital where his heart condition had been stabilised, then immediately transported by the Royal Flying Doctor Service to Royal Perth Hospital where his horrified parents had been waiting.

Two days later, Spud called in. It was eleven o'clock on a Saturday morning.

'Jesus, mate, you gave us all a bit of a scare,' he said.

'I gave myself a bit of scare,' Mike admitted.

'I mean, hell, if that can happen to *you*, then what's on the cards for the rest of us?' Spud looked around the small private ward, pulled a chair up beside the bed and sat. 'Do they mind if you smoke?' he asked, diving a hand into his pocket for his cigarettes.

'I don't know – give it a go and see.'

Spud lit up. 'How long are you going to be in here?'

'I'm not sure. They reckon another day, maybe two.'

'Bugger of a thing to happen, eh.'

A minute or so later, Maggie and Jools arrived. Jools had flown over from Sydney the moment her mother had rung with news of Mike's heart attack.

'G'day, Mrs McAllister. G'day, Jools.' Spud rose, stubbing his cigarette out on the side plate next to the fruit bowl on the bedside table. 'Well, I'll leave you to it, mate.' He gave Mike a pat on the shoulder. 'You look after your-self now.'

'Yeah, thanks for coming in, Spud.'

'No worries. Any time.' And he left.

'I brought you some peaches.' Maggie took them from the bag and put them in the fruit bowl, then bent down and kissed Mike on the cheek.

'We need another plate,' Jools said.

Outside in the car park, Spud climbed into his brand new HD Holden Premier sedan – he'd long since traded in the Austin. He started up the engine and turned on the car radio, thankful for the opportunity to escape. Christ, he hated hospitals, they gave him the creeps.

'Yesterday' was playing and he turned up the volume.

Great. The Beatles' new hit, and his favourite. Poor old

Mike, he thought as he drove out of the car park. He started to sing along. Who'd have thought it, eh? Mike McAllister, of all people!

He continued singing along to The Beatles at the top of his voice as he headed towards Ascot Racetrack.

Spud had been an accredited satchel swinger for over eighteen months now. White money bag slung over one shoulder, the name 'Wetherill' printed on its side, he'd take his place alongside Big Bet Bob regular as clockwork every Saturday afternoon – at the summer track of Ascot or the winter track of Belmont – and then again each Friday night at the Gloucester Park trots. Be it turf or harness, Bob Wetherill's stand was invariably the busiest in the bookie's ring.

Big Bet Bob paid his young clerk well. Christ, the kid was worth it, Bob thought – the clever little bastard had a built-in calculator for a brain – which meant it'd be only a matter of time before he went into business on his own. But what the hell, wasn't that always the way with the smart ones? You trained 'em up and then they shot through on you, it happened every time. Bob was philosophical about it – he liked Spud.

Spud doubled the money Bob paid him by betting carefully and wisely, keeping his eyes and ears open to the main chance. He rarely lost, and occasionally came in for a sizeable win. But he didn't waste his newfound wealth on the good life – there'd be time for that later, he told himself. He'd acquired the requisite wardrobe to go with his new image and he'd bought the Holden on hire purchase, squirrelling away the majority of his earnings. He'd need a healthy sum in the new year. Under the Betting Control Act of 1954 a bond was required to become a registered WA bookmaker, and he'd need to purchase permits from both the WA Turf Club and the Trotting Association. Then, of course, he'd need to buy time while he earned a reputation and built up a following.

Things were going very much according to plan, Spud thought smugly as he walked into the elegance of the world that was Ascot. Christ, he loved Ascot. It was a track truly built for the sport of kings, right by the Swan River with its own natural lake in the middle, stone buildings that reeked of a bygone age and a grandstand to match any. Ascot was in a class of its own. And it was a class to which Spud already felt he belonged.

Johanna hadn't gone down to Manjimup over the Christmas break. Normally she would have – despite dreading the experience, she always returned home during the holidays to play the dutiful daughter. But Mike wouldn't be away in the Abrolhos for long, and she'd wanted to spend as much of the break with him as she could – to eke out their affair for as long as possible. Although they'd been lovers for six weeks, she was no more secure in his feelings for her than she had been at the start. In fact, now more than ever, she felt she was living on borrowed time.

She'd considered going home for the ten days he was away, but at the last moment she'd decided against it and phoned her mother to say that she'd been invited to the coastal town of Rockingham by a girlfriend at uni whose parents had a holiday shack there. She didn't know why she felt the need to invent such an elaborate lie – her mother was probably thankful that she wasn't coming home – but it was typical of their delicate eggshell existence. They trod very carefully around each other – more so than ever these days.

Jo was deeply thankful now that she'd stayed in Perth.

So was Mike. For the first time in their relationship he felt a genuine need for her. And it showed.

Johanna was aware of the change in him the first time they had sex after his release from hospital. She'd been uncertain as to whether they should or not.

'I'm not an invalid, Jo,' he'd said, sensing her doubts,

although, in a way, he was. He'd had strict medical warnings not to overtax himself for the next several months, but he'd decided that didn't include sex.

That night, in the little bedroom of her Kingsway flat, they made love as they never had before. Sex between them had always been satisfying. Mike was a considerate lover, proficient in foreplay, careful to bring her to orgasm before his own climax, but Jo had been aware that to Mike sex was purely sex. It certainly wasn't an act of love – it wasn't even a particularly sharing experience. It was more a highly pleasurable exchange of favours, and she'd come to expect nothing more. Theirs was simply an affair and much as she loved him, she accepted the fact.

Tonight was different. She could sense him giving himself to her wholly, lovingly, and she responded in kind. Tonight it wasn't sex, she thought, tonight they were making love, and as they approached their mutual climax, they looked into each other's eyes. What was it that she saw there, she wondered, as her own love threatened to engulf her. Was it a return of her love? Or merely gratitude to be alive?

As they lay sated in each other's arms, she was still wondering. She suspected the latter. But whatever it was, they had certainly shared something.

They talked that night too – in a way they'd never talked before.

It was a hot, sultry December night. The afternoon sea breeze had not performed its customary rescue mission for the past two days, and many were finding the heatwave uncomfortable. But not Mike and Jo. They sat comfortably cross-legged amongst the rumpled sheets, the bedside lamp illuminating the sweat on their bare skin, while he told her what had happened at the Abrolhos. He'd told no-one else, and he didn't intend to, but he felt the need to unburden himself just the once. Just to her.

'The Abrolhos had a profound effect on me, Jo,' he said.

'I mean, right from the start – before the heart attack. The islands are desolate, and at first they appear insignificant, but they're not. They're dangerous and indestructible. For centuries they've defied erosion, and there they sit, like innocent outcrops of sand and rock, just biding their time, waiting to lay claim to anyone or anything that's foolish enough to underestimate them.' He was aware that he probably sounded fanciful, but he didn't care. 'I'm not talking about a malevolence,' he added thoughtfully, 'I'm talking about nature making a statement. You defy that statement at your own peril, and that's what I did.'

She made no comment, but waited in silence for him to go on. He'd never spoken in this manner before, and she was aware that again he was sharing something intimate with her.

'When I dived on the wreck,' he continued, 'I was over-whelmed by the sight of it. There she was, the *Batavia*, lying right where she had for over four hundred years, stored by the reef like a prize. I didn't want to leave. It was extraordinary – the preservation of the wreck, the beauty of the reef, the sheer power of it!' He shrugged, briefly breaking the moment. 'That's where I went wrong. I didn't respect its power. I stayed down too long, it was as simple as that.'

Mike had said nothing to her about the discovery of his congenital heart weakness. Surprisingly, he'd said nothing to his parents either, having decided that the fact would remain strictly between his cardiologist and himself. He couldn't bear the thought that others might treat him differently, that they might see him as 'fragile'.

'I felt I could breathe underwater,' he said. 'I honestly felt I could open up my mouth and breathe. I could have stayed there forever.'

He remembered the faces of the dead people coming at him from out of the wreck, screaming. He'd remembered them often over the past week, but he wasn't haunted by them. They were a lesson, a warning not to intrude too far, not to overstep the limits. That's what the reef had been telling him, he'd decided.

'I tried to make it to the surface. But I couldn't seem to get there.' He recalled the voices screaming for him to come back and save them. 'I could see the sun shining through the water above, but I couldn't get up there. It was as if the reef was pulling me back – claiming me, just like it had claimed the others.

'I don't remember anything after that,' he said, 'except a massive pain in my chest. I must have made it to the surface and then had the heart attack.' He uncrossed his legs and leaned back thoughtfully against the bedhead. 'You know, it's a weird feeling – it's made me look at things differently.'

Mike was aware that the experience had left him with a heightened sense of the preciousness of life, which he supposed was to be expected, but of far greater impact was the affirmation of purpose he now felt. The field of environment and marine biology was no longer a commitment. To Mike it had become a destiny. The islands of the Abrolhos and the power of the reef had delivered an unmistakable message.

'Well, it'd be weird if you *didn't* look at things differently,' Jo said. 'You nearly died. That's bound to alter your perspective.'

He nodded. 'Yes.' She was right, of course – gratitude to be alive would certainly explain a renewed sense of purpose. But he preferred to believe that his future had been dictated by the environment itself. All of which was too difficult to explain, he decided. 'Yes, I suppose it's that simple.'

'Of course it is,' she said. 'I'm glad that you didn't. Die, that is.'

He smiled as he pulled her to him. Her candour always delighted him. Jo didn't take bullshit from anyone. 'That's my girl,' he said. 'She cuts through the crap and gets right to the point.'

'I didn't think what you were saying was crap at all,' she started to protest.

'I didn't say you did.' He kissed her. 'Thanks for listening.'

They made love again. Very quietly. They heard Kathy come home, she'd been to the movies. They'd known they had the place to themselves until at least eleven. They lay there breathing heavily, giggling a little, hoping she hadn't heard.

'I'm starving,' Mike whispered.

'Give it another five minutes.'

From the slit beneath the door they saw the lounge room lights go out.

'She's gone to bed,' Jo whispered, 'stay there.' And slipping on her towelling robe, she stole out to the kitchen.

It was a farce, she thought as she put the bread in the toaster and cut up the cheese. Kathy knew they were there, it was why she'd gone to the movies. Just as Jo went to the movies or stayed out late when Kath had her boyfriend around.

She remembered the night Mike had tried to tempt her into his side verandah bedroom, as he obviously had many of his previous conquests. They'd already made love that very afternoon, aboard his father's yacht, *Alana*. They'd dropped anchor at Blackwall Reach, just the other side of the river, and he'd taken her into the cabin.

'Alana,' she'd said afterwards as they'd lain entwined, the boat rocking in the wash of the odd passing speedboat, 'it's a pretty name.'

'Yeah, Dad named her after his mother. I can hardly remember Grandma Alana, but you're right, it's a pretty name.'

She'd refused the verandah bedroom later that night, although she hadn't said why – she'd let him think she was merely self-conscious. But that was the evening she'd met his parents – they'd asked her to stay for dinner – and the idea of the verandah bedroom had seemed tawdry. Jo preferred the current arrangement. If it couldn't be *Alana*, then it would be her flat, she'd decided, and Kath would be at the movies.

She returned to the bedroom with the grilled cheese on toast and the mandatory bottle of tomato sauce. Mike couldn't eat cheese on toast without tomato sauce, and she'd recently discovered she couldn't either.

'Did you go down to Manjimup while I was away?' he asked as they sat on the bed demolishing the toast.

'Nope.'

'You said you probably would.'

'I decided against it.'

'Why, Jo?'

'Oh . . . just didn't feel like it.'

'No, I mean you *never* want to go. Why's that?'

He was looking at her keenly. He'd not shown an interest in her home life before, she thought. But then she'd always skirted around the issue – perhaps he'd been respecting her privacy. Given the way he'd just unburdened himself, he probably considered it was time for her to do the same. But she was hesitant, still unsure of how much she should share with him.

'I can't stand my stepfather,' she said simply.

He nodded, and waited for her to continue. She'd told him that her father had died when she was a child and that her mother had remarried, but nothing else.

'He's a perve. But my mother doesn't know it, and I can't tell her.'

Mike studied her for a moment. Johanna's ability to sum up a situation succinctly was a characteristic he admired, but he wasn't about to let her fob him off with so little detail. Not this time. Not tonight.

'Go on,' he said.

She paused, then put aside her plate with deliberation.

'Darren's been perving on me since I was ten years old. When I was a kid, he was always trying to catch me in the bath or while I was undressing. Or he'd invent some excuse to touch me. He'd admire a dress or a new haircut, anything that gave him the opportunity for a bit of a feel-up. God, he's a creep.'

She could have left it there, but she didn't. Instead, she curled up on her side, leaning on her elbow, head propped in her hand, and continued.

'I remember, when I was twelve, wishing that he'd make a definite move and that Mum would catch him at it. Then she'd know the truth about the prick she'd married. But he never did – he was too smart for that. And Mum used to nag me for being sullen. "All Darren wants is to be a good stepfather,"' Jo pulled a face as she mimicked her mother, '"but you won't give him a chance." What the hell could I do? If I'd told her the truth, she would have accused me of lying. She thought I was jealous. When I refused to adopt his name, she told me I was being deliberately spiteful.

'Poor Mum.' Jo shook her head regretfully. 'If she'd only known how I much longed to have a dad. I can barely remember my real father – he died when I was six. Just my luck to cop a dad like Darren.' She was letting it all hang out now, and in a way it was a relief to talk about it.

'He doesn't dare try his tricks on me these days, but the damage has been done. He's ruined the relationship I once had with my mother, and I loathe him for it. I can't stand being near him, I can't stand the games we play, and most of all I can't stand myself.'

There, she'd said it. She'd finally owned up to the truth.

'Why on earth is that?' Mike quietly asked, collecting up the plates and dumping them on the bedside table.

'Because I'm letting him put me through uni. He's paying for the lot. I even get a healthy monthly allowance.'

Her voice was harsh now. 'Darren's a manager for Bunnings Timber Mills – he can afford it, he's quite well off.'

God, she was bitter, he thought.

'Of course, I should have refused to accept his "generous offer" as my mother called it right from the start. But I couldn't do that without destroying the little that Mum and I had left. At least that's what I told myself,' she added with a touch of cynicism. 'But I wanted to study medicine, so perhaps it was a lie.'

It hadn't been a lie at all. She'd longed to tackle her career the hard way – anything rather than be beholden to Darren. She'd work and save up for a year before she went to uni, she'd wanted to tell her mother. She'd wait tables at night while she studied. Why not? Other students did. But if she'd told her mother that, it would have been the end of their relationship. It would have amounted to a choice between Darren and her, and her mother would most certainly have chosen Darren. Why shouldn't she? She loved him.

'The games are even harder now,' Jo said. 'I do my best to play the thankful, appreciative stepchild, but Mum can see through it. She thinks I'm an ingrate for not embracing Darren as a mentor and father figure, and I hate myself for being a liar and a hypocrite.' *So there,* her voice said, it was the end of her story. The story she'd told no-one.

'You're the least hypocritical person I've ever known,' Mike said, nestling beside her and taking her in his arms. It was a hideous situation for a woman of Jo's honesty and integrity, he thought.

She snuggled up to him, aware that she'd bared her soul and wondering if she might regret it later. But for now, she was glad. They'd both bared their souls, hadn't they? And they'd never been closer. Somehow it gave her a vague sense of hope where before there'd been none.

*

When Mike McAllister returned to university the following year, most of his fellow students noted no particular
change in him. He didn't look like a bloke who'd suffered
a near-death experience. He wasn't allowed to play rugby
for three months, which was understandable, but apart
from that, he was the same old Mike.

His close mates, however, did sense a change. Ian and
Muzza and Spud couldn't exactly put their finger on it, but
there was something different about Mike. An added
maturity perhaps – a bit of the lair had gone. But perhaps
it wasn't all that surprising. They'd grown up too. That
year – 1966 – was proving one of change for them all.

Ian Pemberton had joined the workforce. His honours
thesis, 'The Petrography of Telluride Mineralisation in the
Kalgoorlie-Yilgarn Greenstone Belt', had attracted commercial interest as he'd known it would. He'd been offered
a highly lucrative position as an exploration geologist with
Western Mining Ltd, and having attended a month of
briefings at their Perth office was shortly to leave for
Kalgoorlie, where the race for nickel had started in earnest
in the rich greenstone area known geologically as the
Yilgarn Precambrian Block.

Spud had achieved the first of his many goals in
becoming the youngest bookmaker registered in Western
Australia. It had taken him no time to earn a reputation
and gain a following – Big Bet Bob's whiz kid was now
'Farrell, licensed bookmaker', with his own clerk, and his
own white satchel with his own name printed on the side.

But it was Muzza who had been swept up in the radical
change that was affecting the entire nation. Murray
Hatfield had been conscripted. He'd been informed of the
fact in November the previous year – one of many.

It was a new era. Throughout two world wars, Australians had fought as volunteers. During the Great War,
Prime Minister William Morris Hughes had tried, twice,
to force the issue of conscription upon the Australian

people. Both attempts had failed. During World War Two, although compulsory military training had been intro- duced for the defence of the home front, overseas service had remained voluntary. Now, however, allied to America and committed to the war in Vietnam, the Australian government had introduced in 1965 new powers enabling it to send national servicemen on active duty overseas. The issue was dividing the nation.

'You're mad,' Ian told Muzza. 'I thought you were going to defer – that's what you said up at the Abrolhos.'

He and Mike had discussed the matter with Muzza, and they'd all agreed there was only one course of action open to him – the deferment of his national service until he'd completed his degree. Now here he was reneging on the idea. It was too bloody stupid for words.

The three were sitting in the beer garden at Steve's on an early Friday evening. Spud was due to join them, but he was late.

'Christ, you can defer your call-up until you finish med,' Ian went on. 'That's another whole *four years*! The war'll be over by then.'

'What made you change your mind, Muzza?' Mike asked. He wished Pembo would shut up. What was the point in nagging? Muzza had made his decision. Hell, he was off to training camp next week.

'I don't know. My dad, I suppose. He fought in the war, and . . . well . . .' Muzza shrugged. 'I thought I should do the same.'

'But it's not the same *war*, Muzza. It's not *our* war. It never *was* our war. We shouldn't be *in it*, for Christ's sake.'

Well-meaning as his intention was, in his frustration Ian was at his patronising worst. He sounded like his mother, Mike thought.

Muzza realised that his response had been dumb. He shouldn't have made any reference to World War Two, it was inviting Pembo's diatribe. And he wished he hadn't used his father as a scapegoat. His dad hadn't attempted to influence him at all. 'It's your decision, Murray,' he'd said. 'You're one of the lucky ones – you have a legal way out, if you want to take it.'

Muzza wished he had the guts to tell Pembo that he wanted to go to war. He wanted to know what it was like. Simple as that. But he'd be asking for it if he did. It was why he'd appeared to go along with the advice Pembo and Mike had offered up at the Abrolhos.

'You should be taking a *stance*, for Christ's sake!' Ian ranted. 'Jesus, there are people out there who are *risking jail*! Burning their draft cards! Conscientious objectors, who don't have a leg to stand on. You *do*! You can defer while you –'

'Shut up, Pembo,' Mike said.

Ian looked at Mike angrily. He knew Mike agreed that Muzza should defer, and he was about to argue the fact, but he was interrupted before he could get a word out.

'Sorry, I'm late.' Spud threw himself into the chair they'd saved for him. He was looking very smart in a tailored navy sports jacket and red tie. 'Had a bit of business to conduct in the Pen.'

He said it for effect, then sat back, languid, smug and pompous.

'The Pen?' Mike grinned. 'You're moving up in the world.'

The entrance to the small private bar at Steve's, known as the Killing Pen, was situated directly under the grand wooden staircase that led to the hotel's first floor. Entry to the Pen had long been granted by invitation only from Steve McHenry, the pub's owner, but since his relatively recent death, his widow, Hazel, had allowed invitations to be extended by the regulars who'd become fixtures during her husband's time. The bar was run on an honour system, money being placed in a dish to cover the alcohol consumed, and the clientele consisted of successful and select members of the Perth business community, most with right-wing Liberal Party connections and most of whom lived in the affluent Peppermint Grove and Dalkeith-Nedlands areas.

Spud dropped his act and leaned forward, elbows on the table. 'You'll never guess who I scored the invite from, Mikey.' A pause, again for effect. 'Anthony Wilson.'

The two shared a smile of recognition. Several years back, during one of their reminiscing sessions, Spud had admitted that he'd returned Anthony Wilson's wallet. 'He gave me five quid,' he'd said.

'You smart bastard.' Mike had wondered why he hadn't guessed that had been Spud's intention from the start – it was so typical.

'And guess what I did with the money?'

'Wouldn't have a clue.'

'I went to a brothel. My first time, remember? The mystique of the Orient?'

They'd roared with laughter.

Spud had neglected to add that he'd stolen Anthony Wilson's car radio and hub caps. Mike was too bloody honest to find that part funny. Spud thought it hilarious himself – even more so now, given the current circumstances.

'Anthony Wilson, the politician?' Ian asked. Spud nodded. 'He's a dodgy one. What sort of business are you "conducting" with him?'

Ian had forgotten his annoyance. He had a begrudging admiration for Spud's business acumen and was genuinely interested. Spud had told him that he was going to invest his savings. He'd met his expenses, he'd said, and there was no sense in having money sitting in the bank earning piss-weak interest when it could be working for you. 'Property,' he'd announced. 'I'm going to stop leasing – it's dead money anyway. I'm going to put a deposit on a property and set up new offices.'

Spud didn't find Ian's question about his business affairs impertinent. To the contrary; he liked showing off to Pembo.

'I've found the place I'm after,' he said. 'It's in Dalkeith, and I'm looking for a bit of help in changing its residential zoning.'

Ian laughed. 'Sounds to me like you're on the right track,' he said. 'I've heard Wilson's as crooked as a dog's hind leg.'

Just what his old man used to say, Spud thought, but his old man had intended the remark to be derogatory. Ian had hit the nail on the head. Bent as he was, Anthony Wilson was proving an invaluable contact. He had the councillors and the mayor on side, and as a long-serving MP he knew every pollie in town, Liberal and Labor. Convenient that the man had a gambling habit – Spud had renewed their acquaintance when he'd heard that.

He gave Ian a wink, which signalled they were on the same wavelength, then stood.

'Bit of a dry argument. My round,' he said, picking up the empty jug. 'Time to party!'

Then he solemnly announced, 'It's our duty to get right royally pissed tonight.' He raised the jug high. 'To you, Muzza. We salute you – off to fight for king and country.'

'Well, not just yet – not until I've done my training,' Muzza muttered, regretting the fact that he was in the spotlight again. He'd been relieved by the change in conversation. He had the feeling, too, that Spud's reference to king and country was an attempt to rile Pembo.

It was. Spud knew Ian Pemberton's stance on the Vietnam War and he opposed it. In Spud's opinion, they were in the bloody war whether they liked it or not, and the troops should be sent off as heroes, not made to feel guilty because they hadn't burnt their draft cards like the wowsers who called themselves conscientious objectors.

'Off to fight for the President of the US of A, you mean,'

Ian said cuttingly. He'd well and truly risen to the bait. 'Off to make money for the mighty American war machine –'

'Give it a rest, Pembo,' Mike said, with a warning look to Spud. It was Muzza's farewell and not the right time to wind Pembo up, he signalled.

To Muzza's relief, Pembo shut up, albeit sulkily, and Spud stopped stirring and went off to the bar. He'd made his point anyway.

Half an hour later, it was Ian's shout.

He plonked the jug on the table. 'It's a bloody disgrace the way they've put all the prices up,' he said – and decimalisation became the instant topic of conversation.

Ian was convinced there was a conspiracy afoot since Australia's conversion to decimal currency just two months previously. He maintained that the government and private enterprise were using the conversion to their advantage.

Spud disagreed. 'Just teething problems,' he said. He'd embraced the changeover wholeheartedly – it'd make his life a whole lot easier in the long run.

'I know it's a simpler currency,' Muzza said, 'and it won't take long to get used to it, but it's a bit of a bugger having to unlearn a lifetime of schooling.'

'And what's going to happen when they bring in metric across the board?' Mike said. 'How the hell do I know how tall I am in centimetres?'

'So much for a uni education.' Spud threw his head back and roared with laughter.

They all agreed that the times were changing, and they drank to decimal currency and the lowering of the legal drinking age to eighteen.

'At least that's one good thing to come out of conscription,' Mike said.

The Australian government had wisely decided that if young men were to be sent off to war, they should perhaps be allowed into pubs and bars.

They drank to a whole lot of other things after that. To Muzza's safe return from Vietnam, to Mike's narrow escape at the Abrolhos, to Ian's imminent departure for Kalgoorlie, and to Spud's forthcoming property purchase . . . then they started all over again. Jug after jug. As Spud had predicted, they got right royally pissed that night, and out of respect for Muzza, he and Pembo didn't row once, which was quite a record.

The relationship between Ian Pemberton and Spud Farrell was prickly at times, but despite their innate differences, a fierce competitiveness remained their bond. Who would be the richer, and who would get there first? That was the question.

Spud was well on his way. It was his intention to build a syndicate, and already he'd financed several trustworthy mates who visited the hotels and bars of the larger country towns and operated as SP bookies, taking bets from the locals on the big meets in Perth.

'We're making a killing in Kal,' he'd say to Ian, and it was true the cash flowed in from the goldmining township of Kalgoorlie, where men earned big money and weren't afraid to gamble it. Spud had decided that mining towns were the way to go. 'When you get to Kal, you'll be able to while away the time in the bar at the Palace laying bets on the ponies with a Farrell bookie,' he'd say, really rubbing it in.

He enjoyed boasting to Pembo. He didn't bother so much with Mikey, who never seemed particularly impressed, but he knew that Ian Pemberton was frustrated by the fact that although he was earning big money, he was slower out of the starting stalls in his bid for success. It pleased Spud to rub Pembo's nose in it. It was his way of saying 'Who needs a uni degree to make it in this world?'

Several months after their farewell drinks for Muzza, Spud and Ian met once again at Steve's bar – on a wintry

Friday lunchtime. Ian had escaped Kalgoorlie for a long weekend in Perth, as he often did these days. Kal could become a little stifling, he'd found.

Once again, Spud took great pleasure in boasting – this time about the successful acquisition of his new offices.

'You were right,' Ian said as he begrudgingly toasted his mate's latest triumph. 'Wilson's a handy man to know.'

Spud had told him the details, making it sound easy as usual. Anthony Wilson's contacts within the council had paid off, money had changed hands and the property had been rezoned – simple.

Spud could tell that Pembo was envious, and he only wished he could boast about his latest enterprise – the most exciting to date. It'd put him up to his eyeballs in debt – he'd have to borrow big money – but it was a sure-fire winner in the long term. However, as he hadn't pulled off the purchase yet, and was to be a silent partner in the scheme, he decided to keep quiet about it for now. Ruby would probably prefer it that way.

He left Steve's an hour later and set off for Subiaco. Ruby wasn't expecting him, but she was always home on a Friday afternoon and they had a lot to talk about. Spud was raring to go.

Spud Farrell and Ruby Chan were entering into a partnership. The property next door to the Sun Majestic Massage Parlour was up for sale, and it had been Spud's idea to buy it and extend the brothel under Ruby's management. The money it would make would repay the hefty loan he'd need for the purchase, and after that he'd be laughing.

He parked in the street outside Ruby's house, surprised that her car wasn't in the driveway. He should have rung, he thought, but he often popped in on a Friday arvo. Perhaps she was just out shopping. He decided he'd wait.

He walked down the side path and into the small back garden. The grass was freshly mown, he noticed, and he smiled as he wondered whether Ruby had found another young virgin to take under her wing. He doubted it; she was well over forty now – past it for a successful hooker. Not that she wasn't still a good-looking sort, but Ruby was too smart to compete with the young ones. She was a businesswoman these days. And a formidable one at that, with contacts in high places. Hell, Spud thought, the dirt he got on the corporate executives and the pollies who frequented the Sun Majestic made Ruby an even more valuable contact than Anthony bloody Wilson. It was an added incentive to their partnership.

He sat on the back steps and lit up a smoke. Strange that Ruby chose to remain here, he thought, looking at the poky little garden and the wooden dunny, the rotary-blade mower leaning against it – he couldn't believe she still had the old mower. Surely she could afford a place flashier than this. But then perhaps not. All of her money had gone into the Sun Majestic. He hadn't known until recently that Ruby owned the brothel; he'd presumed it belonged to some anonymous fat cat – most of the whorehouses did – and that she merely ran the business. But she'd told him with great pride that she'd recently paid off the last of the mortgage and she now owned the property lock, stock and barrel. Bloody convenient, Spud thought. That's what had inspired him to make a bid for the place next door when it had come on the market. Christ, they were going to make a killing.

'It's Spud, isn't it?'

He'd been so deep in his thoughts that he hadn't heard the back door open behind him. He turned. Jesus, he thought. It's her.

'Spud. That's right. G'day, Mayjay.' He stood.

'You remembered.' She smiled with pretended surprise.

'Yep. Took a second or so, but it came back to me.' He grinned cockily. Christ alive, of course he remembered, and she bloody well knew it.

'You're waiting for Ruby?'

He nodded.

'She's out shopping, she won't be long. Come on in.'

Shit, he thought, stubbing out his cigarette, this is what happened last time.

'We'll have to stop meeting like this, won't we,' she said suggestively as she stood aside to let him in.

Spud had just turned seventeen the first time he'd met Mayjay, and the circumstances had been much the same. He'd come to Ruby's to mow the grass, arriving a little earlier than usual, and she'd been out shopping. He'd stripped down to the waist and started pushing the old mower around, unaware that the back door had opened and that he was being watched.

After a few minutes, he'd stopped to take a breather.

'Hello,' she called.

He looked to the back door, thinking that Ruby had returned, but it wasn't Ruby standing there. It was the most gorgeous-looking creature he'd ever seen in his life. Dark-haired, dark-eyed, her beauty was so dramatically arresting that for a moment he was speechless.

'It's very hot out there,' she said. 'Why don't you come in and have a glass of lemonade? Or there's beer if you prefer.'

He propped the mower against the outhouse, gathered up his shirt and joined her.

'I'm Mary-Jane,' she said, ushering him into the lounge room and offering her hand. 'Mary-Jane Smith. But you can call me Mayjay.'

'Spud,' he replied, finding his voice. She was somewhat taller than he was, and she wore a light cotton dress with shoestring straps, displaying the tanned flawless skin of her shoulders and a shape that was perfect. She had to be a model, he thought. He guessed her age at around eighteen, only a year or so older than him, but she was so self-assured that he felt very young and very clumsy. 'Spud Farrell,' he said with a little more force as they shook hands, he wasn't accustomed to feeling awkward.

Mayjay smiled. She was fully aware of the effect she had upon men. Old, young, they were all the same.

'You're a *friend* of Ruby's, are you?' she asked.

'Yeah, that's right.' Why had she said *friend* like that, he wondered; it sounded very suggestive. 'I mow the grass for her.'

'I bet you do.' The black eyebrows raised a fraction and the perfect mouth curved in a smile that was more than suggestive, it was lascivious.

Spud was bewildered. What was going on? She couldn't be coming on to him – not a bird like her. Where was the lemonade or the beer she'd offered? She was taking the piss out of him, he decided. Well, bugger that.

'Yep, I mow the grass and I fix things around the house – I'm a sort of handyman, see.' He backed away, slipping an arm into his denim shirt, about to shrug it over his shoulders.

'Don't do that.'

He froze. It was an order and he found himself instinctively obeying.

She looked him up and down with a cool objectivity, the way farmers appraise breeding stock, her gaze coming to rest on the light fuzz of ginger curls that had only recently sprouted in the centre of his chest. 'You look much nicer without the shirt.'

Shit, Spud thought, what the hell's going on?

She kicked off her sandals and sat on the sofa, leaning back, heaving her dress up to her thighs. 'And it's so hot, isn't it? Too hot for clothes.'

He could see a glimpse of lace-pantied crotch and the sight was arousing. She *had* to be coming on to him, he thought. But her eyes didn't invite, they mocked – what was she playing at? Was she a hooker? She sure as hell didn't look like a hooker, but what was she doing in Ruby's house?

'You're a good-looking young man, Spud,' she said.

She didn't find him good-looking at all. He was as common as muck, she thought, but cute in a way. And just a kid – little more than sixteen, she guessed. That was what made him so interesting. Mayjay loved to tease.

'I bet you're great in bed.'

She rose and crossed to where he stood, mesmerised, the denim shirt still dangling from his wrist to the floor.

'How do you like it? Kinky?' She smiled a challenge. 'I do. The kinkier the better. Ever tried auto-eroticism?'

Her hands were suddenly on the belt of his jeans, and instinctively he went to ward them off. She was teasing him, playing a game, and, despite his erection, he wasn't sure that he liked it.

'Don't be frightened, Spud,' she said, gently pushing his hands away, undoing the belt, slowly feeding it free. He didn't stop her. He couldn't. Her eyes were hypno- tically locked onto his now, and he couldn't seem to speak, let alone move.

'I can give you the greatest thrill you've ever had,' she said. 'I can fuck you like you've never been fucked before.' She fastened the belt around her neck and pulled it tight, like a noose, holding on to the end of the strap. 'I just bet you'd love doing it my way.'

Mayjay enjoyed teasing, but she liked to shock far more, and she could see the effect she was having on him. He was shocked all right, and fascinated too. She had him under her spell, she was turning him on, and she was beginning to feel quite horny herself. God, she could teach him a trick or two, she thought.

Spud didn't resist as she started undoing his jeans. This was no longer a game. This was something dangerously exciting and his heart was pounding with anticipation.

'Give him his belt back, Mary-Jane.'

Ruby's voice cut the air like a knife and they turned to see her standing in the doorway to the hall, a bag of groceries in her hand.

'Hello, Ruby.'

Mayjay wasn't at all fazed by her mother's arrival. She'd expected Ruby home soon – maybe she'd even wanted to be sprung in the act. She liked to shock her mother. She liked to remind Ruby that the daughter of a whore couldn't be expected to behave like the daughters of proper women.

'I was just filling in for you,' she said. 'Aren't you pleased?' She took the belt from her neck and handed it to Spud, who'd quickly zipped up his jeans.

Ruby ignored her. 'Hello, Spud,' she said. 'Come into the kitchen.'

She left, and Spud obediently followed her.

'I'm sorry, Ruby,' he said as she started briskly unpacking the groceries onto the kitchen table. 'I didn't mean to –'

'I know you didn't, it's not your fault.'

'Well, of course it's not his fault, is it – he's just a kid.' Mayjay lounged against the door frame. 'God, Ruby, you pick them younger by the minute.'

'Go away, Mary-Jane, we'll talk about this later.'

Mayjay shrugged. 'It's one thing to have a mother who's a hooker,' she said to Spud, 'but a paedophile as well . . .?' She raised an eyebrow and slouched off.

Mother? Oh hell, Spud thought. He'd been about to have sex with Ruby's daughter in Ruby's very own home. He hardly dared look at her.

But Ruby appeared unruffled as she packed the groceries away. Mary-Jane was punishing her again. She didn't know why her daughter found it necessary to punish her – Mary-Jane had been protected from the world of prostitution and well educated. Ruby had put her through a June Dally-Watkins modelling course in Sydney and she had a successful career ahead of her. Yet she still

felt the desire to humiliate, and this time she'd been particularly blatant. Probably because she was back in the old
home town with the brothel barely a mile away, Ruby
thought. It was a pity, but the sooner Mary-Jane went
back to Sydney the better. They had a good relationship
when Ruby visited her there – far from the Sun Majestic.

'Mary-Jane's come home for a fortnight's holiday,' she
said, as if nothing had happened. 'She lives in Sydney.
She's a model.'

'Really?' Spud was deeply relieved that Ruby wasn't
mad. 'That's what I thought the moment I laid eyes on her.'

Ruby crossed to the refrigerator with the milk and
butter.

'Honestly, I did. As soon as I saw her, I thought, wow,
she's gotta be a model, with looks like that.' Spud's relief
was getting the better of him, he was running off at the
mouth.

Ruby closed the refrigerator door and turned to him.

'Like mother, like daughter, eh?' He gave a hopeful grin,
but his bravado was deserting him. She didn't seem angry
but her face was set in a warning.

'Hands off, Spud. You don't go near her, do you hear
me?'

The grin disappeared in an instant and he nodded
furiously.

'You don't even know she's my daughter. You tell no-
one, understand?'

'Sure, Ruby. I won't tell a soul. I promise.'

'How long's it been, Spud?' Mayjay sat on the sofa, her
legs curled under her. This time she was wearing a pair of
beige cords and a lightweight turtle-neck sweater. She
looked very elegant – every inch the model.

'Six years,' he said, sitting in the armchair opposite.
She'd offered him a beer but he'd declined. He wasn't sure
how long he was going to stay.

'Six years? Really?' She knew it was six years – she hadn't been back to Perth since that trip, and she wouldn't be here now if it weren't for business. The place was a bloody backwater.

'I've seen you in those skin cream ads on telly,' he said, 'I thought you looked really terrific.'

'Thank you.'

'You've changed your hair though.'

'Don't you like it?'

'Sure,' he said, a little lacklustre. 'It's great.' He thought it looked better the way it had been before. It was shorter and bouncier now, and much lighter – a sort of sandy blonde. He preferred it darker and longer. But hell, you couldn't mess up looks like hers, she was still the most beautiful woman he'd ever seen.

She laughed. He'd grown up, she thought. She didn't alarm him any more. It was a pity he'd lost the cuteness he'd had. He looked like a little thug. She might have fancied him otherwise.

'It's what they're after,' she said, running a hand through her manufactured mane of curls. 'They want the wild beach girl look. They thought the dark hair was too foreign.'

'Oh, right.' He nodded. It was the dark hair and eyes she'd inherited from her mother that gave her that added touch of the exotic. 'Who're *they*?'

'The advertising agency. I'm here to do screen tests – a minimum twelve-month contract starting next year if I get the job.'

'And what's the job?'

'The new face of tourism for Western Australia!' She gave it a dramatic ring. 'But they want more than the face, they want the body too – someone who looks good in a bikini. "Wild, carefree, beach girl beauty", that's what they told my agent.' She stood up, legs astride, hands on hips. 'Do you think I fit the bill?'

'Well, you've sure got the body for it,' Spud said admiringly.

She perched a buttock on the arm of his chair and leaned in to him, her breasts enticing in the turtle-neck sweater.

'Want to pick up where we left off, Spud?' she purred. 'I see you're wearing a belt.'

Jesus, wouldn't he half love to. But she was teasing. Probably hoping Ruby'd spring them again, he thought. Mayjay was trouble. Besides, he didn't dare touch her with a twenty-foot bargepole. Ruby'd have his guts for garters if he did.

'No thanks, Mayjay. I think I'll give it a miss.' He stood. 'Tell Ruby I called in, will you?'

'Chicken.'

'Good luck with the job.'

She was laughing as he made his escape.

CHAPTER SIX

'It's *lovely,* dear. Quite, quite *lovely*!'

Ian was showing his mother around the new apartment he'd purchased in the city. It was to be his pied-à-terre for the weekends when he came into town. Cynthia had been forced to overcome her dismay at the prospect of her son not staying in the family home during his visits to Perth.

'He's twenty-three years old and he wants an apartment in the city,' Gordon had argued in his peremptory fashion. 'For God's sake, Cynthia, he's a *young man.*' The inference being that a *young man* might wish to entertain *young women* in his own apartment.

She'd accepted the inevitable, telling herself it would be fun helping Ian hunt for the apartment of his choice, but she'd been thwarted there too. Ian had said he had 'people in the know', and that he wanted to make his own decisions, and Cynthia had had to satisfy herself with his promise that she would be the first to see the flat he'd selected.

She'd approved of the building the moment she'd laid eyes on it. The block of stone flats in the Esplanade, with arched balconies overlooking the park and the river and ferry terminals, had a pre-war elegance – unlike the modern brickwork monstrosities popping up all over the place and which she abhorred.

'You've shown impeccable taste, I must say.' Her gaze wandered around the spacious lounge room with its high moulded ceilings and solid wooden floors. 'There's a touch of the colonial, isn't there?' She ran her fingers over the polished surface of the mantelpiece and the gleaming tiles of the fireplace. 'Perfectly renovated,' she said admiringly, 'the interior is so beautifully *modernised* without losing its original *character*.' That sort of thing was frightfully fashionable these days, she thought.

'And the furnishings are very much in keeping with the style,' she said, plonking herself briefly in one of the large wicker armchairs. She'd been deeply disappointed when he'd told her the place was furnished; she'd so longed to go shopping with him.

His mother's approval was a huge relief to Ian. The place hadn't actually been furnished at all, but the thought of shopping with Cynthia had been such a nightmare that he'd called in a firm of interior decorators. Thank God they'd got it right. If they hadn't, she would have insisted on replacing everything.

Cynthia gave the kitchen area a full going-over, turning on the taps, opening cupboards and drawers. 'My goodness, you've laid in china and cutlery already.'

Again she was disappointed. She'd wanted to be part of the whole process of decoration and selection, but he'd been very mysterious, and now she was finding that everything had been *done*.

She disguised her hurt at having been so excluded and disappeared to explore the two bedrooms, dismayed to discover that he'd also purchased linen. Then she examined, in minute detail, the separate dining room, the study and the bathroom.

'But are you sure you can *afford* it, dear?' she asked fifteen minutes later when the inspection was over and they'd stepped out onto the balcony to admire the view. The apartment was a highly valuable piece of real estate, she thought, and, lovely though it was, surely it was a little extravagant for a pied-à-terre. 'I mean, you've been working less than a year – you don't want to get yourself too heavily in debt so early in your career. I really do think you should avail yourself of your father's offer.'

Her concern was tinged with annoyance. Although Ian was unaware of it, his father's 'offer' had been a major cause of disagreement between Cynthia and her husband. Gordon had been outraged when she'd suggested they purchase an apartment for their son. 'It could be our Christmas present,' she'd said hopefully.

'Don't be ridiculous.' He dismissed the idea out of hand. 'If the boy needs assistance then he can have an interest-free loan for the amount of the deposit.' Gordon considered the offer most generous. 'He has to make it on his own. I did. No hand-outs, he understands that.'

Ian *did* understand, and he'd delighted his father by refusing the offer. 'Thanks, Dad,' he'd said, 'but I'd rather go it alone.' He'd known it was what his father wanted to hear.

Gordon had basked in his son's display of independence, but Cynthia had been annoyed. She'd given Ian a thousand dollars. 'A little pre-Christmas present, pet,' she'd said, 'just between us,' and Ian had had no compunction whatsoever about accepting the gift. So much for Gordon's stuffy, old-fashioned principles, Cynthia had thought. Her son had far too much common sense to let pride stand in his way.

If Cynthia Pemberton could have bought an apartment for her son herself, without causing major ructions in her marriage, she most certainly would have. And now she was concerned.

'Don't worry, Mum,' Ian said, 'I can afford it. I'm only footing half the cost.'

She looked at him blankly. 'How come?'

'It's an investment. I have a partner in the purchase.'

'Oh.' This was the first she'd heard of it – why hadn't he told her? He'd behaved most mysteriously throughout the whole business, she thought. But she felt a little relieved nonetheless.

'And who *is* this partner?'

'You'll see in a minute – he's out buying champagne to celebrate.'

Ian pulled up a chair for his mother and they sat at the balcony's small wrought-iron table.

'We think it'll really escalate in value,' he continued enthusiastically. 'It's such a great property – the building itself, the view,' he gestured at the river, 'the situation. It's virtually in the heart of the city – a minute's walk up the hill and you're in St Georges Terrace. It's a really good capital investment.'

'Well, you certainly have things all worked out,' Cynthia said approvingly. How very enterprising of Ian, she thought, her worries disappearing.

The front door opened.

'Hello, dear, I'm ho-ome,' a male voice sang out. Then there was the rattle of kitchen cupboards, the clink of glasses, and Spud appeared on the balcony with a bottle and three champagne flutes.

'Here he is,' Ian said, 'my new business partner.'

Oh, Cynthia thought, it's that *awful* little thug.

'G'day, Mrs Pemberton.' Spud dumped the bottle and glasses on the table and thrust out his hand. 'Long time, no see.'

Ian cursed him. Spud could have played it with finesse if he'd wished, but he either couldn't be bothered or he was making a statement. How bloody typical.

'Yes,' Cynthia said, forcing a smile as they shook. 'Ian's twenty-first, I believe.' Taken aback though she was, she made a quick adjustment. She could accept a

thug as a financial associate – over the years she and
Gordon had had any number of dubious connections.
'Um . . .' She racked her brains for the name. 'Patrick . . .
am I right?'

'No . . . Spud.' He grinned amiably – he didn't mean any
offence, he just wanted to get things straight, and if she
couldn't handle it, then tough. And if Pembo, who doted
on his mother, found his behaviour insulting, then that was
too bad as well. Pembo needed him, and both mother and
son would just have to learn. 'Spud Farrell.'

'Yes, I remember now,' she said, trying not to sound
tight. 'Spud. How very nice to see you again.'

Spud picked up the bottle and held it out to her, displaying the label like a waiter. 'Taittinger,' he said in his
best posh voice. 'Vintage. I trust this meets with Madame's
approval?' He winked broadly at Pembo. Pembo had told
him what to get.

'Oh.' Noticing the wink and deciding to play along,
Cynthia gave a girlish laugh. 'How *lovely.*'

Ian relaxed a little.

'No ice bucket, I'm afraid,' Spud said, 'but it just means
we'll have to drink it quickly, doesn't it?' He smiled
winningly at Cynthia. 'And there's another bottle in the
fridge.'

'Oh my goodness,' she said.

'There you go, Pembo.' Spud dumped the bottle in front
of Ian. 'You do the bubbles while I do the tucker.' And he
went off to the kitchen.

Cynthia breathed an inward sigh. The boy seemed nice
enough, but he really was *so* common, and *Pembo* . . . Oh
well, she supposed she'd just have to live with it.

'It was Spud who found the flat,' Ian said as he opened
the champagne. 'He told me the sooner I invested in real
estate the better – he owns two other properties himself.'

'Really? At *his* age.' How very interesting, Cynthia
thought.

'Yes, he has offices in Dalkeith and an investment property in West Perth.'

Spud had told Ian about the Sun Majestic several months previously – he'd been unable to resist – and Ian now wondered how his mother would react to his newly acquired business associate's investment in a brothel.

'What an enterprising young man,' Cynthia said.

Ian poured the champagne and Spud returned with an imported Brie, olives and a smoked salmon pâté.

'How *lovely*.'

They toasted the new apartment.

'Ian tells me you have two other properties, Spud,' Cynthia remarked, and he nodded. 'So what exactly is it that you *do*?'

Ian waited for Spud to say 'I'm a bookie and I own a brothel.' Surely he wouldn't be able to resist the opportunity to shock.

But after a moment's consideration, Spud said, 'I'm an entrepreneur.' He wasn't being evasive – it was the absolute truth, and he liked the word. Why pin a label on himself? There was no business venture he wasn't prepared to tackle.

'An entrepreneur?' Cynthia raised a quizzical eyebrow. It was a term that could cover all forms of nefarious activity, she thought. But then that really was none of her concern. 'How very *adventurous*,' she said.

Three properties and he was only Ian's age – this brash young man was on the way up. She'd known many like him – useful business associates, so long as one distanced oneself from them socially. She found herself reassessing her opinion of Spud Farrell.

Ian could see the glint of admiration in his mother's eyes and he guessed what she was thinking. She probably wouldn't be shocked at all if she knew of Spud's business activities, he thought. His mother was unshockable when it came to the governing factor of her life – money.

They talked about investment properties for a while, then the conversation turned to stocks and shares. Spud had acquired a modest portfolio, he told Cynthia, mainly blue chip investments: he was playing it safe to start with. 'But I'll be keeping an eye open for the main chance,' he said. He was showing off now, aware that he was making an impression.

'Well, with a son in the business, I shall certainly be keeping *my* eye on the mining market,' Cynthia said.

'Come off it, Mum,' Ian laughed. 'There's such a thing as insider trading, you know.'

'Yes, yes, dear,' she gave a frivolous wave of her hand, 'I was joking.'

She hadn't been and Spud knew it. He was recognising the hard-nosed businesswoman beneath the girlish façade. Cynthia Pemberton wasn't stupid at all, he thought.

'I'll get the other bottle, shall I?' He rose from the table.

'Dear me, Spud, I believe you're out to get me *tipsy*,' she said, wiggling a flirtatiously admonishing finger at him.

'That's the general idea,' Spud grinned. They were getting on like a house on fire.

There was a slight hiccup in the proceedings when he returned with the champagne, however.

'And where do you *live*, Spud?' Cynthia asked.

A moment's pause while Spud looked blank. 'Here,' he said. Where the hell did she think he lived?

'*Here?*' She looked around at the balcony and through to the lounge room. Did he mean here in Ian's flat?

'Yes, here – or at least I will be. I'm moving my gear in tomorrow.' He poured the champagne.

Oh, she thought, a *flatmate*. That put a different complexion on things, surely. But then perhaps not, she told herself. Young Spud Farrell was destined for success, and the rough edges were bound to smooth over as he moved up in the world.

'Thank you, dear,' she said as she accepted the glass.

Two glasses later, Cynthia took her leave.

'You *naughty* boy, Spud, you really *have* got me tipsy,' she said. He hadn't. She'd built up a strong resistance to Taittinger over the years, and although she imbibed quite a deal of it, she rarely showed the effects.

They both saw her to the front door, and she shook Spud's hand before offering her cheek to her son.

'I'll see you tomorrow when you collect your things, pet, and I must say I *can't wait* for Christmas.'

Although it was only early November, they'd discussed Christmas at length – or rather Cynthia had. Ian would have a full ten days in Perth and they'd make Christmas Day a real *family* affair – lunch at Kings Park Restaurant – just as they did every year and had done throughout his childhood.

'Oh, and Spud,' Cynthia said, as if the idea had just occurred, which it hadn't, 'why don't you join us for our Boxing Day party? It's quite an annual event, I'm sure you'd enjoy it.'

The Pembertons' Boxing Day party at Peppermint Grove was more than an annual event, it was a line-up of who's who in Perth society, and Spud jumped at the chance.

'Thanks, Mrs Pemberton, that'd be great.'

She left wondering whether, now that he was a business associate of her son's, she might perhaps ask him to call her Cynthia.

After Cynthia had gone, the boys rang Mike as they'd promised they would.

'Family business over,' Ian said. 'We'll meet you at the hospital in half an hour.'

They were off to see Muzza. Mike and Spud visited him regularly, but they considered it an added morale booster when Pembo was in town and the three of them could front up together.

'He needs the old gang,' Spud said. 'Hell, face it, the poor bastard needs all the help he can get.'

Muzza was back from Vietnam. He'd been back for over two months now. But he wasn't the same. Muzza had been wounded in the most ferocious conflict the Australians had yet experienced, and were ever to experience, during the long years of the Vietnam War – the conflict that had already become known as the Battle of Long Tan.

During the late afternoon of 18 August 1966, the members of D Company, 6 RAR had faced an enemy force of some two and a half thousand North Vietnam army regulars and Vietcong guerrillas in the Long Tan rubber plantation of Phuoc Tuy Province. The troops of D Company, 6 RAR, led by a number of army regulars, had been, for the most part, young national servicemen. As dusk had descended they'd fought on bravely amidst the pelting rain and mud and shattered trees of the plantation, and the damage inflicted upon the enemy had been significant. But the Australians had paid a price. Eighteen of their troops had lost their lives. The youngest had been nineteen years of age, the oldest twenty-two.

Many of the wounded had to lie in the mud and rain all night, waiting for dawn when help would arrive. Murray Hatfield had been one of them.

'I didn't know who'd get me first,' he'd told his mates several weeks after his return, when he was deemed fit enough to receive visitors, 'the Vietcong or our own bloody artillery that was still coming in. Then, when things settled down and I waited for morning, I thought, what the hell, it's not going to be either – I'm going to die of thirst. But I didn't, and hey, I'm still here.'

He'd spoken quite openly and with a touch of bravado, or so it had appeared. Actually, it had been desperation. Perhaps, Muzza had thought, if he talked about it to his mates, it might help keep the nightmares away.

He'd copped it early on, he'd told them. The whole

thing had started out as a routine patrol. There'd been some mortars fired in, and the unit was to discover where they'd been fired from.

'I was hoping we wouldn't be out there too long,' he'd said. 'I didn't want to miss out on the concert. Col Joye and Little Pattie were performing that night. Then, when we were only a few kilometres from the base, they came at us from nowhere. The whole world suddenly started blowing up around me. I don't remember anything after that.'

When he'd come to, he'd been unable to move, and he'd lain there all night with a raging thirst while the battle continued.

'Still, I made it,' he'd said, 'and all in one piece – unlike some of the other poor bastards.'

Muzza didn't talk like that any more, because he wasn't in one piece. Another month down the track, he was a whole bunch of fractured pieces now that he knew he'd never walk again.

'I'm one of the lucky ones, aren't I?' he said these days when his mates visited him. 'Hell, yeah! A lot of people with busted spines end up quadriplegics, so they tell me. I just get to lose the use of my legs. Jesus Christ, how lucky's that!'

Mike, Pembo and Spud were sad to discover that today was the same as usual. They'd hoped that Muzza's spirits might have lifted – he was due to leave hospital next week.

'You'll be with your family soon, mate,' Mike said encouragingly. Muzza's was a close-knit family – his parents and his two younger brothers and sister were at the hospital all hours of the day. 'I bet they're looking forward to having you home.'

'Yeah, I'll just bet they are. A cripple! You really need one of those around the house, don't you!'

The boys exchanged a look and Spud rolled his eyes. Jesus Christ, he thought, Muz was worse than ever.

'I'm sorry,' Muzza said. It was good of his mates to visit him, and he regretted having come on so strong – the words had just slipped out. He gave a shrug to suggest that he hadn't really meant it. But he had. He bloody well had! He was dreading going home, having his siblings, whom he adored, waiting on him hand and foot, treating him like an invalid instead of the hero he used to be. He couldn't bear the thought of living twenty-four hours a day with his parents' pain, feeling their sympathy and their own sense of uselessness.

'So, tell me what you've been up to,' he said, changing the subject.

The others chatted on dutifully, aware that Muzza was only pretending an interest. Half an hour later, they took their leave.

'When are you back in town, Pembo?' Muzza tried to lift his game as they said their goodbyes. He knew he'd been a real downer.

'I'm coming home for Christmas.'

'Ah.'

They left awkwardly, Mike and Spud promising they'd call around to Muzza's home in a week or so, and Pembo saying, 'See you at Christmas, Muz.'

'Yeah.' Muzza's mouth was set in a hard, bitter line and his voice dripped sarcasm. 'Christmas. Can't wait.'

Johanna spent Christmas with Mike and his family. She'd needed no excuse to avoid Manjimup this year – Darren had gone on a business trip to New Zealand and had taken her mother with him for an extended holiday. They'd asked her along, but she'd sensed her mother's relief when she'd said that she intended to study during the vacation.

Jo had spent the previous Christmas Day with the McAllisters too, following the drama of Mike's accident in the Abrolhos. She'd had some initial misgivings, wondering whether Mike's parents viewed her as just another in a string of girlfriends. She'd liked them very much on the several times she had met them, but she'd felt that surely they must consider her an intruder on such a family occasion. She'd quickly realised that she had nothing to fear. Maggie and Jim had welcomed her wholeheartedly, and they did so even more this year. Particularly Maggie, who was only too delighted that her son had a regular girl-friend – she considered Johanna a stabilising influence.

Jools liked Jo simply because she was Jo. The two had hit it off instantly.

'She's not stuck up like some of your other uni girl-friends,' she'd said to her brother the previous year. 'You're bloody lucky to have her. She's far too good for you, you know.'

Jools hadn't intended to return to Perth that year. She'd decided to spend a lonely first Christmas away from home in Sydney – possibly as a statement to her father that she was doing fine on her own, or possibly to avoid having to admit that she wasn't – but then her mother had rung with the news of Mike's heart attack.

Things were different this year – there was no need for a statement, and Jools couldn't wait to come home for Christmas. She'd recently relocated to Melbourne and was a trainee with Crawford Productions. She was going to be the first female director in Australian television, she'd decided. Acting was a mug's game.

'So how're you handling it, Jo?' she asked, steadying the huge meat dish on the stove with her oven mitts while Jo basted the turkey. Jo was being treated like one of the family this Christmas. Mike had collected her early and she'd been enlisted to help.

'How am I handling what?'

'My brother's preoccupation with crayfish.'

Jo laughed. Then she said in a mock tutor-like manner, 'You mean his PhD on "The Biology of the *Puerulus* Settling Phase of the Western Rock Lobster, *Panulirus cygnus,* and its Predictive Implications on the Commercial Catch Rate"?'

'Wow,' Jools was impressed, 'and you understand what that means, do you?' Jo nodded. 'Well, you're one up on me. You can sum it up a lot quicker than he can. He tried to explain it to me the other night and it was just so much double Dutch.'

Jools's attention span wasn't her strongest suit – she was flighty and impatient, and when something didn't garner her immediate interest she switched off.

'My brother's turned into a real academic,' she said a little critically as she lifted the meat dish back into the oven and closed the door.

'Well, what do you expect? He *is* an academic.'

That was what Jools liked most about Jo. She didn't muck around, she got right to the point.

'Yes, I s'pose he is,' she said with an element of surprise, as if the thought hadn't occurred to her. Then she grinned, sending herself up. 'I don't bump into many academics in television la-la land. But seriously, don't you reckon he's obsessing just a bit?'

'No,' Jo said. Yes, she thought. Then she chastised herself; she of all people should understand Mike's commitment to his work.

'How's it going?' Maggie bustled in from the dining room where she'd been setting the table.

'Time for the veggies,' Jools said.

'It's ridiculous, isn't it?' her mother remarked as she heaved several bags of vegetables out of the cupboard. 'A whopping great roast dinner in the middle of a blistering hot day.'

'She says that every single year.' Jools grabbed the bag of potatoes. 'I can't remember a year when she hasn't said it. I always tell her to switch to seafood and cold ham, but she won't listen.'

'Your father wouldn't hear of it,' Maggie said. Then to

Jo, 'I blame his Scottish ancestry. Three generations of Perth family and yet the McAllisters remain sticklers for tradition.'

Jo refused Maggie's suggestion that she join the men, who were having a beer on the balcony – she'd like to help with the vegetables, she said. But while she enjoyed the banter between mother and daughter as the three of them chopped and peeled and sliced, her mind was elsewhere. She was thinking of the brief exchange she'd had with Jools. It had been evident, despite Jools's light-hearted remarks, that she'd noticed a change in her brother. And she was right, Jo thought. Mike was obsessed.

It was an exciting time for him, she knew it. Dr Bruce Phillips of the CSIRO was allowing Mike junior co-authorship in his papers, and already their research was providing breakthrough material that would have a profound impact, both in commercial and academic circles. Mike's career path was clearly defined, and she was happy for him. It was ungenerous of her to feel so excluded, she told herself. But whenever he spoke of his future, she didn't appear to be a part of it.

Strange, she thought, how she used to torment herself – she'd been so convinced that she'd be dumped by the wayside when a fresh conquest beckoned. But they'd been together for over a year, and it was no longer other women she worried about. The fresh conquest she now feared was his work.

With the vegetables cooking, the women took a newly opened bottle of beer out to the balcony where they joined the men. Jim was leaning against the railing and Mike was lounging in the hammock. He pulled Jo down beside him, spilling his beer as they rocked about alarmingly, and she laughed. She put her fears aside; she had to, she told herself. Whatever happened, there was nothing she could do about it, so what was the point in worrying? It was just a bloody shame that she loved him so completely. It made the prospect of their parting unbearably painful.

They didn't eat until two in the afternoon, by which time quite a bit of beer had gone down, and lunch turned into a pleasantly raucous affair. They pulled their bon-bon crackers and read out the silly jokes and wore the silly hats that were inside, and Mike opened the chilled bottle of sparkling burgundy while Jim carved the turkey.

'There's white wine if you'd prefer it, Jo,' Maggie said, but Jo declined. 'Sparkling burgundy's another Christmas tradition, I'm afraid.'

'She knows that, Mum, she was here last year, remember?'

Maggie ignored her daughter. 'Jools christened it "the purple stuff that jumps" when she was about ten –'

'She knows that too – you told her last Christmas.'

'Oh. Did I really?' Maggie looked vague.

After the turkey there was fruit salad and ice-cream.

'I used to do a boiled plum pudding and hide three-pences in it when the kids were little,' she said to Jo. 'But then I probably told you that last time,' she added before Jools could interrupt.

'I rather miss the plum pudding,' Jim said. He'd said exactly the same thing last year.

After they'd eaten, they took their coffees out onto the balcony where it was cooler, and Jools called old Baxter up from the back garden where, these days, he spent most of his time sleeping. Baxter was fifteen now, and he climbed the stairs wearily, one step at a time, hating the effort but loving the company when he got there. Tail wagging, he collapsed at Jools's feet.

'Poor old Bax,' she said, squatting beside him and giving him a cuddle. 'He's not allowed inside any more, he's a bit incontinent. Hey, what if I made him a nappy, Mum?' She looked hopefully at her mother.

'Leave the poor animal some dignity,' Maggie said.

A short while later, Jim retired to the boatshed to sand

back the hull of the dinghy and Maggie decided on an afternoon nap, which left Mike and Jools to 'zob' for who'd do the washing up and who'd dry.

'Another tradition,' Mike said to Jo as they held up their fisted right hands. 'Best of three.'

They went through the paper, scissors and stone routine – both vying for the washing up, neither liked to dry – and Jools won.

'She always wins,' Mike said. 'She cheats.'

'I'll do the cutlery,' Jo offered.

When the washing up was out of the way, it was Jools's idea that they go for a swim. Despite the fact that it was late afternoon and a healthy sea breeze was in, the day was still hot and clammy.

Mike would have liked to roar down to North Cott on the bike with Jo, but that would have excluded Jools, so he gave up on the idea. He could have borrowed his father's car, but it didn't hold the same appeal.

'I'm buggered, Jools,' he said, 'and if I try to surf with a gut full of turkey I'll drown.'

'Let's throw ourselves off the end of the jetty then. You brought your bathers, didn't you, Jo?'

'Of course.' Jo always brought her bathers when she came to the McAllisters'. 'I'll be in it.'

It was well after five in the afternoon and, hot as it was, the breeze was squally as they stood on the end of Claremont jetty clutching their flapping towels, hair whipping their faces.

Jo looked down uncertainly at the huge brown jellyfish palpitating like murky hearts in the water below, and thought that she'd rather be getting dumped in the surf at Cottesloe.

'They're harmless,' Mike assured her.

'The idea is to bomb them,' Jools said, climbing up onto one of the jetty's corner pylons. Picking a particularly large cluster, she took off, landing right in the middle.

As she started swimming back towards the iron ladder a little further down the jetty, Mike landed a bombie right beside her, so when he resurfaced she ducked him.

What the hell, Jo thought, as she watched them cavorting like ten year olds, and, aiming for a space between the jellyfish, she threw herself off the jetty. Then they swam to the ladder, climbed up one by one, and did it all over again, Jo's instruction on how to chuck bombies commencing in earnest.

Baxter joined them. He'd followed them when they left the house, but hadn't been able to keep up. Now, finally, he'd plodded his way to the end of the jetty where he lay enjoying the breeze.

Twenty minutes later, they called it a day, breathless and exhausted.

'You two go home and grab the shower first,' Jools said generously. 'Bax and I'll plod back together.' She sprawled beside the dog – Baxter was fast asleep by now. 'And don't use up all the hot water!' she called after them.

She'd give them plenty of time, she decided; with the house clear they might want to sneak into Mike's bedroom. Leaning on one elbow, she watched them walk hand in hand down the jetty. God, Jo was perfect for him, she thought, but Mike was so obsessed with his bloody crayfish he didn't seem to realise it.

Jools considered herself quite an authority on men. She'd recently embarked upon an affair with a television director at Crawfords, whom she found inspirational. She'd had only one previous affair – with an actor shortly after her arrival in Sydney – and it had turned her off actors forever. They were too self-centred. It appeared that academics were somewhat the same, she thought as she lay back on the warm wooden planks to sunbake, although there was very little sun left to bake in. Poor Jo. Mike was so selfish. It was typically male.

*

In the boatshed, Jim had finished sanding back the dinghy and was now applying an undercoat of paint. Mike and Jo walked through the garden and up the back stairs. There was no sign of Maggie, she was still having her nap.

The bathroom was at the end of the balcony, right next to the door that led to Mike's side verandah bedroom. As he took her in his arms, Jo returned his kiss.

'There's no-one around,' he murmured in her ear.

'Let's do a shower first,' she whispered.

He was about to step into the bathroom with her, but she smiled. 'You get second go,' she said.

It was normal for them to share the shower when they were at her flat, but Jo thought how embarrassing it would be if Maggie needed to use the bathroom and they were in there together.

She showered quickly, wondering why the prospect of making love in the side verandah bedroom no longer seemed tawdry. Perhaps it was because she'd sensed Jools's approval. She knew that Jools had deliberately allowed them time to be alone.

During the minute or so while Mike had his hasty shower, Jo sat on the bed gazing at the walls and the memorabilia of his past. She'd seen the room before, he'd shown it to her – it was a real boy's room. Strewn about haphazardly were sporting pennants and trophies, but predominant were the Aboriginal artefacts he'd collected during his outback travels. Propped in corners and hanging from hooks were spears and woomeras, axes and boomerangs, wooden bowls and drinking utensils. He'd spoken to her often and avidly about the Aboriginal attitude towards conservation. He was a great admirer of the Indigenous people and their care for the land that supported them. It was a wonderful room, Jo thought – so indicative of Mike and all he believed in.

They made love with stealth, wary of every sound. But to Jo, it didn't seem furtive. There was a tenderness in their secrecy, as if in so stifling themselves they were expressing something special.

Afterwards, Mike kissed her very gently.

'You're beautiful, Jo,' he said.

He'd said the same thing on occasions in the past. It was the closest he ever came to telling her he loved her.

'You too,' she whispered.

Her remark wasn't flippant, just as she knew his hadn't been, but she always took the lead from him, never telling him she loved him, sure that it wasn't what he wanted to hear.

They dressed and slipped out the other door of Mike's bedroom – the one that led onto the side verandah rather than the balcony. Then they made their entrance to the house via the front door. Jo smiled wryly to herself – Mike had the ideal set-up for illicit dalliances, she thought.

Maggie was making tea in the kitchen, and they joined her. A little while later Jim arrived, and Jools emerged fresh from the shower, and they all adjourned to the balcony to watch the sunset.

With the pinks and oranges fading in the sky, Jo made her farewells. Maggie tried to persuade her into staying for a light dinner.

'I thought I'd do omelettes,' she said. 'No more turkey, I promise.'

But Jo didn't want to overstay her welcome.

'Thank you,' she said, 'it's been the perfect Christmas.'

It had been, she thought. Throughout the entire day, memories of childhood Christmases in Manjimup had come to mind. Darren stroking her in her new party frock. 'Who's a pretty girl?' And then, when she was a teenager, her mother's brittle manner, the vain attempts to drum up a festive atmosphere. Oh, how she envied Mike his family.

They wouldn't hear of it when she said she'd ring for a taxi.

'No, no,' Jim insisted. 'Mike can have the car, he'll drive you home.'

'No, I won't,' Mike said, and his father looked at him askance. 'Jo prefers the bike, Dad.'

'Oh. Right.'

It was dark when they pulled up outside the flat in Kingsway.

'Don't come in, Mike,' she said as she opened the front door.

'Why not?' He was surprised. He'd presumed they'd make love again.

'Go home.'

He looked like a bewildered puppy uncertain of the order, and she laughed, realising that she'd sounded like a dog trainer.

'Maggie's making omelettes,' she said.

'Bugger the omelettes.'

'Go home to your family, Mike.' She kissed him. 'I've had a perfect day, and I'm tired.'

He left with the promise that he'd pick her up at eleven the following morning. Boxing Day at the beach was obligatory, and they were meeting up with a gang at the OBH for lunch.

Mike pondered a little upon his knock-back as he revved up the bike and roared off. Why hadn't Jo wanted sex? She had a healthy libido, and she'd never turned him down before. But then Jo could be quite arbitrary at times. He respected her for it, and he liked her unpredictability, which was probably the reason he hadn't been interested in other women since they'd been together. Then again, other women wouldn't have understood his work and the importance of it. Jo did. He'd never met anyone like Jo, she was a real one-off, he thought.

'I'm thinking of going down to Manjimup for the last fortnight of vacation,' Jo said six weeks later. 'Mum and Darren are back from New Zealand.'

'Oh.' Mike wondered briefly what had prompted her decision, but he didn't enquire. Since the long-ago night she'd told him about her stepfather, she'd made little mention of her family and he never pushed her for details. 'Sure,' he said.

'How did you go with Ray George?' she asked, changing the subject as she brought the coffees to the kitchen table and sat beside him.

Mike had arrived at the Kingsway flat after another full day with one of his supervisors, Dr Ray George, curator of crustacea at the WA Museum. He'd spent much of the holidays working – Jo hadn't seen him for the whole of the past week.

'Terrific!' he said, and launched into a further account of their research and its progression, all of which Jo normally found interesting. But today her mind was elsewhere.

'He asked if I'd like to join a team up north next year –'

Her attention was suddenly captured. 'A team up north?'

'Yep,' he continued eagerly. 'A WA Museum-based team is being sent to the Pilbara. They're going to ecologically map the Dampier Archipelago, and Ray George asked if I'd like to be a part of it.'

'And what did you say?' She tried to make the query sound casual.

'Hell, Jo, what *could* I say?' Mike laughed. In his enthusiasm, he didn't notice the look on her face, or the fact that she seemed to be holding her breath. 'Their interest in me when I've still got a whole year of my PhD to go is one heck of a compliment!'

'Yes, of course it is.'

Well, that just about said it all, she thought. At least she could stop agonising over a decision now. Unwittingly, he'd decided for her. There was only one path she could take, and it terrified her.

'How exciting, Mike. I'm happy for you.' She gave him a peck on the cheek, then rose and crossed to the pantry.

She needed to put some space between them. 'Are you hungry?' she asked, opening a cupboard door. 'Shall I get us something to eat?'

He didn't sense her unrest. 'Not yet. How about you grab your bathers and we go for a burl to North Cott?'

'Fantastic idea. Won't be a tick.'

She disappeared to the bedroom, where she sat for a moment or so, heart pounding wildly as she collected her thoughts. Then she reappeared, all smiles.

'Ready,' she said, towel and bathers rolled up under one arm.

Later that night, after they'd made love, she told him that she'd decided to go to Manjimup the following day.

'Tomorrow?' he queried. 'I thought you said next week.'

'The sooner I get it over with the better.'

'Right.' He was puzzled, it all seemed rather sudden. 'I'll drive you to the train.'

'No, Kathy'll drive me.' She snuggled up beside him and ran a hand over his chest. 'I'd rather say goodbye here, like this.'

He turned to her, but in the darkness of the bedroom he couldn't see the expression on her face. She'd been in a strange mood all evening, he realised – sort of withdrawn. He hoped nothing was wrong. But then Jo was Jo – she'd tell him if something was bothering her. It was probably just the impending trip to Manjimup.

He kissed her. 'I'll miss you,' he said.

'I'll miss you too.'

The new term started in late February, and Mike was concerned. Jo hadn't contacted him upon her return to Perth, and she was nowhere to be found on campus. She must still be in Manjimup, he thought. Perhaps something had happened to cause her to stay down there, perhaps her mother was ill. But surely she would have rung him if that were the case.

He called around to the flat on Saturday morning when he knew Kathy would be there.

'Hi, Mike.'

Kathy wasn't surprised to see him. She'd been expecting him to call.

'Where's Jo?' he asked. 'She hasn't rung me. Is she still in Manjimup?'

'No, she's in Sydney.'

'Sydney?' He was confused. 'What's she doing in Sydney?'

'I've no idea.'

'How long's she going to be there?' His mind was jumbled – why on earth hadn't she told him? 'When's she coming back?'

'She's not.'

'What do you mean?'

'Just that. She's dropped out of uni, she's gone to Sydney and she's not coming back.'

'She's *dropped out of uni*!' He was echoing her foolishly, but he couldn't help it, he was in a state of utter disbelief. 'Why? And why didn't she tell me?'

'I think it's her way of calling things quits.'

He stared at her uncomprehendingly.

'It's over, Mike.'

'Why? Why is it over?'

'I don't know, she didn't say.'

'Where's she staying? What's her phone number?'

'She didn't tell me that either. But she left you a letter. Hang on.'

Kathy disappeared and returned seconds later with an envelope. She handed it to him, expecting him to leave so that he could read its contents in private. But he didn't.

Mike ripped the envelope open and scanned the note, barely taking in Jo's words as he searched for a phone number or an address. But there was none. He was starting to feel desperate.

'She must have left an address. How can I get in touch with her?'

'You can't. I'm sorry, Mike.' Kathy could see the distrust in his eyes. 'I honestly don't have a contact for her. She didn't leave me with one.'

He looked so shattered that she started to feel sorry for him.

'Perhaps she didn't know where she was going to be staying,' she said. 'Perhaps she'll get in touch when she's settled.'

She wouldn't, Kathy thought, remembering the exchange that had taken place when she'd driven Jo to the railway station just three weeks previously.

'I won't be coming back, Kath,' Jo had said as she'd taken her suitcase from the boot of the car. 'I'm arranging for my gear to be shipped from Manjimup and then I'm off to Sydney.' She'd handed Kathy two envelopes. 'There's a month's rent in one. And a note for Mike in the other.'

'Why?' Kathy, too, had been flabbergasted. 'Why are you going?'

'I need to distance myself from him, and I can't do that in Perth.'

'What's wrong? What's happened between you?'

'Nothing – that's just it. I'm not a part of his life. Hang on to the note for me,' she instructed. 'When he comes around to the flat, as I know he will in a few weeks when the holidays are over and I'm not back at uni, give it to him then. Not before.' She'd dropped her brittle manner. Her smile had been a little tremulous and her tone apologetic. 'I'm sorry to land you with this. I know it seems gutless, but I've decided it's the only way.'

Then she'd kissed Kathy on the cheek and picked up her suitcase. 'Thanks for everything. Bye, Kath.' And she'd walked off into the station without a backward glance, leaving Kathy in complete amazement. Jo Whitely had always been a decisive person and a woman of few words, but surely this was taking things to the extreme.

'I'm really sorry I can't be more help, Mike,' Kathy said now, and she meant it. She'd developed a recent antipathy towards men, having been dumped by her boyfriend two months previously, and whatever had gone wrong in the relationship between Mike and Jo, her sympathies had initially been on Jo's side. Now, however, as she looked at Mike, so completely devastated, she couldn't help but feel sorry for him.

'Jo's always been a bit of a mystery, Mike,' she said. 'And now she's decided to disappear. It's weird, I know, but that's the way she wants it.'

Mike wasn't interested in Kathy's views or her sympathy. 'What's her mother's phone number in Manjimup?' Why hadn't he ever thought to ask Jo that, he wondered.

'I wouldn't have a clue. She never talked about her family, and she never stayed in touch when she went home. Odd, don't you think . . .?'

But Kathy's chatter went unheeded. He was leaving without even saying goodbye.

Mike read and re-read Jo's brief note, hearing her voice, but finding no satisfactory explanation in her words.

Forgive me, my darling, for not saying goodbye. It will appear the action of a coward, and that's exactly what it is. I simply don't have the courage to confront you.

You've always admitted that your work takes precedence, Mike, and I've respected your honesty. But I realised, when you spoke of your trip to the Pilbara, that there will never be a place for me in your future. You need to be free. I've probably known it for some time and blindly refused to recognise the truth, but I do now. Just as I recognise that I need to be free too. I have a future of my own to pursue.

I treasure what we've shared, Mike, and I always will. I wish you good luck with the extraordinary career you so rightly deserve.

I love you. There, I've said it.
Jo.

On first reading, Mike felt dismayed by the note's awful finality. It couldn't be over, surely. Not just like that. Then the more he read it, the more the note angered him. How dare she offer him no right of reply. And why should his talk of the Pilbara have been such a catalyst? It was a bloody research trip, for God's sake, he wasn't disappearing from the face of the earth.

The flames of Mike's anger were fuelled by a deep anxiety. He couldn't lose Jo. He mustn't. He loved her. But then he'd never told her so. Was that why she'd left him? Impossible! She knew he loved her. Of course she knew!

Anxiety became desperation, and desperation became panic as Sunday slowly slipped by. Then on Monday he checked with the university. Yes, Johanna Whitely had resigned from her course. She'd simply dropped out. It was a mystery to everyone – she'd been such a good student. He asked around amongst her friends, but they were equally mystified.

He'd try Manjimup, he decided – her mother would know where she was. But Jesus Christ, he thought frantically, I don't even know her mother's name. The stepfather's name was Darren. Darren bloody who? He racked his brains, thinking of the conversation they'd had that night after he'd come out of hospital. She'd been full of self-loathing as she'd told him that the man she detested was putting her through uni. What had she said? *Darren can afford it – he's quite well off.* That was it, he remembered, Darren was a manager for Bunnings Timber Mills.

He rang Bunnings in Manjimup and asked for Darren the manager. 'It's a personal call,' he said to the secretary. She put him through.

'Hello, Darren Collins,' a male voice said.

'Mr Collins, I'm a friend of Jo's, I go to uni with her. My name's Mike McAllister.'

'Ah, yes?'

It was apparent from the man's uninterested tone that he'd never heard the name. So Jo had never mentioned him, Mike thought.

'I'm after a contact address or phone number for her.'

'She's gone to Sydney.'

'Yes, I know that. But she doesn't seem to have left any contact number with her flatmate here in Perth, and I wondered whether –'

'No, I'm sorry, I can't help you there.'

Can't or won't, Mike thought.

'Mr Collins, I'm a very good friend of Jo's, and I really would –'

The voice cut him off irritably. 'Quite frankly . . . um . . . I'm sorry, who is this again?'

'Mike. Mike McAllister.'

'Yes. Mike. Well, quite frankly, Johanna hasn't as yet informed *us* of her exact whereabouts. She's causing her mother a great deal of concern. She's a headstrong girl who follows her own inclinations, and I'm sure if she wants you to know where to find her, she'll inform you.'

'Perhaps if I could speak to her mother –'

'You most certainly may not.'

The man was going to hang up any minute. In desperation, Mike asked, 'Do you know why she dropped out of university and went to Sydney?'

'I've got no bloody idea, boy,' Darren said, dropping the act. 'Your guess is as good as mine.' Then he hung up.

Johanna had disappeared into thin air, it seemed. Mike had nowhere to turn.

CHAPTER SEVEN

Baxter died in late April, just two months short of his sixteenth birthday. It was a peaceful death. Mike discovered him in the early hours of the morning, curled up on the old grey army blanket that served as his bed in the downstairs laundry. He'd had a heart attack during his sleep.

He phoned Jools in Melbourne that night. She was deeply affected, as he'd anticipated she would be.

'Oh . . .' He heard a quick intake of breath and sensed the tears instantly gathering. 'Oh no, not Bax . . .' She was trying to control herself, but with little success. 'Oh . . . oh . . . poor old Bax . . .' Then she caved in altogether. 'When did it happen?' she asked through her sobs.

'I don't know. Sometime during the night, I suppose. I found him this morning.'

'This morning!' There was a gulp of surprise and the sobs halted. 'Why didn't you ring me earlier?'

'You don't like being rung at work. You said they can't even put calls through when you're in the studio.'

'Oh, for God's sake, Mike! This isn't a *social* call! You could have left a message with the switchboard! I could have rung you back!' The sobs started up again.

'This is family . . . This is Baxter . . .'

'This is a *dog*!'

A pause, followed by a series of small gasps while the sobs became sniffles, then Jools's disbelieving voice down the line.

'How can you say that? Baxter's our past. He's our childhood. We grew up together. How can you say he's just a dog?' Her voice was starting to falter again. 'Baxter was more, he was much, much more.'

'I didn't say he was *just* a dog,' Mike replied patiently. 'He was a good mate, I agree.' Jools's reaction was understandable, he supposed – she'd known the animal since she was five years old – but it was silly to be over-emotional. 'The fact is, Jools, he *was* a dog, and he nearly made it to sixteen, which is well over a hundred years in human terms, and that's a pretty damn good innings, and he died in his sleep, presumably without pain, so I don't think there's much cause for grief.'

There was a slight hiccup as Jools gained control of herself, then the timid query, 'Did he look peaceful when you found him?'

'Very. I thought he was asleep. You couldn't tell he was dead.'

'When you realised he was, did you cry?' A brief pause. 'I bet you did. Even you, Mike. Go on. Admit it. I bet you did.'

'Nup.' There *had* been a tear in his eye as he'd patted the old dog goodbye, but he wasn't going to admit it to Jools – he could sense she was starting to get herself worked up again. 'I felt happy for him,' he said. It was the truth.

Mike had chosen the correct tack. His pragmatism and sheer common sense had successfully broken through Jools's instinctive need for drama.

'God, you're a cold fish,' she said, not without affection.

'That's the stupidest saying.'

'Why?' she demanded.

'Ever met a *warm* fish?'

There was a snuffle that could have been a sort of a laugh and then she asked, 'Where is he now?'

'Dad and I buried him down by the grape vines.'

'Oh.'

Was she going to crumple again, he wondered. But she didn't.

'A proper grave?' she asked. 'With a headstone?'

'No.' That hadn't occurred to him.

'Well, I think it's the least you could do for Baxter,' she said peremptorily. 'He deserves that much after what he's meant to the family.'

Mike made no immediate response. How typically melodramatic she was being, he thought.

'Please, Mike.' Jools no longer sounded peremptory; she sounded childlike, vulnerable. 'Please, will you make him a proper grave? Will you do that for him?'

'No, I won't do it for Baxter – he wouldn't give a shit. But I'll do it for you, if you like.'

'You promise?' She was starting to sniffle again.

'I promise.'

The sniffles got louder. She knew he'd keep his promise – Mike always did.

'I could make it a birthday present for next month,' he suggested. 'The headstone could read *Happy Twenty-first, Jools. Love Baxter.* What do you say?'

'Don't you bloody dare.'

As Jools hung up the receiver, she marvelled at the difference between the two of them. She and her brother were chalk and cheese, she thought.

Jools had always considered her way of dealing with things far healthier than Mike's. Surely it was better to openly express one's emotions rather than bottle them up the way he did. But she'd recently decided that Mike didn't bottle up his emotions at all, he simply switched them off. It had certainly appeared that way when she'd rung to offer her heartfelt commiserations about Jo's disappearance.

'It's actually just as well she's gone,' he'd said. 'I'll be heading north next year. I can't afford to be emotionally tied down.'

Convinced as she'd been that her brother was suffering all sorts of inner torment, Jools had found his response quite shocking.

And now old Baxter's death was copping the same reaction, she thought as she sat down with a box of tissues in preparation for a good lengthy bawl. Baxter, like Johanna, had become an episode that belonged to the past. Mike had moved on. It seemed that her brother didn't look back, Jools thought. It seemed that for Mike, the road led in one direction only, and that was ahead.

One Saturday afternoon, Mike called around to see Muzza. Spud was at the racetrack. Mike rarely visited on his own – normally he and Spud called in together on a Sunday – but he felt they'd neglected Muzza of late. Pembo hadn't come to town for over a month, Spud had been extra busy, even on Sundays, and Mike was starting to feel guilty.

Muzza had been out of hospital now for a full five months, but he no longer lived with his family. He'd bought a little house in Shenton Park and moved there in early January, refusing to be a burden to his parents and his younger siblings.

'Mum and Dad are glad to be rid of me,' he'd told his mates at the time. 'Shit, with three teenagers in the house, who the hell needs a useless cripple?' He'd said it in a tough, offhand manner, as if cracking a joke.

His parents hadn't been glad to be rid of him at all, but, recognising their son's fierce need for independence, they'd put up half the money for the weatherboard cottage – Muzza's war pension would meet the further repayments –

and had arranged for the necessary conversions to allow for wheelchair access throughout. It was generous of them as they weren't particularly wealthy, but they'd have gone into debt for their son if need be. They'd even bought Muzza an automatic car with a specially modified hand-brake, and the passenger bucket seat had been removed to house his collapsible wheelchair.

Muzza was grateful, but he never allowed it to show. 'Keeps me out of their hair,' he'd say in that cynical way of his.

Muzza had changed beyond all belief. Gone was the baby-faced, eager-to-please boy he'd once been. He was chain smoking and hitting the booze hard, his mates noted, and from his occasionally bombed-out state, they suspected he was abusing the prescription drugs he took for pain relief. He was barely twenty-one, but, stubble-chinned, unwashed hair pulled back in a ponytail, he looked fifteen years older. They'd tried to tease him about his hair to start with.

'It's time you had a haircut, Muz,' Ian would say, and Mike would add, 'Yeah, mate, you look like a hippie.' The three of them had always taken the mickey out of the hippie set at uni. But Muzza would just shrug and say 'Who gives a shit?' as he downed another slug of Corio whisky. All three found their old mate hard going these days.

Now, as Mike pulled his bike up in front of the Shenton Park house, he saw Muzza in his car in the driveway. He was heaving his collapsible wheelchair out of the open passenger door. Mike watched as Muzza dragged himself across from the driver's side, set up the chair and then hauled himself into it. Laborious though it was, Muzza was very proficient in the exercise, and Mike knew better than to offer any help.

'G'day, Muz,' he said, walking up the driveway. Muzza was lifting something out of the car and into his lap – two bottles of Corio, Mike noticed, and something in a chemist's white paper bag. He'd been laying in the supplies.

'G'day, mate.' Muzza slammed the car door shut, spun the wheelchair about and headed for the ramp that led up to the small front verandah. 'Come on in.'

The ramp was steep, but Muzza zoomed up it, and had the front door open before Mike joined him. His upper body was strong and fit, and in his angry bid for independence the wheelchair had already become an extension of himself. Much as he referred to himself as a useless cripple, Muzza needed no help. Not in the physical sense, anyway.

'Well, well, well, a lone good Samaritan,' he jeered, wheeling himself through the open arch to the kitchen and dumping the bottles and pills on the table while Mike closed the front door. 'I thought you blokes liked to pity in numbers.'

Mike was floored. That was pretty strong even coming from Muzza, he thought. He watched from the archway as Muzza, apparently oblivious to the offensiveness of his remark, lifted two glasses from the cupboard.

'I'll go if you like,' he said.

'Eh?' Muzza turned, puzzled. 'Why?'

'Well, you've got enough pity for yourself, haven't you? You hardly need mine.'

'Oh.' Muzza realised' how insulting he'd sounded, and to Mike of all people. He'd meant it as a joke, but it hadn't come out right at all. He was really glad to see Mike, but he'd got into the habit of playing it tough, as if by anticipating people's pity, he could ward it off. 'It was meant to be a joke,' he said feebly. 'Sorry.'

'Forget it.' Mike grinned as he crossed to the table and sat. 'Have you got a beer? I'm not drinking that muck,' he said, gesturing at the whisky.

They talked for over two hours, and possibly by way of further apology, or possibly because he felt more secure on a one-to-one basis with Mike, Muzza really opened up. He dropped his tough act and the self-derision that masked his sense of uselessness, and spoke with a genuine desire to make contact.

'I didn't serve any fucking purpose, that's the problem. I didn't *do* anything in Nam – just got myself blown up and landed on my back. What's the point in that?'

Mike didn't say anything, but listened attentively. He thought it was healthy the way Muzza was speaking.

'You remember my farewell piss-up at Steve's when Pembo went on about my deferring?' Mike nodded. ' I was so bloody gutless that night. I should have told him that I *wanted* to go to Vietnam.'

Muzza downed a hefty slug of his whisky and lit a cigarette.

'I *did*, you know. I wanted to know what it was like to fight in a war. How bloody naïve can you get?' It was said with a touch of his customary cynicism, then he added in all earnestness, 'But there was something else, Mike. I really did feel I was serving a purpose.'

He dragged heavily on his cigarette before downing the remains in his glass – an automatic gesture. Muzza often seemed unaware of the fact he was drinking.

'Sure,' he continued, 'Spud was sending me up that night with the old king and country toast, but he wasn't far wrong. I thought it was my duty to go and fight, to "do my bit" the way the old man had. But what exactly *was* "my bit"? Bugger all. And now here I am – like this – and for what?' He took a couple more ferocious drags and gave an empty laugh. 'Maybe if I'd lost the use of my legs doing something heroic, I'd handle it better.' Stubbing the cigarette out in an ashtray already crowded with butts, he poured himself another neat whisky. 'Or maybe not. Shit, maybe I'm just looking for an excuse to whinge.'

'I don't think you are.' It was good the way he was letting it all hang out, Mike thought.

Muzza took a swig from his glass and leaned forward, elbows on the table, eyes keenly fixed on Mike's. 'Life has to serve a purpose – you said that yourself up at the Abrolhos, remember?'

Mike nodded warily. He remembered the conversation well. He'd been carrying on about the environment and how he felt such a sense of purpose in his research. *Life has to serve a purpose, Muz*, he'd said, *otherwise why bother living it*? Muzza had been in avid agreement, and Mike had presumed at the time that he'd been referring to his medical studies. But Muz had already decided that he wouldn't defer his call-up, Mike now thought, so the sense of purpose he'd felt must have been the prospect of serving in Vietnam.

Mike wondered whether, if he'd known that at the time, he could have talked Muzza out of his decision. He'd always been aware that Muz looked up to him as a bit of a hero, so it was quite possible, he thought. He felt a sudden stab of guilt. Why, for God's sake, hadn't Muzza said something?

'Well, *you* sure as hell have a purpose,' Muzza continued, unaware of his friend's inner turmoil. Then he laughed, this time without cynicism. 'I'm not so sure about Pembo and Spud, but money certainly talks. Maybe when they've made their millions, they'll do something worthwhile down the track.'

The smile quickly faded. He skolled the whisky in one hit, lit up another cigarette and leaned on the table again. 'But me, Mike – where's my purpose?'

Healthy as Mike considered the conversation to be, and willing as he was to act as a sounding board, he was fearful about making any comment. What if he said the wrong thing? He sat in silence.

'Come on, mate.' Muzza egged him on while he poured himself another drink. The booze was hitting the pills he'd taken earlier and he was feeling good. '*Where* is it? *What* is it?' The questions were rhetorical – he knew no-one had the answers, but having finally let his barriers down, he didn't want to stop. 'Come on. Give me a purpose.'

'I can't. You have to find it yourself.' Mike replied simply because he felt he had to, but once he'd said the words, he felt driven to continue. 'You picked a bummer last time, but you can't give up because it didn't work out. You have to look for something else.'

Muzza stared at him blankly. He wasn't drunk or bombed out enough yet to not recognise that Mike was serious.

'You had a purpose to start with, Muz – you're not like Pembo and Spud, you never were. They think money's the key to everything, but it's not.' Mike mentally crossed his fingers, hoping he wasn't coming up with something Muzza saw as a mere platitude, or worse still a fob-off. 'Hell, mate, you've only been out of hospital five months, you've still got a lot of adjusting to do. Think about the positives – you've already achieved your mobility and your independence, that's a big start.'

He wanted to say 'Stop drinking yourself into the ground and turning into a junkie', but he didn't dare. Besides, what right did he have? If he were in Muzza's situation he might well do the same.

'You need to give yourself time, but you'll find something worthwhile that you really care about. You might want to go back to uni and finish your degree, or you might find something completely different. But you can do it, I know you can.'

Muzza continued to stare at him for a moment or so. Good old Mike with his 'positives', he thought. Good old Mike McAllister, his hero, trying so hard to answer the unanswerable which should never have been asked of him in the first place. God, he loved the bloke. Muzza threw back his head and gave a healthy guffaw of laughter.

'It's that simple, is it, mate?'

Mike, who'd been squirming under the scrutiny, was relieved that he hadn't offended.

'I know it's not,' he said, a little shamefaced. 'I'm sorry, I didn't mean to sound trite.'

'You didn't.' Muzza downed his whisky and picked up the bottle. 'You just sounded like you.'

'Right.' Mike was unsure as to the meaning of Muzza's comment, but he was happy his friend found the whole thing humorous. He held out his empty beer glass. 'Can I have some of that muck now?'

'Sure.' Muzza poured them a hefty slug each. 'Let's get rat-arsed.'

They talked about their mates for a while, both agreeing that Spud was destined to become a wealthy man. 'He's got tentacles everywhere,' Mike said.

Spud's city bookmaking business and the brothel continued to thrive, and his gambling syndicate had expanded to include professional two-up and card games in most country centres, particularly the remote mining towns to the east and far north.

'Christ, the bloke's going to end up running the state,' Muzza said.

'It could well be his intention,' Mike agreed. 'And Pembo's coming up in the world too. Did you know he's left Western Mining?'

Muzza didn't know – he hadn't seen Ian Pemberton for over a month. He was surprised to hear that Pembo had given up such a prestigious job.

'He'll tell you himself – he'll be in town next week – but he says he's learned enough about the business side of things to go it alone.' Mike grinned. 'Which probably means he's nicked a whole heap of top-secret information. He's setting up his own company. He'll be "chief geologist and managing director of Excalibur Nickel Resources Pty Ltd".'

Mike gave it an impressive ring and raised his eyebrows,

but Muzza didn't react. He poured another two stiff whiskies instead.

'Ah well, good luck to them both.' The success of his mates had worn thin, and Muzza, reminded of the emptiness of his own life, felt an irrational surge of irritation. 'They're men who've found their *purpose*, after all,' he said sarcastically. He raised his glass. 'Here's to Pembo and Spud.'

Mike was forced to clink and drink a toast, but his sip was tentative. He didn't really want a second whisky, and he could tell by Muzza's rapid mood swing that the grog and whatever pills he'd popped were taking effect. He quickly changed the subject.

'Spud says that when Pembo arrives, it's party time, starting with a pub crawl next week. We want you to come with us.'

'Party time.' Muzza snorted scornfully as he lit up a cigarette. '*Me? Partying?*' The cynical tone was back.

'Yeah. Why not?'

'Partying involves *women*, doesn't it?'

'A pub crawl doesn't, mate.' Oh shit, Mike thought. He hoped Muzza wasn't about to become aggressive. It often happened quite quickly and for no apparent reason. 'We'd really like you to come, Muz. The four of us, you know – the old gang.'

'Nah, wouldn't want to cramp your style. Christ, even Casanova McAllister'd have trouble scoring with a cripple in tow.' He dragged on his cigarette and the laugh turned into a cough. 'Beats me why you want to root around when you could have had a woman like Jo though,' he said, his tone condemnatory.

Mike heaved a sigh. 'I couldn't have had *a woman like Jo*, Muz. It wasn't a matter of choice, and you know it. She walked out on me, remember?'

He didn't want to talk about Jo, and certainly not while Muz was in his present state. In fact, he'd assiduously

avoided any conversation on the subject following
Muzza's initial reaction.

Muzza had been horrified when he'd heard that Jo had
dropped out of uni and disappeared.

Mike had called around just a few days after Jo's disappearance, and Muzza had been pleased to see him arrive
on his own. When Mike had Spud and Pembo with him,
they'd chat about other mates and the gang from uni –
who was doing what, who sent their regards – and Muzza
would have to pretend an interest he didn't possess, trying
to act 'normal' while he sucked back his cigarettes and
downed his Corio. Perhaps with Mike on his own, they
might be able to skip some of the small talk.

But small talk had been the last thing on Mike's mind.
'Do you know where she is?' he'd asked.

'Who?' Muzza had been completely bewildered.

'Jo. She's gone.'

Mike had been pinning his last hopes on Muzza. Jo was
fond of Muz. She'd visited him regularly when he was in
hospital, preferring to go on her own rather than with the
boys. He'd hoped that Muzza might have some answers.
Plainly he didn't.

'She's dropped out of uni and gone to Sydney.' He
hadn't bothered pulling any punches, there didn't seem
any point. 'Nobody knows where the hell she is.'

Muzza's reaction had been extraordinary. He'd turned
on Mike in direct accusation.

'What did you do to her?'

'Not a bloody thing.' Mike had taken offence. 'She just
left without a word.'

'And you didn't go after her? You didn't *do* anything?'

'How could I? She left no address, no phone number,
nothing. No-one knows where she is. What am I *supposed*
to do, for God's sake?'

Muzza had glared, a mixture of incredulity and con-
demnation, and had been about to say something, but

Mike had been in no mood for further cross-questioning.

'I don't know *why* she went, or *where* she went, she didn't tell me.'

His tone had called a definite halt to the conversation, and he'd left not long afterwards.

The topic had been avoided during Mike's visits over the ensuing two months, particularly as Spud had been with him each time, but Mike knew that Muzza firmly believed he was responsible for Jo's disappearance.

'That's the only trouble with you, mate,' Muzza said now, grinding his cigarette out amongst the butts in the overflowing ashtray. 'You can be a callous bastard when it comes to women.'

Here we go, Mike thought, he's been dying to confront me on my own, and now he's on the attack. Still, he decided, it was healthy that Muzza wanted to talk about something other than himself. Usually when the pills and the booze set in, his self-loathing was at its worst. Mike steeled himself.

'Callous in what way, Muz?' he asked reasonably.

'Well, I can't for the life of me understand how you're not cut up about Jo. Shit, you two were together – how long? Well over a year – more like eighteen months, wasn't it? Didn't you care about her *at all*?'

'Of course I cared. And how do you know I'm not cut up?'

Muzza laughed derisively as he poured himself another whisky, his hand a little unsteady by now. 'Christ, if you are, you've got a strange way of showing it. Spud says you fuck around like there's no tomorrow.'

'So what am I supposed to do? Live like a monk?'

Mike was starting to feel angry. What gave Muzza the right? If it had been anyone else, he'd have told them to mind their own bloody business and he'd have walked out. But he couldn't walk out on Muzza. Muzza was right about a couple of things. He *was* a cripple, and Mike *did* feel sorry for him.

'Fair enough.'

In his gathering bleariness, Muzza sensed his friend's anger, and he supposed it was warranted. But hell, Mike hadn't appreciated Jo – he'd taken her for granted.

He took a slug of his drink – he was starting to feel sorry for himself, he always did around about this stage. It was his own envy talking, and he knew it. Christ, he'd loved Jo. He wondered if she'd ever guessed. Of course she hadn't, who was he kidding? Even though they were the same age, she'd treated him like a kid brother – right from the start, well before she'd met Mike. And of course when Casanova McAllister had arrived on the scene, no-one had got a look in, least of all him. He'd accepted it. Mike was Mike – you could hardly blame the bloke for being fatally attractive to women. But Jo Whitely deserved better than to become just another victim of the McAllister magnetism. What the hell, Muzza thought. Jo was gone, he was a cripple, and Mike sailed through life as always. What was the point in agonising over things that could never have been anyway?

'I'm sorry,' he said. 'It's none of my business. You can tell me to shut up if you like.'

'Shut up, Muz.'

It was said firmly but good-naturedly, and Muzza shrugged agreement, although he would have liked to talk a bit more about Jo. He remembered when she'd come around to see him shortly after he'd moved into the house. She'd brought a pot plant – a housewarming present, she'd said. He looked at it sitting on the window sill – thriving – and recalled how she'd laughed. 'Devil's ivy,' she'd said, 'virtually indestructible. I'm so good at murdering pot plants, I only buy the foolproof variety.'

She'd seemed so happy, he thought. She'd talked about Mike and the wonderful Christmas she'd spent with his family. What had happened? He'd like to hear Mike's side of the story – perhaps to understand things from his perspective. But then, perhaps not, he thought wearily. Shit,

Mike didn't seem to *have* a perspective. Oh, who the hell cares, Muzza thought.

'Okay.' He nodded. 'I've shut up.'

Their eyes met and a truce was called. Mike was thankful to have avoided any further discussion about Jo. He was relieved, too, that Muzza's aggression seemed to have petered out. Muz looked tired now. He'd probably put himself to bed soon – he often did.

But Muzza gained a second wind, hanging on for another two cigarettes and a further large whisky as he vented his anger about the general attitude towards returning Vietnam vets. He saw it in the streets, he said, he watched it on the TV, read it in the papers . . . even the old blokes at the RSL didn't show respect. The lack of recognition was everywhere you looked, and it enraged him.

'The blokes come back shot up and shell-shocked and it's like they're supposed to apologise for having been there. What sort of a welcome home's that?'

Mike sat in silence as Muzza raved on, his words starting to slur, his manner becoming agitated. He was working himself into a frenzy as he usually did when the drink and drugs had taken hold.

'So it's not Gallipoli or the Somme, so it's not Tobruk or the Kokoda Trail, but those blokes over there are fighting on a bloody battlefield, mate, so you tell me the difference! They're looking down the barrel just like all the others did, and they deserve to be bloody well recognised for it.' Then the self-derision set in. 'Of course I'm not talking about *me*! Shit, what did I do? Fuck all. But the *others*! Well, you can see where I'm coming from, can't you? I mean, face it, I'm making sense, aren't I?'

'Sure you are.'

Mike's nod was placating. Muzza was ranting now. His energy would run out soon and he'd crash. He always did when he got himself worked up like this. Sure enough, ten minutes later . . .

'Think I'll have a bit of a lie-down, I'm pissed.' Muzza's voice was weary, he'd come to a halt. He laughed drunkenly. 'No two ways about it, mate, I'm legless.' He said it every single time – he thought it was the funniest thing on earth. 'Bloody legless, I am, and that's a fact.' He laughed again as he wheeled himself off to the bedroom. 'You let yourself out, okay?'

'Sure.' Mike crossed to the front door.

'Hey, Mike . . .' Muzza spun the chair about. 'Thanks for coming, mate, it was beaut to see you.'

'No worries.' It was surprising, Mike thought, how suddenly sober Muzza appeared.

'And thanks for inviting me along on the pub crawl. I appreciate that.'

'So why don't you come? We'd really like you to.'

Muzza smiled, and something in his expression told Mike that he knew there was no 'we' involved in the invitation. Pembo and Spud hadn't asked him on the pub crawl; the idea had been solely Mike's.

'No, I'll give it a miss. I'll leave the partying to you blokes.' Muzza laughed, and all of a sudden he seemed drunk again. 'But *hey*! Call in and we'll have a piss-up, what do you say?'

'We'll come around next week, the three of us, when Pembo's in town.'

Muzza nodded and gave a thumbs up, but before he could wheel himself off, Mike added, 'And I'll call in more often on my own . . . if you'd like me to.'

'Yeah. I would. I'd like it a lot.'

Again he seemed sober; it was extraordinary, Mike thought. 'Right. Well, I'll see you, Muz.'

'See you.' The wheelchair spun on the spot and Muzza disappeared.

Mike rode the bike back to Claremont with caution. He'd skipped lunch and was aware of the effect of two large neat whiskies sitting on an empty stomach.

He thought about Muzza. There was no reason to presume that today represented any particular break-through, but Muzza had certainly responded in a way he never did when Pembo and Spud were present. When the three of them called in, he played it tough, or ranted and raved himself into a state of exhaustion, or else he closed off altogether. Today had been different.

Mike felt guilty that he hadn't visited Muzza more often on his own. He should have made a point of doing so – he knew that Muz had always considered him a closer friend than the others. But it had been easier somehow to pop in en masse.

He recalled how offensive he'd found Muzza's caustic opening remark. He'd nearly turned around and walked out the door, he remembered. *I thought you blokes liked to pity in numbers.* That's what he'd said, and galling though the admission was, Mike realised he'd been right. It had been less confronting to arrive simply as 'one of the mates'.

He'd reached Claremont railway station, and he turned into Bay View Terrace. But when he came to Stirling Highway he didn't cross over and continue down towards the river; he turned right instead and headed for Cottesloe. He'd catch a few waves, he decided.

He picked up speed as he roared down the highway, enjoying the wind raking his hair – as usual he'd ignored the safety helmet. Muzza's whole attitude had been differ-ent today, he thought. The effects of the booze and the pills had been as predictable, but he'd wanted to make contact. Even his aggression, normally aimed at the world in general, had taken the form of a personal attack, and it had resulted in a strange reversal of behaviour. Today it had been Muzza who'd initiated the conversation and he who'd closed off.

He shouldn't have pushed Muz away like that, he thought. He shouldn't have refused to talk about Jo, intrusive as he'd found the line of questioning. He'd sensed that Muzza had wanted to talk about her, and he should have obliged, it would have been good for Muz. After all, the bloke did have some rights – he and Jo had been close friends at uni.

He turned into Eric Street and burned down the hill towards the ocean in the distance. The effect of the whiskies had worn off completely and he was enjoying the power of the bike.

But what could he have told Muzza that he hadn't already? Jo had vanished without a trace and that had been it. He found himself feeling defensive as he recalled Muzza's scathing comments. So he'd got on with his life – what was wrong with that? Was he supposed to go into mourning? Sure, he rooted around – he'd had a number of women in the two months since Jo had gone. He'd even revisited the old Scarborough Beach boatshed. Not with Sophia, but with a girl he'd met at the open-air jazz festival. Just one-night stands, nothing that would inter- fere with his work. But did that make him a callous bastard? It was an unfair remark, Mike thought. He was honest with women, he always had been. He never pre- tended he was after anything other than sex.

Marine Parade was up ahead and as he started to slow down, he felt Jo's arms about him, relaxing their grip. Damn it, he thought, she was back. It had taken him several weeks to get rid of the feeling of her riding pillion. Now she was back and it was all Muz's fault. What was it he'd said? *Didn't you care for her at all?* That was it – and it hadn't been a question, it had been an accusation. Well, bugger you, mate, of course I bloody cared!

Christ alive, he thought, Jo had been the only woman he'd ever seen as a true friend. But he'd been honest with her too. She'd known that his work took precedence over a serious relationship – he'd never led her to believe other- wise. She'd said so herself in the note she'd left him. Did that make him a callous bastard? If so, at least he was an honest one. And Jo had understood that. It had been the greatest thing they'd shared and what he'd loved about her most – her scrupulous honesty and her respect for his.

He pulled up outside the OBH, and felt Jo release her grip, heard her laugh in his ear. By now he was cursing Muzza. He'd closed the book on Jo. He'd told himself that it was just as well she'd left when she had; he'd never wanted to get involved, it was too early in his career. It had been all for the best, he'd persuaded himself, and he'd put her out of his mind. Now Muzza had hit a nerve. Muzza had successfully reminded him just how much he missed Jo.

He took his bathers and towel from the pillion-seat compartment and headed for the changing rooms. Damn you, Muz, he thought, now I'll have to start erasing her all over again. But I will. And if that makes me a callous bastard, mate, then maybe you're right. Maybe that's just what I am.

The following week, Ian Pemberton arrived and the boys' planned pub crawl started out, surprisingly enough, at the Killing Pen.

'Hope you don't mind,' Spud said nonchalantly as the three shared a beer at the flat in the Esplanade, 'but I've arranged to meet Anthony Wilson at the Pen – he wants to introduce me to Gerrard Whitford.'

Mike did mind – why should they all be forced to play Spud's games? 'Why don't Pembo and I catch up with you afterwards?' he said. 'We can meet in the main bar – or the beer garden if it's not too cold.'

'Gerrard Whitford?' Ian's reaction was quite different. Whitford was the WA Minister for Tourism. 'Why didn't you tell me earlier?' He and Spud had been chatting over a beer for a good half hour before Mike's arrival. 'I'd like to meet him.'

'Yes, I thought you might.'

Spud's grin was confident and Mike gave up. He was outnumbered.

'Mind you,' Spud said as he polished off his beer and stood, 'from what I've heard, he's the shag end of nasty.'

The girls at the Sun Majestic didn't have one good word to say about Gerrard Whitford MP, who was a regular client at the brothel. Spud believed the girls implicitly. In his opinion, hookers were great judges of character.

The elite Killing Pen was a poky little bar with standing room only, lean-high benches against the walls and an open window at the far end that gave access to the main bar. Men lounged about, smoking and drinking, while Steve's widow, Hazel McHenry, an extraordinarily attractive Eurasian woman of Indian descent, stood beside the window, greeting her clients and placing their orders with the barman on the other side. Money did not change hands, but was placed in the nearby dish. Anyone suspected of not adhering to the honour system of payment was ostracised forever from the Pen.

On a Friday evening the bar was always crowded, but tonight being Wednesday there were only several men present and business appeared to be the order of the day as they stood in deep discussion.

Anthony Wilson, dapper in his smartly tailored suit, his impeccable black hair minus any hint of grey thanks to the talents of his hairdresser, was chatting to Hazel. A flash of annoyance crossed his face when he saw Spud arrive with his two young mates. How dare the boy so flout the rules. Spud had been a regular at the Pen for little more than a year, and although he no longer required Anthony's personal invitation, it was unbelievably presumptuous of him to turn up with extra guests – particularly guests of no significance.

Anthony muttered an apology as he excused himself

from Hazel – he hoped she wouldn't hold him responsible for the boy's impertinence – and as he crossed to Spud, he wondered exactly how to convey his annoyance. Given their current business relationship and the all-important deal they'd recently undertaken, he could hardly afford to alienate him. Indeed, Spud Farrell held the future of Anthony Wilson MP in his thuggish young hands. But Anthony saw no reason at all why he should be forced to socialise with Farrell's loutish, low-brow mates.

Spud's greeting was effusive. 'Anthony, good to see you. May I introduce Ian Pemberton, chief geologist and managing director of the newly listed Excalibur Nickel Resources. Excalibur went on the Exchange just last week and it has some very prospective leases in both the Kambalda and Laverton areas. By the way, that's a hot tip if you're interested.'

Anthony was extremely interested.

'And this handsome young bloke,' Spud continued without drawing breath, 'is Mike McAllister. Mike's just finishing his doctorate in zoology on our new and lucrative crayfish, or should I say, rock lobster industry. As you're probably aware, Mike's work is very much heralded and supported by the WA Fisheries Department and CSIRO.'

Anthony hadn't been aware, but he was all smiles as he shook hands with the two young men. 'What a pleasure, gentlemen. Welcome to the Pen.'

Spud inwardly smirked as they crossed to Hazel at the bar window. Anthony Wilson was the same smarmy bastard he'd always been.

'Mike,' Hazel said, 'how lovely to see you. How's your dad?'

'Fine thanks, Hazel.'

'Jim McAllister was one of the first regulars at the Pen when Steve first opened the bar,' Hazel explained to the others. 'He used to come here when he was at uni. A wonderful sportsman – Steve so admired him.'

Spud and Ian were surprised that Mike shared such a pally relationship with Hazel McHenry – typical of him not to dine out on it, of course – but neither were as impressed as Anthony Wilson.

So this was Jim McAllister's son, Anthony thought. Old Perth family, the McAllisters, very much respected. And Pemberton. He cast a glance at Ian. Classy-looking young bloke. Could he be the son of the Pemberton who owned *Trusan*? If so, he came from money. Well, well, Spud Farrell was in fine company.

'My round,' he insisted, and ostentatiously placed far more money than was necessary in the dish by the window.

Drinks in hand, the four of them crossed to lean on the benches in the far corner of the bar, Anthony out to impress for all he was worth.

'I don't know if Spud told you,' he said to the others, 'but Gerrard Whitford's popping in to say hello.'

'Yes, I look forward to meeting him.' Ian, too, was laying on the charm.

'He's running a little late, I'm afraid – telephoned me just before I left the office to say he'd be delayed twenty minutes or so.' Gerrard wasn't running late at all. Anthony and Spud had planned to talk business before his arrival, but they could hardly do so in the company of others. 'Of course, it's understandable in a position of importance such as his. He's a dedicated man, it's a twenty-four-hour job.'

Yeah, Spud thought, when he's not behaving like a pig with the girls at the Sun Majestic.

'This is a great opportunity for a young entrepreneur like you, Spud, to meet the man who holds the identity of our state in his hands. In fact, it's a fine opportunity for each of you.' Anthony addressed all three young men. 'Western Australia, in its isolation, needs to firmly establish the strength of its identity in order to attract tourism and the dollar. The world must be made aware of the unique qualities this state has to offer. I believe to achieve our ends with intelligence and integrity we need to marry the talents of a fine minister like Gerrard Whitford with the brilliant minds of tomorrow, like yours.' He was playing the mentor now, seeing himself in the role of elder statesman. 'Gerrard is our man of today, and you are our men of the future. It's an exciting combination, don't you think?' He leaned against the bench and beamed, pleased with his speech.

By now even Ian was irritated by the man's rhetoric, and Mike looked as if he was about to walk out.

'We certainly do,' Spud agreed, 'but in the meantime, maybe we should get another round while the bar's not busy.' The boys were barely halfway through their beers and Anthony hadn't touched his gin and tonic. 'What do you say, Mike? Your shout?'

'Yep.'

Mike disappeared, happy to join Hazel at the window to the main bar. He'd always had a fantasy about Hazel with her smoky complexion and kohl-rimmed eyes, but then, most had. Since Steve's death, his much younger widow had been hotly pursued by many. Hazel had taken it all serenely in her stride. Mike knew he didn't stand a chance – he was just Jim McAllister's son. But the company of a beautiful woman was a welcome escape from the pontificating bore that was Anthony Wilson.

'Now, Anthony, about our current situation . . .' Spud decided to cut through the bullshit. Mike was comfortably out of the way, and he had no compunction about discussing his business in Ian's presence. To the contrary, he relished the opportunity. 'How're we going with the council? Are they going to give me the nod?'

Anthony was horrified by Spud's open reference to their dealings. How dare he bring up the subject in the company of young Pemberton. Word could get around. He tried to signal a warning, but Spud over-rode him.

'Oh, don't worry about Ian,' he said airily. 'Ian lives in Kalgoorlie, he has his own agenda. He's far too busy discovering nickel to bother himself with my paltry business affairs, aren't you, Ian?' Spud flashed a quick glance at Pembo that said there was no need to reply. 'He's another breed of entrepreneur, you see, Anthony, just like me. It's as you said: we're the brains of tomorrow, and as such we can all be of assistance to each other.'

Anthony's ears had pricked up at the mention of nickel discovery. Young Pemberton was a geologist, the managing director of a mining company no less. Anthony himself had his eye on the mining market – what smart investor didn't? Ian Pemberton could prove a handy contact.

'Besides,' Spud continued, 'he knows I've put in a tender for the property.' Then he added meaningfully for Anthony's comfort, 'And that I mean to *restore* it.'

'Ah, right, well . . .' Anthony's smile to Ian was friendly and inclusive, but he chose his words with care. Spud had put him on the spot. 'It's an extraordinarily generous gesture for a businessman like Spud to take on the restoration of a historical building. Don't you think so, Ian?'

'I most certainly do.'

Although Anthony returned his attention to Spud, his choice of words was still for Ian's benefit. 'The council naturally has the good of the community at heart, and from what I've heard, via various sources, it would seem that the tender has been accepted.' He hastily added. 'Of course it's unofficial at this stage. I'm not supposed to know. It's strictly off the record, just between friends.' Still uncomfortable in Ian's presence, his attempt at a comradely smile lacked confidence.

'Excellent.' Spud grinned broadly and shook Anthony's hand. 'So it's full steam ahead. I'm delighted.'

Ian Pemberton was intrigued by the change in Anthony Wilson. In only minutes, Spud had turned the man from an arrogant bore into a bundle of nerves. It wasn't surprising, given the circumstances. Ian knew all about their plans, Spud had told him every detail. An impressive convict-built bond store near Fremantle had been considered for listing as a heritage site, but 'certain members of the council' as Spud had smugly put it, openly inferring they'd been paid off, had decided the restoration would be too costly. The site had therefore been offered up for public sale and the building had faced demolition. Of all the offers tendered, Spud's had been the only one that had come with the promise to restore and preserve the original façade of the store. And now, apparently, his offer had been accepted.

'Congratulations,' Ian said, shaking Spud's hand effusively.

Anthony glanced from one to the other. They were close friends, it was obvious, and the fact worried him. Pemberton knew of the tender for the building. How much else did he know? Spud surely wouldn't have told him everything.

But Spud had. He and Ian trusted each other's silence. Ian also had his secrets, and the two recounted to each other every business deal they undertook, nefarious or otherwise. It was all part of the competition that existed between them.

'This deal's a beauty. I get the place for a song if the council agrees,' Spud had boasted just the previous evening when Ian had arrived from Kalgoorlie. 'All the bribe money's coming from Wilson, although the councillors taking the kickback don't know it. Plus he's footing two-thirds of the purchase price – which of course they don't know either.'

'You mean he's buying the place himself?'

'Virtually. It's his retirement plan for when he leaves politics. I'm supposed to convert the place into an up-market vintage car sales and hire outlet, and he'll buy it back from me when he retires. They won't be able to point a finger at him – the building isn't in his constituency. He's pulling off the deal purely through his connections. Wilson knows every rotten apple in Perth.'

'*Vintage* cars? Why vintage?'

'They're his passion. Always have been apparently. I don't see vintage cars doing big business in Perth myself, but that's his problem. I can't lose. If he goes broke, I'll buy the place back on my own terms and turn it into an all-purpose used-car yard.'

'What about the restoration part?'

'Oh, that'll go by the board. It's just a hook.'

Anthony Wilson was now sipping nervously at his gin and tonic.

'So what do you intend to do with the property once you've restored it, Spud?' Ian asked innocently.

'I'm thinking of turning it into vintage car outlet.'

'*Vintage* cars. Really? I didn't know you were a vintage car freak.'

'Oh yes, they've always been a passion of mine.'

Ian, enjoying Anthony's obvious discomfort, was about to ask him how he felt about vintage cars himself, but Mike arrived with the next round.

'Sorry about the wait,' he said as he unloaded the drinks from the small tin tray, 'the main bar's busy evidently.' It hadn't been, but he'd stayed chatting with Hazel for as long as he thought excusable.

'Gerrard.' Anthony ignored the fresh gin and tonic placed on the bench before him and gave a wave to the new arrival who'd appeared at the doorway.

Gerrard Whitford joined them. A fleshy man in his mid-forties with a well-coiffed head of grey hair, his face bore the stamp of too much good living and his manner the hearty confidence of one who believed himself still in his youthful prime. He dumped his briefcase on the floor beside him and initiated the introductions. 'Gerrard Whitford,' he said as he shook hands heartily all round. 'I didn't know this was going to be a party. I thought I was just coming to meet our young entrepreneurial genius here.' He gave Spud a matey pat on the back. 'You boys out on the town, are you?'

'Yep.' Spud answered for the others. 'We're off on a pub crawl, this is our first port of call.'

'Good for you.' Gerrard laughed. 'I might just tag along. Get up to a bit of mischief somewhere down the track, eh?' A wink.

'What would you like to drink, Gerrard?' Mike asked while Anthony laughed loudly and the others shared a dutiful smile. 'It's my round.'

'Whisky, thanks, Mike. Johnnie Walker'll do, but make it a double.'

Mike thankfully dived off for the bar.

When he returned, Gerrard had just finished telling a joke and the others were laughing uproariously. Gerrard was an accomplished joke-teller.

'Good on you, Mike,' he said, accepting the drink. 'Perfectly timed. Never interrupt a man's punch line, eh? And boy, do I have a reward for you.' He picked up his briefcase and put it on the bench. 'Didn't want to share it with the others until you were back, wouldn't be fair.' He took out a folder.

'What do you think I have here, Anthony,' he said, waving the folder teasingly.

'I've no idea, Gerrard, why don't you tell me.' Anthony gave his most sycophantic oh-you're-such-a-wag smile.

'The new campaign, mate, that's what. It's taken us nearly a year to get it all together, starting with a six-month search for the right subject – and what a pleasure that was I can tell you.' His grin was lascivious. 'And now we're all ready to go. The first series of TV ads are completed and we're about to let the cat out of the bag.' He shoved the briefcase aside, placed the folder ceremoniously on the bench and opened it. 'You lucky lot are the first to feast your eyes on her.' He splayed a series of ten by eight photographs out before them. 'There you go, boys, meet the new face of WA tourism. And the body to go with it.'

They all gazed at the photographs. Some were portraits, others full-length shots of a nubile, bikini-clad girl sprinting across the beach or cavorting in the surf. The sheer animal beauty of her was startling. Like a thoroughbred racehorse, she was perfect.

Well, well, well, Spud thought, Ruby's little girl, Mary-Jane.

Mike was as spellbound as the others, but he couldn't help thinking what a load of bullshit it all was. So this was the strength of the state's identity achieved through intelligence and integrity? What a joke.

'Wild beach girl beauty,' Gerrard said, proud of the effect his unveiling had had on them, 'that was the image the ad agency was after, and I think we've come up with the goods.' He said it boastfully as if the discovery were his own personal triumph, although he'd actually played no part in it. 'Her name's Mayjay. No surname. Dramatic, which is a good thing.'

Spud remained silent as the men started sifting through the photographs, although he couldn't wait to tell his mates that he knew Mayjay. 'How?' they'd ask. 'She's the daughter of a friend of mine,' he'd say. He wouldn't tell them who though. And he certainly wasn't going to say one word in the presence of Gerrard the pig.

But pig or not, Whitford was the Minister for Tourism and a very useful man to know. Spud intended to cultivate his friendship. It wouldn't be difficult. Gerrard and his kind never were – lechers and drunkards were always easy to please.

As he looked at the photographs he wondered how he might incorporate Mayjay in whatever business deal he struck with Gerrard. Spud Farrell Enterprises and the face of WA had an impressive ring.

CHAPTER EIGHT

The university year was over and Mike, having long since completed his thesis, was awaiting the verdict of his examiners, which could take some time. It was a foregone conclusion, however, that his PhD would be granted, the WA Fisheries Department and the CSIRO having embraced the findings of his work with Bruce Phillips.

The face of the vast and highly lucrative Western Australian commercial crayfishing industry was about to change forever due to the intensive research undertaken by Dr Bruce Phillips and his dedicated young PhD assistant Mike McAllister. Their findings had proved that the western rock lobster, *Panulirus cygnus*, took between three and a half to four years to grow from larva to legally sized adult, and their estimates of the numbers settling on various areas of the WA coast gave them the ability to predict, within certain tolerances of natural mortality, the numbers of commercially sized crayfish four years in advance. The WA Fisheries Department would in future be able to determine the levels of fishing effort for the seasons ahead – the numbers of pots, numbers of fishing and processing boats, and, if necessary, even the length of the season itself. The research results also enabled them to keep the whole of the Abrolhos Archipelago region closed over the breeding season to allow an abundant supply of eggs to be released, to hatch, and for the larvae to begin their ten-month drift at the mercy of the currents before being redistributed to settle as *puerulus* along the south-western coastline of the state.

Both the industry and the government regulator were deeply grateful to Dr Phillips and his assistant, and their efforts were widely acclaimed. As a result, the services of the soon-to-be-qualified Dr McAllister had been eagerly sought, but Mike had ignored the offers of research positions, which would have involved principally laboratory work. Instead, he'd agreed to join the WA Museum-based team on their expedition north, which was scheduled for departure in early February the following year.

'Only two months now, I can't wait,' Mike said excitedly. 'I'll be out in the field, it's what I've always wanted.'

'And what you've been working towards for six bloody years. Good on you, mate – you deserve every success.' Muzza was genuinely happy for his friend, although he'd miss Mike. Very much.

The two were seated in Muzza's kitchen, surrounded by the faces that screamed at them from the wall and the twisted shapes of bodies and wreckage strewn amongst shattered rubber trees. During his weekly visits, Mike had become accustomed to the images scrawled on the walls, and these days he ignored them. Spud and Ian, however, who called in less frequently, still found them very unsettling.

'Christ, Muz, they've been there for three months now,' Spud complained. 'You said you were going to paint over them.'

'I am.'

'When?' Ian asked.

'When I'm ready.'

Muzza wasn't sure when that would be. Perhaps never. While the drawings and paintings were there, the images didn't come to haunt him in his sleep.

The artwork had materialised through a suggestion made by the psychiatrist whom Muzza was obliged to visit on a regular basis during his six-month good-behaviour bond.

'I've been advised to seek an outlet through which I can express my anger,' he'd announced one morning when his mates had arrived to discover the lower half of one kitchen wall covered in huge charcoal-drawn faces. Some were Vietnamese, some Caucasian, all demented, all screaming in pain, or rage, it was impossible to tell which. 'They're not bad, are they?' he'd remarked, gazing at them with all the objective appraisal of an art critic. 'I always liked drawing. I should have opted for architecture instead of medicine.'

The drawings were more than 'not bad'. Despite their disturbing element, and scrawled as they were in a primitive way, they were surprisingly good.

The day Murray Hatfield's neighbour had taken him to court had proved a blessing in disguise. Muzza had attacked poor Rodney for no apparent reason, although it later turned out that he'd thought the car parked across his driveway belonged to Rodney. It hadn't been Rodney's car at all, but Muzza had nonetheless called him out into the street, charged his wheelchair at the unfortunate man and hauled him to the pavement, landing on top of him and punching away for all he was worth. Rodney, terrified, had scrambled free and called the police.

The judge had been lenient. Given the fact that Muzza was a war veteran, he'd been let off with a six-month good-behaviour bond under the proviso that he attend regular counselling sessions with a court-appointed psychiatrist.

'The shrink said I should write it all down,' he'd explained as the others had looked askance at the tormented faces on the wall, 'but I decided to draw it instead. I'm going to try painting the next lot.'

Over the ensuing weeks, the kitchen walls steadily became a battleground until Muzza ran out of space. It frustrated him that he couldn't reach higher and cover the entire wall, and he'd been about to start on the living area the other side of the arch. But then Mike had arrived with a load of art supplies, and it had proved unnecessary. Muzza found that he actually preferred an easel and canvas.

Before long, he was visiting the library and combing the bookstores, and soon the kitchen table was littered with books. He studied the work of the masters, concentrating on light and perspective, applying the lessons he taught himself daily, and although the content of his paintings remained disturbing, they began to take on a hauntingly beautiful new form. They were becoming works of art.

Muzza's behaviour was obsessive, his mates agreed, but they also agreed that he seemed much more content in himself lately. And he was certainly less reliant on the grog and the pills.

Yet further evidence of Murray Hatfield's rehabilitation had taken place in mid-November when he'd agreed to attend the grand opening of Farrell Vintage Motors.

'Sure. I'll come,' he'd said. 'The shrink says I should get out more, and I'd like to take a look at the cars.' Muzza had always been interested in vintage cars.

His mates had considered it an absolute breakthrough. Muz never socialised publicly.

'Besides,' he'd grinned, 'I want to see what all the fuss is about, don't I?'

For the past two months there had been considerable coverage in the press about Spud's latest enterprise. The site in Fremantle had been picketed by small groups of angry protesters, and several articles in the *West Aus-*

tralian had referred to 'the desecration of a historical landmark' and 'the greedy opportunism of money-hungry developers with no care for the state's heritage'. The ongoing campaign was led by none other than Natalie Hollingsworth, Mike's old flame during his early university days, now a qualified architect and a passionate spokesperson on the preservation of historical landmarks.

Spud had taken it all in his stride. 'Natalie always *was* up herself,' he'd said to the others. He'd only met the girl on a few occasions, but he knew the type. Old Perth money. Natalie had had it easy all her life. Well, some people had to make it on their own, he'd thought, and Natalie Hollingsworth and her lot could just go and get fucked.

'My God, I can see what she's on about.' Muzza had been aghast as he and Mike had approached the showrooms of Farrell Vintage Motors, where beautiful models in period dress posed by each of the vehicles on display and waiters, also in period costume, passed around trays of vintage champagne. 'It's a bloody monstrosity.'

Only the barest bones of the old bond store's façade remained. Stark remnants of convict brickwork were barely discernible amongst the Italian colonnades and ornate trimmings.

'How could they let him get away with it?'

'It seems, with the exception of Natalie and her followers, few people care about old buildings any more,' Mike had replied caustically. It was a direct quote from Spud, who'd refused to listen to criticism from the outset, and Mike had certainly offered his.

'Stop being over-sensitive,' Spud had said, 'nobody cares any more. It's all about modernising these days. You just need to maintain a bit of the old stuff to keep the wowsers happy and it works every time. Look what they've done to the barracks.'

'Exactly!' To Mike, the comment had proved his point

beyond a doubt. The demolition of the magnificent Perth military barracks was nearing completion, and nothing was left but its lonely arched entrance standing at the top of St Georges Terrace like a miniaturised Arc de Triomphe. It was a travesty. 'It looks bloody ridiculous.'

Spud had remained dismissive. 'Depends on your point of view. I think it looks great myself. And the rest of the stuff was just a waste of space anyway.'

The grand opening of Farrell Vintage Motors had not disappointed. It had been grand to the point of absolute ostentation, and Mike and Muzza had watched the spectacle in open-mouthed amazement.

Spud himself had arrived in a bright red Itala claimed to be one of the original vehicles driven in the 1907 Great Race from Peking to Paris. The vehicle was privately owned and was neither for sale nor hire, but would serve as an exhibition piece and, given its reputed history, a major attraction for a month following the opening. Anthony Wilson had had the Itala flown in at enormous personal expense, and was secretly livid that Spud had not only received the credit but had had the honour of arriving in style when it should have been him. There was nothing he could do about it, however, and Spud's spectacular arrival had been the highlight of the occasion, along with the address from the Honourable Gerrard Whitford, Minister for Tourism, who had officially opened the showrooms, flanked either side by pretty young girls in period costume.

Natalie Hollingsworth and her small band of followers had been plainly visible through the large display windows, chanting slogans and waving placards out in the street, but the minister had appeared unfazed by the sight. He'd personally congratulated Spud Farrell on saving a fine old building from destruction while simultaneously offering an innovative new service to the citizens of Perth and providing a fresh attraction for tourists and locals alike.

'Well,' Muzza had remarked as he and Mike had left the showrooms, 'my first social outing for some time has certainly proved a learning experience. Can't wait to tell the shrink.'

Now the two sat comfortably in Muzza's kitchen, Mike waxing enthusiastic about his forthcoming expedition and Muzza busy at his easel and canvas. He was painting Mike's portrait. He'd been working on it for several weeks and it was nearing completion, but he refused to let Mike see his work.

'Not until it's finished,' he'd repeatedly insisted, but it was obvious he was pleased with his efforts.

Muzza had finally stopped painting the haunted faces and visions of his dreams, and turned his hand to portraits instead – the final proof, in Mike's opinion, that Murray Hatfield had rejoined the world. He'd completed two self-portraits, neither of which he was happy with despite his friends finding them extraordinarily good, but this third piece, his study of Mike, he secretly considered his masterpiece.

'Are you coming to watch the parade with us next Saturday?' Mike asked, sitting back in his chair. He'd talked enough about himself and his work, he decided.

'I've thought about it.' Paintbrush poised, Muzza's eyes flickered from the canvas to Mike. 'Keep leaning on the table.' Mike did as he was told. 'I'd really like to see the cars, but there's bound to be a huge crowd so I reckon I'll give it a miss.' He paused, dabbing at the portrait. 'Besides,' he added, an unpleasantly sarcastic edge to his tone, 'beauty quests are hardly my bag.'

'Fair enough.'

Mike made no further comment. He hadn't assumed that the beauty quest *would* be Muzza's bag. But vintage cars certainly were. Muz was over-reacting again.

Silence reigned for a moment while Muzza regretted his unnecessary dig. The mere thought of women was enough, sometimes, to put him on a downward spiral. And why not? When you couldn't get it up for the rest of your bloody life, women were a thing of the past, weren't they? But that was hardly Mike's fault.

'So what time's it all happening?' he asked, keen to make amends.

'The cavalcade and opening ceremony are mid-afternoon, and the beauty quest starts at four – Spud says they want to avoid the full heat of the day.'

Mike was aware that Muzza's query was tantamount to an apology, although he considered no apology necessary himself. The odd outbursts of bitterness were perfectly understandable. For all of the progress made over the past six months, Muzza was still a damaged man psychologically. Perhaps he always would be. And who could blame him?

'I'll watch it on television,' Muzza said. 'According to the newspapers, it's going to be the biggest thing since sliced bread.'

'Of course it will be.' Mike laughed. 'Spud's at the helm.'

A quarter of an hour later when he took his leave, they were still talking about Spud's audacity.

'Don't ask me how he does it.' Mike shook his head in bewilderment.

'That's Spud,' Muzza said. 'He'll never change.'

Farrell Vintage Motors was one of the minor sponsors involved in the finals of the WA Beach Girl Beauty Quest to be held at Scarborough the following weekend.

For the past month, state-wide competitions had been conducted in the larger beachside towns as far north as Port Hedland and as far south as Albany. The events, promoted by the state Department of Tourism and backed by local businesses, had proved popular, contestants from surrounding coastal areas being joined by dozens of hopefuls who

had travelled hundreds of miles from rural centres, remote
bush townships and even outback cattle stations. The girls'
expenses had been footed by their families and local com-
munities, but the quest's grand final was to be a different
matter altogether. The twenty lucky finalists were to be
flown to Perth courtesy of Ansett Airlines, where they
would be accommodated courtesy of the Ocean Beach
Hotel at North Cottesloe, a venue that perfectly fitted the
ethos of the quest, it had been decided. They would be
transported in chauffeur-driven limousines courtesy of Avis,
and the winner would receive a healthy cash prize, a return
trip to New York courtesy of Qantas, and a guaranteed six-
month photographic modelling contract.

Many large corporations had been only too happy to
join the state government in sponsoring the grand final of
the WA Beach Girl Beauty Quest, particularly as the event
was to be televised. But somehow Farrell Vintage Motors,
in providing its vehicles, had managed to make the event
appear its own.

The contestants were to be transported in a cavalcade of
vintage cars down the Scarborough Esplanade, the driver
of each car in full period costume. Leading the cavalcade
would be the famous 1907 Itala, and *From Paris to Peking
to Perth* was the proud slogan that had featured in recent
advertisements. Driving the Itala would be well-known
Perth identity Spud Farrell, and accompanying him would
be the special guest of honour, none other than the symbol
of Western Australia herself, Mayjay.

For the past seven months, Mayjay had dominated television screens, billboards and magazines, not only across
the state but the entire country. The rest of Australia had
been treated to the image of Mayjay in the glorious surrounds the west had to offer. Mayjay framed by a dramatic
sunset over the Indian Ocean; Mayjay against the
backdrop of stark red rock, which could only be the Kim-
berleys; Mayjay dwarfed by the giant karri trees of the

southern timberlands . . . and on it went.

The lengthy promotional campaign adopted by the state Department of Tourism was proving successful, and the advertising agency's idea to incorporate a beauty quest had been considered a positive brainwave. Glorious girls from all over the state would compete in the WA Beach Girl Beauty Quest, and who better to present the sash and crown to the winning contestant than the face of WA herself – the original beach girl beauty, Mayjay.

'So we finally get to meet her, do we?'

Mike exchanged an incredulous glance with Ian. It was Friday night and Spud had just offered them invitations to the sponsors bash after the following day's event.

'All the contestants will be there,' Spud had said, before casually adding, 'and Mayjay too.'

Both Mike and Ian had been sceptical when Spud had told them, months ago, that he knew Mayjay, particularly as he'd been so enigmatic about the fact. 'She's the daughter of a friend of mine,' he'd said, nothing more, and they'd thought it might be so much bullshit. But the more ubiquitous Mayjay had become – it seemed, as the months passed, she was everywhere they looked – the more Spud had stuck to his story until they saw no reason to disbelieve him. Spud wasn't one for empty boasts, and now it appeared he was going to make good with a personal introduction.

'Oh, you'll get to meet her all right, I guarantee it. But a word of warning: dress like the sponsors, suit and tie. It's a private party and there'll be hundreds trying to crash it.' He grinned. 'The organisers reckon they want to keep the yobbos out, but it's my guess the lecherous bastards want to keep the girls to themselves.'

Scarborough Beach on a hot December day was always crowded – the broad white expanse of sand littered with bodies baking in the sun, the postcard aquamarine of the sea teeming with those cooling off from the heat, or, when the surf was up, riding the waves to shore.

Fronting onto the coastal scrub where the surf club stood, and where the sandhills led down to the main beach, was the broad avenue of the Scarborough Esplanade. It was just three blocks long, the intervening streets leading back to the major link road of the West Coast Highway, but during the height of midsummer, the three short blocks of the Esplanade were, for many, the most exciting place in Perth. Families thronged to Luna Park, drinkers lounged in the beer garden of the Scarborough Beach Hotel, and bathing-costume-clad queues lined up at the hamburger joint of Peters by the Sea. But the attraction that drew the greatest crowds was undoubtedly the Snake Pit, which sat in the middle of the three blocks, Luna Park to the south and the hotel to the north. The Snake Pit was famous. Or rather, it was infamous. Although it hadn't started out that way.

The small, popular eatery aptly named La Spiaggia, meaning 'beach' in Italian, had started out in the fifties as a humble kiosk, until the owner had dug out a large part of the sand dune beside his stall, built a retaining wall on the uphill side and laid in a spacious wooden floor. Then he'd added the major ingredient – the music that was driving the youth of the world wild. Rock'n'roll. News of the live rock bands performing at Scarborough had travelled fast, and before long the innocent open-air dance floor of La Spiaggia had become the hottest place in town. Motorbikes roared up the Esplanade. Bodgies in black leather jackets and desert boots turned up in droves, and with them their companions, widgies, in tight sweaters, hooped earrings and bright red lipstick. Then the hot-rodders arrived and drag-racing became an added attraction, the screech of tyres and the smell of burning rubber mingling intoxicatingly with the beat of rock'n'roll.

For many, the dance remained the thing as they jived themselves into a frenzy on the polished wooden floor that had become known as the Snake Pit. But there was an unruly element which had stamped the place its own. As the fifties had become the sixties and the decade had rolled on, the bodgies and their widgies had become the rockers and their chicks, and other gangs had emerged. The sharpies, surfies, mods and rockers all gathered at the Snake Pit. Occasionally, and inevitably, clashes occurred, but there was a general acceptance that this was common ground. To the gang members, the Snake Pit had become synonymous with the angry rebellion of their youth – this was a place that belonged to them. This was their personal domain.

The Snake Pit had created excitement in Scarborough, but it had brought with it an element of danger.

On this particular hot December day, Scarborough Beach was more crowded than ever, and at lunchtime the numbers swelled as hundreds of others arrived to take up their positions in anticipation of the parade and the beauty quest.

Complex constructions of scaffolding, wood and canvas had been erected on the beach. A huge stage, complete with catwalk, sat in the centre, a red-carpeted wooden walkway leading from the steps at the side to a large brightly striped marquee, which would house the contestants. There was a special grandstand for the official government party and principal sponsors, and opposite it a shaded area with tables and chairs for the panel of judges. There was no seating arranged for the general public, who would quite happily spread their towels and beach mats out on the baking sand, or watch from the elevated position of the sandhills.

Despite the fact that it was still two hours before the military brass band would lead the procession down the Esplanade, Simon from 6PR Radio was already making announcements over the loudspeaker system.

'Just two hours to go, folks! The grand final of the WA Beach Girl Beauty Quest is about to take place right here at Scarborough! And who's hosting it? None other than our very own . . .' A pause for the silent drum roll. '*Dougie Mac*!'

Simon wasn't an on-air personality, although he was doing an excellent imitation. Simon was a hardworking publicist, and today was the promotional opportunity of a lifetime. Douglas 'Dougie Mac' Mackay was 6PR's top-rating disc jockey and the event was to be televised – it was a publicist's dream.

'Presenting the sash and crown to the winner,' Simon continued, spruiking like a true professional, 'will be the face of WA herself, Mayjay, and presenting the cash prize, the Honourable Gerrard Whitford, Minister for Tourism.'

The additional announcement had been a direct order from Gerrard Whitford's assistant, Howard Stonehaven.

'Don't forget the "Honourable",' Howard had said. 'Gerrard likes that.'

'So don't go away, folks, stay right where you are. In just two hours we'll be joined by our very own *Dougie Mac*!'

Simon switched off the PA system – he'd take a fifteen-minute break before starting up again. And, as a gesture of rebellion, he'd continue to give Dougie Mac two plugs each announcement and the 'Honourable' Gerrard Whitford just one.

The Honourable Gerrard Whitford was at that very moment ogling the girls in the showrooms of Farrell Vintage Motors. The huge main showroom floor had been denuded of its vehicles, which all stood waiting in the street, and chairs and benches and mirrors had been set up. Twenty beautiful young women were being buffed and fluffed by make-up artists and hairdressers, and Gerrard was feasting his eyes upon the sight. But he was a little distracted. His trump card wasn't amongst them. Mayjay was late.

'Where the hell is she?' he roared above the surrounding chatter as Howard appeared by his side. 'Did you ring the hotel?'

'Yes. They said she'd left. She must be on her way.'

'I bloody well hope so. She's bloody late.'

'Who? Mayjay?' Spud had emerged from the nearby door that led to the boardroom where a buffet luncheon was set up. He joined them, a beer in his hand. 'She should be here any tick now, her publicist phoned twenty minutes ago saying they were on their way.'

'Why the hell didn't you tell me?'

'I just did.' Spud ignored the man, turning to Howard instead. 'You should grab yourself some lunch, Howard, before the girls demolish it all. I thought beautiful women didn't eat, but I was wrong.'

'I'm fine thanks, Spud, I had a sandwich earlier.'

The smile the two young men shared was one of acknowledgement – neither had much time for Gerrard Whitford.

'How about you, Gerrard?' Spud asked. 'Fancy some lunch?'

'Excellent idea.' Aware that his show of irritation had been unwise, Gerrard quickly pasted on his public persona with a hearty smile – any display of ill humour was reserved for his staff. 'Need to get some food inside us, don't we? It's a big day, we're all a bit jumpy.'

The clumsy excuse Gerrard offered for his rudeness was, strangely enough, true. He was nervous. This was potentially his finest hour and he couldn't afford any slip-ups. Today was an integral part of the most expensive advertising campaign ever undertaken during his tenure. And yet the beauty quest had been funded more by commercial sponsorship than by the government. It was a coup. And it was to be televised. His personal triumph would be witnessed across the state!

Gerrard had conveniently forgotten that the sponsorship

agreements had been put in place by his assistant, Howard Stonehaven, who had also engaged the interest of Channel 9. He'd forgotten, too, that the key points he'd included in his speech of thanks to the sponsors had come from Howard, particularly the line he'd practised as his final quote. *The marriage of government and private enterprise,* Howard had urged. *It's the way of the future, Gerrard.* Gerrard had found it inspirational stuff.

He ran through the words again. He'd deliver them directly to the camera, he decided. My God, but it would make an impact.

Yet again Gerrard thanked his good fortune that David Brand was in Canberra and unable to officiate. But then, had the Premier been in town he may not have attended in any event – his department had shown little interest in the beauty quest. Given the country's current turmoil, and the ever-increasing protests against Australia's commitment to the war in Vietnam, the project had been considered frivolous. Howard Stonehaven had come up with the perfect response to their indifference. 'It's the very frivolity of the beauty quest that makes it so valuable,' he'd retaliated. 'In stressful times people seek an escape.' Gerrard had quickly adopted the argument as his own.

How right he'd been, he thought now with smug satisfaction – the WA Beach Girl Beauty Quest had been embraced across the state. Today he would receive the recognition he so rightfully deserved. It was tremendously exciting. No wonder he was feeling jumpy.

'Grab us a plate of something, will you, Howard?' he said, turning to his assistant. 'Plenty of meat. And a beer wouldn't go astray either.' In a matey aside to Spud, he added, 'Better keep clear of the top shelf until after the speeches, eh?'

Howard obediently left, disguising his contempt as he always did. Gerrard Whitford's days were numbered. The man was a dinosaur – he hadn't had an idea of his own in years. Howard Stonehaven was not alone in his views; others were starting to notice Gerrard's incompetence. And those who didn't soon had their attention drawn to the fact. Discreetly. Howard always appeared supportive.

'But I'm sure Gerrard has things in hand,' he'd say, while informing his confidant of a problem as yet unforeseen, and one which he knew Gerrard would not address.

Howard was driven by the purest of motives – his actions were for the good of the party. It was high time Gerrard Whitford was put out to pasture and new blood introduced. Howard strongly believed in 'the right man for the right job', and he strongly believed the right man was him.

As he piled slices of ham and rare roast beef onto a plate, he wondered which and how many of his personal quotes Gerrard would use in his speech of thanks to the sponsors. The man would be well and truly caught out. Howard had privately shared any number of pithy and memorable catch phrases with Gerrard. He'd also shared them with each of their mutual colleagues and all the major sponsors, when he was quite sure that Gerrard was nowhere within earshot.

'Hello, Spud.'

The voice was in his ear, and Spud turned to discover Mayjay standing right behind him. Beside her was an efficient-looking young woman in a well-cut suit, the miniskirt of which displayed a neat pair of legs. He and Gerrard had been so busy chatting that the women's unannounced entrance had taken them both by surprise.

'Hello, Mayjay.'

'Good to see you.' She smiled her lazy, insolent smile and offered her hand.

'You too.' It was the same extraordinary smile he'd found so disconcerting the very first time he'd met her. Was its intention to seduce or insult? It was difficult to tell, and equally difficult to look away. 'You haven't changed,' he said as they shook hands.

'Mayjay!' Gerrard interrupted loudly, extending his hand so that Mayjay was forced to turn her attention to him. His grin was broad and friendly but he was angry. How dare the bitch greet Spud before she greeted him. He was the minister, it was a shocking breach of protocol.

'You look beautiful, my dear,' he said, shaking her hand. She did. Bare-legged, in high-heeled sandals and a bright red mini dress with shoestring straps, she was bloody gorgeous. 'Absolutely beautiful.'

'I should hope so. It's my job.' Mayjay turned to the neat young woman beside her. 'This is Trish Barraclough.'

'Yes, yes, I know, we've met.' Gerrard gave the woman a perfunctory nod. He'd had numerous meetings and phone conversations with the ad agency publicist assigned to Mayjay.

'I wasn't introducing her to you. I was introducing her to Spud.'

'Of course.' Christ, the bitch was rude, Gerrard thought.

When the introductions were over, he said tightly to Trish, 'We're a little late aren't we?' Still angered by Mayjay's insolence, he took his annoyance out on the publicist.

The pained look on Trish Barraclough's face spoke multitudes. She was sick to death of Mayjay's tardiness herself. The woman was unprofessional and downright arrogant and Trish couldn't stand her. The sooner Mayjay's contract was over the better as far as she was concerned. But she said nothing, prepared to take the blame as always.

'We've been keeping hair and make-up waiting for nearly forty minutes.' Gerrard's tone demanded an apology, and preferably a grovelling one.

'*We* don't need hair and make-up.' It was Mayjay who replied. '*We* do our own.' She thrust her flawless face close to his, eyebrows raised scornfully. 'I'm surprised you haven't noticed.'

Well, well, Trish thought, for once Mayjay wasn't leaving her to shoulder the blame. Not that she was leaping nobly to her publicist's defence, Trish knew that – she was having a dig at Whitford, and who wouldn't want to – but it was a relief to be let off the hook.

'Nevertheless,' Gerrard tried to maintain his dignity while he backed off, 'the schedule was quite clear, everyone was called at the same time –'

'I'm not everyone,' Mayjay replied. She looked about at the girls, noticing that many had a glass in their hands. 'Ah, champagne,' she said with an approving smile to Spud. 'Your idea?'

'Of course.'

'Lead me to it.'

Trish interrupted. 'I think we should introduce ourselves to the contestants first,' she suggested, pleasantly but firmly.

Trish was a tough young woman, successful in a man's world. An active feminist, she was paving the way for others within a forward-thinking firm where she was considered executive material. At twenty-five, she already headed their publicity department and was very good at her job.

'Why?' Mayjay had no desire whatsoever to chat to the contestants.

'Because it's polite and it's friendly . . . and because it's what we're paid to do.'

Mayjay shrugged. She didn't like the publicist any more than the publicist liked her. Trish Barraclough, in her opinion, was a stitched-up little power person who was jealous because she couldn't score with men. Or else she was frigid.

'All right,' she said sulkily, 'if you say so, you're the boss.'

Trish covered the weary resignation she felt with the brightest of smiles. 'Let's get a glass of champagne first, shall we?' It was easier to let the woman have her own way. What was the point in doing the introductions if she remained sullen and uncommunicative.

'An excellent suggestion.' Mayjay smiled happily. She'd won.

'Through there.' As Spud pointed to the door that led to the boardroom, he gave Trish a sympathetic wink. Being Mayjay's publicist was obviously no picnic.

'Let's step outside,' Gerrard said as soon as the women had disappeared. He wanted a private chat, away from the excited natter of the girls and their attendants, and the bustle of the runners delivering drinks and food.

Spud signalled to Ziggy, his general manager, that he'd only be gone five minutes – they'd need to be rounding up the troops shortly. Then he allowed himself to be ushered into the street where an ABC television crew was setting up. Channel 9 was covering the entire event live, but the ABC was shooting footage for a human-interest segment to follow the evening news. One of the two cameramen present was already filming the Itala where she sat ready to lead the procession, gleaming and polished to perfection. Her bodywork was a little camouflaged by the banners strapped to each side that read *From Paris to Peking to Perth,* and in only slightly smaller letters above, *Farrell Vintage Motors,* but she looked splendid nonetheless.

Spud was delighted that Anthony Wilson's ABC contact, a bright young segment producer on the news, had come up with the goods. The ABC had initially been unenthusiastic about the beauty quest, particularly as it was being fully covered by Nine, but the executive producers had found the suggestion of 'local business assists government' most interesting. And they'd readily agreed that the Itala offered a historical element which was right up the ABC's alley.

'I didn't know you'd met her, you didn't tell me that.' Gerrard tried to sound casual as he took Spud to one side.

'Met who?' Spud had been busily studying the camera-man's angle and wondering about the width of the lens – was the bloke getting the showrooms in the background as he filmed the Itala? Probably not. A pity, but it didn't really matter, Spud supposed, he was certainly getting the banner.

'Mayjay, of course.' Gerrard curbed his annoyance. 'You didn't tell me.'

'Tell you what?'

'That you'd *met* her.' The irritation was starting to show.

'Oh. Well, I have.' Spud smiled apologetically. Although he didn't like Gerrard Whitford, there was no sense in alienating the man while he was still in office. And it hadn't been his intention to irritate anyway, he'd simply been distracted. 'I've met her a couple of times actually.'

'Really?' Gerrard wondered when, and why. Spud Farrell had only recently come on board as a sponsor, and he wasn't one of the major players. What did he have to offer? 'Did you score?'

'Eh?'

'Did you fuck her?'

'No.' Spud was mystified. 'Why the hell would you think that I had?'

'Because she's a slut, that's why.' Glad that he now had Farrell's undivided attention, Gerrard was eager to divulge the gossip. 'She's turned it up for a number of the sponsors. Only the major ones – it appears she's choosy. And I've heard she accepts *presents*.'

The innuendo was plain and he smirked lasciviously, but the words had a ring of vitriol. He'd tried it on with the girl himself and she'd knocked him back in no uncertain terms, which he'd found most insulting, given his position. Why the sponsors and not him? He was the minister!

'Professionally trained model, my arse!' Gerrard gave a loud snort of derision. 'She's nothing but a fucking hooker!'

'A bloody good-looking one, you've got to admit.'

Spud checked his watch. He found the news of Mayjay's sexual exploits extremely interesting and he'd have liked to hear more, but they were running out of time.

'I'd better get into my clobber,' he said. 'It'll take a while to round the girls up, and we'll need to be leaving in the next half hour.'

Inside the showrooms, he signalled Ziggy to get things moving and disappeared into his office. As he donned his Peking to Paris khaki, Spud's mind was on Mayjay, recalling the long-ago afternoon in Ruby's lounge room when they'd first met. *How do you like it?* she'd asked as she'd undone his belt. *Kinky?* Her smile had dared him. *I do. The kinkier the better.* She'd fastened the belt around her neck. *I just bet you'd love doing it my way*, she'd said.

He wondered if she'd done it kinky with the sponsors. The thought was intriguing, and, he had to admit, rather titillating.

Twenty minutes later the convoy prepared to set off. The image was a colourful one, albeit bizarre – pretty girls in bright, miniskirted summer dresses being assisted into classic vintage vehicles by drivers in full period costume. The ABC cameramen were careful not to miss a trick.

In his adventurer's khaki and pith helmet, Spud was playing the role to the hilt. Having opened the Itala's passenger door, he stepped aside with a grand flourish of showmanship to make way for Mayjay.

She looked him up and down approvingly. 'Very nice,' she said, her eyes roaming over his knee-high boots and safari jacket before coming to rest suggestively on his crotch. 'Love the jodhpurs.'

Spud felt his pulse quicken. Could he be in with a chance? Then, recalling Ruby's warning, he put the thought out of his mind. He couldn't afford to risk the wrath of Ruby Chan and the powerful heavies she had

at her beck and call. Still, the fact that Mayjay was coming
on to him was immensely flattering.

Her eyes wandered languidly upwards until they came
to rest on the pith helmet. 'I'm not so sure about *that*
though.' There was mockery in her laughter as she climbed
into the Itala.

Spud's ego came crashing down about him. But even in
his humiliation, he felt a stab of anger. Was it her deliberate intention to make him an object of ridicule? How dare
she! He gave a laugh, intimating a joke shared, and prayed
that the cameraman hadn't caught the moment – or if
he had, that it wouldn't go to air. At the same time, he
wondered whether he really did look stupid. Should he get
rid of the pith helmet during the actual ceremony? He was
thankful that he'd brought along his suit for the party
afterwards. He'd contemplated staying in his adventurer's
gear, but he had a nasty feeling now that she'd been having
a dig at the jodhpurs as well.

The police patrol car and two escort motorcycles took
off slowly, the vintage vehicles following at their own pace.
There were eight in all, each and every one in mint condition, including a 1927 Packard and a 1933 Delage. They
were a collector's dream – in this case, Anthony Wilson's
dream, or rather his passion. Anthony had ached to be
included in the procession, but hadn't been able to come
up with a plausible reason why he should be.

Behind the vintage cars came the government chauffeur-
driven vehicle carrying the Honourable Gerrard Whitford,
who, much to the embarrassment of his assistant seated
beside him, waved at passers-by through the open window,
receiving little if any response. Gerrard had thought it
fitting that, as the event's key spokesperson, he should be
part of the parade, although the rest of the official party
would be waiting at Scarborough.

Following the government car were several Avis limousines transporting a bevy of publicists, minders, hair-

dressers, make-up artists, and Ziggy. Siegfried 'Ziggy' Schultz, the general manager of Farrell Vintage Motors, would drive the Itala back to the showrooms after the event. Finally, bringing up the rear of the procession, two more police escort motorcycles added the final touch of pomp and ceremony to a sight that was, all in all, most impressive.

As the convoy travelled down Stirling Highway, people gathered in groups on the pavement to cheer the contestants as they passed. Some of the four-seater vintage cars carried three girls apiece, and they waved and blew kisses in return. But the onlookers' principal cheers were directed at Mayjay, who was leading the procession in the open two-seater Itala driven by Spud. She was enjoying the attention immensely, and as they passed a particularly large crowd, she clasped the windscreen and rose to wave like true royalty.

'Sit down,' Spud ordered, 'there's a corner coming up.'

It would be a little while before they turned the corner, but still smarting from his humiliation he wanted her to know who was boss.

She obeyed instantly, and her smile was radiant as she linked her hand through his arm and gazed at him in what appeared to be genuine admiration. 'This was a great idea, Spud,' she said. 'How boring it would have been in limos. You're an absolute genius.'

He basked in the praise, he couldn't help himself. Christ, the woman was perverse.

At Scarborough, crowds had gathered, the hundreds having swelled to well over a thousand. Police were in evidence, press photographers and camera crews were set up, and 6PR's Dougie Mac, with a roaming mike, was spruiking for all he was worth. The official party had gathered at the north end of the Esplanade, beside the parking area. The lord mayor of Perth, the local mayor and councillors, together with Anthony Wilson – who, despite having nothing to do with the electorate, had somehow managed to be included – were joined by representatives of the major corporate sponsors, and all took up their positions in the cordoned-off area by the main track that led to the beach.

At the southern end of the Esplanade, in the forecourt of Luna Park, the assembled military brass band awaited its signal from the policeman in the nearby patrol car, who in turn awaited the radio message from his colleague leading the procession from Fremantle.

The policeman gave the drum major the thumbs up. The convoy was turning off the West Coast Highway, just one short block away.

Upon command, the band marched out of the forecourt, turned sharp right into the Esplanade and took up its position. There was a minute's silence, musicians poised, then the drum major barked the order and, as the band struck up and began its march down the street, the police car and motorcycles rounded the corner.

The timing was perfect. 'Seventy-Six Trombones' was in full swing as the Itala came into view, Mayjay, the symbol of Western Australia, standing in all her magnificence, saluting the crowds.

The cameras turned over, hundreds roared their approval, and the cavalcade began its slow procession down the fluttering-flag-lined length of the Esplanade. The grand final of the WA Beach Girl Beauty Quest was under way.

CHAPTER NINE

In open cotton shirts, towels slung around their necks and shorts pulled over their bathers, Mike McAllister and Ian Pemberton were lounging in the deserted beer garden of the Scarborough Beach Hotel. The few drinkers who'd been there had left to watch the parade, and in an hour or so the staff would start clearing the place in preparation for the private party that evening. The boys had brought along their suits for the sponsors bash, as Spud had advised, but they'd left them in Ian's car. It wouldn't have been any fun hanging around Scarborough in a jacket and tie on a blistering Saturday afternoon.

The two had arrived around lunchtime, intending to catch a few waves and have a beer and a hamburger before watching the parade, but already the crowds had been gathering. An hour later, when they'd emerged from the surf, it seemed hundreds more had appeared from nowhere. The queue at Peters by the Sea stretched for nearly a block, so they hadn't bothered with the hamburger, and there was no sense in jostling for a position to watch the cavalcade – every vantage point along the street had been taken. They'd opted for the beer garden instead. They'd wait until the procession reached the north end of the Esplanade, they'd decided – they were tall, they'd be able to see over the heads of most people.

Through the beer garden's rear entrance, which opened onto the parking area and the Esplanade beyond, they'd caught glimpses of the official party's arrival, and they were just starting on their fourth beer apiece when 'Seventy-Six Trombones' struck up. They decided not to rush things, however. Why bother wasting a good beer, they agreed, let the parade come to them.

A short while later, as the band, now playing 'Pomp and Circumstance', drew near, they drained their glasses and wandered out through the car park to join the crowds lining the pavement. The first thing they saw, gliding above the heads of the gathered throng, was Mayjay. Standing majestic in the Itala, her hair windswept, her arms outstretched, she acknowledged her worshipping subjects like a pagan princess.

'My God, she's even more incredible in the flesh,' Mike muttered.

'You're not wrong.'

They both craned for a view of the car and its driver, and Ian gave a snort of amusement.

'Do my eyes deceive me or is Spud wearing a pith helmet?'

The band came to a sudden halt before the official party, the cars slowly pulled up in a line, and the drivers helped the girls alight.

'Christ alive, what's he come as?' Ian laughed.

Mike shared a smile – Spud really was too short for jodhpurs and a pith helmet – but he resisted the urge to laugh out loud. 'It's his big day, Pembo. Don't spoil it by taking the piss out of him.'

Ian gave a shrug that said 'why not?' Personally he couldn't wait to take the piss out of Spud. If the situation was reversed Spud would do the same to him.

A brief opening ceremony took place in the cordoned-off area, police keeping at bay the hordes that threatened to surge forward, eager for a clearer view of the contestants and, most particularly, Mayjay. The local mayor made a short speech, before introducing the lord mayor, who made a longer speech officially welcoming the contestants to Perth. Then Mayjay was symbolically presented with the keys of the city, after which the girls were escorted down the main track to the marquee. The official party, now including Spud and Mayjay, followed to take up their seats in the grandstand, and a mad dash over the sandhills ensued as hundreds scrambled for prize positions near the stage.

Mike and Ian didn't join in the rush, but ambled across the street to watch from the higher ground as, on stage, Dougie Mac introduced the members of the local rock band who had been patiently awaiting their big moment.

The band had aptly chosen a bracket of favourites from The Beach Boys, and as 'Surfin' USA' and 'Good Vibrations' blared through the speakers, hairdressers and make-up artists worked frantically in the marquee, repairing the damage that had resulted during the drive from Fremantle. The band would shortly segue into the Little Pattie number, 'He's My Blonde Headed Stompie Wompie Real Gone Surfer Boy', which would be their standby cue. All the contestants would be called up on stage where they'd be briefly interviewed, one by one, before returning to the marquee to don their bikinis for their individual parade on the catwalk.

Up on the sand hills overlooking the beach – not far from where Mike and Ian stood – a gang of some twenty young men had gathered with their girlfriends. They wore boots, jeans and T-shirts and, despite the heat, their signature black leather jackets. The girls were similarly attired, although most had discarded their jackets, dangling them nonchalantly from one finger over a shoulder. The rockers, their chicks riding pillion, had fronted up on their motorbikes a good hour earlier to watch the procession. Like

everyone else they'd appeared to enjoy it, and like
everyone else they now appeared to be enjoying the music,
clapping along with the rest of the crowd.

At the end of the number, the band members took their
bows, then quickly cleared their equipment to the rear of
the stage as, one by one, the contestants were introduced.

'Miss Geraldton! Miss Rockingham! Miss Mandurah!'
Checking out the names in the folder he carried, Dougie,
the jarringly energetic wake-up voice of breakfast radio,
gave it his best hard sell as he called the winners of the
previous competitions up onto the stage.

As the girls paraded along the red carpet from the
marquee to the stage and mounted the steps to join
Dougie, they were cheered and applauded, the rockers up
on the sandhill being particularly vocal.

The rockers' applause, however, differed from that of
the general crowd. While there was nothing specifically
offensive in their catcalls and whistles and cries of 'hubba
hubba', their enthusiasm sounded fake. They were overly
raucous. It was difficult to tell whether they were jeering
or cheering, but one thing was obvious. Their chicks
weren't happy.

When the contestants were all lined up on stage, Dougie
took each girl aside and interviewed her, referring meticulously to the list of questions in his folder. As the girls
would be judged according to their responses, he knew
that he had to get it right.

Some girls, assured and confident, played to the crowd,
and some won fans with a natural charm. Favourites were
quickly establishing themselves, and at the conclusion of
each interview, as the contestant returned to the marquee,
the applause accorded them varied markedly.

The rockers were letting it be known loud and clear who
their favourites were. But they weren't waiting until the
girls had been interviewed. Miss Port Hedland, a bosomy
blonde who hailed from a cattle station three hundred

kilometres from the coast, received a cacophony of catcalls the moment she stepped forward. As did Miss Albany, an equally well-endowed redhead who lived in the remote desert goldmining town of Coolgardie.

'Go home, slag!'

Carol considered it her duty to make a statement, and she screeched the words at the top of her voice. She was Marco's girlfriend, and as Marco was the leader of the gang it made her the chicks' leader and therefore their spokesperson, and the chicks were all thoroughly fed up with the attention being afforded the women on stage.

The other chicks gave her a rousing cheer, and the rockers laughed. It was exactly the reaction they'd been seeking. Along with creating a stir, they liked to rile their women – it was all part of the game.

By the time it came to the individual parade, the rockers were playing their game in earnest, and the chicks, keen to gain their boyfriends' approval, were joining in vociferously. As the bikini-clad contestants made their way down the catwalk, some with the slick assurance of professionals, others with a gaucherie that betrayed their origins, the rockers yelled 'Get it off!' and 'Show us your tits!' while their girlfriends countered with 'Slags!' 'Sluts!' and 'Go home, Molls!'

Although the gang numbered only forty amongst a crowd in excess of a thousand, they were making their mark. The cameramen wisely avoided them, and the spectators tried to pay them no attention in the hope they'd get bored and go away, but it became increasingly difficult to ignore the troublesome group. Others nearby, including Mike and Ian, started yelling at them to shut up, which only spurred them on and added to the disruption. It was a welcome relief when the police closed in.

The rockers were surprisingly acquiescent – taking their lead from Marco, as they always did.

'Just cheering the girls on,' Marco said cockily, draping

his arm around Carol's neck. 'Can't help it if the chicks get jealous, can we?'

He looked around at the rest of the gang, who nodded, shrugging innocence. En masse, they wandered off to their motorbikes. They'd had their fun, they wouldn't push things further – there was no point in being arrested for disturbing the peace. Besides, they'd be back later. Scarborough was their place, particularly after dark.

The rest of the afternoon proceeded smoothly. Miss Bunbury was declared the winner, which very much irritated Miss Perth, a professional catwalk model who'd won the highly contested local competition held at Cottesloe and who'd considered herself a shoo-in.

Dougie Mac called Mayjay to the stage and the audience went wild as she draped the sash over Miss Bunbury's shoulder and placed the crown on her head. Miss Bunbury had been a popular choice.

'Our winner!' Dougie screamed into the microphone, and Miss Bunbury stepped forward, a hand to her head, fighting to maintain possession of her precariously balanced crown, which, if lost, threatened to take her hairpiece with it.

'Miss WA Beach Girl Beauty!'

Upon Dougie's further ear-shattering pronouncement, Mayjay turned to the crowd, arms extended in gracious acknowledgement of the winner. The applause was suddenly overwhelming. It was obvious for whom it was intended. Lovely though she was, the newly crowned Miss WA Beach Girl Beauty didn't hold a candle to the real thing.

Twenty minutes later the show was well and truly over and the cameras had stopped rolling, but up on stage, as he continued his speech, the Honourable Gerrard Whitford seemed unaware of the fact.

'The WA Beach Girl Beauty Quest,' he concluded, soldiering on manfully as families collected children and beach mats and headed off to the car park, 'is proof positive that the marriage of government and private enterprise is indeed the way of the future!'

It was only then that Gerrard noticed there was no cameraman behind the nearby camera. Strange, he thought. Perhaps they were getting it in a long shot from one of the others. Pity. He wanted to finish on a close-up.

In the grandstand, where the captive official party had been forced to lend its attention, Howard Stonehaven led the dutiful applause, blissfully happy in the knowledge that Gerrard had made a thorough fool of himself.

Two familiar figures were standing beside the Itala chatting to Ziggy as Spud and Anthony Wilson strolled up from the beach. One of them held out his hand to Spud.

'Dr Livingstone, I presume?'

'Cut it out, Pembo.' Spud slapped the hand away, and Mike flashed a look of rebuke at Ian, who ignored it.

'Or is it perhaps Henry Morton Stanley himself?'

As Ian looked him up and down in wide-eyed mock admiration, Spud cursed the fact that he was still wearing the pith helmet. Did he really look stupid? He wouldn't normally have allowed Pembo's ridicule to affect him, but he was reminded of Mayjay's scorn. He was about to tell Pembo to fuck off, when Anthony Wilson's need for attention unwittingly saved the day.

'Ian ... Mike ...' Anthony offered his hand, teeth gleaming. 'Good to see you again, boys.'

The three men shook.

'I've been reading about Excalibur in the press, Ian.' Anthony had read one tiny snippet about Ian Pemberton's company in the financial pages, but he was eager to make an impression. 'Most exciting. I believe you're acquiring new –'

'You've met Ziggy, I take it?' Spud addressed his mates, excluding Anthony altogether. Pembo's piss-take was forgivable, Anthony Wilson's obsequiousness was not, and poor Ziggy, whom Spud liked, was being left out of things.

'Yeah, we introduced ourselves,' Mike said. 'We've been admiring the Itala, but he won't let us take her for a test drive.'

'I should bloody well hope not.' Spud was suddenly all smiles as he turned to Anthony. 'I can't remember if you've met Ziggy, Anthony, have you? Siegfried Schultz, Anthony Wilson.'

'Yes, we've met,' Anthony said tightly. 'Hello, Ziggy.'

'Anthony.' Ziggy smiled broadly and offered his hand. 'It is gut to see you,' he said in his thick Bavarian accent.

Anthony returned the smile and the handshake, but he was not amused. He had employed Siegfried Schultz himself and at great expense. It had been a costly exercise enticing the highly skilled mechanic to leave his home in South Australia and relocate to Perth. Indeed, Ziggy would not have succumbed to the offer at all had he not been given Anthony's personal assurance that the vintage cars for which they shared a mutual passion would be solely under his control. All of which had meant that Anthony had had to blow his cover. Siegfried Schultz was aware of his employer's true identity. He knew that Farrell Vintage Motors was principally owned by Anthony Wilson, MP.

'Perhaps if you're really nice to Ziggy,' Spud continued amiably, 'he might let you drive the Itala back to the show-rooms.'

Anthony looked daggers at Spud. That had been the plan from the outset, and he'd been eagerly anticipating the drive to Fremantle in the Itala. Now Spud was forcing him to play out this ridiculous charade in front of his mates.

'What do you say, Ziggy?' Spud's plea to the German appeared in earnest. 'Anthony's really interested in vintage vehicles, and I hear he's a very good driver.'

'Ja, this we could arrange, I think.' Ziggy grinned from one to the other. He hadn't registered the subtlety of the exchange and the power play behind it. He genuinely thought it was a very good joke. 'We drive together, Anthony. Just you and me in the Itala, ja?'

'That's very kind of you Ziggy. Thank you.' There were times, Anthony thought, when he very much regretted having gone into partnership with Spud Farrell.

After retrieving his gear from the trunk of the Itala, Spud retired to the hotel to change, telling Mike and Ian that he'd leave their names with the bouncer at the door to the pub's main lounge. They agreed to meet him there in an hour or so when they, too, had changed. It was after six, the party wouldn't kick off for some time yet, and Mike was keen to catch a few waves before it started to get dark.

'It'll give us a while for the mob to clear,' he said as he and Ian wandered down to the beach. 'The change rooms at the surf club'll be packed.' Mike couldn't wait to get into the surf. He needed to wake up. Four beers on an empty stomach and an afternoon in the sun had left him desperately tired.

An hour later, freshly scrubbed up in their suits and ties, they joined the throng on the Esplanade. The families had gone home and the crowds had thinned dramatically, but the place was still crowded. People were queuing up for hamburgers and flocking to the pub's main bar, preparing themselves for the evening's entertainment, and as night fell there was an air of expectancy. There always was in Scarborough on a Saturday night. Soon the Snake Pit would come alive.

'Let's skip the hamburgers,' Ian said when they found themselves once again confronted by a long queue at Peters by the Sea. 'There'll be food at the party.'

Hungry as he was, Mike agreed and they strolled up the street to the Scarborough Beach Hotel where the lounges and beer garden had been privately booked for the sponsors party. They presented themselves to the bouncer, who checked their names on his list, and were immediately granted entry. Spud, however, was nowhere in sight. Nor was Mayjay. Nor were any of the other girls they were so eager to meet. Instead, in the rather mothy main lounge, which had certainly seen finer days, a score of men in suits stood around sipping champagne and beer, swapping business cards and talking shop.

'Some party,' Ian said, having checked with a passing waiter, 'there's not even bourbon. If you want top shelf you have to buy it in the main bar.'

They stopped another waiter and asked about food. A buffet dinner was being set up in the beer garden, they were told, and the guests would shortly be invited in. Before the man could bustle off, Ian slipped him a note and asked where the girls were.

'They're in there.' Pocketing the five dollars, the waiter gave a jerk of his head to indicate the beer garden. 'With a bunch of bigwigs, doing pictures and stuff for the press. I could sneak you in if you like.'

'No, we'll wait for the food.'

Ian made the decision without consultation, but Mike didn't mind, he was still feeling weary and he couldn't be bothered either way.

'Well at least we know where Spud is,' he said.

'Bugger him.' Ian turned on his heel. 'Let's go to the main bar, I need a bourbon.'

The main bar was open to the public and crowded. While Ian fought his way through the mob to buy the first round, Mike found a niche for them in the corner at the far end of the bar.

'I said I wanted a beer.' He looked askance at the bourbon and Coke Ian handed him ten minutes later.

'It's not a case of what you *want*, it's a case of what you *need*,' Ian countered, 'and you *need* a bourbon.'

Bloody Pembo, Mike thought as he took a sip – it was a double. Pembo was plainly out to get drunk, but Mike wasn't in the mood himself. The swim had freshened him up a little, but not enough. The day had been wearying and he didn't have Pembo's energy. He knew why. He knew exactly where Pembo's energy came from.

'I'll tell you what else you need.' Ian dived a hand into the inside breast pocket of his jacket and produced a small plastic screw-top phial.

'No,' Mike said emphatically, 'I'm not doing those bloody things again.'

He'd recently joined Ian on one of his pill-popping evenings, just to see what it was like. He'd been as high as a kite until six the following morning. It had been fun. But the palpitations he'd experienced later that day hadn't. They'd been an unpleasant reminder that he had a heart condition.

The speed pills were a habit Ian Pemberton had picked up from his business partner – a brash young American financial expert called Phil Cowan. Whenever the two came into town together, they'd party all night.

'We've gotta lotta lost time to account for,' Phil would say in his mock John Wayne accent. 'Let's face it, there ain't much happenin' in Kal.'

Mike and Spud liked Phil well enough, he was good fun, but his boundless energy could be wearing, even when he wasn't on the pills. It was hardly surprising, they'd agreed, that Pembo needed to pop a few himself in order to keep up with the bloke.

'Two each.' Ian held out his hand to reveal four Dexedrine tablets resting in the centre of his palm. He'd downed a couple several hours ago when they'd been drinking in the beer garden, but he could do with a booster. 'They're only Dexies,' he said reassuringly as he slipped the phial back in his pocket, 'they won't do you any harm, just pep you up a bit.' He peered at Mike. 'And you could do with some pepping up – you're not in the mood, are you?' That was the trouble with Mike McAllister, Ian thought. When Mike wasn't in the mood he was no good at faking it. He never pretended he was having a good time if he wasn't – he could be a real downer like that. 'Christ, you look as if you don't even want to be here.'

I don't, Mike thought. The truth was, he didn't want to be anywhere. All he wanted was a feed and a bed.

'Come on,' Ian urged, plonking the pills on the bar in front of them, 'liven up. You don't want to spoil things for Spud, do you?'

'Don't blackmail me, Pembo.'

'Why not?' To Ian it seemed perfectly justifiable that he should. 'You said it yourself. This is Spud's big day, remember?'

The rock band in the nearby Snake Pit struck up 'Time Is On My Side', the first in its Rolling Stones bracket. Mike was a great Stones fan and it seemed like an omen. What the hell, he thought. Pembo was right, he needed to get in the mood. He grabbed two of the pills and downed them, downing most of his bourbon and Coke at the same time. He'd worry about the palpitations tomorrow.

'That's my man,' Ian said, following suit. 'And I tell you what,' he grinned lasciviously, 'if you manage to score tonight you'll thank me. You can go on forever with a couple of Dexies in you.'

Mike bought the next round and he made it two double bourbons. It seemed the way to go, and besides he could hardly switch to beer when it was his shout. Half an hour later, he was no longer hungry and no longer tired, and the music from across the street was enticing.

'Let's go to the Snake Pit,' he said, draining his glass.

Ian readily agreed. He wasn't feeling hungry either, he was just raring to go.

It was nine o'clock, and in the pub's beer garden, now atmospherically draped with fairy lights, guests continued to attack the buffet table. Waiters replenished the platters of meats and prawns and local lobster at breakneck speed, the food disappearing as soon as it was set down. An afternoon in the sun had rendered everyone ravenous.

Spud was wondering where Mike and Pembo had got to. He'd checked in the main lounge, which was also crowded, diners having escaped the feeding frenzy of the beer garden to scoff their meal in comparative comfort, but there'd been no sign of the boys. A waiter had told him they'd gone to the bar, but a check there had also proved fruitless. They were nowhere to be found and Spud was annoyed. He'd had Mayjay all lined up for the introduction, and she'd seemed quite keen.

'Any friends of yours are bound to be interesting, Spud,' she'd said.

Mayjay had even meant it to a certain degree. Anyone would be more interesting, she'd thought, than the bloody journalist and local mayor, with whom Trish-bloody-Barraclough had landed her for the past ten minutes. The photographer from some crappy little local newspaper had clicked away as if it was the *New York* bloody *Times*. Thank Christ the press meeting had finally come to an end and the scumbag journos, photographers and other freeloaders had been let loose on the food and the booze.

Spud, mystified again by Mayjay's contradictory nature, had found her interest in his friends flattering, and had been impatiently awaiting Mike's and Pembo's arrival so that he could show off. But they hadn't turned up, and Mayjay had lost interest, wandering away to chat to the Qantas Chief Executive who'd been literally drooling at the mouth. Now, having explored the pub to no avail, Spud had returned to the beer garden, cross.

Trish Barraclough was relieved that Mayjay hadn't deserted her post. She watched her chatting to the Qantas chief executive and the newly crowned Miss Bunbury, and was pleasantly surprised that Mayjay appeared to be still working the room. A number of the girls, bored with the chat-ups from drink-affected sponsors and government officials, had been lured by the sound of the rock band across the street and had quietly slipped away to seek a bit of action on the dance floor of the Snake Pit. Trish couldn't blame them, but it was one thing for the contestants to disappear to the Snake Pit and another thing altogether for Mayjay. The evening was not a social event for someone as highly paid as the symbol of Western Australia.

Trish checked her watch. She'd give it until ten o'clock, she decided, another half an hour or so, and then she'd rescue Mayjay and take her back to the hotel. She returned her attention to Gerrard Whitford, who, she was aware, suddenly found her attractive. She'd taken off her suit jacket – although lightweight, it had been unpleasantly hot throughout the afternoon – and she knew he found her breasts riveting. She also knew that all the contestants had his number and had successfully avoided him, and that she was the poor sod who had no option but to suffer his company.

Howard Stonehaven was observing Gerrard with distaste. The combined effect of alcohol and a smorgasbord of beautiful young women was bringing out the worst in the man. No wonder so many of the girls were disappearing, Howard thought. But then they'd probably have left even if Gerrard wasn't around – it was a drab party. And that, too, was Gerrard's fault. Howard had strongly argued against the choice of venue. They needed somewhere far more up-market than the shabby Scarborough Beach Hotel, he'd said. But Gerrard had insisted a local venue was essential, maintaining that it would break the mood of the day if they moved the party to another area – and besides, the Scarborough Beach Hotel was atmospheric and colourful.

The argument had sounded not altogether unreasonable, so Howard had hedged his bets, allowing it to appear that the idea may have been his own, just in case Gerrard proved right. Now that the party had turned out a failure, however, he would be sure to remind his colleagues that the Scarborough Beach Hotel had been Gerrard's choice. It would be yet another nail in the man's coffin. And that, at least, Howard thought, would be some compensation for having to endure a dismal evening like this.

Spud was thinking along similar lines. It was a bloody awful party and a big disappointment – he'd really looked forward to tonight. Half the girls had ducked off to the Snake Pit, which was probably where Mike and Pembo were, he thought. Christ, they weren't dumb. They'd no doubt heard the party was a wash-out and headed straight for the rock music, and who could blame them?

Spud picked up his jacket and made for the door.

'Excuse me, Gerrard.' Trish could finally take no more. The man's eyes were firmly fixed upon her breasts and she had a feeling he was about to proposition her. He obviously thought that any woman who spent more than five minutes in his company found him attractive. Hadn't he heard of women's lib? Didn't he know that women loathed his type? That they always had? She'd love to tell him so to his face, but she didn't. She played the game, as always.

'Can't stay chatting, much as I'd love to,' she said, shrugging on her suit jacket. Gerrard's eyes jerked upwards to meet hers. 'Duty calls, I'm afraid.' And she marched off to join Mayjay, Miss Bunbury and the Qantas executive.

Gerrard watched her go, focusing on her backside in its neat pin-striped miniskirt. What a pity, he'd been about to make a move. Great tits, he thought. Good arse too.

'Hello, Brian, having a good time?' Trish gave Brian Tomlinson a particularly bright smile. Qantas was the ad agency's top client, and its sponsorship of the WA Beach Girl Beauty Quest, an account also handled by the agency, was a cross-marketing coup.

'Couldn't be better.'

Trish noted Brian's glance at Mayjay. Another woman-iser out to score, she thought. Well, he'd certainly set his sights high, but it was quite possible he'd make it. Mayjay had already slept with the Ansett representative – perhaps she had a penchant for airline executives.

'And how about you, Penelope?' Trish turned her bright smile to Miss Bunbury. 'It's a big night for you, isn't it?'

Penelope responded enthusiastically. It was very exciting and she was having a wonderful time, she said. This was the biggest night of her life. Penelope was a nice girl.

Mayjay had had enough of the social chat. She'd been weighing up her options. Mr Qantas obviously wanted to sleep with her, but she didn't particularly fancy him. Bored, she'd been contemplating whether or not to head off to the Snake Pit where the bouncer had told her she could score some cocaine. Her own stash had run out – she'd snorted the last line in the ladies' lavatory at Farrell Vintage Motors – and she needed something to alleviate the tediousness of the evening. She'd asked amongst the contestants, but they'd been unable to come up with even a speed pill, let alone coke, they were such a square bunch. Obviously not professionals, she'd thought dismissively – stimulants were rife amongst the modelling set in Sydney, who snorted and swallowed with religious regularity in the knowledge that it kept the weight off.

The Snake Pit had been beckoning Mayjay for the past ten minutes and Trish's intervention was the final clincher.

'I'm off.'

Her interruption of Penelope was appallingly rude. Turning on her heel, she was about to walk away, but Trish was too quick for her.

'Off where?' she asked pleasantly, forcing a halt to Mayjay's flight.

'To the music. To the dance floor.' Mayjay's petulance clearly said 'Where else?' 'I'm bored.'

'I don't think that's such a good idea.' Trish's tone remained pleasant, but her smile was now tight.

'Oh, and why's that?' Go on, Mayjay thought, say it, I dare you. *We're paying you a fortune, you bitch, how dare you knock off early.* She knew exactly what Trish was thinking.

'It would be unwise of you to go to the Snake Pit on your own. It's quite a rough place, I'm told.'

'I won't be on my own. Some of the girls have gone. I'll be with them.'

'Since when have you been *one of the girls,* Mayjay?' For the benefit of the others, Trish laughed lightly, as if joking, but she wasn't. God, the woman had a hide. The girls weren't being paid a fortune like her, and Mayjay had made it plain that she considered them beneath her anyway. How dare she try and play it both ways.

'Besides, the girls don't have a minder and you do.' Trish turned to Brian and Penelope with a self-effacing shrug. 'I'm it, I'm afraid, and I can't neglect my duties.' Then back to Mayjay, still charming, but with a definite reminder that Mayjay, too, had duties. 'I'll be standing by with the limousine at ten o'clock.'

Trish-bitch-Barraclough had gone too far, Mayjay thought. 'I won't need the limo,' she said bluntly. 'And I'm electing a new minder.' She treated the Qantas chief executive to a dazzling smile. Mr Qantas, she thought, what the hell was his name? Ah yes, that was it. 'Brian, will you accept the position? Will you be my minder for the night?' She tucked a hand through his arm, her eyes settling on his mouth, the tip of her tongue running suggestively over her lips. 'It appears I need some looking after.'

Brian Tomlinson was no slouch when it came to women, but he'd never before experienced such an overtly sexual come-on, and all in the space of seconds. 'Well, of course,' he said, hoping his voice sounded normal. 'I'd be only too happy to look after you, Mayjay.'

'Oh good.' Her eyes slid up to meet his and she nestled a breast against his arm. 'That's nice,' she purred.

For one confusing second, Brian thought she meant the touch of their bodies, and he agreed wholeheartedly.

'So you see, Trish,' without drawing breath, Mayjay addressed her publicist with only the subtlest change in her tone, 'you won't be needed after all.' Her eyes and the proprietorial hand tucked through the arm of Brian Tomlinson signalled a definite message. *See, bitch? Your top client is eating out of my hand. Now tell me I'm not doing my job!*

'You can take the limo home all by yourself,' she said sweetly. 'You can even pretend it's just for you.'

Trish said nothing. What *was* there to say? If Mayjay wished to go beyond the call of duty in entertaining the agency's principal client, then who was she to complain? And the woman's intended spite was water off a duck's back. Trish was only too happy to take the limo home herself and get an early night.

Hitching the straps of her small gold evening bag over her shoulder, Mayjay turned to Miss Bunbury, but she couldn't remember the girl's name.

'Goodbye,' she said. 'You're very pretty.'

'Thank you.'

Trish ignored Mayjay's grand exit as she swanned off with Brian Tomlinson. The woman wouldn't last in the business, she thought. Mayjay was a flash in the pan, despite her beauty – just another rank amateur. Trish had seen them come and go with monotonous regularity.

'Come with me, Penelope,' she said, steering the girl towards a group of executives. 'There are some important people you need to chat to.' She'd give Penelope five minutes of her time, she thought. Then she'd sneak out the rear entrance to where the limo was waiting.

*

Brian Tomlinson put his arm around Mayjay as they were
about to step into the street. Presuming that she was
coming home with him and anxious to beat a hasty retreat,
he was ready to guide her to his nearby car. But she halted
at the door.

'I have to see a couple of people before I leave,' she said.
'Why don't you have another drink? I shouldn't be too
long.'

He paused, a flicker of suspicion in his eyes. Was she
having him on? He wasn't in the mood for games. If
she was a prick-teaser he didn't want a bar of her. She
was either going to sleep with him or she wasn't.

Sensing his misgivings, Mayjay was quick with her reassurance.

'They're paying me a lot of money, Brian.' Her apology
sounded not only sincere but eminently reasonable. 'It's
politic of me to say a couple of farewells.'

She wasn't altogether having him on, as he suspected,
but she was certainly using him. Brian Tomlinson had been
handy in getting her away from Trish Barraclough. She
was prepared to sleep with him however – Mr Qantas was
a worthy conquest who could prove useful. But he wasn't
her type. The prospect of sex with him didn't thrill her, and
Mayjay demanded that sex be thrilling. She needed a line
of coke, she told herself – artificial stimulation was essential when fucking a man one didn't fancy. *Boris at the
Snake Pit*, the bouncer had said. *You'll find him hanging
around La Spiaggia.*

'A few minutes, that's all.' She fed Brian's arm around
her and pressed her crotch teasingly against his. 'Five or
ten at the most.'

Her other hand hooked itself about his neck, and Brian
couldn't resist the parted lips on offer. As they kissed, he
felt her tongue dart across his teeth and her pelvis gently
sway against his growing erection.

'Stick to the main bar,' she whispered when their mouths

parted. If Trish-bitch-Barraclough spotted Mr Qantas on his own, she thought, the cow of a woman would be bound to come on the hunt. 'I'll meet you there in ten minutes.'

As she turned to go, her hand fleetingly brushed his groin, as if by accident, and she smiled a promise over her shoulder.

Brian obediently went into the main bar where he caught his breath, ordered a cooling beer and tantalised himself with images of Mayjay naked.

At the Snake Pit, the band was belting out the Chantays' latest surfie hit from the USA. 'Pipeline', with its pumping rhythm and sexual innuendo, was driving youth wild in nightclubs and dance halls all over the world, and the Snake Pit was no exception. The simple wooden dance floor set out on the sand writhed with a sea of bodies. Bare-footed and frantic, sweat flowing freely, dancers jived and twisted and stomped the night away, the hot air charged with a feverish energy.

Spud, upon his arrival, had been quick to forgive Mike and Ian for deserting him. 'Knew I'd find you here, you bastards!' he'd yelled above the din as he joined them in their spot on the sand. He'd spent a good five minutes hunting amongst the crowd.

Mike, bare-footed like the others, trousers rolled up, open shirt flapping, had just come off the dance floor after a rigorous workout, his bare chest drenched in sweat. Ian, collapsed on the sand and swigging back a beer, was in a similar condition.

'Sorry, mate,' Mike had yelled back, flopping beside Ian to look up at Spud.

'It's okay. You didn't miss much. The food was good.'

Spud had known immediately that the boys were on a high, he could see it in their eyes. Well, Pembo was on a constant high these days, with his bloody speed pills.

Unlike Mike to succumb though, he'd thought. What the hell, they were having a good time.

He'd plonked himself next to them, taking off his shoes and his jacket and producing the ubiquitous flask of Jack Daniel's. Might as well join in the fun, he'd thought, passing around the flask and rolling up his trousers.

They now sat companionably, swigging back the bourbon and watching the girls on the dance floor. They compared notes, differing occasionally on who was hot and who wasn't, but they were all in accord about the redhead. Miss Albany should have won the beauty quest, Mike said, and the others agreed.

They watched Miss Albany as she walked off the dance floor to join two other girls, also gorgeous, also contestants, and as they saw them gather up their shoes, the boys, presuming they were leaving, were about to jump to their feet. The opportunity seemed too good to miss.

'So these are your mates, Spud.'

The voice was right overhead, and there was something about it that commanded attention, even in the surrounding din.

All three of them turned and glanced up to where she stood only several feet behind them, legs astride, sandals in hand. She liked to sneak up on people.

'I'm Mayjay,' she said, her eyes focused on Mike. 'Don't get up,' she laughed, although none of them had made a move, momentarily dumbfounded by the tanned legs and the perfect body in its form-fitting red mini dress. 'Mind if I join you?'

She already had, dumping her bag and sandals, seating herself between Spud and Mike, digging her bare toes into the sand.

'You didn't tell me your friends were so good-looking, Spud.' Again she had eyes only for Mike.

Mayjay had seen him the moment she'd arrived. Avoiding the dancers, on her way to the kiosk in search of

Boris, she'd spied Spud passing a flask to a couple of his mates. She'd been about to avoid him also – she liked Spud, but with Mr Qantas waiting it would be unwise to invite a chat – then she'd noticed the young man beside him, smiling as he accepted the flask, tilting his head back as he swigged from it, his dark tousled hair wet with sweat, his bare chest glistening. She couldn't take her eyes off him. This was the man she wanted, she thought. Bugger Brian Tomlinson, and bugger Boris – sex with this one wouldn't require a line of coke.

She'd taken off her sandals and made a beeline through the sand. Mr Qantas would be angry, but he wouldn't come looking for her. He'd get bored waiting and go home on his own, and who the hell cared? Here was her challenge. This was where the night's excitement lay.

'Mike McAllister and Ian Pemberton, otherwise known as Pembo . . .'

Mayjay dragged her eyes from Mike as Spud made the introductions. The other one was good-looking too, she realised. In fact, despite slightly bat ears, he was downright handsome, and although not as well-muscled as his friend, the sweaty bare chest that he, too, displayed through his open shirt was fit and very attractive. A smorgasbord, she thought, the evening was picking up. Even more importantly, she could tell they were both on a high. Given the dilated pupils, she presumed it was coke. What a turn-on. These two were out for excitement. Well, so am I boys, she thought.

She smiled at Mike. 'Want to share it around?' She leaned in close to him so she didn't have to shout above the band.

Mike started guiltily. Had she read his thoughts? The look in her eyes had been so openly inviting that all he'd been able to think of was getting her into bed.

'Share what around?'

'The coke, or whatever it is you're on.'

Ian picked his jacket up from the sand and dived his hand into its inside pocket.

'No coke, only Dexies, I'm afraid.'

'That'll do.' She accepted the two speed pills he offered, Spud passed her the flask and she downed them with a swig of Jack Daniel's. 'Thanks.' Handing the flask back to Spud, she stood. 'Want to dance?' The offer was directed to Mike.

'Sure.'

He scrambled to his feet and they took off for the dance floor. Spud and Ian looked over to where the redhead and her girlfriends had been. They'd gone. Mike had scored Mayjay and they'd lost their opportunity. Damn it, they thought.

A male vocalist had joined the band now, and was offering an excellent rendition of the Fortune's latest hit, 'You've Got Your Troubles, I've Got Mine'.

As they stepped onto the wooden dance floor, Mayjay didn't gyrate independently of her partner as the others were doing, she melded her body to his and they danced in a close embrace. The invitation she'd offered with her eyes, she now offered with her whole body, and Mike, self-conscious of his instant erection, tried at first to steer a little distance between them.

'No, not like that,' she murmured, her breath fanning his ear, her hand at the small of his back, urging him closer. 'Share it, Mike. Share it.' Her body undulated against his in time with the music and her own mantra. 'Share it, Mike. Share it. Share it.'

Self-consciousness forgotten, Mike succumbed to the moment. The pills, the alcohol, the music and, above all, the movement of her body combined in a headiness that made him lost to everything about him. This wasn't dancing, this was sex. And it was the sort of sex that could go on forever, slow, sensual, with no frantic need. He felt

no sense of urgency and no threat of impending ejaculation as his hands slid to her buttocks and their groins
moved in harmony, the pace dictated by her whispers and
the music's rhythm. On it went, on and on, Mike's mind
and body lost in a state of total sensuality.

'We're going to take a short break now, folks. Don't go
away.'

The abrupt cessation of the music shocked him back to
reality and, as the bandleader made the announcement,
he broke away to look around guiltily, wondering if he
should be embarrassed. They'd been having sex right in
the middle of the dance floor! But to his relief, no-one
appeared to have noticed.

As the band played a final riff, the crowd gave them a
rousing round of applause, but Mike was still lost in his
own thoughts. God, he'd been horny. He still was. And
he'd felt as if he could go on forever. It must be the pills –
no wonder Pembo had said they were good for sex.

'I think we need to disappear, don't you?' From the look
in Mayjay's eyes, her feelings matched his. 'I don't care
where to,' she said, 'but somewhere, and quick.'

Mayjay had no compunction about where they did it
or who saw them. In fact, when she was this turned on
she enjoyed an audience. 'Let's go to the beach.'

'I know somewhere.' The boat shed, he thought. The
key had still been in its hiding place the last time he'd
visited, and even if it wasn't there now, the boatshed was
old and ramshackle, it would be easy to break into. He
took her hand and they stepped from the dance floor.

'Slag! Bloody slag!'

'Go on Carol! Give it to her!'

Suddenly, with neither the blare of the music nor the
cheers of the crowd to muffle it, a ruckus in the street
could be clearly heard.

'Fight! Fight! Fight!'

*

Dozens started swarming from the Snake Pit to investigate.

'Come on, let's take a look,' Spud said, he and Ian appearing beside them. Spud handed Mayjay her sandals and evening bag. 'Better take them with you, they'll get nicked for sure if you don't.'

Spud was carrying his own jacket and shoes. He'd told Ian to grab the rest of the gear, but Ian hadn't. It'd been safe all the while they'd been dancing, he'd said, and besides, they needed to save their possie in the sand. Spud thought it was bloody stupid of Pembo to leave designer stuff like his just lying around, but then Pembo was always stupid when he had the pills in him, and the same went for Mike tonight. Serve them both right for getting stuck into the drugs, he thought, I'm not my brother's keeper. But he'd made sure he'd grabbed Mayjay's sandals and bag.

She took them from him, and the four were swept along with the general exodus out into the street.

On the opposite side of the road, a fierce wrestling match was taking place on the grass. Carol, the rocker chick, and the redhead, Miss Albany, were rolling about, grunting and cursing, arms and legs flailing, the gang members, encircling them, urging them on.

'Go on, Carol! Give it to her!' the chicks yelled, while the rockers set up a steady rhythmic handclap.

Miss Albany's flimsy summer dress was ripped to pieces and one magnificent breast exposed, while Carol's leather jacket weathered the storm intact. But appearances were deceptive. Miss Albany, whose name was Bev, hailed from the tough goldmining town of Coolgardie, and her five brothers had taught her every trick they knew. They'd kill anyone who messed with their sister, and if they weren't around then they'd make sure their sister could do the job herself. Carol had picked the wrong adversary.

Flashing a healthy expanse of lacy crotch, Bev flung a leg around Carol and straddled her, pinning her wrists to the ground. Where the hell were the bloody cops, she thought. She didn't mind her dress being ruined, but she wasn't going to let the tart muck up her face – she was a beauty queen, for Christ's sake.

Beneath her, Carol bucked, screaming obscenities, and managed to break one arm free. Bev rose quickly to her feet, backing away to gain some distance.

Carol also stood, her breathing laboured. She was running out of steam. But she nonetheless came in for the kill. Carol was desperate, she was losing face in front of the gang, and she charged, arms outstretched, fingers at the ready, determined to claw Bev's eyes out.

Bev had had enough. If the cops weren't coming she'd have to do it herself. She stepped neatly to one side and, as Carol charged past, she grabbed her arm and spun her around. She waited a second for Carol to gain her balance, then took her by both shoulders and smashed her forehead as hard as she could into the woman's face. Carol sank to her knees, whimpering, clutching her broken nose. The fight was finished before it had begun.

As if on cue, the police arrived and, sport over, the crowd quickly dispersed.

Mayjay, who'd found the spectacle arousing, was eager to pick up where she and Mike had left off. The pills were meeting the remnants of the coke, and she was ready for action. She was aware, too, that Ian, who had been standing beside her openly ogling the girls, had found the fight as erotic as she had.

'We're going for a walk, Pembo,' she said, her arm about Mike's waist, her body pasted against his, unmistakably signalling that 'walk' was a euphemism for something entirely different. 'Want to come along for the ride?'

Neither Mike nor Ian, nor Spud for that matter, were quite sure they'd read the invitation correctly.

They had. Mayjay was quick to clear up any misunderstanding.

'The more the merrier,' she said, eyeing Ian off hungrily. It had been a while since she'd had a threesome and she liked group sex. What the hell, she could give Spud a treat while she was at it. 'Why don't you join us, Spud? You can watch.' She shared a special wink with him – she and Spud went back, after all. 'You might learn something.' It was a promise.

Spud recognised the same dare she'd offered when he was seventeen years old and she'd placed his belt around her neck. Mayjay liked to shock. She'd been playing with him then and she was playing with him now. She was playing with them all. Everything was a game to Ruby's little girl. And yet it wasn't. She was deadly serious.

Mike's laugh was forced. He found the joke a bit off, and he found the fact that Pembo was literally drooling even more so. Jeez, the two of them were spaced out, he thought, but not *that* spaced out, surely.

'She's joking, you stupid bastard,' he said, and he led Mayjay away in the direction of the boatshed.

'Is she?' Ian muttered to Spud as he watched them go. He hadn't thought so himself, she'd seemed to be coming on strong. But then he was pretty bombed, maybe it was wishful thinking.

'No, she's not joking.' Spud noted the look Mayjay cast back at them and knew she was hoping they'd follow.

'Shit.'

Ian didn't even think to ask Spud how he knew the workings of Mayjay's mind. Like a moth to a flame, he followed the pair as they disappeared into the sandhills. He wasn't sure what he was going to do, maybe he'd just wait his turn, but shit, he was in with a chance.

Spud, stone cold sober, knew that he should pull the plug right there and then. Pembo was booze- and drug-affected, and his groin was ruling his head. There was bound to be trouble. But he didn't pull the plug.

'Don't let Mike see you,' he muttered as together they followed the shadowy shapes in the distance. Spud couldn't resist. He wanted to know.

'She likes it kinky,' he said.

CHAPTER TEN

The night was cloudless and the moon near full, its reflection on the sea's still surface casting an eerie half-light across the beach. On the foreshore and dotted about amongst the nearby sandhills people were dimly visible, some huddled in groups passing around a joint or a bottle, some in pairs kissing and petting, one couple openly in the throes of sex. No-one paid the slightest attention to Mike and Mayjay as they made their way to the boatshed.

'Here'll do.' Mayjay halted. She didn't want to wait any longer; she wanted to rut in the sand like the couple they'd just passed. Her hands went to the belt of his trousers, her sandals, looped over her wrists, getting in the way as she fumbled clumsily with the buckle.

Mike stopped her, although he, too, was aroused. God, the woman was on heat.

'It's not far,' he said. 'A bit further down the beach.'

The rambling old boatshed stood on stilts several feet above the sand, a wooden ramp leading down from the side facing the sea. The big double doors allowing access to the ramp were bolted from the inside, and the entrance was via a single door at the front. Mike quickly found the key – it was where it had always been, under the broken ledge of the side window. But it wouldn't have mattered if it hadn't been there. The window was broken, they could easily have climbed in.

He led the way to the front, undid the padlock and slid back the bolt. The door creaked on its rusty old hinges as he opened it, and they stepped inside to the musty smell of wood.

Mayjay's eyes flickered about, taking in her surrounds. Two surf boats, highly polished and heavily adorned with sponsors' logos, stood ready for action, and life-saving equipment hung from the wooden beams either side of the shed. Ropes and pulleys dangled from huge hooks, and from smaller hooks, balls of twine, coiled wire, tools. This was a masculine place, a realm forbidden to women. She was glad they'd come here, it was illicit and exciting.

Mike was about to close the door.

'Leave it,' she said, turning to face him. 'I want to see.'

Dropping her sandals and evening bag to the floor, she hauled the red mini dress up and over her head in one swift movement and stood naked before him but for her silk panties. She wore no brassiere. Mayjay not only wanted to see, she wanted to be seen. She never had sex in the dark, she liked to be looked at. Now, in the moon's dull glow through the window opposite her and the light that filtered through the open door to her left, she knew she could be seen, albeit dimly, by anyone who chose to peer into the boatshed. As she slid her panties down over her buttocks, she wondered whether the others had followed. She hoped they had; she was in the mood for an audience.

The sight of her body sent Mike's pulse racing and he quickly stripped from the waist down. As he reached for her, she stopped him, a hand on his chest.

'This too,' she said, slipping his open shirt off his shoulders. 'I want to feel all of you.'

Both of them now naked, she snaked her body against

his, sliding his hardened penis between her legs, closing her thighs on him, undulating her pelvis, her breasts rubbing against his chest. But Mike was no longer in the mood to be teased. Their foreplay had been conducted on the dance floor. With a hand beneath her buttocks, he hoisted her off her feet, prepared to take her against the wall.

Mayjay wrapped her legs around him, opening herself for him. She liked it standing up, and she wanted it brutal tonight. It was then that she saw the shapes at the window opposite. She couldn't make out who they were, but she knew. Spud and Pembo were watching. Her audience had arrived.

'Wait.' She struggled free, diving for the floor, scrabbling about in the gloom for Mike's trousers and the belt.

Mike watched, bewildered. What the hell was going on? Would she prefer they did it on the floor? He was about to join her, but she stood, his belt in her hand, threading it through the buckle and looping it like a noose around her neck.

'Pull on the belt when I tell you to,' she said, backing against the wall, her eyes on the window. The thought of the two watching was the biggest turn-on of all.

Mike paid no heed to the belt dangling between them as he once again hoisted her onto his hips. He had no idea what she meant and he was past caring as he thrust himself into her.

Mayjay's eyes remained fixed on the window.

'Jesus Christ, does she know we're here?' Ian whispered. All they could see were the two shadowy shapes bucking against the wall, but from the direction of her head, Ian could swear she was looking right at them.

Spud didn't answer. Oh yes, he thought, she knew only too well they were there. He waited to see what she'd do with the belt. He'd been waiting to find out since he was seventeen years old.

Mayjay was steadily working herself towards orgasm. It wasn't far off now, and she was looking forward to sharing the thrill of it with her audience. Watch and learn, boys, she thought.

'Pull on the belt,' she hissed. 'Pull hard on the belt.'

But Mike didn't hear her, or if he did he, chose not to – he was lost in his own sexual drive. Pembo had been right about the pills, he thought as their bodies pounded together mercilessly – even at this rate he felt he could go all night.

She pulled on the belt herself, closing off the carotid artery, waiting for the delicious flood of trapped blood to the brain that would heighten her orgasm tenfold. But it wasn't working, she wasn't able to sustain a constant steady pressure, their sex was too violent, too disruptive. She needed a willing partner.

'Pull on the belt,' she urged again, but still Mike wasn't listening. Damn him, she thought, and reaching up her hand, she ran it along the wooden beam just above her head, searching for a hook or a nail. She'd done it before when a sexual partner wouldn't join in the game, tying a noose to the bedhead, often passing out at the height of her orgasm. That, too, was part of the pleasure – the look of shock on the man's face when she regained her senses.

Mike was distracted. She'd been matching him equally, but she'd broken the rhythm. What on earth was she doing?

She thrust the belt into his hand. 'Hang it from something,' she urged.

He hesitated, confused.

'Do it, Mike!' She started up her own rhythm, clenching her muscles, drawing him into her, then releasing, then drawing him deeper. 'It'll be good for you too, I promise.'

Locked together, he edged her clumsily along the wall, fumbling about above her head, the feel of her driving him on. It was bizarre, but if this was the way she wanted it . . . He found what he was after, and, discarding the ball of twine that hung from the rusty cup hook, he forced one of the belt's eyelets over it.

'Yes,' she hissed, 'yes,' and she pulled her head forward, the belt tight about her neck.

To Mike, the sight was disturbing but intensely erotic.

Spud peered through the grime of the window. 'What's happening with the belt?' he asked in a whisper. He'd seen her put it around her neck, but couldn't make out what was going on. All he could see was their frantic coupling.

'I don't know.' Ian didn't take his eyes from the pair. 'I think they've hung it from something.'

After the initial and impressive sight of Mayjay naked, Spud and Ian hadn't found the spectacle as erotic as they'd anticipated. It had actually been funny to start with, seeing Mike's buttocks thumping away. Now they were only too interested in what was going on with the belt.

'Come on.' Spud crept towards the corner of the shed, heading for the open front door. He turned back as Ian hesitated. 'They won't see us, you silly bastard. Christ, listen to them, they're going at it hammer and tongs.'

Even from where the two stood, they could hear the animal grunts that matched the increasingly urgent pound of bodies against wood. Seconds later, as they peered through the door, the couple inside was so oblivious to the intrusion that Spud and Ian didn't bother disguising their presence, but stood transfixed by the sight.

'Good God, she's strangling herself,' Ian whispered. 'Shouldn't we do something?'

'No.' Spud watched, fascinated. 'She likes it this way.'

Mayjay had forgotten her audience. She was writhing in an orgasmic frenzy. Her circulation cut off, the rush of pleasure overwhelmed her and she started to go into spasm. Waves of ecstasy were engulfing her, she was delirious. Any moment she would faint.

Mike could feel her body shuddering, her muscles clenching around him. The force of her orgasm was bringing him to his own climax.

The old wooden floorboards could take no more. They collapsed under the strain. And Mike, on the threshold of ejaculation, collapsed with them, his feet disappearing through the floor, Mayjay ripped from his grasp as he landed heavily on his backside.

The sight was so ludicrous that Spud and Ian couldn't help themselves – they burst into laughter.

Mike heard his mates laughing uproariously, but he took no notice. Mayjay's feet were right before him, her knees sagging. She was still hanging from the belt – he'd have to get her down before she suffocated. He hauled his legs out of the hole, amazed that she hadn't fallen with him, he wouldn't have thought the hook was that strong.

The moment he saw her face he knew she was dead. Her head was at a hideous angle, her eyes staring at him, her mouth grotesquely open, her tongue lolling out, clown-like.

The hook was certainly strong. Small as it was, it was made of steel, which, over the years, had rusted into the solid timber beam. It had been more than strong enough to withstand the brief, jarring weight of two bodies and the crack of a broken neck.

'Oh God!' Mike's voice was barely recognisable, a hoarse, disbelieving whisper. 'Oh God! Oh God!' he said over and over as he stared in stupefied horror at the twisted mask before him.

Spud and Ian had quickly sobered up. From their vantage point at the doorway, they'd registered that the girl hadn't landed on the floor along with Mike, that her form was still hanging there and that it was very still.

Now, as Mike stood dumbfounded, Spud took over. Jesus, he thought, was Mike that bombed out that he couldn't see the danger? The girl had fainted – they'd have to resuscitate her. If they left it much longer, she could suffocate. Why the hell was he just standing there?

'Come on, mate,' he urged, racing forward. 'We have to get her down before she strangles.'

'She's dead.' Mike couldn't take his eyes from her face. Nor could Spud.

'Oh Jesus!' His voice, like Mike's, was a horrified whisper. 'Oh Jesus, her neck's broken.'

It was Spud who first came to his senses, taking the girl's weight in his arms. 'Get the belt off the hook,' he ordered.

Ian crept tentatively forward, watching as the other two lifted the girl down and took the belt from around her neck. He clapped his hand over his mouth when he saw her lying there, her face contorted, her eyes fixed in a glassy stare. Then he started to whimper.

'Shut up, Pembo.' Spud closed the girl's eyes, he didn't want to look at them either. He pushed her tongue back inside her mouth and closed her jaw too.

Ian turned away, he was going to be sick.

Spud sprang into action, taking instant command. Christ alive, somebody had to, he thought. Pembo was about to throw up and Mike was glazed over like a bloody zombie

'Grab her clothes.' He directed the order at Ian. Then to Mike, 'Put your gear on.'

Ian did as he was told, thankful to be distracted, but Mike remained squatting by the girl, gazing uncomprehendingly at her. How had this happened?

'Get dressed, Mikey.' It was an order. 'Your leg's starting to bleed, we don't want to leave evidence.'

The remark jolted Mike briefly from his stupefied state. 'What do you mean? We have to call the police.'

'Nope, I'll look after things. Leave it to me.'

Spud had decided upon a course of action within seconds, and it didn't involve the police. Police entered Spud's equation only when they could prove useful, and his corrupt copper mates wouldn't be able to help him on this one.

Mike was confused. The girl was dead, surely they had to call the police. His mind was jumbled, he couldn't think clearly.

'Put your pants on – you're about to bleed on the floor.' Spud gathered up Mike's clothes and tossed them to him.

Mike stood, catching them instinctively, then swivelled his head to examine the back of his right thigh which was hurting. There was a gash, superficial, but it was starting to ooze blood. He dressed, still on automatic pilot, letting Spud take command. He didn't know what else to do.

'The belt as well.'

Spud chucked it to him, but Mike didn't instinctively catch it. He stared down to where it had landed at his feet.

'Put it on.' Spud gave the order with authority, watching as Mike slowly stooped to pick up the belt. Jesus, the bloke was on another planet, he thought. Taking the clothes Ian handed him, he fed the girl's feet through the panties. Ian turned away from the sight. Bugger you, Pembo, you could give me a hand, he thought. But he decided not to ask. Pembo'd only throw up. The panties in place, he started hauling the mini dress over the girl's head.

'We're in this together, mate,' he said. 'You know that, don't you?' It was a word of warning.

Spud had quite accurately read Ian's thoughts. Ian Pemberton didn't want any part of what was going on. He certainly didn't want to go to the cops. What would his parents say if he got mixed up in something as sordid as this? But he didn't want to help Spud cover up the girl's death either. He just wanted to run. He wanted to run from the boatshed and never look back. This was nothing to do with him.

'We stick together, Pembo.' Spud pulled the dress down over the girl's hips, lifting her body, grunting a little with the effort. 'It's what mates do.' He looked up at Ian. 'You

understand what I'm getting at, don't you?' This time it
was more than a word of warning; it was a distinct threat.

'Sure, Spud.' Ian turned; the girl was dressed now and
the sight easier to bear. 'I understand.' Their eyes met.
Sometimes Spud scared Ian.

Spud lifted the body from the floor, draping the girl's
arm over his shoulder, her head lolling drunkenly against
his. There was no point in asking the others for help; they
were both useless, in shock and still junked up, neither
thinking clearly.

'Give me her stuff.'

He took the sandals and evening bag Ian handed him
and, half-dragging, half-carrying the girl to the door, he
issued his final instructions. 'Lock the shed and put the key
back, then go to the Snake Pit and make yourselves seen.
Don't forget to take my gear – it's outside by the window.
I'll meet you there as soon as I can. If anyone asks, I'm in
the lavatory.'

Spud prayed that Mike's and Ian's gear would be where
they'd left it. If their jackets and shoes had been stolen, it
could prove an added complication. As he staggered off
towards the sandhills, he prayed, too, that he and Mayjay
looked like any other drunken couple.

He didn't actually need to stagger. He was strong and
bore her weight with ease, but every now and then he
lurched for effect, even muttering drunkenly for the benefit
of anyone who might see them, keeping his head down
all the while. It was a fine performance and he played it
with panache, but he hoped it was unnecessary. He was
heading away from the main beach area and there
appeared to be no-one around.

At the Snake Pit, the male vocalist was once more in full
flight and the activity on the dance floor was as wild as ever.

Mike's and Ian's jackets and shoes were miraculously
just where they'd left them, 'saving their possie in the

sand'. Ian immediately set about doing as Spud had instructed, making himself seen, dancing and flirting with every girl he could, albeit with a touch of desperation. Mike, however, sat by their jackets staring morosely into space, seeing nothing but the girl hanging there, his own belt about her neck. The same belt he now wore around his waist. How had it happened?

Spud returned, and proceeded to play loud and drunk although he was as sober as a judge. He danced with a couple of girls and sang along to 'Heartbreak Hotel', much to the vocalist's annoyance, then he went across the street to the pub where he bribed the barman to refill his flask.

He pretended to drink a lot of bourbon, but actually imbibed very little, encouraging the others to drink up, particularly Mike. Mike was muttering about the police again and Spud needed to keep him distracted.

'Not now, mate,' he murmured in reply. 'Not tonight. You're in no fit state to do anything tonight, we'll talk about it tomorrow. Come on, have another slug.'

They stayed at the Snake Pit until one in the morning and Mike was drunk when the three of them left in Ian's car. As they dropped him off at Claremont, Spud extracted a promise – from Ian too. They would meet here at Mike's place, he said, at ten o'clock, and they would say not one word about what had happened until then.

During the drive back to their city apartment, Spud refused to discuss the matter with Ian. 'I'm not saying anything while you're full of speed. We'll talk about it tomorrow, like I said.' And when they got home, he disappeared to his bedroom with a 'Night, Pembo', as if nothing had happened.

Ian was left with no option but to retire to his own bedroom, where he stared sleeplessly at the ceiling for hours, frightened out of his wits and wishing he'd stayed in Kalgoorlie.

*

The news was on the radio that morning, and on the television too. It hadn't made the newspapers yet, but it certainly would the following day.

Mayjay, the face of Western Australia, had been found dead at Scarborough Beach, her body discovered by two joggers shortly after dawn. The cause of death had been a broken neck and foul play was suspected. Police were keen to interview a gang of rockers who had caused a disturbance outside the Snake Pit the previous night.

The whole of WA was shocked.

'It was on the radio, did you hear it?'

Spud returned to the flat, having been out to buy the *Sunday Times* and a couple of takeaway coffees, to discover Ian pacing about in a state of agitation. Spud hadn't heard the radio report himself, but the people in the milk bar had been talking of nothing else.

'Of course it'll be on the radio. It'll be on the telly too, and tomorrow it'll be headline news all over Australia.'

Spud dumped the paper and coffees on the dining room table. Ian's agitation annoyed him. What the hell had he expected? That Mayjay's death wouldn't rate a mention?

'But they're hinting it was murder!'

'Why wouldn't they? People don't go around breaking their own bloody necks, especially not in the sandhills at Scarborough!' In his exasperation, Spud raised his voice. He was feeling a bit jumpy himself and Ian's semi-hysteria wasn't helping. 'Get a grip on yourself, Pembo, and turn the telly on.'

After they'd watched the television newsflash, which all the channels were running at regular intervals, Ian started ranting again. Spud told him to shut up.

'We don't talk about it until we see Mike,' he said. 'That's what we agreed.'

They left the flat ten minutes later, Ian maintaining his silence but still twitchy.

It wasn't Ian's nervousness that was Spud's main concern, however. Pembo would keep his mouth shut through sheer terror, Spud knew it. Mike was the worry. The drugs and the booze would have worn off by now and Mike would want to do the right thing. Mike always did.

'I'm going to the police. I should have gone last night.'

It was just as Spud had feared.

The three of them stood at the end of Claremont jetty. The jetty had been Mike's idea; he'd seen from the balcony that it was deserted.

'I don't want you to come with me and I won't tell them you were there. It'll be exactly as it happened, just me and the girl.' Mike couldn't bring himself to say her name.

A huge weight lifted from Ian. He was off the hook.

'Oh yeah?' Spud sneered. 'And how did she get into the sandhills?'

'I took her there myself. I was scared, I didn't know what I was doing.'

The sneer faded and Spud spelled it out. 'You need witnesses, Mikey. You'll be dead in the water on your own – they'll have you up on a murder charge.'

'It was an accidental death.'

Like Ian, Mike had been awake most of the night. The effects of the speed pills had deprived him of sleep, but when the drunkenness had worn off, he'd been able to think through the events of the night and he'd prepared himself for the consequences.

'It was a ludicrous, hideous, meaningless death,' he said with deliberation, 'but it was an accident.' This was what he'd told himself, over and over as he'd tried to force the girl's contorted face from his mind.

A ludicrous, hideous, meaningless death? Spud was angry, Mike didn't appear to realise the implications.

'Jesus Christ, Mikey,' he burst out, 'this is Mayjay we're

talking about! The face of WA! It's been a state-wide
campaign, the government's involved! The press'll have a
field day and the coppers are going to need a scapegoat!'
He waited a moment for the penny to drop. 'Don't you
know what that means?'

'No. What does it mean, Spud?'

'It means you need us, mate. It means you need witnesses!'

Ian felt sick again. This was his worst nightmare.

Mike leaned against the corner pylon of the jetty, the
one he and Spud used to chuck bombies from when they
were kids. His knees were weak and the after-effects of the
pills had set in – he could feel the palpitations.

'Sit down, mate, you look bloody terrible.'

They sat, all three of them, Mike leaning against the
pylon, the other two with their knees hunched up. They
looked like overgrown kids in a huddle, planning some
mischievous prank.

'You know I'm making sense, don't you?' Spud asked.

'Yeah . . .' Mike could see that it would certainly look
bad without witnesses. 'But I'll take my chances, I'll go it
alone. Hell, it was me with the girl, wasn't it? You two
weren't involved.'

'Of course we were.'

'No, we weren't,' Ian interjected, seeing a way out. If
Mike wanted to go it alone, they should let him. Anything
rather than be dragged through the mud as a couple of
pervs who'd been watching a sex act that had ended up
going hideously wrong. He'd be labelled forever; his
parents would die of shame. 'Mike's right, Spud. It wasn't
us with the girl.'

'But it could have been, couldn't it?' Spud turned like a
rabid dog. 'Don't tell me you wouldn't have played her
games if she'd asked you to, Pembo – you were red hot for
it. I know I sure as hell would have. It just happened to be
Mike, didn't it? We're involved, *mate*, make no mistake

about that. And we stick together – that's what *mates* are for!'

His use of the word 'mate' was deliberately scathing. Pembo was a mate only when it suited him, and it was time he learned that mateship meant more than that. Much, much more.

Ian fell silent. He was no match for Spud, he'd do as he was told. But his life was shattered and he stared down at the jetty, absently picking at the old splintered wood, picturing it all – his parents' revulsion, the derision of his workmates. He'd never live it down.

'Don't worry, Pembo, you're off the hook.' Spud's tone remained scathing, but his eyes were on Mike as he made his announcement. 'We're not going to the cops, any of us.'

Mike, puzzled by the contradictory new tack, was about to interrupt.

'No, no, hear me out, Mikey, please,' Spud said reasonably, and Mike waited for him to continue.

'If you go to the police, Pembo and I go with you, whether you like it or not. If you try and go on your own then we'll simply front up, so there's no way around it.'

Mike made no reply, and Ian kept picking at his hole in the jetty.

'But have you thought about what it'll do to Pembo's family and career?'

Ian stopped fidgeting and looked up. Had he heard right?

'More importantly, have you thought about what it'll do to your own family? How do you think this'll affect your mum and dad? And what about *your* career, Mikey? You can say goodbye to the Pilbara trip for starters – you'll be in court. Then, even if you get off with some "death by misadventure" plea, it'll have been in every paper all over the country and who's going to want to employ a bloke with a past like yours? All those years of study down the drain.'

Spud had spent much time deliberating upon the argument he'd present, and he could see from Mike's

reaction that he'd taken the right tack. Mike hadn't
thought through the ramifications of this on the rest of his
life and the lives of his family; he'd been too preoccupied
with doing the right thing. Spud congratulated himself on
the added touch – the ruin of Pembo's life along with
Mike's own had been a pure stroke of genius. Personally,
he couldn't give a shit about Pembo's life. And he hadn't
even bothered using his own as leverage – adverse publicity certainly wouldn't ruin *him*. All of which had left him
wondering at his actions. Granted, he'd prefer to avoid
any involvement with the death of Ruby Chan's daughter,
but when it came to the crunch he'd be able to handle
Ruby. Spud had concluded that, for once, his motives were
quite possibly altruistic. He wanted to save Mikey. Mikey
was his mate.

He offered up the final clincher. It was a cliché to be
sure, but it was irrefutable.

'She's dead, Mikey. Ruining two families and two
careers won't change that. It won't bring her back.'

Ian's nod of agreement was concerned and caring, but
he felt like giving Spud a round of applause. God, Spud
was clever.

'So what do we do?' Mike said.

He hated himself at that moment. He couldn't pretend
that he was doing this for Pembo, although it was smart
of Spud to give him that out. He wasn't even doing it for
his family. His parents would be horrified, but they'd
stand by him, knowing that he'd done the right thing in
coming forward. He was doing this for himself. And it was
the act of a coward.

'We do nothing.' Spud got down to business. 'I'll
be interviewed, there's no two ways about that. I knew
Mayjay and I was part of the publicity campaign – the
coppers'll be chasing up everyone connected with her.
But I doubt whether they'll come at you blokes. They can't
interview everyone who was there last night.'

Ian's exhalation was audible, but his relief short-lived.

'Of course, it'll be a different matter if someone personally identifies you two as having been in her company.'

'What do we tell them?'

'You tell them the truth, Pembo. You had a chat with her, Mike had a dance with her.' Spud smiled sardonically. 'You just leave out the nasty bits.'

Extensive interviews were conducted during the investigation into Mayjay's death. The rockers all had alibis, most of which were backed up by the gang members themselves, and the police continued to grill them mercilessly. The rockers remained their principal suspects.

As far as it could be ascertained, the last person to have had any concrete exchange with the deceased was Qantas executive Brian Tomlinson. The deceased's personal publicist, Trish Barraclough, had witnessed the two leaving the sponsors' party, and had herself left the Scarborough Beach Hotel before ten o'clock, presuming her client was safe in the company of Mr Tomlinson. Mr Tomlinson, however, had remained in the main bar for half an hour; the barman, to whom he'd been chatting, observed him depart alone at around ten thirty. At approximately the same time, prominent businessman Spud Farrell had witnessed the deceased, and indeed talked briefly with her, at the Snake Pit.

Random interviews were carried out amongst the hundreds present that night, and several reported having observed Mayjay, both at the Snake Pit and outside in the street watching the fight between the rocker chick and the beauty contestant. No-one had noticed who Mayjay was with, and she'd not been sighted after that.

Mike McAllister and Ian Pemberton were not amongst those interviewed.

Across the entire country, the press was having a field day. With proprietorial dignity, the *West Australian* treated the case as a tragedy. *The shocking and untimely death of a young woman whose beauty symbolised the beauty of our state . . . All Western Australians mourn the loss of Mayjay.* The *West* also informed its readers that Mayjay had truly been one of them, a fact unknown by many who'd presumed she'd come from Sydney. Mayjay, one of the country's foremost models, it was reported, had been Mary-Jane Smith, born and bred in Perth.

No mention of Mary-Jane's mother, Ruby Chan, appeared in any media reportage. The police commissioner, a regular at the Sun Majestic Massage Parlour, had complied with Ruby's request that the press be denied her name and the details of her occupation. He'd agreed that it was only right, in deference to her daughter.

Some of the eastern states' tabloids differed in their approach. *BEACH GIRL BEAUTY MURDER!* was the headline that screamed from the front page of one Sydney daily. *MAYJAY, THE FACE OF WA, FOUND DEAD!*

Western Australians were outraged at the insensitivity, considering it typical of the disrespect displayed by eastern-staters towards the west. Their anger was justified: it was indeed tabloid journalism at its worst, and the editor knew he'd be rapped over the knuckles. A homicide had yet to be proved, but he'd been unable to resist the headline. To him, it was reminiscent of the Pyjama Girl Murder, and that had been a winner for years. It still was. Classics like the Pyjama Girl Murder could be trotted out every decade, particularly if the culprit wasn't found and the case remained a mystery. A good reporter could drum up all kinds of twists and turns, even conspiracy theories, out of unsolved crimes with catchy titles. The Beach Girl Beauty Murder was a journo's dream come true.

Two weeks later, when Ian Pemberton returned to Kalgoorlie, the reportage was still extensive but no longer front page. And a month after that, the police having made no headway with their investigations, things seemed to have reached a stalemate. Even for the press.

'You've got to try and put it out of your mind, Mikey.'

Spud's eyes remained on the road as he drove across the Causeway, but he could feel the tension in Mike seated beside him. It was palpable; it had been ever since that night. Or perhaps it was only when Mike was with him, he thought. It was difficult to tell, they'd stopped going out together socially. Mike had kept pretty much to himself, and the few times Spud had called around, he hadn't been communicative. In Spud's opinion, it was high time they talked.

Mike stared out the window. He'd known Spud would want to talk. They'd *both* known Spud would want to talk. It was why he'd originally refused the offer of a lift to the airport, and why Spud had insisted.

Spud's eyes flickered from the road as Mike remained silent. 'You can't let it wear you down like this, mate. It's not healthy, you know.'

'Yeah, yeah.' Mike's response was testy. 'I know.'

'You don't want to talk about it, do you?'

'You're a mind-reader, Spud.'

'Right.' Spud took his aggression out on the car and they zoomed down Canning Highway well over the speed limit. 'We won't talk then,' he snapped. Fat lot of thanks he got for saving the bloke's hide!

Mike felt guilty as they pulled up at the airport. It wasn't fair of him to take things out on Spud. Rightly or wrongly, Spud had put himself at risk for the sake of his mate. It wasn't Spud who was the coward.

Spud opened the boot and Mike heaved out his gear.

'Thanks for the lift.'

Sensing that Mike didn't want him to come into the airport, Spud's anger turned to hurt. Mikey was closing him out.

'Rightio,' he said abruptly. 'I'll see you then.'

'Listen to me, Spud.' Mike stopped him as he started to move off. 'Things between us haven't changed.' It was a lie, Mike thought, things between them *had* changed. They'd changed because *he'd* changed. He'd changed irrevocably. But that wasn't Spud's fault. 'You're my best friend, you always have been, and I'm grateful for . . . for everything you did.' He had difficulty getting the words out. 'I just can't talk about it, that's all.'

The girl's face was there as he said it, eyes staring, tongue lolling. She'd always be there, with his belt around her neck. He'd wondered whether if he'd given himself up, things might be different; whether he might have found some form of exoneration in admitting his guilt. But then the coward in him had hoped that he'd never know.

Spud grinned his forgiveness. 'Not another word, mate, not another word.' He flung his arms around Mike. 'Mates forever, eh, Mikey?'

'Yep.' Mike returned the embrace. 'Mates forever.'

Mike shouldered his pack and, suitcase in hand, walked into the airport. Spud watched him go. Poor old Mikey, he thought, he was doing it hard. But he'd get over it. Up there in the Pilbara it would all just become a bad dream.

BOOK THREE

CHAPTER ELEVEN

The old wooden rocking chair creaked rhythmically, a comforting sound, as Jo rocked gently back and forth. A tiny, perfect hand encircled her forefinger, tugging in time with the mouth that suckled greedily at her breast, and the blackest of eyelashes fluttered in frenzied ecstasy. Feeding time was always an orgy. Jo laughed, overwhelmed by an indescribable love.

Johanna Whitely had given birth to a baby girl at Sydney's Royal Hospital for Women in September 1967. She called her Alana.

There was no hidden agenda in her choice. She intended to make no claims on Mike, she didn't even expect to see him again. And if she did, and if he mistakenly read some meaning into the fact that she'd named her baby Alana, then she'd simply tell him the truth. It was a pretty name. She'd always loved it.

Jo had her personal reasons for the choice. Her own childhood memories were not happy, and she wanted a past to share with her daughter. That past, she'd decided, would be Mike's. She'd paint pictures for the child of the lovely old house by the river where her father had grown up, and the sailing boats and the jetty and Baxter the dog.

Perhaps, when Alana was old enough, she might even tell her that she'd been conceived on Christmas Day aboard a beautiful yacht. A yacht called *Alana*. It wouldn't altogether be the truth, but it was a nicely romantic white lie. And it *had* happened on Christmas Day.

At first Jo had cursed that afternoon in Mike's side verandah bedroom. It had been one of just two occasions when they'd had unprotected sex – after their first time, she'd had herself fitted with a diaphragm. But she hadn't taken it with her that Christmas Day, she hadn't thought she'd need it.

When her worst fears had been confirmed, she'd been unable to tell Mike. As she'd listened to him talk of his career plans, so excited by the offer of the Pilbara expedition the following year, she'd known finally and conclusively that she held no place in his future. She'd always felt insecure, but she'd lived in hope. Now, carrying his child, she'd been able deceive herself no longer.

During the ensuing fortnight in Manjimup, she'd made her plans, keeping the news also from her mother. Her mother would insist upon her staying at home, and Jo had vowed to herself she would never again live under the same roof as Darren Collins.

Terrifying as the prospect of single motherhood had been, never once had she contemplated abortion as an option. Which rather surprised her. Having always professed herself an agnostic – mainly in order to avoid conversations about religion – she had supposed that she believed, as the feminists advocated, in a woman's right of choice. But when faced with her own personal dilemma, the right of choice had not seemed to apply to her. She'd wondered whether perhaps she was not an agnostic after all. Perhaps she really did believe in divine retribution.

In her characteristically practical fashion, Jo had persuaded herself that it was meant to be. At least it had brought about a decision. She might have waited years, possibly her whole life, in the hope that Mike would recognise the value of the love they shared. For she didn't doubt that, in his own way, he loved her, even though his career overshadowed the fact. But she didn't want to wait forever in the wings of someone else's life. And she couldn't saddle him with a child. Not now. He needed to be free. And so did she. A child wouldn't ruin her life, she'd decided, a child would enrich it. She would do everything she'd intended. She would complete her degree, she would take up a career in medicine, and she would have a child with whom to share it all.

When she'd arrived in Sydney, she'd contacted her aunt, as she'd promised her mother she would.

'As soon as Nora's helped you get settled, you'll let us know where you are, won't you?' her mother had said. Hillary Collins hadn't enjoyed telephoning her younger sister to ask for the favour. She and Nora had been estranged for years, the exchange of dutiful Christmas and birthday cards being their only form of communication. But she'd had little choice: Johanna had been insistent upon going to Sydney. Why on earth the girl would want to continue her studies in the east was beyond Hillary's comprehension, but then Jo had always been wayward and unpredictable. She was probably moving to Sydney out of spite, just to put extra distance between her and Darren, Hillary had thought. If so, it was extraordinarily ungrateful after all the help he'd given her.

'Darren will continue to send your allowance,' she'd said meaningfully.

'Thank you, that's very kind of him.'

Even without her mother's instigating phone call, Jo had intended getting in touch with her aunt. Nora was the only person she knew in Sydney and she'd need a contact. Perhaps even a confidante, although she hadn't been sure how much information she would share with Nora.

Unlike her mother, Jo had kept in touch with Nora over

the years, the two regularly corresponding. She hadn't seen her aunt since she was a child, but Nora had at one time been the most important influence in her life. Moving into the family home in South Perth shortly after the death of Jo's father, it was Nora who had helped Hillary through the grieving process and it had been Nora who had cared for the lonely, devastated little girl. She'd stayed with them for three years, holding the fragile household together while she completed her psychology degree at UWA. Then, not long after Hillary's remarriage, Nora had moved to Sydney, and a year or so after that she herself had married.

Hillary hadn't travelled to Sydney for her only sister's wedding, a fact which Jo, even at the age of eleven, had found strange, particularly as Nora had been such a mainstay in her mother's hour of need. She'd found it strange, also, that as the years progressed Nora had rarely been mentioned, and when she herself had talked of her, her mother had been non-communicative, showing little interest in her younger sister.

'She's a Sydney-sider now,' Hillary had said dismissively. 'You can write if you like, but I can't be bothered myself. I feel we don't have much in common any more. East and west don't mix.' It was as if they existed in two different worlds.

Jo had never known how, or why, the estrangement between the sisters had occurred, but she'd found out shortly after her arrival in Sydney.

Nora had welcomed her with open arms, insisting Jo stay with her and her family in their terrace house in Potts Point.

'At least until we can find you somewhere decent,' she'd said. 'You'll want a place close to uni, I suppose.'

'Yes, I suppose I will.'

Jo hadn't told her aunt that it could be years before she'd be looking at uni. She hadn't really thought about it too much herself. She'd have the baby, then figure out what to do. One step at a time.

Nora was everything Jo remembered: strong, direct, capable, and with a sense of humour that at times enjoyed shocking. Slim and athletically attractive, she hadn't even seemed to have aged, although she appeared a lot smaller than Jo recalled. But then, she supposed, grown-ups always look big to a nine year old, and children take little notice of age.

'How do you get on with Darren?' Nora asked.

'Fine.'

Jo had been in Sydney only a week when Nora had plonked the question into what had seemed like a general conversation about her life in Perth at uni and her holidays spent in Manjimup.

'No. I mean, how do you *really* get on with Darren. Do you like him?'

They were sitting on the back balcony looking out over the tiny cottages of Woolloomooloo, and beyond that the Domain and the city skyline dominated by the massive arch of the Harbour Bridge. Nora's house was one in a long string of impressive terraces that fronted on to Victoria Street and which were currently under threat by greedy developers and corrupt town-planners. 'They're trying to illegally change the residential zoning so they can build high-rise blocks and take advantage of the view,' Nora had said. 'They're offering people a fortune to sell up, but Geoff and I are going to stay put. We'll fight them all the way.' Built on a sandstone ridge overlooking the valley, the terraces had a truly spectacular view from the rear.

Jo became aware that Nora was studying her keenly, already reading something into her reservation.

'No, I *don't* like him much,' she admitted. Then, as her aunt continued to study her, waiting for more, she decided that she might as well tell the truth. 'Actually, I can't stand him.'

'That's what I thought – you've never mentioned him in your letters. Why can't you stand him, Jo?'

'Because he's destroyed my relationship with Mum.'

'Did he ever do anything to you?'

Jo faltered. She'd been about to tell Nora everything, but the question had taken her by surprise. It had been so blunt, so direct. What *was* there to tell? *When I was a child he used to look at me, and make excuses to touch me, and I didn't like him.* It would sound exactly the same as it would have sounded to her mother had she ever told her: the over-reaction of a child still grieving the death of her father and jealous of her mother's new husband. That was surely the way Nora would see it. She might even try to defend Darren. 'But he was only trying to be a good stepfather,' she might say. Jo wasn't having a bar of it.

'No, he never did anything.'

Nora could see that the girl had closed off. 'He did to me,' she said. Good, that had got her attention. 'He raped me in the front room of the house in South Perth while you and your mum were at the Royal Show.'

That had more than got her attention. In fact, Nora found it rather comical the way her beautifully elegant young niece's eyes widened and her jaw gaped. Jo was, understandably, gob-smacked. But there was more to come.

'It was just before Hillary married him,' she said. 'I was twenty-three years old and a virgin.' She smiled, end of shock tactics. 'It was the fifties, remember, we kept ourselves for Mr Right in those days.'

'He *raped* you?' Jo's voice was a barely audible whisper.

'Well, it started out as seduction – a kiss and a cuddle on the front room sofa where Hill served tea to visitors she was trying to impress. I have to admit that I found it so thrillingly wicked I went along with it for a while.

Perhaps I was trying to prove a point to myself,' Nora added in all honesty. 'I used to be jealous of Hill as a kid. She was eight years older than me, a real stunner, and I was the scrawny kid sister, playing the tomboy when I really didn't want to. I'd always wished that boys would flock to me the way they did to Hill. I suppose I was proving some sort of point to myself, letting her fiancé have a bit of a pash. And let's face it, Darren's a very good-looking man.'

Jo made no comment. She'd never found him so personally.

'Anyway,' Nora continued, 'after a few minutes he started to grope me, and when I tried to call a halt he accused me of being a prick-teaser.' Another shrug of honesty. 'I suppose he was right in a way, wasn't he? But at twenty-three, even though I'd looked after you and Hill – who, frankly, was a mess when your dad died – I was still a dumb kid sexually. I tried to reason with him. I said I was sorry, I hadn't meant to lead him on, he was my sister's fiancé and it had been terrible of me . . . But it didn't stop him, and that's when the whole thing got ugly. He told me I was a slut and that I wanted it, and that he was the one who was going to give it to me. He knew I was a virgin.'

Nora had spoken throughout in her customary wry manner, without a hint of melodrama, and she concluded in exactly the same way.

'Afterwards, he warned me that if I told Hill what had happened, he'd say I threw myself at him, that he knocked me back, and that I was making up the story because I was afraid he'd tell her. He was supremely confident. *She'll believe me. You won't have a leg to stand on.* Those were his exact words.'

Nora sat back, story over. 'And that's it, kiddo. Oh, just for the record, let's keep it between ourselves. I've never told Geoff. He hasn't met Hillary, but he may some day, and it's something he doesn't need to know.' She nodded encouragingly. 'We're in agreement, Jo: Darren's not a nice man. So why don't you tell me what he did to you?'

'But you *did* tell Mum, didn't you? What did she say?'

'She believed him, of course. I'd always been jealous . . . I didn't want her to be happy . . . I couldn't get a man of my own so I'd tried to steal hers . . . She got really hysterical. Darren was right – I didn't have a leg to stand on.'

'But why? Why would Mum be so gullible? After everything you'd done for her? For both of us?'

Nora hadn't wanted to go into the details of what she truly believed; she'd told her story only as encouragement for Jo to tell hers. But the girl seemed intent upon hearing the truth, and it might help if she understood her mother's obsession with the man she so detested.

'Hillary did it tough when your dad came home from the war,' she said, treading gently. This was delicate ground.

'So did Dad.'

It was a defensive reaction, and Nora wasn't surprised. Jo had been only six when her father had died. She remembered him as the gentle creature he'd been in his last years; a beautiful man, certainly, but fragile, dying.

'He was gassed in the war, Jo.'

'I know that. I've always known that.' Defensive again. Jo wasn't sure why they were discussing her father.

'Hillary was thrilled when he came home, and seemingly in one piece. She'd been worried sick, of course. She thought that now he was back, everything would return to normal. But it didn't. A year later, the war was over but Hill's own troubles were just beginning. Your dad was a very sick man.'

'What exactly are you trying to say? That Mum was thankful when he died?'

'No, not at all, she loved him very much.' Damn, Nora thought, she'd known this would be difficult. Perhaps she should have left it alone. 'I'm just trying to explain the hold Darren had over your mother. She was in her early thirties, a sensual young woman, and your father had been an invalid for years –'

'I was born in 1945, Nora, Dad couldn't have been impotent.'

'Of course not.'

Well, perhaps not in the euphoria of his homecoming, Nora thought, but didn't the girl recall the constant attacks and the struggle for breath in those final years? Didn't she remember the oxygen tank always at the ready? Was her memory that selective?

No longer merely on the defensive, Jo's reply had carried a touch of belligerence and Nora realised that to explain the reasons for Hillary's blind obsession with Darren was pointless. Jo was too preoccupied with her own obsession, too determined to preserve the image of a man she could barely recall. Nora found the fierce way she clung to the memory of her father intensely moving. It was as if he were all that she had.

'I'm just saying that your mother was vulnerable, Jo,' she continued gently. 'She was a lonely woman, devastated by your father's death, and Darren swept her off her feet.'

He certainly had, she thought, in every sense. Hillary had regaled her with details of Darren's sexual prowess in those days when they'd talked as sisters. *You wanted to know what it was like, didn't you, Nora?* That was another of the vicious accusations Hillary had flung at her after the rape.

'And so she believed him over you, the sister who'd nursed her through her grief? Who'd looked after her daughter?' Jo remained unforgiving. Nora's attempted explanation had only reignited the antagonism she felt towards her mother. 'I'm afraid it doesn't cut any ice with me.'

Well, at least they'd got off the subject of her father, Nora thought, regretful that she'd brought the matter up.

She hadn't realised that Jo would be so zealously overprotective.

'Your turn, kiddo,' she said. 'Tell me about Darren.'

Jo, also relieved by the change of subject, told her
aunt everything, the story of her childhood tumbling out
unchecked, the second time only in the whole of her life
that she'd spoken of it. She'd found a certain relief in the
guarded version she'd shared with Mike, but this was
different, a total unburdening. Nora was far more than
just a caring and sympathetic listener. Nora knew precisely
what she was talking about. Nora knew Darren.

'That's why I hate him,' she said fifteen minutes later.
'Not for what he did to me, but for what he did to me and
Mum. He put a wall up between us.'

Suddenly aware that her story must have sounded in-
adequate in the face of Nora's, Jo stared self-consciously
down at the wooden deck of the balcony. 'I'm sorry, I've
gone on about nothing really, haven't I? I mean, what
did he do to me? He didn't *rape* me, he didn't take my
virginity, did he?'

Nora said nothing but her heart went out to the girl.
No, she thought, he didn't take your virginity, kiddo. He
took much, much more. He took your childhood. Why
had it never occurred to her that Darren might make overtures towards Hillary's daughter, she thought guiltily. Of
course he would. Darren Collins was a monster.

Jo continued to stare miserably at the decking. 'I just
wish I could have told Mum, that's all.'

'She wouldn't have believed you.'

'I know.'

'No, kiddo, you *don't* know.' Nora paused, waiting for
the girl to look up at her. 'It's your mother who knows.'
She let the words sink in before she continued. 'I believe
that Hillary's always known. Just as she knew that I was
telling the truth all those years ago.'

'Then *why*?' Jo was incredulous, it seemed an extraordinary statement. 'Why didn't she believe you? Why wouldn't she have believed me, if I'd told her?'

'She couldn't afford to. She still can't. I doubt whether she'll ever allow herself to face the truth. At least, that's my belief.'

'How can you be so sure?'

'Is she still the same with him? When Darren's in the room, there's no-one else there?'

Jo remembered the times, too innumerable to mention, when she'd seemed invisible to her mother. 'Yes,' she said.

'That's how it was from the moment they first met. Hillary's entire existence revolves around him, it always has. She's blinded herself to anything she perceives as a threat – her sister, her daughter, even the man himself. She can't afford to believe anything bad of Darren, and he knows it. Golly, he could probably get away with murder if he chose to. In Hill's eyes, anyway.'

Jo was no longer incredulous. Everything Nora said rang true. She'd always known her mother wouldn't believe her, but had she sensed that her mother didn't *want* to believe her? Was that why she'd kept silent all those years? She could see herself now, edging away as Darren stroked her pretty new dress, his hands straying across her shoulders and arms. She could see her mother entering the room, Darren continuing to stroke her, less lasciviously, his face bland and paternal, but nonetheless secure in his actions. She could hear both of them commenting on what a pretty dress it was, and she could feel herself wondering why her mother couldn't see that something was terribly wrong.

She felt sickened and angry. Thank God she'd developed her own strength. She remembered how, as she'd got older, she'd stood her ground, staring him down, defying him to go that step further, hoping her mother would catch him out, her boldness scaring him off. Darren had proved a coward, which was just as well, she now thought. What would it have taken for her mother to defend her? A rape, like Nora's? Or would Hillary have turned a blind eye to that too?

'Don't be angry with your mother, Jo. She can't help it, she's her own victim.'

This time Nora didn't regret having spoken as she had. Better that Jo should understand her mother, she thought. Perhaps one day she may even feel sorry for her. Nora certainly did.

'Poor Hillary,' she said, 'it's tragic. She's denied herself friends and family for years. She's built herself a prison, and she'll lock us all out rather than admit to a truth which, deep down, she knows.'

'I wonder if she'll lock out her grandchild.'

It was Jo's turn to shock, although that hadn't been her intention. Today was a day for confessions, and now seemed the perfect time to tell Nora. Besides, it was good to have an ally.

An hour later, the peace of the afternoon was shattered as Stevie and Paula, ten and eight years old respectively, arrived home from school. But by that time, the plans were set in motion.

'Jo's not going to get a flat after all,' Nora announced. 'She's going to be staying with us.'

'Beauty bottler!' Stevie yelled.

Jo had already established herself as a favourite with Nora's children, and Stevie's hug was quickly followed by Paula's before the two raced off to to make themselves Vegemite sandwiches.

'He gets it from old Uncle Ted,' Nora had explained upon Jo's first meeting with the children, 'along with "whacko the diddle-o" and "strike me lucky" and all the rest. I like it.' She'd promised to take Jo to meet old Uncle Ted who lived in the Blue Mountains. He'd been in World War One and was a colourful bloke, she'd said, the kids both adored him. Jo, who had never met her mother's uncle, had realised that she was more surrounded by relatives in Sydney than she'd ever been in her life.

As she watched the children gallop away towards the kitchen, Nora yelling after them, 'It's not a race!', a sense of family overwhelmed her and she fought back the embarrassing threat of tears.

'Don't you think you'd better discuss all this with Geoff first?' she said, looking away and blinking rapidly, hoping that Nora hadn't perceived her moment of weakness. Jo rarely cried, and never in the presence of others.

'Rubbish, there's tons of room and he adores you. He did the moment he met you, and why on earth wouldn't he? We're family.'

That was all it took. Jo's eyes welled, and she focused on the multi-storey car park – the one ugly feature that marred the otherwise perfect view. 'You're right, the car park's an absolute monstrosity,' she said, willing the tears to stay in their sockets.

'Let it out, kiddo.' Nora shifted her chair close and gathered Jo in her arms. 'Come on now, let it out.'

Jo sobbed as she never had before. It had been an afternoon of revelations and she was drained.

'There, there.' Nora, a small woman, considerably shorter than Jo, cuddled the girl to her breast like a gawky child. 'You're not alone any more,' she crooned.

Jo felt ridiculous, and sobbed all the more.

She gathered herself together only minutes later, and Nora, aware that her niece was unaccustomed to such outbursts of emotion, shifted away to give her space.

'Did you really think you could do all this on your own?' she asked.

'Yes.'

Despite the tear-stained face, the look in the hazel-green eyes was one of unwavering resolution, and Nora realised that the girl most certainly would have done it on her own. She was strong, there was no doubt about that.

'Well, now you don't have to,' she said.

'I know. And I'm glad,' Jo admitted. 'Thank you.'

'Why thank me?' Nora grinned wickedly. 'With two kids at school, me not working and Geoff on a government salary, Darren's money will come in handy I can promise you.'

Jo had insisted that if she were to stay with them, she would pay her way, and as she returned Nora's smile, albeit shakily, she realised this was another first. She'd always felt guilty about accepting Darren's money. She didn't any more.

'Why on earth should you?' Nora had said when she'd expressed her guilt. 'You're earning it. He's paying for your silence, placing you in his debt, just in case.'

Nora's smile faded now; there was one other issue they needed to address.

'You must tell your mother about the pregnancy,' she said.

'Not just yet.' Jo's reply was detached. 'I'll leave it for a while.'

'At least let me ring her and let her know you're staying on here with us.'

'No. Mike will be trying to find out where I am. It's better that she doesn't have a contact to give him.'

'What do I say then?'

'That I'm visiting old Uncle Ted in the Blue Mountains.'

'You'll have to tell her sometime, kiddo.'

'I will.'

Jo didn't tell her mother until shortly before the baby was born. She telephoned and they chatted intermittently, but she never said a word about her pregnancy. And her mother didn't question her about why she'd not yet enrolled at Sydney University, accepting Jo's glib explanation that she was taking a year off and working part-time as a receptionist in a doctor's Macquarie Street rooms, which she was. Hillary's main concern appeared to be the accommodation arrangements.

'I thought you were going to get a flat,' she said. 'It doesn't seem right that you should bludge off Nora.'

'I'm not. We've made a business deal. I'm paying her full Sydney rental rates each week. I checked the going price for Potts Point.'

'Oh. Well, I suppose that's all right. I mean, it's very kind of Nora to take you in, but I don't want to be beholden to her.'

The response to the phone call six months later was far less complacent.

'You're *what*?'

'I'm pregnant.'

There was a very long pause. Then: 'What are you going to do about it?'

'What do you mean?'

'Well, you're not married. You're not going to *have* it, surely.'

'I'm due in two weeks, Mum.'

'Oh my God.' An audible gasp followed, then Darren's voice. 'What is it, what's wrong?' Then a muffled exchange between the two, her mother obviously putting her hand over the receiver. Jo couldn't make out the words. But when Hillary's voice came back down the line it was bordering on hysterical.

'Why didn't you tell me? For God's sake, Johanna, why didn't you *tell* me! What did you plan to do? Have a child without telling your own *mother*?' She was working herself into a frenzy. 'Don't I *mean* anything to you? You're my *daughter*, how could you do this to me? To *both* of us? Darren's appalled too. How could you keep it a secret from us?'

Her mother was genuinely distraught, and Jo supposed she should feel guilty, or at least concerned, but she felt very little of anything.

Then Darren came on the line.

'Your mother's pretty upset, Johanna.'

'Yes, I can hear that.'

'You should have told us.'

'Yes.'

'I'll bring her to Sydney, of course. We'll be there for the birth.'

'No. Don't come over. Tell Mum I'll ring her as soon as the baby's born.'

A pause. 'This is very cruel, you know. You're breaking your mother's heart, I hope you realise that.'

'I don't mean to. Tell her I'm sorry.'

Jo hung up. It *was* cruel of her, she thought. But it was necessary.

CHAPTER TWELVE

Shortly after Alana's birth, Jo rang her mother as she'd promised she would. She suggested that Hillary come to Sydney on her own.

'If you don't mind, Mum,' she said. 'I can't wait to see you and show you the baby, but I'm really tired, I don't feel like socialising.'

Hillary was both hurt and offended. 'Darren's your stepfather, I hardly call that socialising.'

'All right, sorry.' Jo didn't have the energy to argue, she'd returned home from hospital just the previous day and was genuinely exhausted. Besides, if she were ever to confront her mother about Darren, it would not be over the telephone. 'But could we keep the first visit just between us? You know, mother, daughter, grand-daughter – it's something special, don't you think?'

The excuse was perfectly plausible and just what Hillary needed to hear. She was more than mollified, she was deeply touched.

'Yes, darling, of course it's something special. It's something very, very special. And I can't wait to see you too, both of you. Alana, what a lovely name.'

*

Hillary didn't stay at the Potts Point house for the four days of her visit, although Nora and Geoff had extended an invitation. She'd made a reservation at the Hilton in the city instead.

'Golly, Hill, it's a bit extravagant,' Nora said after she'd embraced her sister at the front door. Hillary had also refused to let Geoff pick her up at the airport, preferring to get a taxi straight to the hotel in order to freshen up before seeing them. 'Why stay at a posh place when we've got heaps of room here?'

'Oh, you know me, Nor.' Hillary laughed gaily. 'I love staying at posh places.'

'That's true. Come on in.' Nora led the way through to the lounge room.

'This is Geoff,' she said, introducing the pleasant, un-assuming-looking man who, having taken the afternoon off work in order to meet his wife's sister, had been waiting patiently for the past hour or so. 'Geoff, this is Hill.'

'Hello, Hillary.' He offered his hand.

'Geoff, how lovely to meet you at long last.' Hillary laid on the charm as they shook.

'You too. And you're every bit as good-looking as I've been led to believe.'

Geoff laid on the charm in return, but he was really only obeying instructions. 'Flatter her,' Nora had said. 'Hillary needs flattery, although why I don't know, she's an absolute stunner.' Nora hadn't been exaggerating, he thought, it was obvious where Jo got her good looks. Hillary Collins, like her daughter, was a natural beauty. Geoff personally found the streaked and coiffed blonde hair and the meticulously applied make-up rather gilding the lily, but he was relieved that he hadn't had to bullshit.

'You haven't seen her for thirteen years,' he'd said to Nora. 'What if she's changed?'

'Then lie,' Nora had told him, which was unlike her. A clever manipulator, she unashamedly lied herself when it served her purpose, but she never asked him to.

Geoffrey Metcalf had always found it a mystery that his wife, a family-orientated woman, had lost touch with her only sister, but Nora's explanation had been simply that they'd drifted apart, and it hadn't been up to him to question why.

Hillary gave another girlish laugh as she turned to Nora. 'You told him to say that, didn't you?'

'Geoff never lies. You're as gorgeous as ever, Hill.'

Hillary hoped that she was. At forty-seven it got harder every year.

'And you're as fit as ever, Nor,' she said. One compliment always deserved another, although in Hillary's opinion, Nora was showing her age. Good heavens, she was only thirty-nine, why wasn't she colouring the tinge of grey in her hair? In fact, she should get rid of the mousy brown altogether, auburn would be far more flattering. 'Just look at you, not an ounce of fat, the body of an eighteen year old, it's positively obscene.'

They were both trying too hard, Geoff thought, which he supposed wasn't all that surprising.

'Shall I put the kettle on, or is it time to break open the champagne?' he asked.

'Let's go the champagne, shall we? There's a lot to toast.'

'Oh yes,' Hillary agreed, 'champagne definitely. Now where's Jo? Where's the baby?'

'Upstairs, she's feeding. Come on, follow me.'

Geoff disappeared into the kitchen and the women went upstairs, Nora quietly pushing open the door of the small single bedroom they'd converted into a nursery.

Jo didn't hear them at first, she was too engaged in the child at her breast. Seated in the old wooden rocking chair that Nora had donated to the nursery, she was rocking her baby gently back and forth, gazing down at the little mouth, now sucking in desultory fashion, sated, sleepy.

Nora glanced at her sister. Hillary was entranced by the sight. There was even the hint of a tear in her eyes.

'I'll leave you two alone for a while,' she whispered.

Jo looked up, suddenly aware of the women at the door.

'Hello, Mum.' She smiled, 'I'm sorry I didn't come down-stairs. I heard you arrive, but –'

'Good heavens above, darling, don't apologise.' Hillary, having instantly harnessed her emotions, bustled into the room, kissed Jo on the forehead, and seated herself on the small single bed, leaning forward to peer at the baby.

'I'll give Geoff a hand with the champagne,' Nora said unnecessarily, and she left, closing the door behind her.

'So this is Alana. Look at that wonderful black hair, and those eyelashes! She's very beautiful.'

'Yes, isn't she?'

They sat silently admiring the baby, who had lost all interest in the breast and was starting to nod off. Jo burped her, and then, with an impish grin, held the tiny bundle out to Hillary. 'Give Grandma a cuddle,' she said.

'We'll have none of that,' Hillary warned as she took the child, nestling her in the crook of an arm and stroking the silky down of her hair.

'Well, what should she call you then? Nanna? Nan? Gran?'

'Hillary will be quite adequate, thank you.'

Jo laughed, she'd known her mother would say that.

Glancing up from her grandchild, Hillary once again felt a quick rush of emotion, which this time she didn't bother disguising.

'You look radiant, Jo. Motherhood agrees with you.'

'Yes. It does.'

The two women shared a smile, and to Jo the years of bitterness seemed suddenly unimportant. What was the point of dwelling in the past when there was a whole new future to take care of, she thought.

'It's good to see you, Mum.'

'Yes. Oh dear.' Hillary passed the baby back and delved into her handbag. 'Oh dear, how silly. Babies are such an emotional issue, aren't they?' She made a quick recovery, carefully dabbing at the outer corners of her eyes with a lace hanky.

'You're safe,' Jo said.

'Mm?' Hillary, now in search of her compact, looked up from the handbag.

'Your mascara – it's all in place, it hasn't run.' She wasn't having a dig.

'Oh, good.' Hillary put the bag aside and settled herself for a lengthy chat. 'Now, tell me about Alana. It's a gorgeous name, I love it. Where did it come from?'

'A twenty-four-foot yacht.'

'Really? How intriguing.'

Aware that she was about to be interrogated, Jo decided to get in first. She told her mother the basic facts. Alana's father had been a fellow student at uni with whom she'd had an ongoing affair, she said. She hadn't told him she was pregnant and she didn't intend to tell him about the child, at least not straight away. She'd wait until she and Alana were properly settled first. But she'd certainly make contact when the time was right – if he wished to play a part in his daughter's life it was only fair he be given the opportunity.

'But of course you must tell him straight away,' Hillary interjected, 'and the sooner the better. What about maintenance?'

'Don't be bossy, Mum.' Jo was gentle, but adamant. 'I've made my decisions, and I'm going to do it my own way.'

'Well, there's nothing new in that, is there?' The words just popped out and Hillary cursed herself. She tried to make amends. 'He rang, you know. At least, we presume it was him. He said his name was Mike . . .?'

'Yes, Mike, that's right.' Her mother was fishing for the

surname, but Jo didn't offer it. 'What did you tell him?'

'I didn't speak to him myself. Darren did.'

Hillary fidgeted with her handbag, recalling the scene – one of the rare occasions when she'd been openly critical of her husband's actions.

'Why didn't you *tell* me?' she'd demanded. Not once had he mentioned the young man who'd tried to contact her daughter; the subject had only come up after Jo's phone call announcing her pregnancy.

'Mike Somebody-or-other,' he'd said casually. 'Must have been the father.'

'For heaven's sake, Darren, you should have *told* me.'

'Why?' Darren had played the innocent at first.

'*Why*? He was trying to find her, how could you just fob him off? He's the father of her *child*!'

'I wasn't to know that, was I? He could have been anyone.'

'What did you tell him? Did you give him Nora's address?'

'No, why should I? We didn't even know she was staying there, did we?'

'But Nora would have known where to find her.'

'Good God, Hillary, I was only trying to protect you.' A change of tack: he was now the wrongfully accused. 'You'd lost contact with your daughter, you were upset – I didn't want to bother you with every Tom, Dick and Harry who was trying to chase her up.' Aggrieved, wounded. 'I try and do what's best for you, and this is all the thanks I get.'

'I'm sorry.'

He'd successfully worn her down in just one minute; it was an art he'd perfected.

'What did Darren tell him?' Jo asked now. 'Did he give him Nora's phone number?'

'No.' Hillary felt racked with guilt. 'But you see, darling, we didn't know you were staying here, did we? And we didn't know about the pregnancy, or that Mike was the father, how could we? We –'

'It's all right, Mum.' So Darren hadn't told her Mike had phoned, Jo thought. Her mother's desperate attempt to shoulder the blame equally rather than paint her husband in a bad light was obvious. But for once Jo was thankful to her stepfather. 'It's fine, really it is. Darren did the right thing. I'm grateful.'

There was a tap at the door and Nora popped her head in.

'Champagne's all set up if you're ready,' she said.

They went downstairs and joined Geoff on the balcony, where they clinked glasses and toasted the baby. Hillary waxed lyrical about the view, and was horrified to hear that the Victoria Street terraces were under threat from high-rise developers.

'These beautiful buildings,' she exclaimed, 'it's criminal. Mind you, they're doing the same thing in the west – demolishing history and erecting monstrosities. Modern architecture is so ghastly, isn't it?'

Such a blanket statement led to mild disagreement from Geoff. 'Oh, I don't know, there's always the exception. What about the Opera House? I love it myself. I think it's the best thing that could happen to this country, it'll really put us on the map.'

Along with the rest of Australia, Hillary had seen the artist's impressions of the new Sydney Opera House, which had been widely published in the media, and, like many, she hadn't known quite what to make of it.

'It's certainly unconventional,' she said, choosing her words with care in the face of Geoff's obvious enthusiasm.

'Yes, people either love it or hate it – there's been a lot of controversy. I feel sorry for Utzon.'

Nora noticed her sister's slightly glazed expression. 'Jørn Utzon,' she said, 'the architect.'

'Of course.' Caught out, Hillary quickly added, 'He

resigned last year, didn't he?', thankful that she recalled reading the fact. She hadn't really been following the progress of the Opera House. Why should she? It was a long way from Manjimup.

'They forced changes in his design,' Nora said. 'It was bloody unfair.'

Geoff pointed out to the right where the Harbour Bridge towered over the tangle of buildings and the parkland's trees. 'You can't quite see Bennelong Point from where we are, but that's where she's going up, over there. I'll take you to have a look at it while you're here, if you like,' he said.

'Yes, I'd like that very much. Thank you.' It would be quite a talking point when she got home, Hillary thought, to say that she'd seen the Opera House being built.

Nora turned the conversation towards Jo's future – she considered there'd been quite enough social chat.

'I think Jo should enrol at uni next year,' she said bluntly, ignoring the warning glance from her husband who thought she was premature in broaching the subject. 'The sooner she completes her degree, the sooner she can get on with her life.'

Hillary was floored. 'But she's just had a baby.'

'Oh, that doesn't stop women in this day and age,' Nora continued breezily. 'Career and motherhood are the perfect mix according to the women's libbers.'

'Then how come you haven't pursued your own career?' Hillary's tone was a little icy. 'I seem to recall you were very passionate about psychology. How come you're now a housewife and mother?'

'Because I choose to be, and a very noble profession it is, to be sure.' Nora grinned, aware that she was being contrary and ruffling Hillary's feathers in the process. 'I'll go back to work when the kids are both in high school. I'm enjoying their company too much at the moment. Who knows, I might even go back to immigration.' She winked at her husband. It was where they'd first met: Geoff was a senior psychologist at the Immigration Department. 'That is, if the boss'll have me.'

Geoff stood. 'Which reminds me,' he said, 'I brought some paperwork home.' He didn't find Nora's behaviour amusing at all; he thought she was being pushy and that Hillary had every right to be offended. But he wasn't going to interfere; the women were sisters and they could sort it out between themselves. 'If you'll excuse me.' He retired from the balcony, relieved to make his escape.

'Then surely,' Hillary said, eyebrows raised archly, 'like you, Jo should enjoy her child's company before she chooses to embark upon a career.' Nora was being deliberately provocative, she thought, it was typical of her.

'But she doesn't have a career, does she?' Nora wasn't letting up. It was true she'd always enjoyed needling her sister, watching Hillary become progressively more aloof and superior, but she was in earnest now. 'And she won't have a career until she gets her degree. Jo has to have her qualifications before she can make her choice – surely you can see the difference.'

Jo was amused that she was being talked about as if she weren't there, and the friction between the sisters interested her. They'd reverted to type, as if nothing had happened between them. Their typically sibling behaviour was fascinating, and surely healthy, she thought.

'So I suppose she'd just pop out between lectures and breastfeed the baby, would she?' Hillary said mockingly.

'No, she could express her milk and I could do the feeds here.'

Hillary gave a snort of derision, ladylike, but a snort nonetheless. 'You're being silly now, Nora.' Her tone remained dismissive, but she was annoyed that her sister had the hide to even suggest such a thing. Johanna was coming home to Manjimup.

'We've discussed it.' Nora was no longer needling, keen

for Hillary to see the sense of her argument. 'I can't wait myself! It'll be like having another baby of my own after all these years.'

In her enthusiasm, Nora didn't realise how tasteless her statement sounded – that she would, in effect, be taking over her sister's daughter and grandchild. But Hillary heard nothing beyond the fact that this ludicrous arrangement had already come under discussion.

She turned her attention to her daughter. 'You've *discussed* it?' This wasn't possible, she thought. Jo would bring her baby home – she and Darren had talked about it at length. They'd even planned which room they'd convert to a nursery.

Jo was taken aback by her mother's shocked reaction. It had always been her intention to remain in Sydney – hadn't her mother realised that?

'So you want to continue with your medical degree?' Hillary said quietly as she fought to regain her composure. 'And as early as next year.'

Jo nodded. 'Now that it seems possible, the sooner the better. I agree with Nora.'

'Well . . . I suppose a career's quite admirable, so long as you feel you can manage it all. But surely you don't have to set your sights on Sydney, darling. You could continue your studies in Perth, couldn't you?'

'Yes, I suppose I could, but –'

'Then of course you must. Darren will apply for a transfer. We'll move up to the city, and I'll be there to look after the baby.'

There was a moment's silence. Hillary glanced from her sister to her daughter; both said nothing. Well, what *could* they say, she thought, it was the obvious solution.

'I am your mother, after all, Jo, and Alana is my grandchild.' She allowed herself a light laugh of self-mockery. 'Much as I might at times deny being a grandmother. You must forgive me, darling, sheer vanity of course –'

Jo took a deep breath. 'I'm going to enrol here in Sydney, Mum.'

The smile froze on Hillary's face. 'I see.'

She glanced again at Nora, this time with suspicion. Paranoia started to creep in. There was a conspiracy going on, she thought. Her sister intended to rob her of her daughter, and her daughter intended to rob her of her grandchild. Why?

'You'd made up your mind right from the start, hadn't you?' she said accusingly. 'You've intended to stay in Sydney all along.'

'Yes.'

'Why didn't you tell me?'

'I thought you must have known.'

'And why would I have known that, Johanna? Why would it have even crossed my mind that you might wish to deprive me of my grandchild?'

'I don't want to deprive you of your grandchild –'

'But that's what you're doing, isn't it? That's what you're both doing. And I want to know why.'

Oh no, you don't, Nora thought, marvelling at her sister's self-righteousness. You don't want to know at all. With bated breath, she waited for Jo to blurt out the truth.

But, confronted by her mother's injured innocence, Jo felt a sense of hopelessness. What was she to say? *I won't expose my child to a man like your husband.* She couldn't bring herself to do it. Not now. There would no doubt come a time when confrontation would be unavoidable, but not today.

'I can't complete my degree in Perth, Mum,' she said carefully. 'Don't you see? I can't go back to UWA, Mike will be there.' He wouldn't be, she thought. He'd have finished his studies by now, he'd be off to the Pilbara.

Hillary breathed a sigh of relief. There was no conspiracy at all – how silly of her to have thought that there could be. 'Ah, yes, I see. Oh my darling, I'm sorry, I didn't realise.' Everything made perfect sense and she nodded sympathetically. 'You want to avoid the father. Of course.'

Jo didn't dare look at Nora. 'Yes. I want to avoid the father. That's why I have to enrol here in Sydney.'

How sad, Hillary thought. How very sad, but how very understandable. Poor Jo. 'Oh dear me, what a tragic situation,' she said.

Hillary refused Nora's invitation to stay for dinner.

'Thank you, Nor darling, but it was such a long flight and I'm utterly exhausted. Perhaps tomorrow?' she asked hopefully.

'Of course. And the night after that, and the night after that. You've got another whole three days, Hill.'

The flight had been less than four hours, and as there was a two-hour time difference between the cities, it was only five o'clock in Perth. Nora found it difficult to understand how Hillary could be 'utterly exhausted', but then, she supposed, they needed to take things in easy stages.

'See you tomorrow, Mum.' Jo embraced her mother at the front door. Geoff had insisted upon driving Hillary to the Hilton. 'We'll go for a walk up to the Cross and I'll show you around.'

'How wicked,' her mother laughed. 'I can't wait.' Hillary was back on form.

Mother and daughter enjoyed each other's company over the next several days. They explored the colourful red-light district of Kings Cross, Hillary gawking at the strip joints where spruikers touted for trade in the broad light of day. They had coffee in bohemian cafés peopled by artists and students, and she tut-tutted at the prostitutes openly plying their trade from doorways that led to seedy rooms above. She pretended to be shocked, but she found it all titillating.

'A bit of a change from Manjimup,' she said.

They walked down the old Butler Stairs to Woolloo-mooloo. Cut into the rock of the hillside, the stairs led from fashionable Victoria Street to the working-class district in the valley below. Hillary found it most picturesque.

'Good heavens above,' she said, as they wandered through the narrow streets lined with workers' cottages. 'How on earth can people live in such tiny houses?'

During their time together, she didn't attempt any further discussion about Jo's future, nor did she try to elicit promises from her daughter. She left it until the last day of her stay – in fact, until the very last minute, as they were saying goodbye.

'I'll wait outside in case we don't hear the taxi arrive,' Nora said, leaving mother and daughter alone in the front room. Hillary had once again been adamant about refusing her sister's offer of a lift to the airport.

'You'll bring her home to visit during the holidays, won't you?' Hillary said as she cradled the sleeping baby in her arms. 'Darren will pay for the air fares, of course.'

'Well, she's a bit young to travel yet, Mum. I'll leave it for a while.'

'Yes, of course, darling, I understand.' Alana squirmed, and Hillary looked down at the little face twisting into a yawn, the miniature fists clenching the air. The baby was waking up, it was time to be fed. 'But when she's a bit older . . .' Hillary smiled at the tiny, perfect fingers encircling her thumb. 'Oh, Jo, it'll be wonderful, I can't wait.' This was just what they needed, she thought, the baby would bridge the gap between her daughter and her husband. 'We'll be a real family.'

Never, Jo thought. Never. She was saved from answering. Alana let out a hungry wail and Nora called from the front door, 'Taxi's here.'

'Bye, Mum,' she said as she took the baby, 'have a good trip.' And she kissed the cheek her mother proffered.

*

At first, Jo kept to herself at uni. Not altogether by choice. The other fourth-year medical students had journeyed through their course together and friendships were by now firmly established. She endured the inevitable chat-ups from some of the male students who considered themselves studs, but she responded to their attentions with such a remote indifference that, offended by the brush-off, they quickly spread the word that Jo Whitely was 'up herself'.

Jo didn't mind being a loner, she never had. Besides, there was no time for socialising. Having been up since dawn tending to Alana, she would arrive just in time for the first lecture of the day and leave as soon as the last was over. Lunchtimes she usually spent seated on one of the benches nestled against the old stone walls of the university's open central courtyard. She'd chew on a sandwich as she pored over her books, and sometimes, particularly when the weather was inclement, she'd skip the sandwich altogether and spend her lunchtime in the library. Deprived of sleep, she felt constantly weary, but she loved being back at university.

'You're Jo Whitely, aren't you? You're in med, fourth year.'

She was seated on her customary bench. It was a fine day in early spring and she shielded her eyes against the September sun as she looked up at the young man. He wasn't a medical student, but she'd noticed him about the campus. Slim, sandy-haired and average-looking, he was not particularly conspicuous in himself, but for the fact of his obvious popularity. Always, it seemed, he was surrounded by others.

'That's right,' she said, a little guarded.

'Andrew Gaden. Final year, law.' He extended his hand and she was forced to shake it. 'Mind if I join you?'

She did, but it was too late to object. He'd already sat. She waited for the chat-up.

'I'm on a recruitment drive. Would you be interested in joining the debating society?'

'Oh.' Perhaps this wasn't a chat-up at all. 'Well,' she smiled apologetically, 'I'm afraid I can't. I really don't have the time.'

'Why not?' The question was guileless, and seemingly rhetorical as he continued. 'It's only a once-a-month debate, and we have a short meeting every other week. All very casual and a lot of fun, you'd love it. Really.'

He gave an enthusiastic grin, and she realised that he had dimples.

'I'm sure I would.' She knew she would, she'd loved being on the debating team at UWA. 'Thanks for asking me, Andrew, but I'm sorry, I've decided not to take on any extracurricular stuff.'

'Why?'

Again the question was guileless, and the surprise obviously genuine. Andrew was not only president of the debating society, he was a regular contributor to the university newsletter and always wrote sketches for, and appeared in, the annual revue. In Andrew Gaden's opinion, extracurricular activities were the highlight of university life.

'I took last year off,' she said, wondering whether he'd ask 'why?' to that too, 'and there's some catching up to do.'

'Ah, so that's why you've always got your head in a book. I thought it was a case of over-zealous swotting.'

'No, it's a case of making up for lost time.'

'Speaking of time,' he glanced at his watch, 'we've got fifteen minutes. How about a coffee?'

He smiled as he stood, and she automatically stood too. His manner was disarming and his dimples beguiling, but she felt no threat. He wasn't coming on to her, she thought, he was just being friendly, and she could do with a friend. She liked him.

'All right,' she said.

*

Andrew *was* coming on to her. He had a private twenty-dollar bet going with his best friend, Ben, that he'd score with Jo Whitely.

'Not a snowball's chance, Andy,' Ben had said. 'She's up herself.'

They'd kept the bet strictly between themselves; Andrew wasn't one who needed to boast of his conquests. But he found the remote Jo Whitely incredibly attractive, and the challenge she presented irresistible.

Six weeks later he called the bet off, admitting defeat, although he didn't tell Ben why. Having yet to score a date, and without even having kissed her, let alone possessed her body, he found himself smitten with Jo Whitely. So much so that he didn't dare push her too fast. He sensed that she wasn't seeking a relationship, and he himself was no longer interested in a one-night stand.

Jo knew that Andrew Gaden found her attractive, and she was careful to offer him no encouragement. But Andy had flair, he was fun to be with and she enjoyed his company. She hadn't realised how much she'd missed having a friend at uni. She'd even joined the debating society, after discussing it with Nora, who had insisted it was time she start socialising.

'It'll be good for you – you need to make friends,' Nora had said, and when Jo had remained hesitant, she'd eagerly added, 'You could have your meetings here.'

Jo had laughed, presuming she was joking. 'Oh Nora, what in the wide world would I do without you?'

'You'd manage, kiddo. You're tough.'

'Not tough enough to bring the debating society home and introduce them to my illegitimate child, I'm afraid.'

'I don't understand why you're so determined to keep it a secret,' Nora had said blithely. 'Single motherhood doesn't carry the degree of stigma it once did.'

'It does where I come from.'

'Okay then, we'll tell them she's mine.'

Jo hadn't taken Nora up on the offer. The debating society had proved an excellent idea, however: it wasn't too time-consuming and it did gain Jo friends. She now ate her lunch with the others in the canteen, finding their conversation stimulating and enjoying their company, as they did hers. Word soon spread that Jo Whitely wasn't up herself at all.

Andrew, however, was getting nowhere. Jo was blossoming, but without him. He spent less time alone with her than he had when she'd joined him for their solitary lunches, he still couldn't tempt her out to a movie or dinner, and she continued to disappear at the drop of a hat, never staying to socialise after a meeting or debate. It was frustrating and mystifying.

The final term was drawing to a close and the great debate, the society's last for the year, was to be held in the University's Great Hall. Along with the drama society's annual revue, the great debate was always a highlight, its topic invariably satirical, its intention being to ridicule institutions, attitudes, government policies or the like. This year's topic, 'For and Against the Creation of the Sydney Opera House', had been Jo's idea and the other society members had keenly embraced it.

Inspired as she'd been by many a conversation with Geoff and Nora, Jo was looking forward to the debate, and when straws were drawn to determine the teams, she was delighted to score final speaker for the negative. It gave her ample opportunity to be provocative.

The Great Hall was packed with students who'd been cheering and jeering each speaker in turn, and heckling at each point that was made. The debate was coming to its conclusion and Jo was nearing the end of her argument.

'The truth is we are a *sporting* nation. What need do we have for a home-grown culture *at all*? Australians have been happily served by American and British culture for years! The final speaker for the affirmative has talked of

such luminaries as Robert Helpmann and Joan Suther-
land.' The final speaker on the opposing team had been
Andy Gaden. 'Luminaries indeed, but I ask you, where do
they stand in the affections of the general populace when
compared with the likes of Dawn Fraser and Rod Laver?'
More cheers and jeers.

'There is no place for an opera house in this country!' Jo
raised her voice above the din. 'What we need are more
swimming complexes and tennis courts, more cricket
grounds and race tracks. It is our bounden duty to nurture
tomorrow's Frasers and Lavers, to discover our future Don
Bradmans and to breed our new Phar Laps!' Winding the
audience up, she punched her fist in the air with theatrical
emphasis. 'This country is not interested in the arts, and
why should it be? Why bother with an Australian film
industry when we have Hollywood? Why bother with the
opera and the ballet and the theatre when we have our
football and rugby and cricket? Who *needs* the Sydney
Opera House?' She was pitching her voice above the
crowd now. 'Not Sydney! Not Australia! Of *course* we're
against the Opera House. *Any* opera house. It's not part of
our identity! The Sydney Opera House is *un-Australian*!'

She left the podium to resounding applause and
returned to her seat amongst the other speakers who were
lined up either side of the stage. The adjudicator then
called upon each speaker, one by one, to rise to his or her
feet. The outcome of the debate, as always, was to be
decided by the sheer volume of audience reaction.

The crowd gave voice wildly, adding whistles and the
ferocious stamping of feet, and, as was to be expected, the
negative team won hands down. Every one of the students,
even the most sports-devoted, was in favour of the Opera
House, and they'd enjoyed the send-up approach of those
speaking against it. Jo Whitely received the loudest
ovation of all, even from the A grade rugby team.

*

'Oh, come on, Jo,' Andy urged half an hour later. 'You're not doing your disappearing act tonight of all nights – we won't let you.' The gang, fifteen in all, was going to the Dolphin Hotel in Surry Hills, and as usual Jo appeared to be backing out. 'Break the rules, be a devil.'

Jo's hesitation lasted only a second. 'Just one drink,' she said. She was on a high and Nora had told her not to rush home.

'Let your hair down for once, kiddo,' she'd said. 'This is your big night, and Alana'll be fast asleep anyway.'

It was a balmy November evening and the gang took over the little vine-covered courtyard at the rear of the hotel, the middle-aged couple seated there quickly retiring to the lounge upon the students' rowdy arrival. Tables were pulled together, jugs of beer and bowls of chips fetched from the bar, and then they settled down to chatter at the tops of their voices, each trying to top one another as they relived the night's event. Jo wasn't the only one on a high; the great debate had been an unmitigated success.

'I'll get my own thanks, Andy,' she said when he asked her what she wanted to drink. 'I'm only here for the one.'

'It'll be the end of our friendship if you don't let me shout you a drink, Johanna,' he insisted. 'Now what'll it be? Are you happy with beer?' She gave an apologetic shake of her head. 'What then? White wine? Gin and tonic? Rum and Coke?'

'I'm sorry,' she said. 'Port and lemonade?'

He raised an eyebrow and went to the bar.

Jo ended up staying for two drinks. Having eked out her port and lemonade for as long as possible, she slipped away to the bar to buy herself another, together with a jug of beer for the table. She was having too good a time to leave. She didn't actually want a second drink herself, but she knew if she sat with an empty glass in front of her someone would inevitably fill it up with beer. As she stepped back into the courtyard she collided with Andrew.

'Oh,' he said, his relief evident, 'there you are. I thought you'd gone.' He'd been heading out into Crown Street, hoping to catch up with her, presuming that she'd be looking for a taxi.

'Why would I go without saying goodbye?' She plonked the jug in his hands. 'My round.'

They returned to the gang. The group conversation had died down now, every angle of the debate having been discussed. A bunch remained chatting animatedly at one end of the table, but the others were having quieter discussions in twos and threes, and one couple had moved to another table altogether, where, in the darkest corner of the courtyard, away from the fairy lights, their mouths were no longer engaged in conversation.

Andrew put the jug of beer on the table and manoeuvred Jo to the chairs at the far end, which had been vacated by the couple. He wanted to suggest they find another table themselves, but she appeared in such a party mood that he decided not to risk it.

'So what are you doing over the holidays?' he asked, engaging her one on one before she could tune in to the others. There was only a fortnight of uni to go and desperation dictated that this was the night he must make his move.

'My mother's coming over from Perth. We're going to the Blue Mountains.'

The dilemma of the holidays had been easily solved. Old Uncle Ted hadn't seen the baby yet, although he'd been ringing demanding a 'private audience' as he called it, and Hillary herself had suggested she make the trip east, agreeing that Alana was far too young to travel. She'd be coming alone, she'd said, Darren was busy, and she'd welcomed the idea of visiting old Uncle Ted. 'Good heavens above, I haven't seen him since I was a child.'

'The Blue Mountains – that'll be nice,' Andrew

remarked casually. 'For the whole of the holidays?' He hoped not.

'No, Mum's only here for a week.'

'Right. So you'll be in Sydney then . . .?'

'Yep.' She sensed he was going to ask her out so she got in quickly. 'What are *you* doing for the holidays, Andy?'

'Well, they're not really holidays for me, are they? This is my final year. I'll be looking for a job.'

'Hardly.' She laughed. Andy Gaden was a brilliant law student, everyone knew it. He'd probably have the pick of any law firm he wished. 'It's an exciting time for you, isn't it?'

'Yes, I suppose it is.'

She had no idea how beautiful she looked, he thought, her fair hair catching the glow from the fairy lights strung amongst the vines, her eyes sparkling vivaciously. She was so animated. The remote Jo Whitely had certainly been transformed. But then that was just the barrier she put up, he'd known it for some time now.

'I'll miss uni,' he said, swilling back a mouthful of beer, 'it's been a lot of fun.'

'You mean the extracurricular activities have.' She grinned, 'I don't know when you ever got the time to study.'

'Well, they do stimulate the mind, don't they,' he said, frowning at her with mock severity over the rim of his beer glass. 'I hope you'll continue with the debating society next year when I'm not there to boss you around.'

'Oh, I will,' she promised, 'absolutely. I'm so grateful you got me involved. I love it.'

He put the glass down. 'Do you know what I'm going to miss most of all about uni, Jo?'

'What?'

'You.' He took her hand in his. Whether he scared her off or not, it was time to have it out. She didn't pull away, which he found encouraging. 'I want to keep seeing you,

Jo. Not just at debate meetings and lunch in the canteen. I want to get to know you better than that. Why won't you go out with me? I'm not coming on heavy – just dinner, that's a start.'

A start to what, she wondered. She'd been waiting for this to happen, knowing that she couldn't keep avoiding the inevitable, and she felt sad at the thought of losing his friendship: it had meant a great deal to her.

'I like you Andy. I like you a lot. Apart from family, you're the only friend I have in Sydney. Well, let's face it,' she admitted wryly, 'you're about the only friend I have full stop.'

'Then why? Why do you keep closing me out?'

She clasped his hand firmly, a gesture of both friendship and apology. 'I'm not interested in a relationship. I'm sorry.'

'I'm not asking you for one.'

Oh yes, you are, she thought, and she smiled as she withdrew her hand. 'I have to go.'

'You haven't finished your drink.'

'I didn't really want it. I came for just the one, remember?'

She was already on her feet. He stood. 'I'll find you a taxi.'

'No, you stay with the others. I can find one myself.'

'You're determined to emasculate me, aren't you?' He smiled, dimples flashing. 'Come on,' he said as he took her arm.

Jo said her good nights to the others, and then the two of them were out in busy Crown Street, cars zooming past, but no sign of a taxi.

Andrew was glad of the opportunity to buy extra time. 'There's a rank at Taylor Square,' he said, taking her arm once again, prepared to walk the several blocks with her.

'Go back to the gang, Andy.' He refused to budge and she laughed. 'I'm not trying to emasculate you, honestly.

I don't even need a taxi, I can walk to Victoria Street from here.'

Victoria Street, well, that was a start, he thought.

'Through Darlinghurst? I wouldn't hear of it, you'd be mugged. Besides, I've had enough of the gang. I prefer your company, let's go.' Arm in arm, they walked down Crown Street. Arriving at the broad intersection of Taylor Square, where nightclubs and restaurants flashed gaudy neon signs, they crossed over Oxford Street to the lone taxi parked at the rank beside the all-night newspaper and cigarette stand.

'Thanks, Andy,' she said as he opened the car's rear door for her, 'you've saved me from a mugging and I'm deeply indebted.' She kissed him on the cheek.

'I'll drop you home and take the taxi on.' When she hesitated briefly, he added, 'It could be ages before another one turns up.'

'Oh. Of course. Sorry.'

They clambered in, Andrew hoping she wouldn't notice the For Hire signs on the two approaching taxis behind them. She didn't.

'Potts Point, thanks,' she told the driver. 'Victoria Street.'

They travelled in companionable silence. Or so Jo thought. She never felt the need for unnecessary social chat herself. But Andrew had decided to go for broke. Why not? He had nothing to lose. She was obviously prepared to disappear from his life, and at least he had the right to know why. As the lights of Kings Cross appeared directly ahead, he turned to her.

'Why do you find me such a threat?' he asked.

The question was as confronting as he'd intended it to be and she struggled for the answer.

'I don't find you a threat, Andy,' she hedged.

'No? I'm about the only friend you have *full stop*, that's what you said. And yet you want to throw that friendship away. Sounds a bit threatened to me.'

The taxi driver turned into Victoria Street. 'What number, lady?'

'Eighty-five, thanks, down towards the end.'

She knew Andy was waiting for an answer, and he deserved one, it was only fair. But what *was* the answer? No-one at university knew she was a single mother, and she intended to keep it that way. She'd been honest when she'd told him she wasn't interested in a relationship; she couldn't afford to let anyone into her life. Besides, she wasn't in love with him, she didn't wish to sleep with him. But she greatly valued his friendship. What was she to say? She decided to trust him.

'Here's fine,' she said abruptly. The taxi had just passed Nora's terrace.

They pulled up several houses further down the street and Andrew helped her from the car. She took out her purse to pay the taxi fare.

'No, don't, I'll look after it,' he said.

'I'm not asking you in.'

'I know that. Keep the meter running,' he told the driver. 'I'll be going on to Randwick.'

'Right you are, mate.'

He walked her to the front door of eighty-five. 'So what is it, Jo? Tell me.' Her introspection had been obvious and he'd sensed that she'd been trying to come to some form of decision.

Oh well, she thought practically, the truth would seal the matter: he'd certainly stop pursuing her once he knew about the baby. But she hoped it wouldn't mean the end of their friendship. She decided not to beat around the bush, what was the point?

'I have a child,' she said. 'No husband, there never was one, just a child.'

He was too stunned to reply.

'She's over a year old now. Her name's Alana.'

She'd never seen him at a loss for words before. Finally,

he cleared his throat. 'Well . . . um . . . that's certainly a bombshell.'

'Yes, it is, isn't it?'

She wondered why she felt so terribly disappointed; it was unreasonable of her. Of course he'd be shocked – how had she expected him to react? But she also realised it had been foolish of her to expect any continuation of their friendship.

'I'd appreciate it if you didn't tell anyone, Andy.'

'Of course . . . naturally . . . I mean, of course I won't tell anyone.'

'Good.'

Well, that was that, she thought, and she left him standing in the street.

CHAPTER THIRTEEEN

T he huge upstairs verandah was crowded and noisy
as yet more drinkers jostled their way out from
the jam-packed bar, protectively nursing their
jugs of beer. The verandah's dozens of tables and chairs
were occupied and standing room was at a minimum
with barely enough space to throw a punch. But before
long there'd be punches thrown nonetheless. The Mermaid
Hotel was a rough place on a Saturday night.

Despite the crowd, the heat was not unpleasant. Beneath
the corrugated-iron roof, large ceiling fans whirred, and a
breeze drifted in from the sea. It was late July, the middle
of the dry season.

Mike and Dan had found a spot in the far corner by the
wooden-latticed railings, where they'd been drinking
steadily for the past hour with a bunch of miners from
Hamersley Iron. Mike hadn't met the men before, but
then, apart from Dan, Mike didn't really know anyone in
Dampier. His trips into town were rare, and he would
normally have avoided the Mermaid, but this time he
wasn't merely after supplies – he'd run out of funds and
was looking for a job. The pub had seemed as good a place
as any to make enquiries.

Amongst the hard-drinking men were several equally hard-drinking women, which sometimes spelled trouble – the shortage of available women in Dampier could lead to fierce competition. But tonight the crowd's raucousness was good-natured with little evidence of frayed tempers. Everyone seemed bent on having a good time.

Then the Swede arrived.

Her name was Mia. She was very, very blonde, tanned, figure-perfect and extraordinarily good-looking – a true Nordic beauty. She and her two companions, a man and a woman, cut a swathe through the crowd, men openly ogling as she crossed from the bar door to Dan and the miners at the far end of the verandah. One or two in the crowd greeted the man with her, who was carrying two jugs of beer. 'G'day, Eric,' they said, but they weren't looking at Eric. Nor were they looking at the other woman, despite the fact that she was bosomy and the sort who would normally attract a good deal of attention. All eyes were on Mia. Even those who'd seen her before and knew she was Eric's wife.

Once she was ensconced with the bunch in the corner, the general focus returned to drinking and camaraderie, but there had been a subtle change in the tone of the evening. The Swede was a distraction and furtive glances continued to be cast in her direction.

Dan made the introductions – he knew everyone in Dampier – and as he did so, Mike realised, with an involuntary stab of disappointment, that Mia was in the company of her husband. Then he reminded himself that it was just as well. He'd avoided female company for the past six months, and he wanted to keep it that way.

Mia's friend, Eva, however, wasn't going to make it easy.

'Hello,' she said as they were introduced. She'd greeted the other men, all of whom she knew – two of them intimately, a one-night stand apiece. 'I saw you in Woolworths about a month ago.' She cosied up to him, the cramped surrounds serving as a perfect excuse.

Mike smiled. 'You've got a good memory.'

Memory had nothing to do with it, Eva thought, who could forget a bloke this good-looking? She'd been keeping her eye out for him ever since.

'How come you haven't been around town?' she asked. Eva worked in Dampier's busy shopping arcade, the hub of the township where everyone gathered. In fact, the shopping arcade virtually *was* the town. She found it most strange that she'd only seen him the once.

'Mike's a bit of a nomad,' Dan said as Eric topped up everyone's glasses. 'He keeps pretty much to himself.'

Unfazed, Eva continued to invade Mike's space, tucking her arm possessively through his. She was accustomed to having her pick of the men and she'd decided that this one was hers for the night.

Mike found her proximity impossible to ignore, the ample breast that nuzzled his side alerting his body to the fact that he hadn't had sex for eight months. Not since *that* night. He cursed himself. He should have avoided the Mermaid. In fact, he should leave this very minute. But he didn't. He stayed right where he was, Eva's arm snaking about him, her body wriggling enticingly against his. Even when it was his round and he went to the bar, she insisted on going with him under the pretext of helping him carry the jugs back, holding his hand, which announced to the few other women present that he was her property. As the night grew louder and drunker and rougher and tougher, Mike's libido couldn't help but respond to the knowledge that she was his for the taking.

A fight broke out on the verandah, as it inevitably did, and a man was sent sprawling over a table. Freshly filled beer jugs crashed to the floor, which infuriated the drinkers, and both protagonists were hauled out bodily into the street where the brawl, now involving half a dozen men, continued. No-one knew what the original fight had been about, presumably a woman, but they didn't care. It was the waste of good beer that was unforgivable.

Aggression and lust went hand in hand, and Mia, the beautiful Swede, was no longer merely the object of covert admiration. As men grew drunker, looks stopped being furtive and mutters ceased to be inaudible; she'd become a tantalising object of desire. They all wanted her. The air was palpable with lust, and at one table bets were being mysteriously laid.

Mia herself was aware of the effect she was having, and appeared to be basking in the attention. Eva, too, was revelling in the reflected glory of her friend and the sexual undercurrent it aroused. Mia was a useful magnet to be around.

Mike, lately unaccustomed to heavy drinking sessions, was feeling heady and a little bit out of it, but he could sense the tension. He glanced at Eric, the Swede's husband, a tough-looking man, presumably good with his fists. Surely there was going to be trouble. But Eric, far from being offended, seemed proud of the effect his wife was having on the men, even pleased that she might be a source of disruption. Perhaps he was spoiling for a fight, Mike thought. Perhaps he was waiting for someone to make a move.

Then a young man pushed his way through the crowd and thrust a folded piece of paper into Mia's hand. He pointed to the table where the bets were being laid, and disappeared without a word.

Mia opened the note and read it. She laughed lightly and looked over at the table where a mixture of Japanese and Australians were seated. All eyes – eleven men in number – were on her and none said a word as they waited for her answer. Several at nearby tables, obviously in the know, also waited and watched, and the group gathered about Mia fell silent, wondering what was going on.

She lifted an eyebrow, intrigued, and waved the note in the air, querying which one had sent it. All interested eyes were now directed to the table. A squat man seated at the far end, heavily built for a Japanese, raised his hand.

Mia smiled and shook her head, and the table erupted into laughter, the Japanese's comrades slapping him on the back in commiseration. They'd won the bet.

'What the hell was that all about?' Eric asked.

Mia read the note aloud in her attractively broken accent. '*One thousand dollars if you will sleep with me.*' Then she passed it around for the others to see.

Mike cast another glance at Eric; surely this was the signal for a fight. But Eric simply looked over at the Japanese, his expression one of curiosity more than anything. Mike, along with the others, automatically looked back at the table too. The Japanese, who hadn't joined in his companions' laughter, once again raised his hand. Two fingers. The bid had gone up.

Eva ground her pelvis against Mike's leg in an unmistakable signal. She found it all intensely erotic. If the offer had been made to her, she would certainly have accepted. Not that she was a working girl – she'd never prostituted herself, and she never would – but to be openly bid for like this! How flattering, and how sexy!

Once again Mia shook her head, and this time the colleagues of the Japanese didn't laugh. Realising that the game was in earnest, they waited for him to make his next move.

Word had quickly spread from table to table and now every drinker on the verandah was watching the proceedings.

The Japanese slowly held up three fingers. He was the skipper of an iron-ore tanker, he made good money and as a single man he had nothing to spend it on. He was wealthy, he could afford it. He sat back and waited for the Swedish beauty's response.

Word had also reached the bar and men left the queues thronging for drinks and came outside to watch.

Mia glanced at her husband. 'Three thousand dollars,' she murmured. The sum was impressive.

Eric muttered something to her under his breath.

Mia smiled across the verandah to the Japanese, and the Japanese smiled back.

Never had there been silence at the Mermaid Pub on a Saturday night, but there wasn't a word uttered as the entire verandah waited.

Mia held up her hand, five fingers splayed, just as Eric had instructed.

The Japanese nodded and rose from the table.

There was a huge round of applause and the crowd parted to make way for him as he crossed to the Swede in the corner. Some slapped him on the back and made lewd remarks, but he paid them no heed. Tohito was pleased with the outcome of his bid. The purchase had cost him nothing. Each of his companions had bet five hundred dollars that he couldn't buy the girl – wagers that amounted to exactly five thousand. He'd been prepared to go far higher. For a blonde such as this, he would have bid ten thousand.

The Japanese and the Swede left wordlessly arm in arm to the cheers of all, and Eric skolled his beer as if in a toast.

After they'd gone, the drinking and general hubbub returned to normal, but much of the conversation was about the Swede and the Jap. Men were aroused, and the few women present had become the focus of the night. There were bound to be more fights.

Eva knew that she could have had the pick of the bar – they were all as randy as hell. So was she, but she'd made her choice.

'Let's go down the beach,' she said to Mike, and they left.

They didn't make it to the beach. Barely a hundred metres away, amongst the trees and palms that surrounded the tavern, they started tearing at each other's clothes, unable to wait any longer.

Mike lifted her from her feet and took her against the smooth trunk of a lemon-scented gum, the nearby sound of drunken carousing drowning out her rapidly mounting moans. He made little noise himself as he drove into her with a desperate urgency. Their coupling to him was no more than a long-awaited sexual release, and eyes closed, teeth clenched, he grunted slightly as his climax approached.

She was orgasming now, crying out as she thrust herself back at him, and as Mike neared ejaculation he opened his eyes. But the girl bucking wildly, legs wrapped around him, head thrown back in ecstasy, was not the girl from the verandah. It was the dead girl. His belt about her broken neck, her tongue lolling from her mouth, she stared at him in grotesque accusation.

It was over in a matter of seconds and he turned away, pulling up his shorts, not daring to look at the girl whose name he'd suddenly forgotten. He felt sickened.

'Well, we certainly needed that, didn't we?' Eva giggled as she scrambled into her panties. 'A quickie but a goodie, eh? God, I was hot, and you were too obviously. Do you want to come back to my place?' She pushed an exposed breast back into her brassiere. 'I've got plenty of beer. You could stay the night and we could have a repeat perform-ance.'

He didn't reply, which she took for a yes.

'Come on,' she said, grabbing his hand.

'No.' Mike wanted to shake his hand free, but he didn't. It wasn't her fault after all. 'Thanks for the offer, but no.' He forced himself to look at her, and attempted a smile with little success. 'Come on, I'll take you back to the pub.'

'Oh.' Eva looked surprised. 'All right, if that's the way you want it.'

Hand in hand they walked back to the tavern. Eva would have preferred to storm off in a huff, but she didn't want to return alone. She needed it known that she'd made her conquest with the handsome young stranger. But she was insulted nonetheless. So he'd just been after a quick fuck, she thought. She knew the sort. Thought he was too good for her, did he? Well, fuck him.

She was further insulted when he left her at the steps that led up to the verandah.

'I have to go,' he said abruptly.

She watched him walk off to his car. Fuck you, you bastard, she wanted to scream after him, but she didn't. She had her reputation to think of.

Mike drove out of town and into the scrub, to a waterhole where he often camped. He didn't lie on the bank and gaze up at the diamond-studded sky. He didn't marvel at the stillness of the night and hold his breath wondering which of the myriad creatures it might be rustling gently in the nearby spinifex. He didn't even get out of the car. He sat hunched over the wheel staring unseeingly at the windscreen.

How could he have so deluded himself? How could he have presumed that the dead girl had left him?

The Burrup Peninsula and Dampier Archipelago, approximately fifteen hundred kilometres north of Perth, belonged to the region known as the Pilbara, one of Australia's most remote and primitive areas. A rugged landscape of ancient rock formations, treeless islands and harsh interior, the peninsula and its surrounds could seem, to some, an inhospitable place. But none could deny the power of its stark and timeless beauty. The Pilbara could cast a spell. It could get into the blood. Everyone who'd been there knew that. It had got into Mike McAllister's.

At first, he hadn't been sure what had compelled him to stay on in the region after the completion of the museum team's two-month survey. Was it his love for the place? Or was it his need to escape? He still had dreams about the girl. He could see her hanging there in that Scarborough Beach boatshed, his own leather belt about her neck, and he knew that for as long as he lived she'd never leave him. Like Muzza, he'd be visited by the image of a past he wished he'd never known.

Muzza himself had sensed something, Mike remembered. All that time ago when he'd called in to say goodbye.

'What is it, mate?'

Muzza had been puzzled when Mike had phoned a number of times to say he was busy, and hurt that Mike hadn't been around for a whole six weeks and had now only come to say goodbye. He hadn't commented upon the fact though, simply fetching a couple of beers from the fridge as usual, but when he'd positioned himself at his easel and taken up his brush to put the finishing touches to the portrait, he'd been startled by what he'd seen in Mike's eyes. The man before him was different from the man in the painting.

'What's happened?'

'What do you mean, what's happened? Nothing. I told you, I've been busy preparing for the trip, that's all.' Mike had deliberately misunderstood the question. 'No painting today, Muz, I'm not in the mood.' Then, not wishing to be hurtful, he'd added, 'Sorry, mate, too much on my mind.'

'Sure.' Muzza had downed tools and joined him at the table. 'It's finished anyway, you can take a look if you like.'

The portrait *was* finished, Muzza had thought. He could only paint what he saw. And he didn't want to paint what he saw in Mike's eyes.

'It's the best thing you've done, Muz.'

Mike had stared in awe at the painting. It was more than a likeness; Muzza had captured the very essence of him. Or perhaps the him he'd once been, he thought. Things had changed now. He didn't like himself any more.

'Yes, it is good, isn't it?'

An hour later, when Mike left, Muzza had offered him the portrait, but he hadn't accepted it.

'I can't take it up north,' he'd said. 'You look after it for me, Muz.' He'd studied the painting a moment longer. 'I like to think that I'll be here with you.' Then he'd added, as nonchalantly as he could, 'Share a beer with me every now and then, eh?'

After Mike had gone with the empty promise that he'd write, both of them knowing he wouldn't, Muzza had stared at the portrait for a very long time. And he'd prayed that whatever demon was tormenting Mike McAllister might have disappeared when next they met.

The marine biological and ecological survey of the Dampier Archipelago had offered Mike the perfect escape. The museum team had concentrated upon the Hamersley Shoals between the outer islands, from Rosemary Island to the west across to Legendre Island to the east, and each day's diving had found Mike lost in the underwater world he loved, the image of the girl blanked from his memory. And when they'd cruised past the islands' giant granite cliffs and anchored in one of the pristine sandy coves for a leisurely swim, the girl had not been with him. But then nothing had. This primitive landscape rendered one mindless. It obliterated the past and negated the future in its own agelessness.

But ashore, in the township of Dampier, walking the streets in the sweltering heat, or drinking at the Mermaid with mates from the team, things had been different. Whenever he'd caught sight of an attractive woman, the image of the dead girl had flashed startlingly before him. Any alluring aspect of the female body – the shape of a breast, the curve of a buttock – and the girl was there. Just for a second. Until he looked away. He'd taken to avoiding female company.

When the team had finally returned to Perth, there'd been no agony in Mike's decision to stay on. The Pilbara

had changed him. Or perhaps the girl had. Perhaps the
need to escape her memory had enhanced the effect of this
isolated and desolate part of the world – he'd lost sight of
the reason, but his career no longer seemed of the utmost
importance. He'd decided to put everything on hold. He
was single, he was free, and he was in the Pilbara; there'd
be time for a career further down the track. But then,
perhaps not. His burning ambition to serve a purpose in
life seemed to have faded.

He'd bought a second-hand Toyota Scout, stocked it up
and explored the region, camping as he went, travelling
into the hinterland, where the rocky hills gave way to the
clay country with its red earth and dry creek beds. Even in
this forbidding territory, the flora had its own beauty. Seas
of bastard bush, a prickly acacia that would rip a man to
shreds if he walked through it bare-legged, were prettily
clothed in yellow, and the aptly named snakewood tree's
reptilian limbs writhed in a series of lifelike configurations.
After the healthy monsoonal rains, colour had abounded.
The silver-gold of the spinifex was tinged mauve with the
flowering mulla mulla shrub, and clumps of vivid red Sturt
desert peas splattered the land like blood.

He'd followed the dry river beds to the billabongs where,
amongst the cajeput paperbarks, river gums and white-
trunked coolibahs, wildlife abounded. In the late afternoons
he would set up camp and swim away the day's dust, keeping a wary eye out for the large pythons that lay in wait
for any unsuspecting wallaby that might venture down the
bank for a drink at dusk. He'd watch the indefatigable
snakebirds bob out of sight and magically reappear on their
endless fishing patrol, and brown kites circle lazily overhead
while the whistling tree ducks, wary of their presence,
deserted their bank-side perches for the safety of the water.

Never once had he missed the companionship of others,
and solitude had provided peace of a sort, the image of
the dead girl rarely reappearing. But solitude had also lent

itself to introspection, and his thoughts had turned to
Jo. He'd trampled on her love, hadn't he? And when she'd
left him, he'd successfully relegated her to the past. The
one woman he'd loved, the one woman he would *ever*
love, he'd closed from his mind as he'd moved on with his
own all-important career. What sort of a man did that
make him? A callous bastard, according to Muzza, and a
cold fish, according to Jools. He'd come to the conclusion
that they were both right. There was something lacking in
him. He was an emotional desert, as remote and inhospitable as this land, which looked after itself and its own,
but never others. A traveller would die out here. Like this
land, he was incapable of nurture. No wonder Jo had left
him – who could possibly blame her?

Mike's self-analysis was ruthlessly honest, but he found
some gain in confronting the man he was. Even if he
couldn't change himself, it helped him to move on.

Dampier had always held one major attraction when the
need for fresh supplies forced him into town, and that was
Dan. Dan Aitkens, whose slogan was 'Dan's Your Man',
was an enterprising 'local' who'd set himself up in a tidy
business, offering his services, and that of his Cessna 172,
to the big industrial combines. He made a mint flying
reconnaissance trips over the area for Dampier Salt and
Hamersley Iron, he'd told Mike. Sometimes they were just
joy flights for the big boys, but more often than not they
were genuine recces.

The two had met when Mike had first arrived at
Dampier. Dan had flown several reconnaissance trips over
the reef for the museum team, to give them the lay of the
land, and he'd maintained his friendship with Mike when
the others had left. Mike was like him, Dan had decided.
He was here to escape. From what, Dan didn't know and
didn't care, but the Pilbara had got to the bloke just the
way it had him.

Dan wasn't a local at all, he was a crop-duster who'd come north after a failed marriage five years previously. He'd had an instant eye for the potential the recent industrial development of the area offered, and had quickly concocted a local background to give himself added credibility. The claim no longer seemed a falsehood, either to the few in the know or to Dan himself. There was no-one who had a greater knowledge, or love, of the area than Dan did. He enjoyed sharing it with Mike.

'God's country, mate,' he'd say as they flew low over the hills of the peninsula and swooped even lower to skim across the archipelago. 'God's own bloody country.'

Mike never tired of his joy rides with Dan. Viewed from the air, the unique landscape was at its most spectacular, and nature at its most contradictory. The rich red-brown boulders of the diorite hills seemed to grow out of their surrounds, as if erupting in protest of their captive greenery. But the appearance was deceptive – over the centuries exactly the opposite had occurred. Niches in the rock had allowed the steady growth of spinifex and grasses, and the combination made for a breathtaking vision. Stretching as far as the eye could see was a primitive mosaic of unbelievable proportions.

Also viewed from the air was the industrial blot on the landscape, which, according to Dan, grew bigger with each progressive year.

'I'm not knocking it, mate, it's my living,' he'd say to Mike, 'but jeez, just look at the way it's taken over.'

It was true that the denuded earth of the Hamerlsey Iron loading yards, where trains two kilometres long delivered the ore from the inland mines, looked obscenely ravaged, and the docks and jetties of Port Dampier, stretching far out into the clear blue sea, were ugly and intrusive. So, too, the endless ponds of the Dampier Solar Salt Farm, impressive as they were, stretching stark and white over hundreds of hectares, appeared a hideous invasion upon nature.

But to Mike, there was something faintly ludicrous about it all. Man's interference seemed petty in the face of the unconquerable timelessness surrounding it. Ugly though the intrusion might be, this was no more than a momentary blemish, the land seemed to say, it would leave no lasting scar. In millions of years, mankind would cease to exist, but this terrain would not. This land had been here before the existence of man, and would be here long after his demise.

The peace Mike had found in his semi-nomadic existence was shattered following his sexual encounter at the Mermaid Hotel. Was the dead girl to be present every time he touched a woman, he wondered despairingly. Was he destined to copulate with her for the rest of his life? He decided to keep well away from temptation.

Looking further afield, he accepted a job as a deck hand aboard a prawn trawler working out of the small but thriving fishing port at Point Samson, roughly thirty kilometres north-east of Dampier. The Point Samson Peninsula, with its secluded coves and white sandy beaches, was extraordinarily beautiful, and the nearby townships of Roebourne and Cossack, having been the first European settlements in the Pilbara, were picturesque.

Roebourne, established in 1866, remained a busy town, its hospital servicing the area, but its attractive stone buildings reflected a dramatic past, particularly the old jail, whose grim history was a reminder of the atrocities inflicted upon the local Indigenous population. The architecture of Cossack was even more impressive, which made the fact that it stood derelict all the more poignant. Cossack, the once thriving port for pearlers and those seeking their fortunes in the Pilbara gold rush of the 1880s, was a ghost town, finally abandoned by its last stalwart inhabitants in 1950.

The Greek brothers who owned the prawn trawler

FLOODTIDE

allowed Mike to live on board. They were only too happy to have their vessel under constant surveillance while they went home to their families, and the arrangement suited Mike. As the weeks became months, the dead girl ceased haunting him and he was content in his mindless existence. The brothers worked him hard, but he liked them. And they liked him. In fact, Nick and George Kostopoulos considered 'the boy', as they referred to him, a real find, and they told their friends so.

'The boy is fearless,' they boasted. 'He will go over the side and free the net when it catches on the propellers. He has no fear of the sharks at all.' Nick and George were very wary of the sharks themselves. All the fishermen were.

In their early forties, the brothers rather reminded Mike of beefier, Greek versions of Tubby and Fats Lard, the cray fishermen from Geraldton.

Not long after their new deckhand had been in their employ, Nick and George discovered that 'the boy' was far more than a 'find'. He was a veritable goldmine.

'Go in closer to the mangroves, Nick.'

The night was still and the moon was full, perfect conditions for trawling.

Nick, at the helm, was surprised by Mike's suggestion.

'But we always trawl this far from the mangroves. Better we keep a safe distance. We don't want to foul the net.'

'We're on a king tide, you won't foul the net. You can go much closer.'

'Why should I?'

'Because that's where the prawns are.'

'Oh, is that a fact?'

'Yes, it is.' Mike ignored Nick's scorn. 'The prawns feed where the nutrients are, and the nutrients are in the shallower water near the mangroves,' he said patiently. 'It's a full moon and a king tide – you'll be able to get much closer than you can in normal conditions. Go on,' he urged, 'give it a try.'

'Do as he says, Nick.' George jumped in before his brother could say no. Nick didn't like being told what to do. But the boy sounded very sure of himself, George thought. And besides, he was right about the tide, there was no danger of fouling the net. 'What harm is there in giving it a try, eh?' he said jovially, defying his brother's baleful look.

They had a bumper haul that night, the best they'd had all season.

'How did you know?' George asked. 'How did you know about the . . .' he fumbled for the word, '. . . the nutrients?'

Nick nodded, scorn forgotten; he too was eager for the answer.

Mike smiled, but remained evasive. He had no wish to share his past with the brothers. 'The mangroves,' he said enigmatically. 'The mangroves are the powerhouse of the sea.'

From that night on, the brothers fished as close to the mangroves as they dared, and when it was a king tide they always realised a bumper harvest. The boy was not only fearless, they boasted to their friends, he was smart. But they didn't tell their friends why. Their friends didn't need to know that the mangroves were the powerhouse of the sea.

They doubled his salary, they didn't want to lose him, and Nick took to calling him 'genius'. 'Hey genius,' he'd say, 'where shall we trawl tonight?' The boy always seemed to have the right answers.

The nickname reminded Mike of the way Tubby Lard had called him Einstein, and he found it comforting. It was good to recall a part of his past with affection – he'd become accustomed to blocking out all but the present.

Having exchanged his nomadic existence for one of equal isolation aboard the prawn trawler, Mike's lifestyle remained that of a recluse. The nights when they didn't trawl were spent reading books or listening to music on his transistor radio, and his free afternoons were spent diving on the reefs off the northern shores of Point Samson. The reefs teemed with marine life, and he was happiest then. He'd make the occasional trip to Dampier to purchase more books and sometimes to meet up with Dan, but that was the extent of his socialising. Until he met Rupert Crofton-Asher. Ash changed everything.

It was the New Year of 1969. Mike hadn't gone home for Christmas. He'd rung his parents, as he did intermittently, and said he was making good money and intended to work through the holiday period. It wasn't altogether true. The brothers didn't trawl during the monsoon season and had taken their families south for their customary annual vacation. They would normally have laid off their deck-hand, but as they were loath to lose their 'boy genius' they'd kept Mike on a retainer with instructions to oversee the anti-fouling and general maintenance of the vessel. Mike eagerly accepted both the offer and the ready excuse that came with it. The truth was, he wasn't yet ready to return to Perth. He wasn't sure when he would be.

One Sunday afternoon, he took the trawler's tender – a three-metre tinny – out to the reefs well off the shores of Point Samson beach. He left it hanging off the reef on a pick anchor while he dived. During the height of the monsoonal summer he was always careful to choose deep, clear water and to keep a wary eye out for the sea wasps that prevailed at that time of the year. He'd stick close to the reef too, in order to make his escape should the stinging jellyfish or sea snakes, or any of the other creatures known commonly as bities, make an appearance.

Having resurfaced, he recovered his breath, swimming lazily, breathing through his snorkel as he watched a huge loggerhead turtle which had also just surfaced. A boat was cruising not far away, a seven-metre Bluefin Savage. He gave a wave to the lone fisherman on board and the man waved back.

The turtle dived and Mike did too, following the cumbersome creature as it wildly flapped to gain momentum. Then, having built up its speed, the giant animal stopped flapping and used its flippers merely as rudders, gliding like a missile, effortless, powerful, no longer cumbersome but a thing of great beauty.

Mike followed the turtle for as long as he dared. He would have liked to stay down longer, but he knew better than to push himself too hard these days. Depressurising as he went, he made his ascent.

He resurfaced to a hive of activity. Everywhere there were fins, and grey shapes hurtled through the water at breakneck speed. After a brief, startled second he realised they were dolphins, a large pod, several dozen it appeared.

Barely a hundred metres away the Bluefin picked up speed. The man at the helm gave Mike another wave. He'd maintained a safe distance from the reef, keeping his eye out for the diver, and his wave seemed to say 'Watch this'. He revved up the engine and started doing wheelies, turning sharply, ploughing through his own wash, and the dolphins immediately latched on to the game. They followed the boat, and each time it turned they leapt from the water and jumped its wake, then weaved and dodged, trying to second guess its next move. They varied their tactics, some diving beneath the vessel, some swimming beside its bow, but each time it turned they raced for the wake, jumping it in a spectacular display of aerial gymnastics.

Mike sat waist-deep on the edge of the reef and watched as the play continued. It went on for a full fifteen minutes and could have gone on much longer if the Bluefin's skipper hadn't called a halt. The dolphins were tireless and bent on having fun.

The man slowed the boat to a crawl and made his way

over to Mike, the dolphins following, begging for more. He put the engine into neutral and idled about twenty metres from the reef.

'I'll run out of fuel if I go on much longer,' he said.

'Thanks for the show, it was a real treat.'

'They sure are something, aren't they.'

The two watched as the dolphins, realising the game was over, started heading off to seek amusement elsewhere.

'I've never seen a pod as big as that before,' Mike said.

'Yeah, it's a big one all right, but I've seen bigger around here. Where you from?'

'Perth.' Mike guessed from the man's accent that he was American.

'How about a beer? I've got some on ice.'

'Great. Thanks.'

He dumped his flippers, mask and snorkel in the nearby tinny and swam to the boat. Then, using the engine leg as a ladder, he climbed up over the stern. The man handed him a towel.

'Rupert Crofton-Asher,' he said. 'They call me Ash.'

He was a lean, athletic-looking man in his mid-thirties, with a weathered face and a cropped beard that accentuated a strong jawline. His smile was friendly and the soft drawl of his accent pleasing.

'G'day, Ash. I'm Mike McAllister.'

The two men shook and, as Mike dried himself off, Ash put the engine into gear.

'I'll just get a little distance between us and the reef.'

Five minutes later, he cut the engine altogether and they drifted in open water. Ash grabbed a bottle of Swan Lager from the esky in the cabin. He poured two glasses and handed one to Mike.

'Cheers,' he said as they clinked.

'Cheers,' Mike responded.

Swivelling his skipper's seat around to face the stern, Ash settled himself, bare feet up on the gunwales, while

Mike sat on the engine box opposite him, both men swigging thirstily at their beers. The day was hot and sultry, the air moisture-laden with the humidity of the monsoon season.

'It doesn't get much better than this, does it?' Ash wiped a minor beer spillage from his beard and gazed about at the aqua water and the white, white beach of Point Samson.

'God's own country,' Mike agreed, quoting Dan.

'How long have you been here, Mike?'

'Coming up for a year now.'

'Really? That long?' Ash was surprised. He didn't know why, but he'd presumed that the young man was a holiday-maker. 'Strange I haven't bumped into you. I'm a fixture myself, been here over five years.'

'Oh, I've been bumming around a bit, doing a lot of travelling. I'm working on a prawn trawler at the moment.'

Again Ash was surprised. Young Mike McAllister didn't look like a fisherman, and he was very well spoken. Ash would have guessed him to be an educated man. 'So you live here at Point Samson?'

'I live on the trawler.'

'Is that so?' Perhaps he was a uni student taking a year off from his studies, as some did, Ash thought. He was about to enquire further but Mike got in first.

'What about you Ash? Are you American?'

'Canadian, Ontario.' Ash wasn't being nosy, he was always interested in people and their stories, and he now happily launched into his own.

'I came to Perth in '62 for the Empire Games and never left,' he said. 'Fell in love with an Aussie girl. We got married and moved up here, and then I fell in love with the Pilbara, and that was that. No going back now, we're both hooked on the place.'

'The Games? You mean as a competitor?'

'Yeah, I was with the Canadian track team.' Mike looked duly impressed, but before he could respond, Ash laughed. 'No big deal, I assure you. I was reserve runner in the four by one hundred relay, and didn't even get to compete. At twenty-nine I think I was past it.'

He laughed again, and his laugh was so infectious that Mike grinned. Ash was very engaging.

'It must have been an honour to be part of the team though,' he said.

'Oh, most certainly.' Ash drained his glass and fetched the bottle from the esky. 'What about you, Mike?' he asked as he poured them fresh beers. 'Are you a sportsman? You look pretty fit.'

'I was big into rugby at uni.' Suddenly Mike found himself relating his own potted history – there seemed no reason not to, Ash was such an easy conversationalist.

'A marine biologist, eh?' Ash appeared most interested. 'We could do with your kind up here. Industrial development's posing a bit of a threat to marine life.'

'A *bit* of a threat! What about Dampier Salt?' Mike had forgotten, in his self-imposed exile, how much he'd missed conversation, and before he knew it, he'd launched into a diatribe about the creation of the Dampier Solar Salt Farm. 'Hundreds of hectares of prime mangrove swamp flooded and destroyed! It's criminal. Do you realise what that does to the ecology of the area?'

Ash didn't reply, presuming from Mike's impassioned attack that the question was rhetorical. He was right.

'I mean, do you realise how important the mangroves are to the coastal marine environment? That's where all the primary energy conversion starts, to say nothing of their importance as nursery areas for most fish species. The mangroves are the powerhouse of the entire marine system!' Mike spread his arms wide in an all-encompassing gesture, spilling his beer in the process but not noticing. 'Which means Dampier Salt's got one hell of a lot to answer for.'

He trailed off, aware that Ash had been nodding attentively but hadn't said a word. 'Sorry, I got a bit carried
away.'

'Don't apologise, it's good to hear someone so passionate about the environment.'

'Old habits die hard, I suppose.' Mike smiled. 'God, I
haven't mouthed off like that for a long time. Anyway,
enough about me,' he said, changing the subject. 'What are
you doing up here, Ash?'

'I'm a mining engineer for Dampier Salt.'

There was a pause. 'Whoops,' Mike said.

Ash threw back his head and laughed.

'I'm sorry, I didn't mean any offence . . .'

'None taken, I assure you.' Ash grinned. 'Hey, I'm pretty
green myself, I'm Canadian, remember? I'm on your side.'
His smile faded as he continued. 'I've been following
the policies adopted back home. Rachel Carson started the
ball rolling . . .' Mike nodded; he'd read *Silent Spring*,
the revolutionary book on the environment published in
1962 in America. 'And I tell you what, Mike, I'd bet even
money that it's only a matter of time before we see the
introduction of environmental legislation here in WA. Let's
face it, with all this industrial development going on we
sure as hell need to do something.'

He swigged thoughtfully at his beer. To Ash, it seemed
his meeting up with young Mike McAllister was most
opportune.

'You know, the boss was talking just the other day about
the possibility of Dampier Salt developing some potentially profit-making biological side products.'

'It'd be a good idea,' Mike agreed. 'There'd be a lot of
marine activity in the ponds, particular in the primary
levels before the salinity becomes too concentrated.'

'Yeah, it makes sense, doesn't it. Even I can see that.'
Ash smiled self-deprecatingly. 'A civil engineering degree
gives me an understanding of basic geology, but I don't

know shit from clay when it comes to things like man-groves or what attracts fish to where. It seems to me like you're just the guy we need. Hey, why don't I have a word with the boss?' He was eager-eyed and enthusiastic, the prospect was exciting. 'You'd like Maurie, he's a great guy, and I bet he'll just jump at the chance to have you on board. What do you say, Mike?'

The conversation had suddenly snowballed into a job offer and Mike found himself backing off. He wasn't ready to join the work force.

'Well, thanks, Ash, that's very kind of you,' he said, uncertain and self-conscious, 'but I'm happy on the prawn trawler. For the moment, anyway,' he added. He didn't wish to appear ungrateful. 'Perhaps sometime a little further down the track.'

Ash was intrigued. A little further down the track from where? How strange, he thought, that a highly qualified young man with such a passion for his chosen field should decide to opt out. But he didn't pursue the subject.

'Right you are,' he said affably, swilling back the remnants of his glass. 'Help yourself to another beer while I clean the fish.' He lifted up the wet hessian sack covering a bucket in the corner of the cockpit to reveal a healthy catch of coral trout and red emperor.

'Good haul.' Mike stood, polishing off his own beer. 'I'll give you a hand if you like.'

'You're on, but only if you lend a hand with the eating as well.' When Mike hesitated, he added, 'No point in cleaning fish unless you get a feed out of it. How about dinner tonight with me and Beth?'

'Thanks,' Mike smiled, 'I'd love it.'

'Good.'

Ash hauled out a couple of cutting boards and conversation ceased as they immersed themselves in fish guts, pelicans gathering for the heads they threw overboard and seagulls swooping in to squabble noisily over the entrails.

After they'd finished cleaning the fish, they had another beer. Then Ash took the boat back to the reef and Mike's tinny, before heading for the Bluefin's mooring, which was at the far western end of the bay.

Mike slipped over the side and trod water. 'Thanks for the beers. My shout tonight, I'll bring some along.'

He knew the cottage where Ash and his wife lived. It was a converted fisherman's hut; there were several at the far end of the bay. 'The one with the red tin roof,' Ash had told him, 'and the two extra bedrooms tacked on either side.'

Mike swam to the tinny. 'Make it around seven,' Ash called. Then he revved up the engine and the Bluefin took off.

'You're Mike McAllister.'

The woman who opened the flywire door and greeted him as he stood on the small front verandah was in her late twenties. Fair-haired and freckled with a strong, sporty body, she was a little too muscular and her face a little too square-boned to be classed as pretty, but, like her husband, Beth Crofton-Asher was instantly engaging. Her eyes crinkled as she smiled.

'I'm Beth, hello.'

'Hello.'

Mike shifted the bottles he was carrying in a brown paper bag to his other arm and shook the hand she offered. He'd nicked the beers from the supply the brothers kept aboard the trawler; he'd replace them the following day. Before Beth could usher him inside, a ball of energy in the form of a four-year-old child charged across the room behind her and out onto the verandah.

'And this is Pete,' she said as the little boy screeched to a halt and stood gazing up at Mike, huge intelligent brown eyes demanding an introduction. 'Say hello to Mike, Pete.'

'Hi, Mike.' The little boy offered his hand and they shook.

'Hi, Pete.'

'Come on in.'

The interior of the cottage was simple. One comparatively large room served all purposes, with doors leading off either side to the two tiny bedrooms. Armchairs and a sofa sat in one corner, a small Laminex-topped four-seater dining table in the other, and at the far end an island bench divided the kitchen area.

Ash looked up from the bench where he was filleting the fish. 'Hi there, Mike, pull up a pew,' he called, gesturing at one of the nearby stools. 'I'm just about done here. Hey hon,' he said to Beth, 'grab us a beer, will you?'

Beth took the bottles from Mike, opened one and poured glasses for the three of them while Pete clambered up onto another of the stools. He perched precariously, elbows on the bench, chin in his hands, and studied Mike.

'I take it you two have met,' Ash said.

'Yep, we've met.' Mike winked at the little boy, whose face cracked into a smile. 'How old are you, Pete?'

'I'm four. How old are you?'

'Twenty-six.'

'I can read.'

'Wow, that's fantastic!'

'And I can write.'

'That's even more fantastic.'

'He gets special tuition,' Ash explained. 'Beth's a kindergarten teacher with radical methods. She thinks kids should have fully developed literacy skills before they're five.'

'Not *fully* developed,' his wife countered good-humouredly as she positioned herself beside him and started making the salad. 'But they should be able to read, and to write to a certain extent, before school age. If the parents have the wherewithal, of course,' she added. 'Many around here sadly don't, which is a bit of an indictment in my opinion.'

'Beth's a militant when it comes to education.' Ash grinned at Mike and proceeded to talk about his wife as if she weren't there, but his pride in her was evident. 'She runs a kindergarten in Roebourne set up by the community service. The kids are mostly Indigenous and they adore her. They'll do anything she says, which includes learning to read and write. Mind you, she's very clever the way she goes about it – she makes the whole process such fun that they don't even realise they're being educated. It's a total con, but it works. The parents are barely literate and their four and five year olds are regular little Samuel Pepyses.'

Beth laughed, but as she proceeded to talk in more detail of her work, it was quite obvious she was deeply committed. Mike found the discussion fascinating, and he felt very much at home as the couple chatted away. They were easy company. Ash's interjections were more often than not at Beth's expense, but she fobbed him off good-naturedly with an expertise born of practice.

The fish having been filleted and the salad prepared, they adjourned to the small patio Ash had built out the back, where the vestige of a breeze did little to alleviate the sticky heat of the night. The patio was complete with a homemade brick barbecue, which was already smouldering in readiness for the fish, and at the rear of the yard, beside the ramshackle wooden dunny, a single lamp glowed a fluorescent mauve-blue. The air around it was thick with insects, the blue hues of the light attracting the mosquitoes and moths away from the more subdued yellow lighting of the patio.

They sat at the wooden table, Pete eating his dinner of crumbed fish sticks which Beth had fried up on the stove inside. 'He prefers the frozen kind,' she said ruefully. As they picked at the cheese and olives she'd put out, Ash pouring another beer, Mike asked where they'd met.

It had been during the Empire Games, Ash told him,

Beth had competed in the springboard diving. Before Mike could comment, Beth took over. Like her husband, she was surprisingly self-effacing.

'I probably wouldn't have made the team at all if I hadn't been a Perth girl, born and bred,' she said. 'There was a big local contingent – no travel and live-away expenses, you see.'

'Rubbish,' Ash said. 'You were damn good.'

'I didn't get a place.'

'At least you competed! She made the finals too,' he added proudly to Mike.

'Well, you're both far too humble in my opinion,' Mike said. 'If I'd been chosen to represent my country, I'd brag about it.'

'I do,' Ash insisted. 'I brag about her.'

'Me too. I brag about him.' Beth laughed. 'Oh my God, don't we sound like the most awful double act.'

After Pete had been put to bed, they opened a bottle of wine, cooked the fish in foil with butter and lemon, ate two large servings each, and demolished the salad. They talked non-stop, and Mike told them all about himself without feeling in the least threatened. Even when Beth asked him if he had a girlfriend.

'I did once,' he said. 'I mean a *serious* girlfriend. We were together for about a year and a half, but I messed things up. I wish to hell I hadn't now,' he said.

How strongly Jo came to mind in the presence of these two, he thought. Perhaps it was because he envied what they had, or perhaps the wine on top of the beer was making him sentimental. At least that's what he told himself, but he knew it was neither envy nor alcohol. It was regret. Ash and Beth were a reminder of what might have been if he'd acted differently. But then he couldn't have acted differently, could he? He wouldn't have known how. He'd behaved true to form, accepting Jo's love and offering nothing in return. He didn't like himself for it, but there was no going back, so why live with regrets? What was the point? The point was, he missed Jo. He suddenly missed her terribly.

Noting his introspection, Beth felt sorry for Mike McAllister. So it was a broken love affair that had caused him to bury himself away as he had, she thought. Well, they'd just have to find him another girlfriend. Despite a shortage of women in the area, it wouldn't be difficult, he had to be the most eligible man for miles – good company, intelligent, and he looked like a Greek god. What more could a girl want?

An hour later, as Mike took his leave, she set the wheels in motion.

'We're having a bit of a gathering at Skippers next Sunday,' she said, glancing at her husband, who looked surprised – it was the first he'd heard of it. 'Why don't you join us?'

For months Mike had been deliberately avoiding Skippers, the popular local restaurant overlooking the beach – in fact, the only one in the area. He now found himself accepting the invitation with alacrity.

'Great, I'd like that,' he said, and as he did, he realised that he'd been hoping they'd suggest another meeting. He would have done so himself, but he could hardly invite them aboard a prawn trawler.

'Thanks for tonight.' He shook Ash's hand, and as Beth kissed him on the cheek, he said, 'I'll bring you around a load of prawns tomorrow.'

'Is that a promise?'

'It's a promise.'

'Well, it's certainly the way to this woman's heart.'

Half an hour later, as they prepared for bed, Ash disagreed with Beth's theory that a broken heart was responsible for Mike's opting out.

'No, I think he's trying to escape. Don't ask me from

what, but a guy doesn't lose his ambition and throw away a career over an eighteen-month love affair,' he said. 'But if you want to line up a woman for him, you go right ahead, because one thing's for sure: he's lonely.'

Ash climbed into bed naked, pulling the thin sheet over him. 'Mind you,' he continued, 'I'm not sure if it's a woman he's after. I'm going to work on him to accept a job with us. I'll introduce him around at the yacht club too, and take him to the pub with a few of the guys – he could do with some male company.'

Having stripped off, Beth wriggled in beside him – the two always slept naked. 'Spoken like a true misogynist,' she said.

Then they turned out the lights and made love.

CHAPTER FOURTEEN

The Crofton-Ashers had unwittingly revealed to Mike the extent of his loneliness, and as the weeks passed he welcomed the change they brought to his life. He thought he'd been happy enough in his solitary existence, but he knew now that he'd just been marking time.

He'd quickly realised Beth's intentions, however; she'd made them patently obvious right from the outset.

'Heather, this is Mike. Mike McAllister, Heather Gaynor.'

The moment he'd stepped onto the open verandah of Skippers, Beth had cornered him, dragging him to the table where a half dozen diners were seated and plonking him beside the only unaccompanied girl there.

'Hello, Heather.'

'Mike.'

Beth had launched into a resumé. 'Heather's a school teacher in Dampier. She's from Perth and she's been up here three years.' Then she'd noted the couple who'd just arrived. 'Oh, Maurie and Margot are here. I'll leave you two to have a chat.' And off she'd dashed to arrange the final seating.

Mike had enjoyed the evening. The men had been work colleagues of Ash's from Dampier Salt, and the conversation had been stimulating. He'd cringed at first when Ash, having introduced him as a marine biologist, had immediately brought up the subject of environmental protection. Surely such men would regard him as the enemy, he'd thought. But they hadn't. To the contrary, they'd plied him with questions – particularly Maurie, the boss. Mike had curbed his vitriolic attack on the desecration of the past and spoken of future protective methods that could be adopted. Maurie had found his views most interesting. Ash had watched the exchange with satisfaction – his carefully planned campaign was going just as he'd hoped.

Beth's carefully planned campaign hadn't been quite so successful.

Mike had liked Heather. She was an intelligent, personable young woman in her mid-twenties and he'd found her attractive. But at the end of the evening, as they'd all said their good nights, he hadn't asked her out. He'd sensed that she wanted him to, but he hadn't been tempted to test himself. Friendships with women were dangerous. They inevitably led to a sexual relationship, and that would mean the return of the dead girl.

True to his word, Ash introduced Mike to the Hampton Harbour Boat and Sailing Club at Dampier. The club was the exclusive preserve of the upper echelons from Hamersley Iron and Dampier Salt and membership was essential, but nobody bothered to query Mike's credentials. In his signal khaki shorts and shirt, they presumed he was one of them – a new kid on the block whom Ash had taken under his wing – just as Ash had intended they should.

Ash was a contradictory man, Mike had discovered. He chose to live in the comparative isolation of Point Samson rather than Dampier, maintaining it was worth the extra half-hour of travel to and from work. 'I'm a beachcomber,' he'd say, 'Dampier's a company town, too suburban for

me.' Yet, gregarious by nature, Ash enjoyed male camaraderie and a good night's drinking, which meant the
Mermaid Hotel regularly beckoned. For a beachcomber,
he led a very social existence, Mike thought.

Mike himself preferred the boat club bar to the
Mermaid, but the odd raucous night at the pub was
inescapable now that Rupert Crofton-Asher had taken
over his social life.

'Hello, stranger.'

Eva smiled flirtatiously and slipped her arm through
Mike's. She wasn't one to bear a grudge, and certainly not
against a bloke this good-looking. 'I haven't seen you for
ages. Where have you been?' she asked, the pressure of
her breast signalling all was forgiven and that a repeat
performance was still on offer.

'Hello.'

Mike couldn't for the life of him remember her name,
and he was wondering how to introduce her to Ash. But it
proved unnecessary.

'How you going, Ash?'

'Fine thanks, Eva. Can I get you a beer?'

They knew each other of course.

'Actually it's my round,' Mike said. He dived off to the
bar, and for the rest of the evening, much to Eva's annoyance, he assiduously avoided her blatant attempts to
seduce him.

There were times when Ash's mandatory drinking
sessions and Beth's eager matchmaking brought Mike into
contact with women on more than a mere social level.
Several, like Eva, had made it plain they were on offer, and
his body couldn't help but respond. It made life difficult.
Finally, he succumbed. Upon hearing that a couple of 'the
girls' had arrived at Hearson Cove, his sexual drive won
out and he paid them a visit, deciding it would be the least
complicated way to ease his frustration.

The secluded bay of Hearson Cove on the eastern side of the Burrup Peninsula was a popular choice for the enterprising prostitutes who arrived in their camper vans. They'd set up business for the week, word quickly getting around, and would make a small fortune servicing the Hamersley Iron workers. Then they'd move on before the authorities were alerted to their presence.

Mike knew that he was inviting the dead girl's return, and as the camper van rocked to the pounding of their bodies on the narrow bunk he kept his eyes tightly shut. But she was there, in his mind. Afterwards, sated though he was, he didn't feel any better for the experience. But he knew it wouldn't be the last time he'd visit a prostitute. He would need to seek sexual release now and then and a prostitute was his only option. To invite a relationship was to invite the dead girl back into his life on a regular basis, and he couldn't risk that.

'Why on earth doesn't he ask Heather out? It's the fourth time he's met her, and they talked all afternoon, he obviously likes her.'

Following yet another Sunday barbecue and a further attempt at matchmaking, Beth remained mystified by Mike's lack of interest in women.

'It's such a *shame*. Heather's so *right* for him, don't you think?'

Ash said nothing as he lay in bed watching his wife. Seated naked on the little stool in front of the dressing-table mirror, she was brushing her hair with vigorous frustration. Beth had had quite a bit to drink at the barbecue and, on such occasions, her alcohol-fuelled monologues rarely required an answer.

'She's mad about him too, I can tell.' Beth put down the hairbrush and picked up the jar of moisturising cream. 'Maybe he doesn't find her sexy, maybe that's it,' she said as she distractedly dabbed the cream on her face. 'I think she's awfully attractive myself, although it's impossible to tell what turns men on, isn't it?' She shared the thought with her reflection for a second or so. 'But then, what about Wendy? Wendy's as sexy as all get out, and she came on so strong to him, remember?' This time her eyes appeared to be seeking an answer from his reflection in the mirror. 'Don't you remember, Ash? When I introduced them at Maurie's birthday party, she was all over him. *Surely* you remember.'

'Yes, I remember.' Ash smiled as he watched her. He was feeling a little drunk himself and wasn't really listening, but her antics were amusing him, and God, how he loved that healthy, strong body.

'Well, why wouldn't he find Wendy sexy? Any man would, surely.' She'd finished massaging the cream in and now stared demandingly at the mirror. 'I mean, you would, wouldn't you? Be honest.'

'We certainly do have the chats tonight, don't we?'

'Oh my God.' She swivelled about to face him, the stool teetering slightly. 'You don't think he could be queer, do you?' she asked, regaining her balance.

Ash didn't just laugh, he guffawed.

'No, really, I mean it. He couldn't be, surely, he looks so ... *masculine*. But then it's sometimes hard to tell, isn't it? Not that it matters if he is,' she added hastily, 'but golly, if he's queer I'll have to stop lining him up with girls, won't I?'

'He slept with a prostitute last week.' Ash decided to call a halt, it was time she came to bed.

'He what?'

'He visited one of the girls camped out at Hearson –'

'He *told* you?' She interrupted him, her jaw gaping comically.

'No, but word gets around, you know how it is. Half of the guys from Hamersley Iron fronted up.'

'Oh, poor Mike.' Beth's face was a picture of concern. 'Oh, that poor young man.'

What now, Ash thought. He didn't dare ask, but she launched into an explanation anyway.

'He's still pining over that girl. After all this time he's still in love with her! He'd visit a prostitute rather than get involved with anyone else. Oh, how awful for him!'

'Stop worrying about other people's sexual problems and come to bed, hon.'

'But don't you see –'

'No, I don't. Now come to bed.' There was only one way to shut her up.

Beth stopped plying Mike with women after that, although regarding Heather she continued to keep her fingers firmly crossed. He couldn't pine forever, she told herself. Broken hearts had a way of mending themselves, and Heather was the perfect match for him.

Mike was thankful for the breathing space. He adored Beth. She was intelligent, warm, funny and the most generous-spirited person he'd ever met. But he was relieved that she was finally off his case.

The following Christmas he once again didn't return to Perth, but not because he was avoiding friends and family and old haunts. When the Greek brothers had moved south for the monsoon season, he'd left their employ and accepted a position with Dampier Salt. For nearly three months now, he'd been working as a marine biologist monitoring the biological integrity of the solar salt ponds and overseeing the possible commercial development of *Artemia* spp., commonly known as brine shrimp.

Ash's plan had paid off. Mike's life had changed irrevocably.

He'd moved into one of the old fisherman's cottages not far from Ash's. It was a simple weatherboard shack with a corrugated-iron roof, little more than a hovel, but it suited him.

His parents were relieved to hear about the new job and the fact that he finally had a real address, but for different reasons. Jim McAllister had worried that Mike was frittering away his life, having worked so hard to gain qualifications that could serve some worthwhile purpose. 'If he wanted to sow his wild oats, he should have done it before university,' he'd regularly complained over the past two years. But Maggie was simply pleased that her son sounded happy and settled; she'd been deeply concerned about his mental wellbeing.

Mike had re-established his links with Perth, writing regularly to Muzza, waxing lyrical about his love of the Pilbara. Muzza wrote back, sending sketches of his latest work – he was mounting an exhibition, he said.

The phone calls to family were more regular too, but Mike copped a tirade from Jools when he rang on Christmas Day and the phone was passed around. Jools was home for Christmas and furious that he'd once again deserted the family.

'This is two years in a row now,' she said accusingly.

'You weren't home for Christmas last year I heard,' Mike countered good-naturedly.

'That's different. I was interstate.'

Mike looked out from the post office phone box at the dusty and deserted main street of Roebourne.

'I'm a long way away, Jools. This is more than interstate, it's another world up here.'

'That's bullshit!'

Mike heard a muffled comment from his mother about 'language', and Jools's retaliatory 'No, I mean it, Mum,' then her voice came back down the line. 'It's still WA,' she declaimed haughtily.

Mike smiled – Jools was playing the full drama queen. But she was right nonetheless.

'Yes,' he admitted, 'it's still WA.'

There was a pause as she waited for him to go on, but he didn't. 'So why not come home then?' she demanded.

'Because I'm twenty-seven years old and I'm not

supposed to run home every Christmas, Jools,' he said, exasperated. 'Ask Mum and Dad, they don't expect me to!'

'Oh.'

Unbeknownst to Mike his voice had carried down the line and Jim and Maggie were nodding in agreement. Another pause followed.

'Well, it's just that we miss you.'

He wondered why Jools had caved in so quickly. He would have expected more of a fight.

'I've put a cross on his grave,' she said forlornly.

'Whose?'

'Baxter's.'

'Why? You're not religious.'

'Baxter was.'

The pips sounded and Mike dug in his pockets for more change, but it was too late – the phone had cut out. It didn't matter, he'd spoken to his parents.

He laughed as he crossed the street to the Toyota, and he was still smiling as he set off for Ash and Beth's Christmas barbecue. Exasperating as she was, he missed Jools too. He missed them all. He'd make a trip to Perth sometime next year, he decided.

But only several weeks later, Perth made a trip to him instead.

'Well, aren't you going to ask me in?'

Mike had opened the front door of his hut in response to the knock expecting to see Ash or Beth or little Pete. No-one else ever visited him, the door was never locked and he'd wondered why they hadn't simply called out and let themselves in as they always did, particularly Pete, who barged into the place like a miniature tornado.

He stared in stunned disbelief at the young man who stood there, briefcase in hand, his hire car parked on the dirt road behind him.

'Pembo!'

'I've come a helluva long way to see you, it's been a thirsty trip, and I'll never forgive you if you don't have a beer.'

Mike laughed, and the two embraced.

'So what are you *really* doing here, Pembo?' he asked five minutes later when they were settled out the back under the canvas awning he'd rigged up to provide shade. He intended building a patio and front verandah, and even a proper bedroom, as Ash had done, but he hadn't got around to it yet. 'You certainly haven't travelled this far north just to see me, so don't give me that bullshit,' he said with a grin.

'Well, I have in a way. Cheers.' Ian saluted with his glass, then quickly knocked back half his beer before he continued. 'We're doing some pegging and basic surveys, mainly for nickel, but I could have sent my *minions*,' he said with a boastfully raised eyebrow. 'Spud and I agreed, however, that you've been out of touch far too long, and I was elected to come up and check that you're doing all right. You obviously are.' He looked wryly at the ramshackle hut and the canvas awning. 'Heavens above, a veritable *mansion*!' he said, sounding exactly like his mother.

Mike gave a hoot of laughter. Pembo was very amusing when he camped it up.

'What *minions*?' he asked dutifully. It was quite clear that Ian Pemberton was bursting to show off.

'A lot's changed in two years, Mike.' Ian dropped the act. 'For starters, I'm rich and rapidly becoming more so – at least on paper.' He put his beer on the wooden crate that served as a coffee table and leaned forward, elbows on knees, eyes gleaming. 'Excalibur's making a killing. We've gone public, and our stock price has quadrupled in the past month.'

'Good God, really? How come?'

'I take it you know about the Poseidon nickel strikes at Windarra last September?'

'I've heard the odd word,' Mike said with more than a touch of irony. 'I do read the paper occasionally, and this is mining territory.' Of course he knew of the major nickel discovery which had focused global attention upon Western Australia.

His irony was wasted on Ian, who merely shrugged. 'Nice to hear you keep in touch. Muzza told us you'd been working on a prawn trawler.' Then, before Mike could interrupt, he continued. 'Poseidon's shares were trading at eighty cents, but when the discovery was released they went through the roof. They reached twelve dollars thirty by the end of the month and they've been on the rise ever since. They're skyrocketing now due to speculation and they're far too high for the average investor, so everyone's looking for other nickel stocks. Even other mining stocks in general. The world's gone mining mad, Mike, and we're cashing in on it.' He grinned. 'Remember I told you at uni you should have switched to geol? I was right, wasn't I?'

'For you, yes. But I'm happy where I am.'

Really, Ian thought, on a prawn trawler? Then he remembered that Muzza had said something about a job at Dampier Salt. But where was the big money in that?

'So go on,' Mike said encouragingly. 'You were up to where you were cashing in on the boom. But so are a lot of others, I've heard. Isn't it dangerous?'

'Oh, we'll get out of nickel before it crashes,' Ian said, 'and we'll last longer than most, because we're not the shonky ones. There are new listed companies that don't even have mining leases, let alone viable mines. We're the real thing.'

'I thought Excalibur Nickel Resources was an exploration company.'

'It was and it still is, but it's under the umbrella of Excalibur Holdings now – so is Excalibur Mining, we do the lot. Sometimes we prospect for the bigger companies, sometimes we develop the claim ourselves.' He picked up the briefcase that lay at his feet. 'Just take a look at this.' Producing the latest edition of *The Bulletin*, he opened it up at the right spot and proudly laid it out on the wooden crate before Mike. 'What do you think of that?' he said. 'A two-page spread, and cop the header!'

Mike stared down at the picture before him. A sartorially elegant Ian Pemberton and his American partner, Phil Cowan, equally well-attired, were seated at a boardroom table looking the epitome of youthful corporate whiz kids. He read the header out loud: '*The young moguls of mining – two men on the move.* The editor's fond of alliteration,' he said.

'Read on, it's fantastic.'

Picking up the magazine, Mike scanned the article, Ian watching him keenly, disappointed that he wasn't reading every word out loud.

'Well, *The Bulletin*'s certainly taking you and Phil seriously,' he said when he'd finished. He handed the magazine back, but Ian shook his head.

'No, no, keep it, I brought that copy up for you. I've got heaps more.' He smiled happily, Mike's comment had pleased him. 'Oh yes, we're bona fide all right. Even if the crash comes and we get out of nickel, we can't go under. We're sourcing the full suite of base metals like copper, lead and zinc, as well as chasing the old faithful, gold, of course. Hell, we've even got a crew out just south of here near the Munni Munni complex doing a basic search for platinum.'

It was important to Ian that Mike should know he was bona fide. He wasn't quite sure why, but he didn't want Mike McAllister to know of the dubious road he'd travelled to get this far. How he'd pegged alongside Western Mining and other big companies, writing up impressive prospectuses after basic surveys. How he and Phil Cowan had sold the ground to others, even to Western Mining, flogging what were little more than patches of dirt between major claims. The two had made a good team, Phil the ideas man and financial genius, but it had been Ian's expertise as a geologist that had paid off. His reports had never been outright lies. There'd always been enough evidence to suggest potential, and Excalibur could not be held responsible if the mining companies went off half-cocked without requesting a more in-depth survey. Their original intention had been to make money and then move on to another area before they gained a questionable reputation. But following the Poseidon strikes they'd changed their minds. They'd become bona fide instead.

There was no difference in the long run, it was all about making money, but Ian wasn't sure if Mike would understand that. Mike belonged to the university days when academic qualifications had counted for something. And perhaps, Ian thought, they'd meant something to him too at the time, despite his ultimate aim to be rich. Perhaps that's why it was so important that Mike should know he was bona fide.

'I presume you got my address from Muzza,' Mike said, taking advantage of the brief lapse in conversation. He was keen for news from home. 'How is he? We've been writing to each other and he sounds great.'

'He is. Never seen him better.'

'He's getting together an exhibition, he says.'

'Yes, for mid-year. He's working like a madman.'

'Is he still seeing the psychiatrist? I've asked him but he's being very mysterious. He says I have to come to Perth to find out.'

'You mean he hasn't told you?'

'Told me what?'

'Well, he hasn't told us either, but it's pretty obvious.'

'What is?'

'The shrink isn't his shrink any more, she's his girl-friend.'

'She's his *what*?'

'You heard me, his girlfriend. At least that's what Spud and I reckon. He hasn't told us anything, but we pop in every few weeks, always on a Sunday, and she's been there the last two times we've called. Her name's Olga . . . something unpronounceable.'

So that was what Muz had been hinting at, Mike thought. For the past few weeks Muzza had said there was some news he wanted to share, but not over the phone and not in a letter. Mike had presumed it had something to do with the exhibition. But it wasn't that at all. Muzza had a girlfriend. How wonderful.

Ian was still rattling on. 'What he's doing with a woman when he can't get it up's beyond me. Spud reckons she must be a bit of a weirdo, but it's obviously doing him good, so we're happy for him –'

'How's Spud?' Mike changed the subject.

'He said to tell you he's living the life of Riley.'

Mike smiled at the memory of one of Spud's favourite sayings.

'He's breeding thoroughbred racehorses, amongst other things. He's bought a stud farm at Swan Valley.'

'A bookie breeding racehorses?'

'Oh, he's been pretty careful, he wants to be seen as legitimate. The stud farm's under a private company name so that he can maintain his bookmaker's licence. He's kept the gambling syndicate too, but he's watching it closely. If the shit hits the fan, he'll get out.'

'He's sailing close to the wind if he wants to be seen as legitimate,' Mike said wryly. The travelling bookies and card sharps of Spud Farrell's syndicate were well known around the Pilbara, where they did a roaring trade. The local authorities, accepting gambling as a way of life, turned a blind eye, but syndicates like Spud's were hardly legitimate.

'They won't get Spud. He's too smart.' Ian had had enough of talking about the others – he still hadn't told

Mike his greatest news of all. 'Hey, crack another beer open, we have to make a toast.'

'To what?'

'Get the beer and I'll tell you.'

Mike fetched a cold bottle and when their glasses were filled, Ian raised his.

'To Arlene,' he said. 'Go on,' he urged when Mike looked mystified.

'All right. To Arlene.'

They clinked glasses and drank.

'I'm madly in love and I'm going to get married,' Ian announced.

The two of them proceeded to get quite drunk while Ian raved on about his fiancée, and when the beer had run out he left rather unsteadily to drive back to Dampier where he and his team were staying.

After he'd gone, Mike realised that not one word had been spoken about his own life over the past two years. Pembo had shown not a shred of interest, which Mike found typical, but also healthy. He'd been startled to see Pembo standing at his front door, a jolting reminder of that night in Scarborough. He'd expected some uneasiness between them, and had dreaded the thought that Pembo might bring up the subject. But Pembo had been just Pembo. Arrogant, insufferably conceited, self-obsessed, and yet strangely vulnerable. Still desperate for Mike's approval, as he had been throughout their lives, their relationship remained unchanged. Mike was thankful, and a little envious. The dead girl obviously didn't haunt Ian Pemberton.

He wondered if it was the same for Spud. Had Spud successfully put that night behind him? He'd certainly appeared to at the time – he'd been the strongest of the three of them. But then Spud had known the dead girl personally. Did she come back to him now and then? Would she be there between them always, a past that they shared, unspoken of, but ever present? He'd certainly felt that way when Spud had farewelled him at the airport – he'd felt that things between them would never again be the same.

There was only one way to find out, he decided. He'd make a trip to Perth. He'd reneged on the offer of a few weeks' leave over Christmas, but he'd accept it now. It was time to see his family again, and Spud and Muzza. It was time to stop running away.

CHAPTER FIFTEEN

Mike's assumption regarding Ian Pemberton was correct. Ian never thought of the dead girl. He had at first, simply because he'd been scared. After his return to Kalgoorlie he'd lived in terror for months, waiting for some evidence to come to light which would connect him with the Beach Girl Beauty Murder case, which still regularly appeared in the newspapers. But he was well and truly out of the woods now, and there were far too many exciting things happening in his life. The night in Scarborough had become no more than a blur.

Surprisingly enough, things hadn't been quite so easy for Spud. Never one to dwell on the past, he'd quickly put the episode behind him, even congratulating himself on the way he'd got Mike out of a very unpleasant situation. But he hadn't anticipated Ruby Chan and the guilt she would arouse in him.

Ruby had mourned the loss of her daughter. A guarded woman, she rarely shared her feelings, but she'd needed to express her grief, and the only person she'd had to turn to had been Spud. No-one else knew of her relationship to Mayjay.

*

'She was a beautiful little girl, my Mary-Jane,' Ruby said. 'Even as a newborn, people admired her beauty, and newborn babies usually look much the same, don't they?'

Spud nodded.

'Mary-Jane didn't. Mary-Jane was always different.'

This was the third time since Mayjay's death that he'd called around to see Ruby, having promised that he would. She never sobbed or wailed. She didn't even cry, just talked endlessly about her daughter, which made Spud feel most uncomfortable. He was riddled with guilt, knowing that he could have told Ruby the truth about what had happened. But he didn't. He simply sat there while she talked, hoping that when her grief subsided, and the ever-reminding reports in the press died down, Ruby would return to the hard-nosed businesswoman she was.

But it seemed Ruby suffered her own sense of guilt.

'It's all my fault,' she said one day. Unexpectedly, right out of the blue, and at first Spud hadn't known what she was talking about.

They were at the Sun Majestic, sitting in the little back office going over the books for the end of the financial year. Mayjay had been dead for well over six months and Ruby had seemed back to her old self.

'What's your fault?' he asked, presuming she meant the bookwork, which was impeccable as always. Ruby, like himself, was a wizard with figures and he'd never once been able to catch her out. 'Everything's spot-on, Rube, couldn't be better. Jeez, it's been a good year.'

'Mary-Jane always blamed me for being a whore.'

Oh no, Spud thought, here we go again.

'I can't see that there's anything wrong with prostitution myself, so long as a brothel's run good and clean.' Ruby peered at him over the rims of her spectacles; she wore reading glasses these days. 'Whores serve a valuable purpose. There are a lot of lonely men out there. Some just need sex, but some need female company, and a good whore knows that. A good whore's better than any social worker. You just ask some of my old clients, they'll tell you I'm right.'

Why was she so defensive, Spud wondered. Why did she feel the need to justify her existence, and to him of all people? Where was this leading?

'Unfortunately Mary-Jane could never understand that. She saw me as a slut. It's my fault she's dead.'

There was a pause, and Spud felt he should say something, although for the life of him he didn't know what.

'All mothers blame themselves for what happens to their kids,' he said finally, trying to sound wise. 'Even if the kid gets sick the mother'll say it was her fault.' He'd read that somewhere.

But Ruby wasn't listening. She took off her glasses and gazed at the unadorned wall opposite, massaging her brow with her fingertips, trying to ease the headache that threatened.

'Mary-Jane decided very early on to be "bad". It was her way of getting back at me. But I didn't realise she'd learned so many tricks.'

Spud remained silent, still mystified, but realising that she didn't need, and wasn't seeking, any input from him.

'You remember that day when I came home, and she was there with your belt around her neck?'

Jesus, Spud thought, how could he forget? 'Yeah, of course I remember. I didn't know what she was on about.' He smiled, trying to lighten the moment. 'Mayjay liked to shock, that's for sure.'

'*I* was shocked that day.' The almond eyes now focused themselves on him and Spud felt distinctly ill at ease. 'Auto-eroticism, where did she learn that?'

Spud shrugged. How the hell would he know? Did she expect an answer?

Ruby didn't. 'About ten years ago,' she continued, 'there were two girls at the Sun Majestic who specialised in

auto-eroticism. I didn't approve, it's a dangerous game.
But I wasn't the madam then, so what could I do? One
of them was over-zealous with a client one night and he
ended up dead. She clamped the carotid artery for too
long. He had a heart attack.'

The almond eyes continued to observe him, calmly.
'Until that afternoon, when I saw you two together, I had
no idea that Mary-Jane knew about auto-eroticism.'

Christ alive, Spud thought, was she accusing him?
'Jesus, Ruby! She sure as hell didn't learn it from me!'

'Of course she didn't.' Ruby's tone was dismissive and a
trifle impatient. 'She learned it from the Sun Majestic –
from the very place her own mother worked. Spying on the
girls, watching how they did it.' Her eyes wandered, and
she was again staring vacantly at the wall as she pictured
her daughter. 'She would have been only fourteen, fifteen
at the most. How interesting she must have found it.'

Spud breathed a huge sigh of relief, she'd worried him
there for a minute. 'This isn't doing you any good, Rube,'
he said comfortingly. 'There's no point in going over the
past. Mary-Jane's death wasn't your fault, you have to
stop blaming yourself. Besides,' he said, hoping it would
clinch the conversation and they could get back to the
books, 'they'll catch the bastard who did it one day. Just
you wait and see.'

'I hope they don't.'

'Come again?' Spud wasn't sure if he'd heard correctly.

'It wasn't his fault. It was mine.' She turned to face him
once more. 'Mary-Jane wasn't murdered. She'd had a belt
around her neck, so they reckon. There was a wound from
the buckle, that's what the police report said.'

Spud nodded, he'd read it in the papers. He waited for
her to go on.

'They were having sex and things went wrong, that's
what happened. And now some poor bastard is running
around in fear of his life. I feel sorry for him.'

Ruby's composure was deceptive. She wasn't at all confident. She'd given her theory a great deal of thought and she was waiting now for Spud to scoff at her. But she was hoping beyond all hope that he wouldn't.

Spud himself was at a complete loss for words. How easy it would be for him to say 'You're right, Rube,' and tell her the whole story. Surely the truth would comfort her. But he couldn't. He didn't dare.

'Does it make you feel better to think that's the way it was?' he asked.

Ruby shrugged, as if it made no difference. But it did. It made all the difference in the world.

'Well, I'll bet you're right on the money. I'll bet that's *exactly* what happened.'

She said nothing, but Spud sensed he was on the right track. She wanted to be convinced, he could see it in her eyes.

'A sex act that went wrong,' he said emphatically, 'that's just what it was.' His mind searched for the words Mikey had used, what were they? *A ludicrous, hideous, meaningless death, but an accident.* No, that didn't sound right. 'It was a tragic mistake, Rube. It shouldn't have happened. But it was an accident. Nobody's fault – least of all yours.'

Ruby finally cracked. Just a little. She made no movement, but a single tear found its way down her cheek. She'd wanted to believe her theory, even as she'd blamed herself. She'd wanted to know that her daughter hadn't died, terrified, tortured, at the hands of a madman.

Spud stood and, taking her by the shoulders, he raised her gently to her feet. 'Mary-Jane wouldn't have suffered. Her neck was broken. It would have snapped just like that, she wouldn't have felt a thing. You know it's true, don't you, Ruby?'

'Yes,' she said, 'I know it's true.'

He held her close, stroking the still jet-black hair as silent tears streamed down her face. He was relieved, but not entirely absolved of his guilt the way he might have hoped. He felt like a bit of a phoney.

Over the ensuing days, however, Spud quickly shrugged off all remaining vestige of guilt. He conveniently forgot that, without any help from him, Ruby had come up with her own theory. He was pleased with himself. How clever he'd been. Ruby Chan knew precisely how her daughter had died without ever being told the truth.

The mare nuzzled his shoulder, but he kept his hands behind his back, refusing to produce the pieces of carrot she was after. She snuffled down his arm, nostrils aquiver, lips seeking. He was wearing a T-shirt and her velvety softness caressed his bare skin. She started edging around behind him. He turned on the spot, continuing to face her, so she tried the other side. The mare wasn't stupid. He teased her this way and that for a minute or so until she'd had enough. She raised her head, pawed the ground and whinnied. She wasn't going to play any more.

Spud laughed and presented her with a fistful of carrot pieces. When she'd gobbled them out of his open palm, she spoke again. A further whinny, which said 'Now the other hand', and the exercise was repeated.

He loved the mare. She was his favourite. A two-year-old chestnut, her name was Killarney Miss, a tribute to his Irish ancestry which had pleased his father no end, and she was destined to be next season's winner.

Killarney Miss followed him as he walked towards the fence, and when he'd seated himself on the railings she nuzzled him again. She was no longer seeking a reward, she knew the carrots were gone, this was a genuine nuzzle of affection.

Spud scratched the white blaze of the mare's forehead the way she liked him to and gazed across the valley to the distant rolling hills. Behind him, the stud farm and stables and training track were a hive of activity, but this was his favourite spot, where he'd sit surveying the pasture land of his domain feeling like a king.

And he *was* a king, he thought, or he would be soon. Spud Farrell, king of the entrepreneurs. All of this was just the start. The seventies would be his decade – there was no looking back now that he was legitimate. He'd have to relinquish his bookmaker's licence soon, which was a pity, but it was too risky trying to play both sides. And the gambling syndicate – well, he'd hold on to that for a while, but he'd hand the reins over to his junior partner and keep his name out of play. The brothels, the Sun Majestic and the two new ones he and Ruby had bought in Fremantle, could never be traced to him. As for the rest, it was all strictly legit. The stud farm, which was his pride and joy, the offices in Dalkeith which he'd recently extended, the city flat in the Esplanade, which he now owned having bought Pembo out, and Farrell Motors, which had become a real money-spinner.

Anthony Wilson's business scheme had proved an unmitigated disaster. As Spud had privately predicted to Ian Pemberton, Perth was not ready for vintage cars, at least not on the grand scale of Anthony's dreams, and after he'd bought up Anthony's share of the showrooms – for a song, as he'd also predicted – he'd turned the business into a highly profitable Holden car franchise. He'd kept the Itala, however, purchasing it from the original owner, and it sat on constant show proudly bearing its banner *From Paris to Peking to Perth*. Spud considered the vehicle a symbol of prestige, and well worth the hefty sum he'd paid.

The mare was bored now. She was young and needed some action. She frisked off, prancing, tossing her head, enjoying her freedom and the movement of her body. Just as she enjoyed each morning's gruelling work-out. Killarney Miss didn't like to stay still for long.

Spud convinced himself, as he always did, that she was

showing off just for him. That was the only thing missing, he thought as he watched her admiringly. He wanted someone to show off to himself. He wanted a woman. Not a wife, or a partner – he had no wish to share his burgeoning fortune – but he wanted a woman to admire him, to see him as the king of commerce he truly was. He'd been fantasising about a mistress for some time now. She'd be a woman of great beauty so that others would envy him – a symbol of his success – and he'd look after her well. She'd have to be Asian, of course; Ruby had thoroughly spoiled him in that regard.

Spud's early sexual experiences had left him with a lifelong passion for the Oriental. Western women, in his opinion, did not hold the same appeal. He'd briefly considered Lolita, the Chinese-Malay who was his favourite of the girls at the Sun Majestic, but had decided it would be unwise to elevate her to the status of mistress. Her sexual prowess was extraordinary, and she more than qualified in the beauty stakes, but she was too well known as a hooker amongst Perth's corporate and political hierarchy.

He jumped down from the railings. Time to stop daydreaming, there was business to attend to. He'd find his Asian beauty soon enough, but he must be selective. He mustn't rush things just because he felt the desire to show off.

There was a jaunty spring in his step as he walked back to the stables. Besides, he told himself, he'd have someone to show off to only next week. Mike was coming to Perth.

Spud couldn't wait. It had been two whole years. Who better to show off to than his best mate, Mikey? He'd bring him out to the farm the moment he arrived.

But Mike didn't contact Spud the moment he arrived. He climbed on his motorbike and headed for Shenton Park instead.

'G'day, Muz.'

'Mike!' Muzza grabbed the hand that Mike extended and hauled him into a bear-like embrace, Mike losing his balance and sprawling over the wheelchair.

He laughed as he untangled himself and stood. 'It's good to see you, Muz. Gee, you look great.'

Muzza looked more than great, he thought – he looked reborn. Clean-shaven, hair neatly cut, eyes brimming with vitality, he was the baby-faced Muzza of the old days.

'I feel great. Come in and meet Olga.'

The first thing that confronted Mike as he stepped into the open-plan lounge room was his portrait. Now framed, and hung in pride of place, it was magnificent. There were other paintings too. Gone were the agonised faces of Muzza's nightmares; the walls were now covered with works of art. But he had no time to stop and admire them, or even to make a comment, as Muzza eagerly led the way through the arch to the kitchen.

A slim, dark-haired woman was at the sink washing dishes. As they entered, she turned, drying her hands on a tea towel.

'Olga, this is Mike McAllister. Mike, this is Olga.'

Muzza's introduction sounded as if it should have been followed by a fanfare of trumpets – he'd been longing for the moment when the two most important people in his life would meet.

'Hello, Mike.' Olga smiled and offered her hand. 'Murray has told me so much about you. It is good to meet you at long last.'

She spoke with a slight accent. Her voice was attractive, and her smile softened the sharp features of an angular, intelligent face. She was a good deal older than Muzza, who was only twenty-five – Mike guessed her to be in her mid-thirties – and there was no hint of vanity in her appearance. Her hair was tied back in a severe ponytail, she wore no make-up and was minus jewellery except for a single gold chain about her neck.

'Good to meet you too, Olga.' He grinned as they shook. 'Although I must say Muzza's kept you a bit of a secret.'

'He has been waiting for you.'

She draped her arm about Muzza's shoulder and he automatically took her hand in both of his. Mike found the gesture suggestive of a very physical relationship – they looked extraordinarily happy, he thought.

'Olga's my shrink,' Muzza announced. 'All the best shrinks are Polish.'

'I am *not* your shrink,' she corrected him.

'Well, she *used* to be my shrink. She got rid of me as a patient six months ago, said it wasn't ethical.'

'I don't suppose it would be.' Mike smiled – they were so obviously in love.

'Yeah. She said shrinks aren't allowed to treat their own husbands.'

'Their own *what?*'

Muzza laughed, delighted by his best friend's dumb-founded reaction.

'We were married in early November,' he said, and he looked up at his wife.

Olga leaned down to him. Their kiss was one of such tenderness that Mike wondered whether he should turn away. But he didn't, knowing that the two were sharing this moment with him. He felt privileged.

'I haven't told Spud or Pembo, or even the family yet,' Muzza said. 'Nobody knows except the Registrar of Births, Deaths and Marriages. Olga hasn't told anyone either.'

'Murray has been waiting for you, Mike. You are very important to him.'

Mike was moved, but he wasn't sure what to say. He was also a little bewildered. Olga had spoken so meaning-fully. Why had Muzza been waiting for him? Why was he so very important? He covered his confusion by embracing her and then shaking Muzza's hand.

'Congratulations, I'm really happy for you both,' he said, which he thought sounded rather tame, but they beamed with pleasure. Then he thumped Muzza on the back. 'Well, this explains why you look so good.'

'Time for the toast. Grab us the bottle will you, love.'

Olga fetched the vintage Moët et Chandon from the refrigerator.

'We'll get stuck into the beer in a minute,' Muzza said, 'but I thought we should toast ourselves with the real stuff first.'

They sat around the table, clinking glasses to marriage and to friendship, and then Muz got down to business.

'You're here for three weeks, you said on the phone?'

'Yep, arrived yesterday, staying with Mum and Dad. You're my first port of call.'

'Good.' Muzza took his wife's hand in his and their fingers entwined. 'We're going to have a proper ceremony the week after next. Nothing churchy, neither of us is religious, but I've lined up a celebrant and we've decided on Kings Park. Will you be my best man?'

His tone was brisk and efficient, but Mike wasn't fooled. It was plain that the ceremony and his own role as best man were of great importance to Muzza. So this was what Olga had meant, he thought. This was why Muz had been waiting for him.

'Of course I will. I'd be honoured.'

'Fantastic! All set to go.' Muzza smiled excitedly at his wife. 'Tomorrow I'll drop the bombshell on the family.' Then to Mike: 'They'll be over the moon, they're mad about her. They reckon she's the best thing that ever happened to me, and they're not wrong.' He drained his glass, then pulled a face. 'Let's get stuck into the beer, Olga can finish the bottle.'

'Olga is going to the clinic,' she said, rising from the table. It was her day off, but she intended to leave them alone, at least for a few hours. 'You two have a lot to catch up on. Goodbye for the moment, Mike.' She gave him a peck on the cheek. 'I shall leave you with my toy boy.'

Mike found the term oddly amusing from a woman like Olga.

She ruffled her husband's hair. 'Goodbye, my darling.' Then, slinging a voluminous leather handbag over her shoulder, she walked out the door.

Muzza gazed thoughtfully after her. 'She never says that in the company of others.'

'Never says what?'

'She never calls me her toy boy – it's our private joke. She wants me to talk about her. Well, about *us* . . . you know . . .'

Mike's expression was blank. Had he missed something?

Muzza grinned. 'That's the problem with having a wife who's a shrink. She's very, very clever and always one step ahead.' He whirled his wheelchair about and headed for the fridge. 'Grab us a couple of glasses, will you?'

When they were settled with their beers, Muzza started to talk, just as Olga had hoped he would. She'd not openly broached the subject herself. She rarely did when she perceived a problem, choosing instead to hint at a way her husband might find the solution for himself. She'd hoped that he would speak intimately with his best friend. Murray needed to talk to a man, she'd thought. And that man was plainly Mike McAllister.

'Spud and Pembo don't understand Olga and me,' Muzza said. 'Six months ago, when we first started going out together, they really got on my nerves. They didn't say anything, of course, but I could sense it, and I wanted to thump their bloody lights out.' A flash of the old Muzza madness appeared in his eyes. 'Olga told me I was overreacting. She said they were good friends and they were glad to see me happy. She was right, of course.' He relaxed and gave a nonchalant shrug. 'I mean, hell, it's natural for blokes to wonder what a cripple like me gets up to in bed with a woman, isn't it?'

The remark was made without bitterness, a simple statement of fact, but Mike felt uneasy. He hoped Muz didn't include him in those who 'wondered' and he certainly had no desire for detail.

'I don't give a shit what Spud and Pembo think now,' Muzza continued, 'at least, not about me. But it sometimes bugs me that they see Olga as weird.' He laughed. 'Well, they would anyway, wouldn't they? She's hardly their type. They both find intelligent women daunting, have you noticed that? Spud and Pembo can't see beyond the obviously sexual.'

There was a definite touch of sarcasm, he was having a dig at his mates' expense, but the good humour was back as he skolled the remains of his beer and leaned confidentially across the table. 'What they don't realise, Mike, is that Olga is as sexy as all get out.'

Mike was more than uneasy now, he was distinctly embarrassed. He wanted to change the subject, but didn't know how.

'Oh, don't get me wrong,' Muzza continued, oblivious to his friend's discomfort, 'there's been no miracle. I'm not functional, I never will be. But there are other ways to satisfy a woman, particularly a woman as sensual as Olga.' He grinned, and there was an element of insanity in his joy.

Mike decided that it had gone far enough. 'Muz, you don't need to tell me this –'

'But I do! Don't you see? For Christ's sake, man, don't go coy on me! I need to tell just one person on earth, and you're it! I make her happy, Mike! I satisfy her! Do you know what that means?' He thumped his fist on the table in a wild gesture of triumph. 'It makes me feel like a man again! That's what it means!'

Mike felt foolish. How stupid, how shallow he'd been

not to have realised the importance of Murray Hatfield's sexual relationship.

'I'm sorry,' he said. 'I'm really sorry, Muz. I should have understood . . .'

But Muzza wasn't the least bit offended. 'Of course you shouldn't, mate. Why should you?' He grinned to put Mike at his ease. 'Hell, face it, how *could* you? Sex is simple for Casanova McAllister. I'm talking about something more complicated.'

The grin faded as he leaned forward once more, in deadly earnest. 'Olga's changed my life, Mike. I'm overwhelmed when she shares herself with me the way she does. She looks in my eyes and gives herself to me, and I'm lost. Nothing else matters, not even my impotency.'

If only Muzza knew the truth, Mike thought. Sex wasn't simple at all for Casanova McAllister. Casanova McAllister didn't look into the transported face of the woman he loved. Casanova McAllister kept his eyes tightly shut to avoid a dead girl.

'I envy you, Muz,' he said. 'I truly envy you.' He did.

Muzza laughed. He didn't believe Mike for a minute, but it felt so good to have confided in the one man he could trust. 'And so you should, mate,' he said as he poured them both another beer. 'And so you should!' He raised his glass in a toast. 'Thanks for listening, Mike.' Then he downed half his beer and dumped the glass on the table. 'Rightio, we've finished with the sex stuff. Now tell me about the Pilbara.'

They talked for a long time. At least Mike did. And as he spoke of his passion for the Pilbara and the effect it had had on him, Muzza, having satisfied his own need to communicate, observed his friend with an artist's objectivity. He was relieved that Mike no longer appeared tormented as he had upon their last meeting. But he'd changed nonetheless, Muzza thought. He was certainly not the person in the portrait. But then the person in the portrait had been a boy, and this was a man. Perhaps it was as simple as that. He hoped so.

With a couple more beers under their belts, they rang Spud, who'd been waiting for Mike's call.

'Mikey, you're in town! Great! Stay right where you are – I'll pick you up and we'll go out to the farm.'

'I'm at Muzza's.'

'Oh. I see. Muz gets top priority, does he?' It was difficult to tell whether Spud's pique was for real or whether he was joking. 'Okay, we'll take him with us.'

'No, I'll give it a miss today if that's all right, Spud. Could we make it tomorrow?'

'Fine by me.' For one split second Spud *had* been miffed that Mike had chosen to visit Muzza before him. But he'd quickly reproached himself. Mike was playing the good Samaritan – of course he'd call on poor old Muz first, that was Mikey's way. 'Why don't you ask Muz if he wants to come along. He hasn't seen the farm yet.'

'I'll put him on, you can ask him yourself.'

Muzza reneged on the trip to the farm; he had a physiotherapist's appointment, he said. Which wasn't really true, but he thought it best that Spud and Mike have their own private reunion.

He nudged a signal to Mike, who huddled beside him, his ear to the handpiece. 'Hey Spud,' he said, 'want to come to a wedding the week after next?'

'Whose?'

'Mine.'

'Shit! You and Olga are getting *married*?'

The reaction was instinctive and very, very loud. Muzza and Mike shared a grin.

'Yep.'

A moment's pause, then, 'Good on you, mate. I'll be there with bells on.'

After they'd hung up, they rang Ian Pemberton, who'd relocated from Kalgoorlie to Perth where the head offices of Excalibur Holdings were now situated.

Pembo's reaction was a little less crass but equally incredulous.

'*Really?*'

'Yep. Really.'

'Well, of course I'll be there, Muz. I'm very happy for you.'

'Invitations'll be in the post tomorrow,' Muzza said. He laughed as he hung up. 'You see what I mean?'

Mike nodded. 'But they wish you well, Muz.'

'Course they do, I know that.'

Olga arrived home.

'Hello, Mike,' she said. Then she kissed her husband. 'Have you told him?' she asked.

'Told him what?'

'About the portrait, of course.' She smiled. What else could he have possibly thought she meant? But Olga had known the moment she'd walked into the kitchen that her husband had confided in his friend. Murray was positively glowing.

'Yeah, I forgot. The portrait.'

Muzza spun himself around and disappeared through the arch into the lounge room, the others following. He was difficult to keep up with.

They gazed at Mike's portrait, all three of them.

'I want to enter it in this year's Archibald,' Muzza said, 'so long as you don't mind.'

'Of course I don't. It's your creation, do what you will with it. But wouldn't it be better to paint someone famous?'

Mike's casual laugh was a smoke screen. He found the portrait confronting. Here was the person he'd once been: boyish-faced and eager, a young man on the threshold of life. Was it only two years since he'd looked like this?

'Nup. Don't want anyone famous, this is my best piece. I'm calling it *Life's Purpose*.'

Their eyes met for a moment, both of them recalling the conversations of their past. Then Mike looked back at the portrait.

'It's a good title. Spot-on.'

'Yes, isn't it?'

Mike didn't accept Olga's invitation to stay to dinner, much as he'd have liked to.

'Mum's cooking a roast,' he said. 'It's her special treat, she thinks I'm twelve years old.'

'Mothers always do, don't they.' Olga smiled. Then, as she walked him to the door, she said quietly, 'Thank you for being Murray's friend. You are good for him.'

'It works both ways, Olga. He's good for me too.'

'Yes. You are very lucky.' She kissed him on the cheek. 'As am I. We are all lucky to have Murray in our lives.'

Spud picked Mike up in the brand new Land Rover he'd bought for the farm – he drove a Mercedes in the city. The Swan Valley property was only thirty kilometres out of Perth, the roads were excellent, and he didn't actually need a four-wheel-drive vehicle, but he liked the dual image. He freely admitted the fact to Mike, who greeted him with a grin when he arrived at the front door of the McAllister house.

'What's with the Akubra?' Mike looked Spud up and down, taking in the boots, the jeans, the sleeveless T-shirt and, above all, the hat. He'd never seen Spud in an Akubra before.

'Got to look the part, Mikey.' Spud held up his fists and shadow-boxed. 'Gotta create the image, you know what I mean?'

Mike dodged the jabs, then laughed as they embraced.

'I see what you mean, all right,' he said a minute or so later when they walked across the verandah and out the front gate to the spanking new, shiny green Land Rover.

They climbed in, and Spud paused before turning on the

ignition. 'How're you going, Mikey?' he asked meaning-fully. 'Everything okay?'

'Fine, mate. Everything's fine.'

'Good. Just the way it should be.'

Spud started up the engine and switched on the radio. He'd got the message. The night in Scarborough would remain a forbidden topic, just as it had been two years ago. He was more than happy with that.

'Honky Tonk Woman' blared from the speakers, and they drove up Bay View Terrace and onto Stirling High-way singing along to The Rolling Stones.

The day was one of mateship. Spud gave Mike a full guided tour of the stud farm, showing off for all he was worth and revelling in his friend's praise. He had several horses in work, and he introduced Mike to his resident trainer, a beefy man called Gus who was well known and respected in Perth racing circles. They stood at the practice track and watched the two young strappers take the horses through their paces, and Spud remained respectfully silent as Gus gave his instructions.

He was garrulous again, however, as they continued with the tour, starting with the stables where two brood mares were heavily in foal. 'A couple of newcomers in a month or so,' he proudly announced. He was going to have the stables extended, he said with an expansive wave of his hand. 'I'm upgrading everything, right across the board.'

Spud personally greeted each of the stable hands, intro-ducing them on a first-name basis to his good mate Mike. It was apparent that the youngsters all liked the boss. One, a snub-nosed tomboyish girl of around seventeen, was grooming Killarney Miss.

'You're doing a good job, Bec.'

'Thanks, Boss.' Bec beamed.

'Meet next year's Perth Cup winner, Mike,' Spud said boastfully as he scratched the mare's forehead.

They walked down to the paddock and admired the brood mares, then back up to the farmhouse, which wasn't grand. The house itself was the least important item on Spud's agenda, but it was comfortable enough accommodation for Gus and his team. They sat on the front verandah with a couple of beers, eating the meat pies they'd bought on the way. The pies were stone cold by now, but they didn't bother heating them up in the oven of the old wood stove. It would have taken too long and they were starving. The day was hot anyway, and the beers from the icebox were well chilled, which was all that really mattered.

Then they wandered down to Spud's favourite spot where they perched on the railings and looked out over the valley.

'It's beautiful, Spud, truly beautiful.'

'Yeah.' Spud lit up a cigarette. 'And this is just the beginning, Mikey.' Cigarette dangling from his lips, he spread his arms wide, like a jet about to take off. 'This is just the beginning, mate.'

Mike had no doubt that it was. He thought of Spud's early years. His drunken father, his paper runs as a kid, his morning milk deliveries, the way he'd helped support his family even as a schoolboy, and the way he'd scoffed at a tertiary education when Mike had known that, deep down, Spud had envied him and his uni mates.

'You deserve your success, Spud,' he said. 'You've worked hard and you've earned it – good on you.'

That was what clinched the day for Spud. He'd earned Mikey's respect and he felt drunk with pride. Heaven couldn't be much better than this, he thought.

During the drive back to town, Spud brought up the subject of Muzza's impending wedding.

'So what do you think of Olga?' he asked.

He was interested in Mike's opinion. He and Pembo had discussed Olga in detail – they had Muzza's best interests at heart. They'd agreed that she could be quite a good-looking sort if only she did something with herself. Pembo had said that she deliberately presented herself as a 'plain Jane' because sex didn't interest her, which was just as well for Muzza's sake. But Spud had wondered whether perhaps Olga didn't want to present a threat to Muzza by making herself desirable and becoming a possible object of other men's attentions. Spud had thought very deeply on the matter.

'She's a shrink, Pembo,' he'd said. 'Face it, she's smart.'

They'd both decided that Olga was a bit of a weirdo, and left it at that.

'I like her a lot,' Mike said.

'Yeah, well, she's certainly done wonders for Muz, that's for sure,' Spud agreed.

'No, I mean I like her a *lot*. I like her as a woman. I think she's very attractive.'

'Really?'

It wasn't the response Spud had expected. Mike had always had an eye for good-looking women. Hell, Mike McAllister had always been the first to score with the choicest of them all, and he'd certainly been selective. How surprising that he should consider someone as ordinary as Olga attractive, Spud thought.

'I don't see it myself,' he shrugged. 'But horses for courses, eh?'

Mike felt no need to comment and they drove on in silence for a few more minutes. Then Spud said, 'Pembo rang me last night. We both reckon it's really great that they're getting married.'

'Yes, it is, isn't it?' Mike smiled to himself. Olga was right. Muzza was definitely over-reacting.

Spud switched on the radio, but it was 'Je T'aime', not one of his favourites, so he kept the volume down. 'Did you know Pembo's getting married himself next year?'

'Yes, he told me. Arlene. What's she like?'

'Cynthia.'

'What?' Mike looked at him to see whether or not he was joking, but Spud's eyes were on the road ahead and he appeared deadly serious.

'Pembo's marrying his mother.'

'Don't tell me . . . you're Mike . . . I've heard *so* much about you.' Pembo had been about to introduce them, but Arlene had dived in. 'Ian never stops talking about his best friend at uni. How *divine* to meet you, Mike. I'm Arlene.'

Mike caught Spud's eye and wanted to burst out laughing.

'Arlene Johnstone, Mike McAllister.' Ian did the formal introductions. 'Mike, this is my fiancée, Arlene.'

Arlene laughed. 'There's no need to stand on *ceremony*, darling. I feel as if we've known each other for *years*, don't you, Mike?'

'I sure do, Arlene. For years.' He avoided Spud's eyes.

Despite the burning hot February afternoon, it was comfortable enough on the hill of Kings Park amongst the shade of the trees, a light sea breeze coming up from the river. Muzza and Olga had instructed their guests to wear casual gear and everyone had, with the exception of Arlene, who teetered about on ridiculously high heels that sank into the grass with her every step. Not that she minded. Fashion statements were necessary in Arlene's opinion, and she'd willingly freeze in a cocktail frock on the worst winter night whenever the occasion called for it.

Sonny and Cher's 'I Got You Babe' played through the sound system's speakers, and Mike stood beside Muzza and the celebrant as Olga was escorted 'down the aisle' by her friend and colleague, Dr Leo Bradman. Mike thought how very elegant she looked in her simple red dress and flat-heeled sandals. The only make-up she'd applied was a touch of lipstick, but her black hair was loose and fell about her shoulders. She had lovely hair. Strange, he thought, that Spud and Pembo couldn't see what an attractive woman Olga was in her understated way.

The ceremony was charming, and very, very touching. Muzza, surrounded by his family and friends, glowed even more radiantly than the bride.

The two looked into each other's eyes as they recited Shakespeare's 116th sonnet. They'd learned it off by heart, and Olga started.

'Let me not to the marriage of true minds
Admit impediments. Love is not love
Which alters when it alteration finds . . .'

She completed the first stanza perfectly, and it was Muzza's turn. He started out well, but then . . .

'Love's not Time's fool, though rosy lips and cheeks
Within his . . .'

Within his what, Muzza thought. He'd had a sudden mental blackout. Within Time's what?

'. . . bending sickle's compass come.' Olga completed the line for him. She didn't murmur the words, or hiss them under her breath hoping no-one would hear her, she simply completed the line and Muzza continued.

'Love alters not with his brief hours and weeks,
But bears it out even to the edge of doom.'

No-one had laughed at the stumble. Mike was sure that most hadn't even noticed, presuming it was part of the double act. And Muzza was the least worried of all as he grinned, sharing the joke with his wife. He looked so incredibly young, Mike thought.

'If this be error and upon me prove'd,
I never writ, nor no man ever love'd.'

They completed the final couplet together.

The celebrant called upon Mike as best man to produce the ring, which he did, then he and Leo Bradman, who had 'given away' the bride, stepped back amongst the guests as the vows were exchanged. Apart from several friends from the clinic where she worked, Olga had no family present, nor any representatives of her past, which Mike found poignant knowing her story as he did.

Olga had lost touch with her parents and her younger sister, who were in Poland, Muzza had told him. Her Jewish father had disowned her when she'd gone against his wishes and married an Australian whom she'd met at university in Warsaw. A year later, she'd come to Australia with her new husband, but the marriage had lasted for only one further year and she'd been left on her own at the age of twenty-six.

'Tough call,' Muzza had said, 'alone in a foreign country, deserted by a man who'd never really loved her in the first place.' He'd sounded condemnatory as he'd spoken about the husband. 'She doesn't say much, but I can read between the lines. The way I see it, the bastard just wanted to get into her pants. She was a virgin and the only way to do it was to marry her. She loved him. She trusted him enough to leave her homeland and travel halfway around the world! But the novelty wore off and he left her stranded – what a prick!'

It had been the first time Muzza had ever talked about Olga's past and he'd got himself quite worked up. 'She refused to go home though. Her qualifications weren't recognised, so she had to work in a restaurant at night to put herself through uni. But she did it. She's proud. If her family didn't want her, then she didn't want them, she said.'

The wedding ceremony concluded, and there was a round of applause as husband and wife kissed. Then Muzza winked at Mike; a wink that said 'We've been married for three months, if only they knew.'

Well-wishers gathered around the couple, and Muzza's parents, siblings, aunts, uncles and cousins surrounded the bride, embracing her as one of their own.

Well, Olga certainly had a family now, Mike thought. He looked at Muzza who, even as he accepted the con-gratulations and hearty slaps on the back, had eyes for no-one but his wife. And she'd sure as hell found love and a man she could trust.

Waiters popped champagne corks and people mingled while the couple signed the official registration papers and posed for photographs. Muzza and Olga hadn't hired a photographer, but family members and friends had arrived with cameras and were insistent, so they obliged with good humour.

'What a *lovely* ceremony, wasn't it?'

Mike had been about to join Spud and Pembo, who'd parked themselves over beside the help-yourself beer table, but Arlene had latched on to him again.

'Yes, it certainly was,' he agreed.

'You *will* be at *our* wedding, won't you, Mike? We're getting married at Christmas – *promise* me you'll be there.'

'I promise, Arlene. Cross my heart and hope to die.'

She laughed gaily, a laugh very reminiscent of Cynthia's, Mike couldn't help thinking. She even *looked* like Cynthia. A young Cynthia anyway – she couldn't have been more than twenty-one, twenty-two at the outside. But like Cynthia, she was very slim, very blonde and very beautiful, in a synthetic way. It was uncanny. He wondered if, like Cynthia Pemberton, there was a clever woman beneath the façade. He somehow doubted it.

'I'm so glad.' Arlene's smile faded, she was serious now. 'Your friendship is important to Ian, you know.'

It certainly was. Mike was exactly the sort of friend Ian should cultivate, Arlene thought as she glanced over at her fiancé, in conversation with Spud Farrell. Spud was essential because he was well on the way to becoming rich, as indeed was Ian, and the rich naturally gravitated to one another. But men of good family like Mike McAllister, men who had class and commanded respect, were highly advantageous from an image point of view.

'I'm not sure you realise just *how* important,' she added with a meaningful look, which said that *she* did.

Mike found both the look and the attempted sincerity gauche. Here was one area of expertise she hadn't mastered in the Cynthia manner, he thought. Cynthia was so blatantly flirtatious when pretending to sincerity that you couldn't help succumbing even when you knew it was a sham. If Arlene was going to model herself on her future mother-in-law, then she'd better start taking lessons.

'Well, friendships formed at university are usually very lasting, aren't they?' he said, easing his way out of the conversation.

'Isn't that funny,' her face lit up, 'that's exactly what my father says. Daddy always says his closest friends are those he made at uni.' Arlene smiled, pleased that they'd discovered common ground so quickly. 'Flinders University, that is, we're from South Australia. Daddy's an orthopaedic surgeon.' She wanted Mike to know that, like him, she came from good stock.

'Really?'

'Yes, Mummy went to Flinders too, that's where they met, but they came to Perth when I was fifteen. We've been living out at Kalamunda, Daddy likes the country air, but we recently moved into town.' Her smile was that of the confidante. 'He says he got sick of commuting, but I actually think Mummy talked him into it. She told me she felt stranded in the hills.'

'Yes, I suppose she would.'

Mike cast an envious glance towards Spud and Pembo at the beer table; it seemed he was stuck with Arlene for a while.

Spud poured himself a second glass and then topped up Pembo's.

'So Arlene likes the penthouse, does she?' he asked.

The seemingly innocent query was laden with innuendo, and the two shared a smile. Ian had filled Spud in on the facts. Arlene, who lived with her parents at their new

waterside home in Nedlands, played the virginal fiancée to
the hilt, and with great success. Her family and friends had
no idea that the two of them had been sleeping together
for the past three months.

'Yes,' Ian replied. 'She particularly likes the wall-to-wall
mirrors in the master bedroom.'

They laughed.

'Well, I'm glad it paid off for you,' Spud said. 'It's a good
buy too. You won't go wrong there.'

Arlene and her need for secrecy had been the reason
Ian had sold his share in the Esplanade flat to Spud. Arlene
wouldn't sleep with him while the two shared accommodation.

'How could you possibly suggest it, Ian?' she'd said,
horrified.

At the time, he hadn't been sure whether her horror had
been a general reaction to his suggestion they make love
before they were married, or whether it had been merely
the thought of Spud's nearby presence. He'd shopped
around for another apartment, but Arlene had remained
unforthcoming, and he'd resigned himself to the awful fact
that he might have to wait for over a year. He was quite
prepared to do so, he was obsessed with Arlene.

Then the real estate agent had shown them the penthouse, tastefully leaving them alone to explore it for
themselves.

'How *divine*!' she'd said. The kiss they'd shared in the
master bedroom had left Ian in no doubt. She'd never
kissed him like that before. 'How absolutely *divine*!' And
she'd kissed him again, the same way. He'd bought the
place that very afternoon.

Built in 1961, the Mount Eliza apartments at the top
of Mount Street had been Perth's first luxury high-rise
apartment complex, and as such remained extremely con-
troversial. It towered on the hill overlooking Kings Park,
a circular building fifteen storeys high, and had created a

furore at the time of its construction, most considering it
an eyesore. The fuss had eventually died down, although
there were many who still referred to it scathingly as
'the thermos' or 'the spark plug'. There was no denying,
however, the luxury of its interior or the panoramic views
afforded its occupants, particularly those whose apartments took up a whole floor, as Ian's did.

Ian Pemberton's penthouse looked out towards Rottnest
Island to the west and the Darling Scarp to the east. It
looked up and down the Swan River and over Kings Park,
or over the city and the northern suburbs, depending upon
which room or window one chose to look out from.

Arlene had a key to the apartment, and while her fiancé
was away on field trips or working at his Kalgoorlie offices,
as he so often was, she'd pop in. She'd wander, clockwise
or anti-clockwise dependent upon her mood. She adored
the apartment. It must have cost Ian a *fortune*, she thought.

It had. Or rather, it had cost Excalibur Holdings a
fortune.

'Yes, it's a good buy,' Ian agreed with Spud, and the conversation turned to business.

The wedding party and guests were about to retire to the
Kings Park Restaurant just up the path where the reception was to be held. But Muzza wanted a quick break.
He'd had enough of posing for photographs and respond-
ing to toasts with champagne. He was after a beer with his
mates.

'Go on,' Olga urged. 'I will lead the troops and see you
at the reception.'

'Good on you, love.'

He looked about. Spud and Pembo were over by the
beer table, but where was Mike? Olga spied him first,
locked in conversation with Arlene.

'I will send Mike to you,' she said. 'Join your friends,
darling.'

Muzza gratefully zoomed off, and in less than a minute had a beer in his hand.

Arlene was still in full flight. She'd been telling Mike about her interest in fashion design. She'd graduated from her arts course at UWA only last year.

'Just imagine,' she said, 'if I'd gone to uni a few years earlier, I'd have been there with you and Ian. Isn't it funny the way life pans out?'

'Yes, I suppose it is.'

Convinced by now that Arlene was seriously dumb, Mike had resigned himself to the conversation – she was, after all, only trying to be nice. But he was deeply thankful for Olga's interruption.

'We are going to the reception, Arlene,' Olga said.

Arlene found the intrusion extremely rude. Bossy too, she thought. But then Olga was often bossy. And where were her manners? She could at least have said 'excuse me'.

'Lovely.'

Arlene smiled at Mike, presuming they'd walk up to the restaurant together and continue their chat. She must ensure she sat next to him at the reception – she'd switch the place settings if necessary. Her plan to cultivate his friendship on a personal level was going extremely well. But Olga once again interrupted, tucking a comradely arm through Arlene's.

'The boys are going to have a quick beer before they join us,' she said. 'Shall we go with the others?' Olga was always friendly towards Arlene. Sure that, deep down, the girl was insecure, she felt sorry for her.

Arlene was irritated, but left with no choice. 'I'll see you shortly, Mike,' she called over her shoulder as Olga led her away.

Arlene didn't like Olga. Olga was foreign and plain and yet utterly self-assured. The mixture was not right at all, she should recognise her place in the pecking order. And how on *earth* could the woman get around the way she did, without any *make-up*? Ian, strangely enough, refused to encourage any criticism of Olga. He was normally amused when Arlene bitched about other women – he'd laugh with delight and egg her on. But not when it came to Olga. 'Yeah, she's a bit of a weirdo, but she's good for Muz', was all he'd say. Arlene found it most annoying.

Mike, Spud and Ian raised their glasses to Muzza.

'Here's to a long and happy life with a woman who loves you, mate,' Spud said.

'To Muzza and Olga,' Mike toasted.

'To Muzza and Olga,' Ian repeated, and all three drank heartily while Muzza grinned from ear to ear.

He raised his own glass. 'To mateship,' he declared.

'To mateship.' They drank again.

Then, just like the old days, the toasts continued. They kept topping up their glasses as they drank to Mike and his new job with Dampier Salt, to Spud's stud farm and next year's Perth Cup, and to Excalibur Holdings and its fresh enterprise in the Pilbara.

It appeared they'd run out of toasts, but Muzza came up with another.

'To the next matrimonial cab off the rank,' he said. 'To Pembo and Arlene.'

Muzza didn't particularly warm to Arlene, but he'd been influenced by Olga, as was often the case. Olga was a very astute judge of people's character, and if Olga felt the girl was insecure then she was no doubt right. Anyway, he thought, Pembo was mad about Arlene, and that was all that mattered. As mates it was their bounden duty to accept her into the fold.

Mike and Spud were plainly in agreement.

'To Pembo and Arlene,' they said with gusto.

Ian beamed. He wished Arlene was with them so she could hear the toast. She was keen for his friends to like her, and this was proof that they did. Hell, what man wouldn't like a woman as good-looking as Arlene? He couldn't wait to see her walking down the aisle, the most beautiful bride in the world. He'd be the envy of all. And then they could live together as man and wife. He longed for the day, he was sick of the subterfuge. A whole ten months to go! God, he wished it was Christmas.

The four of them were well in the mood to party as they made their way up the path to the restaurant.

'Hey Muzza,' Ian said quietly when they got to the door, 'could you somehow manage to get that toast in towards the end of the reception?'

Muzza looked blank.

'You know . . . me and Arlene and the wedding at Christmas, she'd really like that.'

'Course I will, mate.' Muzza was amused. How very out of character for Ian Pemberton to sound humble. But he found the request touching. There were no two ways about it: the man was in love. Pembo was putty in Arlene's hands.

CHAPTER SIXTEEN

Andrew had been surprised when Jo had announced that she was going home for Christmas, and that furthermore she was leaving in just one week.

'But you never go home for Christmas,' he said. 'Your mother always comes to Sydney. Why the change? And why so soon? It's three weeks until Christmas.'

'Well, I'm not actually going home – not to Manjimup anyway. Mum's moved to Perth.' She appeared a little distracted.

'But surely your mother can come over here? What about Alana?'

Jo smiled in spite of herself. His protective attitude towards Alana was always endearing.

'She's three years old, Andy. She's very excited about the prospect of flying in an aeroplane. I couldn't possibly disappoint her now.'

'You mean you've already told her? Before you talked it over with me?' Andrew was genuinely shocked.

'Yes.' This was the down side, she thought. Andy was under the impression she belonged to him, but she didn't. Perhaps she loved him, she really didn't know, but the more proprietorial he became, the more she retreated into herself. 'I need to go home, Andy,' she said. 'Things have happened. I need to see my mother.'

She'd closed off, he could tell. It annoyed him when she did that, but he'd learned not to push her too hard. Johanna preferred to keep her feelings to herself, and it was difficult to get through to her at times. He wouldn't pursue the conversation now, he decided, but he'd choose the right moment, when she was at her most receptive. He'd need to make his bid before she left for Perth.

Johanna Whitely and Andrew Gaden had been lovers for over a year. He'd initially kept his distance after she'd shocked him with the news of her child – why pursue a woman with a baby, he'd thought. But he'd felt guilty. Jo needed a friend and he was letting her down. He'd realised only several weeks after he'd renewed their friendship that he'd been fooling himself. He was more in love with her than ever, and it wasn't friendship he wanted.

It had been a full six months before they'd made love, and he'd expected things to change after that. But they hadn't really. She was sensual in bed, and openly affectionate, but he still didn't know where he stood with her. Johanna remained a mystery.

Jo remained a mystery to herself in some ways. What was it she wanted? She'd given in to Andrew's sexual overtures during a moment of weakness, never intending to embark upon a full-blown affair. But Andy had proved irresistible. He was fun, he made her laugh, and furthermore he was an excellent lover. She found their sex far more fulfilling than the exchange of favours she'd experienced with Mike. So how come she didn't love him the way she'd loved Mike? Jo had given up asking herself that question.

Despite his repeated requests, she'd refused to move in with him during her final year at university, continuing to stay at Nora's house in Potts Point, but most weekends had been spent at the flat he'd bought in Double Bay.

Andrew, now a highly sought-after lawyer, enjoyed the trappings that went with success, and that included a three-bedroom apartment with harbour views.

He'd reserved one of the spare bedrooms for Alana, fresh toys appearing on a regular basis, and he'd recently had the walls covered with Donald Duck wallpaper. Jo had found it somewhat confronting.

'Andy, you shouldn't have!'

'Why not? Look at her. She loves it.'

Allie was kissing every Donald Duck she could reach.

'You spoil her too much already.'

Jo knew that her response sounded weak, just as she knew that the indulgence of the child was not the problem at all. The problem was her own feeling of entrapment. Andy treated her like some form of acquisition, he was taking over her life. And now, it would appear, her daughter's too.

'I like to spoil her. Hey Allie,' he said, falling to his knees, 'give your Uncle Andy a great big hug.' And Allie charged into his outstretched arms.

The wooing of Alana had initially been part of Andrew's game plan. He had determined to marry Johanna. If in doing so he must inherit a child, then he would shoulder the burden, he'd told himself. But Allie had long since ceased to be a burden. Allie, with her mop of black curls and laughing blue eyes, had won his heart.

He'd decided to wait until Jo had completed her course and gained her degree before proposing. He felt very confident. Surely she must recognise what he had to offer. A man who loved her, a ready father for her daughter and a comfortable lifestyle – the combination was perfect. Besides, she loved him, although she didn't appear to recognise the fact.

Her final year now completed, Andrew had simply been waiting for the results to come through – it was a foregone conclusion that she'd pass. Yet here Jo was, announcing that she and Allie were off to Perth. In a week! Further-more, there appeared no grounds for discussion. Johanna could be very frustrating at times.

He chose the right moment several days later, on a rare Sunday afternoon when they were lolling in bed after having made love. Allie was at the zoo with Nora and Geoff and their children.

'Enjoy a Sunday off for a change,' Nora had laughed to Jo. 'With three kids in the car there's no room for you anyway.'

'How wonderfully decadent.' Jo lay nestled against Andy, her head in the crook of his shoulder, one arm draped over his chest.

'I'll miss you while you're in Perth,' he said, toying with her hair. She wore it a little longer these days, shoulder length. He liked to think she did so in order to please him, but he doubted it. Jo was very much her own woman. Then he casually asked, 'Do you know how long you'll be away?'

'I'm not sure. A month, maybe two.' He deserved to know the reason she was going, she thought, it had been unfair of her to close him out. 'Mum's marriage has broken up,' she said abruptly. 'My stepfather walked out on her. I need to make sure she's all right.'

He waited for any further explanation, but none was forthcoming. Not that he'd really expected it. She never spoke of her family.

'I see.' Now was the time, he thought. 'There's some-thing I want to ask you, Jo, and I'd like an answer before you leave.'

No, no, she thought. Don't ask me, Andy. Not again, please. I don't want to live with you. I'm not your posses-sion. I'm not anyone's possession.

'Will you marry me?'

She lay for a moment in stunned silence.

'You're surprised,' he said, turning to look at her. 'Why?'

She wondered why herself. She'd known that he loved her; why was this unexpected? But it was. Throughout their affair, the thought that he might want to marry her hadn't once crossed her mind.

'I love you, Jo.' He kissed her. 'I love you very much, and I love Allie too. I want to be a husband to you and a father to Allie. What do you think? We'd make a great team.'

She met his gaze with forthright honesty. 'I'm not sure if I'd be a good wife, Andy. I've worked hard and I want a career.'

'Well, of course you do,' he laughed. 'I wouldn't stand in your way. God, Jo, that's what I love about you, your sheer bloody tenacity!'

She sat up and looked at him as he propped on one elbow.

'I'd be a fool to knock back an offer like this, wouldn't I?'

'Yes, you would.'

'Do you want to saddle yourself with a child so early in your career?'

'A child like Allie, yes.'

'Do I love you enough, Andy?'

She thought she'd floored him with that one, but he laughed again.

'Yes, you do, Jo. You love me far more than you realise.'

He was right, she thought. In her obsession to maintain her independence, she'd failed to recognise that she *did* love him.

'Well, I suppose we can take it as read then,' she said.

'May we adjourn the court now?'

He pulled her down on top of him and they rolled about on the bed like children.

They didn't make love – not immediately anyway. Andy was very much in the mood for a return bout, but he opted

for conversation instead. He talked about their future and
Jo's career, doing his best to wind her up and getting himself as excited as a schoolboy in the process. She'd serve
her residency year and then he'd help her set up her own
practice, he said.

'With your very own brass plaque,' he proclaimed theatrically, painting a sign in the air. 'Dr Johanna Whitely,
MD. No, no, that's wrong. Dr Johanna Gaden, MD.'

'Aren't you being a bit premature?' she laughed, 'I
haven't passed yet, let alone been offered a residency.'

But he dismissed any reservations with a careless wave
of the hand. 'You'll come in amongst the top ten, you
always do. There isn't a hospital in Sydney that won't
jump at the chance of scoring an intern like you.'

Andy's excitement was always irresistible, even to a
pragmatist like Jo, so she gave up trying to be the voice of
reason and lay back delighting in his boyish enthusiasm.

Half an hour later, they made love, and afterwards, as
he held her close, he said, 'I'd like to submit a plea on my
own behalf.' She looked a query. 'A shorter sentence?' he
begged. 'Please, Jo? Two months is a very long time.'

'Yes, it is, isn't it.' She kissed him. 'I'll come home in a
month. I promise.'

He smiled to himself. She hadn't realised that it was the
first time she'd referred to Sydney as 'home'– in his
presence, anyway.

The flight was slow, nearly five hours: the plane was flying
into a strong westerly.

After the initial thrill of take-off, Allie had settled down
with her crayons and sketch pad. She was drawing a
picture of the aeroplane for Heely, and even the pockets of
turbulence they hit now and then didn't distract her. Allie
loved drawing and she wanted to impress Heely.

Hillary's insistence, right from the start, that her grandchild call her by name had resulted in 'Heely'. She'd been

unable to make any further inroads, and had resigned
herself to the fact that she'd be Heely from now on. 'Well,
anything's better than Grandma,' she'd said.

Jo was trying to immerse herself in the paperback she'd
bought at the airport, but with little success. She couldn't
help wondering what would await her when she arrived in
Perth. Her mother had sounded so strange on the phone.

'I won't be coming to Sydney this Christmas,' Hillary
had said. 'Besides, it's *your* turn to visit *me*. You promised,
remember?'

Jo had felt cornered. She'd managed to avoid the
problem of Christmas and Manjimup with surprising ease
over the years of her study. 'I'll come over when I've
finished my course, Mum,' she'd said, and Hillary had
been very accommodating.

'I understand, dear, I'll come to Sydney. Unfortunately
Darren won't be with me, he's frightfully busy lately.'

Now it appeared Hillary was taking her up on her
promise. Jo had started to hedge.

'Well, it's a bit difficult for me to come to Manjimup
right now, Mum. My results aren't through yet and –'

'I'm not in Manjimup. I'm in Perth. Darren left me six
months ago.'

'Oh.' Jo was amazed. How come her mother hadn't told
her at the time? How come she wasn't hysterical?

'Is there someone else involved?' She'd posed the
question carefully, gently.

'Yes.' Hillary had sounded strained, but quite in control.
'Someone very pretty and a good deal younger. Twenty-
eight, in fact. It's been going on for some time.'

'I see.' So Darren had traded Hillary in for a newer
model, Jo thought. How surprising that he hadn't done
it sooner.

'He and Yvonne have stayed in Manjimup and I've come
up to Perth. We thought it would be better that way.'

Jo was speechless. How extraordinary that her mother

could discuss the situation so calmly, even referring to the woman by name. She'd have expected Hillary to be reduced to a wreck under such circumstances.

'I have a very nice little flat on the corner of Victoria Street and Adelaide Terrace, lovely and central. And there's a good-sized spare room – you and Allie will be quite comfortable.' Hillary's voice had held a definite plea. 'I'd really like to see you, dear.'

'I'll be there in a week, Mum.'

Hillary appeared very much as she'd sounded on the phone, in total control, but the strain was evident.

'How lovely, darling,' she said of Allie's aeroplane drawing.

'And this is you, Heely,' the little girl said, turning the page to a stick figure with a lot of hair and red lips.

'Goodness me, don't I look pretty.'

'Yes.'

Allie fixed her vivid blue eyes on her grandmother's, pleased that Heely had recognised the likeness. Then she sprawled on the floor with her sketch pad, happily engrossed in another drawing. But within several minutes she was fast asleep so they put her to bed.

'Are you hungry?' Hillary asked. 'There's chicken, and salad, and –'

'No, thanks Mum, we ate on the plane.'

'Right.' Hillary was glad, she wasn't hungry either. 'Coffee? Tea? White wine?' It was clear that she favoured the latter.

'A glass of wine'd be great, thanks,' Jo said, although she would have preferred a cup of tea.

'I like the flat, Mum, it's cosy,' she said as Hillary collected the wine from the refrigerator. The flat was actually more gloomy than cosy, she thought. In a single storey block of only five apartments, each with its own small front porch, it was not unattractive, but the afternoon sun barely penetrated the narrow front windows. 'You don't get much light though, do you?' In typical fashion, Jo couldn't help but comment.

'You know me, darling, I don't like the sun. So bad for the skin.'

They settled themselves in the large comfortable leather armchairs which were far too big for the small lounge room.

'These are from Manjimup,' Jo said. She recognised them, just as she recognised the sideboard and the coffee table, and through the door, the dining setting, also far too big for the room.

'Yes. Darren set the flat up for me. He wanted me to feel at home.'

Out with the old and in with the new, Jo thought. He'd no doubt be acquiring brand new furnishings for his brand new mistress.

'He's been very thoughtful,' Hillary said. 'And extremely generous, I must say. He bought me this flat. It's in my name, I own it.'

What was so generous about that, Jo wondered. Darren was a very wealthy man, he was on the board of Bunnings now. He held shares in the richest timber mills in the state and owned any number of properties. What's more, she'd be willing to bet that much of his capital had been invested in Hillary's name for tax purposes. Darren was robbing his wife blind, Jo thought angrily. Hillary was owed far more than this poky little flat.

'When are you going to get a divorce?' she asked bluntly.

'Not for a while yet.' Hillary took several healthy sips of her wine. 'It's sort of a trial separation while we see how things pan out.' She sounded evasive.

So the bastard was stringing her along, letting her live in hope, Jo thought. She longed to drill some sense into her mother's deluded brain. 'He'll never come back to you

Mum, can't you see?' she wanted to yell. 'You're well rid
of the bastard. Divorce him! Take him to the cleaners, milk
him for all you can get! You've earned it!'

'You need to discuss a proper settlement, Mum,' she said
instead.

'Oh no, dear, it's not necessary. As I said, he's been more
than generous. I receive a very healthy monthly allowance,
far more than I need really. Poor darling, he feels so
terribly guilty.'

Guilty! He feels guilty?

Hillary could see the disbelief on her daughter's face.
Dear Jo, she thought. Dear darling Jo was trying so hard
to be protective, but she didn't understand. She never had.

'He loves me, Jo, and he always will. He told me so.
I'll be his true love for as long as he lives.'

'Then why has he left you?'

'He can't help himself, darling.' Hillary's smile was
fragile, but strangely serene. She'd accepted the tragic
truth of her situation. 'He's obsessed with Yvonne. He's
heartbroken and riddled with guilt, the poor man, but
there's nothing he can do about it.'

That same look of disbelief, Hillary noted. But then it
wasn't within Jo's capacity to understand a man of passion
like Darren. Johanna was too remote, too clinical. Her
daughter had never known, and probably never *would*
know, a love such as she and Darren had shared. Hillary
tried, very gently, to explain the situation.

'Darren has never been able to resist beauty, Jo. It's
the reason he fell in love with me in the first place. He
was always so proud of my beauty, it was my gift to him,
he'd say.'

She finished her glass of wine and stared thoughtfully at
the bottle, finding the words difficult, but wanting to be
honest with her daughter.

'When my beauty faded, it was only natural for his eye
to wander. I've known for some time that he's been

attracted to other women. Younger women. I've even known that lately he's slept with them from time to time.'

Lately? Darren's been sleeping around throughout your entire marriage, Mum.

Hillary gave a rueful shrug. 'I've had to accept it. At fifty there's little one can offer by way of competition. I just didn't anticipate him falling in love,' she said regretfully. 'Nor did he. That's why he's so torn, poor darling.'

Jo was appalled. Her mother was accepting responsibility for her husband's infidelity. Hillary truly believed that the blame lay with her and the loss of her beauty. Were there no limits to Darren's Machiavellian powers?

'But you're beautiful, Mum. You're an extraordinarily beautiful woman.'

'I'm not twenty-eight, dear.'

'You do know that he won't come back to you, don't you?' Jo said brutally.

'Yes, I do believe you're right.' Hillary's hand was shaking a little as she poured herself another glass of wine. 'But we'll always have the past, and he'll visit me regularly.'

Oh no, he won't, Mum. Once he's certain you're out of his hair, he'll wipe you completely.

'A person only has one great love in their life,' Hillary continued, quietly but with utter conviction. 'Darren's been mine, and I've been his. Nothing will change that.'

Jo remembered how she'd longed to confront her mother. How she'd ached to see the look on Hillary's face when she spewed out the truth about the monster she'd married. That day would never come, she now realised. Even if her mother were to believe her, which she very much doubted, the truth would render Hillary's life meaningless.

Hillary decided to change the subject. Her daughter's brutal honesty was disturbing.

'How long will you be staying, dear?'

'I was planning on a month, but I could make it a bit longer if you like.' She'd be breaking her promise to Andy, she thought. He'd be disappointed. She was disappointed herself, she'd wanted to get home to him. But she'd noticed the rate at which her mother had drunk the wine. And she'd seen the shaky hand on the bottle. 'Perhaps two months?'

'Two months would be lovely. I'd like that very, very much.'

Mike stepped out of the exclusive drapery store into London Arcade, hoisting the bulky gift-wrapped box under his arm. It wasn't heavy, but it'd be a bastard getting it home on the bike, he thought. He should have had the bed linen set delivered, but Pembo's wedding was only five days away, and with the Christmas rush the store wouldn't guarantee the package's early arrival, so he hadn't dared risk it. Just as well he hadn't undertaken the crystal glasses or the bone china dinner service which had also been on Arlene's wedding gift list, he thought. Spud had fortunately taken on the major breakables. 'You can't afford them anyway, mate,' Spud had said. 'Go for the bed linen.'

He started down the Arcade towards St Georges Terrace, dodging the Christmas shoppers and tourists. London Arcade, with its mock Tudor design, was a picturesque link between Hay Street and the Terrace and a popular attraction to both locals and visitors.

The aroma of fresh coffee wafted from a nearby crowded café, and Mike plonked himself at the one vacant table outside. It was crammed next door to a cigarette kiosk and he nearly upset the rack of postcards as he dumped his package on the seat beside him.

'What'll it be?' the young waitress asked through her chewing gum.

He ordered a coffee and a toasted ham sandwich, then

sat back to watch the passing parade, feeling like a tourist himself. The city and its busyness was a far cry from the outback townships of Roebourne and Dampier.

As he looked about, his eye was caught by the woman seated several tables away. Of indeterminate age, probably in her forties, she was extremely beautiful and seemed somehow familiar. He was sure he didn't know her, but who did she remind him of? Then he realised, with a shock, that it was Johanna. The woman was an older version of Jo, he thought as he openly stared at her.

His coffee arrived.

'The sandwich'll only be a few minutes.'

He barely heard the young waitress. He remained transfixed by the woman. She was seated alone, several shopping bags piled on the chair beside her, and as she sipped her coffee her eyes were focused on the gift store opposite.

Mike followed her gaze and through the passers-by he saw a little girl staring into the window, entranced by the display.

'Allie,' the woman called, and Mike looked back at her. She beckoned to the child. The child joined her.

'Stay where I can see you, darling,' the woman said.

The little girl peered around for something of nearby interest. 'Can I look at the postcards?' she asked.

'Yes. You can buy one if you like.'

Taking the coin the woman handed her, the child skipped happily over to the kiosk and the rack of postcards beside Mike.

The woman's eyes, following her, suddenly met Mike's gaze and he felt caught out. Then she smiled. He smiled back, thankful that she apparently presumed it was the child who had intrigued him, and that she hadn't thought he was ogling her. He turned his attention to the child, who was closely examining the postcards, and with another sense of shock he realised that she, too, seemed familiar.

The little girl, aware that she was being watched, turned and smiled.

'Hello,' she said, electric blue eyes locking into his.

'Hello,' Mike replied. He knew this child.

'Which one do you like the best?' she asked, jabbing a forefinger at the postcards. 'The koala or the kangaroo?'

'The koala, I think.' Her face belonged to photographs from his childhood. Her face was *his* face.

'Me too.'

She took the card from the rack and held it up to the man in the kiosk, the coin in her other outstretched hand, but he leaned down and ruffled her hair.

'You can have it for nuthin', sweetheart,' he said. 'Call it a Christmas present.'

'Thank you.' She turned back to Mike with a happy and all-too-familiar grin. 'He gave it to me for nothing,' she said.

Mike hadn't moved a muscle, he hadn't even dared think. It was too bizarre.

She held the postcard out for his inspection. 'See?' she said. 'It's got a baby on its back.'

'So it has.'

Allie beamed at the nice man. Then she kissed the post-card. Allie always kissed things she liked, and she very much liked koalas.

'What's your name?' Mike asked.

'Alana.'

He froze.

'What's yours?'

'Mike.'

'I'm named after a boat,' she said proudly. 'A beautiful, beautiful yacht.'

'Yes,' he heard himself say, 'I know.'

'Do you really?' Allie looked at him, wide-eyed. She'd thought that no-one else but her mother knew about the boat. 'Have you seen it?'

'Yes, I have. And you're right, it's a very, very beautiful

yacht.' He looked towards the woman, whom he knew to be Johanna's mother, and again the woman smiled at him. 'That lady's your grandmother, isn't she?' he asked the little girl.

'That's Heely,' she said.

'Do you think she'd mind if I said hello?'

'No.'

The child took his hand, and he stood.

Hillary shared a smile with her grand-daughter as Allie led the handsome young man over to her table. She'd found their exchange charming.

'You've made a new friend I see, Allie.'

'Look, Heely,' she held out the postcard. 'The man over there,' she pointed at the kiosk, 'gave it to me for nothing.'

'That was very nice of him.'

'You're Jo's mother, aren't you?' Mike asked, but it wasn't a question.

'Yes.' Hillary's concentration had been upon the child. Now, as she focused upon the young man, she was startled by the resemblance between the two.

'I'm Mike,' he said. 'Mike McAllister.'

She hadn't heard the surname before. 'Of course you are,' she said. 'Hello, Mike.' She extended her hand. 'I'm Hillary Collins. I've been hoping we'd meet some day.'

They shook.

'I think you'd better sit down,' she said. 'We have a lot to talk about.'

In a daze, Mike collected his package and his coffee and joined Hillary, who, after admiring the koala, sent Allie off to buy another three postcards.

'She's my daughter, isn't she?' he asked, unable to take his eyes from the child.

'Yes.'

'One toasted ham sandwich?'

The young waitress's query was pointed. She was actually saying 'So you're sitting *here* now, are you?'

'Yes, thanks.'

Mike ordered another coffee for Hillary, who refused anything to eat.

'Allie and I had lunch half an hour ago,' she said.

The waitress openly smirked as she walked back into the café. What a smooth operator, she thought, it had taken him less than ten minutes to chat up the blonde. Mind you, it was a wonder he'd bothered. Gorgeous-looking the blonde might be, but she was old enough to be his mother. No accounting for taste, she supposed.

Mike ignored the sandwich while they talked, and twenty minutes later, as they left the café, it remained untouched. He was no longer hungry.

The three of them stepped out of London Court and set off down St Georges Terrace, Hillary and Allie hand in hand and Mike, package tucked under one arm, carrying the shopping bags.

'She's bound to be home by now,' Hillary said as they crossed Pier Street. Then in a whispered aside, she added, 'She went out on her own to get Allie's Christmas present.'

They reached Victoria Street and Hillary pointed to the block of flats on the opposite corner. 'That's us,' she said.

Mike recognised the place. It had been outside this very block of flats that he and Spud had watched the Brown brothers and Ivan the Pole divvy up the money from Anthony Wilson's wallet. He could see the five of them now, huddled under the streetlamp.

'You wait here,' Hillary said conspiratorially as they arrived at the small front porch. 'I'll only be a few minutes.' She took the shopping bags from him and she and Allie disappeared into the flat.

Every fibre in Hillary's body was tingling with anticipation. She was about to reunite Johanna with the father of her child. What could possibly be more romantic?

Mike had told his story circumspectly, trying to shoulder the blame, saying that he should have sensed Jo's predicament, but Hillary had drawn her own conclusions. No man ever sensed a woman's needs, she'd thought, and it had been foolish of Johanna to disappear mysteriously without a word. That was the problem with Jo, of course. She was too proud, too single-minded and independent, often with little thought for the feelings of others. Hillary had no idea where she got it from. But her daughter had left that poor boy desperate and broken-hearted with nowhere to turn. It really wasn't fair. And he was so *handsome*!

Putting down his package, Mike perched himself on the low brick wall that surrounded the porch, trying to look relaxed, even nonchalant, but his heart was pounding. He didn't share Hillary's confidence.

'Just tell her you love her and all will be forgiven, Mike,' Hillary had said. 'Good heavens above, the father of her child? Her first true love? She won't be able to resist.'

Mike wasn't sure that it worked that way. Not with Johanna.

Jo was making a cup of tea when they entered.

'Hello, Mum, had a good day's shopping?' She winked to say that Allie's tricycle was well hidden away. Allie was a tomboy who wanted to ride a bike like the older kids, so the tricycle had been inevitable. It'd be a bugger of a thing to get back to Sydney, Jo thought, but she'd manage.

'Look!' Allie raced to her mother, holding out her postcards. 'This one's my favourite,' she said, sifting through them, 'It's a koala with his baby.'

'*Her* baby,' Jo automatically corrected.

'Yes. It's on her back, see? And we met a nice man, and he likes koalas too, and he's waiting –'

'Allie and I are going for a walk down to the river,' Hillary interrupted.

'But you only just got home.'

'And now we're going out again. You'd like to feed the seagulls, wouldn't you, Allie?'

Allie nodded vigorously.

'Go and get some bread then.'

The child scampered off to the kitchen.

'Wouldn't you like a cup of tea first, Mum?'

'No, thank you, darling. I had a coffee, two actually, in London Arcade. Do you need the toilet before we go, Allie?' she asked as the little girl galloped back with a loaf of fresh bread. But Allie shook her head, eager to be on her way.

'Hang on, I just bought that. I'll get you some stale stuff.'

Jo started for the kitchen, but Hillary grabbed Allie's hand.

'No, no, don't worry. I'll buy some more while we're out.' The two of them headed for the door. 'By the way,' Hillary added, 'Allie's nice man is waiting outside.'

'Bye, Mum,' Allie yelled as she was yanked out the door.

They were gone, leaving Jo bewildered by the speed of it all.

'Bye, Mike,' she heard Allie call.

Mike? She stood motionless. Did this mean what she thought it did? Yes, knowing Hillary. Her mother's passion for romance had got the better of her – how very typical. Damn you, Mum, Jo thought, you could have said something.

She took a deep breath and walked very slowly to the open front door. He was sitting on the low brick wall just outside, and he smiled when he saw her. The same winning grin, she thought, the same supremely confident Mike McAllister of old. She didn't return the smile.

'Hello, Mike,' she said.

'Hello, Jo.'

Jo looked at her mother and Allie, who were standing barely twenty metres away at the lights waiting to cross Victoria Street. Hillary waved back.

'I've been set up, haven't I?'

'It would seem so.'

'You'd better come in.'

He followed her inside to the flat and she closed the door after him.

'I was making a cup of tea. Would you like one?'

She set off immediately for the kitchen and Mike was obliged to follow.

'No, thanks. I had coffee with your mother.'

'Ah yes. In London Arcade.'

She put the pot of tea she'd planned to make for Hillary aside, took a cup from the cupboard and poured the boiling water from the electric jug over a teabag. She avoided looking at him as she busied herself. The initial sight of him had had a profound effect on her and she felt decidedly unsettled, which annoyed her.

How detached she was, Mike thought, how indifferent; irritated even. He felt like an intruder who'd disturbed her day. Things weren't going to be as easy as Hillary had predicted, but then he hadn't expected they would be. He longed to take Jo in his arms and tell her he was sorry for who he was. He hadn't meant to close her out, he wanted to say. He loved her – he'd always loved her. But it wouldn't work, he knew it. The best way with Jo was to be direct. At least, it had been four years ago.

'You should have told me, Jo.'

'Told you what?' she hedged as she fetched the milk from the refrigerator.

'You know damn well what.'

'I see.' She squeezed out the teabag and added the milk to the cup. 'Hillary's been talking.'

'She didn't need to, for God's sake. One look and it's pretty obvious – you'd hardly need to be Sherlock Holmes to figure it out.' He found her remoteness infuriating. 'Jesus, Jo, how was I to know? How could I have guessed? You should have told me.'

The accusatory edge to his voice compelled her to look at him.

'Why?' she demanded, relieved that they were avoiding sentimentality and getting straight to the point. 'Why should I have told you? What would you have done?'

'I would have married you, of course.'

For the first time, she smiled. How simple he made it sound. 'You would have done the right thing, you mean.'

'Naturally.'

This time she laughed, but not unkindly, and Mike felt flummoxed.

'That's what you'd have wanted, isn't it?' he asked.

She ignored the question. 'You would have willingly saddled yourself with a child so early in your career?' She'd asked Andy exactly the same thing only ten days ago, she recalled.

'Yes.' She was staring at him whimsically and he started to flounder. 'Well, I would have had to, wouldn't I? I mean, there wouldn't have been any choice, would there?'

She laughed again, fondly this time. She respected his honesty, she always had.

Mike relaxed. Emboldened by her laughter he decided to turn the tables.

'So you didn't want to be a hindrance to my career, is that it? Don't you think that's being a little overly noble, Jo?'

'Yes, if that had been my sole motive,' she agreed. 'But it wasn't.'

Mike nodded. He didn't think it had been.

'I didn't want to marry a man who didn't love me.'

She'd turned the tables right back on him.

'But I *did* love you,' he protested. He had, hadn't he? He'd never told her so, but surely she must have sensed it with her woman's intuition. Of course he'd loved her. 'You must have known, surely,' he said with a touch of desperation.

She smiled at the panic she saw in his face. 'Yes, I knew that you loved me,' she said. 'The trouble was you didn't know it yourself, and I wasn't prepared to wait around long enough for you to find out.'

Jo had a sudden sense of déjà vu. She'd played a similar scene with Andy, she realised, except the roles had been reversed. *You love me far more than you realise, Jo*, she could hear him saying, and she'd believed him. But did she? The mere sight of Mike had been enough to raise her doubts.

'Well, I know now,' Mike said, 'and I still love you.' The words that had once seemed so difficult now came with surprising ease. He was prepared to lay his cards on the table. What did he have to lose? 'I've always loved you, and I always will.'

How she'd longed to hear him say that all those years ago, she thought, but she steeled herself. It would be foolish to alter all her well-laid plans just because of a romantic over-reaction.

'Do I get another chance?' he asked.

As he waited hopefully, even a little breathlessly, for her answer, Jo realised that she'd been wrong. He wasn't the same supremely confident Mike McAllister. For all of his apparent assurance, there was something lost about him. He'd changed. He was vulnerable.

'I'm getting married next year, Mike.'

'Oh.' It was as if she'd slapped him in the face.

'I don't know exactly when.' She picked up her forgotten cup of tea and sipped at it. 'We haven't set the date yet.'

'I see.'

'I'm glad you're here though. It's time Allie met her natural father. I'd planned to introduce you sooner or later.' She had, but his unexpected appearance made her realise she'd been putting off the moment. 'I'd like you two to become friends.'

'Yes, so would I.' He wondered how she could possibly sound so clinical. 'Why did you call her Alana?' he asked. Surely the choice signalled something.

'It's a pretty name. I've always liked it. You know that.' She'd had the response ready for years.

Apparently the name meant nothing. 'Of course,' he said.

'We'll do the introductions as soon as Mum and Allie get home, shall we?'

'Fine.'

'I'll make a pot of tea – Hillary'll want one.'

She topped up the electric jug, which didn't need topping up, and put the tea leaves in the pot, forgetting that it already had four spoonfuls in it. How would Allie react, she wondered, and felt a flutter of nerves verging on panic. Things were happening altogether too quickly.

Allie's reaction to the fact that the nice man who liked koalas was her father turned out to be remarkable in its lack of drama.

'So that's how you knew about the boat,' she said with a three year old's logic.

'Yes.'

'The beautiful yacht belonged to Mike's father, Allie,' Jo started to explain but her daughter wasn't listening.

'Can I see it?' The question was directed at Mike.

'I'll take you out on it if you like.'

'When?'

Mike looked at Jo. 'Tomorrow?'

She hesitated. A trip on the yacht wasn't as simple as it sounded – surely it would involve a meeting with Jim and Maggie McAllister. Of course, it was only right the child should get to know her grandparents, she told herself, but not now. Not yet. She felt railroaded.

'Just the three of us,' Mike said. He knew what she was thinking. 'Mum and Dad are in Sydney spending Christmas with Jools.'

She nodded gratefully. 'Tomorrow would be fine.' Allie

jumped up and down, and Hillary beamed. Everything
was going so well, she thought.

'I'm afraid *Alana*'s not as beautiful as she once was,' Mike
said apologetically as they rowed out to the mooring.
'She's twenty-five years old now, showing a bit of wear
and tear.'

But Allie could see no signs of wear and tear at all. To
her, *Alana* was every bit as beautiful as the yacht her
mother had painted in her mind.

The three of them sailed over to Blackwall Reach, then
downriver to look at the big ships berthed at the Fremantle
docks. Jo and Allie sat up the bow, holding their hats on
firmly with both hands, the wind threatening to whip them
away, Allie asking questions about every landmark they
passed, Jo yelling the queries back to Mike at the helm.

On the way back, they tied up to the jetty at Point
Walter and Mike threw bombies off the pylon, but Allie,
wary of the deep water, was too frightened to jump in.

'She's not a strong swimmer,' Jo said. 'Well, not *yet*,' she
added hastily, aware that a child's inability to swim was
probably criminal in Mike's eyes. 'I'm enrolling her in
classes next year.' She really must, she told herself, she'd
been very slack.

'Why don't we start now?' he said, and he took Allie to
the shallows where he proceeded to teach her.

With her feet firmly planted on the sandy bottom, the
child's fear of the water quickly subsided, and before long
Mike had her floating, supported by his hand. He taught
her how to breathe out with her head submerged, blowing
the air through her mouth and nose. He was gentle but
persuasive, and the little girl placed her complete trust in
him. Allie was eager to please and quick to learn.

Jo, watching from the beach, thought how any onlooker
would find it impossible to believe that this obvious father-
daughter pair had met only yesterday.

As they sailed back towards the mooring at Claremont, she gazed about at the beauty of Freshwater Bay thinking how perfect the afternoon had been. But its very perfection made her wary. It had been reminiscent of all those other perfect days she'd spent with Mike on the water, and she didn't want to step back into the past. She couldn't afford to allow the developing relationship between Mike and Allie, affecting as she found it, to take over her life. She had plans of her own, she told herself, and her plans involved Andy, not Mike.

'Pembo's getting married next Saturday.'

She was seated in the cockpit, Allie beside her, Mike at the tiller, and his voice jolted her from her thoughts.

'A huge affair, half of Perth'll be there,' he said. 'I was going to take Jools, but she's showing off her new fiancé to Mum and Dad in Sydney. Would you like to come?'

The invitation was offered casually, but he was praying she'd accept. He could sense that she'd put her guard up again.

'Pembo'd love it if you were there, and we don't need to tell anyone the full story.' He glanced at Allie, who was clutching the mainsheet convinced she was sailing the boat single-handed, although the rope was firmly held by a cleat. 'Just that you're in town.'

Jo was hesitant.

'The whole gang from uni's going,' he added, 'including Muzza.' Surely Muzza would be the clincher, he thought, they'd been very close.

'I saw his portrait of you at the New South Wales Gallery,' she said. 'I think it should have won.'

'Yes, a lot of people did, even some of the critics.' He sensed she was avoiding the invitation, but he went along with the flow anyway. 'Muzza didn't care, he was just thrilled that he'd been hung in the Archibald.'

'What an amazing talent.'

She recalled the effect the portrait had had on her. She

must have stood gazing at it for over half an hour. The young Mike McAllister she remembered so vividly, eager for all life had to offer. Muzza had captured him to perfection.

'How is he?' she asked. 'I think of him a lot.' She had over the years. She would have liked to keep in touch with Muzza, but she hadn't dared for fear word would get back to Mike.

'Muzza's great. He's married.'

'Really? How wonderful.'

'Yep, a stunning Polish woman called Olga who adores him nearly as much as he adores her.' He looked at her hopefully. 'They'll be at the wedding. Will you come?' Then he added, 'Muzza'd really love you to meet Olga.'

She laughed. 'What a blatant piece of blackmail, but yes, of course I'll come,' she said, chastising herself. There was no threat in the invitation, she was being over-dramatic. 'It'll be good to catch up with the old gang.'

Jo rang Andy that night. He'd telephoned her every few days since she'd been in Perth, but this time she took the onus upon herself. She wasn't sure why, but she felt the need to hear his voice. Besides, it would be wrong not to keep him abreast of the news.

'I'll just pop into the kitchen,' Hillary said as her daughter started to dial. Hillary always retired to the kitchen with her glass of white wine whenever Jo talked to Andy.

'Don't be silly, Mum,' Jo started to protest.

'Couples need their privacy, dear.' And Hillary disappeared without another word.

'What a pleasant surprise,' Andy said when he heard her voice. He sounded ridiculously young, like a kid at Christmas. 'I was going to phone you tomorrow.'

'I thought I'd get in first.'

'How's Allie? Behaving herself?'

'She's dead to the world.' Jo looked at her daughter, fast asleep on the couch. It was around the time Andy normally rang and he always had a quick chat with Allie. 'I couldn't wake her if I tried.'

'So early?' There was a pause and Jo could see him checking his watch. 'But it's only seven o'clock Perth time.' Andy knew only too well that it took a great deal of bargaining power to get Allie to bed. Her energy always lasted until nine, after which, having exhausted herself, she was out like a light.

'She's been on a boat all afternoon. I think I've discovered the secret – buckets and buckets of sea air.'

'We'll have to buy a boat then,' he said.

'It wouldn't be a bad idea. But you'll never guess *which* boat we've been out on, Andy. Oh my God, things have happened so fast, there's so much to tell you . . .'

He knew which boat. He'd heard the child say it often enough, hadn't he? And Jo had told him just as much as she felt he had a right to know.

'*Alana*,' he said, trying to keep the smile in his voice. 'You've been out on the beautiful, beautiful yacht, have you?'

The yacht that belonged to the child's father, wasn't that what she'd told him?

He waited for Jo to go on, which she did, excitedly.

'Yes, isn't that amazing? Mike turned up just yesterday . . .'

Mike, that's right. She'd said his name was Mike. She'd never mentioned the surname.

'. . . Hillary bumped into him in town and she brought him home with her. I could have killed her at the time, but it's turned out well. I mean, it's right for Allie to meet her natural father, don't you think?'

'Of course it's right.'

Somewhere down the track, Jo, yes, but not now! It's too soon! Far too soon!

'Anyway, I was so nervous when I introduced Allie to him, I didn't know what to expect. But you wouldn't believe how easy it was, Andy. She was more interested in the boat than she was in him. So Mike took us out on it this afternoon . . .'

Good old Mike.

'. . . I was worried that it might mean meeting up with his parents again, which I'd dreaded – the boat actually belongs to Mike's father – but they're in Sydney with his sister for a couple of weeks, so we escaped all that. Not that it'll be a problem when they come back – Mike says they'll be mad about Allie.'

She gave a brief laugh, the words were tumbling out. 'It's terrible of me, but do you know, I'd completely forgotten that Mike's father named the boat *Alana* after his mother. When I see him I'll have to pretend I remembered, he's bound to read something special into it. But it'll be good for Allie to form a bond with her grandparents, won't it?'

Marvellous. A ready-made family.

'Yes of course, Jo. I'm very happy for you.'

She was halted mid-stream. 'Not me, Andy. Allie. I'm talking about Allie. I think it's only right that she knows where she comes from. That she isn't named after some mythical yacht, that it's all very real.'

Don't you know how you sound, Jo? Can't you hear your own voice?

'Are you going to sleep with him?'

The words just sprang out, and he cursed himself the moment he'd said them. But it was too late, useless to retract the question.

A deathly pause. And he waited.

'Of course I'm not going to sleep with him.'

The shocked reaction was exactly as he'd expected – very honest and very real. Johanna, for all her fierce intelligence, was pulling the wool over her own eyes,

Andy thought. The sheer joy he could hear down the line – did she truly believe it all related to her child?

'Why on earth would you ask me something like that?' She was more than shocked, she was appalled.

'I'm sorry. Touch of male jealousy, I suppose. I miss you.' He backed off immediately. No point in discussing it.

'But I love you, Andy.'

'I know you do. And I love you too. Let's forget I said it, shall we?'

They talked for a while longer, but things were strained and it was a relief to them both when Jo called a halt.

'I'd better put Allie to bed,' she said.

'Give her a big cuddle from me.'

'Of course.' She smiled. 'Butterfly kisses and everything. I'll speak to you in a few days.'

She expected him to ring, he thought, but he wouldn't. He'd wait for the phone call he dreaded.

'Yes, in a few days. Good night, Jo. Sweet dreams.' He'd inherited the saying from his parents as a child, and he said it to her every night they spent together. She liked it.

'You too, Andy. Sweet dreams.'

Jo hung up confused, feeling that she'd hurt him, but wondering how.

Andy hung up knowing it was over.

Mike and Jo made love three days later. Neither had planned it. But Hillary had.

They arrived back at the flat shortly before nine. They'd left Ian Pemberton's wedding reception early so that Jo could put Allie to bed.

'What do you make of Arlene?' Mike asked as he joined her at the front door after paying off the taxi.

'I'm not sure. Is she dumb or is she smart? I found it hard to tell. But she's rather like Pembo's mother, don't you think?'

He laughed. Jo had met Cynthia for the first time only that afternoon, but she'd picked it in one.

'Anyway,' she shrugged, 'Pembo worships her, so it doesn't really matter, does it?' She unlocked the door and they stepped inside. 'As for Olga – you're right, she's stunning. How wonderful for Muzza, I've never seen him so happy.'

The lounge room light was on, but no-one was there. Jo put a finger to her lips – Hillary was probably putting Allie to bed. She crept off to check, but the bedroom was empty.

She came back to discover Mike holding the note her mother had left on the coffee table. He read it out loud. '*Allie and I have gone to* Hello Dolly. *Back at eleven.*'

'The movies at *this* time of night?' She took the note from him and stared at it incredulously. 'Why on earth would Mum bother? She's already seen *Hello Dolly*, and Allie'll sleep right through it.'

'I think you've been set up again, Jo.'

She looked at him, expecting to see a smile, presuming he was joking. But he wasn't.

'I think we both have,' he said.

'Oh.' She felt silly for not having registered the fact herself. How typical of Hillary. But she wished he hadn't openly commented upon her mother's ridiculous attempt to manoeuvre them into bed. The effect had been instantaneous. The tone of the evening had changed dramatically.

'Would you like a cup of coffee while I ring you a taxi?' They would have had a cup of coffee with Hillary if she'd been here, wouldn't they? So why did the invitation seem to offer something more?

'I'll get a taxi in the street,' he said. But he made no move towards the front door, just as she had made no move to the kitchen. Did she want him to go?

They stood barely two metres apart, staring at each other.

'Do you want me to go?' he asked.

'I think it would be best.'

Both remained motionless.

'I'm getting married next year, Mike.' She said the words firmly, with resolve, as if she dared him to differ.

'So you told me. What's his name?'

'Andrew. Andrew Gaden. He's a lawyer.'

'What about Allie?'

'Oh, Andy adores Allie.' She looked away, flicking back her hair with a toss of her head. A rare gesture; she only did it when she was self-conscious, which was not often. 'In fact, Allie's probably one of the reasons he wants to marry me – he's put Donald Duck wallpaper up in the spare room.' She faltered slightly, realising that she was talking for the sake of talking.

He'd noticed the falter, just as he'd noticed the flick of the hair. He took a pace towards her and, leaning down, he kissed her, very gently.

She didn't respond, but then she didn't resist either.

'I'm getting married, Mike,' she repeated, although it didn't carry the same ring at all.

'Yes. Next year. To me.'

He kissed her again. She responded this time, her mind vaguely trying to encompass the complications. What about her plans? Her career? Andy? Then everything became blurred by the thought that perhaps Hillary, in her foolish romanticism, had been right all along. Perhaps a person only had one great love in their life. Poor Andy, she thought, she'd have to ring him tomorrow. But then Andy had known, hadn't he? Andy had known this would happen.

As they made love, Mike looked into her eyes. He'd never done so in the past.

'I love you, Jo,' he said.

She whispered her love back to him, over and over, the way she'd longed to in the old days but had never dared. Not for one moment did her eyes leave his, and she saw there something else besides love. She saw need. His need for her eclipsed everything, and she was transported.

She couldn't offer him enough of herself. To Jo, love and need had become inexplicably entwined.

When it was over, they lay silently in each other's arms, both overwhelmed, both lost in their own thoughts.

Jo had never known how desperately she longed to be needed. She'd steadfastly refused to need any*one* or any*thing* herself. Why should she? *She* wasn't needed. So she'd put up her walls. But she was needed now. Mike needed her. And for the first time in her life, she was prepared to admit to a need in herself. She needed Mike.

Mike was thinking of the dead girl and how she hadn't been there. She hadn't been there for one second. There'd been only Jo and the love he felt for her and the love that he'd seen in her eyes. Even now, when he thought of the dead girl, marvelling at her absence, her image was no more than a blur from a past to which he didn't belong.

'Jo . . .' He turned on his side to face her. He hadn't known that he had a capacity for such love, and he wasn't sure how to express himself.

Apparently he didn't need to.

'Yes,' she said. 'Yes, I know.'

CHAPTER SEVENTEEN

The seventies was proving to be Spud's decade, just as he'd anticipated. Within five years, Farrell Enterprises had become the Farrell Corporation, and, at the age of thirty-two, Spud Farrell was not only a wealthy and successful businessman, but one of integrity – a fact that several of his contemporaries, who'd thought him dangerously on the edge of the law, found surprising. During the 1974 WA Royal Commission into Gambling, however, the name Farrell had not even received a mention. Spud was apparently as clean as a whistle. Furthermore, it was well known that he contributed generously to worthwhile charities and supported local youth sports groups and community projects like Rotary, the Lions Club and APEX.

Not so widely known was his largesse when it came to State Government campaign funds. The WA Labor Party had benefited very nicely from his contributions for several years, but he'd recently swapped allegiance. When the Liberals had come into power in 1974, their party campaign funds had received a healthy boost in the form of a personal cheque from Spud Farrell.

Spud had reaped the benefits of his support in any

number of ways, from advance information to practical assistance. The government tenders received from Farrell Constructions – a major arm of the Farrell Corporation – regularly undercut the tenders submitted by other companies, there was rarely any trouble with development planning, and the normal petty objections to rezoning were quickly overcome.

'To the marriage of government and private enterprise, Howard,' Spud said with a brief salute of his champagne glass. He and Howard Stonehaven, MP, Minister for Lands and Works, were dining at the Oyster Beds in Fremantle. They'd become great mates.

'I've said it all along, Spud,' Howard smiled, joining in the joke, 'as well you know.'

They were both recalling Gerrard Whitford and how he'd been set up with the quote all those years ago, everyone knowing it to be Howard's personal catch phrase. The man had looked like the fool he was.

Howard forked the last oyster from his platter into his mouth. Poor long-forgotten Gerrard, he thought as he sat back and gazed contentedly through the window at the flotilla of craft passing by.

The restaurant was built out over the water, and they'd arrived there by boat themselves. Spud's company launch was berthed at the Oyster Beds' jetty, the skipper on board waiting to take them back to the pen at Royal Freshwater Bay Yacht Club. The Oyster Beds was a favourite haunt of Spud's. He regularly brought guests there in the company launch. It impressed them.

'You must come up to Queensland for the long weekend next month,' he said, nodding to the waitress to collect their platters. 'We're opening the new hotel at Surfers Paradise. Nothing too lavish to start with, only forty rooms, but great views. I'm sure you'll like it.'

'Got a finger in every pie, haven't you, Spud,' Howard said with begrudging admiration. He envied the lifestyle of businessmen like Farrell who travelled to lunch on corporate launches and popped overseas regularly for the tennis at Wimbledon or the cricket at Lord's.

'Oh . . . just feeling my way, sounding things out, you know how it is,' Spud said airily. 'The hotel trade's lucrative, but it's my guess resorts are the way of the future.' He downed the last of his champagne and poured himself a glass of white wine from the bottle in the ice bucket. 'This country just cries out for resorts.'

He poured a glass for Howard as well, although Howard was barely halfway through his champagne. Then he leaned back in his chair, expanding upon his theme, a man of vision.

'Look at Fiji,' he said, 'we should be following their example. We've got the beaches and the climate, all we need to do is chuck in the palm trees and the swimming pools. Lots of glitz, gloss and glamour, that's what the punters want. The locals think they're in Hollywood and the tourists go apeshit.'

'You may have a point, Spud.' Howard's ears had pricked up. 'We need to attract overseas interest.' He'd have a chat to Max, the Minister for Tourism – there was bound to be something in it for them both, he thought. 'A resort would certainly be a boost to state tourism – where exactly did you have in mind?'

Western Australia hadn't featured in Spud's immediate plans, he'd been contemplating Queensland for his first venture into resorts, but noting Howard's interest he did a quick rethink. No harm in paving the way.

'Well, look at our coastline,' he said. 'North, south, take your pick.' It sounded too vague, as if he hadn't given the matter much consideration, so he added, 'And then there are the city beaches . . . Scarborough . . . Cottesloe . . .' He grinned. 'Hell, we could mow down the old OBH and build a whopping great resort right there at North Cott. That'd rattle a few locals, wouldn't it?'

Howard's smile in response was smug; it seemed to say, *Nothing's impossible.*

'Ah, the lobster.' Spud greeted the waitress, who placed two obscenely large crustaceans before them, and conversation came to a halt as they tackled their respective thermidor and mornay.

They skipped dessert and, over coffee and cognacs, got down to the purpose of their lunch – a feasible site for Farrell Towers. The high-rise office block, which would one day house the new corporation's headquarters, was in its early 'talk' stages as yet, but it was only a matter of time. Farrell Towers was Spud's personal dream.

One and a half hours later, the company launch safely penned, Spud and Howard shook hands in the yacht club's car park.

'Don't forget the long weekend and the hotel opening,' Spud said. 'I'll send you the official invite next week. I'm flying a gang of twenty up, and I can promise you three days you won't forget.' He winked lasciviously. 'And I mean real partying – wall-to-wall Gold Coast birds with big tits, you know what I mean.'

'Thanks Spud, sounds fun.' Howard smiled politely. He found Spud's manner truly gross at times, but he'd accept the invitation – it was one of the perks of his trade. And he'd accept all that the invitation inferred. The mention of Gold Coast birds meant high-class call girls – Spud Farrell certainly knew how to entertain. Howard just wished he wouldn't voice things so blatantly.

Spud grinned as he drove off; he'd deliberately bunged on the uncouth act. Howard was a snob and a hypocrite. His responsible MP image was that of a happily married man with three children, but he was always the first to avail himself of the call-girl service provided at Spud's events. Spud didn't mind, he was happy to oblige. What the hell, he thought, go for it, mate, just don't piss from such a bloody great height.

Spud never availed himself of the call girls he provided for others – he'd made it his policy over the years. He'd always been content with the service provided by his own girls at his own brothels, where discretion was guaranteed. But he no longer slept with his girls these days, not even Lolita, who said she was missing him when he called around at the Sun Majestic to talk business with Ruby. Spud didn't need the girls and he didn't need Lolita. Spud had Cora.

Cora Santos had been Spud's mistress for well over a year, although he hadn't intended to keep her for that long.

'You bring them in on a six-month visa, mate,' Len had advised, 'then you get shot of them. Saves any complications down the track.'

Len Baker was a mining magnate who'd cleaned up in the nickel boom. Like Spud and Pembo, he was one of the clique. Perth's rapidly burgeoning circle of wealthy gravitated to each other like members of an exclusive club. A seemingly classless society, their money was their bond.

'A quick turnover, that's the way to go,' Len had said. He had it down to a fine art himself, regularly importing a housekeeper from the Philippines to double as a mistress, then sending her home after six months and bringing out the next one. 'Don't hang on to them for more than a year at the most – you don't want to risk a de facto claim. And watch them with your money. They like to support their family on the sly and they'll bleed you for all they can get if you don't keep your eye on them.' Just when it had all started sounding too complicated for Spud's liking, Len had added with a leer, 'But I tell you what, mate, it's worth it. They're a horny bunch, those Filipinas. Best sex I've had in my life. Good lookers too, every one of them.'

Spud had taken on board Len's advice, which had appeared sound, and he'd intended to adhere to the six-month turnover. But he hadn't counted on Cora.

She was every bit as beautiful as her photograph, which

he'd found surprising; he'd suspected that it might be touched up. She was smaller than he'd expected, indeed petite, and at first he'd been disappointed, until he'd discovered that her breasts were perfect, and proportionately large for a girl of her size. She wore her hair short and that, too, had been an initial disappointment. He'd told her to grow it long, the way it had been in the photograph, but he doubted it would achieve the desired length within six months. No matter, he'd told himself as heads turned in the street and he saw the envy in men's eyes, the impact of Cora's beauty on others was achieving exactly the desired effect. And she was amazing in bed – even better than Lolita.

But it was the impact of Cora herself that Spud hadn't taken into consideration. He found her personality utterly irresistible. She played her public role to perfection the way she knew he wanted her to – the shy, inaccessible beauty – but in private, Cora was fun. She was playful and effervescent. She bubbled with a simple, child-like vitality. Everything seemed a delight to Cora.

Spud had spent the first several months trying to figure her out. Was she clever? Was it all an act? Was she taking him for a ride? He really didn't know. But when the six-month term had come to an end, he hadn't sent her home, he'd been too intrigued.

Now, over a year down the track, he'd given up questioning her motives. He'd accepted that to Cora, life was genuinely uncomplicated. What the hell, he'd decided, she was great sex and good to be around – despite Len's dire warnings, he'd give her a while yet.

After leaving the yacht club, Spud didn't go back to the office. He had a good hour before his four o'clock meeting with Pembo and Phil Cowan, and he decided to pop home instead. Cora would be waiting for him and there'd be time for a quickie.

He drove down Bay View Terrace, taking in the old

Claremont jetty dead ahead as he turned left into Victoria Avenue. It pleased him the way the jetty never seemed to change – their old stamping ground, Mikey's and his. He could still see them chucking bombies off the end. He passed the McAllister house, which looked shabby these days, he thought, but then perhaps it always had been. It certainly wasn't as imposing as his own house only several kilometres away. Who would have believed, all those years ago, when he'd lived in envy of Mikey, that he, Spud Farrell, would own one of the grandest riverside homes in Victoria Avenue?

Spud had built his two-storey mansion, which sloped down to the river, only the previous year. Befitting his station in life, it was his pride and joy, boasting marble pillars at the entrance, huge balconies overlooking the water, and landscaped gardens that ran from the down-stairs level right to the shoreline. He even employed servants. Not that he'd ever *call* them servants – he wasn't up himself like some of his mates. But if a live-in house-keeper and gardener weren't servants, then what the bloody hell were they, he asked himself. Hell, fancy having servants! How posh was that!

Natalija and Josef, the Yugoslav couple whose quarters were downstairs at the rear of the house, actually found Spud a most amenable employer. Josef sometimes doubled as a chauffeur, the requisite outfit hanging in his wardrobe, and Natalija was sometimes called upon to greet guests at the front door, but such occasions were rare. Spud pre-ferred to drive himself, and he didn't stand on ceremony when entertaining his mates. Any show of pomp was strictly reserved for times when he felt it advantageous to impress prospective business associates.

As he pulled into the four-car garage, the double front doors of the house opened. Cora had heard the Merc's arrival, she'd been waiting.

He was barely out of the car before she'd run to him and

covered him with kisses. Then they walked hand in hand
to the house, Cora plying him with questions. He'd told
her he was lunching at the Oyster Beds and she'd sulked
when he'd said it was a business meeting and that she
couldn't come along. But she'd only been pretending.

'You have oysters?' she asked excitedly as she skipped
along beside him. 'You have oysters? Yes?'

'Yes, I had the oysters.'

'And lobster? You have lobster?'

'Yes, I had the lobster.'

'Thermidor?'

'Yes, thermidor.'

He'd promised he'd have the oysters and the thermidor,
they were Cora's favourites. Cora was obsessed with food.
She ate voraciously, morning noon and night, her appetite
seemingly endless, but she never gained weight. She even
loved talking about food. After a full lunch, Cora could
quite happily discuss in detail exactly what she planned to
have for dinner.

'And ice-cream? You have ice-cream?'

'No, I didn't have ice-cream. I had coffee and cognac
instead.'

'Ah.' Cora would have had ice-cream herself.

As they stepped inside, a pleasant sea breeze wafted
through the open doors to the balcony, and beyond the
massive plate-glass windows the wind-rippled river glis-
tened silver-grey.

Natalija greeted him in her broken English as she passed
by with a wicker basket of bed linen. She headed for the
rear stairs that led down to the laundry, making herself
scarce as she usually did. Her employer and his mistress
didn't restrict their lovemaking to the bedroom, nor to any
particular time of day.

Spud took off his jacket and tie and draped them over
one of the leather lounge chairs. 'Did you buy anything
this morning?' he asked.

'Yes. I go shopping like you say. And look, Spud . . .'

She disappeared into the main bedroom and he heard her voice calling back to him.

'You look what I get. Is beautiful . . .'

Spud took a Montecristo from the humidor on the sideboard and clipped the end. He'd given up cigarettes lately. He found he preferred a good Cuban cigar anyway, and they suited his image. He had them imported.

'Which you like best? Red? Yellow?'

She appeared, holding the dresses up one by one against her body and twirling about before him. The vivid colours looked glorious against her dusky skin. Cora loved bright colours.

'Very beautiful, yes? Very expensive. Which you like best?'

'They're both nice,' he said, striking a match and dragging on the cigar, seeing the end glow. The dresses weren't expensive. They were pretty little summer frocks, couldn't have been more than fifty bucks each, he thought. He'd given her five hundred in cash that very morning when he'd dropped her in St Georges Terrace on his way to the office. He knew where the rest of the money had gone. She'd sent it home to her family. Well, Len had warned him, hadn't he? Spud had been annoyed by the deceit at first, but it didn't bother him these days. He told himself that he respected the way she supported her family.

'And for you. Look . . .' She dumped the dresses on the sofa and once again raced off to the bedroom, reappearing with a tie which she held out to him. 'For you, I buy this. Very, *very* expensive.'

It was. Pure silk, imported. Cora knew the difference. She never bought him cheap presents.

Spud threaded the tie beneath his collar. 'It's great,' he said. 'I like it.'

'Yes.' She took over for him, tying an expert Windsor knot, then stepped back, thoughtfully appraising the effect. 'Is good colour for you, this blue, I think.'

She looked so adorably serious. He was about to kiss her, but she turned away and picked up one of the dresses.

'I put on for you. Both dress I put on.' When she turned back to him, the light of play was in her eyes and her smile was cheeky. 'Red . . . yellow . . . you say what you like best.'

Then, very slowly and teasingly, she started to strip.

Spud poured himself a generous nip of Hennessy XO from the bottle beside the humidor and settled back on the sofa to watch.

He was over half an hour late for his four o'clock meeting.

As he pulled up in the car park of the city office block, three floors of which constituted the head offices of the Farrell Corporation, Spud was annoyed with himself. He was a stickler for punctuality and demanded it in others. His tardiness would therefore require an apology, and he never apologised to business associates unless it was absolutely necessary. He blamed the cognacs. Cora's strip and its aftermath had been a distraction admittedly, but it was the cognacs that had done it. He rarely drank spirits in the middle of the day and they'd affected him, he'd lost track of the time.

When he arrived on the fifth floor, he found that his secretary had settled Ian Pemberton and Phil Cowan comfortably in the boardroom and was in the throes of serving them a second pot of coffee.

'Thanks, Marge,' he said with gratitude, then briskly to the others, 'Pembo, Phil, I'm sorry to keep you waiting. The lunch with Howard went longer than I'd intended. Inexcusable nonetheless, my apologies to you both.'

Ian wasn't in the least bothered. 'What the hell, Spud, it's only us, hardly a meeting of the board.'

But Phil Cowan wasn't about to let such an opportunity slip by. An apology from Spud Farrell was rare, and he decided to make the most of it. He looked ostentatiously at his watch, then at the pot of percolated coffee hovering in Marge's hands.

'Does a thirty-five-minute wait warrant the offer of something a little stronger?' he asked in his New York twang, perfect teeth flashing a grin that was meant to charm, but which grated on Spud.

'Of course it does, Phil.' *You piece of shit.* Spud would have liked to say, 'Bit early in the day, mate, got a problem with the grog, have you?' Christ, he thought, Phil had a problem with far more than the grog. Under the circumstances, however, he was left with no option.

'Marge, would you do the honours? And how about you, Pembo, fancy a beer?'

'Sure.' Ian was worried. He'd suddenly realised why Phil had made a quick trip to the lavatory only ten minutes ago. Bugger it, he thought. Phil had been straight as a die when they'd arrived.

'Grab us a couple of beers too, thanks, Marge,' Spud said as his secretary crossed to the concealed bar in the corner with its drinks cabinet and refrigerator. 'The usual for you, Phil?' he asked. He kept every one of his business associates' favourite tipples in the bar, and Phil was a bourbon man, Jack Daniel's on the rocks.

'You're a good man, Spud.'

Again the grin that grated, but then Phil Cowan's flashy charm had been grating on Spud for some time now. In the early days, along with everyone else, he'd been taken in by the likeable American. Phil was fun, a party animal, although his constant energy was at times exhausting. But Phil had ceased being fun, and the source of the man's indefatigable energy had become a genuine worry to Spud. He was regretting now that Ian had brought Phil Cowan in on their joint business ventures.

Spud and Ian no longer competed. There was no point – their strength lay in joining forces. Spud had made a fortune in the nickel boom through Ian's expert advice, both blithely ignoring the insider trading laws, and when the Farrell Corporation had been formed, Ian had invested, becoming a major shareholder. The only fly in the ointment appeared to be Phil.

Spud had voiced his worries only several months previously, after Phil had arrived at a board meeting suspiciously high.

'Isn't he a bit old to be popping pills?' he'd said derisively. 'I thought that sort of stuff was for kids.'

Ian had recognised the direct reference to his own use of amphetamines and had tried to make light of it. 'I wouldn't worry, Spud. He'll grow out of it. I did.'

Spud had considered the response far too blasé. 'Well, if you want an addict for a partner, that's your business,' he'd said, 'but you keep him on the straight and narrow when he's anywhere near me. We don't tolerate junkies on the board of the Farrell Corporation.'

'Sure, Spud. Don't worry. Phil's fine.'

Phil wasn't fine, and there was every cause for worry. Phil had developed a heavy cocaine habit. But Ian didn't dare tell Spud that.

Ian Pemberton had been in a quandary for the past several months. He felt sorry for Phil Cowan. Phil was a man with a brilliant mind – he'd topped his course at Harvard and had been the power behind the throne in the creation of Excalibur Holdings – but he was ruining his life. Ian didn't know what to do. He couldn't afford to risk any damage to his relationship with Spud and the Farrell Corporation. He'd warned Phil to keep himself clean when he was around Spud, and Phil had seemed to toe the line for a while. Yet here they were, just the three of them, and Phil was as high as a kite.

'How did the lunch with Howard go?' he asked, hoping that Spud hadn't noticed Phil's dilated pupils and the telltale signs, which he himself recognised only too well.

'Excellent – had him eating out of my hand. Literally.

Champagne, oysters, lobster, cognac – he loves the good life, that one.'

Phil brayed a laugh that was unnecessarily loud. Having downed his bourbon in one swift gulp, he held his empty glass out to Marge, who was about to leave with the coffee tray.

'Hey, Marge, honey, any chance of a second? That one didn't touch the sides.'

Marge glanced at her boss. Ian watched anxiously, waiting for Spud to blow a fuse. The brassy laugh, the hyped-up behaviour, they were dead giveaways.

Spud had noticed the signs all right, but he decided to wait for Phil to hang himself. He gave Marge a curt nod.

'Good on you, sweetheart,' the American said amiably as she crossed to the bar with his glass. 'You're a national treasure, that's what you are.'

Just one step further, you slimy piece of shit, and I'll throw you right out on your junkie arse.

'Thanks, Marge,' Spud said when she'd prepared the drink and was about to leave.

For the next ten minutes, Phil appeared to be on his best behaviour. He didn't say a word while Spud and Ian discussed the two locations Howard Stonehaven had suggested as possible sites for Farrell Towers. Instead, he gazed across the boardroom table through the windows that looked out over the city waters. Something had caught his attention. A small sailing boat with a lone man at the helm was battling against a stiff sea breeze, tacking back and forth, gaining just a little distance each time, inexorably making its way downriver. Phil found the sight mesmerising. The lone yachtsman's fight against the elements was noble, profound. It was an allegory for life. It symbolised man's struggle through the winds and tides of his existence.

'So what do *you* think, Phil?' Spud stood and leaned

across the table, barking the query right into Phil's face. He wanted to punch the man's lights out. The vacant stare had annoyed him even more than the hyped-up performance.

'Eh?' Phil was jolted back to the real world. He was expected to reply. But what had they been talking about? He hadn't heard a word.

'Farrell Towers . . .' Spud pushed back his chair and started pacing the boardroom, as he often did when expounding upon a theory or revving up his colleagues. 'Farrell Towers will one day become the symbol of the Farrell Corporation. It will also house the headquarters of Excalibur Holdings. I'd say it's a pretty important project for us all, wouldn't you?'

'Yeah . . . sure . . .'

'So what do you think about the sites we've discussed?' He'd circled the table now and was beside Phil's chair. 'We'd like your input, wouldn't we, Pembo?' His smile was dangerous and he didn't look at Ian. His eyes, glinting ominously, were focused on Phil. Ian made no reply, but cringed, waiting for the inevitable.

'Come on, Phil, old buddy boy, whiz kid, genius,' Spud said with fake heartiness. 'Let's hear from you, what are your views?'

Phil appeared to register neither the danger in the smile nor the glint in the eyes.

'God Almighty, Spud, you don't need *my* input.' He laughed. 'Christ, man, *you're* the whiz kid. *You're* the genius.' He'd forgotten the question – what the hell had they been talking about? He'd found it boring. So what? Who cared? Spud had it all figured out. 'I mean, look at you, man! Spud Farrell, youngest corporate boss in the country. Hell, youngest corporate boss in the whole god-damned *world*. You got it made, buddy, you don't need *my* input.'

'You're dead bloody right I don't.' Spud exploded. He

grabbed Phil by the lapels of his jacket and hoisted him to his feet, the chair toppling over on its side. 'Get out of here, you useless piece of junkie shit.' He hauled the American several paces from the table and swung him with all his might at the closed wooden door.

Phil staggered forward, losing his balance. He crashed into the door and ended up on the floor, bewildered. What had gone wrong? What had he done? He climbed to his feet.

Spud squared up to him in a fighting stance, fists clenched. He was a lot shorter than the American but barrel-chested and pugnacious. Phil wouldn't have stood a chance if he'd dared to take him on.

Phil looked at Ian. What's happening, his eyes asked. What's this all about? But Ian wasn't saying a thing.

'Go on, you useless bastard,' Spud snarled. 'Piss off before I beat the crap out of you.'

Phil fumbled for the door handle. Whatever the hell was going on, whatever the hell was bugging Spud, he was far better off out of here, he decided. He left as quickly as he could.

Spud closed the door calmly, his anger abated. 'You've got to get rid of him, Pembo,' he said. 'You've got to get rid of the prick – he's no use to you.'

Ian picked up the chair that had toppled over, wishing that the whole situation would simply go away. Of course he wanted to get rid of Phil – Phil was even more of a wild card than Spud realised. But the man was his partner. They'd built their business up together from absolutely nothing. He owed Phil Cowan.

Spud was studying him shrewdly; he could read Ian's mind. Of course Pembo wanted to get shot of Phil Cowan, he just didn't have the guts. Poor old Pembo, that was always his problem.

'You don't owe him a cent, mate,' he said. 'Do whatever you have to do. Phase him out, buy him up, pay him off

– doesn't matter how you go about it, but get rid of him, Pembo. He'll bring you down if you don't, I'm warning you.'

Ian didn't take any immediate action. He didn't know how to. Spud had made it sound easy, but it wasn't. Instead, he advised Phil Cowan to sever all relations with the Farrell Corporation. Phil happily obliged. He resigned from the board and brokered his personal shares over to his partner for cash – he needed the ready money anyway. Ian left it at that for the moment. At least it kept Phil away from Spud.

Then something occurred that put the problem of Phil Cowan right out of his mind. It happened on a Sunday, during the family roast dinner at the house in Peppermint Grove.

The weekly roast had become mandatory, Cynthia gathering together her son, his wife and their children the way all good families did. To everyone's surprise, not least her own, she'd embraced grandparenthood. She adored the twins, and when she took little Gordy and Fleur to play on the grassy riverside banks of Peppermint Grove, she delighted in telling people, 'No, I'm not the mother, I'm the grandmother', knowing that it seemed barely believable.

Gordon was seated at the end of the table, waiting to carve the leg of lamb, the twins perched on the edge of their seats either side of him. Gordy and Fleur were nearly four years old now and no longer needed high chairs. Ian had just finished pouring the shiraz when Cynthia arrived with a platter of vegetables, closely followed by Arlene with a bowl of peas and the gravy boat, which she placed beside Gordon. Gordon was particularly fond of gravy.

'Arlene made the gravy today,' Cynthia announced, seating herself at the other end of the table, 'with rosemary and red wine, it's absolutely delicious.'

Cynthia always went out of her way to praise Arlene, whom she considered the perfect daughter-in-law. Ian couldn't have found a better wife if she'd handpicked one for him herself, she thought.

'Uh-uh,' Gordon said, 'naughty.'

A little hand had crept out to grab a fistful of peas, and Gordon rapped his grandson over the knuckles with his bread knife. Not hard enough to hurt, but hard enough to discipline. Gordon believed in discipline. For boys, anyway. Particularly feisty little boys like Gordy.

Gordon was inordinately fond of his grandson, and he was pleased beyond measure, although he never let on, that Ian had named the child after him. The idea had actually been Arlene's, but she allowed her father-in-law to believe it had been his son's. She considered it wise to keep the old man indebted to Ian and aware of his obligations to the next generation.

Cheeky little bat-eared Gordy looked up at his grand-father, bold, unfrightened, and Gordon tried not to smile. He wasn't feeling particularly well, he hadn't been all day, but the boy gave him unprecedented pleasure. The child was so unlike his father at that age, he thought. Ian had always been a mummy's boy – he recalled how it used to annoy him. But he had to admit, his son had done very well for himself. He'd certainly made a lot of money, and a man's accumulation of wealth was the measure of his standing in society. Gordon flickered a look at his son who was tucking a napkin into little Fleur's collar. Yes, he was proud of Ian.

'I think we're ready now, darling,' Cynthia prompted gently. Everyone was waiting, it was time to carve, but her husband appeared strangely preoccupied.

'Of course, my dear. I'm sorry.'

Gordon quickly stood. A little too quickly it seemed: he felt dizzy and rather peculiar. He steadied himself, plunging the carving fork into the meat, anchoring the leg of lamb, and thereby himself. Or so he thought. He picked up the knife and started to carve. Then he gave a stifled grunt. His face twisted and he dropped the knife, his right hand clutching at his chest. His left hand remained clenched around the carving fork, and as he fell he dragged the leg of lamb with him, along with the bowl of peas, the gravy boat and his glass of red wine.

Arlene screamed, the twins screamed, and Cynthia sat frozen in horror.

Ian rushed to his father's side. Gordon lay on the floor, embracing the lamb, his face fixed in a grimace, his eyes staring glassily at nothing. Still twitching, he was sur-rounded by peas and gravy and drenched in red wine. He looked like a traffic accident.

Ian did everything he could to revive his father while Arlene rang for the ambulance. He gave mouth-to-mouth resuscitation and frantically pumped Gordon's chest for a full ten minutes, but there was no sign of life. Gordon Pemberton's heart attack had been massive. He'd died the moment he'd hit the floor.

Cynthia was a mess in the days that followed. At the funeral, she broke down completely. Everyone was deeply sympathetic. The poor woman, they thought, Gordon had been her life.

As the weeks passed, she ceased to be distraught, but remained inconsolable. She wandered about the big house lost and distracted, as if in search of her husband. Arlene, who visited daily with the children, found it most disturbing.

'Poor Cynthia, it's so sad,' she said. 'We must do some-thing, Ian.'

'There's nothing we *can* do, poppet, it's perfectly natural. The grieving process can take a very long time. She'll get over it eventually.'

'But she's so lonely there without Gordon and that place is far too big for her. Shouldn't we buy her somewhere smaller?'

Ian found the suggestion a strange one. Surely moving his mother would be the worst possible idea. The house she and Gordon had designed themselves was very precious to Cynthia. But then Arlene didn't know that.

'No, I think she's best off where she is.'

'Well, perhaps a little further down the track,' Arlene said. 'It's something to bear in mind. I worry about her terribly.'

'I know you do, poppet.' Thank God for Arlene, he thought. Arlene had been a tower of strength throughout the whole tragic business. He didn't know what he'd do without her. Ian himself was very worried about his mother. Arlene regularly voiced her concern that Cynthia might be becoming mentally unstable and it preyed on his mind. Surely Arlene was wrong. Surely his mother was simply experiencing grief. These were very troubling times.

Several weeks later, his troubles were dramatically compounded.

'Didn't you collect the paper?' he asked as Arlene walked in from the lounge room having settled the twins in front of the television set.

He'd seated himself at the kitchen table where the *Sunday Times* was normally laid out beside his bowl of fruit. He always slept in on a Sunday while Arlene took the twins for a walk in Kings Park – Gordy and Fleur were awake at six – and she always collected the newspaper from their mailbox in the downstairs foyer, laying it out on the table for him. But this morning, for some reason, it wasn't there. The fruit was, but no newspaper.

'Of course I did.' She dumped it on the table in front of him, still rolled up.

'What's wrong, poppet?'

She'd been grumpy a lot lately. He suspected it had something to do with the fruitless search for the new house. Arlene had become dissatisfied with the penthouse over the past year or so. She was obsessed with finding the perfect home – with a sizeable backyard for the children, she said – which Ian found quite understandable. He was doing his best, but every place they saw seemed unsatisfactory to Arlene. Just yesterday they'd looked at a property by the river in South Perth, which was rapidly becoming quite fashionable. He'd thought it ideal himself, but Arlene hadn't. He couldn't understand the problem.

'Nothing's wrong,' she shrugged. 'I didn't sleep well, that's all.'

Arlene's response was the standard one she gave whenever she was annoyed, and she was doubly annoyed when Ian unquestioningly accepted it. He was blind to the obvious solution. His demented mother was crashing around in a huge home with perfect views of the river, a swimming pool and a gloriously landscaped garden. Arlene found it a matter of immense frustration that she couldn't, by way of suggestion, inveigle some common sense into her husband. But she didn't dare make the proposition outright. Ian wouldn't be able to see the practicality of it at all. He positively worshipped his mother.

'Oh dear,' he said sympathetically, 'that's no good.' Arlene hadn't been sleeping well for quite some time, it was worrying. 'Why don't you have a lie-down? I'll look after the kids.'

He unrolled the newspaper, furling it back on itself to get rid of the irritating bend, and Arlene stomped off to have a shower.

BEACH GIRL BEAUTY SUSPECT APPREHENDED! the headline shrieked, and beneath the headline, taking up half the page, was a huge picture of Mayjay.

Ian felt sick. He flicked through to page four for the details, but there were very few. A man had been arrested after accosting two girls at Scarborough Beach early the previous evening and was being held for questioning in regard to the Beach Girl Beauty Murder.

He popped his head around the bathroom door and

called above the hiss of the shower, 'I have to go out for a while, won't be long.'

So much for 'Have a lie-down, I'll look after the kids', Arlene thought irritably.

'It's a beat-up,' Spud said. 'Pure sensationalism, nothing to worry about. '

Spud had seen the newspaper and had appeared very calm when Ian arrived at his front door. They'd walked through the side gate, past where Josef was working in the rockery, and down to the very rear of the garden where they now sat on the bench by the foreshore, Spud doing his best to talk Ian out of his agitated state.

'One-upmanship, that's all it is. The bloke was picked up on a Saturday so the *Sunday Times* is running with a scoop. When the proper story comes out in the *West*, I bet the editor'll cop it for a premature headline like that.'

'*Premature?*' Spud's attempt at pacification wasn't working. 'So you *do* think they're going to charge this bloke?'

'Nah. Some insider's dropped a bit of info that the coppers are questioning him about the Beach Girl case. It doesn't mean a thing.'

'Why would they question him if they didn't think they had some hard evidence?'

Spud shrugged. 'Why *wouldn't* they?'

'But it happened over eight years ago!'

'And they'll still be asking questions *twenty*-eight years from now, Pembo. These things don't just go away, you know.' He stood. 'Come on, let's go up to the house and have a coffee. We'll talk about all this when we know the full story.'

The *Sunday Times* did indeed come in for some criticism, but the editor didn't care. They'd achieved massive sales that day, and the headline, it appeared, had not been a complete furphy. The police had genuine cause to connect the man, whom they'd arrested for indecent behaviour, with the Beach Girl Beauty Murder case.

A picture of the man – in his early thirties, bearded and wild-eyed – appeared in the *West Australian*, with a request from police for anyone knowing his identity to come forward. The accompanying report stated that the offender had exposed himself to two girls on the beach at Scarborough during the early hours of Saturday evening. His behaviour had been demented.

He had a belt around his neck and he was tugging on it like he was hanging himself, the girls had stated. *He kept saying, 'Come and have some fun, come and have some fun,' over and over. He was mad. We were terrified.*

In searching the man's rented room at a nearby boarding house, police had discovered no form of identification. Items suggestive of deviant behaviour had been evident: a leather whip, a set of handcuffs, and ropes tied to the bedhead and the door handle. Every inch of wall space had been pasted with pictures of beautiful girls – Mayjay, the face of WA, featuring prominently. And pasted beside the pictures of Mayjay had been newspaper articles relating to the Beach Girl Beauty Murder.

'So he's a perve and he's into auto-eroticism,' Spud said. 'So what? They can't pin a murder on him for that.'

Ian had once again rushed around to Spud's in a panic, and Spud was once again reassuring him as they sat on the balcony overlooking the river. This time, however, Spud wasn't as confident as he tried to make out.

'The bloke's a fruitcake. They'll let him go, they'll have to.'

But would they, he wondered. The police might be only too happy to pin the crime on the poor bastard – they needed a scapegoat. The situation presented a dichotomy and Spud's feelings were mixed. If the loony went down for the count, it'd clear the decks forever of the Beach Girl Beauty Murder. But there was one major problem. Mike.

Ian was thinking exactly the same thing.

'And if they don't let him go, what do you reckon Mike'll do?'

They both knew full well what Mike would do. He'd tell the whole story. And even if the death was declared accidental, they'd have the book thrown at them for failing to report it. The adverse publicity would ruin them all.

'Relax, Pembo,' Spud said reassuringly – Pembo's nerves were getting the better of him. 'It's a storm in a teacup. They won't charge the bloke, I tell you.'

But Ian had worked himself into a highly anxious state. 'You know the moment Mike reads about this he's going to come charging down to Perth, don't you? He's probably booking his flight already.'

'Nah, he won't see the papers. It's a backwater up there. Christ, you said yourself he lives in a fisherman's hut! Stop worrying about nothing.'

'Don't kid yourself, Spud. It's not a backwater up there any more, it's a bloody metropolis. God, there's a whole new town! Have you been to Karratha lately?'

Spud had. He knew Karratha well. The gambling syndicate, in which he was now a silent partner, did very good business in the rapidly expanding new township. It appeared there was no placating Pembo, so he gave up trying.

'Listen, mate,' he said, 'whatever happens, you leave Mikey to me. I know how to handle him.'

Ian looked dubious.

'I handled him all right the last time, didn't I?' Spud landed a comforting pat on Ian's shoulder and rose from his chair. 'Now, you go home to your wife and kids and put this out of your mind. I'll look after things.' He grinned confidently. 'I always do, don't I?'

'Yeah.' Ian stood. 'Okay, Spud.'

He had no option but to place his trust in Spud. And Spud did, when all was said and done, have a way of looking after things.

Left on his own, Spud set about boosting his own confidence. He returned to the balcony where he sat staring unseeingly out at the river, his mind ticking over at a furious rate. Mike was bound to have read the newspaper reports. In fact, Spud was surprised that he hadn't already received a phone call. Pembo, for all his jumped-up nervy state, was probably right, he thought. Mike was probably booking a flight to Perth at this very moment. He'd no doubt arrive on the front doorstep tomorrow with the announcement that he was going to the police.

Spud started to plan his strategy. He'd get around Mikey, he told himself. It wouldn't be easy, but he'd done it before and he'd do it again. It was just a matter of choosing the right angle . . .

CHAPTER EIGHTEEN

But Mike hadn't read the newspaper reports. He'd been too busy.

Sunday was always a busy family day, Mike devoting his time to Jo and Allie, and they'd spent that particular Sunday morning fossicking in the mudflats near the ghost town of Cossack with Ash and Beth and their young son, Pete.

The families had become very close. After two years in residence at Roebourne Hospital, Jo had set up a medical clinic at the community centre where Beth taught, and both women shared a deep commitment to their work, particularly with the local Indigenous population. As a result, their children, who attended school at the centre, had become virtually inseparable. Pete, now a beefy nine year old, was the perfect older brother to Allie.

Fossicking in Cossack was a favourite family pastime, particularly for the children. The remains of the township consisted of no more than a derelict stone courthouse and the impressive curved façade of its old bond store, but amongst the mangroves and mudflats lay a wealth of small treasures, proof of a once thriving community.

Over the years, the children had garnered a fine collection, and Mike had had to build extra shelves in Allie's bedroom to house the rows of old medicine bottles and jars, and the carefully stacked coins that sat alongside the brass buckles and all forms of cutlery and utensils.

This particular Sunday had proved most fruitful.

'It's a porcelain pipe . . .' Ash examined the object closely as the six of them squatted on the mudflats admiring Allie's find. 'I'd say late nineteenth century.' He passed it around. 'Well done, Allie.'

'I'll bet it was used to smoke opium,' Jo said with a wink to Mike. She liked to fire up her daughter's lively imagination.

'Yep, opium for sure,' Mike agreed.

Both children were suitably impressed and stared at the pipe in awe.

'Wow,' Pete whispered, breathless with envy. 'An opium pipe.' He handled it carefully as it was passed to him, running a reverent finger around the chipped rim of the bowl. 'Do you want to do a swap, Allie? I'll give you my penny for it.'

Allie looked at him in wide-eyed amazement. Pete's 1901 Federation penny had been the greatest discovery of all time. His offer meant her pipe was of inestimable value.

Beth laughed. 'I'd give that a bit of thought if I were you, love,' she said. 'The penny's actually worth something, you could sell it one day.'

Her practicality was tantamount to sacrilege, and the looks from both children were scathing. As if either of them would ever part with a single one of their treasures!

'No,' Allie said firmly, taking the pipe from him. 'You keep the penny and I'll keep the pipe.' Then, as his face fell, she added, 'But we can do a swap every now and then, if you like.'

'Okay.' Pete grinned, appeased. The two always sorted things out amicably.

They returned to Point Samson, where this time the barbecue took place at Mike and Jo's, and the rest of the day, for the most part anyway, was spent in the water. With the exception of Jo, they were all very strong swimmers. They held diving competitions from the end of the jetty, Beth acting as judge. She'd taught the children back dives and inward dives and somersaults. Pete even managed a clumsy one and a half, but Allie always won. She was agile in the air and pretty to watch.

Allie's favourite experiences, however, were below the water's surface. In her mask and flippers she'd swim beside her father, sharing in the marvels he pointed out to her. Their love of the underwater world had become their bond, and at seven years of age Allie had already decided she wanted to be a marine biologist, just like her dad. Her dad was her hero.

Jo sprawled on the jetty, exhausted. She'd given up competing with the limitless energy of the others. Ash, too, had called it a day. He'd disappeared with his fishing rod and was nowhere to be seen. She leaned back on her elbows and watched them all cavorting. Beth was trying, with little success, to improve upon Pete's one and half somersault. 'Legs straight, lock them together, and dive for the bottom,' she repeatedly instructed, but each time he rolled into the water a gangly mess.

Mike and Allie were snorkelling. With no reefs to hand, there wasn't all that much marine activity, but Allie had nagged her father into it. They'd dive and resurface, and she'd pull her snorkel from her mouth to squeal news of each fresh discovery up to her mother before once again disappearing in a flurry of flippers.

Thank God for Allie, Jo thought. She'd thanked God for Allie virtually every day for the past twelve months. The complications that had followed the stillbirth a year ago meant there would be no more children and the knowledge saddened her immensely. How Mike would have loved a son. But there was always Allie, she told herself. Allie was the son Mike would never have.

Finally, Mike called a halt to the snorkelling. He would far rather have been up on the jetty with Jo anyway, but he'd been indulging Allie as he always did.

'I want you to show me a perfect back dive,' he said when they'd dumped their gear and joined Jo.

Allie ran off, only too eager to oblige, and Mike flopped wetly on the jetty beside his wife.

'Do you know how gorgeous you look?'

He kissed her with passion enough for her to taste the salt on his tongue. She was wearing the new, bright red bikini he'd bought for her in Dampier, its scantiness accentuating the lean, tanned curves of her body, its vivid colour highlighting the blondeness of her sun-streaked hair. Of course she didn't know how gorgeous she looked, he thought. She never did. He was in awe of her lack of vanity.

Jo smiled. 'I look like an absolute slut,' she said.

'Yes. A gorgeous one.'

He kissed her again, and this time the kiss was one of infinite tenderness. Jo responded with mock passion, running her fingers through his hair, opening her mouth greedily, pulling him down on top of her, and suddenly they were wrestling on the jetty. Then she broke away laughing.

'Well, if I look like a slut I might as well behave like one,' she said. He was still treating her with kid gloves, she thought. She wished he wouldn't. When he kissed her so tenderly, she felt a sense of pity, unintentional though it was, and she didn't want pity.

Mike got the message. He did every time, her signals were plain enough. Jo refused to share the pain of her loss. She'd cried just the once, racking great sobs, as she'd held their dead son in her arms. He'd never seen her cry before and he doubted he would again. She was incredibly strong. He sometimes wished that she wasn't.

'Time to go home soon,' he said, tracing the curve of her

hip with his fingertips. 'Do you reckon we could palm Allie off on Ash and Beth for an hour?'

'I think that could be arranged.'

Sunday had come and gone with no sight of a newspaper, but they rarely read the paper on a Sunday anyway. Then, the following day, things went mad.

As a rule, Mike left for Dampier at around five thirty in the morning – he'd become obsessed with the experiments he'd been conducting in the laboratory and liked to have the place to himself for at least an hour. But on this particular Monday he varied the pattern, and as he sat down to his breakfast at the relatively respectable hour of six forty-five, he was unaware of the drama unfolding barely thirty kilometres away.

The *Leonardo da Vinci*, a Dutch vessel and the largest cutter-section dredge in the world, had been chartered by Hamersley Iron to redredge the inshore part of its main shipping channel from East Lewis Island to the loading berths at Parker Point and East Intercourse Island near Dampier.

A series of irritating complications had surrounded the arrival of the *Leonardo*. Firstly, she needed refuelling, having come direct from a job in Brunei for Royal Dutch Shell. However, the tanker normally used for refuelling had replenished Dampier's diesel power plant tanks only the previous week and had returned to the BP refinery at Fremantle. Hamersley had therefore been forced to spot-charter a small coastal tanker doing the inter-island Indonesian run, but they were further hampered by the fact that the loading berths at both Parker Point and East Intercourse Island were currently occupied by iron ore tankers taking on cargo. One of the tankers, moreover, was the massive 420,000-tonne *Tanika Maru*, which meant the loading would take several days to complete. As a consequence, it had been decided that the refuelling

of the *Leonardo* would have to take place at the desig-
nated moorings near Conzinc Island, eight nautical miles
north-north-east of the town and port of Dampier, and
approximately halfway up Mermaid Sound, the entrance
to the port.

Refuelling at sea was a delicate operation, and both the
Dutch crew and the Pakistani crew of the Panamanian-
registered tanker had been fully briefed on the exercise.
The bunkering of the diesel onboard the *Leonardo* was
scheduled to start at first light when meteorological and
oceanographic conditions would be at their mildest.
Particular emphasis had been placed upon the need for
care, given the proximity of Dampier and the environmental sensitivity of the adjacent coral reefs and mangrove-
lined embayments.

At 0600, conditions were just as had been predicted: a
very light north-east wind of six to eight knots and a gentle
sea state of ripple conditions only. The tides were in the
last stages of neap flood with a current speed of approximately one knot towards the town of Dampier.

It was a glorious morning. The archipelago was bathed
in the clear first light of day and the islands' rugged splendour captured in all its glory. But the Pakistani crewmen
were oblivious to the beauty that surrounded them. They
wanted their breakfast. They were impatient as they
attached the coupling mechanism to the dredge's on-take
line. The sooner they could get the fuel offloading under
way, the sooner they could eat. They worked quickly. It
didn't take long. Then, the coupling connected, they
started to pump diesel. They checked the pressure gauges.
All was running smoothly, so they reported for breakfast.

But all was not running smoothly. The work had been
sloppy. The coupling mechanism had not been properly
connected and diesel was leaking into the sea at two
hundred litres per minute. No-one bothered to check over
the side.

Forty-five minutes later, from his watch on the bridge, the first mate of the *Leonardo* noticed the ominous and telltale signs, but by that time it was too late. Nine thousand litres of diesel had made its way into the sea. And the slick was heading directly for Dampier.

'Mike!' Ash barged into the cottage without bothering to knock. It was shortly before seven and the family was seated at the table having breakfast. 'Thank God you're still here.' He'd rung the lab and been told Mike hadn't reported in early as usual, and he'd panicked at the thought he might not be able to find him. 'We need you, buddy.'

'What's up?'

'There's been an oil spill off Conzinc Island and it's heading for Dampier.'

'Jesus Christ! The intake gates at Pond Zero are open.'

Ash's response had been exactly the same when Maurie Healey, Dampier Salt's general manager had phoned him with the news relayed by the harbour master.

'Christ alive, Maurie, we're pumping in fresh seawater to replenish the farm. If the spill gets down there and into Pond Zero, we're in deep shit!'

Mike was already grabbing his gear. 'How long before it reaches East Intercourse Island?' he asked, slinging his backpack over one shoulder.

'About three hours providing sea conditions don't change. They've called an emergency meeting at the harbour master's office in half an hour. Leave your keys,' he added as Mike picked up his car keys from the island bench, 'we'll go in the Landcruiser, it's quicker. Sorry about this, Jo,' he yelled over his shoulder as they both dashed out the door.

Ash drove like a maniac to Dampier.

'Maurie's organising a team,' he said, his eyes glued to the road, the barren landscape zooming past at an alarming rate. 'I've told them to close the gates and cease pumping.' He risked a quick glance at Mike, 'But we're still in big trouble, aren't we?'

'Bloody oath we are. If the spill gets into the mangroves behind West Intercourse Island near our main intake channel, it'll be there for months, even longer. We won't be able to pump until it biodegrades. The whole of Dampier Salt's operations will come to a halt for at least six months, and if it leaches into the farm's water intake, possibly years.'

'Shit, I didn't know it was that bad.'

Maurie didn't either, Ash thought. In fact, Maurie had sounded rather complacent on the phone – at first, anyway.

'Surely if we close the gates and stop pumping we'll be fine,' Maurie had said.

Ash had disagreed. 'I don't think it's that simple. What the hell we do I've no idea, but Mike McAllister's the best one to advise us. I'll bring him to the meeting.'

'Mike? He's a biologist, for God's sake.' Maurie's tone had been dismissive. 'He knows bugger all about engineering and the salt business –'

'But he knows what oil in the environment does. He's our best bet. In fact, he may well be our *only* bet.'

'I see.' Ash's sense of urgency appeared to have finally hit home. 'Well, I'll leave the decisions up to you. I'm not experienced in these areas; my background's in finance.'

Ash had recognised the veiled implication. In registering that the incident could have far-reaching repercussions, Maurie was absolving himself from any further responsibility.

As he'd rung through to the laboratory in search of Mike, Ash had felt disillusioned. He'd never considered Maurie the sort of man who would 'wash his hands' like that. But then, Maurie had never been put to the test before, had he? None of them had. That's what was so bloody scary.

Twenty minutes after they'd embarked upon their mad dash from Point Samson, Mike and Ash were speeding across the connecting causeway from Dampier to East Intercourse Island, a kilometre or so off the coast. They arrived only five minutes late for the meeting.

The office and control room of Captain Gary Hayman, head of Pilbara Harbour Services (PHS) and official harbour master, was huge and imposing. Situated on the third floor of the port control tower on East Intercourse Island, its floor-to-ceiling windows overlooked the whole of the port area. On one wall was a large-scale map of the port of Dampier and the surrounding archipelago, and at the far end was an array of SSB and VHF radios that connected the harbour master to all ships and PHS tugboats within the Port of Dampier.

A large conference table dominated the centre of the room, and when Ash and Mike were shown in, seven people were seated there: six men studying an Admiralty chart and a middle-aged woman taking notes upon instruction from the man seated at the head. Another younger woman was sitting inconspicuously against the wall, well away from the table; notepad in hand, she too was taking notes. It appeared the meeting was already under way.

Introductions were made. The assembly consisted of Gary Hayman, two of his deputies and his ever-faithful secretary, Marge; and the big guns included Maurie Healey, general manager of Dampier Salt, Jack Smythe, deputy general manager of Hamersley's operations in Dampier, and Fred Acorn, the West Australian government's regional coordinator based in the fledgling town of Karratha.

The young woman seated against the wall was not introduced and appeared quite happy to be ignored. She was Kay Freeman, an enterprising local reporter for *The Karratha Klarion*, who also hosted the breakfast news session on Radio 6KA. Kay had relegated the morning's brekkie show to her nervous production assistant who'd never performed on radio before. She knew mousy little Alice was bound to muck things up, but Kay didn't care. She couldn't believe her good fortune. The fact that she'd managed to inveigle her way into this meeting was nothing short of a miracle.

'I can promise you, Mr Harbour Master, not one word will be printed until I have your say-so,' she'd assured Gary Hayman, 'but it would be so much easier if I could be there from the start. I want to make sure I get all my facts right.'

'You'd better, Miss Freeman,' had been the stern reply, 'or I warn you, you and your newspaper will be in big trouble.'

Kay was keeping a very low profile, scribbling away for all she was worth, sure that at any moment Gary Hayman would kick her out. But the harbour master seemed to have forgotten she was there.

'So you're a marine biologist, Mike?' he queried, when Ash had completed the introductions – Ash knew everyone in the room. Gary Hayman's tone was pleasant enough, but he was plainly bemused by Mike's presence.

To Mike's surprise, Maurie Healey answered for him. 'Dr McAllister is in charge of all environmental operations for Dampier Salt, Gary,' he said. Then, flashing a confident smile at Ash, he added, 'Ash is of the opinion Mike's input could be of great value to us, and I'm sure he's right.'

Ash nodded, grateful that Maurie had backed up Mike's credentials, but aware that the man was once again placing the ball in his court should things go wrong. Maurie Healey was steadily taking a dive in Ash's estimation.

'Well, be that as it may,' Gary said briskly, he saw no value in a marine biologist's input himself. 'Take a seat, gentlemen.'

The meeting was called to order, and there was silence as Gary Hayman outlined the situation.

'At a speed of up to two knots under the prevailing

conditions, the spill will reach the town site in approximately two and half hours, possibly sooner if the wind speed strengthens . . .'

Mike, aware that he'd been mentally dismissed, studied the man. Despite an air of arrogance, he was an impressive figure. In his middle years, strongly built and commanding, the harbour master was plainly accustomed to the authority his position demanded.

'. . . However, the tide is due to change in the next two to three hours, which means it's just possible we may escape it altogether. An ebb tide will take the spill out to sea where it will disperse, causing minimal damage.'

Alarm bells started sounding in Mike's brain. Surely the harbour master wasn't underestimating the dangers they faced?

'All necessary authorities have been notified,' Gary concluded, 'and while this is a relatively minor spill, I propose we treat it as a full-scale emergency. . .'

Ash and Mike exchanged a quick glance. *Relatively minor?* their eyes asked each other. *In whose estimation?*

'. . . We'll deploy what oil-spill equipment we have, and treat the whole opportunity as a practice oil-spill contingency exercise. We might as well get some value out of the incident, although I don't think it can really do any serious damage.'

Mike was about to jump to his feet in protest, but Ash, sensing his frustration, got in first.

'I beg to differ, Gary,' he said diplomatically. 'I believe the spill could cause some *very* serious damage.' Aware as he was that the chain of command must be observed, Ash's voice was nonetheless firm – someone had to rattle the harbour master out of his complacency. 'If that oil gets into our salt farm,' he said with great deliberation, 'we can kiss goodbye to all domestic product and possibly half our synthetic stock-feed lines for at least a year. It could cost the company millions of dollars.'

Gary Hayman didn't respond directly, but looked a query at Dampier Salt's general manager. 'Is this so, Maurie?'

'We've closed the intake gates to Pond Zero and ceased pumping,' Maurie said, 'but Ash believes there's still a grave danger, and he's the expert.'

Maurie's level of concern was perfect. If Ash proved an alarmist, then he'd bear the brunt of the blame. If he proved correct, then Maurie had appointed the right man.

'I don't see a huge cause for concern myself,' Gary countered. 'The spill probably won't get that far. We're talking about diesel, after all. Correct me if I'm wrong, but diesel disperses fairly quickly, isn't that so? Jack? Fred?'

This time the query was directed towards the Hamersley Iron deputy manager and the regional coordinator. Both men nodded agreement.

'That's right,' Jack said, 'diesel's at the light end of the oil fractionation column. It disperses far more quickly than oils of a heavier fraction –'

'Exactly!' Mike could stand it no longer. He leapt to his feet. 'And that's the whole problem, for God's sake!'

His voice had been unnecessarily loud, and the silence that followed was broken only by the frantic scratching of Kay Freeman's felt pen. She stopped abruptly, not wishing to call attention to herself and wishing she'd brought her ballpoint biro.

All eyes were focused on Mike.

'What exactly do you perceive as the problem, Dr McAllister?' Gary Hayman's tone was icy. Who the hell was this young upstart?

Mike glanced at Ash whose eyes were encouraging him to take the floor, but to do so with care. *You're at the bottom of the pecking order, buddy,* his eyes said. *There's a pyramid of power sitting around this table. Watch it.* Mike read the message loud and clear.

'With all due respect, Mr Harbour Master, the very fact that diesel *is* so light means that it spreads quicker and travels faster than a spill of a heavier oil fraction. Furthermore, being light, it consists of much smaller molecules and shorter chains of hydrocarbons, many of which, especially the aromatics like benzene, are extremely toxic to marine life. This spill could have disastrous results environmentally.'

He'd gained their attention. Christ, Ash thought, where had Mike learned all that? Gary Hayman, too, was impressed. So the upstart knew what he was talking about, he thought. Good for him. But where was the potential disaster in a spill of only nine thousand litres?

'We're talking of a small spill by oil-spill standards, Mike,' he said, just a little patronisingly. 'The 1967 *Torrey Canyon* spill was in the order of millions of litres to have the disastrous effects it did.'

'Yes, I'm aware of that, Mr Harbour Master. But there was another factor, along with the size of the spill, which contributed to the *Torrey Canyon* disaster.' Mike forced himself to remain dispassionate, although he wanted to scream at them all. Jesus Christ, he thought, didn't they realise the urgency of the situation? 'The *Torrey Canyon* spill was of crude oil and in a very cold sea, which made the oil congeal and persist for months. This spill, although much smaller, is of a very light fraction and it's been released in warm tropical waters, which presents us with a very different, but equally dangerous, scenario. It will not only spread and travel faster, it will dissipate into the water column at a far greater speed and penetrate the fine mangrove mud more easily, thereby killing the burrowing in-fauna, like crabs and worms . . .'

Ash watched in admiration as Mike spelled out the facts calmly. Keep going the way you're going, buddy, he thought. Don't burst into a fit of passion, whatever you do.

'. . . The in-fauna are necessary to keep turning the mud over so that the mangroves can utilise the nutrients contained there,' Mike explained, 'and with the in-fauna dead, the mangroves themselves will also eventually die, along with the juvenile fish and prawns for which they form a nursery area . . .'

Don't you realise the vital importance of the mangroves to the entire marine ecosystem, you stupid bastards? Haven't you done enough damage already!

'. . . This, of course, will have a vast impact upon the local fishing and prawning industry.'

Mike decided to continue his argument along economic lines. After all, he thought with disdain, to men of industry such as these, financial loss spoke louder than any environmental concerns.

'Furthermore, the fine hydrocarbons in the oil will reside in the mud for a long period of time. So if the diesel gets down as far as the mangroves outside Pond Zero, which it very well might, then on each successive incoming tide, when Dampier Salt opens the gates to bring in fresh seawater to flood the evaporation ponds, traces of the oil will enter and pollute the salt.'

There was no longer an air of complacency in the room. All, including Gary Hayman, were listening attentively.

'As Ash has pointed out, this would mean the closure of Dampier Salt for quite some time and the loss of millions of dollars.'

Mike sat abruptly, aware that Ash was giving him a silent round of applause. Both awaited the outcome.

'I see,' Gary said after a moment's silence. 'Well, gentlemen, it appears this is no longer an exercise. According to our young expert, we have a potential economic and environmental disaster on our hands.'

'Yes, Mr Harbour Master.' Mike couldn't resist the last word. 'We most certainly do.'

'Let's dispense with the formalities, shall we? Given the circumstances, I suggest you call me Gary like the rest of our colleagues.' The offer was made not in the manner of friendship, but rather snappily, Mike thought. He presumed he must have offended the man. Well, too bad, he thought. At least he'd made his point.

Gary Hayman stood, barking out instructions. 'Crews are gathering and loading our oil-spill booms onto two of the tugs even as we speak. They'll be ready to depart at short notice once we determine where we want these booms deployed. Meanwhile, I've raised the regional co-ordinator at Port Hedland, and four 205-litre drums of oil dispersant are being trucked here. They should arrive within the next thirty to forty minutes.'

He addressed his deputies, who had remained silent throughout the meeting, awaiting their orders. 'Bill and Trev, you're to return immediately to your tugs, PHS1 and PHS3 – I'm having the oil-spill booms loaded onto them. I'm holding PHS2 for the dispersant when it gets here. When we work out the placement of the booms, I'll be in contact with you on Channel 76. We'll use 76 for all maritime communications and 77 for all land-based oper-ations. Is that understood?'

He didn't wait for a reply as he looked around the table.

'Mike, I want you here in the control room with me. Everyone else can return to their duties, but maintain radio contact with me at all times. Any questions?'

'Yes, I have one.' Mike put up his hand and Gary gave a curt nod. 'What exactly is it that you have in the way of oil-spill booms?'

'Five 200-metre lengths of small Vikoma Estuary boom, and two 100-metre lengths of Oil Mop boom.'

Mike nodded. 'Right. Well, the Oil Mop won't be effec-tive in the open waters of Mermaid Sound, especially if the sea state picks up, but it'd be of great use at Dampier Salt. We could put it across the gates into Pond Zero as an added protection to stop any diesel seeping past, if it gets that far.'

The harbour master made no direct response to Mike, but turned to his deputy. 'Trev, the Oil Mop's been loaded onto PHS3. When you get to your vessel, have it offloaded and transported immediately to the gates at Pond Zero. Anything else, anybody?'

Maurie darted a look to Ash as he spoke. 'Yes, Gary, if it's all right with you, I'd like Ash to remain here with Mike. As Dampier Salt's maintenance manager he knows far more about any mechanical equipment and civil material that may be called upon. Mike's a bit of a novice in these areas.'

Maurie had observed Gary Hayman's attitude. The harbour master was not accustomed to taking advice from an underling. Ash was much higher in the chain of command than Mike and would serve as a buffer.

The harbour master made no acknowledgement of Maurie's diplomatic gesture. 'Right. Ash, you stay. Now, if there's nothing more, let's all get busy.' Everyone rose from the table. 'Marge, some coffee, thanks,' he called to his secretary as she opened the door for the others.

They started filing out of the room. Kay Freeman hung back in her chair by the wall, unobserved, awaiting her turn. When everyone had gone, and she was left alone with the three men, she stood.

'Excuse me, Mr Harbour Master . . .'

Gary whirled about to face her. He'd forgotten she was there.

'Am I free to report this on the local radio at the lunchtime session, and can I put copy in tomorrow's *Klarion*?'

'You most certainly may not, Miss Freeman.'

'But the public has the right to know the facts.'

'We don't know them ourselves yet, and until we do, you and your paper will risk serious litigation if you print one erroneous word. Now, please leave the control room.'

'You'll let me know, won't you, as soon as –'

'Yes, yes,' he literally bundled her outside. 'I'll personally inform you when I'm ready to release information to the media.'

Kay found herself staring at the closed door. She wandered over to the reception area and parked herself there. She certainly wasn't leaving until she had her story. She'd wait all day if necessary.

Inside the control room, Gary's manner, although still efficient, was markedly more amiable. 'Ash, Mike, make yourselves at home. Marge'll be in with the coffee shortly. I'll just put some calls through to Perth, let them know what's happening. Then I'll be on the radio to the tugs, after which we'll get down to the deployment of the booms. Shouldn't be too long.'

He disappeared to the far end of the room, which housed the communications, and Mike and Ash sat side by side at the conference table.

'Jesus, Mike, where'd you learn all that stuff?' Ash whispered.

'I've been reading up – since the *Torrey Canyon* there's quite a lot of published information out there.' Mike was eager to share his discoveries. 'I've been running my own experiments in the lab most mornings too,' he added. 'The chief chemist's given me some large aquaria to play with, and it's been fascinating. I've tested a few of the established theories, as well as a few unestablished ones, and –'

Ash interrupted. Mike had obviously unearthed a whole new passion and was likely to go on for some time. 'I knew you were up to something, but why oil spills?' he asked.

'Why not? With the cavalier attitude of industry around here, this kind of thing was bound to happen. Someone has to know what to do about it.'

'Well, I've got to say, your timing's spot on, buddy. Talk about devotion to duty! You're a godsend.'

'There's a bit more to it than devotion to duty.' Mike found himself forced to admit the truth – he did after all have an ulterior motive.

'And what's that?'

'The Burmah Oil Company, now Woodside-Burmah – they've been fossicking around this region for years. They're starting to make some interesting gas discoveries in the deep waters off here and –'

'Yeah, I've heard the rumours. They've been running their exploration out of Broome, but they'll make their way down to Dampier any day now. And I tell you what, it'll be an enormous operation when they do.'

'Of course it will. And don't you reckon they'll just love a marine biologist who's an expert in oil-spill behaviour and its impact on the environment?'

Ash cut short his guffaw of laughter with a glance to Gary at the far end of the room.

'You sly bastard,' he grinned. 'So altruism isn't your sole motivation, there's a touch of ambition involved.'

Mike returned the grin. 'Just a touch.'

The door opened and Marge arrived with the coffee. Gary signalled from the end of the room to leave his on the table, and after serving Ash and Mike, Marge sat wordlessly, pencil and notepad at the ready. Conversation ceased.

'I take it this one's mine,' Gary said as he joined them fifteen minutes later. 'Thanks, Marge.' He picked up the by now cold mug of strong black into which Marge had stirred two spoons of sugar.

'The oil booms,' he continued, sitting opposite Ash and Mike. 'I've had them linked together, and I've instructed the tugs to hook up to each end and form a loop at the leeward end of the slick in order to capture it and keep it immobile until the dispersant arrives. Who knows, we might even be able to hold it there until the tide turns, providing the sea state doesn't change. I take it you're both in agreement with that?' He downed half the coffee in one go.

Ash saw no reason to differ, but he looked to Mike for confirmation.

'No,' Mike said firmly. 'I don't agree with that at all.'

Gary stared across the conference table, plainly taken aback, and Marge's eyes darted up from her notepad. Subordinates didn't use such a tone when addressing the harbour master.

'What do you mean, no?' Gary put down the mug. 'That's a standard oil-spill manoeuvre.'

'Yes, it's a standard oil-spill manoeuvre all right, but this isn't oil. It's diesel.'

'So?'

'Diesel spreads very thinly over the water's surface, and with the combined effects of both the wind and incoming tide, that surface water is travelling at a speed of well over a knot. At such a speed, the diesel will simply eddy underneath the boom and continue on its way.'

'How do you know this?'

Gary's challenge sounded belligerent, and Ash, aware that Maurie had placed him in the control room to act as a buffer, came to the rescue. He was sure, just as Marge was, that the harbour master found Mike's peremptory manner disrespectful.

'Mike's been studying up on oil spills, Gary, and he's been conducting experiments that –'

'No need to speak for him, Ash, he can tell me himself. Come on, Mike, fill me in on what I don't know. How do we lay these booms? I need your advice.'

As it happened, Maurie Healey, Ash and Marge had all read Gary Hayman's reactions incorrectly. Gary was impressed by young Mike McAllister. Any brusqueness of manner on his part was simply that of a man in command. He'd recognised not only Mike's superior knowledge, but a quality of leadership that he very much respected.

Well, I'll be damned, Ash thought, and he swivelled around in his chair as Mike rose and crossed to the large-scale map on the wall.

'The two major water courses to the harbour itself and

the solar ponds inlet further to the south are either side of this very island we're on.' Mike indicated the positions on the map. 'Here between Parker Point on the mainland and East Intercourse to the north-west, and here between East Intercourse and Mistaken Island to the south-west.'

Gary's impatient nod said 'Tell me something I don't know', but Mike refused to be rattled. His plan was audacious and needed to be spelled out with care.

'I'd keep the booms in their five separate 200-metre lengths and I'd put the first one around here – about a kilometre north of the west end of Parker Point. Then I'd angle it back in a south-westerly direction. This places it not only at an acute angle to the spill, but also at an acute angle to the wind and current, which means the oil wouldn't eddy under it, but rather slide along the length of the boom.'

Well, let's *hope* it would, Mike thought. This was one hell of a jump from his laboratory experiments.

'Then I'd place the next boom here,' he continued, 'a few hundred metres behind the first, at the same acute angle but reaching further to the west, and the third one behind that, each boom deflecting the spill further out into Mermaid Strait. By the time the spill reaches the end of the third boom, it will have passed the harbour entrance.'

'And we follow the same procedure with the other two booms.' Gary was way ahead of him. He'd picked up a red chinagraph pencil and was already marking the positions on the Admiralty chart that sat in the middle of the table. 'We set the other two booms here, from the south-west tip of East Intercourse, lying out past Mistaken Island to the west.'

'Exactly,' Mike said, joining him and looking over his shoulder. 'If we get it right, by the time the diesel reaches these points, the tide will have changed. That means the spill would go out on the ebb tide.' He indicated the directions on the chart. 'Either back north, up Mermaid Sound, or out west, through Mermaid Strait, and into the open sea. That's when we can hit it with the dispersant.'

Both men appeared excited by the plan, but Ash was confused.

'I'm having a bit of trouble visualising it,' he said, stroking his beard methodically as he studied the map. 'Why stagger the booms in that way?' He pointed to the five red lines Gary had drawn.

'Ever seen professional snooker players doing trick shots?' Mike asked. Ash stared back in bewilderment and continued to stroke his beard. 'Picture a snooker table. When you hit a snooker ball at an angle towards the cushion of the table, the ball bounces off at another angle, right?' Ash nodded. 'But if you lay a wooden snooker cue along that same cushion and hit a ball at it, the cue negates the bounce effect. The ball maintains contact with the cue and runs straight down the table parallel with the cushion. If you could stagger another couple of cues behind it, the same thing would happen.'

'So the booms are snooker cues and the spill's the ball?' Ash finally left his beard alone.

'That's it in a nutshell.'

Gary thumped Mike on the back. 'The man's a bloody genius.'

Jesus, Mike thought, I sure hope so.

'Marge, photocopy this section of the map.' Gary slid the Admiralty map across the table to his secretary. 'Three copies, quick as you can, thanks. Ash'll collect them from you in a couple of minutes.'

Marge took the map and disappeared silently. Mike wondered whether perhaps she was mute.

'I'll issue instructions to the tug crews,' Gary said, 'but Ash, I want you to take the maps down to the wharf and give them to Bill and Trev, and I'd like you to go out on PHS1 to help with the booms' placement. Bill's an experienced hand but he's got a raw crew, young kids mostly, he could use a steadying influence on the stern deck. Okay with you?'

'Sure, I'm on my way. Good luck with the snooker, buddy.' Ash gave Mike a wink and left.

As Gary Hayman radioed through to the tugs, Mike picked up the set of binoculars sitting on the end of the table and crossed to the huge windows that looked out in all directions over the harbour. Everything was riding on a theory of his that had never been put to the test. He prayed he was right.

Fifteen minutes later, when Gary joined him, he was still staring through the binoculars.

'The dispersant's arrived,' Gary said. 'The truck's down at the wharf and they're loading it onto PHS2.' Then he added with concern, 'But can we use it safely, Mike? I've heard that dispersants can be as harmful as oils to some forms of marine life.'

How cheering, Mike thought. A man who actually cared about the marine environment. He'd thought only money counted around here.

'It's okay to apply it in open water. That's why we have to deflect the spill and wait for the ebb tide. When the spill's out of the danger area, we'll hit it with the dispersant.'

'So now we play the waiting game?'

'That's right.'

They both glanced at the clock. It was eight forty-five.

Once again, Mike raised the binoculars to his eyes, and for the following half-hour he watched the live action unfold before him.

The booms were now in place. He could see them, lying at jagged angles from the north-east and the south-west. Just like giant snooker cues, he thought, tension mounting as he awaited the outcome.

Then, shortly after nine o'clock, through the glare of the mid-morning sun, he saw it. The sheen of diesel. A broad, glistening path heading towards the booms. No black, coagulated mass of oil, but a thin, reflective gloss, pretty in a way. Pretty and deadly, Mike thought, his eyes straining to maintain focus.

Gary joined him with another set of binoculars, and they watched together as the slick crept steadily closer.

'By my reckoning the tide's at full flood,' Gary said. 'It should be on the turn in the next half-hour or so.'

Mike didn't take his eyes from the binoculars. 'Fingers crossed,' he muttered.

Nine forty-five the clock said, and now the slick was licking at the first of the booms. Gary was no longer watching; he was busy on the radio with traffic coming in on the marine channel. But he kept calling out intermittently, 'Anything happening?'

'Can't tell yet,' Mike called back each time.

His eyes were playing tricks on him. One moment he was sure he could see the sheen on the water, the next there was nothing but a blur of blue ocean. He felt beads of perspiration forming on his brow. It was warm and close in the control room, but he wasn't sweating from the heat. He put down the binoculars and placed the palms of his hands over his eyes, forcing himself to slowly and steadily count a full sixty seconds. Then he raised the binoculars and once again looked out the windows.

The picture painted before him was as clear as the day itself, everything etched to perfection. The glossy sheen of diesel had coursed along one boom and was spilling down to the next, where it was edging along that too. The spill was slowly and steadily being deflected out into the Strait.

My God, it's working, Mike thought.

'Ash just radioed through from PHS1.' Gary was grinning broadly as he joined Mike at the windows. 'He said your snooker game's working a treat.'

'Take a look for yourself.' Mike handed him the binoculars.

Peering through them, Gary gave a whoop of triumph, then pumped Mike's hand. 'You're a bloody genius, mate.'

'Now we have to work on the dispersant,' Mike said, and they both sobered up quickly. There was more to be done.

'How do you suggest we go about it?' Gary wasn't making one single move without Mike McAllister's say-so.

'When we've contained the spill out in the deep water, we can hit it with the dispersant, but not until the tide's changed.'

'It's on the turn right about now.'

'Good.' Mike took another quick look through the binoculars. 'Another half an hour should do it, I'd say. Does your number two tug have spray booms?'

'Yes.'

'Do you have any other tugs you can use as well?

'No. We only have the three, and the others are deployed as you know. But the stuff's all loaded onto PHS2 and ready to go – why do we need more tugs?'

'Dispersants are far more effective if they're mechanically mixed into the seawater,' Mike said, 'bit like a washing machine really. Oil dispersants are the same as washing detergents in principle,' he explained. 'They're just surfactants that help break down the forces of cohesion.'

He looked out the windows to where the slick was still steadily edging into Mermaid Strait. 'The tug's propellers and spray booms will do a certain amount, but it'd be a help if we had more craft out there.'

Then the thought hit him. Of course. The local boating population. The area boasted Australia's highest number of recreational vessels per capita.

'Private boats,' he said.

'Eh?'

'We put out a call for volunteers.' He turned to Gary. 'We get all the locals involved in the mixing process.'

'*All* of them?' Gary looked horrified. 'Do you know how many cowboys there are out there? They'd kill each other.'

'Okay,' Mike agreed, 'but a couple of dozen power boats – the bigger the craft the better. How do we put the call out? What about that newspaper reporter? She does the local radio show . . .'

Gary picked up his office phone and pressed the inter-com button. 'Marge, can you contact that reporter, whatever her name is, the one who was in here?'

'She's right outside your office, Gary. Here in reception.'

Marge speaks, Mike thought. She sounded very nice.

'Her name's Kay Freeman, by the way.' Marge offered a quiet reminder.

'Send her in.'

'Miss Freeman . . .' Gary was expansive as Kay was ushered into the room, and he was even more expansive when she left five minutes later.

'Volunteers with boats over six metres.' Kay repeated her instructions. 'Only those from Dampier, and they must be launched from the Hampton Bay Boat and Sailing Club ramp.'

'That's right. The harbour will be closed to all other boating. And we only want *one* dozen boats,' Gary added with a warning glance at Mike. 'Too many cowboys other-wise. I'll have marshals at the club to oversee things.'

'It'll be on the air in fifteen minutes,' Kay promised.

'Well done, Miss Freeman, I knew I could rely on you.'

She hoped she could rely on him too: he'd promised her an exclusive interview. But then the harbour master seemed a man of his word, Kay thought as she raced down the stairs to the car park. By God, she'd be in with the scoop of the year – her feature would be syndicated all over the state, perhaps even nationally.

The first boat was out on the water within half an hour. Mike recognised the vessel, which was penned at the sailing club. A huge pleasure craft, it was the 'gin palace' owned by one of the bosses of Hamersley Iron. How appropriate, he thought. Others swiftly followed and soon the water was teeming with boats. He watched through the binoculars as they swarmed about the tug. Surely there were more than a dozen.

'An accident just waiting to happen,' Gary muttered ominously.

But there were no mishaps. Amongst the apparent chaos, order prevailed, all skippers bent on a common purpose. The boating fraternity of Dampier was coming to the rescue. It was a grand sight, Mike thought.

'You want to be down there, don't you?' Gary said, reading his mind.

'Yep,' Mike admitted. 'I'd like to be part of the action.'

'You have been, my friend. You most certainly have been.'

The rest of the day was a blur to Mike. A general press conference was called, during which Gary Hayman gave brief details about the spill and announced that the danger had been averted. He then honoured his promise to Kay Freeman and granted her an exclusive interview. On both occasions, he demanded that Mike be present and gave him full credit for the success of the exercise. In fact, he made a point of referring every second question asked of him to Mike. 'Dr McAllister's the expert,' he said.

Kay's article, which was picked up by the syndicate that very afternoon, prominently featured the brilliant young marine biologist who had saved the day.

Gary also insisted upon Mike's presence during the lengthy meetings that followed with the upper echelons of power. Full investigations were to be held into the reason for the spill, and the legal eagles needed to know every aspect.

Mike didn't get home to Point Samson until after dark.

The following morning, he didn't report in early, but
fronted up at Dampier Salt around nine, only to discover
himself besieged by reporters and photographers who'd
travelled from miles for a personal interview. Kay's
syndicated feature had appeared across the nation, and
it seemed everyone wanted a piece of Mike McAllister.

Mike made his excuses and headed for the laboratory
as quickly as he could, but there was no escape. Maurie
burst in on him.

'The ABC's sent a crew up from Perth – they're after a
one-on-one interview for *Statewide Live* to go to air
tonight. Are you all right with that?'

'Sure.' Mike shrugged. The question had been rhetorical, he obviously had no choice.

'They're waiting in my office.' Maurie started leading
the way. 'The reporter's a bit of a looker,' he added with a
wink.

'Dr McAllister.'

She rose from her chair as they entered, a leggy redhead
in her late twenties with a figure her power suit couldn't
disguise.

'Sally Jordan, *Statewide Live*. How do you do.' Her
handshake was strong, masculine.

'Hello, Sally. Call me Mike.'

'Right.' She smiled. 'Mike it is. This is Willie and Jasper.'
She introduced the two crew members with her, then turned
briskly to Maurie. 'Okay if we do the interview here?'

'Yes. Fine. I'll have some coffee sent in.'

'Thanks, that'd be great.' She nodded to Willie and
Jasper who started unzipping bags of equipment. 'Take a
seat, Mike, while the boys set up.'

'Right,' Maurie said, it was plain he was superfluous,
'I'll leave you to it.'

Sally Jordan didn't even notice him go. Her full attention was now focused upon Mike. She pulled up a chair
and sat opposite him.

'So tell me, Mike, how does it feel to be an instant celebrity?'

Her smile was warm and, the brittle efficiency discarded, her manner now friendly and relaxed. Sally liked to build a personal rapport with her interview subject before the camera started rolling.

'I didn't know I was one.'

'Oh God, yes. The Abe doesn't send a team all this way unless the story's really crash hot. And believe me, you're the hottest ticket in town now that the Beach Girl Beauty killer's off the hook. That's the way it should be too, in my opinion. Environmental issues are of far greater relevance than –'

'Excuse me? Now that what's off the hook?' Mike wasn't sure if he'd heard correctly.

'The Beach Girl Beauty killer. Well he wasn't ever really *on* the hook, was he?' She gave an abrupt laugh. 'Much as the cops might have hoped that he was.'

'I'm sorry, I don't know what you're talking about.' He had heard correctly. What the hell was going on?

'You mean you haven't read about it?'

Mike shook his head.

Sally smiled. 'Understandable, I suppose, you've been a bit busy. They caught a bloke and tried to pin the Beach Girl Beauty Murder on him – it's been headlines for the past couple of days.' His blank expression rather surprised her. 'Don't you remember the case? December, '67? Mayjay, face of WA? It was a huge story. Nationwide.'

'Yes. Yes, I remember it.'

'So they thought they had the killer.' She shrugged. 'But it turned out they didn't.'

'Who was he?'

'Some poor schizophrenic, off his medication.'

'And what happened?'

'They let him go. The whole thing was quite sad really.' This time her laugh was more a snort of derision. 'Sadder

for the cops though, they thought they had a scapegoat.'
Sally's view of the police was a little jaundiced, she'd been
arrested as a demonstrator twice during the Vietnam anti-
war protests. 'I don't think they were too happy about it,'
she said. 'In fact –'

'We're ready, Sal,' Jasper interrupted, and Sally jumped
to her feet to check on the lights and the camera shot.

Mike had trouble concentrating throughout the interview. His mind was elsewhere. He wasn't surprised that he
hadn't heard the news from Pembo. Pembo would have
buried his head in the sand hoping it would all go away.
But why hadn't Spud been in touch? Perhaps he had, Mike
thought. Perhaps there was a message at the switchboard.
He certainly hoped so. The implications of any deliberate
silence on Spud's part were highly disturbing.

'That's a wrap,' Sally announced. 'Set up for the
cutaways, thanks, guys. Great interview, Mike,' she said as
she shook his hand effusively. 'Really great.'

Was it? He couldn't remember a word he'd said.

Sally dug a compact out of her handbag and started
refreshing her make-up.

'I need to make a quick call,' Mike said, picking up the
phone on Maurie's desk. 'Only take a tick, then I'll be out
of your hair.' He rang through to the switchboard. 'Mike
McAllister here, Janie. Any messages for me?'

'Tons.' There was a moment's pause while Janie con-
sulted her list. 'The Environmental Protection Authority
and the WA Mines Department both rang you directly, but
Mr Healey's said they have to go through him. And the
media's gone mad, they all want to speak to you personally. The *West* rang from Perth, there's a Jim Forrest from
the *Sydney Morning Herald*, someone from the *Age* in
Melbourne who didn't leave a message but said they'd call
back, and the local radio wants –'

'Any personal calls?'

'Nope.'

'Thanks.' He hung up.

Leaving Sally doing her seriously-in-depth-journalist nods to the camera, Mike stepped out of the office. Maurie was waiting for him.

'The EPA's calling an immediate conference with the Mines Department and they want you and Ash there – particularly you. Can you head down to Perth tomorrow?'

Mike nodded. Oh yes, he could head down to Perth all right. He'd already planned to take the first available flight.

'Hello, Mike. How good you are here.' Cora greeted him vivaciously with a kiss on the cheek, she liked Mike very much. 'I do not see you for long time,' she said as she led the way inside. 'You happy? Your family good, yes?'

'Yes, we're all very well, thanks, Cora.'

'Hey, it's the star himself!' Spud appeared from nowhere, embracing Mike in his customary boisterous hug. 'Saw you on *Statewide* last night, you were great! And what about this morning's headlines? Mike McAllister, Saviour of the Environment!'

'I haven't seen the papers this morning.' Mike didn't react to Spud's exuberance. 'I haven't seen the papers for the past several days,' he added meaningfully, which wasn't altogether true. He'd bought back issues of the *West Australian* and read up on the reports about the Beach Girl Beauty Murder case.

'Right.' Spud ignored the pointed comment and turned to Cora. 'How about some coffee, love? There's a good girl.' She trotted obligingly off to the kitchen, and he took Mike's arm, ushering him towards the balcony. 'It's so great to see you, mate.'

But as he slid the plate-glass door closed behind them, he dropped the hearty manner. He saw little point in keeping up the pretence. Mike was obviously seeking a confrontation.

'Okay, Mikey, spit it out.'

'Why didn't you tell me what was going on?'

'I presumed that you knew. It was in all the papers. Even the *Australian* picked up on the story.'

'So you just waited for me to contact you, is that it?' Mike was surprised by Spud's attitude; he seemed unperturbed.

'Yep. That's about it.'

'And when I *didn't* contact you, it didn't occur to you to call me?'

Spud had contemplated lying. He'd considered telling Mike that he'd called any number of times, but that in all the dramas of the oil spill his messages had obviously gone astray. He'd decided against it, however. Better to stick to the truth, he'd thought – at least, as far as was possible.

'Didn't want to worry you, mate. I knew it'd all blow over.'

'That's not what the newspapers said. They were about to charge the bloke.'

'I thought you didn't read the newspapers?'

'I didn't at the time. I have now.' Mike's look was accusatory, even damning. 'If they'd charged him, Spud, would you have watched him go down without even telling me?'

'No way, Mikey. No way in the world.' Spud eyeballed him back, meeting the accusation head-on. He was being put to the test, and he knew it. 'I might be a bit of a con, mate, but I don't stand by while innocent people take the rap. You know me better than that.'

Yes, Mike thought, that wasn't Spud's way. But he wasn't entirely convinced.

'How could you be so sure it'd blow over?'

'My circle of spies, mate, they're everywhere.' Spud grinned boldly with an air of confidence he hoped was convincing, but he had his fingers firmly crossed. This was where the lies came in, and Mike wasn't as easy to deceive as most. 'It's all about contacts, Mikey, always has been. I can get inside info on whatever I want.'

Spud had sought no information from his network of contacts – he hadn't wished to draw attention to himself by showing interest in the case – but his explanation certainly held the ring of truth. He could see the suspicion in Mike's eyes lessen just a little.

'A copper mate told me that the schizo's parents had come forward as witnesses – they'd sworn he'd been with them in Adelaide at the time of the killing.' A copper mate had told him no such thing. Like everyone else, Spud had read the news when it had eventually been published in the *West Australian*, but Mike would have no way of knowing that. Thank Christ things had turned out the way they had, Spud thought.

'I knew right from the start that the bloke had an alibi,' he said, leaning back in his chair, hands behind his head, a picture of self-righteousness. Time to clinch the argument and he'd be home and hosed. Everything had, after all, rectified itself extraordinarily well.

'The publicity was the best thing that could have happened to that poor schizo bastard. His parents hadn't seen him for five years. They didn't know where the hell he was. Then, right out of the blue, there was his picture on the front page of the *Australian*. Now he's home in Adelaide in the bosom of his family, and back on his medication. How fantastic is that?'

He jumped up to open the door for Cora who'd arrived with the coffee. Perfect timing, he thought.

'Ah, the power of the press, what a wonderful thing.' Taking the tray from her he dumped it on the table. 'And now you've got your own press to consider, Mikey.'

Then off Spud went, full steam ahead, waxing rhapsodic the way only Spud could. 'Carpe diem, mate. Carpe diem. This is just the beginning! I can see an international career beckoning. The world's going to sit up and take notice of

Mike McAllister, I'd put all of my money on it, every god-damned cent. You're a star, Mikey, a veritable star!'

'Yes, Mike,' Cora said as she started to pour, 'you are very famous man.'

Mike realised that the conversation was at an end and there was no point in pursuing it. As always, Spud's reasoning had all the elements of believability. But was he telling the truth? Mike was certain of only one thing. He would never know.

BOOK FOUR

CHAPTER NINETEEN

The challenger had made an unexpected comeback. At the fourth mark, *Australia II* had closed the gap on *Liberty* to just under one minute, and as the giant yachts raced neck to neck on the final of the downwind legs, the 1983 America's Cup became a battle royal between master tacticians.

From the day's first dawning, the crowds gathered at Newport, Rhode Island, had been in a fever of excitement, as indeed had the millions all over the world who were now glued to their television sets. Before it had even begun, this twenty-fifth America's Cup match had created history. For the first time in over one hundred years, a defender had been forced by a challenger to sail the maximum number of races. Now, with three victories apiece under their belts, the Americans and the Australians were set for a 'winner takes all' seventh and final showdown.

'We can do it, Pembo! We can bloody well do it!' Watching from the flying bridge of *Ophelia*, the fifteen-metre luxury cruiser he'd chartered for the week, Spud could barely contain his excitement. 'This is history in the making, mate, the stuff of legend!'

The other twenty guests aboard, courtesy of the Farrell

Corporation, were viewing the race from *Ophelia*'s cock-pit and foredeck, but, with the exception of the skipper, Spud had reserved the flying bridge exclusively for himself, Cora, Pembo and Arlene.

'Conner can't cover Bertrand!' Ian Pemberton, whose eyes were trained unwaveringly upon the yachts, studying their crews' every move, was just as excited as Spud. 'Jesus, look at it, he's going to make the pass, Spud. He's going to make the pass!'

The Australian skipper John Bertrand's tactics had paid off. *Australia II* was slowly but steadily pulling away from *Liberty*.

Spud and Ian cheered and jumped up and down like boisterous children, despite the scowls from the skipper at the helm. He normally didn't allow such behaviour on the bridge, but what the hell, he thought, the money Farrell was paying gave him the right.

At forty, age had lent a few changes to Spud and Pembo. Spud, although still strong and nuggety, had developed a distinct paunch, and Ian's hair was thinning to the extent that he had a bald patch at the back, which he found most worrying.

The two quickly sobered up and continued to discuss the tactics of the American and Australian skippers, ignoring their women, as they had throughout the race. Cora wasn't in the least bothered, but Arlene was infuriated. By now looking decidedly green around the gills, she'd told them a number of times that she wasn't at all well.

'No, poppet, we can't,' Ian had said when she'd hissed a request to be taken ashore. 'It'd spoil everyone's day.'

'It'll spoil their day more if I vomit all over them.'

'Aren't the pills working?'

'Obviously not.'

'Oh, that's a pity. Perhaps you should take some more.'

Ian wished Arlene hadn't insisted upon coming out on the boat – she suffered acute motion sickness in the calmest of conditions. She hadn't joined them during the preliminary races, for which he'd been thankful, but she'd refused to stay at the hotel today of all days. She couldn't watch the final match on *television*, she'd said. She had to tell her friends that she'd actually *been there*.

'I'm going downstairs,' she'd announced half an hour later, very loudly and for the benefit of Spud, who, as their host, should know that one of his guests was unwell.

'Why?' Spud had asked. 'Much better view up here.'

'She's sea sick.'

Arlene had been outraged by Ian's tone. How dare he sound apologetic!

'How come? It's not rough.'

'She just is, Spud.'

'I'll have a lie-down in the cabin.' Arlene's air had been martyr-like – heavens above, she was dying, but she didn't want to put anyone to any *trouble*.

'You'll be much worse off below,' Spud had said. 'Concentrate on the horizon, that's the best thing.' Then he'd ignored her and turned back to the race.

Arlene had been concentrating on the horizon for the past hour, but she wasn't feeling in the least bit better.

'You are still sick, Arlene?' Cora's whispered enquiry was sympathetic.

Arlene nodded.

'When we get back to the hotel, I will make you herb tea. Is very good for the stomach.'

'Thank you, Cora.' How nice that someone was showing concern, she thought, even if it was only Cora.

For years, Arlene had taken no notice whatsoever of Cora. But when Spud had married the girl twelve months ago, she'd been forced to recognise the legitimacy of the relationship. To her surprise, she'd discovered she quite liked Cora.

Cora herself had fully understood the reason for Arlene's aloofness, just as she had understood the reason for Arlene's change of attitude. Filipina mistresses were unacceptable, Filipina wives were tolerated – that was the way Australian society worked. She personally didn't care whether Arlene liked her or not. But today she was very sorry for Arlene. It was not nice to feel sick.

Before long, Arlene disappeared to the cabin and the lavatory. The horizon had not worked, she needed to vomit. Neither Spud nor Pembo noticed her go. *Australia II* and *Liberty* were turning for the final upwind battle, the multitude of spectator boats following.

'Stay with them for a while, then head for the finishing line,' Spud directed the skipper. 'I want to be right there when they cross the mark.'

Having vomited, Arlene felt considerably better. She lay down on the double bed in the master cabin and waited for the interminable race to finish, too drained to be cross any more. She was actually glad that this week away had proved such a distraction for Ian. It was good to see him happy, she thought selflessly. The poor dear had been in such turmoil for months, but at least the decision had been made. And not before time, she thought. Dear God, it had been eight whole years since Gordon had died.

Arlene had resigned herself to the five-bedroom house they'd bought in South Perth, but she'd never given up the battle for Peppermint Grove. It had become a deep-seated obsession with her. Ian owed her that home. So did Cynthia, for that matter. After all, she'd done the right thing by the family. She'd borne two children, a boy and a girl, just as she'd planned – thank God they'd been twins and she'd got it over with in one go, she'd so hated being pregnant – and it really was incredibly selfish of Cynthia to remain all alone in that big house. Surely she could see that it was the perfect home for her grandchildren.

Ian didn't seem to register the fact at all – not that she'd ever put it to him directly.

'I worry about Cynthia, sweetie. Her mind wanders so, and she's a danger to herself all alone in that big house.'

'God, Mum'd rather die than leave the place.'

Arlene wished that she would.

'But if you're really worried, poppet, I could arrange a live-in companion for her.' Ian had thought his mother was coping quite well now, several years after Gordon's death. She'd even taken up bridge again, just once a week.

'But she'd hate having a stranger in the house,' Arlene said.

'We could get rid of the pool and build a granny flat down the back.'

'And ruin the landscaping? Cynthia adores the garden – she designed it herself. It'd break her heart.'

Ian had found his wife's arguments both contradictory and confusing, and he'd given up trying to follow them. Arlene, finally forced to change her tactics, had decided to concentrate her efforts on Cynthia instead.

'You seem a little weary, Cynthia. Are you sure you're not taking on too much? This house is so big, the up-keep must be a constant strain, and of course there's the garden . . .'

'Oh no, dear, I leave everything to the cleaners. And I enjoy pottering around in the garden, it's so peaceful. A man comes in once a week to do the heavier duties.'

All of which Arlene knew, but she remained resolute in her concern. 'I worry about you nonetheless. You're looking so terribly *tired* lately.'

'Am I really?'

'Yes, and you seem a bit jumpy. I feel something's not right.'

'It's true, my nerves do get the better of me at times.' Cynthia started to feel worried herself. 'I haven't been sleeping all that well lately.'

'I knew it.' Arlene nodded sympathetically. 'Why don't I make an appointment with the doctor? He'll prescribe a nice mild sedative.' When Cynthia hesitated, she added, 'I'll come along with you, if you'd like the company.'

'Would you?' Cynthia smiled. 'Oh my dear, how very kind.' She really didn't deserve a daughter-in-law like Arlene, she thought gratefully.

Valium and Normison became the order of the day, and a year or so down the track, when the Normison no longer had the desired effect, Cynthia switched to Nembutal upon Arlene's advice. On the occasions when the doctor was reluctant to renew the prescription, it didn't seem to matter. Arlene always had a regular supply.

Cynthia gave up bridge; she couldn't seem to concentrate. Then, one Saturday afternoon, she had a fall in the garden. That was when the conversation turned to nursing homes.

'But it's only a sprained ankle,' Ian protested.

'And the next time it could be a broken femur,' Arlene countered. 'She could be lying there in agony unable to get to the phone and no-one around to help her. For God's sake, Ian, she's your *mother*! Don't you *care*?'

Of course he cared. He was sick with worry. His mother was aging before his very eyes. Over the past several years she'd become shockingly vague and at times even dotty.

Arlene dutifully checked out all the best nursing homes, and having found the ideal one, she reported back to Ian with enthusiasm.

'You could hardly even *call* it a nursing home, sweetie. She'll have a *divine* little unit all to herself, with her very own verandah, and someone at her beck and call whenever she needs it. They have a communal garden too, with a little fountain in the middle – she can sit there with the others. Just think, she'll have a whole new group of friends. Won't that be lovely? The poor darling, she must be so *lonely*.'

Ian still hedged. Months went by and he was unable to make the decision. Then one morning, while Arlene was at the hairdresser, he called in unexpectedly on his mother. He had the twins in tow, having picked them up from their tennis coaching session.

'Darling, what a pleasant surprise.' Cynthia greeted him at the door, a little glassy-eyed, then smiled charmingly at Gordy and Fleur. 'And who do we have here?' she asked, waiting to be introduced.

When Ian, shocked to the core, reminded her that they were her grandchildren, she covered magnificently.

'But good heavens above, haven't you both *grown*. How old are you now?'

'Nearly twelve,' Gordy said with a look to Fleur. They'd seen their grandmother only the previous week.

'My, how time flies,' Cynthia laughed.

Arlene had breathed a sigh of relief when Ian told her the story.

'You don't see her as often as I do, sweetie,' she said sadly. 'Cynthia's like that a lot these days.' There were tears in his eyes and her heart went out to him. 'I know, I know,' she said, putting her arms around him and cuddling him close. 'Old age is a terrible thing, isn't it?'

But his mother was only sixty-six, Ian thought as he wept on his wife's shoulder.

He made the booking with the nursing home, but decided not to inform Cynthia of the move until after they'd returned from their overseas trip. Then, leaving the twins with Arlene's parents, they took off for the America's Cup.

Home tomorrow, Arlene thought, staring up at the cabin's polished wood ceiling. Poor Ian, how he was dreading the confrontation with his mother. Yes, this trip had been an excellent idea, she decided. The diversion had done him the world of good.

From the deck and the cockpit, the cheering was reaching a peak. What a relief, she thought, they must be nearing the end of the race. She really should drag herself outside and pretend to join in the fun. She sat up gingerly, aware of a slight headache. That's exactly what she'd do – she'd put on a brave face. She mustn't spoil Ian's day, it wouldn't be fair.

She went into the bathroom to refresh her make-up.

The final upwind battle had seen no less than forty-seven tacks, and *Australia II* and *Liberty* were now racing for the finishing line.

The raucous cheers and yells from the spectator boats suddenly stopped. All waited in breathless anticipation for the winning gun, which would sound from *Black Knight*, the New York Yacht Club Race Committee vessel.

It was five twenty in the afternoon. The sun was just starting to set over Block Island and for one brief moment there was utter silence on the water.

Then the gun sounded. *Australia II* had crossed the finishing line forty-one seconds ahead of *Liberty*.

The silence was broken by a cacophony of noise. People screamed themselves hoarse, but they could barely be heard as foghorns hooted, whistles shrieked and firecrackers erupted over the water.

'Bondy's done it!' Spud yelled, whirling Pembo around in a wild dance on the bridge. 'He always said he would and he has!' Spud was good mates with Alan Bond, the Perth businessman who had mounted the Cup challenge. 'Third time lucky! A man of his word!' Spud shouted. 'What a legend!'

Pembo didn't bother screaming back above the noise, but nodded wildly and joined in Spud's insane dance. After three attempts at the Cup, Alan Bond and his team had indeed become the stuff of legend. In bringing to an end a hundred and thirty-two years of American supremacy, they had carved a place for themselves in the annals of sailing history.

Arlene arrived on the bridge.

'I take it we won?' she asked. But nobody heard her.

Mike, Jo and Allie watched the America's Cup on television in their hotel suite in Frankfurt. Given the different time zones, it made for a late night. They stayed up until nearly two thirty in the morning, yelling their encouragement at the screen, urging the Aussies to win.

Spud had invited Mike to join him on the boat he'd chartered out of Newport, but Mike had agreed to speak at the three-day International Oil Spill Conference which was to be held at the Intercontinental Hotel in Frankfurt. Much as he'd longed to be there for the Cup, it hadn't once crossed his mind to opt out of his commitment. He and Jo had planned a two-week holiday around the conference to coincide with Allie's sixteenth birthday, he told Spud. She'd worked really hard to warrant the fortnight off school and this was her first trip overseas. He couldn't possibly disappoint her.

'So take her away on her *seventeenth* birthday! What's the difference?' Spud had been appalled, Mikey was a yachting man from way back. 'This is the opportunity of a lifetime, mate.'

'I know it is, Spud, and thank you but I'll watch it on television.'

'You're mad, Mikey. You're plain fucking mad!'

Yes, Mike thought, Spud might well be right, he might possibly regret having missed the experience. But there was one thing Spud didn't quite understand. Of course Jo and Allie would have let him off the hook; they wouldn't even have allowed their disappointment to show. But he'd undertaken a commitment. The conference had been co-ordinated by CONCAWE, the Oil Companies International Study Group for Conservation of Clean Air and Water in Europe, together with the US Environmental Protection Agency. Sponsored by Shell International Petroleum, BP

International and hosted by the German subsidiary
Deutsche BP, it was of major significance. Environmental
and oil industry personnel from all over the world would
be in attendance, and Mike had agreed to take part a
whole six months ago. Having given his word, he had no
intention of letting them down. But if he told Spud that,
he knew what the reply would be: *Jesus, Mikey, you go
all over the world doing that crap. And for what? All
expenses paid? Where's the deal? Where's the money in it?*

Spud was always at him. It was far easier, Mike thought,
to let Spud believe that his wife and daughter were the
governing factors in this case. There were some things he
and Spud would never see eye to eye on.

They'd arrived in Frankfurt on the Sunday before the
America's Cup race, and Allie had fallen instantly in love
with the Interconti, as it was affectionately known. From
the moment the taxi had pulled up outside the towering
building's grand main entrance and they'd stepped into the
huge open-plan lobby, her jaw had seemed permanently
agape. Allie had never stayed in a luxury hotel before.

After a full investigation of their suite on the fifteenth
floor, she'd disappeared to catch the lift up and down,
exploring every nook and cranny the hotel had to offer.
She'd given the fitness centre a good going-over, then the
beautician and hair salon, followed by each of the restaurants, coffee shops and bars, and even those conference
areas to which she could gain access.

Half an hour later, she burst back into the suite waving
a pamphlet in the air. 'Look! The man at reception gave
me a map.'

Her mother, having finished unpacking, was sprawled
on the bed, and her father, having poured himself a scotch,
was sitting at the table by the windows, gazing out at the
river. Allie, in her excitement, had failed to succumb to
the effects of jet lag, but the long flight from Perth, with its

brief stop in Singapore, had taken its toll on Mike and Jo.

Allie spread the pamphlet out on the table. 'We're right here. See?' She jabbed her finger at the biro-marked cross on the map. 'Wilhelm-Leuschner-Strasse.' She said each word with care, having asked the man for the proper pronunciation, then repeated exactly what he'd told her. 'The hotel is in the heart of the city, on the banks of the River Main.' The man's English had been perfect, but then Allie, in typically gregarious fashion, had talked to quite a number of the staff and it seemed they all spoke excellent English. She'd determined to learn as many German words as she could during her stay. It was only right that she should make the effort.

Mike had been to Frankfurt before on a brief business trip and roughly knew the layout of the city, but Jo didn't. She hauled herself from her weary state on the bed to study the map over her daughter's shoulder.

'If you go down here,' Allie said, 'you come to the river, and you can walk all the way along it, see?' She traced her finger across the map, then cast a hopeful look to her mother, who was a very keen walker. 'What do you say, Mum?'

'Not right now, darling. Tomorrow, I promise.'

'Okay.' Allie, pretending indifference, tucked the map in the hip pocket of her jeans. 'I'll go on my own then.'

Jo recognised the tone with its typically teenage hint of insolence.

'No, you won't,' Mike said, the voice of authority. 'You'll wait until tomorrow and go with your mother.'

Allie's brief rebellion disappeared in an instant; she never pushed the boundaries with her father. The occasional defiance she displayed towards her mother was purely competitive – the bravado of the female adolescent.

'Can I just go down to the river?' she begged, 'It's only a block away.'

'That's up to your mother.' Mike's voice still held a reprimand.

'Can I, Mum? Pleeease?'

Jo couldn't help but smile to herself. Allie, in her bud-ding womanhood and already a true beauty, still had so much of the child about her. The mixture was beguiling, particularly as Allie herself was utterly unaware of it.

'Yes, you may,' she said with a dignified nod.

Allie gave her a quick hug and belted for the door.

'Be careful,' Jo called, but she was already gone.

'Where on earth does she get the energy?' Mike asked.

On the Monday and Tuesday, while Mike was locked away in the conference, Allie and Jo walked everywhere. Firstly along the banks of the river, and then back through the city centre where they window-shopped endlessly, ogling all the latest fashions. Jo wanted to buy Allie a smartly tailored designer-label trouser suit, which she found very elegant herself, but Allie wasn't interested. 'It's great, Mum. I mean it's really fantastic . . .' She didn't want to be hurtful. 'But it's not really *me*, is it?' Jo was forced to admit that her daughter was still a tomboy at heart, so they settled for a number of T-shirts instead.

They visited the magnificent Old Opera House, recon-structed just two years previously following its annihila-tion during World War Two. Like so many German cities, much of Frankfurt's early architecture had been destroyed by the bombs and was only now in the throes of recon-struction. The Old Town itself had been destroyed, which Jo found shocking. Buildings testament to a bygone era, architecture centuries old, long predating the settlement of her own country, had been obliterated forever. How terrible, she thought, that war should wreak such havoc on a city's history.

As they lunched at one of the crowded outdoor cafés in the busy boulevard of Fressgass, they were enthralled by the pageantry of the passing parade. A major world centre for trade and commerce, Frankfurt was a vibrant, cosmopolitan city. 'It's even more buzzy than Sydney,' Allie said.

Jo had taken Allie to Sydney just the previous year for a week's holiday with Nora. She'd told her daughter of the past, never intending to lie, but Allie had had no memory at all of Nora, or of Nora's children who'd played with her when she was a little girl. Nora had laughed. 'How could she possibly remember us, Jo? She was only three.'

Allie recalled nothing of her infant years, but she'd thought that surely there could be no city in the world as buzzy as Sydney. She wasn't so sure now. Mentally, she listed the cities she knew. Or rather those she'd been to: there were only three. Perth, where they now lived, was very pretty, sitting on the banks of the Swan River. And Sydney, with its harbour, was very dramatic, she thought. But Frankfurt was something else altogether. Frankfurt was truly international. Allie was developing a worldly streak.

On the Monday night, Mike took them out to dinner, to a beautiful restaurant overlooking the River Main and the glittering lights of the city skyline. Then, on the Tuesday evening, they ordered room service and settled down to watch the America's Cup.

Jo glanced at Mike as she snuggled beside him on the sofa. How he must long to be there, she thought. She'd urged him to accept Spud's offer. 'Allie would understand, you know.' He'd simply replied that he was committed to the conference. She'd believed him. He was an honourable man and she loved him for it. But she was nagged by a vague sense of unease. Did he have regrets? She hoped not. It somehow placed a dampener on the holiday if he did.

The following day was Allie's birthday, and she was thrilled with the Seiko watch her parents gave her. She put it on, angling her wrist so that the silver and gold caught the light streaming through the windows.

'It's very stylish,' Jo said. 'You'll be able to wear it with everything.'

'You'll be able to wear it a hundred metres down too,' Mike said. 'It's a diver's watch.'

That clinched the deal as far as Allie was concerned – the Seiko had her absolute seal of approval.

Mike wasn't needed for the third and final day of the conference, or rather he'd taken himself out of the running to spend time with his daughter. They'd decided to go sightseeing for Allie's birthday, before attending the official dinner that evening.

The three of them walked the several blocks from the Intercontinental to Frankfurt's huge main railway station and caught the train to Eltville am Rhein. Mike, knowing nothing of the surrounding countryside, had made enquiries of the concierge.

'Rheingau,' he'd been told, 'the wine region, very beautiful. Take the train to Wiesbaden and change there for Eltville.'

The train trip itself was an experience. Allie sat glued to the windows, gazing out at the little garden plots zooming endlessly by, each with a character of its own. Some boasted orderly immaculate rows of vegetables, some were ablaze with riotous blossom, and some were simply an indiscernible mess of vegetation.

'Gardens are a bit like dogs, aren't they,' she said thoughtfully, 'they look like their owners.'

Eltville took Allie's breath away. But she wasn't alone. The little medieval township on the banks of the River Rhein had the same effect upon every tourist who visited it. Dominated by an elegant five-storey tower, the only functioning remnant of its once magnificent castle, Eltville was indeed picture-book beautiful. As the three of them walked its narrow cobbled streets, Mike and Jo shared their daughter's wonderment.

The streets were lined with half-timbered houses evocative of fairy tales, and tiny alleys led through arches into small stone squares – community centres where people gathered. In many a square was a little wine garden, and on many a corner a cosy pub, all offering the local wines, particularly riesling. The region was famous for its rieslings, they were told.

After thoroughly exploring the township itself, they spent a further hour wandering through the rambling gardens of the old castle ruins. They leaned over the sides of its ancient stone well, calling into the depths, hearing their voices reverberate. They criss-crossed the little stone bridges that forded the moat, and on reaching the highest vantage points of the castle's ramparts, they looked out over the whole of the village and the River Rhein below.

By now starving, they made their way down the hill, passing cafés and restaurants all doing a brisk trade. But they'd decided to pick a place with a view of the river.

'That one,' Allie said, pointing ahead to a restaurant whose verandah projected out over the Rhein.

'Well, we couldn't get a better spot if we tried, could we?' Mike said as the waitress led the way to a table by the railings.

They sat, admiring the view. The River Rhein appeared to meander gently by, but its tranquillity was deceptive. Given the efforts of a rowing eight crew as they hauled on their oars heading upriver, the current was immensely strong. A cruise ship passed barely thirty metres from the restaurant: a long, low-lying riverboat, one of the many that plied their trade up and down the Rhein during the tourist season. Passengers were leaning over the railings taking in the sights. Allie waved to them and they waved back.

Mike ordered a bottle of the local riesling.

'When in Rome,' he said.

They placed their food orders, and the waitress offered Allie a word of warning about her choice. 'It is not cooked,' she said. 'The fish is raw.'

'Oh.' After the briefest of pauses, Allie looked at her father. 'When in Rome,' she said and smiled. Then she turned to the waitress. 'I'll have the matje herrings, thank you,' she said firmly.

'What are they like?' Mike asked half an hour later when they were all tucking into their meals.

'Absolutely fantastic.' Allie was loving every mouthful. 'But they don't go with the orange juice.'

Mike leaned over and grabbed a fresh wine glass from the nearby table. 'They'll go with this.' He poured her a small measure of riesling, then raised his own glass in a toast.

'To Eltville and riesling and matje herrings.'

'I'll drink to that,' Allie said. 'Prost.' And they clinked.

Watching the exchange between father and daughter, Jo felt relieved of all doubt. Mike plainly had no regrets at all about missing the America's Cup. How could he, she thought. This day would live in his mind forever.

Allie caught her mother's eye and gave her a wink, sharing the moment. She knew all about the America's Cup offer and she knew exactly what her mother was thinking. Allie herself had only one misgiving. Matje herrings would never, whenever or wherever she ate them, taste quite the same as they had today.

The official dinner at the Intercontinental that night was a grand affair. Delegates' partners had been invited and over five hundred people were seated to table. The dress was formal but the atmosphere relaxed; they'd come to know each other during the conference.

Mike, Jo and Allie had been placed at the VIP table down the front near the podium, along with the Honourable Klaus von Gottfried, chief executive officer of CONCAWE, Dr Matt Shipman of the US EPA, Hans Bauer of Deutsche BP, and representatives from BP and Shell International. Also at the table were delegates from the American Petroleum Institute, the BP Oil Spill Training Centre at South Hampton in England, and the Oilton Field Studies Centre at Pembroke in Wales.

Seated at the head was an elderly gentleman whom Jo

recognised. He was Professor Morris Stanton from the University of Miami's Mangrove Studies Centre and he was famous in his field. She'd met him when she'd accompanied Mike on a trip to Florida where he'd delivered a paper at the university.

'Johanna.' Morris rose to greet her with his customary old-world charm. 'How delightful to see you again,' he said, taking her hand in both of his.

Jo smiled. 'Morris.' He was very entertaining and she liked him, although she had a feeling he'd been a bit of a roué in his day. 'This is our daughter, Alana.'

'Enchanting,' he said as he took Allie's hand in both of his.

Several of the men were accompanied by their wives, and when introductions had been made all round, talk turned to the America's Cup. Mike, being an Australian, was congratulated as if he'd won a personal victory.

'I guess we'll never live it down, eh?' Morris said with a good-humoured smile.

'Well, it was high time someone took the thing off you, Morris.' Mike returned the smile. 'I'm just glad it happened to be the Aussies.'

Klaus von Gottfried rose to make a brief welcoming speech from the podium, and announced that after the main course there would be an address from their special guest speaker, Dr Mike McAllister of the McAllister Research Institute in Western Australia. Upon his return to the table, entrées were served and the topic amongst the men reverted to oil-spill procedures and the conference in general.

Mike was having trouble concentrating on his colleagues' conversation as he looked across the table at Jo and Allie seated opposite. He felt inordinately proud of them. The elegant blonde dressed in beige, patrician, intelligent, listening attentively, and the raven-haired girl in her simple black dress, chatting away, lively and animated.

They were the most beautiful women in the room, he thought. Then he realised, with a sudden sense of shock, how very womanly Allie looked. He could see men's admiring glances. His instinctive reaction was to take a punch at every one of them, but he knew he was over-reacting. Well, well, he thought, his little girl had grown up and he hadn't even noticed.

Allie, having engaged two of the wives in conversation, was busily telling them all about her day. Neither of them had been to Eltville am Rhein, but they agreed it sounded delightful.

'And have you ever eaten matje herrings?' she asked. They hadn't. 'Well, you'll have to give them a go, they're absolutely fantastic.'

One of the women decided the young Australian was gauche and garrulous, but the other found her a breath of fresh air. She'd been bored witless by the complexities of oil-spill behaviour.

After the main course, Professor Morris Stanton was called upon to introduce Mike. Morris, well known to most of the delegates, took to the podium with panache, rambling for several minutes before launching into his introduction.

'I've known Mike McAllister for several years now,' he said, finally getting to the point. Then he went on to give Mike a huge rap: '. . . recipient of the Order of the British Empire . . . in my firm opinion, and that of many, the world's foremost expert on oil-spill management . . .' In true form, Morris's introduction was overly theatrical, and Jo sensed Mike cringe. He himself never mentioned the OBE he'd received three years ago.

'Need I say, there is none better qualified to sum up the whole purpose of this conference,' Morris concluded dra-matically. 'And so, my friends, fellow scientists, regulators, ladies and gentlemen, without further ado, I give you . . . Mike McAllister.'

The room applauded and as Mike crossed to the podium, Allie nudged her mother. 'He looks great, doesn't he?' she said in an audible whisper.

Jo nodded. He certainly did. More so than ever, she thought; age had lent him an added dignity. But then, she remembered, Mike had always looked unbelievably handsome in a dinner suit, much as he hated wearing them.

'When we close our eyes and envisage an oil spill,' Mike said in opening, 'we, and certainly the general public, picture something like the *Torrey Canyon* spill of 1967 or the *Amoco Cadiz* of 1978. Rocky shorelines and sandy beaches inundated with a black, tarry, sticky mess: oil coagulated, seals gasping for breath, dead or dying sea-birds covered with a black, homogenised ooze. It's a graphic picture, isn't it? But as we've come to learn, spills that appear less damaging can have equally disastrous results . . .'

Jo glanced at her daughter, but received no response. Allie, her face glowing with child-like adoration, remained gazing at her father. Jo returned her eyes to the podium. Mike was a commanding presence and had the audience in the palm of his hand. She was proud of him, she thought. It had all been worth it. Hadn't it? She remembered when she'd had her doubts.

There had been times when she'd missed the Pilbara almost unbearably. During that first year or so in Perth, how she'd ached to be back in the little cottage at Point Samson. She'd missed her early morning walks along the deserted beach, watching the first rays of the sun rise over the ocean, and she'd missed Ash and Beth and their raucous weekend barbecues. But most of all, she'd missed working those long, grinding days at the community centre clinic in Roebourne, feeling that her life served a purpose.

She'd adjusted eventually. She'd had to. And as Mike's wife, her life *did* serve a purpose, she'd told herself –

indeed, a purpose greater than her work at the community centre.

Johanna McAllister had been invaluable to her husband during the founding days of the McAllister Research Institute. Mike, with funding from the Department of the Environment and a number of commercial sponsors, had thrown himself wholeheartedly into the enterprise, and Jo, aware that he needed all the allies he could get, had given up medicine to lend him her full support. Mingling in government circles, she'd discovered that she'd developed quite a flair for diplomacy – it was a little like being a politician's wife, she'd thought. And she'd become skilled at fundraising events, her charms of persuasion winning many a benefactor and many a sponsorship. She'd refused a position as a founding member of the board, but it had become quickly evident that, even in her unofficial capacity, she'd embraced a whole new career.

When the Institute had become established, however, her career had taken yet another turn. Her medical background and contacts had provided the perfect foil to broaden her husband's consultancy yet further, into the field of human eco-toxicological research. The study, devoted to the health implications and accumulated effects of environmental stresses and contaminants, had received huge amounts of research funding, particularly from the government.

Not altogether the 'hands on' medical career she'd planned, Jo thought ruefully as she watched her husband at the podium, but certainly a worthy one. Mike's work and the Institute were of the utmost importance, and now, given his international reputation, the Institute was thriving.

'It is imperative we fully understand not only the eco-logical sensitivities of our local environments,' Mike was saying, 'but also the eco-toxicity, and the spreading and evaporative behaviour of our oils . . .'

Glancing once again at her daughter's rapt face, Jo cast aside any remnants of regret. She would always miss the Pilbara and her work there; they'd been the happiest years of her life. But of course it had all been worth it, she told herself. Mike was an inspiration to his daughter, just as his own father had been an inspiration to him. Allie would be facing her matriculation next year and she had her sights firmly set on university. She was planning to study marine biology, and wanted to become an environmentalist like her father. Perhaps even, like him, a world-renowned expert, who could tell? But Allie had set her sights high, Jo knew that much.

'The north-west coast of the state of Western Australia is proving to be one of the next great hydrocarbon provinces of the world.' Mike was nearing the completion of his speech. 'But here the crudes are all light – no waxy component and virtually no heavy tarry end to the product. Which brings me to my overall point . . .' He smiled as he looked around at the audience. 'I'm sure Castrol Oil won't mind if I conclude by quoting their popular advertising slogan: *All Oils Ain't Oils*. And that's a fact.'

He left the stage to a healthy round of applause. He'd covered the salient points and spoken just long enough. Succinct and authoritative was his forte.

Allie was bursting with pride as her father returned to the table. She wanted to jump to her feet and hug him and yell out at the top of her voice, 'You were fantastic, Dad!' But fighting back the impulse, she retained her composure.

They skipped the coffee following dessert. It had been a big day and all three of them were tired, even Allie, so they made their farewells.

As they headed for the lift, Mike put his arm around his wife and whispered in her ear, 'You drifted off a bit, didn't you? I could tell.'

'Just a bit,' she admitted.

'You're allowed to – you've heard it all before.'

'I wasn't bored,' Jo said, 'I was watching her.' She nodded towards Allie, who'd gone ahead of them to the lift. 'You should have seen her face while you were talking, Mike. She worships you. She's so very proud of you. And so am I.'

'The feeling's mutual.'

They paused for a moment, watching their daughter.

'She's grown up, hasn't she?' he said. 'It shocked me to see men looking at her tonight.'

Jo smiled. 'They've been looking at her for the past year.'

'Really?' He was plainly surprised. 'God, how life's moved on.'

Yes, Jo thought, life had certainly moved on. But Mike, in his obsession with his work, rarely seemed to notice the fact.

'And tomorrow it's London,' she said, kissing him lightly. 'London and Muzza and Olga. I can't wait.'

'Hurry up, you two,' Allie called, 'the lift's here.'

They'd booked into 22 Jermyn Street, a boutique hotel just around the corner from Piccadilly Circus. It boasted a 'home away from home' atmosphere and Mike regularly stayed there. Jo, having accompanied him on two previous trips to London, also enjoyed the cosy familiarity of the place.

Mike had no official duties in London. This leg of their holiday had been arranged to coincide with Muzza's big day – two of his paintings were to be hung in the National Portrait Gallery. As a result, Mike had no valid excuse to beg out of the marathon walk demanded of him, and they'd barely unpacked before he found himself marching along Piccadilly on his way to Buckingham Palace. From there, it was down the Mall to St James's Park, on to the Houses of Parliament and Westminster Abbey, then back up Whitehall to Trafalgar Square. Allie, once again in seventh heaven, seemed inexhaustible.

'How the hell do you do it?' he said to Jo when they finally returned to the hotel and he collapsed on the bed.

'I've been in training,' she laughed. 'I copped the same thing in Frankfurt.'

'Thank God tomorrow's the gallery,' he said. The National Portrait Gallery, in Trafalgar Square, was a brief ten-minute walk from the hotel.

But he wasn't about to escape that easily. After her first day's exploration, and having made a thorough study of the map she'd bought, Allie had discovered the layout of the West End. She'd planned very thoroughly the route for tomorrow, and she showed them on the map.

'See?' she said. 'If we go up Shaftesbury Avenue, we can branch off here to Chinatown, and then further up here there's Soho, and then we can go along here to Charing Cross Road and cut through here into St Martin's Lane, and then down to Trafalgar Square. Isn't that fantastic – we can look at every single one of the theatres along the way.'

'I think we'd better leave at nine o'clock,' Jo said. The ceremony at the gallery was scheduled for midday.

Having walked for well over two hours, with a brief coffee break in Soho, they arrived fifteen minutes early, Mike vetoing Allie's suggestion of a quick detour via the Covent Garden markets. They were to meet Muzza and Olga outside the entrance to the National Portrait Gallery at eleven forty-five, and he refused to be late.

Muzza was already there, as baby-faced as ever and neatly spruced up in a suit and tie. Olga was standing beside his wheelchair. Her black hair, now dramatically streaked with grey, was tied back in a severe bun and she was wearing a trim skirt and jacket. They shared hugs all round.

'We're a bit under-dressed, aren't we,' Mike said apologetically. Jo, looking svelte as always, was wearing a trouser suit, but he was in corduroys and Allie in jeans. 'I thought you said it was casual.'

'It is. Blame Olga. She made me get all tarted up – the suit's brand new.' Muzza pulled a face at his wife, who remained supremely unruffled.

'He's the guest of honour, I thought it only right he should look the part,' Olga said.

They made their way into the gallery and headed for the modern section, where Muzza's paintings had been hung earlier that morning, and where the official ceremony was to take place.

When they entered the large gallery room, Mike was relieved to find that, amongst the many suits, quite a few were in casual gear. He quickly realised, however, that although casual dress was acceptable, the function itself was no modest affair. Trays of champagne were being handed around, more and more guests were arriving, and the official party had already gathered on the small dais at the far end.

'Jeez, Muz, I didn't know it was going to be this big.'

'I didn't either, mate.' Muzza's eyes were darting around at the rapidly burgeoning numbers. He was a little jumpy; he didn't like crowds.

Allie was paying no heed at all to the people; her own eyes were trained dead ahead. She was staring at the portrait.

'It's you, Dad.' She hadn't even known of the painting's existence. She was transfixed. Her father as a young man!

Jo was equally taken aback. She remembered how she'd gazed at the portrait in the New South Wales Art Gallery all those years ago, and how it had so vividly brought back the past. She'd not seen it since.

'My God, you didn't tell me,' Mike said.

Muzza grinned. 'I thought I'd leave it as a surprise. I've had it under lock and key for years. You gave it to me, remember? You said, "It's your creation, do with it what you want," and I have.' He looked towards the portrait, although through the crowd and from his wheelchair he could see only glimpses. 'My best work. Incredible, isn't it? Virtually my first portrait, and yet it's my best. Amazing, really.'

'I like the other one better.'

The second painting was of Olga, a large full-length portrait. In a bright red dress, grey-black hair loose about her shoulders, she was seated at a table, her feet bare, her head resting on the palm of one hand, and her eyes were gazing into the eyes of the artist.

'It's beautiful,' Jo said. Even from this far away, the painting, in the simplicity of its lines, was more than beautiful, she thought, it was extraordinary.

Olga tapped her husband on the shoulder. 'I think you'd better join them, my darling,' she prompted gently. She'd noticed that, up on the dais, one of the official party was checking his watch.

'Yeah, rightio,' Muzza said, a little reluctantly, not relishing pushing his way through the crowd. He pointed out two of the dignitaries to Mike. 'The one in the pin-stripe's the Australian ambassador and the bloke next to him's the curator of the gallery. Olga and I met them last night.'

'At a cocktail party held in Murray's honour, what's more.' Olga did the boasting on her husband's behalf. 'Now go along, darling, they're waiting.'

'Come and find a place down the front,' Muzza urged, wheeling his way through the crowd, flustered, apolo-gising as he ran over a man's foot. But his wife and his friends, including young Allie, knew better than to try and pave a path for him. Muzza always tackled obstacles his own way.

The curator and the Australian ambassador led a round of applause as he wheeled himself up the ramp to the dais, Olga following to stand beside him. Muzza had insisted right from the start that she was to remain by his side throughout the ceremony.

'But it's *your* moment, Murray,' she'd argued. 'Why should I be there?'

'Because you're my wife and I want them all to see you.'

'They'll see me in the portrait.'

'And they'll see you in the flesh,' he'd said, putting on one of his sulky turns, 'or I won't go to the ceremony at all.'

As the curator stepped forward to open proceedings, Muzza looked up at his wife and, reaching out, he took her by the hand.

'Works such as these two portraits we see here before us,' the curator said, 'are an asset to the National Gallery and we are honoured to have them in our collection.' He commented with the opinion of an expert upon the individual merits of both paintings, then went on to speak glowingly of Murray Hatfield's rising prominence as an artist of international standing. He talked of the awards the artist had won, and of the various major galleries in which he was hung, and at the conclusion of his speech he introduced the Australian ambassador.

The ambassador, after admitting with all due humility that he was not a connoisseur of fine art, chose the safely patriotic path. 'This is a proud day for Australia . . .'

Jo wasn't listening to the speeches, she was gazing at the portraits. The descriptive plaque on the wall beside Mike's read: *Life's Purpose. Oil on canvas, 1967. The young Mike McAllister. Life's Purpose*, she thought, how apt. Mike had certainly fulfilled his purpose in life. And his purpose had become hers too – strange how things worked out.

The plaque beside Olga's portrait read simply: *Olga. Oil on canvas, 1980*. Jo found the painting extremely moving. The intimate body language, the look in Olga's eyes, the very sensuality of the brush strokes – the feeling between artist and model was palpable, she thought.

Beside her, she was aware that Mike, too, was staring at the portrait.

'There's so much love there,' she whispered. 'You can actually feel it, can't you?'

'Are you surprised?' he whispered back. 'Just look at them.'

Up on the dais, Muzza and Olga remained hand in hand, each other's lifeline.

'On behalf of my fellow countrymen,' the ambassador concluded, 'I heartily congratulate Murray Hatfield. And I thank the National Gallery,' he nodded humbly to the curator, 'and Murray,' he nodded just as humbly to Muzza, 'for the honour bestowed upon all Australians.'

Muzza and Olga exchanged a squeeze of hands. The speech had been a mixture of pomposity and sycophancy that they both found cringe-making. The ambassador stepped back, graciously accepting the polite patter of applause, and the curator called upon the artist to 'say a few words'.

Muzza took him up on the offer – literally. 'It's a great honour to be hung in such company,' he said, looking around at the other portraits surrounding them, many of which he considered true masterpieces. 'And I thank you very much.' They were few words indeed, but he meant each one of them.

The ceremony had come to an end and Muzza couldn't wait to get away from the crowd, but as he wheeled himself down the ramp, Olga following, an elderly gentleman with thinning grey hair materialised from where he'd been standing quietly up the back. He introduced himself. Unnecessarily.

'Magnificent pieces,' he said, shaking Muzza's hand, 'quite magnificent.' He shook Olga's hand too. 'My congratulations,' he said. Then he and Muzza started talking art.

Mike, Jo and Allie hung back watching as the two held

an animated discussion for a full ten minutes, the curator and the ambassador standing to one side respecting the artists' conversation.

'Who is he?' Allie whispered, gathering it was someone important.

'Sidney Nolan,' Jo whispered in reply.

Twenty minutes later, having said their dutiful goodbyes to the curator and the ambassador, Muzza and Olga joined them. Muzza's face was glowing with pleasure and he made no attempt to disguise his sheer delight.

'Did you see who I was talking to?'

'We sure did,' Mike replied.

'He likes my work. *Sidney Nolan* likes my work!'

'He didn't just *like* your work,' Olga corrected him. 'He said the portraits were "magnificent pieces".'

'Yeah,' Muzza grinned. 'Do you reckon it was bullshit?'

'No.'

He laughed – he didn't reckon it was either. Sir Sidney Nolan was one of Muzza's heroes and today was one of the best days of his life.

He glanced around the gallery. Much as he wanted to have a proper look at the exhibition, the place was still crowded. 'Let's get out of here,' he said. 'I'll come back later when everyone's gone.'

The five of them wandered up St Martin's Lane, where they had lunch at an outdoor restaurant, talking nineteen to the dozen. Since Mike's return to Perth, he and Muzza saw a great deal of each other on a regular basis, but conversation never ran out, and Jo and Olga had formed a very close friendship. Mike didn't find it in the least surprising – they were alike in so many ways: strong, intelligent women. The bond between Olga and Allie had confused him a little, however. While at times rebelling against her mother, Allie seemed to unquestioningly accept Olga as the voice of reason.

Far from finding the relationship a threat, Jo had

encouraged it. She'd tried to explain the phenomenon to him. 'Adolescent girls need an older female influence who isn't their mother,' she'd said. 'It's healthy.'

Mike had accepted her reasoning – she obviously knew what she was talking about – but Jo herself had questioned her right to speak as if from personal experience. Hers was hardly the background from which to quote, she'd thought with irony. Certainly, there'd been Nora in her early child-hood, and Nora again when she was in her twenties, but there'd been no-one during those in-between years. She'd wished there had been. Jo welcomed Olga's relationship with her daughter.

They dawdled over lunch, much to Allie's chagrin – she was eager to explore more of London. It was nearly three o'clock when they finished their coffees and paid the bill. Jo had quelled her daughter's impatience by promising a visit to the Covent Garden markets and then a walk down Fleet Street to the old City of London, and Muzza planned to return to the gallery. The mob from the ceremony would be well gone by now, he said, and the lunchtime visitors would have left.

'I'll come with you,' Mike offered as they left the restaurant.

'No need.'

'I want to, believe me. They've run me ragged all morning.'

'Rightio.' Muzza was secretly pleased.

Olga opted to join Jo and Allie on their walk. 'Well, perhaps just the Covent Garden part,' she said, heeding Mike's warning look. 'I'll see you back at the gallery in an hour or so, my darling.' She kissed her husband and left the men to enjoy each other's company, as she invari-ably did.

Apart from the several students wandering about the modern section of the gallery, Muzza and Mike had the place pretty much to themselves.

Ignoring his own paintings, Muzza examined each piece

in the room, positioning himself at various angles, studying every nuance. Here were some of the greatest painters in the modern art world, he thought as he slowly circled the gallery. Max Beckmann, Chuck Close, Francis Bacon, Frank Auerbach, Lucien Freud . . . the list went on.

Forty minutes later he joined Mike, who, not wishing to intrude, had left him to his own devices.

'My God, but the company I'm in,' Muzza said, obviously overwhelmed.

'You deserve to be here, Muz.'

Mike, having also wandered about the gallery, had found himself once again drawn to the portrait of Olga.

'I don't pretend to know anything about art,' he said, 'but surely this has to be the best thing in the whole exhibition.'

'I don't agree.' Muzza wheeled his chair back several paces, studying the painting analytically. 'As a piece of artwork it's good, yes, but there's something missing. I haven't really captured all that she is. Her freedom . . . the inner essence that's Olga . . . maybe just her sexiness.' He shrugged. 'I don't know what it is.' He was edgy, unable to put his finger on what he felt was lacking.

Mike didn't know what to say, he thought the painting was terribly sexy himself. 'Well, you've certainly captured the love,' he said.

'Yeah, maybe that's the problem. I'm too close to the subject.' Muzza's eyes remained critically focused upon the portrait. 'Too much of me and my love in it. Not enough of Olga herself.'

Mike gave up. Who was he to be talking art anyway?

'The one of you is much better, I think,' Muzza said, turning his attention to the other painting. 'I sure as hell captured the young Mike McAllister.'

Swivelling his chair around, he suddenly directed his full focus upon Mike himself. 'I should paint you again.' He studied the face objectively: the grooves in the cheeks, the tinges of grey at the temples – it was a strong face. But there was something more, he thought. There was an integrity, a commitment. This wasn't a man brimming with expectation; this was a man who had arrived. 'You've changed, you know, and it's not just age.'

He turned to look at his earlier portrait.

'*Life's Purpose,*' he said, 'the picture of a young man on the brink.' Then he turned back to Mike. 'We could call the new one *Life's Achievement.*' He grinned. 'The picture of a man who's made it.'

Mike laughed. Muzza was joking.

But Muzza wasn't.

Spud and Cora had stayed on in Newport for the official presentation of the America's Cup, which was to take place in two days, but Ian and Arlene Pemberton had departed for Australia, as planned, the day after the race.

They'd arrived in Perth relatively early in the morning, but by the time they'd got through customs, collected their luggage and caught a taxi home to South Perth it had been nearly ten o'clock. Being a week day, the twins were at school, delivered there by their dutiful grandparents, and after unpacking Ian had suggested to Arlene they go and see his mother.

'Oh, for heaven's sake, can't we leave it until tomorrow? I'm so *tired*!'

Ian couldn't understand why. They'd travelled business class and, with the help of a Normison, she'd slept nearly all the way.

'Mum knows we're coming back today, poppet,' he said. 'I told her we'd call around. She'll be expecting us.'

'Then *you* go,' she replied petulantly. 'I'll stay here.'

'No, you won't, Arlene.' Ian surprised them both. 'I want to get this over and done with as quickly as possible and I need your back-up.'

Goodness, she thought, he was being assertive.

'I want Mum to know that this is a decision we've both
come to, and that it's a decision we've made because we
love her and we care about her. She can take all the time
she wants before she makes the move, but I have to tell her
now. I have to get it off my chest. And I need you there
with me.'

'Of course, sweetie.' Oh well, Arlene thought, if she
must. 'I'm sorry, it was jet lag talking. I know how difficult this is for you.'

She put her arms around him and Ian responded gratefully. Then he rang his mother, but there was no answer.

A reprieve, Arlene thought, how fortunate. 'Tomorrow?'
she queried.

'No, she's probably just having a walk by the river. She'll
be home by the time we get there.'

Arlene heaved a sigh and followed him to the car.

There was no answer when they rang the front doorbell.

'She might be asleep, sweetie,' Arlene said a little testily
after he'd rung several times. 'She gets so tired these days
– we shouldn't disturb her. Let's call around tomorrow.'

'No.' He opened the door with the spare key which he
kept purely for emergencies. He never used it, not wishing
to invade his mother's privacy, but he had a strange feeling
that this might be an emergency.

'Mum?' he called as they stepped into the hall.

There was no answer. He went through to the garden.

'Mum?' Again no answer.

'I told you she'd be sleeping,' Arlene said as he bounded
up the stairs two at a time. She refused to follow; he was
being tiresomely over-dramatic. Then, seconds later, she
heard his howl of anguish.

When she entered the upstairs master bedroom, she discovered her husband on his knees beside the bed, his
mother's hand in both of his. He was stroking her palm
against his cheek and sobbing like a baby.

Cynthia lay in state. Her hair coiffed, her make-up

perfect, she was dressed in a satin lace-trimmed night-
gown, which Arlene recognised as Givenchy. She looked
immaculately beautiful and very, very regal. She also
looked very dead.

'Oh my goodness.' Arlene remained frozen at the
bedroom door. 'Is she . . .?'

'She's so cold,' Ian sobbed, rocking backwards and
forwards, his mother's palm pressed against his cheek.
'She's so cold, Arlene. She's so cold.'

Coming quickly to her senses, Arlene wondered what
she should do. Should she ring for an ambulance? She felt
the dead woman's throat for any sign of a pulse, knowing
that there wouldn't be one, but feeling it was the correct
procedure, and discovered that Cynthia's skin was indeed
icy cold. She'd obviously been dead for some time. The
ambulance could wait, Arlene decided. Her duty was to
comfort her distraught husband.

As she knelt beside him and cradled him in her arms, she
noted the empty bottle of Nembutal sitting on the bedside
table.

Oh dear, she thought, she'd certainly never expected it
to come to this. She'd considered she was doing the right
thing when she'd told Cynthia about the nursing home.
She'd popped around to see her the afternoon before
they'd left – Ian had already said his goodbyes. She'd
thought Cynthia might like to use the week they were
overseas to plan what she wanted to take with her. It was
only fair she should be prepared, Arlene had thought, and
besides, it would save time.

She remembered the scene. It hadn't been easy for her,
she'd had to be very, very firm. Cynthia hadn't believed
her at first.

'But this is my home,' Cynthia had said. 'Ian would
never expect me to leave this house.'

'I'm afraid he's absolutely adamant, he won't budge on
the matter.' Arlene had considered it kinder to be firm. It

would be cruel, she'd thought, to leave the woman with false hope.

'But he's said nothing to me.'

'No, he plans to tell you when we get back from our trip.' The look on Cynthia's face had remained one of incredulity. 'Everything's settled, I'm afraid,' Arlene had said even more firmly; there needed to be no misunderstanding. 'The booking was made some time ago. Ian's already paid for the unit, and they're expecting you to move in any time now.'

She'd seen that the penny had finally dropped. She had to give Cynthia her due: there'd been no argument, no histrionics, no tears. Cynthia had said absolutely nothing. But she'd looked as though she'd just had a dagger plunged into her heart.

'I do feel for you, Cynthia.' Arlene had regretted having sounded so brutal, even though it had been necessary. 'Ian is doing what's best for you, really he is. He's been so very worried about you lately.' She'd kissed her mother-in-law on the cheek as she'd gathered up her handbag. 'But then he'll tell you all this himself when we get home. I just thought you might like to plan what you want to take with you.'

And now it had come to this, Arlene thought, as she rocked her husband gently in her arms. How absolutely dreadful.

'Sssh, sweetie, there, there.'

Ian's sobs were gradually subsiding, although he still clung to his mother's hand.

Arlene gazed at Cynthia where she lay, immaculate, on her death bed. No, she certainly hadn't anticipated anything like this, she thought. But then Cynthia did look so composed in death, didn't she? So serene and peaceful. Perhaps it was for the best when all was said and done. Cynthia really wouldn't have been happy in a nursing home.

CHAPTER TWENTY

Alan Bond and his America's Cup team arrived home to a heroes' welcome across the nation. The whole of Australia was infected by cup fever, but none more so than the citizens of Perth. They claimed the America's Cup as their own, and why shouldn't they? The challenge had been mounted right here on their own turf, and the fabled Cup itself, a giant silver chalice, was to be on exhibition at the Royal Perth Yacht Club. The celebrations went on for weeks.

'To Bondy,' Spud toasted, and the twenty seated about the table rose to their feet.

'To Bondy,' they said, glasses raised.

Alan Bond remained seated. With the broadest of grins he raised his own glass in acknowledgement. He'd been raising his glass and acknowledging tributes for the past month since his return from New York, but he hadn't got sick of it yet, and he knew he never would.

They were at the Mediterranean Garden Restaurant in Rokeby Road, Subiaco. The Mediterranean, owned by Laurie Connell, a highly successful businessman known for his aggressive company takeover tactics, was one of the favourite gathering places for Perth's entrepreneurial and

political elite. Laurie and his wife, Liz, were seated beside
Alan and Eileen Bond, and the political contingent
included the WA Premier, Brian Burke, together with his
close ally and Parliamentary Minister, Julian Grill.

Lang Hancock, the aging iron ore pioneer, had arrived
with his Filipina companion, Rose Lacson. Thirty-nine
years his junior, Rose had taken up employment in his
household as a maid, but had rapidly come to mean a
great deal more to the recently widowed Hancock. Rose
was not the only Filipina at the table. Len Baker, a fellow
mining magnate and good mate of Lang's, had turned up
with his new twenty-five-year-old mistress, who hailed
from Santa Cruz. Her name was Juliet, and she'd been in
Perth for barely a month. And, of course, Cora Farrell,
Spud's wife, was there.

Ian and Arlene Pemberton, normally present at such
gatherings, were conspicuous by their absence. Ian was
still grieving over his mother's death, which Spud found
most unhealthy. Jesus, he thought, they'd all been sympathetic at the time – everyone knew how much Pembo
adored his mother. They'd turned up at the funeral and
paid their respects, carefully saying nothing about the fact
the poor cow had suicided. But that was over a whole
bloody month ago! And Pembo was still on a downward
spiral! The man was neglecting his business, it was bloody
indulgent.

'For Christ's sake, mate, get a grip on yourself!' Spud
had urged. 'You've got a life to live, a business to run!'

But his well-meaning tirade had made no impression.
Ian Pemberton remained deeply depressed. His was more
than a state of mourning; he was plagued with remorse.
Ian blamed himself for his mother's death.

'You told her?' He'd been astounded when Arlene had
admitted to the truth. 'You told her about the *nursing
home*? Why the fuck would you do a thing like that!'

How dare he use such language, she'd thought. But the anger she'd seen in his eyes had warned her not to take issue. 'I did it for your sake,' she'd said, aggrieved. 'I wanted to take some of the pressure off you. I knew you were dreading telling her yourself.'

Arlene had felt it necessary to admit the truth. Ian had been in torment as to the reason for his mother's overdose. Could it possibly have been a mistake, he'd agonised. He knew she took sleeping pills occasionally – perhaps she'd had too much champagne, as she was wont to do, and had then doubled up on the Nembutal forgetting she'd already taken some ... Arlene, wishing no investigation into Cynthia's drug use, and having cleared the medicine cabinet of its abundant supplies, had told her husband the obvious and very simple reason for his mother's suicide. She'd even admitted to having been very firm with Cynthia – again, for his sake. She'd wanted to save him from any possible combat upon their return.

'How could you do it, Arlene? How could you fucking well *do* it!'

Again the language, which appalled her, but she hadn't made her distaste evident. She'd started to cry instead.

'I'm sorry, sweetie. I'm so sorry. I was only thinking of you.'

Her tears had paid off, and the first serious altercation in the thirteen years of their marriage had been successfully avoided. But in the days and weeks that had followed, Ian had spiralled into a deep depression.

Arlene wasn't to blame, he thought. The problem was him and his sheer bloody weakness. He should never have agreed to the nursing home, he should have stood firm. If he had, his mother would still be alive. He was spineless, he told himself, bloody spineless. Just like he had been with Phil Cowan. But for his cowardice, Phil Cowan, too, might still be alive.

'I don't know what to do, Spud,' he remembered

whining. Christ, but he'd been a wimp. 'Phil needs money, big money, and he wants my help.'

Phil Cowan, Ian's long-time friend and business partner, had by then been mainlining for years, and Ian had finally admitted the truth to Spud. 'His dealers are after him and he's gone into hiding. God only knows what they'll do if he can't pay up.'

Spud hadn't said 'I told you so', but his contempt had been plain, and Ian had known that it was directed at him as much as at Phil.

'I presume the useless prick's run off to his weekender?' Ian had nodded. 'What'll I do, Spud?'

'Don't give him a cent. Go home and let him stew in his own juice.'

Spud had said no more than that, and Ian had done as he was told.

Phil Cowan had been discovered at his holiday shack in Mandurah barely a week later, dead of an overdose which was presumed accidental.

Spud hadn't been at all surprised when he'd heard the news. 'Bound to happen,' he'd shrugged. 'A man owes big money, goes into hiding, word gets around he can't pay – a recipe for disaster.'

They'd had no further discussion. Spud hadn't invited it and Ian hadn't pursued it. They'd both known that Spud had had no direct involvement in the sordid episode of Phil Cowan's death. He'd simply utilised his grape vine of contacts. Horrified as he'd been by the death of his friend and partner, Ian's reaction had been tempered with relief, and, although he could barely bring himself to admit it, a sense of gratitude.

Now, all these years later, guilt-ridden over his mother's suicide, the memory of Phil Cowan returned to haunt him. He'd betrayed Phil just as he'd betrayed his mother. They were both dead because he was gutless. Ian was consumed with self-loathing.

The celebratory lunch was a long one – their lunches at the Mediterranean always were. In fact, as Spud and Cora took their leave at five o'clock, it was obvious that the hard-core drinkers would remain at the restaurant for dinner – an occurrence that was not altogether unusual.

Spud was mellow but not drunk as they climbed into the Mercedes – he very rarely allowed alcohol to get the better of him. Cora didn't drink at all, but he certainly wasn't about to trust her at the wheel. He'd taught her to drive, and she'd gained her licence after her third attempt, but Cora was a truly dreadful driver.

'Juliet, she is very nice,' Cora remarked. Today was the first day they'd met Len Barker's new mistress and Cora had liked her a lot. 'She is very pretty too.'

'Yep.' Spud kept his eyes on the road. His mind wasn't on Cora's chatter, he was thinking about the interesting discussion he'd had with Brian Burke when he'd been able to pry him away from Laurie Connell. Laurie and Brian were permanently joined at the hip – Laurie had been boasting for months that he was the one who'd got Burke into power. But then, Spud thought, a little prime ministerial assistance from Burke's old mate Bob Hawke hadn't gone astray.

'Rose, she is nice,' Cora said, with a little less certainty; she wasn't altogether sure about Rose. 'And she is pretty also.'

'Yep.' He really needed to talk things over with Pembo – if only he could get him out of his current doldrums.

'It is funny, Spud, three Filipina at lunch today and I am the only wife.' Cora laughed. The knowledge filled her with pride. But there was no answer from Spud.

'You do not think this is a good thing?' Her face reflected her disappointment; she'd expected some response.

'Sorry, love. I don't think what's a good thing?'

Oh, it was all right, she thought, he just hadn't been listening. She was used to that.

'Me, I am the only Filipina at lunch who is married,' she said.

'Of course.' Spud leaned over and kissed her on the cheek. 'You're married because you're very special.'

Cora beamed happily. She was secure in his love. Not that he ever actually told her he loved her, but he showed it in so many ways.

She settled back to chat about the lunch – she'd varied her choice and had the dhufish today, which had been excellent. Juliet had had the lobster salad, which had also been excellent. Cora knew this because she'd often had the lobster salad herself.

'I tell Juliet that one day I take her to the Oyster Beds. The Oyster Beds, they have the best lobster thermidor, I think.'

Spud smiled. He wasn't listening to the chatter itself, but the sound of her voice pleased him. Everything about Cora pleased him.

'Juliet, she is very nice, I would like her for my friend. But she will not be here long.' Cora's tone was practical, although tinged with regret. 'Len, he will send her back to the Philippines. This is sad, I think.'

She glanced at Spud, but again there was no reply. He wasn't listening. Cora didn't mind. Spud would never send *her* home, she thought, gazing contentedly out the window. They had been together for a whole eight years, and now they were married. Spud was an excellent husband. Cora considered it her duty to be an excellent wife in return. She would never make eyes at other men and flirt the way she saw some wives do. Such behaviour was disloyal. She would never be disloyal to the man she loved.

To Cora, gratitude and love amounted to much the same thing, and not once had it occurred to her to question the difference. The sleepy hollow of Perth was a far cry from the seething back streets of Manila, where she'd never known the luxury of all she could eat and ready money to buy what she wanted. At first, much as she'd revelled in her new life, she'd found it difficult to adjust. She'd gorged herself on the food, but had been unable to bring herself to spend the money he gave her. She still couldn't. She accepted with delight the gifts he lavished upon her, but most of the cash still found its way back to Manila. Her little brother was at university now – the first member of her family ever to have an academic education – and her mother received new shoes every year. As many pairs as she wanted, Italian leather too.

Cora was grateful to Spud beyond measure. She perceived her gratitude as love, and the perception was quite possibly correct. Cora's gratitude, and therefore her love, was reflected in a loyalty so fierce it was akin to devotion. If Spud were threatened, she would quite likely lay down her life for him.

They were driving along Victoria Avenue now, past the wealthy new mansions that were rapidly replacing the rambling old houses by the river. They'd be home soon. She wondered what she should instruct Natalija to prepare for dinner. Natalija always awaited her instructions. But she didn't ask Spud his preference; she could see he was still thinking.

Spud certainly was. Over lunch, he'd pledged a 200,000-dollar donation to the Labor Party, intimating it would be the first of many, and he and Brian Burke had come to an understanding. Spud needed to move and he needed to move quickly – a whole new world was opening up. But he wanted Ian Pemberton by his side. Ian had a brilliant business mind.

You've got just one more fortnight to get your act together, Pembo, he thought. If you're not back on board by then, you can go and get fucked. I'll find another bloody partner.

Spud knew that he wouldn't. For better or for worse, and much as Pembo often infuriated him, they were mates. You didn't give up on your mates.

Like Cora, Spud was a firm believer in loyalty. He was worried about Pembo. How the hell could he get him back on track?

The one to get Ian Pemberton back on track proved to be Arlene, which was surprising because, unlike Spud, she *had* given up on her husband.

Arlene was frustrated beyond all reason. She wanted desperately to shift into the Peppermint Grove house, but when she'd made a tentative suggestion a fortnight or so after the funeral that perhaps they should start considering the move, he'd all but snapped her head off. 'How bloody tasteless,' he'd said. *Tasteless*! *Her*!

It had been a whole five weeks now and she'd done everything herself, with no help from Ian. She'd sifted through Cynthia's personal belongings, and she'd sorted out the furnishings, selling those she didn't want. The house stood ready and waiting for them, but when she hinted at the fact he just glared at her. He was so moody and morose lately, it was getting on her nerves. He even ignored the twins. Which wasn't like him at all, she had to admit. Ian had always been a good father, interested and caring. He loved his children. But young Gordy and Fleur had become virtually invisible. These days she was the one who had to drive them to tennis coaching and footie practice and ballet and singing lessons. She was heartily sick of it.

Now and then he'd go into the office, but according to his secretary he was the same at work: he just sat at his desk and did nothing. His secretary was worried about him. Well, good for her, Arlene thought, but his secretary didn't have to live with him, did she?

Arlene had come to a decision. If Ian chose to ignore his wife and his children, then his wife and his children would ignore him. Besides, there were issues to address, the first of which was Gordy's ears. He was twelve now, and she'd always planned to have his ears done when he was twelve, before he started high school. She'd decided to book the operation for the start of the school holidays, but the plastic surgeon needed a consultation first so she made an appointment for the following week. Then she broke the news to Gordy, very gently.

'All the men in your family have pronounced ears, darling, it's genetic. There's nothing wrong with pronounced ears, of course, but aesthetically it would be to your advantage to have them pinned back.'

Her son stared blankly at her. He didn't seem to understand.

'It's a simple operation . . .' She'd actually heard that recovery from the procedure could be quite painful, but they'd face that part when they came to it. 'And it'll serve you well in the long run, I promise.'

But Gordy, to her infinite surprise, still didn't get her drift.

'Why?' he demanded in his bolshie way.

'Well, you don't want to be called Mickey Mouse, do you, sweetie?' she said reasonably. Heavens above, didn't the boy realise the kindness she was doing him?

'Nobody calls me Mickey Mouse.' Gordy looked at his mother as if she came from another planet.

'But they might at high school, darling. Adolescents can be very cruel.'

'I don't want to have my ears pinned back. They're fine the way they are.'

'They won't be later in life, Gordy,' she said sternly. God, how she wished Cynthia had had Ian's done. 'You'll thank me for it, believe me.'

Gordy made no further reply, but marched into the nearby bathroom where, through the open door, she could see him studying himself in the mirror. He pressed his ears back against the side of his head, then released them to their normal bat position. Good, she thought, he'd got the message.

But Gordy hadn't. He stormed off to his father's study.

Ian was sitting mindlessly at his desk, miserable and self-pitying as he had been all day, when his son burst into the room.

'I don't want to have my ears pinned back,' Gordy announced.

'What?'

'I don't care if it's genetic.' Gordy looked at his father's ears. They did stick out a bit – he'd never really noticed before. Why should he? His dad was just his dad. And Grandpa Gordon *had* had big ears. Not that Gordy remembered himself, but they sure were big in the picture on the lounge room dresser. But Grandpa Gordon had been an old man and old men always had big ears.

'You don't care if what's genetic?' Ian asked, confused.

'Your ears stick out, and Grandpa's did too. What's wrong with that?'

'What are you talking about, Gordy?'

'Mum's booked me in with a plastic surgeon. I've got an appointment next week.'

'Oh?' Ian was raised from his torpor.

'Nobody's ever called me Mickey Mouse. Nobody. Ever.'

'Fine.' The boy was very defensive, Ian thought, what was going on? 'Who said that they did?'

'Mum. Well, she reckons they will. But I'd just like to see them try.' Gordy, the apple of his grandfather's eye, stood defiant. 'I don't want to have my ears done, Dad. And I won't.'

That was the night Ian and Arlene *did* have their first serious altercation.

'How could you call the poor kid *Mickey Mouse*!' Ian had been outraged. 'You could have undermined the boy's confidence for the rest of his life. Thank God he's got guts.'

'Oh, for goodness' sake, I didn't call him Mickey Mouse. I simply pre-empted the cruelty of others. You know what school children are like.'

'Well, let him cope with it in the playground. He doesn't need stuff like that from his own bloody mother!'

Arlene had applied her customary feminine wiles, turning tearful at being so sorely misunderstood. She was doing it purely for the boy's sake, she said.

'No, you're not, Arlene, you're doing it for yourself. God only knows why.'

She took umbrage at that. How dare he!

'I have nothing but Gordy's future happiness at heart,' she declared haughtily.

'He's happy the way he is, can't you see that? He *likes* the way he looks. Leave him alone.'

Arlene, finally realising that her husband was not putty in her hands, which in itself was a revelation, admitted defeat and left the room in a huff.

But the true realisation was Ian's. He realised that he'd ignored his family to the point where his son's wellbeing had been threatened. He further realised, for the first time in his marriage, that his wife had a tendency to manipulate.

Arlene had successfully, albeit unwittingly, got her husband back on track.

The following day Ian reported in to Farrell Towers. But he didn't go to the Excalibur Holdings offices on the third floor; he went straight to Spud's main office suite on the ninth.

'Sorry I've let you down,' he said. 'I'm ready to go to work now.'

'Welcome back to the land of the living, mate.' Spud circled his desk and shook Ian's hand, then led the way through to the lounge room and bar. He was greatly relieved. 'What brought about the change?' he asked as they sat in the comfortable armchairs by the huge window with its panoramic views of the city and the river.

'I had a row with Arlene.'

'Really?' That'd be a first, Spud thought, Pembo never said boo to his wife. 'What about?'

Ian decided not to mention Gordy's ears, it wouldn't be fair to the boy. 'She wants to move into the Peppermint Grove house, and I don't.'

Well, of course she'd want to move in, Spud thought, she'd probably been lusting after the house for years. He wouldn't have been surprised if she'd shoved the pills down poor old Cynthia's throat herself. Spud couldn't stand Arlene. The cold-shoulder treatment she'd given Cora for years had been unpardonable. But the woman was more than a snob and a racist, in his opinion. She was dangerous. Pembo, of course, was blind to the fact. He couldn't see that his wife was a real cunt.

'Anyway, it shook me out of myself,' Ian said. Then he changed the subject; he really didn't want to discuss Arlene. 'So what's happening? You said on the phone we had big things to talk about.'

'We sure do, mate. There are major times ahead. We've never had it so good.' He told Ian about the party donation he'd made. 'Just the first of many, Pembo, and believe me, we'll see a return on it. Burke's making his intentions plain right from the start.'

The Labor Party had come into power in WA in February, ousting the Liberals after a nine-year reign, and the new Premier, former television journalist Brian Burke, was indeed aligning himself with the hard-core circle of Perth's entrepreneurs.

'You should have heard him carry on at lunch last week,' Spud said. 'I think he was practising his speech for the media. Of course, everyone was half-pissed and they all applauded him, but he was dead bloody serious.'

Spud rose and struck a stance in mockery of Brian Burke, who had indeed waxed loquacious. '*An elite of the able,* that's what he calls it. He's going to create a *new order* where the government works closely with business *for the advantage of the state.*' Spud gave Burke's quotes their full oratorical ring of passion. '*It'll be the salvation of WA and the salvation of the country!*' Then he flopped back in his armchair. 'You're bound to read all that and a whole heap more in the press – he's got the media in his pocket, particularly television. All his old journo mates are on side.'

Taking a cigar from the humidor that sat on the coffee table, Spud carefully clipped the end off into the large ceramic ashtray. 'Of course, he's a total wanker and it's a load of bullshit, he's in it for himself, but that's fine by me,' he said, lighting up. 'After lunch, when we were mingling, I offered the donation and we had a bit of a chat.' He pulled heavily on the cigar, watching the plumes of smoke rise. 'Like I said, Pembo, we've got it made.'

Spud had been paying money into the coffers of successive governments for years, but he'd never received quite such unashamedly blatant promises in the past. Brian Burke's *elite of the able* was right up his alley, he'd decided.

He and Ian spent the next half-hour considering the various favours they might call in and the advantages they might seek in exchange for their generous party donation.

'There's another angle too,' Ian said thoughtfully, after they'd discussed sundry possible business or property acquisitions, and which government building contracts were up for tender. 'What about the Institute? It's an open conduit for funding, has been for several years. And we're on the board.'

The Farrell Corporation and Excalibur Holdings had been the first sponsors to offer donations in the founding days of the McAllister Research Institute. Spud and Ian had been keen to help Mike, of course, but their very public donations had been an excellent tax write-off, and their involvement so beneficial to their respective public profiles that they'd even become honorary executive directors.

'What exactly did you have in mind?' Spud asked,

looking shrewdly at Ian. God but it was good, he thought, to have Pembo back.

The first hint of Brian Burke's corrupt regime was discovered by none other than journalist Sally Jordan.

By 1985, Sally Jordan had risen in rank to become the senior reporter on ABC Television's *Statewide Live*, which was not surprising. Now in her late thirties, she'd been with the show for over a decade. She produced her own segments and essentially had carte blanche in the choice of her material, although she naturally conferred with her executive producer.

During this particular day's conference with Patrick, her EP, she ran past him the two major stories that she planned for that week. The second was to be a segment about heritage buildings currently under threat by real estate developers, to which Patrick gave his immediate approval. In running through the first of her intended stories, however, Sally was a little close-lipped. She had her doubts about Patrick. Brian Burke had been in power for over two years now and yet Patrick seemed reluctant to go with any story that criticised the government. She suspected no sinister motive on his part, but he'd worked closely with Burke in the past and any possible hint of mateship in his reticence met with Sally's strong disapproval.

'I'm going to cover the protest meetings by the Nursery Growers Association,' she said. 'They're up in arms about the virtual takeover of WA Flower Power Pty Limited.'

The cutely named Flower Power Company had in the short year of its existence cornered the major export market for the growth and sale of flowers both wild and domestic. The Nursery Growers, having just eighteen months previously contributed money for a government bureaucrat's overseas trip to find viable markets for their produce, were naturally not happy about the Flower Power takeover.

'Fine,' Patrick said. He knew of the fracas and it sounded like a good local story, although he was surprised Sally was interested in wild flowers. Sally wasn't, but she'd done her homework. Patrick hadn't.

The bureaucrat, a man called Dan Scully from the Department of Agriculture, had returned from his trip, funded jointly by the WA government and the Nursery Growers, and had promptly retired from the public service. Within six months, he'd set up his own private company, a nursery which he'd called WA Flower Power Pty Limited, and had picked up virtually every major overseas contract in the offing.

Sally filmed the public protest meetings, getting the cameraman to zoom in close on the angry faces and the placards reading *Give us our money back* and *Government pays to put us out of business.*

She visited the Flower Power nursery and attempted her trademark foot-in-the-door approach, but met with little success in the form of direct confrontation. Dan Scully's repeated 'no comment' responses from behind his firmly locked flywire screen, however, spoke multitudes. And when he finally slammed the inner door shut, she took great satisfaction in barrelling to the camera: 'Well, I think that just about sums it up, don't you?'

She wrote her own voiceover material to go with the footage, as she always did, but this time she didn't give it to Ryan, her assistant producer, to transfer to autocue. Young Ryan was ambitious and a bit of a toady. She thought, in his haste to ingratiate himself, he might run off to Patrick.

'It's all visuals,' she said. 'I'll just read from my notes.'

The segment was hard-hitting, a definite indictment.

'Is this where our taxpayers' money should be going?' Sally's voice queried over footage of the lavish Flower Power Nursery. 'To feather the nest of an ex-public servant?' Over a shot of the protesters: 'These people have every right to be angry.' Over a shot of Dan Scully behind his flywire door: 'This man used their hard-earned cash to gain knowledge of the overseas market, then set himself up in direct competition.'

At the end of the segment, when they returned to studio, Sally directed her closing statement down the barrel, summing up the state of play as she saw it.

'Dan Scully should answer for his betrayal of the trust placed in him during his employment as a public servant. And the government should answer as to how and why such an abuse of funding, both public and private, was ever allowed to occur.'

Sally left the studio that night pleased with herself. She was aware that Ryan was looking at her askance, and that she'd probably cop a talking-to from Patrick the following day about why she hadn't warned him she was doing an exposé. But who cared, it had been a bloody good segment.

'What the hell did you think you were doing?' She copped far more than a talking-to from Patrick.

'The Premier called the ABC manager at his home last night. Burke's furious, he wants you sacked.'

'Well, that'd be dumb, wouldn't it?' Sally said boldly. 'It'd only add fuel to the fire.'

She was taken aback at such a knee-jerk reaction, but the mention of dismissal didn't alarm her unduly. They couldn't possibly sack her – they'd have to know that she wouldn't leave quietly. By God, she thought, she'd go public with a vengeance if they dared give her the boot. Their hands were tied, there was nothing they could do.

But as it turned out, there was.

Several nights later, Sally's story on heritage-listed buildings under threat went to air. Again, most of the segment was visual footage shot on location with her studio voiceover. This time, she'd given her notes to Ryan for transferral to autocue as she normally did.

'These grand old buildings that stand as monuments to

the past,' she read, 'are under threat from greedy developers with no care for our city's history . . .'

At first she didn't notice the changes in the footage, she was too busy concentrating on the autocue. Then, from the corner of her eye, she caught the monitor. That wasn't the building she was speaking about, she thought, horrified. It wasn't even one of the buildings she'd filmed. She read on, glancing regularly at the monitor. Much of the footage was different. Shots of other old buildings had been salted in amongst the carefully documented heritage-listed architecture that was under threat.

She tried to ad-lib. 'And here's another fine example of our early architecture,' she said. She didn't even know what building it was.

At the close of the segment, when the studio camera light came on, she was completely flustered. Normally she rounded off her story with a personal pithy comment, but she was at a loss. What should she do? She did nothing, simply read the autocue introduction to the lighter segment that always ended the program.

'And now for a report from the fashion show in Sydney, here's Alison Summers with the latest designer trends in store for us this coming winter.'

She fronted Ryan the moment they were off air.

'What the fuck's going on?' she demanded. 'What happened to my footage?'

'What do you mean?' He obviously took offence at her belligerent tone. 'That was the tape that came up from the editing suite. I naturally presumed that you'd looked at it.'

Sally had. She'd run the footage and written her notes accordingly. But someone had switched the tape.

The ABC received a number of complaints, and the next morning Patrick demanded she apologise on air that night. It was Friday and *Statewide Live* didn't air again until Monday, so the problem had to be rectified immediately, he said. He was furious.

'We can't afford sloppy work and badly researched material, Sally. Do you realise the damage this sort of thing could do to the ABC's image?'

'But the tape was switched,' she said. 'Half of the shots weren't mine. I didn't even film some of those buildings.'

He looked incredulous, and Sally knew herself that it sounded pretty far-fetched. But she continued vehemently.

'Come on, Patrick, you know me. I don't fuck up like that. I've *never* fucked up like that. And if I ever *do* make a mistake, I bloody well take the rap for it.'

Her argument rang true. Patrick had to admit that Sally Jordan's research was invariably spot-on, and she was certainly never one to pass the buck.

'How the hell could a thing like that happen?'

'Don't ask me, but it was an act of sabotage. Someone's out to discredit me.'

'And in doing so, they're discrediting the ABC. I'm sorry, Sal, but you'll have to make a personal on-air apology. The general manager's already insisted on it, and I'm afraid I have to agree. Regardless of the circumstances, we've no other option.'

She tried to protest, but Patrick, although genuinely sympathetic, remained insistent.

'We can't just announce there was a mix-up with the footage. Be reasonable, Sal, we'd look like absolute fuck-wits. The only way out is for the journalist to take full responsibility. And that journalist is you.'

That night Sally felt sick as she faced the camera.

'In my story last night on the threat to our historical buildings, I'm afraid some of the facts were not as they should have been.' The words stuck in her craw. 'As viewers may have noticed, I referred to one or two build-ings incorrectly, and much of the architecture shown in the footage has proved not to be heritage listed. I take full responsibility for these errors, and I sincerely apologise for the flaws in my research.'

Sally Jordan's credibility had been totally undermined.

She sweated it out through the weekend, fielding the odd phone call but keeping her mouth shut. Then on Monday, determined to get to the bottom of the matter, she paid a visit to Greg, the film editor whose studio was in the bowels of the building.

Yes, Greg said, he *had* made some changes. There'd been a number of stock shots Ryan had wanted added to the original footage. He'd thought nothing of it at the time, he said – assistant producers often liked to put their personal thumbprint on a story. Greg personally found the practice a bit cheeky. Shit, he said, most of the time the APs didn't even go out on location. How could they know the full story?

'I heard there was a bit of a kerfuffle. Did Ryan bugger it up?' he asked mildly.

'Yes,' Sally retorted, 'and he may well have successfully buggered up my career.'

She stormed off to confront Ryan, but he was nowhere to be found. She'd forgotten that she'd already sent him out to do some field research on her latest story. So she reported her findings to Patrick, who immediately informed the general manager.

The next day, Ryan was called upon to explain his actions in Sally's presence. He'd found the segment short on time, he told the general manager, so he'd added some stock shots. He was very sorry if he'd got it wrong, but he presumed Sally had seen the final edit and given it the go-ahead.

'You bloody well knew that I hadn't, you little bastard,' she said. Beneath her fury, she was mystified. What the hell was he playing at? Why was he out to discredit her? Was he after her job?

No action was taken against young Ryan Bromley, which Sally considered strange. In the past, she'd always found the ABC protective of their staff and quick to right an injustice. But the general manager deemed it unnecessary to take action. Ryan had made a mistake, it was agreed, he should have conferred with his senior producer, but he'd learned a lesson, it wouldn't happen again. To keep the peace, however, it was decided he be assigned to another producer.

A month later, Ryan Bromley resigned. He left the ABC to take up a position as press officer with the Premier's Department.

Shortly afterwards, Sally found herself out of a job. She wasn't dismissed. Her contract was up and the ABC was not going to automatically renew it as they had done in the past. They were sorry to see her go, the general manager said, she'd been one of the best journalists they'd ever had.

The delicately inferred reason she was given was the sad demographic reality that viewers these days preferred younger reporters. At least younger *female* reporters. Sally was powerless to contest the fact. She was, after all, looking forty in the face.

But she knew the truth. She had no doubt she was paying the price for her exposé, and there was nothing she could do about it. The WA Flower Power story had dwindled to zero, the press hadn't followed up on the issue, it was yesterday's news. If she tried to go public and fight her dismissal, she'd simply be joining the whinge of all aging female reporters who found themselves replaced by fresh-faced twenty-something cabs off the rank.

Sally Jordan realised that she'd collided with an iceberg, and that WA Flower Power was only the tip of it.

CHAPTER TWENTY-ONE

Jools returned to Perth that summer of 1985, her first trip in over six years. She was 'coming home for Christmas' she announced, which Mike found a bit strange. His sister and her writer husband had been settled in Ireland for years and he'd presumed she'd embraced Dublin as home.

'It'll be just like the old days, Mike,' she bubbled enthusiastically over the phone. Henry wasn't coming with her, which was just as well, she said, things weren't crash hot between them at the moment.

Well, he supposed that explained why Dublin wasn't home.

Jools was thirty-nine years old, childless and her second marriage was crumbling. Going the way of the first, she said, but so what? She refused to give in. She was growing old disgracefully and proud of the fact.

There was a touch of desperation about Jools these days. She drank too much and she smoked a lot, but somehow she still managed to be fun, albeit, Mike discovered, as infuriating as ever.

'My God, what an atrocity,' she said as she stood with her brother in Victoria Avenue looking at the high-rise apartment block that sat where the family home had once been. 'Why on earth did Dad do it?'

'He didn't exactly build the thing himself, Jools,' Mike said a little tersely. He found the implied accusation offensive.

'You know what I mean. Why on earth did he sell?' Undeterred by the reprimand, Jools was still accusing.

How like her, Mike thought. She was oblivious to the circumstances and yet totally opinionated. But he decided not to allow it to irritate him. Jools was just being Jools, and it was good to see her again.

'He sold because the bloke next door did.' He patiently repeated exactly what he'd said over the phone years ago when she'd expressed her horror at their parents' plan to sell the old Claremont house. 'Dad couldn't bear the thought of living next door to a bloody great high rise, which is pretty understandable.'

'Yes,' she said, vaguely recalling that he'd told her. She looked at the apartments with added distaste. 'So the developers ended up getting practically the whole block from the jetty to where the old baths used to be. How criminal.' Then, in typically mercurial fashion, she turned to him with a huge smile. 'But I'm glad Mum and Dad are happy where they are.'

'Come on,' he said, 'time to go. Jo and Allie'll be waiting.'

Mike had picked his sister up from the airport on his own. It had been Jo's idea. The siblings hadn't seen each other for over six years and she'd thought they might like some time together.

'No, no, wait, Mike, wait.' Jools looked at him beseechingly. 'Just a walk to the end of the jetty? Please?'

He gave in with good humour, and together they walked to the end of the old Claremont jetty.

Jools took off her sandals, feeling the sun-warmed, weathered planks beneath her bare feet, not bothered by the threat of splinters or the splatter of bird mess. She looked out across the bay to Point Walter where she used to sail her little boat, and she peered down at the jetty's pylons where she and Mike had gathered the mussels they'd cooked up in the old laundry tub.

'Let's go for a swim,' she said. 'I can get my bathers from the car. They're in the very top of my suitcase, it'll only take a tick.' She had a desperate desire to throw bombies off the pylons.

'I don't have mine with me.'

'Then go in your underpants – you've done it before.'

'Not now, Jools, Mum and Dad are expecting us.'

They'd already be late, he thought, having stopped off at her insistence for this trip down memory lane. And after picking up Jo and Allie in Nedlands it was a further forty-minute drive to Shoalwater Bay. But Mike understood his sister's nostalgic longing. Indeed, he understood it the way no-one else could.

'We'll come back, I promise,' he said. 'We'll come back before you leave, just you and me, and we'll chuck bombies off the jetty the way we used to.'

'Goody,' she said, 'I'd like that,' and she threaded her arm companionably through his as they walked back to the car.

Words couldn't express Jools's gratitude for the past they shared, she and Mike. Her memories of their childhood by the river had become more precious than ever over the last year or so. As they walked beneath the big Norfolk Island pine which stood at the bottom of Jetty Road, she looked up through its branches. She'd been living a lot in the past lately, she thought. And why shouldn't she? The present didn't seem to have much going for it.

'God, we were lucky little bastards, weren't we,' she said. The understatement of the year, she thought. 'And we never knew it – we took it all for granted.'

'Kids always do.'

They exchanged a smile.

Jools was surprised when they pulled up outside Mike's modest single-storey house in Nedlands with its neat little garden and river glimpses from the far corner of the front verandah.

'Surely a world-famous scientist should have something more posh,' she said. As usual, she wasn't shy in voicing her opinion. 'Where's the luxury? Two storeys at least, panoramic river views, a huge launch on a mooring – I was expecting that sort of thing.'

Mike laughed, she was incorrigible. 'We don't need all the trimmings, and there're plenty of launches and views at the Institute,' he said. 'You've never seen it, have you?'

Jools shook her head, shamefaced. She'd been to Perth several times during the early years of the Institute, when they'd been working out of an old corrugated-iron shed at Woodman Point. Or so Mike had told her. 'It used to be a Water Board storage depot in the days when the main city sewage discharge was from a pipe out into Cockburn Sound,' he'd said, which hadn't particularly enthralled Jools. Besides, her trips had been fleeting ones, just for Christmas, so she hadn't considered herself obliged to pay a visit. She felt decidedly guilty now.

'I sort of never got around to it,' she said apologetically.

But Mike didn't seem at all bothered. 'There have been a few changes – you'll be impressed.'

The front door opened and Jo appeared, Allie by her side.

'Jools, how wonderful to see you.' The two women embraced fondly.

'My God, but you're ageless,' Jools said, 'it's bloody disgusting. And just look at you, Allie.' She stood back admiringly, 'You're going to be a model, I can tell. Well, you probably are already. How old are you now? Seventeen?'

'Eighteen.'

'Eighteen, and a knockout.' She gave her niece a fierce hug. 'I bet you don't remember me.'

'Yes, I do.' Allie had met Jools only the once. She'd been nine years old and they'd come down from the Pilbara for a family Christmas at her grandparents' house. Her aunt had made a very vivid impression upon her, as had been Jools's intention at the time. 'You gave me a book, remember?'

Jools looked a little blank.

'By Patrick Dennis?' Allie added meaningfully.

'That's right, of course I did.' Jools laughed, delighted. '*Auntie Mame*, I thought it was apt.'

'It was,' Allie said. And it still is, she thought. Jools was obviously bent on the madcap aunty image. But Allie reserved judgement; Jools seemed nice.

'So are you a model? You ought to be.'

'No, I'm a uni student.'

'Allie's just topped her first year at UWA,' Mike boasted. He'd told Jools several times that Allie was at uni, but she obviously hadn't been listening, which was par for the course. 'She's going to be a marine biologist.'

'Well, I got that one wrong, didn't I?' Jools gave a comical shrug. Personally she thought the girl was mad. Why on earth wasn't she cashing in on her looks?

They piled into the car, Jo insisting Jools take the front seat so that she could see better, and Mike drove them down the old coast road.

Jools enjoyed the drive south, it brought back childhood memories of picnics and crabbing at Mandurah. Even the stench from the abattoirs and skin-drying sheds as they passed Robbs Jetty evoked happy, anticipatory times.

Roughly ten kilometres south of Fremantle, Mike pointed out the turn-off to the Institute.

'We're just down there,' he said, 'on the south side of Woodman Point. The location's ideal. Ours is the most northerly of the industrial leases so we have access to deep clean water for intake into the laboratories and aquaria. I'll collect you from Mum and Dad's tomorrow and give you the personal guided tour, if you like.'

'Great.'

They passed the country town of Rockingham, roughly thirty-five kilometres south of Fremantle, and as they turned off the main link road, the territory became new to Jools. During all her childhood trips south, she couldn't remember her parents ever having taken the short detour to Shoalwater Bay. And now they lived there. Extraordinary, she thought. She somehow couldn't picture them anywhere but the old house in Claremont. Then they turned the corner into Arcadia Drive.

Arcadia Drive, Shoalwater Bay, was as picturesque as it sounded. The road followed the broad sweep of the bay, which was spectacular: the sand a startling white, two tiny islands sitting in the vivid aquamarine of the Indian Ocean barely half a kilometre offshore.

'Oh, how beautiful,' Jools breathed. 'No wonder they're happy here.'

Mike nodded. 'They hardly go into town at all these days. And when they do, Mum says turning that corner to home is her sanity.'

'Do those little islands have names?'

'They sure do.' It was Allie who replied from the back seat, with a chortle that Jools found attractive. 'And whoever came up with them had a vivid imagination.' She pointed out the open window. 'That one's Seal Island, and most summers there's a small colony sprawled on the beach. And that one's a nesting sanctuary for gulls and terns so it's called Bird Island. And the bigger one, right down the end, just off the point, that's Penguin Island, but they got it a bit wrong. They should have been more specific and called it *Fairy* Penguin Island, because guess what nests there?' She gave another chortle. 'You should go and have a look at it while you're here, Jools, it's so pretty. You can actually walk out across the sandbar on a really low tide.' Allie had been coming to Shoalwater Bay for summer holidays every year since she was twelve. She loved the place.

The house was a comfortable low-slung bungalow facing onto Arcadia Drive and the sandhills that led to the beach beyond. As soon as Mike pulled into the driveway, Maggie and Jim appeared. He'd rung to say they'd be an hour late so that his parents wouldn't worry, but they'd been keeping an impatiently eagle eye out nonetheless.

The reunion was as dramatic as Mike had anticipated, certainly from Jools anyway. She wept unashamedly as she hugged her mother and then her father, and then she hugged them both all over again. Maggie laughed with sheer delight, and Mike noticed that his father had the glint of an uncharacteristic tear in his eye, which he hastily blinked away hoping no-one had noticed. But then his father was becoming fragile lately.

Jim McAllister put his failing fitness down to old sports injuries. 'The price you pay as you get older, Mike,' he said, trying to shrug it off. He'd been forced to sell *Alana* years ago. Sailing was not the sport for a man with a chronic lower back problem, he'd admitted, and he'd replaced the yacht with a small cabin cruiser. 'Who'd ever have thought I'd end up with a stink boat,' he'd joked to his son. But recently the launch too had had to go – he'd become annoyingly prone to sea sickness, which he blamed on his stomach ulcer. Jim's principal pleasure these days was gained from his garden, where vegetables and vines and fruit trees thrived, just as they had at the old house.

Mike had at first wondered whether retirement perhaps didn't suit a man like Jim McAllister – the rapid aging process had seemed to coincide with his parents' move to Shoalwater Bay. But of late he'd decided, sadly, that he was wrong. His father was simply growing old.

Jools remarked upon the fact an hour or so later when
the two of them were seated, beers in hand, on the back
patio watching their father tend the barbecue. Jo and Allie
were helping Maggie with the salads in the kitchen and
Jools, presumed to be jet-lagged, had been barred. Mike
was naturally barred from the barbecue, which had always
remained Jim McAllister's fiercely protected personal
domain.

'Time to turn the steaks,' Jim had said as he'd eased himself from his chair, trying to disguise the pain in his back.
'Meat should be turned only once during the cooking.'

Mike smiled. He'd forgotten how many times he'd
heard his father say that.

'Hasn't Dad *aged*,' Jools muttered as she lit up another
Stuyvesant.

'Oh, give him a break, he's seventy-one.' She always
managed to arouse the defensive in him, Mike thought.
Why was that? She was only voicing his own thoughts,
but it was the way she said it.

'I know, but Mum hasn't aged. She's just the same, isn't
she?' Jools said unperturbed, studying her father. 'Dad
looks so *old*, don't you think?'

As Mike stifled a retort, Jools realised she'd irritated
him. She'd merely been making an observation; she'd
intended no criticism of their father. But then she'd got
over her hero worship, hadn't she? Mike hadn't. Jim
McAllister remained up there with barely a crack on his
pedestal. Oh well, she thought, sibling differences. Some
things never change.

Lunch was loud, Jools holding court, talking about the
old days and being very funny. But when lunch was over
and they were onto their coffees, Jools was still revisiting
her personal blasts from the past, which was beginning to
pall on Mike.

'Do you remember when Baxter went clean off the
jetty?' she said. 'He was half-blind, the poor old thing, and

he just kept walking until he tripped over the end. Remember, Mike? He dived in head first, it was amazing. And I went hysterical, didn't I?'

Mike nodded. He remembered, yes, she'd gone hysterical.

'But he just swam ashore like the old trouper he was. Bax could swim better than he could walk,' she laughed.

'You did show her, didn't you, Mike?' Maggie asked.

'Show her what?'

'Baxter's gravestone.'

'No.' He'd forgotten it was there. 'No, I didn't.'

'You brought him here? To Shoalwater Bay?' Jools finally came to a halt, staring at her brother in amazement.

'Of course I didn't – he'd have been dust, for God's sake,' Mike said irritably. He felt foolish in front of his wife and his now adult daughter; he hadn't even mentioned his sentimental gesture to them – why on earth would he? 'I just brought the headstone from Claremont and shoved it up the back. I thought you might like it.'

'Oh, Mike, where is he?'

'*He* isn't anywhere. *It's* up in the back corner by the grape vines.'

'Show me. Please.'

She stood and offered her hand. Mike didn't take it, but he reluctantly rose and led the way out into the back garden.

Jo and Allie smiled as they watched them go.

They walked between the corn crop and the bean trellises to the grape vines which grew in the far corner, their unripened muscatels hanging in clusters.

'There,' he said, pointing.

'*Baxter. 1951–1967. RIP.*' Jools read out the inscription her brother had carved all those years ago. She'd built a little garden around the headstone at the old Claremont house, she remembered, and she'd tended it regularly each Christmas she'd come home. It just stood on an old pile of bricks now, but that didn't matter.

'Thank you, Mike,' she whispered, tears streaming down her face. 'This is so wonderful. I love you, you know.'

She was clearly touched, and Mike didn't doubt the tears were genuine, but Jools could never resist the drama of the moment.

'I love you, too, Jools,' he said. He did. She drove him mad, but he loved her.

The following day, as promised, Mike returned to collect Jools for her guided tour of the Institute. When they pulled up in the car park, which seemed to Jools huge, she scrambled eagerly out of the car.

'My God!' she exclaimed, staring at the marina. 'Are all those boats yours?'

'No way,' Mike laughed. 'That's the Cockburn Power Boat and Yacht Racing Club, and the combined Sea Rescue Base, but we have access to their ramps and slips which is perfect for us. That nearest jetty,' he pointed, 'the one with just a half a dozen pens, that's our mini marina. We pay rental to the Cockburn City Council and a nominal fee to the club, but they're very generous. We even share the club's car park, so it's a handy set-up all round.'

Jools stared at the massive vessel hauled up on the nearby slips – it must belong to some millionaire, she thought. She was about to ask Mike, but he was already on the move.

'Let's go,' he said. 'I'll show you the boats later.'

He led the way towards the main entrance of the modern office block to their left. From the car park it appeared single storey, but there was a second level below, built into the slope that led down to the foreshore.

Jools halted at the front doors and read out loud the name emblazoned above. 'The McAllister Research Institute.' She turned to him with a huge smile. 'Gosh, I bet Dad's proud.'

'Yes, I think he is.' Mike returned the smile. He knew only too well how proud his father was. Jim McAllister had been uncharacteristically lavish in his praise.

'What an achievement, Mike,' he'd said. 'What a worth-while testament to your life and the goal you set yourself all those years ago. You deserve your success. I'm proud of you.'

In the past, Jim had rarely praised his son, preferring to lead the way by example. To Mike, such a tribute coming from the man who'd been an inspiration to him through-out his life was extraordinarily precious.

'Come on,' he said to Jools, opening the door, 'there's a lot to see.'

He showed her briefly around the offices, introducing her to people here and there, and then they stepped out onto the rear balcony.

'Wow,' Jools exclaimed.

The Institute was nestled in the crook of Jervoise Bay and overlooked the vast expanse of Cockburn Sound. To the north, the view was pristine, with the adjacent marina and nearby Woodman Point. But far to the south of the sound, the factories and plants and chimneys of heavy industry had rendered the natural landscape virtually unrecognisable.

'Yes, it's an impressive view,' Mike agreed. Different as the coastline was, its ravaged state reminded him in a strange way of Dampier. Ugly and beautiful at the same time.

They proceeded to the lower level, which was Mike's true domain, where the laboratories and experimental aquaria were housed. As they went, he gave her a rundown on some of the local projects they were currently involved in.

'We're doing some work with Cockburn Cement at the moment. Cockburn dredges up the lime-rich sand from the sea bed of the sound and the sea grasses that are destroyed in the process need to be re-established.' He opened a door to one of the aquaria. 'The sea-grass beds are essential for the ecological integrity and biodiversity of the sound and the various fisheries it supports...'

Jools was trying to take in everything he was saying, but she was getting a little distracted along the way. She was in awe of the size of the place. It was so deceptive from the outside, she thought. And all the sophisticated research equipment – it must have cost a fortune!

'And here,' Mike said ten minutes later as they entered yet another laboratory, 'we have a project that's a bit of a mixed bag.' He introduced her to the computer operator, one of many, and explained the program he was working on. 'We're trying to show, through marine computer modelling, that the phosphate and heavy metal effluent from CSBP's superphosphate works further south is dispersed evenly throughout the major part of Cockburn Sound. But as well as serving CSBP, we're also serving the government.'

It was a case scenario that typified the McAllister Institute, and Mike was proud of the fact. In serving industry and government he was creating an all-round awareness and responsibility for the environment.

'The bioaccumulation of heavy metals in the black mussel has been a sore point with the Department of Fisheries for years – it's such a highly commercial area. The discharge from CSBP has been the main worry, but through our advice they've lifted their game, and we're willing to prove it.' He smiled, resting his case. 'So, as you can see, we're really serving two masters.'

'Where does all the money come from?' Jools asked as she followed him out into the corridor.

Mike halted abruptly. 'Government and industry, of course.' Had she taken in a word he'd said, he wondered – he couldn't have simplified things more. But then he supposed he shouldn't blame her. He'd never been particularly interested in *her* work, had he? Why should she be interested in his?

But Jools was. Or rather, she was interested in how the

Institute had come into being. How had her brother managed to create all this, she wondered, and in such a relatively short space of time?

'How have you done it, Mike? The whole thing's extraordinary. How on earth have you done it?'

He could tell she was in awe, and he was pleased. She didn't need to know the actual details of his work, he thought, it was enough that she recognised his achievement.

'Things were tough at the start,' he admitted. 'All we had was some modest government funding and we had to rely a lot on benefactors. The university was helpful, and the Cockburn Yacht Club, of course, with its marina – both the chancellor and the commodore are honorary members of the board. But it was actually commercial sponsorship that got the ball rolling – Spud put us on to that tack.'

'Spud Farrell?'

'Yep,' he said with a grin, 'the very same.'

'But he's a crook.' She laughed. 'He always has been.' She regretted the words the moment she'd said them. She could see he was annoyed.

'Perth hasn't been your home for the past twenty years, Jools,' he said evenly. 'You don't know this town any more. You don't know this town, and you don't know its people.' Mike was more than annoyed, he was angry.

'I'm sorry.' Jools cursed herself and her big mouth. She hadn't meant anything by the comment, it had just slipped out.

'Spud's been generous to a fault. He was our first major sponsor. He's an honorary director on the board! He's devoted himself tirelessly to the Institute!' Mike was getting himself wound up, he couldn't seem to stop. 'How dare you barge in with your uninformed opinions and incorrect moral judgements. What gives you the right –'

'I'm sorry, honestly!' God, he was mad, she thought. 'It was just a flippant remark. I'm really, really sorry.'

She was genuinely contrite, and Mike had no option but to accept her apology, although he did do so with ill grace.

'I'll show you the boats now,' he said abruptly, and he strode off down the corridor towards the stairs, Jools forced to run after him. His sister should keep her flippant remarks for the superficial world of entertainment where both she and they belonged, he thought.

Mike's anger soon abated, however. Once outside, as he led the way to the slips, Jools following, subdued, he realised that he'd over-reacted. He shouldn't have allowed her to get to him that way, he told himself. In fact, he wondered why he had. She hadn't meant to offend, she'd simply been thoughtless.

'This is the pride of our fleet,' he said as they stood before the slips, the huge fifty-metre vessel Jools had admired earlier towering above them. 'Pity I can't show you around, but she's undergoing her annual service.'

'That's not a boat, that's a ship.' Jools attempted to sound her jokey self, but didn't quite pull it off. She was feeling very guilty.

'Yep, she sure is. She has all the latest radar, sonar, GPS gear aboard, a laboratory, the works. We have a permanent skipper, a crew of ten, and she has guest accommodation for a further ten.'

Jools couldn't help wondering where the money came from to fund a ship like this – Spud and his corporate mates? But she didn't dare ask, and, as Mike kept talking, the tension between them eased until she felt herself finally relax.

'We're real trouble-shooters in the region,' he explained. 'The WA government hires us out to Indonesia and the Papua New Guinea government and we can even assist in sea rescue if necessary.'

'*Carina*.' She read out loud the name on the vessel's side.

'One of the brightest constellations in the southern hemisphere,' Mike said. 'Rather apt, I think.'

'Is that a heli-pad?' she asked.

'Yep. We don't actually have our own helicopter, but the pad's there for emergencies.'

'Wow!' She was deeply impressed. 'It's real Jacques Cousteau time, isn't it?'

'Yeah, I suppose it is a bit, only we don't make movies.'

They walked down to the jetty, Mike showing her the Institute's various vessels in their pens – the dinghies and the larger aluminium trailer craft, a Savage and a Quintrex – and finally he pulled up before the pen that housed his personal pride and joy.

'This is my favourite, isn't she a beauty? Step aboard, I'll take you for a run.' By now he felt a genuine need to make up for his outburst.

'Pretty flash. What is she?' Jools slipped off her sandals and clambered aboard.

'She's a 6.8-metre Kevlar Cat powered by twin 180 HP Mercury outboards and she goes like the wind.' He stepped aboard himself and started up the engines, letting them idle in neutral. 'Hey, guess what I've called her?'

'Not *Alana*, surely?'

'Yep. *Alana II*.' He grinned. 'It's a win situation all round. Dad thinks she's named after Grandma and the old boat, and Allie thinks she's named after her.'

Jools laughed, relieved that things between them seemed back to normal.

'We use her for deeper offshore research work,' he said. 'We've taken her up to Broome and down to Albany by trailer – she goes all over the state. You want to release the bowline?'

Jools went forward and unhitched the rope which was attached to a bollard on the marina's jetty. 'Say when,' she called.

'When,' he called back.

She slung the line onto the jetty. Then, as she clambered back into the cockpit, Mike set the engines in reverse.

'You take the portside,' he said, and between them they released the port and starboard stern lines as Mike slowly reversed out of the pen.

Jools was reminded of the days aboard *Alana* when she'd been a nimble forward hand to her father.

They set off out of the marina at a slow pace, but once in open water Mike increased the speed. 'We'll just go to Freo and back,' he said. Then he revved up the engines full bore.

'What did I tell you?' he called above the roar as they planed across the surface of the water. 'She goes like the wind.'

Having shown off the boat's power, he cut back on the revs and as they motored up the coast to Fremantle, he pointed out the landmarks, some of which Jools recognised and some of which were quite new to her.

Her hair whipping about her face and the salty smell of the sea in her nostrils, Jools was exhilarated. She was on a boat with her brother just like the old days and, as she looked across the ocean to the dim outline of Rottnest Island on the horizon, she felt that she'd truly come home. But all too soon it was over and they were quietly chuffing back into the marina. What a pity, she thought. She could have stayed out on the water all day.

Several days later the McAllister family once again congregated at Shoalwater Bay, this time for Christmas lunch. Mike, Jo and Allie arrived mid-morning laden with presents which they placed alongside those already sitting beneath the large weeping fig in its tub on the patio. Maggie decorated the fig each year, and Allie loved the fact that they had a living Christmas tree.

Jools had helped Maggie with the laborious preparation of vegetables, thankful that her parents had maintained the baked dinner tradition. She recalled how she'd tried to nag her mother into switching to salads and seafood. She was glad that Maggie hadn't. Jools wanted everything to be the same as it once was.

They drank champagne and opened their presents, Allie demanding the privilege of handing them around as she always did, and Jools giving in with good grace, remembering that it had once been her job.

Then they adjourned to the table where Jim carved the turkey and Mike opened the wine.

'Look, Jools.' He held up the bottle.

'Oh my God,' she shrieked, 'sparkling burgundy! I haven't had sparkling burgundy for years!'

Maggie smiled; nor had they. 'Mike bought it specially for you. I didn't even know they still made it.'

'The purple stuff that jumps.' Jools beamed as she held out her glass.

They pulled their Christmas crackers and wore their silly paper hats and gorged themselves on turkey, and after the sparkling burgundy Jools segued on to the shiraz. She was drinking far too much, but who cared? She felt she couldn't be happier.

Shortly after lunch, Mike and Allie went over to the beach for a swim, but Jools didn't join them. She weaved her way off to the spare bedroom instead.

Jo helped Maggie with the washing up, Jim too having wandered off for a lie-down, and they talked about Jools.

'She's actually very unhappy,' Maggie said. 'She sees herself as a failure with a second marriage going down the drain, but I think she's giving up too soon. She's so proud of Henry and his work – he's a very successful playwright – and they have such a lot in common. It's a marriage well worth fighting for in my opinion.'

Jo felt sorry for Jools and was glad Mike had invited her to stay with them in Nedlands for a few days, so Jools could explore her old home town.

'Are you sure you don't mind having Jools with us?' Mike asked as they drove back to Perth. 'She can be a bit much, particularly when she hits the grog, and she can always stay on at Mum and Dad's, you know.'

'Of course I'm sure, I'm looking forward to her company.' Mike's ambivalent attitude towards his sister intrigued Jo. On the one hand he was so critical and on the other so caring. Baxter's gravestone . . . the sparkling burgundy . . . They were a strange pair, Mike and Jools, she thought. She rather envied them their differences. She would have liked to have had a sibling.

'So what did you have in mind for today?' Jo asked as she and Jools sat over coffee at the kitchen table the following week.

'I thought I'd catch the bus to Freo. Mike drove me through on the way in from Shoalwater Bay and I can't believe how the place has changed.'

'I've got a better idea. Why don't I drive us into Fremantle tomorrow? We can go to the Saturday markets.'

Jo seemed genuinely keen, so Jools nodded happily. 'Great,' she said.

'And I need to pop into town this afternoon, do you want to come with me?'

'Sure.'

'There's only one catch.'

'Oh?'

'You have to have coffee with my mother.'

'Oh no, I wouldn't want to intrude.'

'You won't be intruding, believe me,' Jo said drily.

The comment sounded caustic and Jools raised an eyebrow.

'Mum comes in from Mount Lawley for her shopping fest each Friday, which I avoid like the plague,' Jo explained. 'Shopping with Hillary is an absolute nightmare. But I do feel obliged to meet her for coffee, and sometimes even that's an uphill battle. I could use a bit of back-up. Is it a bargain?'

Jools had never heard Jo speak of her mother before, and the arch tone was so uncharacteristic. How intriguing, she thought.

'It's a bargain,' she said.

'Good. I'll take you for a drive around first, and we'll have a bite of lunch in Northbridge'

'Northbridge?' Jools was surprised. 'That used to be North Perth, didn't it?'

'Yes, it's the trendy place to dine these days.'

'Really? It was the grotty end of town when I was at tech.'

'Not any more. Come on, get your gear together and I'll show you your old home town.'

Jools studied Hillary closely, looking for the telltale signs of a facelift. She could usually pick them; she'd worked with any number of aging actresses who'd had nips and tucks. But she couldn't find one giveaway trace. Jo's mother looked no more than fifty at the outside – how was it possible? She did a quick bit of arithmetic. Jo herself had turned forty last year . . . she was two years younger than Mike . . . that meant Hillary had to be in her sixties . . . unless she'd given birth at some ridiculously young age, and even then . . .

'Excuse me, dear,' Hillary said tightly, 'but do I have a smudge on my nose or lettuce in my teeth? I wish you'd tell me.' She found the way Johanna's sister-in-law was staring at her frightfully rude.

'No. No.' Jools was appalled, she hadn't realised she'd been openly gawking. 'Oh God, I'm sorry. It's just that you're so incredibly beautiful and so unbelievably *young*.'

'Oh.' Hillary laughed and flicked back her hair, which she wore shortish to mid-length these days. She'd eschewed the stark blonde coiffure, adopting a warm honey colour and a more casual style which she knew suited her well. 'How kind.'

Well, you've won a lifelong friend there, Jo thought. Good work, Jools.

'It's all in the genes,' Hillary said, and she smiled at her daughter. 'Johanna will age well too.'

'Yep,' Jools agreed, 'I'd go along with that.'

Hillary decided, after all, that she very much liked Johanna's sister-in-law, although the tomboyish look in a woman of her age, presumably late thirties, really should be avoided.

'How's Basil?' Jo asked, changing the subject.

'As well as can be expected for a man his age with high blood pressure,' her mother answered dismissively.

Hillary had finally married the man who had loved her dearly for the past five years. She'd met Basil, a widower, at a book club she'd joined and they'd discovered they had a great deal in common – they shared the same taste in music and they both loved the theatre and the cinema. Hillary's life had become a social whirl of activity, but she'd kept Basil firmly at arm's length, refusing to marry him, while at the same time intimating that perhaps one day she might. Jo had considered her behaviour disgraceful.

'For God's sake, Mum, either marry him or get out of his life,' she'd said. 'The poor man wants a wife, can't you see that?'

Hillary had eventually succumbed, for fear that Basil might start looking elsewhere.

'I see that *you're* married, Jools,' Hillary now said. She always took note of a woman's ring finger.

'Yes.' Jools's answer was glib, she didn't want to talk about her marriage. 'Second time around.'

'Oh, I'm one step ahead of you, I'm afraid. I'm on my third.' Hillary gave one of her girlish laughs, then leaned forward conspiratorially. 'And which one was your great love?'

'I beg your pardon?' Jools said, bewildered.

'Which of your husbands was your great love? The first or the second?'

'Well . . .' Jools didn't know what to say, she found the question highly intrusive. 'I loved them both.'

'Ah,' Hillary smiled knowingly, 'a woman has only one great love in her life.'

Here we go, Jo thought. She'd been waiting for the inevitable.

'My second husband was mine. Of course, I loved Johanna's father deeply,' Hillary added, 'but I was young, so very, very young . . .'

What a terrible phoney the woman was, Jools thought as she listened to Hillary ramble on. And how awful of her to dismiss Jo's father like that, in the very presence of his daughter.

But the comment had gone unheeded by Jo. She was only thankful that her mother had a fresh audience, and that she didn't have to listen to Hillary's romantic nonsense, which she voiced to all and sundry, even her own husband.

It was obscene, Jo thought. Hillary had seen Darren just once in the past ten years, and that was only because he'd heard that she'd married. He'd fronted up demanding the return of the flat in Victoria Street, and Hillary would no doubt have signed the place over to him – she'd accepted his story of having 'fallen upon hard times'. But fortunately Darren had been too late. Basil had sold the flat and invested the money in his wife's name. It was 'her own little nest egg', he'd said, and no-one else was to touch it. Good old Basil, Jo had thought. He wasn't stupid.

Jo had long ceased worrying about her mother. She suffered the filial duty of a weekly coffee in the Hay Street Mall, but the only feelings she could muster were for her mother's husband. Basil was a fine man, and one who deserved a far better wife than Hillary in Jo's opinion.

After their coffee and cake, Jo and Jools saw Hillary and

her shopping bags into a taxi, then walked the several blocks to where Jo had parked the car.

As they set off for Nedlands, Jools supposed that she should make some comment about Hillary, but she wasn't sure what to say. How very unalike Johanna and her mother were, she thought. Apart from their beauty, they had nothing at all in common – the practical, unpretentious daughter and her preposterous caricature of a mother.

'Hillary's very beautiful,' she said, but as it turned out, she didn't need to go any further.

'Hillary's deluded, she lives in her own world.' Jo smiled reassuringly. 'There's really no need to say anything, you know.'

The following day, the two of them explored Fremantle, enjoying each other's company as they visited the markets and wandered down High Street, stopping off for a coffee in one of the cafés. They admired the maxi yachts in the huge marina and had lunch at the nearby fish markets, which had become very fashionable with outdoor restaurants overlooking the water.

'How amazing,' Jools said, 'the good old Freo fish markets, who would have believed it? This place used to be the pits.' That's what she'd loved about it, she thought, remembering when she was ten how they'd bought their fish and chips rolled up in newspaper and how they'd sat by the sea wall throwing the remnants to the seagulls. 'Fremantle's certainly changed.'

'They're gearing up for the America's Cup,' Jo said, 'only a year or so to go now.' She had to admit that even she was surprised at the apparent overnight change in Fremantle; she hadn't visited the port for some time. 'It'll change even more over the next twelve months.'

'The whole of Perth's changed,' Jools said thoughtfully. 'The very *feel* of the place is different. It's more than just the new buildings and the modernising of the old parts of town, it's something in the air – the pace of the place, the people themselves.' Mike was right, she thought. Perth hadn't been her home for twenty years. Her Christmas visits hadn't kept her in touch with the city's progress; they'd merely enhanced the memories of her childhood. She no longer knew Perth.

'You can't go back, can you?' she said. 'It's silly to try.'

The remark was puzzlingly enigmatic and Jo looked a query.

'Sorry.' Jools smiled, she hadn't intended to sound mysterious. 'I've just realised the futility of what I've been doing.'

'And what's that?'

'I've been clutching at the past to avoid the present. I can see that now. It's time I moved on.'

Jools, the ultimate party girl, surprised her brother by declining his invitation to a New Year's Eve party in town, choosing instead to return to Shoalwater Bay and see in the new year with Jim and Maggie. A party was a party was a party, she said, and she'd planned to spend the last few days of her holiday with her parents anyway.

Three days later, Mike picked her up to take her to the airport. The farewells were subdued.

'You look after yourself, Dad,' Jools whispered as she hugged first her father, then her mother. 'You too, Mum.'

As Maggie returned her daughter's embrace, she said with heartfelt meaning, 'Give my love to Henry, won't you?'

'I will.'

During the drive to the airport, Jools seemed in a contemplative mood, and Mike, having expected the customary ceaseless chatter, was surprised and somewhat concerned. 'You're very quiet,' he said. 'Are you all right?'

'Yeah, fine. Sorry, I was a million miles away.' She hadn't meant to be rude, she was grateful to her brother.

'Thanks for everything, Mike, all the ferrying around, looking after me the way you have. You've been really terrific.'

'What are big brothers for?' he grinned. 'Hey!' He clicked his fingers as he suddenly recalled his promise. 'I forgot the bombies off Claremont jetty. Why didn't you remind me?'

'I forgot myself.' She smiled. 'Don't worry, it was only a momentary whim.'

'Next time, eh?'

'Yep, next time.'

'Are you sorry to be leaving?' he asked. She was once more looking pensively out the window.

'No, I'm rather looking forward to getting home,' Jools said. She'd been thinking of Henry.

Mike didn't reply, but he found the reference to 'home' a healthy sign.

When they arrived at the airport, Jools was adamant that he drop her out the front of the terminal. Much easier, she said, otherwise they'd have to park in the car park and it was all too complicated. She was accustomed to travelling by herself, she was perfectly self-sufficient, and besides, she hated airport farewells. Jools had reverted to her old self.

'Now, Mike, I want you to do one thing for me,' she said when he'd lifted her suitcase out of the boot.

'What's that?'

'I want you to promise me you'll get Dad to see a doctor.'

'Oh, come on, Jools, you know Dad. You can't get him to do anything he doesn't want to do, and he doesn't want to see a doctor – he's made that quite clear.'

'So Mum said, but someone has to –'

'Have you been worrying Mum?' he demanded.

'What?'

'Have you been nagging her about getting Dad to a doctor?'

'No, I haven't been *nagging* her!' Jools took offence at the accusation. 'I just said a couple of times that I thought he didn't look well.'

A couple of times, Mike thought, that meant she'd been nagging. She just couldn't help herself, could she? He took a deep breath and tried to keep the irritation from his voice.

'Look, Jools, I'll have a word with Dad, one on one, I promise.' Fat lot of good it'd do, he thought, his father wouldn't listen. 'But *please, please* don't nag Mum about it when you speak to her on the phone. You'll only worry her. Dad accepts the fact that he's growing old, and you have to too.'

Jools knew that once again she'd exasperated him, but too bad, she thought.

'He's not growing old, Mike,' she said. 'He doesn't know it, but he's sick. I can see it in his eyes. Promise me you'll speak to him.'

'I just said I would, didn't I?'

'Right.' There was a moment's tense silence. 'Well, thanks again for everything.'

They shared a perfunctory hug and Jools wheeled her suitcase through the terminal doors without looking back. She'd said her bit, it was over to Mike now. She had a marriage to sort out herself, and it wasn't going to be easy.

Bloody Jools, Mike thought as he climbed into the car.

Four months later, Jim McAllister was diagnosed with a highly invasive cancer, which, by that time, was inoperable. Another month later, he died. But Jools had been wrong about one thing. Jim McAllister had known his days were numbered, and had had no wish to extend his life.

'I don't need someone else to give me the news, Mike,' he'd said when Mike had honoured his promise and suggested his father see a doctor. 'I'll go when my time's up, and that won't be long now. It's unfair on your mother,

I know – for her sake I should try and hang around longer, but I have no desire to.'

Mike had been shocked by his father's obduracy, and even more so by Jim's refusal to share the knowledge of his condition with his wife. 'She'd want me to opt for surgery, and I don't relish the thought of being carved up like so much meat on a butcher's slab. A man's never the same afterwards. My father never was.'

'Procedures have changed a lot over the last forty years, Dad.'

'Oh yes, I'm quite aware of that. But it's my decision. Death's a personal thing. You must promise not a word to your mother.'

Mike had respected his father's wish, saying nothing, and Jim McAllister had remained uncompromising to the end. He'd continued as normal, never confiding in Maggie until his final collapse and hospitalisation. Mike had considered his father's exclusion of his wife of over forty years a selfish act, and he'd wondered, even as he'd mourned the man who had been his hero for as long as he could remember, whether perhaps the trait was genetic.

CHAPTER TWENTY-TWO

S ally Jordan slammed the latest edition of *The Bulletin* down on her desk and gave a hoot of triumph.

'That'll get them where it hurts,' she said out loud to herself.

Sally now worked for the *West Australian* and she'd been covering the select committee inquiry into the government sale of the Midland Abattoir and Saleyards, but had been frustrated by her editor's firm directive. 'Just the facts, Sal, report the findings, nothing more. You're not there to draw conclusions.'

Well, she bloody well *should* be, she'd thought, she was an investigative journalist, for Christ's sake, and the whole thing was as dodgy as all get out. But Sally couldn't afford to lose another job so she'd done as she was told and toed the line. For the moment anyway. Her time would come.

The local media in general seemed hesitant to pass judgement on the abattoir sale, Sally had found, either as a favour to Burke or because they were intimidated by him, she wasn't sure which. As for the Premier himself – well, that was a different story. There was nothing hesitant about Brian Burke. In true arrogant style, Burke continued to thumb his nose at the select committee, openly scoffing at its findings.

'Try scoffing at that, you smug bastard,' she said as she looked at the magazine sitting on her desk. 'WA Inc won't get out of this one in a hurry.'

WA Inc was the commonly used journalistic term that referred to the state government's dealings with private businessmen, and Sally was only too delighted that its latest outrage had been exposed for the whole country to see. The 2 September issue of *The Bulletin* had painted the larger picture in all its true colours, she thought with satisfaction. The iceberg was finally emerging. Brian Burke's government was in trouble.

The private sale six months previously of the government-owned Midland Abattoir and Saleyards had led to an outcry from members of the opposition, and also from a number of Perth businessmen, in particular the highly respected Ric New, a leading figure in the state's commercial life.

The abattoir and saleyards sat on twenty-nine hectares of prime industrial land situated near Ric New's Midland Brickworks, and had been sold for a fraction of the site's true value. The buyer, Peter Ellett, had proved to be a former employee of New's, and the sale had been conducted in secret, no tenders having been provided for other interested parties. It further materialised that the government had been aware from the outset of Ellett's intention to build a high-technology brickworks on the site, in direct competition with his former employer.

Many amongst the opposition saw the government's actions as a direct attack upon Ric New, who was not only well known as a loyal Liberal supporter, but who had loudly condemned the Burke Labor government's blatant appeals to businessmen for financial support. Burke was out to get Ric New, they said.

The Legislative Council had appointed a select committee to carry out an inquiry, the opposition maintaining that the sale had been illegal, and the situation had been steadily snowballing ever since.

'Listen to this, Spud. Just listen to this.' Ian Pemberton burst into Spud's office waving a copy of the latest *Bulletin*.

Realising that he had no option, Spud settled comfortably back in his chair.

'*More than bricks are flying in a heated political row in Western Australia involving a number of the state's leading personalities,*' Ian read, with a significant look to Spud, who just shrugged. '*What might well have passed off as simply a property sale by the WA Development Corporation, a state government instrumentality, has over the past six months evolved into a formidable challenge to the Burke Labor government's credibility, with the potential of blowing up into a major political scandal.*'

'So?' Spud said when Ian dumped the open magazine on the desk in front of him.

'What do you mean "so"? We're talking about *The Bulletin*, Spud! And *The Bulletin*'s intimating that this brickyards fiasco could bring down the state government.'

'Bullshit. Brian knows what he's doing, he's got it all in hand.'

Spud had great faith in Brian Burke, they'd become good mates. The bloke had balls, he thought. He admired the way Burke was standing his ground and telling everyone to go and get fucked. Good for him! But Pembo was after reassurance, as always.

'C'mon, mate, you know the story,' Spud said. 'The site was sold to Ellett in good faith and for a good purpose. The state needs an alternative brickworks! Brian's sticking to that and they won't be able to prove otherwise. Now stop worrying, and let me get back to work.'

Spud refused to discuss the matter any further, and Ian left with dire misgivings about the whole predicament.

Those in the know didn't believe for one minute the argument put forward by Brian Burke and his newly appointed Minister for Agriculture, Julian Grill. The two maintained that a cartel had been set up to create a monopoly on the production and distribution of clay bricks in Western Australia. The government sale of the abattoir site to Peter Ellett for the sole purpose of creating fresh competition, they said, was for the good of the state. But many saw a more sinister purpose in their claim of a cartel. Brian Burke and Julian Grill were out to besmirch the good character of Ric New, a highly ethical business-man and one of the state's principal brick manufacturers.

The situation continued to career in a series of danger-ously lunatic directions. Peter Ellett's criminal record was revealed, a Liberal backbencher on the select committee had his car sabotaged, and the committee chairman claimed that witnesses had been pressured by the govern-ment. Finally, in October, one thousand citizens petitioned the Governor. Things were definitely getting out of hand.

But Brian Burke remained defiant throughout. He launched a scathing attack on the Legislative Council, bringing the two houses of parliament into direct conflict, and he openly dismissed the inquiries as 'a waste of money'.

It was eventually decided that the select committee's findings were of insufficient substance, and in November the sale of the abattoir site to Peter Ellett was announced legal and formally registered.

A storm ensued. On 3 December the opposition moved that a new select committee be formed to inquire into alle-gations of government impropriety. But the motion was defeated. Burke had triumphed.

'What did I tell you?' Spud laughed.

Ian Pemberton breathed a massive sigh of relief. Brian Burke's Labor government was their nest egg. They were too involved with Burke and too reliant upon his favours to see him topple.

America's Cup fever once again consumed the nation, and as the new year of 1987 dawned, the host city Perth and its port of Fremantle became the focus of world-wide attention. People flocked from interstate and abroad, the streets bustling with the rich and famous, accommodation at a premium. Luxury hotels were booked out by politicians and sports stars and Hollywood actors, all paying exorbitant amounts, and the mere average mortal found that even the cheapest motel or boarding house had quadrupled its rates.

'Bloody good for business,' Spud said as he and Ian drove at a snail's pace through the crowded streets of Fremantle on their way to the marina. 'Everyone's making a bundle.'

'And we might well be left with a string of white elephants when it's all over,' Ian replied dourly, looking at the endless array of new and refurbished shops and restaurants, bars and cafés.

'Yeah, the old Freo's had more than a facelift,' Spud agreed, 'she's had the full makeover. Let's just hope it pays off and we win. If we keep the Cup, Freo'll go the way of Newport, Rhode Island – we'll be the yachting centre of the world.'

But the Australians didn't keep the Cup. On Wednesday, 2 February, in the final of four hard-fought races, Dennis Conner skippered *Stars & Stripes* to victory, defeating Iain Murray's *Kookaburra III* and sweeping the series. The Americans had unequivocally reclaimed the Cup as their own.

Pity about the businesses that were bound to go broke, Spud thought, but he wasn't too worried himself. He'd bet hugely on the Yanks to win.

*

'What a bummer about the Cup, eh?' Muzza said, brush poised over the canvas, eyes flicking to Mike then back to the painting.

'Ah well . . .' Mike shrugged. 'The best man won. Conner and his team were magnificent.'

Mike had finally and reluctantly agreed to sit for the portrait Muzza had been nagging him about for years. 'You drop in most weekends anyway,' Muz had said, 'you might as well let me daub away while we chat.'

Knowing how restless Mike became under scrutiny, Muzza kept up a chain of conversation to maintain his interest, sometimes about things that held little appeal for him personally. Such was the case right now. Muz didn't care one iota about the America's Cup. Spud had invited him to join the gang aboard his corporate launch for the series, but he'd declined, saying that wheelchairs and boats didn't mix. 'Even wheelchairs and bloody great gin palaces like yours, Spud,' he'd said with a laugh, no dig intended. 'I'll watch it on the telly.' But he hadn't. Murray Hatfield was perhaps the only person in Perth to whom the America's Cup was simply another yacht race, and yachts were of no interest to him. If it had been cars . . . well, now that would have been a different matter.

'So was Spud slitting his wrists?' he asked as he worked on the perfect arc of light that was hitting Mike's left cheekbone. God, it was a strong face, he thought.

'No way. In fact, he seemed to expect defeat right from the beginning. Of course, come the fourth race, we could all see the writing on the wall, but Spud wasn't fazed for one minute.'

'He probably had money on the Yanks.'

'Probably,' Mike agreed. They both knew Spud well.

'How's Allie? Looking forward to fourth year?'

Muzza noted that Mike was getting fidgety and Allie was always a sure-fire topic, he'd found. Having come close to topping her course three years in a row, she was an inordinate source of pride to her father. 'She's a brilliant student,' Mike would boast. 'So committed! Incredible in one so young!' It always made Muzza smile. 'I wonder where she gets it from,' he'd say.

But today, Mike's response was far from glowing.

'She's sleeping with her bloody boyfriend,' he growled. 'At least, I'm pretty sure she is. Jo won't talk about it, and she refuses to ask her outright. She says that *if* Allie's having an affair, she'll tell us when she feels the time's right. And of course I can't ask the kid myself – that's a mother's job, for Christ's sake.'

'Well, she's not exactly a kid any more, is she? I'm sure Jo's is the way to go,' Muzza said diplomatically.

Allie was nineteen years old and she'd had a steady boy-friend for the past six months. Losing her virginity was a fairly natural progression in his opinion.

'Has she said anything to Olga?' The thought suddenly occurred to Mike that perhaps she had. Olga had become Allie's true confidante.

'Wouldn't have a clue, mate.'

The lie came easily to Muzza. Any confidence Olga and he shared remained strictly between the two of them and he felt not a vestige of guilt as he concentrated his brush upon the light in the eyes, which had suddenly taken on a whole new meaning.

'She shouldn't be distracted from her studies.' Mike frowned. 'Besides,' he added with a touch of petulance, 'I don't like the young bloke she's seeing.'

Muzza couldn't help himself; he burst out laughing. 'Is there a young bloke you *would* like?'

The predatory passion of Mike's youth was coming back to haunt him, he thought. Mike, of all people, would know the sole motive uppermost in the mind of every young man confronted by a girl like Allie.

'Give her a break, Mike,' he said reasonably. 'She's fought them off for long enough, and she's got a regular bloke. Nineteen must be some sort of record in this day and age.'

But when it came to his daughter, Mike appeared to have lost his sense of humour.

'I don't think it's a laughing matter, Muzza,' he replied.

Muz backed off. He put down the paintbrush – time to call it a day, he thought – and changed the subject to Pembo's forthcoming party, which, rather than the Cup Celebration originally intended, had now become a Cup Commiseration.

'Spud says it's just an excuse for another lavish Pemberton Peppermint Grove piss-up,' he said. 'I wouldn't know myself, I haven't been to one, but I gather Arlene's big into entertaining these days.'

But Mike wasn't prepared to be mollified, and when he left ten minutes later, he was still a little terse. 'I'll see you at Pembo's on Saturday,' he said.

'Rightio, see you at Pembo's.'

Muzza wasn't particularly bothered, it would all blow over, although he supposed he shouldn't have laughed. Mike's behaviour was that of the stereotypical father: overprotective and convinced that no man was good enough for his little girl. But if the bloke only knew it, he had nothing at all to worry about. Muzza couldn't tell him that though. He'd be betraying a confidence if he did.

'I'm not in love with Greg,' Allie had told Olga, 'and I'm quite sure he's not in love with me. Well, he's in lust,' she'd admitted, 'but that's a bit different, isn't it? Anyway, I thought it was time I lost my virginity. I seemed to be the only one in my whole year who hadn't.'

'Are you on the pill?' Olga, as always, had cut right to the chase.

'Oh yes, of course.' Allie hoped that she hadn't sounded overly clinical, she hadn't meant to. 'Don't get me wrong,' she added, 'Greg and I really do have something going for us. We're in the same year, and we both love uni. We help each other with our work, and we even vie for who's going to top the course. We share a lot more than sex. It's just . . . well . . .' She shrugged. 'Just not the right time to get serious, you know?'

'Yes I do, and I think you're being very sensible. Have you told your mother yet?'

'No, but Mum knows. What's more, she knows that I know she knows.' Allie laughed; her rebellious attitude towards her mother was a thing of the past. 'We have this unspoken language, Mum and I. She probably even knows I'm telling you. In fact, I get the feeling she wants me to.'

'Why the subterfuge, then?'

'I don't want it out in the open because of Dad, and I think Mum knows that too. She's keeping him at arm's length, acting as a buffer, which is really great.' Allie paused thoughtfully, she enjoyed baring her soul to Olga. 'It'd worry Dad if he knew I was having an affair – not just in your run-of-the mill protective-father way – it'd worry him that I might lose focus on my career.'

Was that the true motive for her silence, Allie wondered. She wasn't sure herself. She only knew that she didn't want things to change between her and her father.

'You have a life to live as well,' Olga said. 'Surely he must understand that.'

'I'm not sure if he does really. Dad lives for his work. He always has.'

'And he expects you to do the same?'

'Possibly.' Allie considered the matter for a moment or so. 'Yes, probably deep down, he does,' she said. Then she smiled. 'But I don't mind. I only hope I can live up to his expectations. Dad's my inspiration.'

In his daughter's eyes, Mike McAllister's pedestal remained firmly intact: unblemished and without the merest hint of even a hairline fracture.

*

Muzza enjoyed Pembo's party, although he hadn't expected to. He wheeled himself through the side gates of the Peppermint Grove house into the garden with its fairy lights and fountains, accepting a beer from the tray of one of the several waiters. A string quartet was playing and a food marquee had been erected, and he was reminded of Pembo's twenty-first birthday. Except he hadn't been in a wheelchair then, had he? And he hadn't had Olga by his side. He smiled up at her. There was not one shred of bitterness left in Murray Hatfield.

He'd been reticent at first about accepting the invitation, but he'd knocked Pembo back so many times that he was starting to feel guilty. He was glad he'd come now. It was good to be together, he thought as he looked at the old gang. He'd taken himself off for 'a stroll around the garden' as he liked to put it, and he now sat quietly in a corner of the rockery watching the guests mingle. There must have been forty or so, and the numbers were burgeoning as yet more arrived. Many he knew, some from as far back as his uni days, and many he'd never seen before, but his eyes kept straying to the old gang.

Spud, holding hands with his effervescent child bride – God, Cora must be over thirty by now, Muzza thought, but exotic, doll-like, she still looked nineteen. And Allie – well, of course Allie was the true beauty. He watched her throw back her head and heard her laugh that gutsy, uninhibited laugh of hers. He'd like to paint Allie. She'd brought her boyfriend along – he'd chatted to Greg briefly, a nice young man, vaguely reminiscent, Muzza had thought, of a shorter, less handsome version of the young Mike McAllister. As the two of them shared whatever the joke had been with Gordy and Fleur, the Pemberton twins, he saw Greg put his arm around Allie, and his eyes darted to where Mike stood near the pool in conversation with Jo and Pembo and two other couples. Sure enough, Mike was glowering at his daughter's boyfriend. Muzza grinned.

Poor old Mike, he thought. He didn't realise that Allie could have chosen a great deal worse. Greg was nowhere near as dangerous to women as Mike had been in his youth.

'Are you hiding?'

Olga had crept up behind him and he jumped, startled by her sudden appearance.

She laughed. 'Come on,' she said, 'time to mingle.'

'Rightio.'

They joined Mike and Jo and Pembo.

'There you are, Muz, I wondered where you'd got to.' Ian Pemberton greeted him heartily, then introduced Muzza and Olga to the university chancellor and the commodore of the Cockburn Yacht Club and their wives. He called over two waiters, drinks were topped up and canapés passed around, and they were all enjoying each other's company when Arlene suddenly swooped upon them.

'Come along, everyone,' she said gaily with a clap of her hands, oblivious to the fact that she'd just ruined the commodore's punch line. 'Time to see the renovations.'

Arlene had been marshalling people for the past hour and trooping them upstairs in groups to show off the new third floor they'd added to the house. 'Upstairs, please.' She attempted to shoo them all before her as if they were sheep, but no-one made a move. Then she noticed Muzza in his wheelchair. 'Oh,' she said, looking him up and down as if he were some terrible inconvenience.

There was a moment's awkward silence which Arlene found annoying. Why were they staring at her as if she'd done something wrong? Even Ian seemed embarrassed. She couldn't help it if Muzza was a cripple.

But Muz grinned his disarmingly baby-faced grin, quickly putting them all at ease.

'For God's sake, don't mind me,' he said.

'Of course we won't,' Olga chimed in. 'You stay down here and mingle, darling, we won't be long.' And she herself led the way to the house. Didn't Arlene realise, she thought, that the wheelchair was not a factor at all. It was Arlene's manner, or rather her lack of manners, which had created the moment.

Ian, who was playing no part in his wife's guided tours, watched as they obediently trooped off. 'Sorry, Muz,' he said.

'What for? Come on, let's have a beer with Spud.'

Muzza spent a pleasant fifteen minutes with Spud and Cora and Ian while Olga and the others endured Arlene's mandatory guided tour with its running commentary.

'There was a bit of a to-do with the neighbours when we put the plans in,' Arlene said as they trudged upstairs. A *bit* of a to-do, she thought, heavens above, they'd come out of the woodwork *screaming*. 'But fortunately Ian has friends in high places.' She led them through the sitting room and out onto the huge upper balcony. 'And it was certainly worth the fight,' she said triumphantly. 'Just look at that for a view.'

Yes, Olga thought, at the expense of everyone else's.

'Well, you can't really see much at the moment,' Arlene added apologetically as they gazed across Freshwater Bay to the dots of lights on the other side of the river. 'But during the day it's absolutely magnificent.'

They were shown the new master bedroom and its en suite with the latest in massive spa baths.

'Fleur has the original master bedroom and en suite on the second floor now,' Arlene said with a proud mother's laugh. 'A sixteen-year-old girl needs her own bathroom, don't you agree?'

No-one really did, but the chancellor's wife, a very polite woman, made some murmur as if she might.

Arlene wasn't particularly satisfied with this group, they weren't as appreciative as the last, so she sped through the rest of the tour: her dressing room, her study and the library which housed her personal favourite artworks.

'The top floor is very much my space,' she said as she led the way downstairs, eager to round up the next lot.

'What was it like?' Muzza murmured when Olga had joined him and they'd left the others to have a quiet chat on their own.

'Indulgent,' she said.

'They've ruined the look of the place from the outside.' He gazed up at the bald silhouette of the upper floor. 'It was quite a gracious home, I remember. Oh well,' he shrugged, 'each to his own. Let's go and eat.'

And they joined the commodore and the chancellor and their wives who'd headed for the buffet in the food marquee.

The tone of the party changed an hour or so later with the arrival of the Premier and his entourage of around a dozen, including a very loud Laurie Connell. It was evident that all of them had had a few drinks. By now it was well after ten o'clock, but Arlene, who would have considered such tardiness in others unbelievably rude, was quick to accept their perfunctory apology. They'd had a business meeting and couldn't get away earlier, they said.

'Of course,' she replied, 'I *quite* understand. How *lovely* to see you all.' Having the Premier at her soirees was always a coup, and she'd been worried for the past hour that Brian Burke and his friends weren't going to show up. 'Do help yourselves to the buffet, you must be *starving*.'

They weren't – their business meeting had been conducted over dinner – but with drinks in hand, and a waiter standing by at the ready, they ensconced themselves in the pool area where they were quickly joined by others, including Spud and Pembo. This was the clique. This was where the hard-core drinking and the hard-core conversation would take place as the night wore on.

The string quartet that had welcomed the guests' arrival had long been replaced by stereo music piped from the house through the garden's speakers, and Gordy had turned up the volume on Madonna. He, Fleur and several of the other younger guests were dancing to 'Papa Don't Preach' on the back verandah.

Things were getting progressively noisier, and there was a minor exodus shortly after eleven. The commodore and the chancellor and their wives departed, along with a number of others. Muzza and Olga also decided to leave, and they said their farewells to Mike and Jo before seeking out Arlene.

'Yes, we're taking off too,' Mike said. He glanced towards the verandah where Allie and Greg, along with half a dozen others, were throwing themselves around to 'True Blue'. Gordy, who'd retained control of the music, was a Madonna freak. 'Allie's staying on for a while.'

'Well, of course she is,' Jo said lightly to the others. 'It's a Saturday night, no uni tomorrow, and she's having a wonderful time.'

Mike was impossible lately, she thought, as the four of them went off in search of their hostess. He'd actually expected Allie to come home with them.

'No, Mike,' she'd said when he'd been about to inter-rupt the couple on the verandah. 'Allie arrived with her boyfriend and she'll leave with her boyfriend. Don't humi-liate her, she's not a ten year old.'

'Yeah, yeah, all right, I'm sorry,' he'd said brusquely, knowing she was right but irritated nonetheless.

Jo was beginning to feel like the ham in the sandwich when it came to her husband and daughter. She was tired of the subterfuge; it was causing tension between her and Mike. She wished that Allie would admit to her affair, and that Mike would let his daughter grow up, but they both seemed reluctant to upset the status quo. They'd shared a world of their own, father and daughter, each idolising the other – in fact, she sometimes wondered just who was the greater hero to whom. But Allie was a woman now; times had changed.

'Thank you *so* much for coming, the party wouldn't have been the *same* without you.' Arlene was vociferous in her farewell to them, ignoring the elderly couple who'd been waiting to say goodbye. 'Ian's closest and dearest friends, he would have been *devastated* if you hadn't been here.'

Considering they'd seen neither hair nor hide of Ian since the arrival of the Premier's entourage, they doubted whether they would have been missed, but they all smiled and thanked her for a lovely night.

Arlene brushed cheeks lightly with each and every one. 'And *Muzza*,' she said, clasping his hand with fervour as she bent down to him, 'it's so *lovely* to see you out and about.'

'Thanks, Arlene, great party.'

The four managed to contain themselves for the several seconds it took Arlene to direct her attention to the elderly couple still patiently waiting, but when Muzza looked up at Olga and crossed his eyes, her stifled snort of laughter got them all going.

As they made their way along the path towards the side gate, Muzza and Mike cast a glance at the poolside area, prepared to give Pembo a wave, but there was no point. Amongst the plumes of spiralling cigar smoke, both Pembo and Spud were in deep debate with the company of twenty or so, most vying to be heard, the conversation already threatening to drown out Madonna.

'Yep,' Muzza grinned, 'the party sure wouldn't have been the same without us.'

By three in the morning, the mob still gathered around the pool was decidedly drunk, with the exception of Spud. He was a little bleary, but comparatively sober, having stayed on beer while the others had got stuck into the cognac and port. Everyone was pouring their own now from the bottles Ian had ordered the waiters to leave on the tables when they'd knocked off an hour previously.

Spud stubbed out his cigar in the overflowing ashtray. He'd leave soon, he decided, he'd had a good time and the evening had served its purpose. He and Pembo had had a very productive chat with Brian Burke, and another healthy injection of government funding had been promised to the McAllister Institute. But Pembo was now legless and the conversation had come full circle. They were all drunkenly back on the Cup and how the loss of it was bound to destroy some businesses. Well, fair enough, Spud supposed – it was a commiseration party after all – but the company had become boring, he thought, as he watched Laurie Connell holding the floor, the way Laurie always did.

'It's a dog-eat-dog world,' Laurie was saying, enjoying the sound of his own voice. 'You've got to fight your way back when times get hard – you can't take things lying down. Those who go under just don't have the guts . . .'

Laurie was a loudmouth in Spud's opinion.

Spud Farrell didn't much like Laurie Connell, which was odd because they had a lot in common. Both were pugnacious, self-made men, highly successful entrepreneurs who employed aggressive business tactics, and both were devoted horse-racing enthusiasts. Some presumed there was an element of jealousy in Spud – Laurie's horses had met with far more success than his had. Indeed, little more than a month previously Connell's Rocket Racer had taken out the Perth Cup. Spud Farrell had been bridesmaid many times, but he'd never won the coveted Perth Cup. And he never would, Spud had decided, if it meant he had to employ Connell's methods. Rocket Racer had come in a full nine lengths ahead of the field and then galloped another whole lap before the jockey had been able to pull the animal up. It had collapsed and died several weeks later, but the whole business had never been investigated. Spud cared too much for his horses to do that to them. Sure, he bribed jockeys whenever he could, but he'd never doped a horse and he never would.

'You need more than guts, Laurie.' Bram Midford had taken offence to Connell's comments and he interrupted, slurring his words but determined to make his point. He was sick of the man's empty bravura. Bram had put a lot of money into outlets reliant upon the tourist dollar, and the loss of the Cup could see them all go down the tube. 'You need more than guts in my fucking business. You need fucking tourists, mate! That's what you need!'

'Well, I guess you'll have to weather the storm, won't you, Bram?' Laurie said condescendingly. 'You'll have to weather the storm and see it through, just like the rest of us.'

Oh yeah, Spud thought, and exactly what storm will *you* be weathering, Laurie? Your bank'll be the first port of call for businesses needing to buy time.

Laurie Connell was a smart bastard, Spud had to give him that much. Rothwells Merchant Bank was known in business circles as a lender of last resort, and as such Laurie was bound to make a tidy profit out of the tourism slump that threatened. Rothwells would fork money out hand over fist to desperate businesses 'weathering the storm' as Laurie so succinctly put it, and they'd quickly foreclose on those who couldn't pay back. That was the way Laurie worked. As a businessman, Spud had to admit, albeit begrudgingly, that he admired Connell's tactics.

'There may well be hard times ahead for all of us,' Laurie continued, still at his bravura best, still determined to maintain centre stage.

But Spud had had enough of the bullshit. It was time to go. He stood.

'Oh Laurie, you poor bugger,' he said with feeling. 'Face it, mate, things just couldn't get worse for you, could they?'

Someone had to take the piss out of the bastard.

Spud's irony proved incorrect, however. Things did get worse for Laurie. They got a whole lot worse for everyone, but particularly for Laurie Connell.

The brief slump in tourism following the loss of the America's Cup was a drop in the ocean compared with the economic chaos wrought by the stock market crash in October of that year. Many major businesses based in Perth found themselves in difficulties, and many would ultimately face bankruptcy, but Rothwells Merchant Bank was the most instantly affected. There was an immediate run on the bank by local investors and Rothwells was forced to close its doors. Laurie Connell was the first of the major players to go under – or so it appeared at the time.

Spud Farrell and Ian Pemberton wasted no sympathy on Connell; they had their own problems to worry about. Excalibur Holdings was in dire trouble and possibly beyond rescue, but of far greater consequence, the entire Farrell Corporation threatened to topple like a house of cards. Ian, as always, was in a frenzy of panic.

'Jesus, Pembo, give it a rest.' Spud, feeling the strain himself, found Ian's hysteria intensely annoying. 'If we go down the tube you're hardly likely to lose the roof over your head, are you? Neither of us is going to end up broke, for Christ's sake.'

For tax reasons, Ian had transferred much of his property to his wife, including the Peppermint Grove house, and he'd set up offshore trust accounts in his children's names. Spud, too, had transferred a great deal of his personal wealth to Cora, also in the form of offshore trusts. When they'd married, he'd insisted she take out Australian citizenship for the very purpose.

'If the corporation goes into bankruptcy, we'll still be in front,' he said scathingly. 'We'll bloody well start again from scratch if we have to.' God, he wished Pembo would develop some balls.

Spud spared no thought whatsoever for the small-time investors who might face the loss of their life's savings. Why should he? When he'd gone public, everyone had grabbed at the chance to get rich quick. They'd all wanted a piece of the action and he'd given it to them. There were leaders and there were followers, and in Spud's opinion, if the followers couldn't stand the heat, they shouldn't have opened the kitchen door. But he had every intention of fighting to the bitter end. Spud wasn't about to admit defeat yet.

Nor, apparently, was Laurie Connell. True to his word, Laurie wasn't taking things lying down, he was fighting back tooth and nail. Having put together a rescue package involving numerous Australian businessmen, Connell appealed directly to his good mate, the WA Premier, Brian Burke.

'My God, I don't believe it!' Spud said when he heard the news. 'I don't bloody well believe it!'

Brian Burke had promised a 150-million-dollar government guarantee to provide short-term relief to Rothwells Merchant Bank. The madness of WA Inc had attained new heights of lunacy. Even in Spud's eyes.

'Brian could be brought to task for this, Pembo,' he said. 'It could be the end.'

But Burke wasn't brought to task. Not yet. Early the following year, Brian Burke was posted as ambassador to Ireland and the Holy See by his friends in Bob Hawke's federal Labor government, and Peter Dowding became the new Labor Premier of Western Australia.

It wasn't the end. But it was the beginning of the end.

CHAPTER TWENTY-THREE

Andrew Gaden strolled into the main bar and lounge of the Parmelia Hotel at a quarter to seven. He'd arrived that very day. Having stepped off the plane into the crisp, dry heat typical of a Perth afternoon in late November, he'd headed straight for the hotel and, as he'd checked in at the front desk, he'd noticed the sign in the lobby. *The Parmelia Hilton welcomes delegates to the 1990 McAllister Research Institute's Environmental Convention.*

The famous Mike McAllister, he'd thought, Johanna's husband. He'd made enquiries of the receptionist and had learned that this was the final day of the convention and that a formal dinner was to be held that night in the main function room on the first floor. The dinner was to start at seven thirty, the receptionist said, but the delegates were bound to gather for a drink in the lounge – they usually did before a convention dinner, particularly those from interstate and overseas who were staying at the hotel.

Andrew ordered a beer from the waiter and found a seat in the corner. Most of the men in the lounge were wearing dinner suits, presumably they were delegates, and a number of women were present. Was it likely Jo would accompany her husband tonight, he wondered, and if so, would they have a drink beforehand or would they head straight upstairs to the function centre? Perhaps he should have hung around in the hotel lobby. But that would have been far too obvious.

His eyes searched the crowded room but there was no sign of her. He sipped his beer and watched the main entrance to the lounge, willing her to appear. He wouldn't say anything to her, he'd decided, he didn't wish to intrude, but for some strange reason he longed to see her again. It had been twenty years. She would surely have changed, he thought. Perhaps he wouldn't even recognise her.

He finished his beer and glanced down at his watch. Seven fifteen. When he looked up, she was suddenly there, standing at the main doors, and of course he recognised her. How could he fail? Jo had always stood out in a crowd.

She wore a dove-grey cocktail dress with a silvery sheen – she favoured pastel colours, he remembered – and her mid-length fair hair was drawn back from her face. Unconsciously elegant, she was as striking as ever.

He recognised the husband too: he'd seen Mike McAllister's face on many a television report and in many a newspaper. But the raven-haired young woman by their side – was that really Allie? Of course it was, he thought. The little girl he'd known had always borne the promise of true beauty.

Andrew rose from his chair, his decision not to intrude forgotten. He simply had to speak to her. He didn't interrupt though; he waited to one side until Jo and Mike had finished their brief chat with the group by the door. As the couple turned to mingle with others of the delegates, Andrew stepped forward.

'Hi Jo,' he said with a grin. Then it occurred to him that perhaps *she* might not recognise *him*, and he was about to introduce himself, just in case.

'Andy! Andy Gaden!' She didn't offer her hand or kiss

his cheek, but embraced him warmly instead. 'Good heavens, you haven't changed at all.'

He hadn't, Jo thought, it was the dimples that did it. His smile took her back twenty years.

'Bit greyer,' he laughed, 'bit more weathered.' Close to, he loved the way the porcelain skin around her eyes crinkled as she smiled.

'Oh, aren't we all,' Jo said. 'Andy, this is my husband, Mike McAllister. Mike, Andy Gaden.'

'*The* Andy Gaden I take it.' Mike's grin was friendly as he offered his hand; there was no mistaking his knowledge of their shared past.

Andy shook Mike's hand and glanced at Jo, a little taken aback.

'No need to be self-conscious, Andy,' she laughed, sharing a fond look with her husband. 'Face it, I've never been a woman of mystery.'

Really, Andy wondered. He'd always found Jo a woman of great mystery himself.

'You remember Allie, of course?' she said.

'How could I forget?' Andy offered his hand. 'You wouldn't remember *me*, Allie, I belong to the era of Donald Duck wallpaper.'

'Yes, I do remember,' Allie said as they shook.

'Really?' he asked, astounded.

'Well, no, I don't remember you. Sorry,' she said. Should she, she wondered. 'But I do remember Donald Duck wallpaper.' Allie had had sudden visions of Donald Ducks looming everywhere as she kissed them. Where had that come from? How amazing.

'What are you doing in Perth, Andy?' Jo asked. Open as she'd been with her husband, there was no need to share with her daughter the fact that this was the man she'd once intended to marry.

'Oh, federal government business, nothing exciting.' He shrugged awkwardly. Mike was looking around, probably wanting to mingle. 'I'm staying at the hotel, just wanted to say hello. Sorry, Mike,' he said, 'didn't mean to intrude. I'm sure you want to have a drink with your colleagues. Good to see you again, Jo.' And he started to back away.

Mike was aware that his unintentional distraction had embarrassed the man. 'You're not intruding at all, Andy. We hadn't planned on having a drink with the gang, we were just going to say a few brief hellos before getting locked in at the dinner table.' He looked at his watch. 'But I'm afraid we do have to head upstairs now.'

'Goodbye, Andy,' Jo said. 'It's been lovely to see you again.' She kissed him lightly on the cheek. 'It really has.'

'How long are you in Perth?' Mike queried.

'Just for the week, but I'll be popping over regularly – it's an ongoing contract.'

'Well, why don't you two catch up tomorrow? Or the day after? Jo's got time on her hands these days.'

Once again Andy was taken aback, but he jumped at the opportunity.

'Sounds like a good idea to me,' he said. 'How about it, Jo? Lunch tomorrow?'

'Lovely. I'll meet you here in the lobby. Say around one?'

'I'll look forward to it.'

As they walked upstairs, Jo whispered to Mike, out of Allie's hearing, 'Why on earth did you do that?'

'Why shouldn't I? It was perfectly obvious that the two of you enjoyed seeing each other.' Mike, too, lowered his voice to a whisper. 'But you'd better watch out, the man's still in love with you.'

'Don't be ridiculous.'

'I'm serious.'

'If you're serious, you'd hardly suggest we meet,' she said with a wry smile.

'Why not? Why should I feel threatened – you chose me, not him.' Mike grinned as he took her hand. 'I obviously got things right somewhere along the line.'

Jo laughed.

'Is someone going to share the joke?' Allie demanded. She'd felt decidedly left out during their whispered exchange.

'Andy's your mother's ex-lover. She was going to marry him at one time.'

The remark rendered both Jo and Allie speechless, but there was no time for further conversation anyway. They'd arrived at the top of the stairs where, outside the function room, guests were mingling and waiters were proffering trays of champagne.

'Bit unusual, isn't it? The husband suggesting the wife have lunch with her ex.' Andy's opening remark echoed Jo's initial reaction. They were dining at the Parmelia's main restaurant, he'd booked a table for one o'clock. 'Mike's obviously not the possessive type.'

'No, he certainly isn't,' she agreed with a smile. 'Particularly given the fact that he's convinced you're still in love with me.'

'Is he really? My goodness, how extraordinarily perceptive.'

'Oh, stop being silly, Andy, it's been twenty years.' He still had that air of theatricality about him which she'd always found amusing.

'I'm not being silly. I'm fully aware it's been twenty years, and at the risk of sounding frightfully Noel Coward, I've loved you for every single one of them. That's a touch of Elyot from *Private Lives*, by the way, just in case you hadn't recognised it.'

His manner may have been theatrical, and his intention to amuse, but Jo realised with a start that he meant what he said.

'Dear me,' she replied. She wasn't sure which surprised her most: his declaration or Mike's perception. 'Then perhaps it's not really wise for us to have lunch.'

'Oh, Jo,' he laughed. 'You're so complex and so simple at the same time – it's your greatest charm, always was. Don't worry, I'm not about to make overtures. I know a happily married woman when I see one. Besides,' he added, with more than a touch of flippancy, 'I'd never allow you to break my heart a second time.'

The waiter arrived with the menu and wine list.

'Well, I think I've done Coward to death, haven't I,' he said. 'Shall we order?'

'Yes, let's.'

'Is it still port and lemonade or have you developed a palate?'

'I've been known to take a glass of white wine now and then,' she smiled. She'd forgotten how much she enjoyed his company.

Andy ordered a Margaret River sauvignon blanc, they both decided upon the grilled dhufish, and when the waiter had gone, he dropped the mask of theatricality.

'So tell me, why do you have time on your hands these days?'

'How do you mean?'

'That's what Mike said. He said you had time on your hands these days, his exact words. But surely you're working?'

'Yes, of course I am.' Her response was instinctively defensive, although she didn't know why. 'I work at the Institute. Mike's established a whole department devoted to human eco-toxicological research, which naturally requires medical input.'

Andy appeared interested, expecting her to go on, but Jo found herself admitting the truth.

'Well, I report in several days a week, but there's not really much for me to do any more. Certainly not the way there was in the early days. They employ full-time experts now.'

'I see.' What had happened to the ambitious, dedicated

Johanna Whitely, Andy wondered. Swallowed up by her husband's career? But he'd noted the defensiveness, so he changed the subject. 'Tell me about Allie,' he said. 'She's as beautiful as I'd expected, but what's she up to?'

The move had been a wise one, he realised, as Jo launched into a proud account of her daughter's academic achievements. Allie had completed her course in marine biology and was currently in the second year of her PhD, she told him. Her primary supervisor was the estuarine research coordinator for the WA Environmental Protection Authority, a Dr Ernest Hodgkin, but much of her work was being conducted at the Institute.

'Which means Mike's really acting as her secondary supervisor,' she said. 'It's fantastic for them both, they love working together.'

'What's her PhD subject?' he asked.

'I can't remember the full title, but it involves the importance of nutrient flow and balance in the estuarine river systems of WA's south-west.'

'I'm impressed.' He was. 'So does she have time for a love life?' he asked with a dimpled grin. 'I imagine she'd have to fight them off.'

'Oh, they come after her in droves, but she doesn't need to fight them off – they give up when she doesn't notice them. Allie's like her father: career-focused and totally tunnel-visioned.'

The wine arrived.

'She did have a boyfriend a while back,' Jo continued as the waiter poured Andy a taster. 'A very nice young man called Greg. They were doing the same course at uni and they became very close, but she dropped him after about a year. Poor Greg, he's still very much in love with her.'

Andy gave a nod to the waiter, who proceeded to pour the wine.

'So she's a heartbreaker like her mother,' he quipped.

'Yes, possibly.' Jo smiled, she didn't perceive any dig in the remark; it was just Andy being funny. 'Greg's working with Mike at the Institute now, and I'm sure he accepted the position so that he could be near Allie. He graduated brilliantly – he could have gone anywhere.'

How things had changed, she thought. No longer was Greg a threat in Mike's eyes, far from it. In Mike's opinion, young Greg Saunders was a highly committed marine biologist, the perfect man to have on their team, and quite possibly the perfect partner for his daughter had she been so inclined. But Allie, much as she genuinely cared for Greg, was oblivious to all but her work. Just as her father had been at her age, Jo remembered. Strange, she thought, how the relationship between Allie and Greg rather reminded her of Mike and herself when they were at university. Only the roles were reversed.

'Well, here's to two women practised in the art.'

Andy's toast jolted her back to the moment. What had he said?

'Heartbreakers, the pair of you.' He raised his glass. 'To you and Allie.'

She laughed, as she was sure he'd intended her to, but for just one moment she wondered whether she'd registered a touch of bitterness.

'Your turn, Andy. Tell me about yourself.'

'I married on the rebound.' His manner continued flippant, but she sensed he was serious. 'A nice woman called Tanya who really deserved better. It only lasted four years, but long enough to produce two children.'

They talked about his son and his daughter and it was Andy's turn to boast. They were both at Sydney University and he plainly adored them. 'At least something worthwhile eventuated from a marriage doomed to fail,' he said.

The dhufish arrived and, as they ate, Jo asked him about his work. She was beginning to think it was safer to avoid personal subjects.

'Business for the federal government, you said – that covers a multitude of sins.'

'Gaden, Birch & Hall, Law and Accountancy,' he announced with all due solemnity. 'I joined forces ten years ago with a couple of financial geniuses and that's the name of our company. We're trouble-shooters known as GBH, which is pretty hilarious when you think about it.'

She looked mystified.

'GBH? Grievous bodily harm?'

'Right,' she laughed. 'Sorry, I didn't get it.'

'Everyone quakes in their boots when we turn up to audit the books and cast a legal eye over what's been going on,' he said, tucking into his meal with relish. 'Most of our work is with major corporations but we accept the odd government contract. God, I wish you could get dhufish in Sydney.'

'So what exactly are you *doing* for the government?' Jo was intrigued.

'Oh, just the usual – our team's running a check on the various federal departments. We're doing Health this week, then we'll be back for Tourism, then Foreign Affairs, Defence, Vet Affairs – a sort of ongoing audit. All pretty mundane stuff.'

'Really?' She looked sceptical. 'Isn't it a little coincidental that an "ongoing audit" has been ordered right at this time? I mean, given the current situation in Perth?'

'You mean the inquiries into WA Inc?'

'Exactly. They're mounting a Royal Commission – Carmen Lawrence announced it just last week. Surely that's why you're here?'

'Good God, no, we're an independent company under contract to the federal government.' His expression was one of mock horror. 'And the federal government never involves itself in state affairs, everyone knows that.' He took a sip of his wine. 'My presence in Perth has no connection at all with the current fracas.'

She smiled and raised a dubious eyebrow. She didn't believe him for a minute.

'Well, one does keep one's eyes and ears open, of course,' Andy admitted, returning her smile. 'Everyone's naturally interested in what's going on in WA.' *Interested*, he thought, they were terrified! Bob Hawke's federal Labor government was as worried as all hell – and justifiably so. The fiasco in WA could backfire on the lot of them.

'We lawyers do talk amongst ourselves, you know how it is. I mean, word does get around.'

Jo laughed. He was outrageous, he'd all but confessed to the fact. 'Face it, Andy, you're a spy.'

'What a terrible thing to suggest. Are you up for dessert?'

They both decided upon the crème caramel.

The political situation in WA had indeed reached epic proportions, which now reverberated around the country.

The final liquidation of Rothwells Merchant Bank had caused huge losses, not only to its investors, but to the Western Australian government. The subject of the 150-million-dollar government guarantee to Rothwells had come in for heavy questioning, and attention had been drawn to many other government involvements with private businessmen during Brian Burke's premiership.

Carmen Lawrence, having replaced Dowding as WA Labor Premier earlier that year, had just announced her government's intention to hold a Royal Commission to 'inquire into certain matters'. Heads were plainly set to roll.

'How was lunch today?' Mike asked that night when he arrived home from the Institute shortly before seven thirty.

'We ate at the Parmelia, the dhufish was excellent, and I had crème caramel for dessert.'

'Come on,' he laughed, 'you know what I mean.' He crossed to the sideboard and poured himself a scotch. Jo was sipping a cup of tea as she watched the ABC News. 'How was your old mate Andy?'

She put down her cup, picked up the remote and turned the television set off. The news was nearly over and she very much wanted to talk anyway.

'He was funny actually. The whole thing started out as a scene from *Private Lives* – I'd forgotten just how funny Andy can be. But you were right.'

'About what?'

'He's still in love with me.'

The news itself was no surprise to Mike, but the man's declaration most certainly was.

'He didn't *say* so, surely!'

'Oh yes. *I'm fully aware it's been twenty years, and I've loved you for every single one of them.*' She gave the words their full theatrical flair. 'As I said, he was playing Noel Coward, or Elyot, or both. But he meant every word.'

Bloody cheeky, Mike thought, taking a swig of his scotch. 'Are you going to see him again?'

'Oh, I don't know,' she said teasingly as he sat beside her on the sofa. 'Why do you ask? Are you jealous?'

'Not a bit,' he replied. 'I trust you. But if the bloke tries to come on to you I'll knock his bloody lights out.'

Realising he was serious, she stopped playing games. 'Andy wasn't coming on to me, Mike. In his own way, he was just letting me know how much I'd hurt him. I must say I was surprised – it was all so long ago – but let's face it, I did leave the poor man virtually at the altar.'

She leaned in to him and kissed him gently. 'I didn't really have much option though, did I?' she murmured, and as she looked into his eyes her smile was brazen. 'It's all your fault, you know. You broke Andy's heart. I didn't.'

He would have liked to make love to her there and then, but she rose from the sofa.

'What do you want for dinner?' she asked, well and truly breaking the mood of the moment. Jo hadn't yet

broached the subject uppermost in her mind, but she felt
it wise to get off the topic of Andy before she did. 'I could
defrost some chops. It'll just be the two of us – Allie's gone
to the movies.'

'Do you really feel like cooking?'

'Nope.' She didn't, after the dhufish and crème caramel;
lunch was normally a sandwich. 'Shall we go decadent?'
Go decadent was their shorthand for pizzas.

'Good idea.' He downed the scotch and stood. 'I'll order
a couple of family size. I'm starving, and Allie'll wolf down
whatever's left when she gets home. Name your poison,'
he said as he crossed to the phone.

'Don't care. Anything with anchovies.'

He rang and ordered the takeaway, after which Jo
decided that the moment was right.

'Mike,' she said, 'how would you feel if I were to go
back to work?'

'What do you mean? You *do* work.' He was puzzled.
'You work at the Institute. You're invaluable to us.'

'I'm not any more, not these days.' Surely he'd noticed,
she thought. Then she realised that he probably hadn't. 'I
report in several times a week, but my duties are token,
you must know that. I want to go back to medicine. Full-
time. I thought I might apply to the Royal Perth Hospital
in the new year. They need doctors.'

'Do they?' he asked, simply for want of something better
to say. He was at a loss – this had come completely out of
the blue. How could she call her duties *token*? And what
difference did it make whether she worked several or seven
days a week? She was devoted to the Institute, she always
had been.

'Every hospital needs doctors, Mike. And that's what
I am. A doctor.'

The words were Andy's. 'You're a doctor, Jo,' he'd said.
'Surely you're not happy working part-time in a laboratory? Don't you miss medicine? You were so dedicated.

What happened?' She hadn't pursued the conversation he'd introduced over coffee, but he'd made his point anyway. He'd successfully stirred up the hornets' nest of longing which, although dormant for some time, hadn't needed much awakening.

'I take it this is Andy's doing,' Mike said coldly. Of course it was, he thought, it had to be.

'Partly,' she admitted. She sensed he was annoyed, but she wanted to be honest. 'I hadn't realised how compliant I'd become, Mike. I need inspiration, I need to work. My work's who I am. Or who I used to be,' she corrected herself.

'Well, well, well . . .'

He crossed to the sideboard to pour himself a rare second scotch, biding time, trying to control his growing anger. *Compliant?* Compliant to whom? To what? To him? To the Institute? They'd shared a dream, the two of them. Surely the McAllister Institute was inspiration enough for her.

'It appears Andy Gaden has a lot to answer for,' he said tightly. The presumption of the man astounded him. Not content with declaring his undying love, he'd aroused dissatisfaction in Jo. What gave him the right to meddle in their lives?

'Don't blame Andy, Mike, please.' She crossed to him. 'He simply asked if I missed medicine, and I realised how very, very much I did. I'm grateful to Andy, and I'd like you to be too. I'll be happier working at the hospital, I know I will.'

His anger died in an instant and he turned to face her.

'Have you been *un*happy, Jo?' Surely not. How could she have been unhappy? He would have noticed.

She smiled her reassurance; she could see he was concerned. 'Not unhappy, my darling,' she said gently. 'Not unhappy, I promise you, but perhaps a little unfulfilled – lately, anyway. I need to rediscover a life of my own.'

'I see.' He put down the glass of scotch, he didn't want it anyway. Had he really deprived his wife of a life of her own? If so, he certainly hadn't realised it. Should he feel guilty? Mike was confused. 'I'm sorry,' he said. He didn't know what else he *could* say.

'What on earth for?' She laughed – he looked so boyish in his confusion, like a child who'd been chastised for a wrong he couldn't comprehend. 'There's nothing to be sorry about. I just need a change, that's all.'

The doorbell rang.

'That'll be the pizzas. Excellent timing. End of conversation.'

She grabbed her wallet and disappeared into the hall, and he was left wondering how he'd allowed himself to become so completely out of touch. It appeared Andy Gaden knew his wife better than he did.

'Time to eat,' she announced when she returned minutes later with the pizzas. He followed her into the kitchen where she dumped the boxes on the table.

'Oh, by the way,' she said, lifting the plates out of the cupboard, 'I forgot to tell you. Andy's a spy.'

'He's a what?'

'Well, he's not *actually* a spy, and yet he is in a way.' She handed him the plates. 'His team of legal eagles is here to run a check on the books of federal government departments, but he's obviously expected to sniff around and report back on the WA Inc debacle.'

'Really?'

'Yes, really.'

She fetched a roll of paper towels and they sat at the table.

'Well, it's hardly surprising that they're worried in Canberra. Bob Hawke was good mates with Burke and Connell – according to Spud, anyway. He says Hawke was primarily responsible for Burke getting into power in the first place.'

Jo lifted out a wedge of seafood pizza. 'Spud was pretty matey with Burke himself,' she said. 'How does he feel about the Royal Commission?'

'He's not talking about it much, not to me anyway. He just shrugs it off, saying it's the politicians who'll suffer. They're the crooks, he says, all *he* ever did was donate funds to the party.' Mike tackled the pepperoni. 'I suppose we'll have to wait and see what happens in the new year, but Spud'll be fine, I'm sure.'

CHAPTER TWENTY-FOUR

The Royal Commission's first principal witness, Laurie Connell, didn't shy away from telling the facts as they were. He was quite blunt, even boastful, about his relationship with Brian Burke and their joint business dealings. He was open also about the dealings of others, and of Brian Burke's 'new order', his 'elite of the able'.

The fresh allegations that arose from Connell's evidence revealed the true extent to which Western Australia, under Burke's premiership, had become an executive state with no constitutional balance maintained. The government and those with powerful vested interests had acted unchecked and in total collusion, undermining the very principles of the Westminster system of democratic rule.

Political shockwaves reverberated around the country.

Prime Minister Bob Hawke was under mounting pressure to recall Burke from his position as ambassador to Ireland and the Holy See. Hawke refused. But a month into the hearings, the heat generated was so intense that Foreign Minister Gareth Evans announced Brian Burke would return to Australia, having been granted three weeks' paid leave, and that he would give evidence to the WA Royal

Commission. Shortly afterwards, Prime Minister Hawke agreed at a press conference that he, too, was prepared to appear before the Commission if asked to do so.

In May 1991, Brian Burke took the witness stand, pale, puffy-eyed and nervous, a shadow of his former braggart self.

Burke and Connell remained central figures crucial to the proceedings, but they were only two of many witnesses, from both the political and private business sectors, who would be called upon to give evidence over the twenty-one months of inquiries and hearings. And they would not be the only ones left facing criminal charges.

'I've stood by you through it all, Ian.'

Arlene Pemberton was trembling with justifiable rage. She'd been a good wife, she told herself, she'd behaved nobly. She'd stood by him when Excalibur Holdings had gone into liquidation, and she'd stood by him these past months with the Farrell Corporation facing bankruptcy. But *this*? This was going too far. She couldn't be expected to stand by him through *this*.

'I've watched our entire *world* crumble around us. I've watched as we've lost *everything*, and I haven't said a word.'

She'd actually said a great deal, and, as her husband's remaining assets were in her name, she actually *owned* a great deal, but none of that was pertinent to Arlene under the current circumstances.

'But I warn you, if you're charged I will seek an instant divorce and you will never see your children again. Do you understand me?'

Arlene refused to succumb to the hysteria that threatened. Ultimatums lacked conviction if delivered hysterically.

'You will move out of this house until the hearings are over,' she said. 'And if you end up facing charges, Ian, don't bother coming back.'

She lost control just a little before she swept out of the

room. 'How could you have let it come to this?' she hissed. 'The *shame*! How could you *do* it to me? How could you do it to the *children*?'

Ian Pemberton and Spud Farrell were to be the next cabs off the rank. Laurie Connell had continued to testify before the commission until the end of November. A lengthy array of politicians and businessmen, including Alan Bond, had been called to give evidence, and now, in the new year of 1992, it was Spud's and Pembo's turn.

Spud watched with an element of distaste as Ian, his head in his hands, sobbed uncontrollably.

'She's kicked me out of the house, Spud. She says if I end up being charged, she'll divorce me.'

Good riddance, Spud thought, you'd be better off without the bitch. But he didn't say anything. He knew he should feel sorry for Pembo: this wasn't the customary Pemberton panic, this was a man on the verge of a nervous breakdown. But he wished Pembo would stop blubbering; they needed to form a strategy.

'She says I'll never see the children again.'

'Your kids are nineteen, for God's sake! They're adults! They can make up their own minds.'

'She'll turn them against me, I know she will.' Ian fought to control himself, wiping his runny nose with the back of his hand. 'What am I going to do, Spud?' He looked up in despair, a quivering mess. 'I can't go to jail, I'll lose everything. What am I going to do?'

'You're going to pull yourself together, that's what you're going to do.' Spud disappeared to the nearest bathroom and returned with a box of tissues. 'Where are you staying?' he asked.

'I booked into the Sheraton.' Ian took a fistful of tissues from the box Spud handed him and blew his nose loudly.

'Right. Well, for starters, we'll collect your stuff. You can move in here.'

'Thanks, Spud. I really appreciate that.' Wiping his tear-stained face, Ian attempted a tremulous smile. He'd more or less gained control now. 'You're a good mate to have around,' he sniffed.

'It's not as if Cora and I don't have enough space.'

Spud gave a comradely grin as he looked about at their lavish surrounds, but the offer hadn't really been made in the true spirit of mateship. Spud knew that Pembo would go to pieces completely in a hotel room on his own. And he couldn't afford to have Ian Pemberton go to pieces. They needed to work as a team.

'Come on,' he said, 'let's go and grab your gear, then we'll figure out a plan. Nobody's going to jail if I can help it.'

Ian felt a whole lot better as they drove into the city. Spud'd get them out of this mess, he thought. Spud always did.

But later that afternoon, as they sat in Spud's study with the pot of coffee Cora had made them, Ian was astounded by Spud's apparent reluctance to take the course of action which he himself considered their only escape route.

'I was rather hoping to leave Mike out of things altogether,' Spud said.

'You *what*?'

'Well, he hasn't been a part of it, has he?'

'Of course he has. Maybe not by act, but by omission he's as guilty as we are.'

'Yeah, yeah, rightio.'

'And he owes us more than a few favours – he must know that.'

'I'm sure he does. Of *course* he does. But I was hoping the Institute wouldn't come under investigation. It might not, you know,' he added hopefully, 'it's a very creditable organisation.'

'Are you insane, Spud?' Ian looked at him as if he were. 'Are you completely out of your mind? The Institute's our biggest danger. We cooked the fucking books! If it doesn't come under investigation, then fine, but what if it does? We can try to talk our way around the million dollars we donated to the Labor Party – hell, we weren't alone there. We can even try to talk our way around some of the kick-backs we scored in exchange, although it's bound to lead to conspiracy claims. But if the Institute comes under the microscope – and why the hell wouldn't it, given the amount of funding that's been shovelled its way – then we're *really* in the shit.'

'Yeah, yeah,' Spud said, 'take it easy.' Pembo was getting the jitters again, but he was nonetheless correct. 'You're right, I know.'

Spud was thankful that Pembo had regained his senses, but at the same time regretful Mike was being drawn into the whole thing. Sorry, Mikey, he thought, I tried to save you, mate.

'You're dead bloody right, Pembo,' he said. 'We need Mike on side.'

'He's our only chance, for Christ's sake.'

'I know, I know. We'll go down and see him first thing tomorrow.'

'Spud . . . Pembo . . .' Mike greeted them warmly when they arrived at the Institute shortly after nine the following morning. They'd reported straight to his office and he was pleased to see them, albeit a little puzzled. Board meetings were held at two in the afternoon, and there wasn't one planned for another three weeks anyway.

'What a pleasant surprise,' he said. 'Do you want a coffee?'

'Yeah, coffee'd be good, thanks.' Spud glanced at Mike's secretary who was sitting in the glass-windowed reception area, its open door too close for comfort. 'Can we have it on the balcony? I want a cigar.'

'You want a cigar at nine o'clock in the morning?'

'Don't preach.'

'Right.' Mike led the way, nodding to his secretary as they passed. 'Coffee, thanks, Bev. We'll be outside.'

'To what do I owe the honour?' he asked as they seated themselves around the table on the balcony overlooking the marina and the whole of Cockburn Sound. The two of them seemed edgy, he thought. Customary for Pembo, of course, but even Spud appeared a little uptight, which was unusual.

'We need to have a chat, Mikey,' Spud said, lighting up his cigar. 'Things are not looking too good and we think you can help us.'

'Yes, I've heard you're in trouble.' In trouble, Mike thought, the Farrell Corporation was going bankrupt – it was in all the papers. But how on earth could he help?

'It's to do with the Royal Commission. We've been called to give evidence.'

'I see.' Mike still didn't compute. Of what possible help could he be?

'We need you to stand by us,' Ian said bluntly.

'Ah. Well, yes, of course, I'd be happy to act as a character witness. The work you've done for us is bound to go in your favour – you've been the mainstays of the Institute. I'm sure the chancellor and the commodore would vouch for that too, and the other board members –'

'Bugger the board members,' Ian interjected. 'We need more than character witnesses, we need your total back-up.'

Not the way to go about things, Spud thought.

'Don't take any notice of Pembo, Mikey, he's just a bit jumpy. Although in essence he's right: we do need your support.' He took a hefty drag on the cigar, smoke billowing into the clear morning air. 'It would be a big help to us if the commission was assured that all government funding to the Institute was put to good use, and that we had your full permission as chairman of the board to handle the finances as we saw fit.'

'But the funding *was* put to good use and you *did* have my permission.' Mike was more confused than ever. 'You had the permission of the whole board.' He grinned. 'Good God, imagine the mess we'd be in if we'd left the financial administration in the hands of the commodore or the chancellor, or for that matter the rest of us academics.'

'Oh, for Christ's sake, Spud,' Ian burst out, frustrated. 'Will you just get to the bloody point!'

'All *right*, Pembo, all *right!*' Spud issued Ian a warning glare. Mike needed to be handled with kid gloves. A few home truths were bound to come as a shock, they had to tread carefully.

Ian got the message. He would far rather have spat it all out and had it over and done with quickly – Mike would agree, he'd have no option – but Spud's methods invariably paid off, so he sat back and bit his tongue.

'Get to what bloody point?' Mike asked.

'Well, all this for starters.' Spud held his arms out in an expansive gesture that embraced the whole of the Institute. 'And *that*, of course,' he added, waving his cigar in the direction of *Carina* which sat in the farthest pen of the jetty below. 'You've got to admit, Mikey, you've had it good.'

'In what way?'

'Government funding, of course. You've had some pretty big handouts.'

'Yes, I agree,' Mike said carefully. 'The government's been very generous over the years.' Just what was Spud hinting at?

'And which particular government got everything up and going? Burke's Labor government, right?'

'Right.'

'So you've really been in on things all along, haven't you?' Spud leaned back complacently, dragging on his cigar. 'I mean, face it, you've had your kickbacks like the rest of us.'

'What exactly are you inferring?'

'Oh come on, Mikey, don't play the total innocent, it makes you look dumb,' Spud retaliated with a sudden flash of exasperation. 'How the hell do you think you scored your bloody great ship? Do you know any other research centre with a state-of-the-art thing like that?'

Mike was silent. He could think of nothing by way of reply.

'Private enterprise and government, mate. Kickbacks all along the way – everyone had a finger in the pie back then. Pembo and I donated hundreds of thousands to Burke's Labor Party, close to a million all up. You must have known the government funding was a return of favours.'

But he hadn't, Mike thought. The notion had never once crossed his mind.

Spud took his silence as acquiescence.

'Of course you did,' he laughed indulgently. 'Christ, Mikey, you know the way I play the game, you of all people – you always have . . .'

Spud's a crook, he always has been. That was what Jools had said, Mike remembered. He also remembered how fiercely he'd sprung to Spud's defence.

'And you played the game yourself – you finally took a leaf out of my book. And why shouldn't you? Hell, when it comes to an enterprise like the Institute, all ends justify the means, don't they?'

Mike remained utterly speechless.

'Jesus, mate, you're preserving the environment! You're serving humanity! We're proud to have been a part of it, aren't we, Pembo?'

'We sure are,' Ian agreed.

Christ, Spud was clever, he thought, a bloody genius when it came to manipulation. Mike was cornered. He had guilt written all over him.

'So you see, we need you to testify to the commission that applications for government funding came directly from *you*. They mustn't know that the money was a payout for party donations. We've got hold of some original application forms. You can sign them and we'll back-date them – easy as pie. Burke's going along with it, naturally – it's to his advantage.'

'But it would be a lie.' Mike finally found his voice, although he remained in a state of shock. This couldn't be happening.

'A white lie, Mikey – for the good of the Institute.'

There was a tap at the balcony door and Spud rose to open it for Bev, who'd arrived with the coffee. She put the tray down on the table and picked up the coffee pot.

'Do you want me to –'

'No,' Mike said. 'We'll serve ourselves.'

'Sure.' Bev left, closing the door behind her. It wasn't like him to be brusque, she thought.

'I'll play mother, shall I?' Spud said as he sat. Someone had to. Mike hadn't moved a muscle. Cigar clenched between his teeth, he poured the coffee, then sat back, mug in hand.

'However, there's one aspect to this whole business which you *don't* know about, Mikey, and for which I really do feel the need to apologise. We both do, don't we, Pembo?'

Ian nodded. No word from him was necessary. Spud was going great guns.

'I won't cut any corners, you need to know the truth. We've been using the Institute's funding for our own purposes.'

It was true, they'd been rorting the McAllister Institute for years. They'd invested the healthy government grants they'd scored from Brian Burke, then returned the cash and doctored the books accordingly, pocketing the profits themselves.

'I'm not proud of the fact,' Spud said, which was a bald-faced lie; he'd been supremely proud of the whole operation, it had been as smooth as silk. The dills on the board had had no idea – they were children when it came to financial management. 'But what's done is done, I'm afraid. Burke was throwing money around like a man with no arms in those days. The problem is, we now have to cover up the fact – for the good of the Institute, of course,' he added. 'That's why we need you to sign and back-date those funding application forms.'

Mike sat frozen, his mind numbed by the revelations that were unfolding.

Spud ground his half-finished cigar into the ashtray and continued, relieved that Mike appeared to have accepted the inevitability of the case at hand.

'The money has to be seen to have come through legitimate channels upon your request. Otherwise the Royal Commission might want to examine the books, and believe me,' he said warningly, 'that's the last thing *any* of us need.'

He sipped at his coffee, awaiting Mike's reaction.

'Did you really think that I'd go along with this?' Mike hardly trusted himself to speak.

'Why not?' Spud put down the coffee mug and looked him directly in the eye. 'You owe us, Mikey. You owe us big time.'

'How could you expect, for one minute, that I'd be a part of what you've done?'

'You already are, mate. You're up to your neck in it. Christ alive, we're only asking for a few back-dated signatures. Do you realise how many *other* forms you've signed over the years? Do you have any idea what they were *for*? You gave us carte blanche to play around with Institute money! Where does that place you? Where does that place the *Institute*? If we go to jail, mate, then so do you. And your precious Institute might well go down the gurgler – you've got to bear that in mind too.'

Spud could see by Mike's shocked reaction that the full impact of the truth had finally registered.

'But if you sign the papers, Mikey, none of that'll happen,' he said reassuringly. 'We'll get away with it, don't you worry. We'll get away with it on the strength of your good name.'

Mike stood and looked from one to the other, his life-long friends, Spud and Pembo. They'd betrayed him. He felt sick with anger.

'You've used my life's work as a front for your criminal activities,' he said, his voice shaking with barely controlled rage, 'and you expect to get away with it on the strength of my *good name*? Well, I won't lie for you, Spud. If I have to go to jail, then so be it. You can rot in hell for all I care. I hope you do. I hope you both do.'

Spud was suddenly deflated. He'd thought he'd been so close. For a moment there, he'd got quite carried away. But how the hell could he have kidded himself? How could he have expected Mike McAllister, of all people, to lie? Mike never lied.

Ian knew in that split-second that Spud had given up the argument, and he stared at the two of them in disbelief. He'd assumed that much as Mike may have found the task odious, he'd help them – through a sense of obligation if nothing else. Now he felt the knot of fear gnawing once more.

'You mean you'd just stand by and let us go to jail?'

'Why would I do otherwise? You betrayed me and now you expect me to *lie* for you? You're scum, Pembo. Jail's where you belong.'

Ian Pemberton's future flashed before him and he sprang to his feet.

'You've been living a lie for years, you sanctimonious bastard! You've been as crooked as us and you bloody well know it. We *made* you! You and your bloody fancy Institute. How dare you turn your back on us now!'

Spud stood, prepared to intervene. Pembo was hysterical.

'And as for your *good fucking name*, well, I'll tell you

something else,' Ian trumpeted, holding back nothing in his attack. 'Where will your *good fucking name* be when the world finds out about Mayjay – ever thought of that?'

The words hung there. Then Ian hissed his threat in manic earnest. 'Because that's what I'll do, Mike, I'm warning you. I'll tell the press, I'll tell everyone. I'm not going down on my own, I can promise you that. If I go, I'll take you with me. *Mike McAllister, Beach Girl Beauty Killer* – that'd look good on the front page, wouldn't it? Mayjay, the face of WA, dead at the hands of Mike-God-Almighty-McAllister! Try dining out on your *good fucking name* when that gets around –'

'Okay, Pembo, enough.' Spud stepped forward and grabbed Ian by the arm. 'You've said your piece.'

But Ian shook his arm free. 'Your whole life's been one fucking lie from the start,' he snarled, spittle flying from his mouth. He was demented in his fear. 'You're a fraud, mate! You're a fucking fraud!'

Spud dragged him aside and slammed him against the heavy glass doors of the balcony.

'I said, that's enough!'

Ian regained his balance and cowered before them, glaring like a caged wild animal. But his hysterical tirade was over.

'Go and wait in the car,' Spud ordered.

He remained for a second or so, the hint of rebellion in his eyes, then he turned and left.

Alone on the balcony, Spud and Mike faced each other in silence.

'He'll do it, you know.' Spud was the first to speak. The insanity of Ian's outburst had astonished him, but he decided to make one last-ditch stand on the strength of it.

'Pembo's going over the edge, as you can see. He'll dredge up the past – either to take you down with him, as he says, or to undermine your credibility and make you appear a part of the whole Institute rort. Which, let's face it, Mikey, you were – whether you knew it or not.'

Even as he asked, with the last vestige of hope, Spud knew what the answer would be. 'I don't suppose Pembo's threat makes you want to rethink things?'

'No,' Mike said coldly. 'It doesn't.'

'Nah, didn't think it would. Well, we'll just have to wait and see what happens, I suppose.'

He crossed to the door, then lingered for a moment.

'I'm sorry everything's turned out the way it has.'

Sorry? Mike thought. He was *sorry*?

'You're a bastard, Spud. You'd sell your grandmother down the river, you're rotten to the core.'

'Yeah, but then you've always known that, haven't you?' Spud said reasonably. 'You know me better than anyone, Mikey. I took advantage of you, I admit it, and I'm sorry. But you let it happen. Deep down you must have known I was out for what I could get. I always am, that's my way.'

'You're saying *I'm* responsible?'

The look in Mike's eyes was murderous, but Spud didn't flinch.

'No, of course I'm not, you had no idea what was going on. But as chairman of the board of the McAllister Institute, you *should* have. I'm saying that you turned a blind eye. We scored the money for you, and you never asked how and you never asked why. That's what I'm saying.'

He opened the balcony door.

'For what it's worth, I'll promise you one thing. Whatever happens to us, I'll do all I can to stop the Institute copping the flak. I owe you that much, and you have my word on it.'

There was no response.

When Spud had gone, Mike stood motionless for quite some time, his cold fury ebbing to be replaced by a terrible, terrible doubt.

Was it possible there was some truth in what Spud had

said? Certainly, he'd never once asked for accountability;
he'd left the entire financial administration in their hands.
He was ignorant when it came to economics. He'd told
them that right from the start. He was the academic, they
were the experts. But had it been ignorance? Or had he
deliberately blinded himself to the fact that the Institute
had been funded by corrupt money?

He walked down the rear steps that led to the beach and
stared out across Cockburn Sound. He looked at *Carina*
where she sat in her berth at the jetty, and he looked back
at the Institute, where it sloped impressively down to the
shore. Doubt slowly became a reality as their words
stabbed dagger-like in his brain.

All ends justify the means, don't they . . .

Could that have been his own deep-seated reasoning? If
so, then for all of his high moral principles, he was no
better than they were.

You've been as crooked as us and you know it . . .

He had been, surely. Blinding himself to the truth had
made him a part of it.

You've been living a lie for years . . .

The realisation horrified him. It was true, he thought.
He was to blame. He'd placed Spud and Pembo in a
position of trust because it had been to his advantage.

Then Pembo's words, screamed in hysteria as they had
been, hit home with a devastating vengeance.

*Where will your good fucking name be when the world
finds out about Mayjay? Your whole life's been one
fucking lie from the start . . . You're a fraud, mate! You're
a fucking fraud!*

Pembo was right. He'd been living a lie ever since that
fatal night. He'd been a fraud from the moment he'd failed
to report Mayjay's death. Oh, he remembered the tremen-
dous guilt he'd suffered at the time, seeing it as an act of
cowardice, but even that had been a lie. Cowardice was a
common human trait, contemptible perhaps, but under-

standable, forgivable. His crime had been far greater. His actions had been governed by self-interest and ambition. Nothing must threaten his career. And nothing had, had it? Mike McAllister, saviour of the environment! He'd been dining out on his reputation for years, accepting the accolades, living his life as a man of dedication and un-impeachable character. And now he was about to be exposed. The whole world would know him for the fraud he was.

Mike left the beach and returned to the laboratory, where he worked through the rest of the day in an agony of self-recrimination.

That evening, at home over dinner, he tried to appear as if nothing out of the ordinary had happened. He joined in Allie's excited conversation about the expedition planned for the following month. They were to take *Carina* north, a job for the Papua New Guinea government, and for the first time Allie was to be a member of the team. As she chatted away, animated, eyes sparkling with anticipation, he tried to match her enthusiasm, but all the while his mind was plagued by questions.

How will she feel when she discovers her father's a coward? How will she feel when she finds out that the man she's perceived as a hero her entire life is a fraud and a liar? How will she feel when I go to jail? What look will I see in her eyes then?

Allie, in her excitement, didn't notice her father's dis-traction. But Jo did. Something was bothering him, she thought. She wondered what it could be, but said nothing. He would tell her in his own good time.

Later that night, as they prepared for bed, Mike still seemed preoccupied, but she didn't question him, waiting instead for him to confide in her, as he always did. She switched off the bedside lamp and snuggled close, silently encouraging him to talk, sensing in the darkness that he wanted to.

Mike was wondering how on earth he should begin. He knew that he must warn Jo of what lay ahead. But how? What words could possibly prepare her?

'How were things at the hospital today?' he finally asked.

She found the question surprising. She'd been practising full-time at Royal Perth Hospital for over a year now, but they rarely discussed her work. Their conversations always revolved around the Institute, in which she still took a great deal of interest.

'Fine,' she said. 'Busy, as always.'

'You're happy there, aren't you?'

'Yes, I am.' Where was this leading, she wondered.

'I'm glad,' he said. He was. He only hoped that the hospital would prove salve enough when her world collapsed around her.

'Do you regret all the years you lost working for the Institute, Jo?'

'Of course not.' She was puzzled. 'Why would you ask me that? They weren't lost years, why should I regret them? The Institute's been the most worthwhile cause of my life.'

'But it was my cause, wasn't it? Selfish of me to insist it become yours.'

Jo leaned over and turned the bedside lamp on.

'Do you want to tell me what's bothering you?' she asked, rolling on her side to face him.

Now was the time, he thought.

'Spud and Pembo came to see me today. They're being called up before the Royal Commission. They're to give evidence in two weeks.'

So that was it. He was worried for his friends.

'Well, we always thought Spud would be called up, didn't we? He and Brian Burke were very pally, remember?'

'Yes. Yes, they were.' Of course they were, he thought, and to his own personal advantage, but how could he tell her that?

She could see he was troubled. But he shouldn't be.

'Mike,' she said, sitting up, cross-legged and business-like, prepared as always to get straight to the heart of the matter. 'You have to be practical about this. I know the three of you have been best friends all your lives, but if Spud and Pembo have dealings to answer for, then that's their concern. You mustn't worry yourself.'

He'd always admired her honesty and her directness. Just as she'd always admired his – that was what made it so impossibly difficult.

'But I do worry. I worry that their involvement with the Institute might reflect badly upon us.' He fumbled his way awkwardly towards the truth, trying to break the news as gently as possible. 'I worry that some link may be made between their dealings and the Institute. Our reputation could suffer . . .'

'Oh, for goodness' sake,' she laughed, 'the Institute's reputation's beyond reproach. And what possible detrimental link could there be? If anything, Spud's and Pembo's involvement with the Institute will stand them in good stead. I presume you'll offer yourself as a character witness?'

'I already have.'

'There you are then. You've done everything you can.' She flopped back on the bed. 'If they've been up to no good then they'll just have to face the music, won't they?'

'Yes, I suppose they will.'

He couldn't tell her. He knew what he should have said. *I have my own music to face, Jo.* But the words simply wouldn't come out.

'I suppose they'll have to.' He kissed her. 'You're right.'

'Of course I am. Now stop worrying.' She leaned over and switched off the bedside lamp. 'Good night, my darling.'

'Night.'

He turned away, quickly feigning sleep, but for hours he stared into the darkness. He'd made a mockery of her life, he thought. She'd devoted herself to the Institute. She'd given up her career for his personal dream, and now her name, along with his, would be dragged through the mud. A woman of honour like Jo! Mike was consumed by a fresh agony of guilt.

The following morning was a Saturday and he took himself down to North Cottesloe for a swim. He didn't take his surfboard for fear Allie would want to join him; they often surfed together.

'Just going for a dip,' he said, 'lot of paperwork to do when I get home,' and he left very quickly. He needed to be on his own.

The beach was already crowded, the day promising to be a scorcher typical of late January.

He swam beyond the breakers, strong, even strokes, further and further out into the open sea, wishing he could just swim and swim and finally disappear. But he couldn't do that. There was nowhere to hide, and what would be the point anyway? Even the drastic measure of suicide wasn't an option. It would only mean further implication. Disappearance or death – both would be seen as a sure sign of guilt. He had his own music to face, and face it he must, whether he wanted to or not.

In a strange way, Mike *did* want to answer for his actions. He would have found a form of relief in unburdening himself about the death of Mayjay, as he should have done all those years ago. And he would somehow have liked to have acknowledged his deliberate ignorance of the Institute's source of funding. To publicly purge himself of his guilt would at least be the action of an honest man. But the disastrous effect his admissions would have upon the Institute, and even more importantly upon his wife and his daughter, remained a torment.

He heard the siren and came to a halt, treading water as he looked back towards the beach. In the distance he could see people scrambling from the surf, desperate in their bid to reach the shore, and he could hear the screams of panic-stricken women calling to their children – a common occurrence on a hot weekend when the shark alarm sounded.

Only a minute or so later, he saw the shark, its fin cleaving the water barely ten metres from him, quite large for a grey nurse, but harmless. He smiled ironically as the thought crossed his mind. If it had been a hungry white pointer that chose to mistake him for a seal, then all his problems would have been solved. An accidental death would have been perfect.

Then he saw one of the surf club's rubber duckies roaring in his direction. It slowed down to idle alongside him.

'Get aboard,' one of the two young crewmen urged, leaning forward to help drag him over the side. 'Get aboard.'

'It's a grey nurse,' Mike said, avoiding the helping hand, 'harmless, don't worry. Thanks, fellas, but I'll find my own way ashore.'

'Get aboard, please, sir.' The young man's voice was now officious and his hand was still firmly on offer.

'Right you are.' Mike accepted the hand, the kid was only doing his job. He allowed himself to be hauled aboard.

'You should have made for shore. Didn't you hear the shark alarm?'

'Yes, I did,' Mike said as the rubber ducky headed for the beach at speed.

'You shouldn't have been this far out anyway.'

Young Sean Brougham was cursing himself. He'd been on watch and he hadn't noticed the swimmer well beyond the breakers; he'd been keeping his eye on the tourists in the shallows. There was a bit of a rip and he'd presumed they'd be the ones in trouble. Christ, when the spotters had seen the shark and the alarm had sounded . . .

'Sorry.' Mike could tell the kid was a bit shaken.

'Okay,' Sean said, 'all's well that ends well.' He was still playing his role, still a little officious, but he appreciated the bloke's apology, it had sounded genuine. Then he suddenly realised who the bloke was. 'Hey, you're Mike McAllister, aren't you?'

'Yes.'

'Well, how's about that?' He grinned. 'How do you do, sir, I'm Sean Brougham.' He offered his hand and they shook, but they didn't talk any further, grasping firmly to the rubber ducky's rope handles as it caught the breakers and surfed its way ashore.

All three clambered out and Mike shook hands with the other surf club crewman. 'Thanks, boys,' he said, as if they'd saved his life. He felt it his duty to do so. 'Sorry to be a trouble. You do a great job, keep up the good work.' And he started to walk away.

But Sean wasn't about to leave his side. 'I know who you are,' he said, following, 'you're pretty famous and all that . . .' The officiousness had gone, he was just an eager kid. 'But you actually know my mum. She went to uni with you.'

'Yeah? Who's your mum?'

'Natalie Brougham. She was Natalie Hollingsworth then. She still talks about you whenever you're in the papers. Says you're an inspiration.'

Natalie Hollingsworth, Mike thought, one of his first girlfriends, how could he forget? Natalie with all her causes – heritage buildings, the Vietnam War, women's rights. He'd always admired Natalie's passion. He wondered why he hadn't seen her around. Everyone knew everyone in Perth, even these days.

'Good to meet you, Sean,' he said, shaking the young man's hand again. 'How *is* your mum? I haven't seen her in years.'

'We've been living in Albany – Dad was a teacher there.

He died a year ago. Things were pretty tough on her then.'

The kid dug his heel into the sand. Things were obviously pretty tough on him too, Mike thought. He couldn't have been more than eighteen.

'But she's got on with her life.' Sean smiled. 'She works with Greenpeace now, that's why you're one of her heroes.'

'I'm sorry to hear about your father.'

'Yeah. Heart attack. Right out of the blue. He was only forty-six, came as a bit of a shock.' Sean concentrated on his heel and the sand for a second or so; he still wasn't over his father's death. 'Anyway,' he said looking up, 'Mum's okay, and that's the main thing.'

'Give her my best, won't you.' Mike needed to get away. 'She's a fine woman, your mother.'

'Yes, I will, sir.'

'Mike'll do.'

'Yeah, thanks.'

The kid stood there waving as Mike walked off down the beach to where he'd left his towel on the sand.

'See you, Mike,' he called.

But Mike didn't turn and wave back. He was too lost in thought.

Forty-six. The kid's father had been a whole three years younger than he was. A heart attack right out of the blue. That was the answer, he thought. He didn't need to be mistaken for a seal by a hungry white pointer; he had a heart attack at his beck and call.

A congenital heart weakness, that's what the doctor had told him when he'd had his attack at the Abrolhos all those years ago. If he'd been older and less fit he might not have survived, the doctor had said. Well, he was certainly older, and presumably less fit, although he felt as strong as ever. He'd had not one twinge of a warning in all this time. In fact, he'd virtually forgotten that he *had* a weakness. He'd even ignored medical advice – he'd been diving for years. But then he'd never pushed himself to the absolute limit, had he? Not as he had at the Abrolhos.

Mike picked up his towel and dried himself off. Then he sat on the sand, oblivious to the midsummer frolic all about him, the shrieks of children, the bat of a nearby tennis ball.

He felt no fear as he thought of his death; his mind was too preoccupied with the consequences that would follow it. What exactly would happen if he were no longer a part of the equation? Pembo certainly wouldn't bring up the subject of Mayjay – there would be no purpose. And if he were tragically struck dead by a heart attack, Spud and Pembo wouldn't dare try to implicate him in any investigation of the Institute's funding. It would appear an attempt to besmirch his good name in a desperate bid to save themselves.

Then his ego presented him with a further thought. Would there be any investigation at all? He was Mike McAllister, founder of the McAllister Institute, world-renowned for its scientific and environmental research. His death would be widely mourned, and most particularly by Western Australians. They would perceive the Institute as his personal monument, and Western Australians didn't like their monuments tarnished. No, he thought, there would be no investigation. No-one would dare. Through his death, the good name of the McAllister Research Institute would not only survive, it would thrive and prosper.

With a start, Mike was jolted back to reality. In his analytical state, he'd forgotten he was sitting on the beach. The shrieks of the children and the bat of the tennis ball were all too vivid now. He looked about him at the carefree clamour of Cottesloe on a blistering Saturday morning, just as it was every summer, just as it would be every summer to come. Every summer that he wouldn't see, Mike thought, suddenly overwhelmed by the magnitude of his decision.

He felt the heat of the sun on his back and the tingle of salt on his skin, and a mortal fear pervaded him. Did he really have the courage to end it all? Was he prepared to no longer exist? To become nothingness? For he didn't believe in life after death. His life had been devoted to science; there'd been no place for a welcoming God.

He tried to comfort himself in the only way he knew how. He would live on through the Institute, he told himself. The Institute was a testament to the value of his life. His own father had said as much. And he would live on in the memories of his wife and daughter. The blameless memories, he reminded himself, the memories that must be preserved at all cost.

His reasoning made sense and strengthened his resolve. But it didn't eradicate the fear. Nothing could do that.

Decision made, Mike stood. Time for one last surf.

He dolphin-dived through the shallow breakers, making for the deeper waves beyond, and for the next half-hour his mind was blissfully blank as his body became one with the surf.

But afterwards, jogging up the beach on his way to the car, he was once again busily making plans. No time for the revisitation of his fear, he told himself, things had to be arranged with care. There was no room for error.

Mike drove directly to the Institute where he knew young Greg Saunders and several members of the team were working on *Carina* in preparation for next month's expedition.

'Ahoy there,' he called from the jetty to where he could see Greg up on the ship's foredeck.

'Mike.' Greg turned and gave him a wave. 'Come to join us workers, have you?'

'I'll swap you for the paperwork any day.' Mike grinned. 'Do you fancy a trip to Rotto tomorrow?' The two of them often took the cat out for a spot of fishing on a Sunday.

'Do I ever,' Greg called back.

'Right you are. Fill her up for me this afternoon, and we'll take off around eight.'

'You're on.'

They exchanged another wave and Mike walked back along the jetty.

All was now set in motion. Greg would be a witness to his death. There must be no element of doubt. He must be seen to have died of natural causes and under the most normal of circumstances.

Mike returned home. He showered and then shut himself away in his study immersed in his paperwork, trying as hard as he could to distract himself, but meeting with little success. There was time to think now.

The fear returned, and along with the fear came thoughts of his wife and daughter, and the realisation that he hadn't really dwelt upon the emotional impact his death would have on Jo and Allie. He'd been too busy trying to protect them from the ignominy of the truth. How typical of him not to have viewed his actions from their perspective – they'd be emotionally devastated.

He remembered how he'd considered his father selfish in excluding his wife from the final months of his life. 'Death is a personal thing,' Jim McAllister had said. But death wasn't a personal thing at all, Mike thought. Not when a man deliberately deprived a woman of a husband and a child of a father. His was surely the most selfish of all acts. But then, grief had a way of healing itself, didn't it? Dishonour did not. He steeled himself.

He was glad that Allie was off to a party that evening; keeping up normal appearances was proving difficult. Then Jo asked if he'd like to go out to dinner – the two of them often did on a Saturday evening.

'What about a quiet night at home,' he said. 'We could go decadent, what do you say?'

'Perfect,' she smiled.

Curled up together on the sofa, they ate pizzas and mindlessly watched television. Mike registered nothing at all on the screen; as he felt Jo's body beside him, he drank in the nearness of her.

Later, they made love. The last time, he thought, the very last time. It was impossible to conceive that he would never make love to her again.

Afterwards, as they lay in each other's arms, he thought how very unfair he was being to her. But then, when had he ever been fair to Jo? He'd been so consumed by the importance of his own life that he'd ignored hers. But he had loved her. He'd loved her as much as it was within his capability to love.

'I love you, Jo,' he whispered.

She hadn't heard him say it in years and the words rather surprised her. The sentiment, however, did not.

'I know,' she whispered in return. She'd always known.

Over breakfast the following morning, Mike looked at the two women most precious in his life and wished he could tell them how much they meant to him. He would have liked to take his daughter in his arms and tell her how proud he was of her, and that he was sorry for what he was about to do and the unhappiness it would cause her. But everything must appear normal.

'You could have asked me along,' Allie said with a mock show of petulance.

'It's a blokes' fishing trip, and you'd only be a distraction to Greg.'

She pulled a face.

'Will you forgive me if I come home with some crays?'

'Yes,' she said. 'Six crays and you're forgiven.'

'Six. Right. It's a promise.'

He kissed Jo on the cheek and gave Allie a wave as he crossed to the door.

'See you,' he said.

*

Aboard the cat on their way to Rottnest, he kept up a similar semblance of normalcy. Greg must suspect nothing out of the ordinary.

They talked about the forthcoming trip to New Guinea. Greg was as excited as Allie. This was the first time he, too, would be accompanying the team on one of their international expeditions. Mike found his enthusiasm engaging. Greg was a fine young man, just right for Allie, he thought. They had so much to share and he loved her a great deal. Perhaps, now that Allie had gained her doctorate, she might take time out to register the fact. But if she did, he wouldn't be there to see it, would he?

'Take over the helm will you, Greg. I'll start rigging the lines.' He needed to distract himself.

Ten minutes later, he saw Carnac Island up ahead, tiny, a colony of seals dozing on the beach of its white sandy cove. Carnac was a keen source of interest to the Institute these days. An important part of the marine coastal environment, it was a valuable habitat for Australian sea lions, one of the world's rarest seal species.

But Mike wasn't thinking of the Institute and its studies as they neared the island. He was recalling how he and Jools had swum with the seals as children. Carnac had been a regular stopping-off point on the family trips to Rottnest. He remembered those special days when the seals had been playful. Each time he and Jools had ducked and dived and somersaulted in the water, the seals had done the same. Jools used to get hysterical with laughter.

He concentrated on rigging the lines.

The crossing was gentle, the swell mild, *Alana* up on the plane breasting the waves with ease, and soon Rottnest Island loomed before them.

'Head for North Point,' Mike said. 'We'll drift for snapper and dhuey.'

When they reached the deep reefs off North Point, they

cut the engines, leaving the boat to slowly drift at the mercy of the wind and the tide.

They fished with handlines, and before long they'd hauled in several snapper and two excellent-sized dhufish. They noted the spots along the reef where the catch had been most plentiful.

Mike started up the engine and circled the boat to do another drift.

'Let's head back to where we picked up the dhueys,' he said.

They didn't drift into the spot as they would normally have done, Mike headed directly for it instead.

'Do you mind if we drop anchor? I want to go over the side and pick up some crays. I promised Allie I would.'

'Sure,' Greg grinned. 'Gives me more time to up the score.'

They always competed, especially for dhufish. Whoever hauled in more dhueys won the day.

When they'd dropped anchor, Mike stripped down to his bathers and fastened the mesh dive bag around his waist. He pulled on his flippers and took the rock lobster snare loop from the open storage locker in the cockpit. Then, mask and snorkel in hand, he slipped over the side. He trod water while he rinsed the mask.

'Good luck,' Greg said. He already had his line in the water.

'Yeah, won't be long.'

Mike donned the mask, inhaled and dived. He swam for the reef below, pressurising as he went, deeper and deeper into the overwhelming silence.

The visibility was perfect, the water crystal clear, and as he reached the reef, he was aware of the colour and activity that surrounded him. But he didn't lose himself in the wonder of it all as he normally did. He remained focused, he had to get this right.

He was around ten metres down, he thought, that should do it, and he locked himself into the side of the reef.

Wedging each end of the snare loop's stainless-steel handle into the rocks, he positioned himself there like a sentinel. Then he waited, counting the seconds until his lungs would need air, monitoring his heart rate as he did so.

He was oblivious to all but the needs of his body as the seconds ticked by. Then more and more seconds. Now was the time he would normally go up, he thought. He'd go slowly and steadily, depressurising on the way. But he didn't go up. He held on, his pulse quickening, his brain sounding an alarm which he ignored. Not yet, he told himself, not yet. A further warning was followed by a sense of panic. Go up! Go up, his brain said, but he fought against the impulse to swim for the surface. He needed to be absolutely sure he had pushed himself beyond his body's limits.

Alarm bells were now ringing, his heart was pounding. Yes, he thought, it was time. Any longer and he might risk the possibility of drowning, and he mustn't drown. Drowning could be seen as a purposeful act. People would query why Mike McAllister, so experienced a diver, had drowned.

He pushed away from the reef, swimming with all his strength for the silvery, dappled light above.

It happened when he wasn't far from the surface. The pain was crippling and he doubled over, clutching at his chest, unable to use his arms further. He resisted the involuntary impulse to scream, keeping his mouth clamped shut, kicking his legs, feebly now, but his powerful diver's flippers moved him ever upwards as the fierce iron fist closed around his heart. The pain was unbearable and the light above unattainable as he craned his neck to look up.

Just a few seconds more, he thought. He couldn't give in. He was close, so close . . .

Then he broke through to the light and felt the sun on his face. A strangled cry escaped him as he opened his mouth for air. But there was no air to be had. No air, no sun, no light, just blackness. Oblivion.

His body bobbed like a cork on the ocean's vast surface.

EPILOGUE

Johanna McAllister had decided that her husband's funeral should be open to the public. The decision was a brave and generous one – it would mean the accompanying intrusion of the media, and she would far rather have had a small private service with family and friends. A private person herself, Jo had no wish to parade her grief, but she knew there would be many who would wish to pay their respects.

Mike's mother and sister were in agreement. A public service was only fitting for a man in Mike's position, particularly given the overwhelming reaction to his death, although Maggie and Jools, too, would have preferred a small affair.

Mike's daughter had no qualms at all about a public service. Allie considered it not only fitting, but mandatory. If she'd had her way, her father would have been given a state funeral.

The reaction to Mike McAllister's death had indeed been extraordinary. He and his work had been internationally recognised for well over a decade, and media around the globe were quick to pick up on the news that was headlines throughout Australia. Dr Mike McAllister, eminent scientist, environmentalist and founder of the renowned McAllister Research Institute in Western Australia, had died unexpectedly of a heart attack. He'd been only forty-nine. Condolences poured in from all parts of the world.

Jo was moved by the tributes, but dreaded the ceremony. She'd shared her emotions with no-one but Allie, even then maintaining a show of strength, feeling that she must for her daughter's sake.

Allie herself had wept for days, a raw outpouring of grief that Jo had found healthy. She'd rather wished she could have done the same, but she'd kept her own tears for the nights when the bed had seemed such a desolate place. Allie had quickly developed her own form of strength, however. 'At least he died the way he would have wanted,' she'd said with a sort of proud defiance. Jo couldn't refute that, and she was glad her daughter found some comfort in the thought. But it didn't take away the emptiness, did it?

Mike's personal secretary, the ever-capable Bev, took over the funeral arrangements. The service was to be delayed a week longer than the family would have pre-ferred, but Bev maintained it necessary to allow those coming from overseas to make flight arrangements, which they agreed was practical.

Then Bev's instructions were issued. They were abun-dantly clear to all, particularly the media:

Press are welcome on the understanding that the privacy of the McAllister family be respected, and that no photo-graphs be taken inside the church.

Television cameras are to remain outside the church's boundaries.

There are to be no flowers delivered to the church or to the bereaved, but in lieu of floral arrangements donations to the World Wildlife Fund will be gratefully accepted. Following the service, transport will be provided for those

who wish to attend the gathering which will be held at
the McAllister Research Institute.

All are welcome, but members of the press are to respect
the fact that the gathering is a private affair. Unless they
have any connection with the family, they are not invited
to attend.

Bev was highly efficient and she was running the event like
a military exercise, for which Jo was eternally grateful.

The day arrived, and the members of the press were
apparently mindful of their instructions. Photographers'
cameras clicked and whirred from a discreet distance, and
journalists made no approaches, biding their time for
perhaps a brief statement from one or two of the mourners
following the funeral service.

Television media, too, maintained a certain sense of
decorum, cameras having been set up in the street well
away from the church's courtyard. But their zoom lenses
homed in on each car as it arrived and each new high-
profile figure who alighted, and the running commentary
from one particular female reporter, although hushed, was
audible to those standing nearby.

Then came the moment of the family's arrival. The black
stretch limousine pulled up, the chauffeur alighted to open
its doors, and the reporter's voice took on a new reverence.

'The crowd gathered is silent as the McAllister family
arrives,' she said. 'Johanna McAllister and her daughter,
Alana, and, with them, stepping out of the car now, is
Dr McAllister's mother and his sister, Julie, accompanied
by her husband.'

Sally Jordan looked down the street to check that the
camera was following the family as the crowd parted to
create a path for them. The soundman standing beside
the camera gave Sally the thumbs up.

'As they make their way towards the church, we wish
them our deepest sympathy in their hour of grief,' she said.

Sally was aware that some present considered she was overstepping the mark. The nearby ABC reporter was making dutiful notes and, when his segment went to air that night during the news, he would read his commentary over the footage his cameraman was currently filming. But Sally was hosting her own current affairs show these days – on commercial television what's more. She'd been welcomed back by a network only too happy to overlook her age in preference for her maverick approach, and Sally was determined to record everything live. It added impact.

The cameraman was giving her the signal that he'd zoomed in on her. He'd lost sight of the family, now swallowed up by the crowd, which had closed ranks as they passed.

'We're here to pay our respects to a great Western Australian . . .'

She ignored the critical glances of those close by and continued her report, filling in time until the next car and the next VIPs arrived. She'd edit it all together later.

Jo was amazed by the numbers of mourners gathered outside the church as she walked towards the entrance, which seemed so very far away. She tried not to catch the sympathy in people's eyes, but amongst the strangers she glimpsed faces she knew. Some she'd met in faraway places, in Frankfurt and Florida and London and Wales – and yet she'd accompanied Mike on relatively few of his trips. There must be many others from all over the world, from places she'd never seen. Mike would have liked that, she thought. He wouldn't have cared at all about the presence of the Prime Minister and the other high-ranking politicians and celebrities, but he would have welcomed such a turnout of his colleagues.

There was standing room only in the church as more and more people filed in, and by the time the service started the place was packed and already stiflingly hot.

The next hour for Jo was interminable. The priest seemed to drone on and on about things Mike would have hated, and she wondered if she'd made the right decision in allowing such pomp and ceremony. Forgive me, my darling, she thought. Her mind switched off for a lot of the proceedings; she could think of nothing but Mike. There were many tributes paid by his colleagues and by longstanding friends, and she thought vaguely that, yes, he would have liked them. The final eulogy was delivered by Allie.

'My father was, and always will be, my hero,' Allie pronounced loudly and clearly from the pulpit. 'He led the way for others to follow. He was a pioneer before the importance of environmental preservation was even considered. I'm proud to have had a father like that . . .' Her voice quavered a little, but she recovered herself and continued in much the same vein.

Oh yes, Jo thought. Oh yes, Mike, you would have liked this. You would have liked this so very, very much, my darling.

For the first time, tears threatened and she stared up at the ceiling, blinking rapidly, willing them away, and as the service came to an end she remained resolutely dry-eyed.

It was a relief to escape the stifling confines of the church, even into the burning breezeless heat of the courtyard. Jo stood with the family, accepting the condolences offered with gracious dignity, but her responses were standard, mechanical. 'Thank you so much for coming . . . Yes, it was a lovely service . . .' She was hardly aware of what she was saying or to whom. She couldn't wait to get away from the church and the awful finality it represented.

'Time to head off, I think.'

Bev to the rescue. Thank God for Bev, she thought.

The family climbed into the black limousine and the car headed off, shortly to be followed by a long procession of vehicles all bound for the Institute.

Sally Jordan found herself a seat in one of the luxury coaches provided. She was aware that she was the only member of the media to flaunt the rules, but then the rules didn't really apply to her, did they? It was true she didn't have a connection with the family, but she'd known Mike McAllister and that was qualification enough. Pity she couldn't film the proceedings, she thought, but she'd be able to deliver a personal report on air, and she might get a few good quotes.

The welcoming arrival of the Fremantle Doctor made conditions at the Institute comfortable, the fresh sea breeze off the water easing the oppressive mid-afternoon heat.

After a sombre beginning, the general atmosphere relaxed and the gathering started to become the party Bev had planned. She'd laid in ample supplies of beer and champagne and finger food, and soon guests were mingling and chatting and rekindling old friendships, the talk principally about Mike and his work. Many of the international visitors were keen to be shown over the Institute, and Bev, in full sergeant major mode, elected Greg the official tour guide leader.

The old gang had gathered in the main entrance foyer away from the crowd in order to pay their own special tribute – Muzza and Olga, Spud and Cora, and Pembo conspicuously minus Arlene.

'To Mike,' Spud said, raising his stubby of beer.

The others did the same. 'To Mike,' they said, and together they saluted the portrait.

Muzza had refused the offer he'd received from the National Portrait Gallery in London, who'd wanted the work as a companion piece to his earlier portrait. Instead, he'd donated the painting to the Institute, where it dominated the foyer in truly spectacular fashion.

Yes, he thought, as they all drank to Mike's portrait, this was certainly where it belonged. He was proud of the piece. He'd captured all of the commitment, all of the integrity, and something else besides. A touch of the steely hardness he'd sometimes seen in Mike's eyes, resolute and unwavering in purpose. Jo herself had commented on the fact. 'You've caught an element of Mike most people don't see, Muz,' she'd said admiringly. 'He can be a hard man.'

Strange, Muz thought, how Mike had inspired his two finest works. But then perhaps not. Mike McAllister had been an inspiration to many.

I'll miss you, Mikey, Spud was thinking. And I'm sorry, mate. I'm really sorry about everything.

Spud wasn't sorry for his actions. He'd done what he'd done and he'd been prepared to pay the price. Guilt wasn't a consideration. But he was extremely sorry that he'd had to involve Mike. If he could have taken the rap on his own he would certainly have done so, but Mike had been so inextricably tied up with the whole business there'd been no other way out. Bloody shame about that, he thought. He hated the fact that they'd parted with bad feelings, or rather that Mike had. He wished he could somehow have made things up between them. But he couldn't now, could he? The poor bastard was dead. What a bugger of a thing to have happened.

Pembo's thoughts were altogether different. As he looked at the portrait, he was riddled with guilt. Not for what he'd done, but for who he was. It seemed the eyes of the portrait were staring at him in personal accusation, and he felt compelled to look away, aware that, beside him, Spud knew why.

Ian Pemberton had been as shocked as any by Mike's death. But he'd been unable to disguise the relief that had swiftly followed with the sure knowledge that, given the tragic death of its founder, the Institute's funding would no longer be questioned.

'The Institute won't come under investigation now, will it? We'll be off the hook, won't we?' They were the first words he'd uttered to Spud upon hearing the news.

The question hadn't, as yet, occurred to Spud. It would have eventually, but there'd have been no joy in it. Christ, he'd rather have served three times the sentence and had Mikey alive. Spud had looked at Ian as if he were some sort of insect that had crawled out from under the nearest rock, which was exactly the way Spud saw him.

'You're just a worm, aren't you, Pembo,' he'd said.

Ian had felt every bit as insignificant and worthless as Spud had intended him to. He still did. He couldn't help himself. The awful truth was that he was still relieved, and the eyes of the portrait seemed to know that. Ian Pemberton's burden in life was the knowledge that he was a coward, and that he always would be.

'Dry argument,' Muzza said, breaking the mood. Everyone was being altogether too quiet, the women respecting the men's silence, and he hoped the portrait wasn't making them all maudlin. It certainly wasn't meant to. He drained his stubby.

'I'll go,' Olga said. 'It's a bit crowded inside.'

'I will help you,' Cora offered and, taking the empty beer bottles from the men, the two women disappeared.

'So it all starts next week, eh?' Muzza said. Spud had told him about their imminent appearance before the Royal Commission, even admitting quite openly that they were likely to end up facing criminal charges as a result of the findings. 'Are you nervous?'

'Nah.' Spud shrugged. 'What will be, will be. Pembo's shitting himself, of course.'

Ian squirmed, wishing Spud would stop putting him down at every opportunity. Muzza pretended not to notice.

'What do you think the final outcome will be?'

'My guess is we might cop a two-year sentence.' Spud's contemptuous glance at Ian said, *Aren't we lucky? Probably would have been six if our best mate hadn't carked it.* 'Could be out in nine months.'

Spud was quite prepared for jail. He'd decided that he

might write a book while he was inside. He'd thought of
taking up painting, but Muzza was too hard an act to
follow. Anyway, he'd keep himself busy, and then when he
was out he'd rise like a phoenix from the ashes.

'Shouldn't be too difficult,' he said. 'What do *you*
reckon, Pembo?' His voice was mocking; he knew Pembo
was terrified. Jail would probably kill Pembo.

'Speak for yourself,' Ian spat back. He was heartily sick
of the digs at his expense. He pulled himself together and
ignored Spud as he turned to Muzza, trying to muster up
some semblance of bravado. 'Arlene's kicked me out,' he
explained, 'doesn't want a bar of what's in store. But
Gordy's sticking by me, which I think says something.'

Ian had moved back to the Sheraton. The strained
relationship between him and Spud had made life intolerable, and his son's support was all that was keeping him
together.

'He's refused to side with his mother,' Ian said with
pride. 'We have a special relationship, Gordy and I.'

Young Gordy Pemberton had certainly rebelled. He'd
even shifted from the Peppermint Grove house into a poky
flat in Crawley with several other students from his
economics course at uni. If his dad was going to jail, then
he'd stick by him, Gordy had announced to his mother's
dismay.

'Yeah,' Spud interjected, 'your *kid*'s got guts, I'll admit
that much.'

He wondered how long it would be before young Gordy
woke up to the fact that his father was the spineless
wonder of the world.

What was going on, Muzza wondered. He felt sorry for
Pembo – he could tell he was frightened, and Spud was
certainly getting the boot in. He wondered why.

'You'll cope, Pembo.' He smiled comfortingly as he
tapped the arm of his wheelchair. 'You can cope with just
about anything if you put your mind to it,' he said.

Pembo gave a wan smile in return, grateful for the show of support, but he knew he wasn't made of that stuff.

Sally Jordan was accompanying a group of international visitors on one of Greg's tours, keeping well in the background, making surreptitious notes as he showed them around the aquaria and laboratories. Some of the visiting scientists were making notes too, so she didn't look out of place.

Sally had been keeping a low profile throughout the afternoon, avoiding locals who might recognise her from television, but she'd copped the odd glance and was expecting at any moment that she'd be asked to leave. Her gatecrashing exercise had proved most successful, however. She'd chatted to quite a few of Mike's overseas colleagues who'd come up with some very useful quotes, which, later in a secluded spot, she'd scribbled verbatim in her notepad. And now she'd had the full guided tour, all of which was most useful, she thought.

As the group returned upstairs, she quickly slipped her notepad into her jacket pocket and decided that now was perhaps the right time to beat a retreat. Cars were on regular standby for those guests who might wish to return to the city.

Then she saw the lone figure standing on the balcony looking out to sea, and she wondered if she dared.

What the hell, of course she did, she couldn't resist. They could only kick her out, and she already had what she'd come for.

She stepped outside, quietly closing the door behind her.

'Dr McAllister,' she said, 'I do hope you don't mind my intruding, but I wondered whether I might have a quick word with you.'

Jo had been sitting on the bench at the foreshore for some time, barefooted, her arms wrapped around her knees. The sea breeze, now fresh and vigorous, whipped at her hair and dress, and somehow also through her brain, seeming to clear away the cloud of depression that had enveloped her.

She'd felt more at ease the moment she'd arrived at the Institute. She'd had no difficulty at all conversing with people as she had at the church. Even Andy was there, which had rather surprised her.

'I wanted to pay my respects at the church, but you seemed a bit surrounded, so I . . .' he'd begun awkwardly.

'Thank you for coming, Andy.'

She'd realised that the words no longer sounded empty and mechanical. She was glad to see him. He'd quickly disappeared into the throng and she'd realised that she was glad to see all the others too. She'd actually enjoyed chatting about Mike to old friends and accepting tributes from so many of his colleagues. It was as if Mike himself had been present. But she'd eventually felt the need to be on her own.

Now, here, gazing about at the Institute and the marina, she felt that Mike was all around her. And he was, she thought. This was where he would always live on. The thought was comforting. It lent her strength. Strength enough even to think of her own future.

She stood, resolved. Not happy – that would take some time, she knew – but she would be able to get on with her life. And Mike would always be with her. He'd be with her in the Pilbara. Because that's where she would go, she'd decided. She would stay in Perth for as long as Allie needed her, and then she would go back to the Pilbara and her work at the clinic. It was where she'd been happiest, where she was needed. She hoped Allie would understand.

As she neared the rear stairs to the balcony, she saw Allie directly above, alone, staring out to sea, others obviously respecting her privacy. A figure joined her, a woman.

Jo didn't know the woman, but she looked vaguely familiar. Then she realised that she'd seen the face on television.

She made for the back stairs; Allie needed rescuing.

'You're a reporter, aren't you?' Allie recognised the woman, a current affairs journalist, she'd seen her on air.

'Yes,' Sally admitted. 'But I did know your father,' she added hastily. 'I was the first to report on the Dampier oil spill in '75. He was a fine man, a very fine man.'

'Yes, he was.'

Sally had intended to start out by offering her condolences, but the young woman's startling blue eyes were shrewdly sizing her up, and she realised that the bullshit approach wouldn't work. Wiser to get straight to the point, she decided.

'As I said, Dr McAllister, I don't wish to be intrusive, but I wondered whether you might like to make some comment.'

'About my father, you mean?'

Sally nodded. 'And perhaps your own plans? Just a brief statement I can quote on air?'

She was probably pushing the envelope now, she thought, and she waited to be told to leave.

'Don't you have a notebook or something? Shouldn't you write it down?'

Sally dived a speedy hand into her jacket pocket.

'My father founded this Institute. This Institute is the measure of his life's work, and I intend to continue that work . . .'

Allie waited calmly, allowing the journalist time to scribble down her words, neither of them noticing the motionless figure at the top of the stairs.

Jo's breath caught in her throat as she watched her daughter. The look in Allie's eyes was exactly that which Muzza had captured in Mike's portrait, even down to the touch of steely hardness. She was watching Mike himself, she thought.

Allie gazed out at the dichotomy of Cockburn Sound, at the beauty of its waters, the sweep of its bay, and the smoke belching from the heavy industry on its shores to the south.

'I intend to devote my life to the McAllister Research Institute and everything it stands for, just as my father did.'

As she turned back to the journalist, whose head was still buried in her notebook, Allie caught sight of her mother, and her face broke into a cheeky grin. She gave Jo a wink, but the tone of her voice retained its edge.

'Did you get that word for word?' she asked.

'I most certainly did, Dr McAllister.' Sally looked up, about to say thank you, but she wasn't allowed the chance.

'Good,' Allie said briskly. 'I wouldn't like to be mis-quoted.'

Realising she was being dismissed, Sally beat a hasty retreat.

When she'd gone, Jo and Allie shared a smile.

'Did you like the act?' Allie said.

'Very impressive. The new Dr McAllister.'

'Yep. That's me.'

'Wouldn't he be proud.'

'I hope so.'

They hugged, holding each other close, words unnecessary.

Allie didn't need her to stay in Perth, Jo thought. Allie's future was predestined. And Mike would be with them both. He'd be here at the Institute where his work would continue, and he'd be up in the Pilbara, where it had all started.

Judy Nunn
Heritage

In a time when desperate people were seizing with both hands the chance for freedom, refugees from more than seventy nations gathered beneath the Southern Cross to forge a new national identity. They came from all over wartorn Europe to the mountains of Australia to help realise one man's dream: the mighty Snowy Mountains Hydro-Electric Scheme. One of the greatest engineering feats of the 20th century, the Snowy Scheme was being built with pride from the sweat and blood of displaced people.

People of all races and creeds tunnelled through a mountain range to turn the course of a majestic river, trying to put to rest ghosts from the inferno of history: buried memories, unimaginable pain and deadly secrets.

From the ruins of Berlin to the birth of Israel, from the Italian Alps to the Australian high country, *Heritage* is a passionate and fast-paced tale of rebirth, struggle, sacrifice and redemption, and a tribute to those who gave meaning to the Australian spirit.

Judy Nunn
Pacific

After fulfilling her dream of performing on the London stage, Australian actress Samantha Lindsay is thrilled when she scores her first Hollywood movie role. She's to play Sarah Blackston, a character loosely based on World War II heroine Mamma Tack, an English nurse who was invaluable to the US forces and native population of the New Hebrides during the conflict in the Pacific. It's the role of a lifetime.

On location in Vanuatu, uncanny parallels between history and fiction emerge and Sam begins a quest for the truth. Just who was the real Mamma Tack? And what was the tragic secret that threatens to destroy people in the present day? The answers reveal not only secrets of the past but Sam's own destiny.

A masterful interweaving of the lives of two passionate women and two worlds, *Pacific* is Judy Nunn at her enthralling best.

Judy Nunn
Territory

Territory is a story of the Top End and the people who
dare to dwell there. Of a family who carved an empire
from the escarpments of Kakadu to the Indian Ocean and
defied God or Man to take it from them. Of Spitfire pilot
Terence Galloway, who brings his English bride, Henrietta,
home from the Battle of Britain to Bullalalla cattle station,
only to be faced with the desperate defence of Darwin
against the Imperial Japanese Air Force.

It is also a story of their sons, Malcolm and Kit, two
brothers who grow up in the harsh but beautiful environment of the Northern Territory, and share a baptism of fire
as young men in the jungles of war-torn Vietnam.

And what of the Dutch East Indies treasure ship which
foundered off Western Australia in 1629? How does the
Batavia's horrific tale of mutiny and murder touch the lives
of the Galloways and other Territorians – like Foong Lee,
the patriarch of the Darwin Chinese community, and
Jackie Yoorunga, the famous Aboriginal stockman? What
is the connection between the infamous 'ship of death' and
the Aborigines that compels a young anthropologist to
discover the truth?

From the blazing inferno that was Darwin on 19 February
1942 to the devastation of Cyclone Tracy, from the red
desert to the tropical shore, *Territory* is a mile-a-minute
read from one of Australia's best loved writers.

Judy Nunn
Beneath the Southern Cross

'A night of debauchery it was . . .'

Thomas Kendall stood with his grandsons beside the massive sandstone walls of Fort Macquarie. He smiled as he looked out across Sydney Cove, '. . . that night they brought the women convicts ashore . . .'

In 1783, Thomas Kendall, a naive nineteen-year-old sentenced to transportation for burglary, finds himself in Sydney Town and a new life in the wild and lawless land beneath the Southern Cross.

Thomas fathers a dynasty that will last beyond two hundred years. His descendants play their part in the forging of a nation, but greed and prejudice see an irreparable rift in the family which will echo through the generations. It is only when a young man reaches far into the past and rights a grievous wrong that the Kendall family can reclaim its honour.

Beneath the Southern Cross is as much a story of a city as it is a family chronicle. With her uncanny ability to bring history to life in technicolour, Judy Nunn traces the fortunes of Thomas Kendall's descendants through good times and bad, two devastating wars and several social revolutions to the present day, vividly drawing the events, the ideas and issues that have made the city of Sydney and the nation of Australia what they are today.